The Flying Man and Other Stories

H. G. Wells

Om Books International

This edition first published in 2020 by

Om Books International

Corporate & Editorial Office
A-12, Sector 64, Noida 201 301
Uttar Pradesh, India
Phone: +91 120 477 4100
Email: editorial@ombooks.com
Website: www.ombooksinternational.com

Sales Office
107, Ansari Road, Darya Ganj,
New Delhi 110 002, India
Phone: +91 11 4000 9000
Fax: +91 11 2327 8091
Email: sales@ombooks.com
Website: www.ombooks.com

ISBN: 978-93-53763-61-9

Printed in India

10 9 8 7 6 5 4 3 2 1

HERBERT GEORGE WELLS was born on 21 September 1866, in Bromley, England. In 1874, Wells, the son of domestic helpers-turned-shopkeepers, had an accident that left him bedridden for months. It was during this time that an avid reader was born. His father would bring him books from the local library and Wells would spend hours devouring the written word. Later, when his mother returned to working as a maidservant in a country house in Sussex, Wells found himself in the owner's magnificent library, immersed in the works of stalwarts like Jonathan Swift, Charles Dickens, Sir Thomas More, Plato, Daniel Defoe and others.

As a teenager, Wells worked as a draper's assistant but eventually quit. Later, he won a scholarship to the Normal School of Science (later, The Royal College of Science) where he learned about astronomy, biology, chemistry, and physics, among other subjects. All through, Wells nursed the secret desire to become a writer someday.

In 1895, following the publication of *The Time Machine*, Wells became an overnight sensation. The story of an English scientist developing a time travel machine earned him the title of 'Father of Futurism'. Wells' successive books, often termed as 'scientific romances' included *The Island of Doctor Moreau* (1896), *The Invisible Man* (1897) and *The War of the Worlds* (1898).

Wells' short stories too reflected his futurist ideas and presented fantastical imageries that continue to enthral readers even today.

The visionary author, sociologist, journalist, and historian breathed his last on 13 August 1946, aged 79.

Contents

1

A Deal in Ostriches

"Talking of the prices of birds, I've seen an ostrich that cost three hundred pounds," said the taxidermist, recalling his youth of travel. "Three hundred pounds!"

He looked at me over his spectacles. "I've seen another that was refused at four."

"No," he said, "it wasn't any fancy points. They was just plain ostriches. A little off colour, too—owing to dietary. And there wasn't any particular restriction of the demand either. You'd have thought five ostriches would have ruled cheap on an East Indiaman. But the point was, one of 'em had swallowed a diamond.

"The chap it got it off was Sir Mohini Padishah, a tremendous swell, a Piccadilly swell you might say up to the neck of him, and then an ugly black head and a whopping turban, with this diamond in it. The blessed bird pecked suddenly and had it, and when the chap made a fuss, it realised it had done wrong, I suppose, and went and mixed itself with the others to preserve its *incog.* It all happened in a minute. I was among the first to arrive, and there was this heathen going over his gods, and two sailors and the man who had charge of the birds laughing, fit to split. It was a rummy way of losing a jewel, come to think of it. The man in charge hadn't been about just at the moment, so that he didn't know which bird it was. Clean lost, you see. I didn't feel half sorry, to tell you the truth. The beggar had been swaggering over his blessed diamond ever since he came aboard.

"A thing like that goes from stem to stern of a ship in no time. Every one was talking about it. Padishah went below to hide his feelings. At dinner—he pigged at a table by himself, him and two other Hindoos—the captain kind of jeered at him about it, and he got very excited. He turned round and talked into my ear. He would not buy the birds; he would have his diamond. He demanded his rights as a British subject. His diamond must be found. He was firm upon that. He would appeal to the House of Lords. The man in charge of the birds was one of those wooden-headed chaps you can't get a new idea into anyhow. He refused any proposal to interfere with the birds by way of medicine. His instructions were to feed them so-and-so and treat them so-and-so, and it was as much as his place was worth not to feed them so-and-so and treat them so-and-so. Padishah had wanted a stomach-pump—though you can't do that to a bird, you know. This Padishah was full of bad law, like most of these blessed Bengalis, and talked of having a lien on the birds, and so forth. But an old boy, who said his son was a London barrister, argued that what a bird swallowed became ipso facto part of the bird, and that Padishah's only remedy lay in an action for damages, and even then it might be possible to show contributory negligence. He hadn't any right of way about an ostrich that didn't belong to him. That upset Padishah extremely, the more so as most of us expressed an opinion that, that was the reasonable view. There wasn't any lawyer aboard to settle the matter, so we all talked pretty free. At last, after Aden, it appears that he came round to the general opinion, and went privately to the man in charge and made an offer for all five ostriches.

"The next morning there was a fine shindy at breakfast. The man hadn't any authority to deal with the birds, and nothing on earth would induce him to sell; but it seems he told Padishah that a Eurasian named Potter had already made him an offer, and on that Padishah denounced Potter before us all. But I think the most of us thought it rather smart of Potter, and I know that when Potter said that he'd wired at Aden to London to buy the birds, and would have an answer at Suez, I cursed pretty richly at a lost opportunity.

"At Suez, Padishah gave way to tears—actual wet tears—when Potter became the owner of the birds, and offered him two hundred and fifty right off for the five, being more than two hundred percent on what Potter had given. Potter said he'd be hanged if he parted with a feather of them—that he meant to kill them off one by one and find the diamond; but afterwards, thinking it over, he relented a little. He was a gambling hound, was this Potter, a little queer at cards, and this kind of prize-packet business must have suited him down to the ground. Anyhow, he offered, for a lark, to sell the birds separately to separate people by auction at a starting price of L80 for a bird. But one of them, he said, he meant to keep for luck.

"You must understand this diamond was a valuable one—a little Jew chap, a diamond merchant, who was with us, had put it at three or four thousand when Padishah had shown it to him—and this idea of an ostrich gamble caught on. Now it happened that I'd been having a few talks on general subjects with the man who looked after these ostriches, and quite incidentally he'd said one of the birds was ailing, and he fancied it had indigestion. It had one feather in its tail almost all white, by which I knew it, and so when, next day, the auction started with it, I capped Padishah's eighty-five by ninety. I fancy I was a bit too sure and eager with my bid, and some of the others spotted the fact that I was in the know. And Padishah went for that particular bird like an irresponsible lunatic. At last the Jew diamond merchant got it for L175, and Padishah said L180 just after the hammer came down—so Potter declared. At any rate the Jew merchant secured it, and there and then he got a gun and shot it. Potter made a Hades of a fuss because he said it would injure the sale of the other three, and Padishah, of course, behaved like an idiot; but all of us were very much excited. I can tell you I was precious glad when that dissection was over, and no diamond had turned up—precious glad. I'd gone to one-forty on that particular bird myself.

"The little Jew was like most Jews—he didn't make any great fuss over bad luck; but Potter declined to go on with the auction until it was understood that the goods could not be delivered until the sale was over. The little Jew wanted to argue that the case was exceptional, and as the discussion ran pretty even, the thing was postponed until the next morning. We had a lively dinner-table that evening, I can tell you, but in the end Potter got his way, since it would stand to reason he would be safer if he stuck to all the birds, and that we owed him some consideration for his sportsmanlike behaviour. And the old gentleman whose son was a lawyer said he'd been thinking the thing over and that it was very doubtful if, when a bird had been opened and the diamond recovered, it ought not to be handed back to the proper owner. I remember I suggested it came under the laws of treasure-trove—which was really the truth of the matter. There was a hot argument, and we settled it was certainly foolish to kill the bird on board the ship. Then the old gentleman, going at large through his legal talk, tried to make out the sale was a lottery and illegal, and appealed to the captain; but Potter said he sold the birds as ostriches. He didn't want to sell any diamonds, he said, and didn't offer that as an inducement. The three birds he put up, to the best of his knowledge and belief, did not contain a diamond. It was in the one he kept—so he hoped.

"Prices ruled high next day all the same. The fact that now there were four chances instead of five of course caused a rise. The blessed birds averaged L227, and, oddly enough, this Padishah didn't secure one of 'em—not one. He made too much shindy, and when he ought to have been bidding he was talking about liens, and besides, Potter was a bit down on him. One fell to a quiet little officer chap, another to the little Jew, and the third was syndicated by the engineers. And then Potter seemed suddenly sorry for having sold them, and said he'd flung away a clear thousand pounds, and that very likely he'd draw a blank and that he always had been a fool, but when I went and had a bit of a talk to him, with the idea of getting him to hedge on his last chance, I found he'd already sold the bird he'd reserved to a political chap that was on board, a chap who'd been studying Indian morals and social questions in his vacation. That last was the three hundred pounds bird. Well, they landed three of the blessed creatures at Brindisi—though the old gentleman said it was a breach of the Customs regulations—and Potter and Padishah landed too. The Hindoo seemed half mad as he saw his blessed diamond going this way and that, so to speak. He kept on saying he'd get an injunction—he had injunction on the brain—and giving his name and address to the chaps who'd bought the birds, so that they'd know where to send the diamond. None of them wanted his name and address, and none of them would give their own. It was a fine row I can tell you—on the platform. They all went off by different trains. I came on to Southampton, and there I saw the last of the birds, as I came≈ashore; it was the one the engineers bought, and it was standing up near the bridge, in a kind of crate, and looking as leggy and silly a setting for a valuable diamond as ever you saw—if it was a setting for a valuable diamond.

"How did it end? Oh! Like that. Well—perhaps. Yes, there's one more thing that may throw light on it. A week or so after landing I was down Regent Street doing a bit of shopping, and who should

I see arm-in-arm and having a purple time of it but Padishah and Potter. If you come to think of it—

"Yes. I've thought that. Only, you see, there's no doubt the diamond was real. And Padishah was an eminent Hindoo. I've seen his name in the papers—often. But whether the bird swallowed the diamond certainly is another matter, as you say."

2

Aepyornis Island

The man with the scarred face leant over the table and looked at my bundle.

"Orchids?" he asked.

"A few," I said.

"Cypripediums," he said.

"Chiefly," said I.

"Anything new? I thought not. I did these islands twenty-five—twenty-seven years ago. If you find anything new here—well, it's brand new. I didn't leave much."

"I'm not a collector," said I.

"I was young then," he went on. "Lord! How I used to fly round." He seemed to take my measure. "I was in the East Indies two years, and in Brazil seven. Then I went to Madagascar."

"I know a few explorers by name," I said, anticipating a yarn. "Whom did you collect for?"

"Dawson's. I wonder if you've heard the name of Butcher ever?"

"Butcher—Butcher?" The name seemed vaguely present in my memory; then I recalled Butcher vs. Dawson. "Why!" said I, "You are the man who sued them for four years' salary—got cast away on a desert island..."

"Your servant," said the man with the scar, bowing. "Funny case, wasn't it? Here was me, making a little fortune on that island, doing nothing for it neither, and them quite unable to give me notice. It often used to amuse me thinking over it while I was there. I did calculations of it—big—all over the blessed atoll in ornamental figuring."

"How did it happen?" said I. "I don't rightly remember the case."

"Well... You've heard of the Aepyornis?"

"Rather. Andrews was telling me of a new species he was working on only a month or so ago. Just before I sailed. They've got a thigh-bone, it seems, nearly a yard long. Monster the thing must have been!"

"I believe you," said the man with the scar. "It was a monster. Sindbad's roc was just a legend of 'em. But when did they find these bones?"

"Three or four years ago—'91, I fancy. Why?"

"Why? Because I found them—Lord—! It's nearly twenty years ago. If Dawson's hadn't been silly about that salary they might have made a perfect ring in 'em...I couldn't help the infernal boat going adrift."

He paused. "I suppose it's the same place. A kind of swamp about ninety miles north of Antananarivo. Do you happen to know? You have to go to it along the coast by boats. You don't happen to remember, perhaps?"

"I don't. I fancy Andrews said something about a swamp."

"It must be the same. It's on the east coast. And somehow there's something in the water that keeps things from decaying. Like creosote it smells. It reminded me of Trinidad. Did they get any more eggs? Some of the eggs I found were a foot and a half long. The swamp goes circling round, you know, and cuts off this bit. It's mostly salt, too. Well... What a time I had of it! I found the things quite by accident. We went for eggs, me and two native chaps, in one of those rum canoes all tied together, and found the bones at the same time. We had a tent and provisions for four days, and we pitched on one of the firmer places. To think of it brings that odd tarry smell back even now. It's funny work. You go probing into the mud with iron rods, you know. Usually the egg gets smashed. I wonder how long it is since these Aepyornises really lived. The missionaries say the natives have legends about when they were alive, but I never heard any such stories myself.* But certainly

* No European is known to have seen a live Aepyornis, with the doubtful exception of Macer, who visited Madagascar in 1745.—H. G. W.

those eggs we got were as fresh as if they had been new laid. Fresh! Carrying them down to the boat one of my nigger chaps dropped one on a rock and it smashed. How I lammed into the beggar! But sweet it was, as if it was new laid, not even smelly, and its mother dead these four hundred years, perhaps. Said a centipede had bit him. However, I'm getting off the straight with the story. It had taken us all day to dig into the slush and get these eggs out unbroken, and we were all covered with beastly black mud, and naturally I was cross. So far as I knew they were the only eggs that have ever been got out, not even cracked. I went afterwards to see the ones they have at the Natural History Museum in London; all of them were cracked and just stuck together like a mosaic, and bits missing. Mine were perfect, and I meant to blow them when I got back. Naturally I was annoyed at the silly duffer dropping three hours' work just on account of a centipede. I hit him about rather."

The man with the scar took out a clay pipe. I placed my pouch before him. He filled up absentmindedly.

"How about the others? Did you get those home? I don't remember—"

"That's the queer part of the story. I had three others. Perfectly fresh eggs. Well, we put 'em in the boat, and then I went up to the tent to make some coffee, leaving my two heathens down by the beach—the one fooling about with his sting and the other helping him. It never occurred to me that the beggars would take advantage of the peculiar position I was in to pick a quarrel. But I suppose the centipede poison and the kicking I had given him had upset the one—he was always a cantankerous sort—and he persuaded the other."

"I remember I was sitting and smoking and boiling up the water over a spirit-lamp, business I used to take on these expeditions. Incidentally I was admiring the swamp under the sunset. All black and blood-red it was, in streaks—a beautiful sight. And up beyond the land rose grey and hazy to the hills, and the sky behind them red, like a furnace mouth. And fifty yards behind the back of me was these blessed heathens—quite regardless of the tranquil air of things—plotting to cut off with the boat and leave me all alone with three days' provisions and a canvas tent, and nothing to drink whatsoever beyond a little keg of water. I heard a kind of yelp behind me, and there they were in this canoe affair—it wasn't properly a boat—and, perhaps, twenty yards from land. I realised what was up in a moment. My gun was in the tent, and besides, I had no bullets—only duck shot. They knew that. But I had a little revolver in my pocket, and I pulled that out as I ran down to the beach.

"'Come back!' says I, flourishing it.

"They jabbered something at me, and the man that broke the egg jeered. I aimed at the other—because he was unwounded and had the paddle, and I missed. They laughed. However, I wasn't beat. I knew I had to keep cool, and I tried him again and made him jump with the whang of it. He didn't laugh that time. The third time I got his head, and over he went, and the paddle with him. It was a precious lucky shot for a revolver. I reckon it was fifty yards. He went right under. I don't know if he was shot, or simply stunned and drowned. Then I began to shout to the other chap to come back, but he huddled up in the canoe and refused to answer. So I fired out my revolver at him and never got near him.

"I felt a precious fool, I can tell you. There I was on this rotten, black beach, flat swamp all behind me, and the flat sea, cold after the sun set, and just this black canoe drifting steadily out to sea. I tell you I damned Dawson's and Jamrach's and Museums and all the rest of it just to rights. I bawled to this nigger to come back, until my voice went up into a scream.

"There was nothing for it but to swim after him and take my luck with the sharks. So I opened my clasp-knife and put it in my mouth, and took off my clothes and waded in. As soon as I was in the water I lost sight of the canoe, but I aimed, as I judged, to head it off. I hoped the man in it was too bad to navigate it, and that it would keep on drifting in the same direction. Presently it came up over the horizon again to the south-westward, about. The afterglow of sunset was well over now and the dim of night creeping up. The stars were coming through the blue. I swum like a champion, though my legs and arms were soon aching.

"However, I came up to him by the time the stars were fairly out. As it got darker I began to see all manner of glowing things in the water—phosphorescence, you know. At times it made me giddy. I hardly knew which was stars and which was phosphorescence, and whether I was swimming on my head or my heels. The canoe was as black as sin, and the ripple under the bows like liquid fire. I was naturally chary of clambering up into it. I was anxious to see what he was up to first. He seemed to be lying cuddled up in a lump in the bows, and the stern was all out of water. The thing kept turning round slowly as it drifted—kind of waltzing, don't you know. I went to the stern and pulled it down, expecting him to wake up. Then I began to clamber in with my knife in my hand, and ready for a rush. But he never stirred. So there I sat in the stern of the little canoe, drifting away over the calm phosphorescent sea, and with all the host of the stars above me, waiting for something to happen.

"After a long time I called him by name, but he never answered. I was too tired to take any risks by going along to him. So we sat there. I fancy I dozed once or twice. When the dawn came I saw he was as dead as a door-nail and all puffed up and purple. My three eggs and the bones were lying in the middle of the canoe, and the keg of water and some coffee and biscuits wrapped in a Cape Argus by his feet, and a tin of methylated spirit underneath him. There was no paddle, nor in fact, anything except the spirit tin that I could use as one, so I settled to drift until I was picked up. I held an inquest on him, brought in a verdict against some snake, scorpion, or centipede unknown, and sent him overboard.

"After that I had a drink of water and a few biscuits, and took a look round. I suppose a man low down as I was don't see very far; leastways, Madagascar was clean out of sight, and any trace of land at all. I saw a sail going south-westward—looked like a schooner but her hull never came up. Presently the sun got high in the sky and began to beat down upon me. Lord! It pretty near made my brains boil. I tried dipping my head in the sea, but after a while my eye fell on the Cape Argus, and I lay down flat in the canoe and spread this over me. Wonderful things these newspapers! I never read one through thoroughly before, but it's odd what you get up to when you're alone, as I was. I suppose I read that blessed old Cape Argus twenty times. The pitch in the canoe simply reeked with the heat and rose up into big blisters.

"I drifted ten days," said the man with the scar. "It's a little thing in the telling, isn't it? Every day was like the last. Except in the morning and the evening I never kept a lookout even—the blaze was so infernal. I didn't see a sail after the first three days, and those I saw took no notice of me. About the sixth night a ship went by scarcely half a mile away from me, with all its lights ablaze and its ports open, looking like a big firefly. There was music aboard. I stood up and shouted and screamed at it. The second day

I broached one of the Aepyornis eggs, scraped the shell away at the end bit by bit, and tried it, and I was glad to find it was good enough to eat. A bit flavour—not bad, I mean—but with something of the taste of a duck's egg. There was a kind of circular patch, about six inches across, on one side of the yoke, and with streaks of blood and a white mark like a ladder in it that I thought queer, but I did not understand what this meant at the time, and I wasn't inclined to be particular. The egg lasted me three days, with biscuits and a drink of water. I chewed coffee-berries too—invigorating stuff. The second egg I opened about the eighth day, and it scared me."

The man with the scar paused. "Yes," he said, "Developing.

"I daresay you find it hard to believe. I did, with the thing before me. There the egg had been, sunk in that cold black mud, perhaps three hundred years. But there was no mistaking it. There was the—what is it—? Embryo, with its big head and curved back, and its heart beating under its throat, and the yolk shrivelled up and great membranes spreading inside of the shell and all over the yolk. Here was I hatching out the eggs of the biggest of all extinct birds, in a little canoe in the midst of the Indian Ocean. If old Dawson had known that! It was worth four years' salary. What do you think?

"However, I had to eat that precious thing up, every bit of it, before I sighted the reef, and some of the mouthfuls were beastly unpleasant. I left the third one alone. I held it up to the light, but the shell was too thick for me to get any notion of what might be happening inside; and though I fancied I heard blood pulsing, it might have been the rustle in my own ears, like what you listen to in a seashell.

"Then came the atoll. Came out of the sunrise, as it were, suddenly, close up to me. I drifted straight towards it until I was about half a mile from shore, not more, and then the current took a turn, and I had to paddle as hard as I could with my hands and bits of the Aepyornis shell to make the place. However, I got there. It was just a common atoll about four miles round, with a few trees growing and a spring in one place, and the lagoon full of parrot-fish. I took the egg ashore and put it in a good place, well above the tide lines and in the sun, to give it all the chance I could, and pulled the canoe up safe, and loafed about prospecting. It's rum how dull an atoll is. As soon as I had found a spring all the interest seemed to vanish. When I was a kid I thought nothing could be finer or more adventurous than the Robinson Crusoe business, but that place was as monotonous as a book of sermons. I went round finding eatable things and generally thinking; but I tell you I was bored to death before the first day was out. It shows my luck—the very day I landed the weather changed. A thunderstorm went by to the north and flicked its wing over the island, and in the night there came a drencher and a howling wind slap over us. It wouldn't have taken much, you know, to upset that canoe.

"I was sleeping under the canoe, and the egg was luckily among the sand higher up the beach, and the first thing I remember was a sound like a hundred pebbles hitting the boat at once, and a rush of water over my body. I'd been dreaming of Antananarivo, and I sat up and halloaed to Intoshi to ask her what the devil was up, and clawed out at the chair where the matches used to be. Then I remembered where I was. There were phosphorescent waves rolling up as if they meant to eat me, and all the rest of the night as black as pitch. The air was simply yelling. The clouds seemed down on your head almost, and the rain fell as if heaven was sinking and they were baling out the waters above the firmament. One great roller came writhing at me, like a fiery serpent, and I bolted. Then I thought of the canoe, and ran down to it as the water went hissing back again; but the thing had gone. I wondered about the egg then, and felt my way to it. It was all right and well out of reach of the maddest waves, so I sat down beside it and cuddled it for company. Lord! What a night that was!

"The storm was over before the morning. There wasn't a rag of cloud left in the sky when the dawn came, and all along the beach there were bits of plank scattered—which was the disarticulated skeleton, so to speak, of my canoe. However, that gave me something to do, for, taking advantage of two of the trees being together, I rigged up a kind of storm-shelter with these vestiges. And that day the egg hatched.

"Hatched, sir, when my head was pillowed on it and I was asleep. I heard a whack and felt a jar and sat up, and there was the end of the egg pecked out and a rum little brown head looking out at me. 'Lord!' I said, 'You're welcome'; and with a little difficulty he came out.

"He was a nice friendly little chap at first, about the size of a small hen—very much like most other young birds, only bigger. His plumage was a dirty brown to begin with, with a sort of grey scab that fell off it very soon, and scarcely feathers—a kind of downy hair. I can hardly express how pleased I was to see him. I tell you, Robinson Crusoe don't make near enough of his loneliness. But here was interesting company. He looked at me and winked his eye from the front backwards, like a hen, and gave a chirp and began to peck about at once, as though being hatched three hundred years too late was just nothing. 'Glad to see you, Man Friday!' says I, for I had naturally settled he was to be called Man Friday if ever he was hatched, as soon as ever, I found the egg in the canoe had developed. I was a bit anxious about his feed, so I gave him a lump of raw parrot-fish at once. He took it, and opened his beak for more. I was glad of that for, under the circumstances, if he'd been at all fanciful, I should have had to eat him after all.

"You'd be surprised what an interesting bird that Aepyornis chick was. He followed me about from the very beginning. He used to stand by me and watch while I fished in the lagoon, and go shares in anything I caught. And he was sensible, too. There were nasty green warty things, like pickled gherkins, used to lie about on the beach, and he tried one of these and it upset him. He never even looked at any of them again.

"And he grew. You could almost see him grow. And as I was never much of a society man, his quiet, friendly ways suited me to a T. For nearly two years we were as happy as we could be on that island. I had no business worries, for I knew my salary was mounting up at Dawsons'. We would see a sail now and then, but nothing ever came near us. I amused myself, too, by decorating the island with designs worked in sea-urchins and fancy shells of various kinds. I put 'Aepyornis Island' all round the place very nearly, in big letters, like what you see done with coloured stones at railway stations in the old country, and mathematical calculations and drawings of various sorts. And I used to lie watching the blessed bird stalking round and growing, growing; and think how I could make a living out of him by showing him about if I ever got taken off. After his first moult he began to get handsome, with a crest and a blue wattle, and a lot of green feathers at the behind of him. And then I used to puzzle whether Dawsons' had any right to claim him or not. Stormy weather and in the rainy season we lay snug under the shelter, I had made out of the old canoe, and I used to tell him lies about my friends at home. And after a storm we would go round the island together to see if there was any drift. It was a kind of idyll, you might say. If only I had, had some tobacco it would have been simply just like heaven.

"It was about the end of the second year our little paradise went wrong. Friday was then about fourteen feet high to the bill of him, with a big, broad head like the end of a pickaxe, and two huge brown eyes with yellow rims, set together like a man's—not out of sight of each other like a hen's. His plumage was fine—none of the half-mourning style of your ostrich—more like a cassowary as far as colour and texture go. And then it was he began to cock his comb at me and give himself airs, and show signs of a nasty temper...

"At last came a time when my fishing had been rather unlucky, and he began to hang about me in a queer, meditative way. I thought he might have been eating sea-cucumbers or something, but it was really just discontent on his part. I was hungry too, and when at last I landed a fish I wanted it for myself. Tempers were short that morning on both sides. He pecked at it and grabbed it, and I gave him a whack on the head to make him leave go. And at that he went for me. Lord...!

"He gave me this in the face." The man indicated his scar. "Then he kicked me. It was like a cart-horse. I got up, and seeing he hadn't finished, I started off full tilt with my arms doubled up over my face. But he ran on those gawky legs of his faster than a race-horse, and kept landing out at me with sledgehammer kicks, and bringing his pickaxe down on the back of my head. I made for the lagoon, and went in up to my neck. He stopped at the water, for he hated getting his feet wet, and began to make a shindy, something like a peacock's, only hoarser. He started strutting up and down the beach. I'll admit I felt small to see this blessed fossil lording it there. And my head and face were all bleeding, and—well, my body just one jelly of bruises.

"I decided to swim across the lagoon and leave him alone for a bit, until the affair blew over. I shinned up the tallest palm-tree, and sat there thinking of it all. I don't suppose I ever felt so hurt by anything before or since. It was the brutal ingratitude of the creature. I'd been more than a brother to him. I'd hatched him, educated him. A great gawky, out-of-date bird! And me a human being—heir of the ages and all that.

"I thought after a time he'd begin to see things in that light himself, and feel a little sorry for his behaviour. I thought if I was to catch some nice little bits of fish, perhaps, and go to him presently in a casual kind of way, and offer them to him, he might do the sensible thing. It took me some time to learn how unforgiving and cantankerous an extinct bird can be. Malice!

"I won't tell you all the little devices I tried to get that bird round again, I simply can't. It makes my cheek burn with shame even now to think of the snubs and buffets I had from this infernal curiosity. I tried violence. I chucked lumps of coral at him from a safe distance, but he only swallowed them. I shied my open knife at him and almost lost it, though it was too big for him to swallow. I tried starving him out and struck fishing, but he took to picking along the beach at low water after worms, and rubbed along on that. Half my time I spent up to my neck in the lagoon, and the rest up the palm-trees. One of them was scarcely high enough, and when he caught me up it he had a regular Bank Holiday with the calves of my legs. It got unbearable. I don't know if you have ever tried sleeping up a palm-tree. It gave me the most horrible nightmares. Think of the shame of it, too! Here was this extinct animal mooning about my island like a sulky duke, and me not allowed to rest the sole of my foot on the place. I used to cry with weariness and vexation. I told him straight that I didn't mean to be chased about a desert island by any damned anachronisms. I told him to go and peck a navigator of his own age. But he only snapped his beak at me. Great ugly bird, all legs and neck!

"I shouldn't like to say how long that went on altogether. I'd have killed him sooner if I'd known how. However, I hit on a way of settling him at last. It is a South American dodge. I joined all my fishing-lines together with stems of seaweed and things, and made a stoutish string, perhaps twelve yards in length or more, and I fastened two lumps of coral rock to the ends of this. It took me some time to do, because every now and then I had to go into the lagoon or up a tree as the fancy took me. This I whirled rapidly round my head, and then let it go at him. The first time I missed, but the next time the string caught his legs beautifully, and wrapped round them again and again. Over he went. I threw it standing waist-deep in the lagoon, and as soon as he went down I was out of the water and sawing at his neck with my knife...

"I don't like to think of that even now. I felt like a murderer while I did it, though my anger was hot against him. When I stood over him and saw him bleeding on the white sand, and his beautiful great legs and neck writhing in his last agony... Pah!

"With that tragedy loneliness came upon me like a curse. Good Lord! You can't imagine how I missed that bird. I sat by his corpse and sorrowed over him, and shivered as I looked round the desolate, silent reef. I thought of what a jolly little bird he had been when he was hatched, and of a thousand pleasant tricks he had played before he went wrong. I thought if I'd only wounded him I might have nursed him round into a better understanding. If I'd had any means of digging into the coral rock I'd have buried him. I felt exactly as if he was human. As it was, I couldn't think of eating him, so I put him in the lagoon, and the little fishes picked him clean. I didn't even save the feathers. Then one day a chap cruising about in a yacht had a fancy to see if my atoll still existed.

"He didn't come a moment too soon, for I was about sick enough of the desolation of it, and only hesitating whether I should walk out into the sea and finish up the business that way, or fall back on the green things...

"I sold the bones to a man named Winslow—a dealer near the British Museum, and he says he sold them to old Havers. It seems Havers didn't understand they were extra large, and it was only after his death they attracted attention. They called 'em Aepyornis—what was it?"

"Aepyornis vastus," said I. "It's funny, the very thing was mentioned to me by a friend of mine. When they found an Aepyornis, with a thigh a yard long, they thought they had reached the top of the scale, and called him Aepyornis maximus. Then some one turned up another thigh-bone four feet six or more, and that they called Aepyornis titan. Then your vastus was found after old Havers died, in his collection, and then a vastissimus turned up."

"Winslow was telling me as much," said the man with the scar. "If they get any more Aepyornises, he reckons some scientific swell will go and burst a blood-vessel. But it was a queer thing to happen to a man, wasn't it—altogether?"

3

The Diamond Maker

Some business had detained me in Chancery Lane, until nine in the evening, and thereafter, having some inkling of a headache, I was disinclined either for entertainment or further work. So much of the sky as the high cliffs of that narrow canon of traffic left visible, spoke of a serene night, and I determined to make my way down to the Embankment, and rest my eyes and cool my head by watching the variegated lights upon the river. Beyond comparison the night is the best time for this place; a merciful darkness hides the dirt of the waters, and the lights of this transitional age, red glaring orange, gas-yellow, and electric white, are set in shadowy outlines of every possible shade between grey and deep purple. Through the arches of Waterloo Bridge a hundred points of light mark the sweep of the Embankment, and above its parapet rise the towers of Westminster, warm grey against the starlight. The black river goes by with only a rare ripple breaking its silence, and disturbing the reflections of the lights that swim upon its surface.

"A warm night," said a voice at my side.

I turned my head, and saw the profile of a man who was leaning over the parapet beside me. It was a refined face, not unhandsome, though pinched and pale enough, and the coat collar turned up and pinned round the throat marked his status in life as sharply as a uniform. I felt I was committed to the price of a bed and breakfast if I answered him.

I looked at him curiously. Would he have anything to tell me worth the money, or was he the common incapable—incapable even of telling his own story? There was a quality of intelligence in his forehead and eyes, and a certain tremulousness in his nether lip that decided me.

"Very warm," said I; "but not too warm for us here."

"No," he said, still looking across the water, "it is pleasant enough here...just now.

"It is good," he continued after a pause, "to find anything so restful as this in London. After one has been fretting about business all day, about getting on, meeting obligations, and parrying dangers, I do not know what one would do if it were not for such pacific corners." He spoke with long pauses between the sentences. "You must know a little of the irksome labour of the world, or you would not be here. But I doubt if you can be so brain-weary and footsore as I am...Bah! Sometimes I doubt if the game is worth the candle. I feel inclined to throw the whole thing over—name, wealth and position—and take to some modest trade. But I know if I abandoned my ambition—hardly as she uses me—I should have nothing but remorse left for the rest of my days."

He became silent. I looked at him in astonishment. If ever I saw a man hopelessly hard-up it was the man in front of me. He was ragged and he was dirty, unshaven and unkempt; he looked as though he had been left in a dust-bin for a week. And he was talking to me of the irksome worries of a large business. I almost laughed outright. Either he was mad or playing a sorry jest on his own poverty.

"If high aims and high positions," said I, "have their drawbacks of hard work and anxiety, they have their compensations. Influence, the power of doing good, of assisting those weaker and poorer than ourselves; and there is even a certain gratification in display."

My banter under the circumstances was in very vile taste. I spoke on the spur of the contrast of his appearance and speech. I was sorry even while I was speaking.

He turned a haggard but very composed face upon me. Said he: "I forgot myself. Of course you would not understand."

He measured me for a moment. "No doubt it is very absurd. You will not believe me even when I tell you, so that it is fairly safe to tell you. And it will be a comfort to tell someone. I really have a big business in hand, a very big business. But there are troubles just now. The fact is...I make diamonds."

"I suppose," said I, "you are out of work just at present?"

"I am sick of being disbelieved," he said impatiently, and suddenly unbuttoning his wretched coat he pulled out a little canvas bag that was hanging by a cord round his neck. From this he produced a brown pebble. "I wonder if you know enough, to know what that is?" He handed it to me.

Now, a year or so ago, I had occupied my leisure in taking a London science degree, so that I have a smattering of physics and mineralogy. The thing was not unlike an uncut diamond of the darker sort, though far too large, being almost as big as the top of my thumb. I took it, and saw it had the form of a regular octahedron, with the curved faces peculiar to the most precious of minerals. I took out my penknife and tried to scratch it—vainly. Leaning forward towards the gas-lamp, I tried the thing on my watch-glass, and scored a white line across that, with the greatest ease.

I looked at my interlocutor with rising curiosity. "It certainly is rather like a diamond. But, if so, it is a Behemoth of diamonds. Where did you get it?"

"I tell you I made it," he said. "Give it back to me."

He replaced it hastily and buttoned his jacket. "I will sell it to you for one hundred pounds," he suddenly whispered eagerly. With that my suspicions returned. The thing might, after all, be merely a lump of that almost equally hard substance, corundum, with an accidental resemblance in shape to the diamond. Or if it was a diamond, how came he by it, and why should he offer it at a hundred pounds?

We looked into one another's eyes. He seemed eager, but honestly eager. At that moment I believed it was a diamond he was trying to sell. Yet I am a poor man, a hundred pounds would leave a visible gap in my fortunes and no sane man would buy a diamond by gaslight from a ragged tramp on his personal warranty only. Still, a diamond that size conjured up a vision of many thousands of pounds. Then, thought I, such a stone could scarcely exist without being mentioned in every book on gems, and again I called to mind the stories of contraband and light-fingered Kaffirs at the Cape. I put the question of purchase on one side.

"How did you get it?" said I.

"I made it."

I had heard something of Moissan, but I knew his artificial diamonds were very small. I shook my head.

"You seem to know something of this kind of thing. I will tell you a little about myself. Perhaps then you may think better of the purchase." He turned round with his back to the river, and put his hands in his pockets. He sighed. "I know you will not believe me."

"Diamonds," he began—and as he spoke his voice lost its faint flavour of the tramp and assumed something of the easy tone of an educated man—"are to be made by throwing carbon out of combination in a suitable flux and under a suitable pressure; the carbon crystallises out, not as black-lead or charcoal-powder, but as small diamonds. So much has been known to chemists for years, but no one yet had hit upon exactly the right flux in which to melt up the carbon, or exactly the right pressure for the best results. Consequently the diamonds made by chemists are small and dark, and worthless as jewels. Now I, you know, have given up my life to this problem—given my life to it."

"I began to work at the conditions of diamond making when I was seventeen, and now I am thirty-two. It seemed to me that it might take all the thought and energies of a man for ten years, or twenty years, but, even if it did, the game was still worth the candle. Suppose one to have at last just hit the right trick before the secret got out and diamonds became as common as coal, one might realize millions. Millions!"

He paused and looked for my sympathy. His eyes shone hungrily. "To think," said he, "that I am on the verge of it all, and here!

"I had," he proceeded, "about a thousand pounds when I was twenty-one, and this, I thought, eked out by a little teaching, would keep my researches going. A year or two was spent in study, at Berlin chiefly, and then I continued on my own account. The trouble was the secrecy. You see, if once I had let out what I was doing, other men might have been spurred on by my belief in the practicability of the idea; and I do not pretend to be such a genius as to have been sure of coming in first, in the case of a race for the discovery. And you see it was important that if I really meant to make a pile, people should not know it was an artificial process and capable of turning out diamonds by the ton. So I had to work all alone. At first I had a little laboratory, but as my resources began to run out I had to conduct my experiments in a wretched unfurnished room in Kentish Town, where I slept at last on a straw mattress on the floor among all my apparatus. The money simply flowed away. I grudged myself everything except scientific appliances. I tried to keep things going by a little teaching, but I am not a very good teacher, and I have no university degree, nor very much education except in chemistry, and I found I had to give a lot of time and labour for precious little money. But I got nearer and nearer the thing. Three years ago I settled the problem of the composition of the flux, and got near the pressure by putting this flux of mine and a certain carbon composition into a closed-up gun-barrel, filling up with water, sealing tightly, and heating."

He paused.

"Rather risky," said I.

"Yes. It burst, and smashed all my windows and a lot of my apparatus; but I got a kind of diamond powder nevertheless. Following out the problem of getting a big pressure upon the molten mixture from which the things were to crystallise, I hit upon some researches of Daubree's at the Paris Laboratorie des Poudres et Salpetres. He exploded dynamite in a tightly screwed steel cylinder, too strong to burst, and I found he could crush rocks into a muck not unlike the South African bed in which diamonds are found. It was a tremendous strain on my resources, but I got a steel cylinder made for my purpose after his pattern. I put in all my stuff and my explosives, built up a fire in my furnace, put the whole concern in, and—went out for a walk."

I could not help laughing at his matter-of-fact manner. "Did you not think it would blow up the house? Were there other people in the place?"

"It was in the interest of science," he said, ultimately. "There was a costermonger family on the floor below, a begging-letter writer in the room behind mine, and two flower-women were upstairs. Perhaps it was a bit thoughtless. But possibly some of them were out.

"When I came back the thing was just where I left it, among the white-hot coals. The explosive hadn't burst the case. And then I had a problem to face. You know time is an important element in crystallisation. If you hurry the process the crystals are small—it is only by prolonged standing that they grow to any size. I resolved to let this apparatus cool for two years, letting the temperature go down slowly during the time. And I was now quite out of money; and with a big fire and the rent of my room, as well as my hunger to satisfy, I had scarcely a penny in the world.

"I can hardly tell you all the shifts I was put to while I was making the diamonds. I have sold newspapers, held horses, opened cab-doors. For many weeks I addressed envelopes. I had a place as assistant to a man who owned a barrow, and used to call down one side of the road while he called down the other.

"Once for a week I had absolutely nothing to do, and I begged. What a week that was! One day the fire was going out and I had eaten nothing all day, and a little chap taking his girl out, gave me sixpence—to show-off. Thank heaven for vanity! How the fish-shops smelt! But I went and spent it all on coals, and had the furnace bright red again, and then—Well, hunger makes a fool of a man.

"At last, three weeks ago, I let the fire out. I took my cylinder and unscrewed it while it was still so hot that it punished my hands, and I scraped out the crumbling lava-like mass with a chisel, and hammered it into a powder upon an iron plate. And I found three big diamonds and five small ones. As I sat on the floor hammering, my door opened, and my neighbour, the begging-letter writer came in. He was drunk—as he usually is, 'Nerchist,' said he. 'You're drunk,' said I. 'Structive scoundrel,' said he. 'Go to your father,' said I, meaning the Father of Lies. 'Never you mind,' said he, and gave me a cunning wink, and hiccupped, and leaning up against the door, with his other eye against the doorpost, began to babble of how he had been prying in my room, and how he had gone to the police that morning, and how they had taken down everything he had to say—'siffiwas a ge'm,' said he. Then I suddenly realised I was in a hole. Either I should have to tell these police my little secret, and get the whole thing blown upon, or be lagged as an Anarchist. So I went up to my neighbour and took him by the collar, and rolled him about a bit, and then I gathered up my diamonds and cleared out. The evening newspapers called my den the Kentish-Town Bomb Factory. And now I cannot part with the things for love or money.

"If I go in to respectable jewellers they ask me to wait, and go and whisper to a clerk to fetch a policeman, and then I say I cannot wait. And I found out a receiver of stolen goods, and he simply stuck to the one I gave him and told me to prosecute if I wanted it back. I am going about now with several hundred thousand pounds-worth of diamonds round my neck, and without either food or shelter. You are the first person I have taken into my confidence. But I like your face and I am hard-driven."

He looked into my eyes.

"It would be madness," said I, "for me to buy a diamond under the circumstances. Besides, I do not carry hundreds of pounds about in my pocket. Yet I more than half believe your story. I will, if you like, do this: come to my office to-morrow..."

"You think I am a thief!" said he keenly. "You will tell the police. I am not coming into a trap."

"Somehow I am assured you are no thief. Here is my card. Take that, anyhow. You need not come to any appointment. Come when you will."

He took the card, and an earnest of my good-will.

"Think better of it and come," said I.

He shook his head doubtfully. "I will pay back your half-crown with interest some day—such interest as will amaze you," said he. "Anyhow, you will keep the secret...? Don't follow me."

He crossed the road and went into the darkness towards the little steps under the archway leading into Essex Street, and I let him go. And that was the last I ever saw of him.

Afterwards I had two letters from him asking me to send bank-notes—not cheques—to certain addresses. I weighed the matter over and took what I conceived to be the wisest course. Once he called upon me when I was out. My urchin described him as a very thin, dirty, and ragged man, with a dreadful cough. He left no message. That was the finish of him so far as my story goes. I wonder sometimes what has become of him. Was he an ingenious monomaniac, or a fraudulent dealer in pebbles, or has he really made diamonds as he asserted? The latter is just sufficiently credible to make me think at times that I have missed the most brilliant opportunity of my life. He may of course be dead, and his diamonds carelessly thrown aside—one, I repeat, was almost as big as my thumb. Or he may be still wandering about trying to sell the things. It is just possible he may yet emerge upon society, and, passing athwart my heavens in the serene altitude sacred to the wealthy and the well-advertised, reproach me silently for my want of enterprise. I sometimes think I might at least have risked five pounds.

4

The Flowering of the Strange Orchid

The buying of orchids always has in it a certain speculative flavour. You have before you the brown shrivelled lump of tissue, and for the rest you must trust your judgment, or the auctioneer, or your good-luck, as your taste may incline. The plant may be moribund or dead, or it may be just a respectable purchase, fair value for your money, or perhaps—for the thing has happened again and again—there slowly unfolds before the delighted eyes of the happy purchaser, day after day, some new variety, some novel richness, a strange twist of the labellum, or some subtler coloration or unexpected mimicry. Pride, beauty, and profit blossom together on one delicate green spike, and it may be, even immortality. For the new miracle of Nature may stand in need of a new specific name, and what so convenient, as that of its discoverer? "Johnsmithia!" There have been worse names.

It was perhaps the hope of some such happy discovery that made Winter-Wedderburn such a frequent attendant at these sales—that hope, and also, maybe, the fact that he had nothing else of the slightest interest to do in the world. He was a shy, lonely, rather ineffectual man, provided with just enough income to keep off the spur of necessity, and not enough nervous energy to make him seek any exacting employments. He might have collected stamps or coins, or translated Horace, or bound books, or invented new species of diatoms. But, as it happened, he grew orchids, and had one ambitious little hothouse.

"I have a fancy," he said over his coffee, "that something is going to happen to me to-day." He spoke—as he moved and thought—slowly.

"Oh, don't say that!" said his housekeeper—who was also his remote cousin. For "something happening" was a euphemism that meant only one thing to her.

"You misunderstand me. I mean nothing unpleasant, though what I do mean I scarcely know.

"To-day," he continued, after a pause, "Peters' are going to sell a batch of plants from the Andamans and the Indies. I shall go up and see what they have. It may be I shall buy something good, unawares. That may be it."

He passed his cup for his second cupful of coffee.

"Are these the things collected by that poor young fellow you told me of the other day?" asked his cousin as she filled his cup.

"Yes," he said, and became meditative over a piece of toast.

"Nothing ever does happen to me," he remarked presently, beginning to think aloud. "I wonder why? Things enough happen to other people. There is Harvey. Only the other week—on Monday he picked up sixpence, on Wednesday his chicks all had the staggers, on Friday his cousin came home from Australia, and on Saturday he broke his ankle. What a whirl of excitement—! Compared to me."

"I think I would rather be without so much excitement," said his housekeeper. "It can't be good for you."

"I suppose it's troublesome. Still...you see, nothing ever happens to me. When I was a little boy I never had accidents. I never fell in love as I grew up. Never married...I wonder how it feels to have something happen to you, something really remarkable.

"That orchid-collector was only thirty-six—twenty years younger than myself—when he died. And he had been married twice, and divorced once; he had, had malarial fever four times, and once he broke his thigh. He killed a Malay once, and once he was wounded by a poisoned dart. And in the end he was killed by jungle-leeches. It must have all been very trouble-some, but then it must have been very interesting, you know—except, perhaps, the leeches."

"I am sure it was not good for him," said the lady, with conviction.

"Perhaps not." And then Wedderburn looked at his watch. "Twenty-three minutes past eight. I am going up by the quarter to twelve train, so that there is plenty of time. I think I shall wear my alpaca jacket—it is quite warm enough—and my grey felt hat and brown shoes. I suppose—"

He glanced out of the window at the serene sky and sunlit garden, and then nervously at his cousin's face.

"I think you had better take an umbrella if you are going to London," she said, in a voice that admitted of no denial. "There's all between here and the station coming back."

When he returned he was in a state of mild excitement. He had made a purchase. It was rare that he could make up his mind quickly enough to buy, but this time he had done so.

"These are Vandas," he said, "and a Dendrobe and some Palaeonopsis." He surveyed his purchases lovingly as he consumed his soup. They were laid out on the spotless tablecloth before him, and he was telling his cousin all about them as he slowly meandered through his dinner. It was his custom to live all his visits to London over again in the evening for her and his own entertainment.

"I knew something would happen to-day. And I have bought all these. Some of them—some of them—I feel sure, do you know, that some of them will be remarkable. I don't know how it is, but I feel just as sure as if someone had told me that some of these will turn out remarkable.

"That one—" he pointed to a shrivelled rhizome—"was not identified. It may be a Palaeonopsis or it may not. It may be a new species, or even a new genus. And it was the last that poor Batten ever collected."

"I don't like the look of it," said his housekeeper. "It's such an ugly shape."

"To me it scarcely seems to have a shape."

"I don't like those things that stick out," said his housekeeper.

"It shall be put away in a pot to-morrow."

"It looks," said the housekeeper, "like a spider shamming dead."

Wedderburn smiled and surveyed the root with his head on one side. "It is certainly not a pretty lump of stuff. But you can never judge of these things from their dry appearance. It may turn out to be a very beautiful orchid indeed. How busy I shall be to-morrow! I must see to-night, just exactly what to do with these things, and to-morrow I shall set to work.

"They found poor Batten lying dead, or dying, in a mangrove swamp—I forget which," he began again presently, "with one of these very orchids crushed up under his body. He had been unwell for some days with some kind of native fever, and I suppose he fainted. These mangrove swamps are very unwholesome. Every drop of blood, they say, was taken out of him by the jungle-leeches. It may be that very plant that cost him his life to obtain."

"I think none the better of it for that."

"Men must work, though women may weep," said Wedderburn, with profound gravity.

"Fancy dying away from every comfort in a nasty swamp! Fancy being ill of fever with nothing to take but chlorodyne and quinine—if men were left to themselves they would live on chlorodyne and quinine—and no one round you but horrible natives! They say the Andaman islanders are most disgusting wretches—and anyhow, they can scarcely make good nurses, not having the necessary training. And just for people in England to have orchids!"

"I don't suppose it was comfortable, but some men seem to enjoy that kind of thing," said Wedderburn. "Anyhow, the natives of his party were sufficiently civilised to take care of all his collection until his colleague, who was an ornithologist, came back again from the interior; though they could not tell the species of the orchid and had let it wither. And it makes these things more interesting."

"It makes them disgusting. I should be afraid of some of the malaria clinging to them. And just think, there has been a dead body lying across that ugly thing! I never thought of that before. There! I declare I cannot eat another mouthful of dinner!"

"I will take them off the table if you like, and put them in the window-seat. I can see them just as well there."

The next few days he was indeed singularly busy in his steamy little hothouse, fussing about with charcoal, lumps of teak, moss, and all the other mysteries of the orchid cultivator. He considered he was having a wonderfully eventful time. In the evening he would talk about these new orchids to his friends, and over, and over again he reverted to his expectation of something strange.

Several of the Vandas and the Dendrobium died under his care, but presently the strange orchid began to show signs of life. He was delighted and took his housekeeper right away from jam-making to see it at once, directly he made the discovery.

"That is a bud," he said, "and presently there will be a lot of leaves there and those little things coming out here are aerial rootlets."

"They look to me like little white fingers poking out of the brown," said his housekeeper. "I don't like them.

"Why not?"

"I don't know. They look like fingers trying to get at you. I can't help my likes and dislikes."

"I don't know for certain, but I don't think there are any orchids I know that have aerial rootlets quite like that. It may be my fancy, of course. You see they are a little flattened at the ends."

"I don't like 'em," said his housekeeper, suddenly shivering and turning away. "I know it's very silly of me—and I'm very sorry, particularly as you like the thing so much. But I can't help thinking of that corpse."

"But it may not be that particular plant. That was merely a guess of mine."

His housekeeper shrugged her shoulders. "Anyhow I don't like it," she said.

Wedderburn felt a little hurt at her dislike to the plant. But that did not prevent his talking to her about orchids generally, and this orchid in particular, whenever he felt inclined.

"There are such queer things about orchids," he said one day; "such possibilities of surprises. You know, Darwin studied their fertilisation, and showed that the whole structure of an ordinary orchid-flower was contrived in order that moths might carry the pollen from plant to plant. Well, it seems that there are lots of orchids known, the flower of which cannot possibly be used for fertilisation in that way. Some of the Cypripediums, for instance; there are no insects known that can possibly fertilise them, and some of them have never been found with seed."

"But how do they form new plants?"

"By runners and tubers, and that kind of outgrowth. That is easily explained. The puzzle is, what are the flowers for?

"Very likely," he added, "my orchid may be something extraordinary in that way. If so, I shall study it. I have often thought of making researches as Darwin did. But hitherto I have not found the time, or something else has happened to prevent it. The leaves are beginning to unfold now. I do wish you would come and see them!"

But she said that the orchid-house was so hot it gave her the headache. She had seen the plant once again, and the aerial rootlets, which were now some of them more than a foot long, had unfortunately reminded her of tentacles reaching out after something; and they got into her dreams, growing after her with incredible rapidity. So that she had settled to her entire satisfaction that she would not see that plant again, and Wedderburn had to admire its leaves alone. They were of the ordinary broad form, and a deep glossy green, with splashes and dots of deep red towards the base. He knew of no other leaves quite like them. The plant was placed on a low bench near the thermometer, and close by was a simple arrangement by which a tap dripped on the hot-water pipes and kept the air steamy. And he spent his afternoons now with some regularity meditating on the approaching flowering of this strange plant.

And at last the great thing happened. Directly he entered the little glass house he knew that the spike had burst out, although his great Palaeonopsis Lowii hid the corner where his new darling stood. There was a new odour in the air, a rich, intensely sweet scent, that overpowered every other in that crowded, steaming little greenhouse.

Directly he noticed this he hurried down to the strange orchid. And, behold! The trailing green spikes bore now three great splashes of blossom, from which this overpowering sweetness proceeded. He stopped before them in an ecstasy of admiration.

The flowers were white, with streaks of golden orange upon the petals; the heavy labellum was coiled into an intricate projection, and a wonderful bluish purple mingled there with the gold. He could see at once that the genus was altogether a new one. And the insufferable scent! How hot the place was! The blossoms swam before his eyes.

He would see if the temperature was right. He made a step towards the thermometer. Suddenly everything appeared unsteady. The bricks on the floor were dancing up and down. Then the white blossoms, the green leaves behind them, the whole green house, seemed to sweep sideways, and then in a curve upward.

At half-past four his cousin made the tea, according to their invariable custom. But Wedderburn did not come in for his tea. "He is worshipping that horrid orchid," she told herself, and waited ten minutes. "His watch must have stopped. I will go and call him."

She went straight to the hothouse, and, opening the door, called his name. There was no reply. She noticed that the air was very close, and loaded with an intense perfume. Then she saw something lying on the bricks between the hot-water pipes.

For a minute, perhaps, she stood motionless.

He was lying, face upward, at the foot of the strange orchid. The tentacle-like aerial rootlets no longer swayed freely in the air, but were crowded together, a tangle of grey ropes, and stretched tight, with their ends closely applied to his chin and neck and hands.

She did not understand. Then she saw from one of the exultant tentacles upon his cheek there trickled a little thread of blood.

With an inarticulate cry she ran towards him, and tried to pull him away from the leech-like suckers. She snapped two of these tentacles, and their sap dripped red.

Then the overpowering scent of the blossom began to make her head reel. How they clung to him! She tore at the tough ropes, and he and the white inflorescence swam about her. She felt she was fainting, knew she must not. She left him and hastily opened the nearest door, and after she had panted for a moment in the fresh air, she had a brilliant inspiration. She caught up a flower-pot and smashed in the windows at the end of the greenhouse. Then she re-entered. She tugged now with renewed strength at Wedderburn's motionless body, and brought the strange orchid crashing to the floor. It still clung with the grimmest tenacity to its victim. In a frenzy, she lugged it and him into the open air.

Then she thought of tearing through the sucker rootlets one by one, and in another minute she had released him, and was dragging him away from the horror.

He was white and bleeding from a dozen circular patches.

The odd-job man was coming up the garden, amazed at the smashing of glass, and saw her emerge, hauling the inanimate body with red-stained hands. For a moment he thought impossible things.

"Bring some water!" she cried, and her voice dispelled his fancies. When, with unnatural alacrity, he returned with the water, he found her weeping with excitement, and with Wedderburn's head upon her knee, wiping the blood from his face.

"What's the matter?" said Wedderburn, opening his eyes feebly, and closing them again at once.

"Go and tell Annie to come out here to me, and then go for Doctor Haddon at once," she said to the odd-job man so soon as he had brought the water; and added, seeing he hesitated, "I will tell you all about it when you come back."

Presently, Wedderburn opened his eyes again, and seeing that he was troubled by the puzzle of his position, she explained to him, "You fainted in the hothouse."

"And the orchid?"

"I will see to that," she said.

Wedderburn had lost a good deal of blood, but beyond that he had suffered no very great injury. They gave him brandy mixed with some pink extract of meat, and carried him upstairs to bed. His housekeeper told her incredible story in fragments to Dr. Haddon. "Come to the orchid-house and see," she said.

The cold outer air was blowing in through the open door, and the sickly perfume was almost dispelled. Most of the torn aerial rootlets lay already withered amidst a number of dark stains upon the bricks. The stem of the inflorescence was broken by the fall of the plant, and the flowers were growing limp and brown at the edges of the petals. The doctor stooped towards it, then saw that one of the aerial rootlets still stirred feebly, and hesitated.

The next morning the strange orchid still lay there, black now and putrescent. The door banged intermittently in the morning breeze, and all the array of Wedderburn's orchids was shrivelled and prostrate. But Wedderburn himself was bright and garrulous upstairs in the glory of his strange adventure.

5

The Jilting of Jane

As I sit writing in my study, I can hear our Jane bumping her way downstairs with a brush and dustpan. She used to, in the old days, sing hymn tunes, or the British national song, for the time being, to these instruments, but latterly she has been silent and even careful over her work. Time was when I prayed with fervour for such silence, and my wife with sighs for such care, but now they have come, we are not so glad as we might have anticipated we should be. Indeed, I would rejoice secretly, though it may be unmanly weakness to admit it, even to hear Jane sing "Daisy," or, by the fracture of any plate but one of Euphemia's best green ones, to learn that the period of brooding has come to an end.

Yet how we longed to hear the last of Jane's young man before we heard the last of him! Jane was always very free with her conversation to my wife, and discoursed admirably in the kitchen on a variety of topics—so well, indeed, that I sometimes left my study door open—our house is a small one—to partake of it. But after William came, it was always William, nothing but William; William this and William that; and when we thought William was worked out and exhausted altogether, then William all over again. The engagement lasted altogether three years; yet how she got introduced to William, and so became thus saturated with him, was always a secret. For my part, I believe it was at the street corner where the Reverend Barnabas Baux used to hold an open-air service after evensong on Sundays. Young Cupids were wont to flit like moths round the paraffin flare of that centre of High

Church hymn-singing. I fancy she stood singing hymns there, out of memory and her imagination, instead of coming home to get supper, and William came up beside her and said, "Hello!" "Hello yourself!" she said; and etiquette being satisfied, they proceeded to converse.

As Euphemia has a reprehensible way of letting her servants talk to her, she soon heard of him. "He is such a respectable young man, ma'am," said Jane, "you don't know." Ignoring the slur cast on her acquaintance, my wife inquired further about this William.

"He is second porter at Maynard's, the draper's," said Jane, "and gets eighteen shillings—nearly a pound—a week, m'm; and when the head porter leaves he will be head porter. His relatives are quite superior people, m'm. Not labouring people at all. His father was a greengrosher, m'm, and had a chumor, and he was bankrup' twice. And one of his sisters is in a Home for the Dying. It will be a very good match for me, m'm," said Jane, "me being an orphan girl."

"Then you are engaged to him?" asked my wife.

"Not engaged, ma'am; but he is saving money to buy a ring—hammyfist."

"Well, Jane, when you are properly engaged to him you may ask him round here on Sunday afternoons, and have tea with him in the kitchen;" for my Euphemia has a motherly conception of her duty towards her maid-servants. And presently the amethystine ring was being worn about the house, even with ostentation, and Jane developed a new way of bringing in the joint so that this gage was evident. The elder Miss Maitland was aggrieved by it, and told my wife that servants ought not to wear rings. But my wife looked it up in Enquire Within and Mrs. Motherly's Book of Household Management, and found no prohibition. So Jane remained with this happiness added to her love.

The treasure of Jane's heart appeared to me to be what respectable people call a very deserving young man. "William, ma'am," said Jane one day suddenly, with ill-concealed complacency, as she counted out the beer bottles, "William, ma'am, is a teetotaller. Yes, m'm; and he don't smoke. Smoking, ma'am," said Jane, as one who reads the heart, "do make such a dust about. Beside the waste of money. And the smell. However, I suppose it's necessary to some."

Possibly it dawned on Jane that she was reflecting a little severely upon Euphemia's comparative ill-fortune, and she added kindly, "I'm sure the master is a hangel when his pipe's alight. Compared to other times."

William was at first a rather shabby young man of the ready-made black coat school of costume. He had watery gray eyes, and a complexion appropriate to the brother of one in a Home for the Dying. Euphemia did not fancy him very much, even at the beginning. His eminent respectability was vouched for by an alpaca umbrella, from which he never allowed himself to be parted.

"He goes to chapel," said Jane. "His papa, ma'am—"

"His what, Jane?"

"His papa, ma'am, was Church: but Mr. Maynard is a Plymouth Brother, and William thinks it Policy, ma'am, to go there too. Mr. Maynard comes and talks to him quite friendly when they ain't busy, about using up all the ends of string, and about his soul. He takes a lot of notice, do Mr. Maynard, of William, and the way he saves string and his soul, ma'am."

Presently we heard that the head porter at Maynard's had left, and that William was head porter at twenty-three shillings a week. "He is really kind of over the man who drives the van," said Jane, "and him married, with three children." And she promised in the pride of her heart to make interest for us with William to favour us so that we might get our parcels of drapery from Maynard's with exceptional promptitude.

After this promotion a rapidly increasing prosperity came upon Jane's young man. One day we learned that Mr. Maynard had given William a book. "Smiles' Elp Yourself, it's called," said Jane; "but it ain't comic. It tells you how to get on in the world, and some what William read to me was lovely, ma'am."

Euphemia told me of this, laughing, and then she became suddenly grave. "Do you know, dear," she said, "Jane said one thing I did not like. She had been quiet for a minute, and then she suddenly remarked, 'William is a lot above me, ma'am, ain't he?'"

"I don't see anything in that," I said, though later my eyes were to be opened.

One Sunday afternoon about that time I was sitting at my writing-desk—possibly I was reading a good book—when a something went by the window. I heard a startled exclamation behind me, and saw

Euphemia with her hands clasped together and her eyes dilated. "George," she said in an awe-stricken whisper, "did you see?"

Then we both spoke to one another at the same moment, slowly and solemnly: "A silk hat! Yellow gloves! A new umbrella!"

"It may be my fancy, dear," said Euphemia; "but his tie was very like yours. I believe Jane keeps him in ties. She told me a little while ago, in a way that implied volumes about the rest of your costume, 'The master do wear pretty ties, ma'am.' And he echoes all your novelties."

The young couple passed our window again on their way to their customary walk. They were arm in arm. Jane looked exquisitely proud, happy, and uncomfortable, with new white cotton gloves, and William, in the silk hat, singularly genteel!

That was the culmination of Jane's happiness. When she returned, "Mr. Maynard has been talking to William, ma'am," she said, "and he is to serve customers, just like the young shop gentlemen, during the next sale. And if he gets on, he is to be made an assistant, ma'am, at the first opportunity. He has got to be as gentlemanly as he can, ma'am; and if he ain't, ma'am, he says it won't be for want of trying. Mr. Maynard has took a great fancy to him."

"He is getting on, Jane," said my wife.

"Yes, ma'am," said Jane thoughtfully; "he is getting on."

And she sighed.

That next Sunday as I drank my tea I interrogated my wife. "How is this Sunday different from all other Sundays, little woman? What has happened? Have you altered the curtains, or rearranged the furniture, or where is the indefinable difference of it? Are you wearing your hair in a new way without warning me? I clearly perceive a change in my environment, and I cannot for the life of me say what it is."

Then my wife answered in her most tragic voice, "George," she said, "that—that William has not come near the place to-day! And Jane is crying her heart out upstairs."

There followed a period of silence. Jane, as I have said, stopped singing about the house, and began to care for our brittle possessions, which struck my wife as being a very sad sign indeed. The next Sunday, and the next, Jane asked to go out, "To walk with William," and my wife, who never attempts to extort confidences, gave her permission, and asked no questions. On each occasion

Jane came back looking flushed and very determined. At last one day she became communicative.

"William is being led away," she remarked abruptly, with a catching of the breath, apropos of tablecloths. "Yes, ma'am. She is a milliner, and she can play on the piano."

"I thought," said my wife, "that you went out with him on Sunday."

"Not out with him, m'm—after him. I walked along by the side of them, and told her he was engaged to me."

"Dear me, Jane, did you? What did they do?"

"Took no more notice of me than if I was dirt. So I told her she should suffer for it."

"It could not have been a very agreeable walk, Jane."

"Not for no parties, ma'am."

"I wish," said Jane, "I could play the piano, ma'am. But anyhow, I don't mean to let her get him away from me. She's older than him, and her hair ain't gold to the roots, ma'am."

It was on the August Bank Holiday that the crisis came. We do not clearly know the details of the fray, but only such fragments as poor Jane let fall. She came home dusty, excited, and with her heart hot within her.

The milliner's mother, the milliner, and William had made a party to the Art Museum at South Kensington, I think. Anyhow, Jane had calmly but firmly accosted them somewhere in the streets, and asserted her right to what, in spite of the consensus of literature, she held to be her inalienable property. She did, I think, go so far as to lay hands on him. They dealt with her in a crushingly superior way. They "called a cab." There was a "scene," William being pulled away into the four-wheeler by his future wife and mother-in-law from the reluctant hands of our discarded Jane. There were threats of giving her "in charge."

"My poor Jane!" said my wife, mincing veal as though she was mincing William. "It's a shame of them. I would think no more of him. He is not worthy of you."

"No, m'm," said Jane. "He is weak.

"But it's that woman has done it," said Jane. She was never known to bring herself to pronounce "that woman's" name or to admit her girlishness. "I can't think what minds some women must have—to try and get a girl's young man away from her. But there, it only hurts to talk about it," said Jane.

Thereafter our house rested from William. But there was something in the manner of Jane's scrubbing the front doorstep or sweeping out the rooms, a certain viciousness, that persuaded me that the story had not yet ended.

"Please, m'm, may I go and see a wedding to-morrow?" said Jane one day.

My wife knew by instinct whose wedding. "Do you think it is wise, Jane?" she said.

"I would like to see the last of him," said Jane.

"My dear," said my wife, fluttering into my room about twenty minutes after Jane had started, "Jane has been to the boot-hole and taken all the left-off boots and shoes, and gone off to the wedding with them in a bag. Surely she cannot mean—"

"Jane," I said, "is developing character. Let us hope for the best."

Jane came back with a pale, hard face. All the boots seemed to be still in her bag, at which my wife heaved a premature sigh of relief. We heard her go upstairs and replace the boots with considerable emphasis.

"Quite a crowd at the wedding, ma'am," she said presently, in a purely conversational style, sitting in our little kitchen, and scrubbing the potatoes; "and such a lovely day for them." She proceeded to numerous other details, clearly avoiding some cardinal incident.

"It was all extremely respectable and nice, ma'am; but her father didn't wear a black coat, and looked quite out of place, ma'am. Mr. Piddingquirk—"

"Who?"

"Mr. Piddingquirk—William that was, ma'am—had white gloves, and a coat like a clergyman, and a lovely chrysanthemum. He looked so nice, ma'am. And there was red carpet down, just like for gentlefolks. And they say he gave the clerk four shillings, ma'am. It was a real kerridge they had—not a fly. When they came out of church there was rice-throwing, and her two little sisters dropping dead flowers. And someone threw a slipper, and then I threw a boot—"

"Threw a boot, Jane!"

"Yes, ma'am. Aimed at her. But it hit him. Yes, ma'am, hard. Gev him a black eye, I should think. I only threw that one. I hadn't the heart to try again. All the little boys cheered when it hit him."

After an interval—"I am sorry the boot hit him."

Another pause. The potatoes were being scrubbed violently. "He always was a bit above me, you know, ma'am. And he was led away."

The potatoes were more than finished. Jane rose sharply with a sigh, and rapped the basin down on the table.

"I don't care," she said. "I don't care a rap. He will find out his mistake yet. It serves me right. I was stuck up about him. I ought not to have looked so high. And I am glad things are as things are."

My wife was in the kitchen, seeing to the cookery. After the confession of the boot-throwing, she must have watched poor Jane fuming with a certain dismay in those brown eyes of hers. But I imagine they softened again very quickly, and then Jane's must have met them.

"Oh, ma'am," said Jane, with an astonishing change of note, "think of all that might have been! Oh, ma'am, I could have been so happy! I ought to have known, but I didn't know...You're very kind to let me talk to you, ma'am...for it's hard on me, ma'am...it's har-r-r-r-d—"

And I gather that Euphemia so far forgot herself as to let Jane sob out some of the fullness of her heart on a sympathetic shoulder. My Euphemia, thank Heaven, has never properly grasped the importance of "keeping up her position." And since that fit of weeping, much of the accent of bitterness has gone out of Jane's scrubbing and brush-work.

Indeed, something passed the other day with the butcher-boy—but that scarcely belongs to this story. However, Jane is young still, and time and change are at work with her. We all have our sorrows, but I do not believe very much in the existence of sorrows that never heal.

6

The Lord of the Dynamos

The chief attendant of the three dynamos that buzzed and rattled at Camberwell, and kept the electric railway going, came out of Yorkshire, and his name was James Holroyd. He was a practical electrician, but fond of whisky, a heavy red-haired brute with irregular teeth. He doubted the existence of the Deity, but accepted Carnot's cycle, and he had read Shakespeare and found him weak in chemistry. His helper came out of the mysterious East, and his name was Azuma-zi. But Holroyd called him Pooh-bah. Holroyd liked a nigger help because he would stand kicking—a habit with Holroyd—and did not pry into the machinery and try to learn the ways of it. Certain odd possibilities of the negro mind brought into abrupt contact with the crown of our civilisation Holroyd never fully realised, though just at the end he got some inkling of them.

To define Azuma-zi was beyond ethnology. He was, perhaps, more negroid than anything else, though his hair was curly rather than frizzy, and his nose had a bridge. Moreover, his skin was brown rather than black, and the whites of his eyes were yellow. His broad cheek-bones and narrow chin gave his face something of the viperine V. His head too, was broad behind, and low and narrow at the forehead, as if his brain had been twisted round in the reverse way to a European's. He was short of stature and still shorter of English. In conversation he made numerous odd noises of no known marketable value, and his infrequent words were carved and wrought into heraldic grotesqueness. Holroyd tried to elucidate his religious beliefs, and—especially after whisky—

lectured to him against superstition and missionaries. Azuma-zi, however, shirked the discussion of his gods, even though he was kicked for it.

Azuma-zi had come, clad in white but insufficient raiment, out of the stoke-hole of the Lord Clive, from the Straits Settlements, and beyond, into London. He had heard even in his youth of the greatness and riches of London, where all the women are white and fair, and even the beggars in the streets are white, and he arrived, with newly-earned gold coins in his pocket, to worship at the shrine of civilisation. The day of his landing was a dismal one; the sky was dun, and a wind-worried drizzle filtered down to the greasy streets, but he plunged boldly into the delights of Shadwell, and was presently cast up, shattered in health, civilised in costume, penniless and, except in matters of the direst necessity, practically a dumb animal, to toil for James Holroyd and to be bullied by him in the dynamo shed at Camberwell. And to James Holroyd bullying was a labour of love.

There were three dynamos with their engines at Camberwell. The two that had been there since the beginning were small machines; the larger one was new. The smaller machines made a reasonable noise; their straps hummed over the drums, every now and then the brushes buzzed and fizzled, and the air churned steadily, whoo! whoo! whoo! Between their poles. One was loose in its foundations and kept the shed vibrating. But the big dynamo drowned these little noises altogether with the sustained drone of its iron core, which somehow set part of the ironwork humming. The place made the visitor's head reel with the throb, throb, throb of the engines, the rotation of the big wheels, the spinning ball-valves, the occasional spittings of the steam, and over all the deep, unceasing, surging note of the big dynamo. This last noise was from an engineering point of view a defect, but Azuma-zi accounted it unto the monster for mightiness and pride.

If it were possible we would have the noises of that shed always about the reader as he reads, we would tell all our story to such an accompaniment. It was a steady stream of din, from which the ear picked out first one thread and then another; there was the intermittent snorting, panting, and seething of the steam-engines, the suck and thud of their pistons, the dull beat on the air as the spokes of the great driving wheels came round, a note the leather straps made as they ran tighter and looser, and a fretful tumult from the dynamos; and over all, sometimes inaudible, as the ear tired of it, and then creeping back upon the senses again, was this trombone note of the big machine. The floor never felt steady and quiet beneath one's feet, but quivered and jarred. It was a confusing, unsteady place, and enough to send anyone's thoughts jerking into odd zigzags. And for three months, while the big strike of the engineers was in progress, Holroyd, who was a blackleg, and Azuma-zi, who was a mere black, were never out of the stir and eddy of it, but slept and fed in the little wooden shanty between the shed and the gates.

Holroyd delivered a theological lecture on the text of his big machine soon after Azuma-zi came. He had to shout to be heard in the din. "Look at that," said Holroyd; "where's your 'eathen idol to match 'im?" And Azuma-zi looked. For a moment Holroyd was inaudible, and then Azuma-zi heard: "Kill a hundred men. Twelve per cent on the ordinary shares," said Holroyd, "and that's something like a Gord!"

Holroyd was proud of his big dynamo, and expatiated upon its size and power to Azuma-zi until heaven knows what odd currents of thought, that and the incessant whirling and shindy, set up within the curly black cranium. He would explain in the most graphic manner the dozen or so ways in which a man might be killed by it, and once he gave Azuma-zi a shock as a sample of its quality. After that, in the breathing times of his labour—it was heavy labour, being not only his own, but most of Holroyd's—Azuma-zi would sit and watch the big machine. Now and then the brushes would sparkle and spit blue flashes, at which Holroyd would swear, but all the rest was as smooth and rhythmic as breathing. The band ran shouting over the shaft, and ever behind one as one watched was the complacent thud of the piston. So it lived all day in this big airy shed, with him and Holroyd to wait upon it; not prisoned up and slaving to drive a ship as the other engines he knew—mere captive devils of the British Solomon—had been, but a machine enthroned. Those two smaller dynamos, Azuma-zi by force of contrast despised; the large one he privately christened the Lord of the Dynamos. They were fretful and irregular, but the big dynamo was steady. How great it was! How serene and easy in its working! Greater and calmer even than the Buddhas he had seen at Rangoon, and yet not motionless, but living! The great black coils spun, spun, spun, the rings ran round under the brushes, and the deep note of its coil steadied the whole. It affected Azuma-zi queerly.

Azuma-zi was not fond of labour. He would sit about and watch the Lord of the Dynamos while Holroyd went away to persuade the yard porter to get whisky, although his proper place was not in the dynamo shed but behind the engines and, moreover if Holroyd caught him skulking he got hit for it with a rod of stout copper wire. He would go and stand close to the colossus and look up at the great leather band running overhead. There was a black patch on the band that came round, and it pleased him somehow among all the clatter to watch this return again and again. Odd thoughts spun with the whirl of it. Scientific people tell us that savages give souls to rocks and trees—and a machine is a thousand times more alive than a rock or a tree. And Azuma-zi was practically a savage still; the veneer of civilisation lay no deeper than his slop suit, his bruises, and the coal grime on his face and hands. His father before him had worshipped a meteoric stone, kindred blood it may be had splashed the broad wheels of Juggernaut.

He took every opportunity Holroyd gave him of touching and handling the great dynamo that was fascinating him. He polished and cleaned it until the metal parts were blinding in the sun. He felt a mysterious sense of service in doing this. He would go up to it and touch its spinning coils gently. The gods he had worshipped were all far away. The people in London hid their gods.

At last his dim feelings grew more distinct, and took shape in thoughts and at last in acts. When he came into the roaring shed one morning he salaamed to the Lord of the Dynamos, and then when Holroyd was away, he went and whispered to the thundering machine that he was its servant, and prayed it to have pity on him and save him from Holroyd. As he did so a rare gleam of light came in through the open archway of the throbbing machine-shed, and the Lord of the Dynamos, as he whirled and roared, was radiant with pale gold. Then Azuma-zi knew that his service was acceptable to his Lord. After that he did not feel so lonely as he had done, and he had indeed been very much alone in London. And even when his work-time was over, which was rare, he loitered about the shed.

The next time Holroyd maltreated him, Azuma-zi went presently to the Lord of the Dynamos and whispered, "Thou seest, O my Lord!" and the angry whir of the machinery seemed to answer him. Thereafter it appeared to him that whenever Holroyd came into the shed a different note mingled with the sounds of the dynamo. "My Lord bides his time," said Azuma-zi to himself. "The iniquity of the fool is not yet ripe." And he waited and watched for the day of reckoning. One day there was evidence of short circuiting, and Holroyd, making an unwary examination—it was in the afternoon—got a rather severe shock. Azuma-zi from behind the engine saw him jump off and curse at the peccant coil.

"He is warned," said Azuma-zi to himself. "Surely my Lord is very patient."

Holroyd had at first initiated his "nigger" into such elementary conceptions of the dynamo's working as would enable him to take temporary charge of the shed in his absence. But when he noticed the manner in which Azuma-zi hung about the monster he became suspicious. He dimly perceived his assistant was "up to something," and connecting him with the anointing of the coils with oil that had rotted the varnish in one place, he issued an edict, shouted above the confusion of the machinery, "Don't 'ee go nigh that big dynamo any more, Pooh-bah, or a'll take thy skin off!" Besides, if it pleased Azuma-zi to be near the big machine, it was plain sense and decency to keep him away from it.

Azuma-zi obeyed at the time, but later he was caught bowing before the Lord of the Dynamos. At which Holroyd twisted his arm and kicked him as he turned to go away. As Azuma-zi presently stood behind the engine and glared at the back of the hated Holroyd, the noises of the machinery took a new rhythm, and sounded like four words in his native tongue.

It is hard to say exactly what madness is. I fancy Azuma-zi was mad. The incessant din and whirl of the dynamo shed may have churned up his little store of knowledge and his big store of superstitious fancy, at last, into something akin to frenzy. At any rate, when the idea of making Holroyd a sacrifice to the Dynamo Fetich was thus suggested to him, it filled him with a strange tumult of exultant emotion.

That night the two men and their black shadows were alone in the shed together. The shed was lit with one big arc-light that winked and flickered purple. The shadows lay black behind the dynamos, the ball governors of the engines whirled from light to darkness, and their pistons beat loud and steady. The world outside seen through the open end of the shed seemed incredibly dim and remote. It seemed absolutely silent too, since the riot of the machinery drowned every external sound. Far away was the black fence of the yard with grey shadowy houses behind, and above was the deep blue sky and the pale little stars. Azuma-zi suddenly walked across the centre of the shed above which the leather bands were running, and went into the shadow by the big dynamo. Holroyd heard a click, and the spin of the armature changed.

"What are you dewin' with that switch?" he bawled in surprise. "Han't I told you—"

Then he saw the set expression of Azuma-zi's eyes as the Asiatic came out of the shadow towards him.

In another moment the two men were grappling fiercely in front of the great dynamo.

"You coffee-headed fool!" gasped Holroyd, with a brown hand at his throat. "Keep off those contact rings." In another moment he was tripped and reeling back upon the Lord of the Dynamos. He instinctively loosened his grip upon his antagonist to save himself from the machine.

The messenger, sent in furious haste from the station, to find out what had happened in the dynamo shed, met Azuma-zi at the porter's lodge by the gate. Azuma-zi tried to explain something, but the messenger could make nothing of the black's incoherent English, and hurried on to the shed. The machines were all noisily at work, and nothing seemed to be disarranged. There was, however, a queer smell of singed hair. Then he saw an odd-looking crumpled mass clinging to the front of the big dynamo, and approaching, recognised the distorted remains of Holroyd.

The man stared and hesitated a moment. Then he saw the face, and shut his eyes convulsively. He turned on his heel before he opened them, so that he should not see Holroyd again, and went out of the shed to get advice and help.

When Azuma-zi saw Holroyd die in the grip of the Great Dynamo he had been a little scared about the consequences of his act. Yet he felt strangely elated, and knew that the favour of the Lord Dynamo was upon him. His plan was already settled when he met the man coming from the station, and the scientific manager who speedily arrived on the scene jumped at the obvious conclusion of suicide. This expert scarcely noticed Azuma-zi, except to ask a few questions. Did he see Holroyd kill himself? Azuma-zi explained that he had been out of sight at the engine furnace until he heard a difference in the noise from the dynamo. It was not a difficult examination, being untinctured by suspicion.

The distorted remains of Holroyd, which the electrician removed from the machine, were hastily covered by the porter with a coffee-stained tablecloth. Somebody, by a happy inspiration, fetched a medical man. The expert was chiefly anxious to get the machine at work again, for seven or eight trains had stopped midway in the stuffy tunnels of the electric railway. Azuma-zi, answering or misunderstanding the questions of the people who had by authority or impudence come into the shed, was presently sent back to the stoke-hole by the scientific manager. Of course a crowd collected outside the gates of the yard—a crowd, for no known reason, always hovers for a day or two near the scene of a sudden death in London; two or three reporters percolated somehow into the engine shed, and one even got to Azuma-zi; but the scientific expert cleared them out again, being himself an amateur journalist.

Presently the body was carried away, and public interest departed with it. Azuma-zi remained very quietly at his furnace, seeing over and over again in the coals a figure that wriggled violently and became still. An hour after the murder, to anyone coming into the shed it would have looked exactly as if nothing had ever happened there. Peeping presently from his engine-room the black saw the Lord Dynamo spin and whirl beside his little brothers, and the driving-wheels were beating round, and the steam in the pistons went thud, thud, exactly as it had been earlier in the evening. After all, from the mechanical point of view, it had been a most insignificant incident—the mere temporary deflection of a current. But now the slender form and slender shadow of the scientific manager replaced the sturdy outline of Holroyd travelling up and down the lane of light upon the vibrating floor under the straps between the engines and the dynamos.

"Have I not served my Lord?" said Azuma-zi inaudibly, from his shadow, and the note of the great dynamo rang out full and clear. As he looked at the big whirling mechanism the strange fascination of it that had been a little in abeyance since Holroyd's death, resumed its sway.

Never had Azuma-zi seen a man killed so swiftly and pitilessly. The big humming machine had slain its victim without wavering for a second from its steady beating. It was indeed a mighty god.

The unconscious scientific manager stood with his back to him, scribbling on a piece of paper. His shadow lay at the foot of the monster.

"Was the Lord Dynamo still hungry? His servant was ready."

Azuma-zi made a stealthy step forward; then stopped. The scientific manager suddenly ceased his writing, walked down the shed to the endmost of the dynamos, and began to examine the brushes.

Azuma-zi hesitated, and then slipped across noiselessly into shadow by the switch. There he waited. Presently the manager's footsteps could be heard returning. He stopped in his old position, unconscious of the stoker crouching ten feet away from him. Then the big dynamo suddenly fizzled, and in another moment Azuma-zi had sprung out of the darkness upon him.

The scientific manager was gripped round the body and swung towards the big dynamo. Kicking with his knee and forcing his antagonist's head down with his hands, he loosened the grip on his waist and swung round away from the machine. Then the black grasped him again, putting a curly head against his chest, and they swayed and panted as it seemed for an age or so. Then the scientific manager was impelled to catch a black ear in his teeth and bite furiously. The black yelled hideously.

They rolled over on the floor, and the black, who had apparently slipped from the vice of the teeth or parted with some ear—the scientific manager wondered which at the time—tried to throttle him. The scientific manager was making some ineffectual attempts to claw something with his hands and to kick, when the welcome sound of quick footsteps sounded on the floor. The next moment Azuma-zi had left him and darted towards the big dynamo. There was a splutter amid the roar.

The officer of the company who had entered, stood staring as Azuma-zi caught the naked terminals in his hands, gave one horrible convulsion, and then hung motionless from the machine, his face violently distorted.

"I'm jolly glad you came in when you did," said the scientific manager, still sitting on the floor.

He looked at the still quivering figure.

"It's not a nice death to die, apparently—but it is quick."

The official was still staring at the body. He was a man of slow apprehension.

There was a pause.

The scientific manager got up on his feet rather awkwardly. He ran his fingers along his collar thoughtfully, and moved his head to and fro several times.

"Poor Holroyd! I see now." Then almost mechanically he went towards the switch in the shadow and turned the current into the railway circuit again. As he did so the singed body loosened its grip upon the machine and fell forward on its face. The core of the dynamo roared out loud and clear, and the armature beat the air.

So ended prematurely the Worship of the Dynamo Deity, perhaps the most short-lived of all religions. Yet withal it could at least boast a Martyrdom and a Human Sacrifice.

7

The Triumphs of a Taxidermist

Here are some of the secrets of taxidermy. They were told me by the taxidermist in a mood of elation. He told me them in the time between the first glass of whisky and the fourth, when a man is no longer cautious and yet not drunk. We sat in his den together; his library it was, his sitting and his eating-room—separated by a bead curtain, so far as the sense of sight went, from the noisome den where he plied his trade.

He sat on a deck chair, and when he was not tapping refractory bits of coal with them, he kept his feet—on which he wore, after the manner of sandals, the holey relics of a pair of carpet slippers—out of the way upon the mantelpiece, among the glass eyes. And his trousers, by-the-bye—though they have nothing to do with his triumphs—were a most horrible yellow plaid, such as they made when our fathers wore side-whiskers and there were crinolines in the land. Further, his hair was black, his face rosy, and his eye a fiery brown; and his coat was chiefly of grease upon a basis of velveteen. And his pipe had a bowl of china showing the Graces, and his spectacles were always askew, the left eye glaring nakedly at you, small and penetrating; the right, seen through a glass darkly, magnified and mild. Thus his discourse ran: "There never was a man who could stuff like me, Bellows, never. I have stuffed elephants and I have stuffed moths, and the things, have looked all the livelier and better for it. And I have stuffed human beings—chiefly amateur ornithologists. But I stuffed a nigger once.

"No, there is no law against it. I made him with all his fingers out and used him as a hat-rack, but that fool Homersby got up a quarrel with him late one night and spoilt him. That was before your time. It is hard to get skins, or I would have another.

"Unpleasant? I don't see it. Seems to me taxidermy is a promising third course to burial or cremation. You could keep all your dear ones by you. Bric-à-brac of that sort stuck about the house would be as good as most company, and much less expensive. You might have them fitted up with clockwork to do things.

"Of course they would have to be varnished, but they need not shine more than lots of people do naturally. Old Manningtree's bald head...Anyhow, you could talk to them without interruption. Even aunts. There is a great future before taxidermy, depend upon it. There is fossils again...."

He suddenly became silent.

"No, I don't think I ought to tell you that." He sucked at his pipe thoughtfully. "Thanks, yes. Not too much water."

"Of course, what I tell you now will go no further. You know I have made some dodos and a great auk? No! Evidently you are an amateur at taxidermy. My dear fellow, half the great auks in the world are about as genuine as the handkerchief of Saint Veronica, as the Holy Coat of Treves. We make 'em of grebes' feathers and the like. And the great auk's eggs too!"

"Good heavens!"

"Yes, we make them out of fine porcelain. I tell you it is worth while. They fetch—one fetched L300 only the other day. That one was really genuine, I believe, but of course one is never certain. It is very fine work, and afterwards you have to get them dusty, for no one who owns one of these precious eggs has ever the temerity to clean the thing. That's the beauty of the business. Even if they suspect an egg they do not like to examine it too closely. It's such brittle capital at the best.

"You did not know that taxidermy rose to heights like that. My boy, it has risen higher. I have rivalled the hands of Nature herself. One of the genuine great auks—"his voice fell to a whisper—"one of the genuine great auks was made by me.

"No. You must study ornithology, and find out which it is yourself. And what is more, I have been approached by a syndicate of dealers to stock one of the unexplored skerries to the north of

Iceland with specimens. I may—some day. But I have another little thing in hand just now. Ever heard of the dinornis?

"It is one of those big birds recently extinct in New Zealand. 'Moa' is its common name, so called because extinct: there is no moa now. See? Well, they have got bones of it, and from some of the marshes even feathers and dried bits of skin. Now, I am going to—well, there is no need to make any bones about it—going to forge a complete stuffed moa. I know a chap out there who will pretend to make the find in a kind of antiseptic swamp, and say he stuffed it at once, as it threatened to fall to pieces. The feathers are peculiar, but I have got a simply lovely way of dodging up singed bits of ostrich plume. Yes, that is the new smell you noticed. They can only discover the fraud with a microscope, and they will hardly care to pull a nice specimen to bits for that.

"In this way, you see, I give my little push in the advancement of science.

"But all this is merely imitating Nature. I have done more than that in my time. I have—beaten her."

He took his feet down from the mantel-board, and leant over confidentially towards me. "I have created birds," he said in a low voice. "New birds. Improvements. Like no birds that was ever seen before."

He resumed his attitude during an impressive silence.

"Enrich the universe; rather. Some of the birds I made were new kinds of humming birds, and very beautiful little things, but some of them were simply rum. The rummest, I think, was the Anomalopteryx Jejuna. Jejunus-a-um—empty—so called because there was really nothing in it; a thoroughly empty bird—except for stuffing. Old Javvers has the thing now, and I suppose he is almost as proud of it as I am. It is a masterpiece, Bellows. It has all the silly clumsiness of your pelican, all the solemn want of dignity of your parrot, all the gaunt ungainliness of a flamingo, with all the extravagant chromatic conflict of a mandarin duck. Such a bird. I made it out of the skeletons of a stork and a toucan and a job lot of feathers. Taxidermy of that kind is just pure joy, Bellows, to a real artist in the art.

"How did I come to make it? Simple enough, as all great inventions are. One of those young genii who write us Science Notes in the papers got hold of a German pamphlet about the birds of New Zealand, and translated some of it by means of a dictionary and his mother-wit—he must have been one of a very large family with a small mother—and he got mixed between the living apteryx and the extinct anomalopteryx; talked about a bird five feet high, living in the jungles of the North Island, rare, shy, specimens difficult to obtain, and so on. Javvers, who even for a collector, is a miraculously ignorant man, read these paragraphs, and swore he would have the thing at any price. Raided the dealers with enquiries. It shows what a man can do by persistence—will-power. Here was a bird-collector swearing he would have a specimen of a bird that did not exist, that never had existed, and which for very shame of its own profane ungainliness, probably would not exist now if it could help itself. And he got it. He got it.

"Have some more whisky, Bellows?" said the taxidermist, rousing himself from a transient contemplation of the mysteries of will-power and the collecting turn of mind. And, replenished, he proceeded to tell me of how he concocted a most attractive mermaid, and how an itinerant preacher, who could not get an audience because of it, smashed it because it was idolatry, or worse, at Burslem Wakes. But as the conversation of all the parties to this transaction, creator, would-be preserver, and destroyer, was uniformly unfit for publication, this cheerful incident must still remain unprinted.

The reader unacquainted with the dark ways of the collector may perhaps be inclined to doubt my taxidermist, but so far as great auks' eggs, and the bogus stuffed birds are concerned, I find that he has the confirmation of distinguished ornithological writers. And the note about the New Zealand bird certainly appeared in a morning paper of unblemished reputation, for the taxidermist keeps a copy and has shown it to me.

8

Through a Window

After his legs were set, they carried Bailey into the study and put him on a couch before the open window. There he lay, a live—even a feverish man down to the loins, and below that a double-barrelled mummy swathed in white wrappings. He tried to read, even tried to write a little, but most of the time he looked out of the window.

He had thought the window cheerful to begin with, but now he thanked God for it many times a day. Within, the room was dim and grey, and in the reflected light, the wear of the furniture showed plainly. His medicine and drink stood on the little table, with such litter as the bare branches of a bunch of grapes, or the ashes of a cigar upon a green plate, or a day old evening paper. The view outside was flooded with light, and across the corner of it came the head of the acacia, and at the foot, the top of the balcony-railing of hammered iron. In the foreground was the weltering silver of the river, never quiet and yet never tiresome. Beyond was the reedy bank, a broad stretch of meadow land, and then a dark line of trees ending in a group of poplars at the distant bend of the river, and upstanding behind them, a square church tower.

Up and down the river, all day long, things were passing. Now a string of barges drifting down to London, piled with lime or barrels of beer; then a steam-launch, disengaging heavy masses of black smoke, and disturbing the whole width of the river with long rolling waves; then an impetuous electric launch, and then a boatload of pleasure-seekers, a solitary sculler, or a four from some rowing club. Perhaps the river was quietest of a morning or late at night. One moonlight night some people drifted down singing, and with a zither playing—it sounded very pleasantly across the water.

In a few days Bailey began to recognise some of the craft; in a week he knew the intimate history of half-a-dozen. The launch Luzon, from Fitzgibbon's, two miles up, would go fretting by, sometimes three or four times a day, conspicuous with its colouring of Indian-red and yellow, and its two Oriental attendants; and one day, to Bailey's vast amusement, the house-boat Purple Emperor came to a stop outside, and breakfasted in the most shameless domesticity. Then one afternoon, the captain of a slow-moving barge began a quarrel with his wife as they came into sight from the left, and had carried it to personal violence before he vanished behind the window-frame to the right. Bailey regarded all this as an entertainment got up to while away his illness, and applauded all the more, these moving incidents. Mrs. Green, coming in at rare intervals with his meals, would catch him clapping his hands or softly crying, "Encore!" But the river players had other engagements, and his encore went unheeded.

"I should never have thought I could take such an interest in things that did not concern me," said Bailey to Wilderspin, who used to come in, in his nervous, friendly way and try to comfort the sufferer by being talked to. "I thought this idle capacity was distinctive of little children and old maids. But it's just circumstances. I simply can't work, and things have to drift; it's no good to fret and struggle. And so I lie here and am as amused as a baby with a rattle, at this river and its affairs.

"Sometimes, of course, it gets a bit dull, but not often.

"I would give anything, Wilderspin, for a swamp—just one swamp—once. Heads swimming and a steam launch to the rescue, and a chap or so hauled out with a boat-hook...There goes Fitzgibbon's launch! They have a new boat-hook, I see, and the little blackie is still in the dumps. I don't think he's very well, Wilderspin. He's been like that for two or three days, squatting sulky-fashion and meditating over the churning of the water. Unwholesome for him to be always staring at the frothy water running away from the stern."

They watched the little steamer fuss across the patch of sunlit river, suffer momentary occultation from the acacia, and glide out of sight behind the dark window-frame.

"I'm getting a wonderful eye for details," said Bailey: "I spotted that new boat-hook at once. The other nigger is a funny little chap. He never used to swagger with the old boat-hook like that."

"Malays, aren't they?" said Wilderspin.

"Don't know," said Bailey. "I thought one called all that sort of mariner Lascar."

Then he began to tell Wilderspin what he knew of the private affairs of the house-boat, Purple Emperor. "Funny," he said, "how these people come from all points of the compass—from Oxford and Windsor, from Asia and Africa—and gather and pass opposite the window just to entertain me. One man floated out of the infinite the day before yesterday, caught one perfect crab opposite, lost and recovered a scull, and passed on again. Probably he will never come into my life again. So far as I am concerned, he has lived and had his little troubles, perhaps thirty—perhaps forty—years on the earth, merely to make an ass of himself for three minutes in front of my window. Wonderful thing, Wilderspin, if you come to think of it."

"Yes," said Wilderspin; "isn't it?"

A day or two after this Bailey had a brilliant morning. Indeed, towards the end of the affair, it became almost as exciting as any window show, very well could be. We will, however begin at the beginning.

Bailey was all alone in the house, for his housekeeper had gone into the town three miles away to pay bills, and the servant had her holiday. The morning began dull. A canoe went up about half-past nine, and later a boatload of camping men came down. But this was mere margin. Things became cheerful about ten o'clock.

It began with something white fluttering in the remote distance where the three poplars marked the river bend. "Pocket-handkerchief," said Bailey, when he saw it "No, too big! Flag perhaps."

However, it was not a flag, for it jumped about. "Man in whites running fast, and this way," said Bailey. "That's luck! But his whites are precious loose!"

Then a singular thing happened. There was a minute pink gleam among the dark trees in the distance, and a little puff of pale grey that began to drift and vanish eastward. The man in white jumped and continued running. Presently the report of the shot arrived.

"What the devil!" said Bailey. "Looks as if someone was shooting at him."

He sat up stiffly and stared hard. The white figure was coming along the pathway through the corn. "It's one of those niggers from the Fitzgibbon's," said Bailey; "or may I be hanged! I wonder why he keeps sawing with his arm."

Then three other figures became indistinctly visible against the dark background of the trees.

Abruptly on the opposite bank a man walked into the picture. He was black-bearded, dressed in flannels, had a red belt, and a vast, grey felt hat. He walked, leaning very much forward and with his hands swinging before him. Behind him one could see the grass swept by the towing-rope of the boat he was dragging. He was steadfastly regarding the white figure that was hurrying through the corn. Suddenly he stopped. Then, with a peculiar gesture, Bailey could see that he began pulling in the tow-rope hand over hand. Over the water could be heard the voices of the people in the still invisible boat.

"What are you after, Hagshot?" said someone.

The individual with the red belt shouted something that was inaudible, and went on lugging in the rope, looking over his shoulder at the advancing white figure as he did so. He came down the bank, and the rope bent a lane among the reeds and lashed the water between his pulls.

Then just the bows of the boat came into view, with the towing-mast and a tall, fair-haired man standing up and trying to see over the bank. The boat bumped unexpectedly among the reeds, and the tall, fair-haired man disappeared suddenly, having apparently fallen back into the invisible part of the boat. There was a curse and some indistinct laughter. Hagshot did not laugh, but hastily clambered into the boat and pushed off. Abruptly the boat passed out of Bailey's sight.

But it was still audible. The melody of voices suggested that its occupants were busy telling each other what to do.

The running figure was drawing near the bank. Bailey could now see clearly that it was one of Fitzgibbon's Orientals, and began to realise what the sinuous thing the man carried in his hand might be. Three other men followed one another through the corn, and the foremost carried what was probably the gun. They were perhaps two hundred yards or more behind the Malay.

"It's a man hunt, by all that's holy!" said Bailey.

The Malay stopped for a moment and surveyed the bank to the right. Then he left the path, and breaking through the corn, vanished in that direction. The three pursuers followed suit, and their heads and gesticulating arms above the corn, after a brief interval, also went out of Bailey's field of vision.

Bailey so far forgot himself as to swear. "Just as things were getting lively!" he said. Something like a woman's shriek came through the air. Then shouts, a howl, a dull whack upon the balcony outside that made Bailey jump, and then the report of a gun.

"This is precious hard on an invalid," said Bailey.

But more was to happen yet in his picture. In fact, a great deal more. The Malay appeared again, running now along the bank up stream. His stride had more swing and less pace in it than before. He was threatening someone ahead with the ugly krees he carried. The blade, Bailey noticed, was dull—it did not shine as steel should.

Then came the tall, fair man, brandishing a boat-hook, and after him three other men in boating costume, running clumsily with oars. The man with the grey hat and red belt was not with them. After an interval the three men with the gun reappeared, still in the corn, but now near the river bank. They emerged upon the towing-path, and hurried after the others. The opposite bank was left blank and desolate again.

The sick-room was disgraced by more profanity. "I would give my life to see the end of this," said Bailey. There were indistinct shouts up stream. Once they seemed to be coming nearer, but they disappointed him.

Bailey sat and grumbled. He was still grumbling when his eye caught something black and round among the waves. "Hullo!" he said. He looked narrowly and saw two triangular black bodies frothing every now and then about a yard in front of this.

He was still doubtful when the little band of pursuers came into sight again, and began to point to this floating object. They were talking eagerly. Then the man with the gun took aim.

"He's swimming the river, by George!" said Bailey.

The Malay looked round, saw the gun, and went under. He came up so close to Bailey's bank of the river that one of the bars of the balcony hid him for a moment. As he emerged the man with the gun fired. The Malay kept steadily onward—Bailey could see the wet hair on his forehead now and the krees between his teeth—and was presently hidden by the balcony.

This seemed to Bailey an unendurable wrong. The man was lost to him for ever now, so he thought. Why couldn't the brute have got himself decently caught on the opposite bank, or shot in the water?

"It's worse than Edwin Drood," said Bailey.

Over the river, too, things had become an absolute blank. All seven men had gone down stream again, probably to get the boat and follow across. Bailey listened and waited. There was silence. "Surely it's not over like this," said Bailey.

Five minutes passed—ten minutes. Then a tug with two barges went up stream. The attitudes of the men upon these were the attitudes of those who see nothing remarkable in earth, water, or sky. Clearly the whole affair had passed out of sight of the river. Probably the hunt had gone into the beech woods behind the house.

"Confound it!" said Bailey. "To be continued again, and no chance this time of the sequel. But this is hard on a sick man."

He heard a step on the staircase behind him and looking round saw the door open. Mrs. Green came in and sat down, panting. She still had her bonnet on, her purse in her hand, and her little brown basket upon her arm. "Oh, there!" she said, and left Bailey to imagine the rest.

"Have a little whisky and water, Mrs. Green, and tell me about it," said Bailey.

Sipping a little, the lady began to recover her powers of explanation.

One of those black creatures at the Fitzgibbon's had gone mad, and was running about with a big knife, stabbing people. He had killed a groom, and stabbed the under-butler, and almost cut the arm off a boating gentleman.

"Running amuck with a krees," said Bailey. "I thought that was it."

And he was hiding in the wood when she came through it from the town.

"What! Did he run after you?" asked Bailey, with a certain touch of glee in his voice.

"No, that was the horrible part of it." Mrs. Green explained. She had been right through the woods and had never known he was there. It was only when she met young Mr. Fitzgibbon carrying his gun in the shrubbery that she heard anything about it. Apparently, what upset Mrs. Green was the lost opportunity for emotion. She was determined, however, to make the most of what was left her.

"To think he was there all the time!" she said, over and over again.

Bailey endured this patiently enough for perhaps ten minutes. At last he thought it advisable to assert himself. "It's twenty past one, Mrs. Green," he said. "Don't you think it time you got me something to eat?"

This brought Mrs. Green suddenly to her knees.

"Oh Lord, sir!" she said. "Oh! Don't go making me go out of this room sir, till I know he's caught. He might have got into the house, sir. He might be creeping, creeping, with that knife of his, along the passage this very—"

She broke off suddenly and glared over him at the window. Her lower jaw dropped. Bailey turned his head sharply.

For the space of half a second things seemed just as they were. There was the tree, the balcony, the shining river, the distant church tower. Then he noticed that the acacia was displaced about a foot to the right, and that it was quivering, and the leaves were rustling. The tree was shaken violently, and a heavy panting was audible.

In another moment a hairy brown hand had appeared and clutched the balcony railings, and in another the face of the Malay was peering through these at the man on the couch. His expression was an unpleasant grin, by reason of the krees he held between his teeth, and he was bleeding from an ugly wound in his cheek. His hair wet to drying stuck out like horns from his head. His body was bare save for the wet trousers that clung to him. Bailey's first impulse was to spring from the couch, but his legs reminded him that this was impossible.

By means of the balcony and tree, the man slowly raised himself until he was visible to Mrs. Green. With a choking cry she made for the door and fumbled with the handle.

Bailey thought swiftly and clutched a medicine bottle in either hand. One he flung, and it smashed against the acacia. Silently and deliberately, and keeping his bright eyes fixed on Bailey, the Malay clambered into the balcony. Bailey, still clutching his second bottle, but with a sickening, sinking feeling about his heart, watched first one leg come over the railing and then the other.

It was Bailey's impression that the Malay took about an hour to get his second leg over the rail. The period that elapsed before the sitting position was changed to a standing one seemed enormous—days, weeks, possibly a year or so. Yet Bailey had no clear impression of anything going on in his mind during that vast period, except a vague wonder at his inability to throw the second medicine bottle. Suddenly the Malay glanced over his shoulder. There was the crack of a rifle. He flung up his arms and came down upon the couch. Mrs. Green began a dismal shriek that seemed likely to last until Doomsday. Bailey stared at the brown body with its shoulder blade driven in, that writhed painfully across his legs and rapidly staining and soaking the spotless bandages. Then he looked at the long krees, with the reddish streaks upon its blade, that lay an inch beyond the trembling brown fingers upon the floor. Then at Mrs. Green, who had backed hard against the door and was staring at the body and shrieking in gusty outbursts as if she would wake the dead. And then the body was shaken by one last convulsive effort.

The Malay gripped the krees, tried to raise himself with his left hand, and collapsed. Then he raised his head, stared for a moment at Mrs. Green, and twisting his face round looked at Bailey. With a gasping groan the dying man succeeded in clutching the bed clothes with his disabled hand, and by a violent effort, which hurt Bailey's legs exceedingly, writhed sideways towards what must be his last victim. Then something seemed released in Bailey's mind and he brought down the second bottle with all his strength on to the Malay's face. The krees fell heavily upon the floor.

"Easy with those legs," said Bailey, as young Fitzgibbon and one of the boating party lifted the body off him.

Young Fitzgibbon was very white in the face. "I didn't mean to kill him," he said.

"It's just as well," said Bailey.

9

In the Avu Observatory

The observatory at Avu, in Borneo, stands on the spur of the mountain. To the north rises the old crater, black at night against the unfathomable blue of the sky. From the little circular building, with its mushroom dome, the slopes plunge steeply downward into the black mysteries of the tropical forest beneath. The little house in which the observer and his assistant live is about, fifty yards from the observatory, and beyond this are the huts of their native attendants.

Thaddy, the chief observer, was down with a slight fever. His assistant, Woodhouse, paused for a moment in silent contemplation of the tropical night before commencing his solitary vigil. The night was very still. Now and then voices and laughter came from the native huts, or the cry of some strange animal was heard from the midst of the mystery of the forest. Nocturnal insects appeared in ghostly fashion out of the darkness, and fluttered round his light. He thought, perhaps, of all the possibilities of discovery that still lay in the black tangle beneath him; for to the naturalist the virgin forests of Borneo are still a wonderland full of strange questions and half-suspected discoveries. Woodhouse carried a small lantern in his hand, and its yellow glow contrasted vividly with the infinite series of tints between lavender-blue and black in which the landscape was painted. His hands and face were smeared with ointment against the attacks of the mosquitoes.

Even in these days of celestial photography, work done in a purely temporary erection, and with only the most primitive appliances, in addition to the telescope, still involves a very large amount of cramped and motionless watching. He sighed as he thought of the physical fatigues before him, stretched himself, and entered the observatory.

The reader is probably familiar with the structure of an ordinary astronomical observatory. The building is usually cylindrical in shape, with a very light hemispherical roof capable of being turned round from the interior. The telescope is supported upon a stone pillar in the centre, and a clockwork arrangement compensates for the earth's rotation, and allows a star once found to be continuously observed. Besides this, there is a compact tracery of wheels and screws about its point of support, by which the astronomer adjusts it. There is, of course, a slit in the movable roof which follows the eye of the telescope in its survey of the heavens. The observer sits or lies on a sloping wooden arrangement, which he can wheel to any part of the observatory as the position of the telescope may require. Within it is advisable to have things as dark as possible, in order to enhance the brilliance of the stars observed.

The lantern flared as Woodhouse entered his circular den, and the general darkness fled into black shadows behind the big machine, from which it presently seemed to creep back over the whole place again as the light waned. The slit was a profound transparent blue, in which six stars shone with tropical brilliance, and their light lay, a pallid gleam, along the black tube of the instrument. Woodhouse shifted the roof, and then proceeding to the telescope, turned first one wheel and then another, the great cylinder slowly swinging into a new position. Then he glanced through the finder, the little companion telescope, moved the roof a little more, made some further adjustments, and set the clockwork in motion. He took off his jacket, for the night was very hot, and pushed into position the uncomfortable seat to which he was condemned for the next four hours. Then with a sigh, he resigned himself to his watch upon the mysteries of space.

There was no sound now in the observatory, and the lantern waned steadily. Outside there was the occasional cry of some animal in alarm or pain, or calling to its mate, and the intermittent sounds of the Malay and Dyak servants. Presently one of the men began a queer chanting song, in which the others joined at intervals. After this it would seem that they turned in for the night, for no further sound came from their direction, and the whispering stillness became more and more profound.

The clockwork ticked steadily. The shrill hum of a mosquito explored the place, and grew shriller in indignation at Woodhouse's ointment. Then the lantern went out and all the observatory was black.

Woodhouse shifted his position presently, when the slow movement of the telescope had carried it beyond the limits of his comfort.

He was watching a little group of stars in the Milky Way, in one of which his chief had seen or fancied a remarkable colour variability. It was not a part of the regular work for which the establishment existed, and for that reason perhaps Woodhouse was deeply interested. He must have forgotten things terrestrial. All his attention was concentrated upon the great blue circle of the telescope field—a circle powdered, so it seemed, with an innumerable multitude of stars, and all luminous against the blackness of its setting. As he watched he seemed to himself to become incorporeal, as if he too were floating in the ether of space. Infinitely remote was the faint red spot he was observing.

Suddenly the stars were blotted out. A flash of blackness passed, and they were visible again.

"Queer," said Woodhouse. "Must have been a bird."

The thing happened again, and immediately after the great tube shivered as though it had been struck. Then the dome of the observatory resounded with a series of thundering blows. The stars seemed to sweep aside as the telescope—which had been unclamped—swung round and away from the slit in the roof.

"Great Scott!" cried Woodhouse. "What's this?"

Some huge vague black shape, with a flapping something like a wing, seemed to be struggling in the aperture of the roof. In another moment the slit was clear again, and the luminous haze of the Milky Way shone warm and bright.

The interior of the roof was perfectly black, and only a scraping sound marked the whereabouts of the unknown creature.

Woodhouse had scrambled from the seat to his feet. He was trembling violently and in a perspiration, with the suddenness of the occurrence. Was the thing, whatever it was, inside or out? It was big, whatever else it might be. Something shot across the skylight, and the telescope swayed. He started violently and put his arm up.

It was in the observatory then, with him. It was clinging to the roof apparently. What the devil was it? Could it see him?

He stood for perhaps a minute in a state of stupefaction. The beast, whatever it was, clawed at the interior of the dome, and then something flapped almost into his face, and he saw the momentary gleam of starlight on a skin like oiled leather. His water-bottle was knocked off his little table with a smash.

The sense of some strange bird-creature hovering a few yards from his face in the darkness was indescribably unpleasant to Woodhouse. As his thought returned he concluded that it must be some night-bird or large bat. At any risk he would see what it was, and pulling a match from his pocket, he tried to strike it on the telescope seat. There was a smoking streak of phosphorescent light, the match flared for a moment, and he saw a vast wing sweeping towards him, a gleam of grey-brown fur, and then he was struck in the face and the match knocked out of his hand. The blow was aimed at his temple, and a claw tore sideways down to his cheek. He reeled and fell, and he heard the extinguished lantern smash. Another blow followed as he fell. He was partly stunned, he felt his own warm blood stream out upon his face. Instinctively he felt his eyes had been struck at, and turning over on his face to save them, tried to crawl under the protection of the telescope.

He was struck again upon the back, and he heard his jacket rip, and then the thing hit the roof of the observatory. He edged as far as he could between the wooden seat and the eyepiece of the instrument, and turned his body round so that it was chiefly his feet that were exposed. With these he could at least kick. He was still in a mystified state. The strange beast banged about in the darkness, and presently clung to the telescope, making it sway and the gear rattle. Once it flapped near him, and he kicked out madly and felt a soft body with his feet. He was horribly scared now. It must be a big thing to swing the telescope like that. He saw for a moment the outline of a head black against the starlight, with sharply-pointed upstanding ears and a crest between them. It seemed to him to be as big as a mastiff's. Then he began to bawl out as loudly as he could for help.

At that the thing came down upon him again. As it did so his hand touched something beside him on the floor. He kicked out, and the next moment his ankle was gripped and held by a row of keen teeth. He yelled again, and tried to free his leg by kicking with the other. Then he realised he had the broken water-bottle at his hand, and snatching it, he struggled into a sitting posture, and feeling in the darkness towards his foot, gripped a velvety ear, like the ear of a big cat. He had seized the water-bottle by its neck and brought it down, with a shivering crash upon the head of the strange beast. He repeated the blow, and then stabbed and jabbed with the jagged end of it, in the darkness, where he judged the face might be.

The small teeth relaxed their hold, and at once Woodhouse pulled his leg free and kicked hard. He felt the sickening feel of fur and bone giving under his boot. There was a tearing bite at his arm, and he struck over it at the face, as he judged, and hit damp fur.

There was a pause; then he heard the sound of claws; and the dragging of a heavy body away from him over the observatory floor. Then there was silence, broken only by his own sobbing breathing, and a sound like licking. Everything was black except the parallelogram of the blue skylight with the luminous dust of stars, against which the end of the telescope now appeared in silhouette. He waited, as it seemed, an interminable time.

Was the thing coming on again? He felt in his trouser-pocket for some matches, and found one remaining. He tried to strike this, but the floor was wet, and it spat and went out. He cursed. He could not see where the door was situated. In his struggle he had quite lost his bearings. The strange beast, disturbed by the splutter of the match, began to move again. "Time!" called Woodhouse, with a sudden gleam of mirth, but the thing was not coming at him again. He must have hurt it, he thought, with the broken bottle. He felt a dull pain in his ankle. Probably he was bleeding there. He wondered if it would support him if he tried to stand up. The night outside was very still. There was no sound of any one moving. The sleepy fools had not heard those wings battering upon the dome, nor his shouts. It was no good wasting strength in shouting. The monster flapped its wings and startled him into a defensive attitude. He hit his elbow against the seat, and it fell over with a crash. He cursed this, and then he cursed the darkness.

Suddenly the oblong patch of starlight seemed to sway to and fro. Was he going to faint? It would never do to faint. He clenched his fists and set his teeth to hold himself together. Where had the door got to? It occurred to him he could get his bearings by the stars visible through the skylight. The patch of stars he saw was in Sagittarius and south-eastward; the door was north—or was it north by west? He tried to think. If he could get the door open he might retreat. It might be the thing was wounded. The suspense was beastly. "Look here!" he said, "If you don't come on, I shall come at you."

Then the thing began clambering up the side of the observatory, and he saw its black outline gradually blot out the skylight. Was it in retreat? He forgot about the door, and watched as the dome shifted and creaked. Somehow he did not feel very frightened or excited now. He felt a curious sinking sensation inside him. The sharply-defined patch of light, with the black form moving across it, seemed to be growing smaller and smaller. That was curious. He began to feel very thirsty, and yet he did not feel inclined to get anything to drink. He seemed to be sliding down a long funnel.

He felt a burning sensation in his throat, and then he perceived it was broad daylight, and that one of the Dyak servants was looking at him with a curious expression. Then there was the top of Thaddy's face upside down. Funny fellow, Thaddy, to go about like that! Then he grasped the situation better, and perceived that his head was on Thaddy's knee, and Thaddy was giving him brandy. And then he saw the eyepiece of the telescope with a lot of red smears on it. He began to remember.

"You've made this observatory in a pretty mess," said Thaddy.

The Dyak boy was beating up an egg in brandy. Woodhouse took this and sat up. He felt a sharp twinge of pain. His ankle was tied up, so were his arm and the side of his face. The smashed glass, red-stained, lay about the floor, the telescope seat was overturned, and by the opposite wall was a dark pool. The door was open, and he saw the grey summit of the mountain against a brilliant background of blue sky.

"Pah!" said Woodhouse. "Who's been killing calves here? Take me out of it."

Then he remembered the Thing, and the fight he had, had with it.

"What was it?" he said to Thaddy—"The Thing I fought with?"

"You know that best," said Thaddy. "But, anyhow, don't worry yourself now about it. Have some more to drink."

Thaddy, however, was curious enough, and it was a hard struggle between duty and inclination to keep Woodhouse quiet until he was decently put away in bed, and had slept upon the copious dose of meat extract Thaddy considered advisable. They then talked it over together.

"It was," said Woodhouse, "more like a big bat than anything else in the world. It had sharp, short ears, and soft fur, and its wings were leathery. Its teeth were little but devilish sharp, and its jaw could not have been very strong or else it would have bitten through my ankle."

"It has pretty nearly," said Thaddy.

"It seemed to me to hit out with its claws pretty freely. That is about as much as I know about the beast. Our conversation was intimate, so to speak, and yet not confidential."

"The Dyak chaps talk about a Big Colugo, a Klangutang—whatever that may be. It does not often attack man, but I suppose you made it nervous. They say there is a Big Colugo and a Little Colugo, and a something else that sounds like gobble. They all fly about at night. For my own part, I know there are flying foxes and flying lemurs about here, but they are, none of them very big beasts."

"There are more things in heaven and earth," said Woodhouse—and Thaddy groaned at the quotation—"and more particularly in the forests of Borneo, than are dreamt of in our philosophies. On the whole, if the Borneo fauna is going to disgorge any more of its novelties upon me, I should prefer that it did so when I was not occupied in the observatory at night and alone."

10

POLLOCK AND THE PORROH MAN

It was in a swampy village on the lagoon river behind the Turner Peninsula that Pollock's first encounter with the Porroh man occurred. The women of that country are famous for their good looks—they are Gallinas with a dash of European blood that dates from the days of Vasco da Gama and the English slave-traders, and the Porroh man too, was possibly inspired by a faint Caucasian taint in his composition. (It's a curious thing to think that some of us may have distant cousins eating men on Sherboro Island or raiding with the Sofas.) At any rate, the Porroh man stabbed the woman to the heart as though he had been a mere low-class Italian, and very narrowly missed Pollock. But Pollock, using his revolver to parry the lightning stab which was aimed at his deltoid muscle, sent the iron dagger flying, and firing, hit the man in the hand.

He fired again and missed, knocking a sudden window out of the wall of the hut. The Porroh man stooped in the doorway, glancing under his arm at Pollock. Pollock caught a glimpse of his inverted face in the sunlight, and then the Englishman was alone, sick and trembling with the excitement of the affair, in the twilight of the place. It had all happened in less time than it takes to read about it.

The woman was quite dead, and having ascertained this, Pollock went to the entrance of the hut and looked out. Things outside were dazzling bright. Half a dozen of the porters of the expedition were standing up in a group near the green huts they occupied, and staring towards him, wondering what the shots might signify. Behind the little group of men was the broad stretch of black fetid mud by the river, a green carpet of rafts of papyrus and water-grass, and then the leaden water. The mangroves beyond the stream loomed indistinctly through the blue haze. There were no signs of excitement in the squat village, whose fence was just visible above the cane-grass.

Pollock came out of the hut cautiously and walked towards the river, looking over his shoulder at intervals. But the Porroh man had vanished Pollock clutched his revolver nervously in his hand.

One of his men came to meet him, and as he came, pointed to the bushes behind the hut in which the Porroh man had disappeared. Pollock had an irritating persuasion of having made an absolute fool of himself; he felt bitter, savage, at the turn things had taken. At the same time, he would have to tell Waterhouse—the moral, exemplary, cautious Waterhouse—who would inevitably take the matter seriously. Pollock cursed bitterly at his luck, at Waterhouse, and especially at the West Coast of Africa. He felt consummately sick of the expedition. And in the back of his mind all the time was a speculative doubt where precisely within the visible horizon the Porroh man might be.

It is perhaps rather shocking, but he was not at all upset by the murder that had just happened. He had seen so much brutality during the last three months, so many dead women, burnt huts, drying skeletons, up the Kittam River in the wake of the Sofa cavalry, that his senses were blunted. What disturbed him was the persuasion that this business was only beginning.

He swore savagely at the black, who ventured to ask a question, and went on into the tent under the orange-trees where Waterhouse was lying, feeling exasperatingly like a boy going into the headmaster's study.

Waterhouse was still sleeping off the effects of his last dose of chlorodyne, and Pollock sat down on a packing-case beside him, and lighting his pipe, waited for him to awake. About him were scattered the pots and weapons Waterhouse had collected from the Mendi people, and which he had been repacking for the canoe voyage to Sulyma.

Presently Waterhouse woke up, and after judicial stretching, decided he was all right again. Pollock got him some tea. Over the tea, the incidents of the afternoon were described by Pollock, after some preliminary beating about the bush. Waterhouse took the matter even more seriously than Pollock had anticipated. He did not simply disapprove, he scolded, he insulted.

"You're one of those infernal fools who think a black man isn't a human being," he said. "I can't be ill a day without you must get into some dirty scrape or other. This is the third time in a month that you have come crossways-on with a native, and this time you're in for it with a vengeance. Porroh, too! They're down upon you enough as it is, about that idol you wrote your silly name on. And they're the most vindictive devils on earth! You make a man ashamed of civilisation. To think you come of a decent family! If ever I cumber myself up with a vicious, stupid young lout like you again—"

"Steady on, now," snarled Pollock, in the tone that always exasperated Waterhouse; "steady on."

At that Waterhouse became speechless. He jumped to his feet.

"Look here, Pollock," he said, after a struggle to control his breath. "You must go home. I won't have you any longer. I'm ill enough as it is, through you—"

"Keep your hair on," said Pollock, staring in front of him. "I'm ready enough to go."

Waterhouse became calmer again. He sat down on the camp-stool. "Very well," he said. "I don't want a row, Pollock you know, but it's confoundedly annoying to have one's plans put out by this kind of thing. I'll come to Sulyma with you, and see you safe aboard—"

"You needn't," said Pollock. "I can go alone. From here."

"Not far," said Waterhouse. "You don't understand this Porroh business."

"How should I know she belonged to a Porroh man?" said Pollock bitterly.

"Well, she did," said Waterhouse; "and you can't undo the thing. Go alone, indeed! I wonder what they'd do to you. You don't seem to understand that this Porroh hokey-pokey rules this country, is its law, religion, constitution, medicine, magic...They appoint the chiefs. The Inquisition, at its best, couldn't hold a candle to these chaps. He will probably set Awajale, the chief here, on to us. It's lucky our porters are Mendis. We shall have to shift this little settlement of ours... Confound you, Pollock! And, of course, you must go and miss him."

He thought, and his thoughts seemed disagreeable. Presently he stood up and took his rifle. "I'd keep close for a bit, if I were you," he said, over his shoulder, as he went out. "I'm going out to see what I can find out about it."

Pollock remained sitting in the tent, meditating. "I was meant for a civilised life," he said to himself, regretfully, as he filled his pipe. "The sooner I get back to London or Paris the better for me."

His eye fell on the sealed case in which Waterhouse had put the featherless poisoned arrows they had bought in the Mendi country. "I wish I had hit the beggar somewhere vital," said Pollock viciously.

Waterhouse came back after a long interval. He was not communicative, though Pollock asked him questions enough. The Porroh man, it seems was a prominent member of that mystical society. The village was interested, but not threatening. No doubt the witch-doctor had gone into the bush. He was a great witch-doctor. "Of course, he's up to something," said Waterhouse, and became silent.

"But what can he do?" asked Pollock, unheeded.

"I must get you out of this. There's something brewing, or things would not be so quiet," said Waterhouse, after a gap of silence. Pollock wanted to know what the brew might be. "Dancing in a circle of skulls", said Waterhouse; "brewing a stink in a copper pot." Pollock wanted particulars. Waterhouse was vague, Pollock pressing. At last Waterhouse lost his temper. "How the devil should I know?" he said to Pollock's twentieth inquiry what the Porroh man would do. "He tried to kill you off-hand in the hut. Now, I fancy he will try something more elaborate. But you'll see fast enough. I don't want to help unnerve you. It's probably all nonsense."

That night, as they were sitting at their fire, Pollock again tried to draw Waterhouse out on the subject of Porroh methods. "Better get to sleep," said Waterhouse, when Pollock's bent became apparent; "we start early to-morrow. You may want all your nerve about you."

"But what line will he take?"

"Can't say. They're versatile people. They know a lot of rum dodges. You'd better get that copper-devil, Shakespear, to talk."

There was a flash and a heavy bang, out of the darkness behind the huts, and a clay bullet came whistling close to Pollock's head. This, at least, was crude enough. The blacks and half-breeds sitting and yarning round their own fire jumped up, and someone fired into the dark.

"Better go into one of the huts," said Waterhouse quietly, still sitting unmoved.

Pollock stood up by the fire and drew his revolver. Fighting, at least, he was not afraid of. But a man in the dark is in the best of armour. Realising the wisdom of Waterhouse's advice, Pollock went into the tent and lay down there.

What little sleep he had was disturbed by dreams, variegated dreams, but chiefly of the Porroh man's face, upside down, as he went out of the hut, and looked up under his arm. It was odd that this transitory impression should have stuck so firmly in Pollock's memory. Moreover, he was troubled by queer pains in his limbs.

In the white haze of the early morning, as they were loading the canoes, a barbed arrow suddenly appeared quivering in the ground close to Pollock's foot. The boys made a perfunctory effort to clear out the thicket, but it led to no capture.

After these two occurrences, there was a disposition on the part of the expedition to leave Pollock to himself, and Pollock became, for the first time in his life, anxious to mingle with blacks. Waterhouse took one canoe, and Pollock, in spite of a friendly desire to chat with Waterhouse, had to take the other. He was left all alone in the front part of the canoe, and he had the greatest trouble to make the men—who did not love him—keep to the middle of the river, a clear hundred yards or more from either shore. However, he made Shakespear, the Freetown half-breed, come up to his own end of the canoe and tell him about Porroh, which Shakespear, failing in his attempts to leave Pollock alone, presently did with considerable freedom and gusto.

The day passed. The canoe glided swiftly along the ribbon of lagoon water, between the drift of water-figs, fallen trees, papyrus, and palm-wine palms, and with the dark mangrove swamp to the left, through which one could hear now and then the roar of the Atlantic surf. Shakespear told in his soft, blurred English of how the Porroh could cast spells; how men withered up under their malice; how they could send dreams and devils; how they tormented and killed the sons of Ijibu; how they kidnapped a white trader from Sulyma who had maltreated one of the sect, and how his body looked when it was found. And Pollock after each narrative cursed under his breath at the want of missionary enterprise that allowed such things to be, and at the inert British Government that ruled over this dark heathendom of Sierra Leone. In the evening they came to the Kasi Lake, and sent a score of crocodiles lumbering off the island on which the expedition camped for the night.

The next day they reached Sulyma, and smelt the sea breeze, but Pollock had to put up there for five days before he could get on to Freetown. Waterhouse, considering him to be comparatively safe here, and within the pale of Freetown influence, left him and went back with the expedition to Gbemma, and Pollock became very friendly with Perera, the only resident white trader at Sulyma—so friendly, indeed, that he went about with him everywhere. Perera was a little Portuguese Jew, who had lived in England, and he appreciated the Englishman's friendliness as a great compliment.

For two days nothing happened out of the ordinary; for the most part Pollock and Perera played Nap—the only game they had in common—and Pollock got into debt. Then, on the second evening, Pollock had a disagreeable intimation of the arrival of the Porroh man in Sulyma by getting a flesh-wound in the shoulder from a lump of filed iron. It was a long shot, and the missile had nearly spent its force when it hit him. Still it conveyed its message plainly enough. Pollock sat up in his hammock, revolver in hand, all that night, and next morning confided, to some extent, in the Anglo-Portuguese.

Perera took the matter seriously. He knew the local customs pretty thoroughly. "It is a personal question, you must know. It is revenge. And of course he is hurried by your leaving de country. None of de natives or half-breeds will interfere wid him very much—unless you make it wort deir while. If you come upon him suddenly, you might shoot him. But den he might shoot you.

"Den dere's dis—infernal magic," said Perera. "Of course, I don't believe in it—superstition—but still it's not nice to tink dat wherever you are, dere is a black man, who spends a moonlight night now and den a-dancing about a fire to send you bad dreams... Had any bad dreams?"

"Rather," said Pollock. "I keep on seeing the beggar's head upside down grinning at me and showing all his teeth as he did in the hut, and coming close up to me, and then going ever so far off, and coming back. It's nothing to be afraid of, but somehow it simply paralyses me with terror in my sleep. Queer things—dreams. I know it's a dream all the time, and I can't wake up from it."

"It's probably only fancy," said Perera. "Den my niggers say Porroh men can send snakes. Seen any snakes lately?"

"Only one. I killed him this morning, on the floor near my hammock. Almost trod on him as I got up."

"Ah!" said Perera, and then, reassuringly, "Of course it is a—coincidence. Still I would keep my eyes open. Den dere's pains in de bones."

"I thought they were due to miasma," said Pollock.

"Probably dey are. When did dey begin?"

Then Pollock remembered that he first noticed them the night after the fight in the hut. "It's my opinion he don't want to kill you," said Perera—"at least not yet. I've heard deir idea is to scare and worry a man wid deir spells, and narrow misses, and rheumatic pains, and bad dreams, and all dat, until he's sick of life. Of course, it's all talk, you know. You mustn't worry about it...But I wonder what he'll be up to next."

"I shall have to be up to something first," said Pollock, staring gloomily at the greasy cards that Perera was putting on the table. "It don't suit my dignity to be followed about, and shot at, and blighted in this way. I wonder if Porroh hokey-pokey upsets your luck at cards."

He looked at Perera suspiciously.

"Very likely it does," said Perera warmly, shuffling. "Dey are wonderful people."

That afternoon Pollock killed two snakes in his hammock, and there was also an extraordinary increase in the number of red ants that swarmed over the place; and these annoyances put him in a fit temper to talk over business with a certain Mendi rough he had interviewed before. The Mendi rough showed Pollock a little iron dagger, and demonstrated where one struck in the neck, in a way that made Pollock shiver, and in return for certain considerations Pollock promised him a double-barrelled gun with an ornamental lock.

In the evening, as Pollock and Perera were playing cards, the Mendi rough came in through the doorway, carrying something in a blood-soaked piece of native cloth.

"Not here!" said Pollock very hurriedly. "Not here!"

But he was not quick enough to prevent the man, who was anxious to get to Pollock's side of the bargain, from opening the cloth and throwing the head of the Porroh man upon the table. It bounded from there on to the floor, leaving a red trail on the cards, and rolled into the corner, where it came to rest upside down, but glaring hard at Pollock.

Perera jumped up as the thing fell among the cards, and began in his excitement to gabble in Portuguese. The Mendi was bowing, with the red cloth in his hand. "De gun!" he cried. Pollock stared back at the head in the corner. It bore exactly the expression it had in his dreams. Something seemed to snap in his own brain as he looked at it.

Then Perera found his English again.

"You got him killed?" he said. "You did not kill him yourself?"

"Why should I?" said Pollock.

"But he will not be able to take it off now!"

"Take what off?" said Pollock.

"And all dese cards are spoiled!"

"What do you mean by taking off?" said Pollock.

"You must send me a new pack from Freetown. You can buy dem dere.

"But—'take it off'?"

"It is only superstition. I forgot. De niggers say dat if de witches—he was a witch—But it is rubbish...You must make de Porroh man take it off, or kill him yourself...It is very silly."

Pollock swore under his breath, still staring hard at the head in the corner.

"I can't stand that glare," he said. Then suddenly he rushed at the thing and kicked it. It rolled some yards or so, and came to rest in the same position as before, upside down, and looking at him.

"He is ugly," said the Anglo-Portuguese. "Very ugly. Dey do it on deir faces with little knives."

Pollock would have kicked the head again, but the Mendi man touched him on the arm. "De gun?" he said, looking nervously at the head.

"Two—if you will take that beastly thing away," said Pollock.

The Mendi shook his head, and intimated that he only wanted one gun now due to him, and for which he would be obliged. Pollock found neither cajolery nor bullying any good with him. Perera had a gun to sell (at a profit of three hundred per cent), and with that the man presently departed. Then Pollock's eyes, against his will, were recalled to the thing on the floor.

"It is funny dat his head keeps upside down," said Perera, with an uneasy laugh. "His brains must be heavy, like de weight in de little images one sees dat keep always upright wid lead in dem. You will take him wiv you when you go presently. You might take him now. De cards are all spoilt. Dere is a man sell dem in Freetown. De room is in a filthy mess as it is. You should have killed him yourself."

Pollock pulled himself together, and went and picked up the head. He would hang it up by the lamp-hook in the middle of the ceiling of his room, and dig a grave for it at once. He was under the impression that he hung it up by the hair, but that must have been wrong, for when he returned for it, it was hanging by the neck upside down.

He buried it before sunset on the north side of the shed he occupied, so that he should not have to pass the grave after dark when he was returning from Perera's. He killed two snakes before he went to sleep. In the darkest part of the night he awoke with a start, and heard a pattering sound and something scraping on the floor. He sat up noiselessly, and felt under his pillow for his revolver. A mumbling growl followed, and Pollock fired at the sound. There was a yelp, and something dark passed for a moment across the hazy blue of the doorway. "A dog!" said Pollock, lying down again.

In the early dawn he awoke again with a peculiar sense of unrest. The vague pain in his bones had returned. For some time he lay watching the red ants that were swarming over the ceiling, and then, as the light grew brighter, he looked over the edge of his hammock and saw something dark on the floor. He gave such a violent start that the hammock overset and flung him out.

He found himself lying, perhaps, a yard away from the head of the Porroh man. It had been disinterred by the dog, and the nose was grievously battered. Ants and flies swarmed over it. By an odd coincidence, it was still upside down, and with the same diabolical expression in the inverted eyes.

Pollock sat paralysed, and stared at the horror for some time. Then he got up and walked round it—giving it a wide berth—and out of the shed. The clear light of the sunrise, the living stir of vegetation before the breath of the dying land-breeze, and the empty grave with the marks of the dog's paws, lightened the weight upon his mind a little.

He told Perera of the business as though it was a jest—a jest to be told with white lips. "You should not have frighten de dog," said Perera, with poorly simulated hilarity.

The next two days, until the steamer came, were spent by Pollock in making a more effectual disposition of his possession.

Overcoming his aversion to handling the thing, he went down to the river mouth and threw it into the sea-water, but by some miracle it escaped the crocodiles, and was cast up by the tide on the mud a little way up the river, to be found by an intelligent Arab half-breed, and offered for sale to Pollock and Perera as a curiosity, just on the edge of night. The native hung about in the brief twilight, making lower and lower offers, and at last, getting scared in some way by the evident dread these wise white men had for the thing, went off, and passing Pollock's shed, threw his burden in there for Pollock to discover in the morning.

At this Pollock got into a kind of frenzy. He would burn the thing. He went out straightway into the dawn, and had constructed a big pyre of brushwood before the heat of the day. He was interrupted by the hooter of the little paddle steamer from Monrovia to Bathurst, which was coming through the gap in the bar. "Thank Heaven!" said Pollock, with infinite piety, when the meaning of the sound dawned upon him. With trembling hands he lit his pile of wood hastily, threw the head upon it, and went away to pack his portmanteau and make his adieux to Perera.

That afternoon, with a sense of infinite relief, Pollock watched the flat swampy foreshore of Sulyma grow small in the distance. The gap in the long line of white surge became narrower and narrower. It seemed to be closing in and cutting him off from his trouble. The feeling of dread and worry began to slip from him bit by bit. At Sulyma belief in Porroh malignity and Porroh magic had been in the air, his sense of Porroh had been vast, pervading, threatening, dreadful. Now manifestly the domain of Porroh was only a little place, a little black band between the sea and the blue cloudy Mendi uplands.

"Good-bye, Porroh!" said Pollock. "Good-bye—certainly not au revoir."

The captain of the steamer came and leant over the rail beside him, and wished him good-evening, and spat at the froth of the wake in token of friendly ease.

"I picked up a rummy curio on the beach this go," said the captain. "It's a thing I never saw done this side of Indy before."

"What might that be?" said Pollock.

"Pickled 'ed," said the captain.

"What!" said Pollock.

"'Ed—smoked. 'Ed of one of those Porroh chaps, all ornamented with knife-cuts. Why! What's up? Nothing? I shouldn't have took you for a nervous chap. Green in the face. By gosh! You're a bad sailor. All right, eh? Lord, how funny you went...! Well, this 'ed I was telling you of is a bit rum in a way. I've got it, along with some snakes, in a jar of spirit in my cabin what I keeps for such curios, and I'm hanged if it don't float upsy down. Hullo!"

Pollock had given an incoherent cry, and had his hands in his hair. He ran towards the paddle-boxes with a half-formed idea of jumping into the sea, and then he realised his position and turned back towards the captain.

"Here!" said the captain. "Jack Philips, just keep him off me! Stand off! No nearer, mister! What's the matter with you? Are you mad?"

Pollock put his hand to his head. It was no good explaining. "I believe I am pretty nearly mad at times," he said. "It's a pain I have here. Comes suddenly. You'll excuse me, I hope."

He was white and in a perspiration. He saw suddenly very clearly all the danger he ran of having his sanity doubted. He forced himself to restore the captain's confidence, by answering his sympathetic inquiries, noting his suggestions, even trying a spoonful of neat brandy in his cheek, and that matter settled, asking a number of questions about the captain's private trade in curiosities. The captain described the head in detail. All the while Pollock was struggling to keep under a preposterous persuasion that the ship was as transparent as glass, and that he could distinctly see the inverted face looking at him from the cabin beneath his feet.

Pollock had a worse time almost on the steamer than he had at Sulyma. All day he had to control himself in spite of his intense perception of the imminent presence of that horrible head that was overshadowing his mind. At night his old nightmare returned, until, with a violent effort, he would force himself awake, rigid with the horror of it, and with the ghost of a hoarse scream in his throat.

He left the actual head behind at Bathurst, where he changed ship for Teneriffe, but not his dreams nor the dull ache in his bones. At Teneriffe, Pollock transferred to a Cape liner, but the head followed him. He gambled, he tried chess, he even read books, but he knew the danger of drink. Yet whenever a round black shadow, a round black object came into his range, there he looked for the head, and—saw it. He knew clearly enough that his imagination was growing traitor to him, and yet at times it seemed the ship he sailed in, his fellow-passengers, the sailors, the wide sea, was all part of a filmy phantasmagoria that hung, scarcely veiling it, between him and a horrible real world. Then the Porroh man, thrusting his diabolical face through that curtain, was the one real and undeniable thing. At that he would get up and touch things, taste something, gnaw something, burn his hand with a match, or run a needle into himself.

So, struggling grimly and silently with his excited imagination, Pollock reached England. He landed at Southampton, and went on straight from Waterloo to his banker's in Cornhill in a cab. There he transacted some business with the manager in a private room, and all the while the head hung like an ornament under the black marble mantel and dripped upon the fender. He could hear the drops fall, and see the red on the fender.

"A pretty fern," said the manager, following his eyes. "But it makes the fender rusty."

"Very," said Pollock; "a very pretty fern. And that reminds me. Can you recommend me a physician for mind troubles? I've got a little—what is it—? Hallucination."

The head laughed savagely, wildly. Pollock was surprised the manager did not notice it. But the manager only stared at his face.

With the address of a doctor, Pollock presently emerged in Cornhill. There was no cab in sight, and so he went on down to the western end of the street, and essayed the crossing opposite the Mansion House. The crossing is hardly easy even for the expert Londoner; cabs, vans, carriages, mail-carts, omnibuses go by in one incessant stream; to anyone fresh from the malarious solitudes of Sierra Leone it is a boiling, maddening confusion. But when an inverted head suddenly comes bouncing, like an indiarubber ball, between your legs, leaving distinct smears of blood every time it touches the ground, you can scarcely hope to avoid an accident. Pollock lifted his feet convulsively to avoid it, and then kicked at the thing furiously. Then something hit him violently in the back, and a hot pain ran up his arm.

He had been hit by the pole of an omnibus, and three of the fingers of his left hand smashed by the hoof of one of the horses—the very fingers, as it happened, that he shot from the Porroh man.

They pulled him out from between the horse's legs, and found the address of the physician, in his crushed hand.

For a couple of days Pollock's sensations were full of the sweet, pungent smell of chloroform, of painful operations that caused him no pain, of lying still and being given food and drink. Then he had a slight fever, and was very thirsty, and his old nightmare came back. It was only when it returned that he noticed it had left him for a day.

"If my skull had been smashed instead of my fingers, it might have gone altogether," said Pollock, staring thoughtfully at the dark cushion that had taken on for the time the shape of the head.

Pollock at the first opportunity told the physician of his mind trouble. He knew clearly that he must go mad unless something should intervene to save him. He explained that he had witnessed a decapitation in Dahomey, and was haunted by one of the heads. Naturally, he did not care to state the actual facts. The physician looked grave.

Presently he spoke hesitatingly. "As a child, did you get very much religious training?"

"Very little," said Pollock.

A shade passed over the physician's face. "I don't know if you have heard of the miraculous cures—it may be, of course, they are not miraculous—at Lourdes."

"Faith-healing will hardly suit me, I am afraid," said Pollock, with his eye on the dark cushion.

The head distorted its scarred features in an abominable grimace. The physician went upon a new track. "It's all imagination," he said, speaking with sudden briskness. "A fair case for faith-healing, anyhow. Your nervous system has run down, you're in that twilight state of health when the bogles come easiest. The strong impression was too much for you. I must make you up a little mixture that will strengthen your nervous system—especially your brain. And you must take exercise."

"I'm no good for faith-healing," said Pollock.

"And therefore we must restore tone. Go in search of stimulating air—Scotland, Norway, the Alps—"

"Jericho, if you like," said Pollock—"where Naaman went."

However, so soon as his fingers would let him, Pollock made a gallant attempt to follow out the doctor's suggestion. It was now November. He tried football, but to Pollock the game consisted in kicking a furious inverted head about a field. He was no good at the game. He kicked blindly, with a kind of horror, and when they put him back into goal, and the ball came swooping down upon him, he suddenly yelled and got out of its way. The discreditable stories that had driven him from England to wander in the tropics shut him off from any but men's society, and now his increasingly strange behaviour made even his man friends avoid him. The thing was no longer a thing of the eye merely; it gibbered at him, spoke to him. A horrible fear came upon him that presently, when he took hold of the apparition, it would no longer become some mere article of furniture, but would feel like a real dissevered head. Alone, he would curse at the thing, defy it, entreat it; once or twice, in spite of his grim self-control, he addressed it in the presence of others. He felt the growing suspicion in the eyes of the people that watched him—his landlady, the servant, his man.

One day early in December his cousin Arnold—his next of kin—came to see him and draw him out, and watch his sunken yellow face with narrow eager eyes. And it seemed to Pollock that the hat his cousin carried in his hand was no hat at all, but a Gorgon head that glared at him upside down, and fought with its eyes against his reason. However, he was still resolute to see the matter out. He got a bicycle, and, riding over the frosty road from Wandsworth to Kingston, found the thing rolling along at his side, and leaving a dark trail behind it. He set his teeth and rode faster. Then suddenly, as he came down the hill towards Richmond Park, the apparition rolled in front of him and under his wheel, so quickly that he had no time for thought, and, turning quickly to avoid it, was flung violently against a heap of stones and broke his left wrist.

The end came on Christmas morning. All night he had been in a fever, the bandages encircling his wrist like a band of fire, his dreams more vivid and terrible than ever. In the cold, colourless, uncertain light that came before the sunrise, he sat up in his bed, and saw the head upon the bracket in the place of the bronze jar that had stood there overnight.

"I know that is a bronze jar," he said, with a chill doubt at his heart. Presently the doubt was irresistible. He got out of bed slowly, shivering, and advanced to the jar with his hand raised. Surely he would see now his imagination had deceived him, recognise the distinctive sheen of bronze. At last, after an age of hesitation, his fingers came down on the patterned cheek of the head. He withdrew them spasmodically. The last stage was reached. His sense of touch had betrayed him.

Trembling, stumbling against the bed, kicking against his shoes with his bare feet, a dark confusion eddying round him, he groped his way to the dressing-table, took his razor from the drawer, and sat down on the bed with this in his hand. In the looking-glass he saw his own face, colourless, haggard, full of the ultimate bitterness of despair.

He beheld in swift succession the incidents in the brief tale of his experience. His wretched home, his still more wretched schooldays, the years of vicious life he had led since then, one act of selfish dishonour leading to another; it was all clear and pitiless now, all its squalid folly, in the cold light of the dawn. He came to the hut, to the fight with the Porroh man, to the retreat down the river to Sulyma, to the Mendi assassin and his red parcel, to his frantic endeavours to destroy the head, to the growth of his hallucination. It was a hallucination! He knew it was. A hallucination merely. For a moment he snatched at hope. He looked away from the glass, and on the bracket, the inverted head grinned and grimaced at him... With the stiff fingers of his bandaged hand he felt at his neck for the throb of his arteries. The morning was very cold, the steel blade felt like ice.

11

The Argonauts of the Air

One saw Monson's Flying Machine from the windows of the trains passing either along the South-Western main line or along the line between Wimbledon and Worcester Park—, to be more exact, one saw the huge scaffolding which limited the flight of the apparatus. They rose over the tree-tops, a massive alley of interlacing iron and timber, and an enormous web of ropes and tackle, extending the best part of two miles. From the Leatherhead branch this alley was foreshortened and in part hidden by hill with villas; but from the main line one had it in profile, a complex tangle of girders and curving bars, very impressive to the excursionists from Portsmouth and Southampton and the West. Monson had taken up the work where Maxim had left it, had gone on at first with an utter contempt for the journalistic wit and ignorance that had irritated and hampered his predecessor, and had spent (it was said) rather more than half his immense fortune upon his experiments. The results, to an impatient generation, seemed inconsiderable. When some five years had passed after the growth of the colossal iron groves at Worcester Park, and Monson still failed to put in a fluttering appearance over Trafalgar Square, even the Isle of Wight trippers felt their liberty to smile. And such intelligent people as did not consider Monson a fool stricken with the mania for invention, denounced him as being (for no particular reason) a self-advertising quack.

Yet now and again a morning trainload of season-ticket holders would see a white monster rush headlong through the airy tracery of guides and bars, and hear the further stays, nettings and buffers snap, creak, and groan with the impact of the blow. Then there would be an efflorescence of black-set white-rimmed faces along the sides of the train, and the morning papers would be neglected for a vigorous discussion of the possibility of flying (in which nothing new was ever said by any chance), until the train reached Waterloo, and its cargo of season-ticket holders dispersed themselves over London. Or the fathers and mothers in some multitudinous train of weary excursionists returning exhausted from a day of rest by the sea, would find the dark fabric, standing out against the evening sky, useful in diverting some bilious child from its introspection, and be suddenly startled by the swift transit of a huge black flapping shape that strained upward against the guides. It was a great and forcible thing beyond dispute, and excellent for conversation; yet all the same, it was but flying in leading-strings, and most of those who witnessed it scarcely counted its flight as flying. More of a switchback it seemed to the run of the folk.

Monson, I say, did not trouble himself very keenly about the opinions of the press at first. But possibly he, even had formed but a poor idea of the time it would take before the tactics of flying were mastered, the swift assured adjustment of the big soaring shape to every gust and chance movement of the air; nor had he clearly reckoned the money this prolonged struggle against gravitation would cost him. And he was not so pachydermatous as he seemed. Secretly he had his periodical bundles of cuttings sent him by Romeike, he had his periodical reminders from his banker; and if he did not mind the initial ridicule and scepticism, he felt the growing neglect as the months went by and the money dribbled away. Time was when Monson had sent the enterprising journalist, keen after readable matter, empty from his gates. But when the enterprising journalist ceased from troubling, Monson was anything but satisfied in his heart of hearts. Still day by day the work went on, and the multitudinous subtle difficulties of steering diminished in number. Day by day, too the money trickled away, until his balance was no longer a matter of hundreds of thousands, but of tens. And at last came an anniversary.

Monson, sitting in the little drawing-shed, suddenly noticed the date on Woodhouse's calendar.

"It was five years ago to-day that we began," he said to Woodhouse suddenly.

"Is it?" said Woodhouse.

"It's the alterations play the devil with us," said Monson, biting a paper-fastener.

The drawings for the new vans to the hinder screw lay on the table before him as he spoke. He pitched the mutilated brass paper-fastener into the waste-paper basket and drummed with his fingers. "These alterations! Will the mathematicians ever be clever enough to save us all this patching and experimenting? Five years—learning by rule of thumb, when one might think that it was possible to calculate the whole thing out beforehand. The cost of it! I might have hired three senior wranglers for life. But they'd only have developed some beautifully useless theorems in pneumatics. What a time it has been, Woodhouse!"

"These mouldings will take three weeks," said Woodhouse. "At special prices."

"Three weeks!" said Monson, and sat drumming.

"Three weeks certain," said Woodhouse, an excellent engineer, but no good as a comforter. He drew the sheets towards him and began shading a bar.

Monson stopped drumming, and began to bite his finger-nails, staring the while at Woodhouse's head.

"How long have they been calling this Monson's Folly?" he said suddenly.

"Oh! Year or so," said Woodhouse carelessly, without looking up.

Monson sucked the air in between his teeth, and went to the window. The stout iron columns carrying the elevated rails upon which the start of the machine was made rose up close by, and the machine was hidden by the upper edge of the window. Through the grove of iron pillars, red painted and ornate with rows of bolts, one had a glimpse of the pretty scenery towards Esher. A train went gliding noiselessly across the middle distance, its rattle drowned by the hammering of the workmen overhead. Monson could imagine the grinning faces at the windows of the carriages. He swore savagely under his breath, and dabbed viciously at a blowfly that suddenly became noisy on the window-pane.

"What's up?" said Woodhouse, staring in surprise at his employer.

"I'm about sick of this."

Woodhouse scratched his cheek. "Oh!" he said, after an assimilating pause. He pushed the drawing away from him.

"Here these fools...I'm trying to conquer a new element—trying to do a thing that will revolutionise life. And instead of taking an intelligent interest, they grin and make their stupid jokes, and call me and my appliances names."

"Asses!" said Woodhouse, letting his eye fall again on the drawing.

The epithet, curiously enough, made Monson wince. "I'm about sick of it, Woodhouse, anyhow," he said, after a pause.

Woodhouse shrugged his shoulders.

"There's nothing for it but patience, I suppose," said Monson, sticking his hands in his pockets. "I've started. I've made my bed, and I've got to lie on it. I can't go back. I'll see it through, and spend every penny I have and every penny I can borrow. But I tell you, Woodhouse, I'm infernally sick of it, all the same. If I'd paid a tenth part of the money towards some political greaser's expenses—I'd have been a baronet before this."

Monson paused. Woodhouse stared in front of him with a blank expression he always employed to indicate sympathy, and tapped his pencil-case on the table. Monson stared at him for a minute.

"Oh, damn!" said Monson suddenly, and abruptly rushed out of the room.

Woodhouse continued his sympathetic rigour for perhaps half a minute. Then he sighed and resumed the shading of the drawings. Something had evidently upset Monson. Nice chap, and generous, but difficult to get on with. It was the way with every amateur who had anything to do with engineering—wanted everything finished at once. But Monson had usually the patience of the expert. Odd he was so irritable. Nice and round that aluminium rod did look now! Woodhouse threw back his head, and put it, first this side and then that, to appreciate his bit of shading better.

"Mr. Woodhouse," said Hooper, the foreman of the labourers, putting his head in at the door.

"Hullo!" said Woodhouse, without turning round.

"Nothing happened, sir?" said Hooper.

"Happened?" said Woodhouse.

"The governor just been up the rails swearing like a tornader."

"Oh!" said Woodhouse.

"It ain't like him, sir."

"No?"

"And I was thinking perhaps—"

"Don't think," said Woodhouse, still admiring the drawings.

Hooper knew Woodhouse, and shut the door suddenly with a vicious slam. Woodhouse stared stonily before him for some further minutes, and then made an ineffectual effort to pick his teeth with his pencil. Abruptly he desisted, pitched that old, tried, and stumpy servitor across the room, got up, stretched himself, and followed Hooper.

He looked ruffled—it was visible to every workman he met. When a millionaire who has been spending thousands on experiments that employ quite a little army of people suddenly indicates that he is sick of the undertaking, there is almost invariably a certain amount of mental friction in the ranks of the little army he employs. And even before he indicates his intentions there are speculations and murmurs, a watching of faces and a study of straws. Hundreds of people knew before the day was out that Monson was ruffled, Woodhouse ruffled, Hooper ruffled. A workman's wife, for instance (whom Monson had never seen), decided to keep her money in the savings-bank instead of buying a velveteen dress. So far-reaching are even the casual curses of a millionaire.

Monson found a certain satisfaction in going on the works and behaving disagreeably to as many people as possible. After a time even that palled upon him, and he rode off the grounds, to every one's relief there, and through the lanes south-eastward, to the infinite tribulation of his house steward at Cheam.

And the immediate cause of it all, the little grain of annoyance that had suddenly precipitated all this discontent with his life-work was—these trivial things that direct all our great decisions—! Half a dozen ill-considered remarks made by a pretty girl, prettily dressed, with a beautiful voice and something more than prettiness in her soft grey eyes. And of these half-dozen remarks, two words especially—"Monson's Folly." She had felt she was behaving charmingly to Monson; she reflected the next day how exceptionally effective she had been, and no one would have been more amazed than she, had she learned the effect she had left on Monson's mind. I hope, considering everything, that she never knew.

"How are you getting on with your flying-machine?" she asked. ("I wonder if I shall ever meet any one with the sense not to ask that," thought Monson.) "It will be very dangerous at first, will it not?" ("Thinks I'm afraid.") "Jorgon is going to play presently; have you heard him before?" ("My mania being attended to, we turn to rational conversation.") Gush about Jorgon; gradual decline of conversation, ending with—"You must let me know when your flying-machine is finished, Mr. Monson, and then I will consider the advisability of taking a ticket." ("One would think I was still playing inventions in the nursery.") But the bitterest thing she said was not meant for Monson's ears. To Phlox, the novelist, she was always conscientiously brilliant. "I have been talking to Mr. Monson, and he can think of nothing, positively nothing, but that flying-machine of his. Do you know, all his workmen call that place of his 'Monson's Folly'? He is quite impossible. It is really very, very sad. I always regard him myself in the light of sunken treasure—the Lost Millionaire, you know."

She was pretty and well educated—, indeed, she had written an epigrammatic novelette; but the bitterness was that she was typical. She summarised what the world thought of the man who was working sanely, steadily, and surely towards a more tremendous revolution in the appliances of civilisation, a more far-reaching alteration in the ways of humanity than has ever been effected since history began. They did not even take his seriously. In a little while he would be proverbial. "I must fly now," he said on his way home, smarting with a sense of absolute social failure. "I must fly soon. If it doesn't come off soon, by God! I shall run amuck."

He said that before he had gone through his pass-book and his litter of papers. Inadequate as the cause seems, it was that girl's voice and the expression of her eyes that precipitated his discontent. But certainly the discovery that he had no longer even one hundred thousand pounds' worth of realisable property behind him was the poison that made the wound deadly.

It was the next day after this that he exploded upon Woodhouse and his workmen, and thereafter his bearing was consistently grim for three weeks, and anxiety dwelt in Cheam and Ewell, Maldon, Morden, and Worcester Park, places that had thriven mightily on his experiments.

Four weeks after that first swearing of his, he stood with Woodhouse by the reconstructed machine as it lay across the elevated railway, by means of which it gained its initial impetus. The new propeller glittered a brighter white than the rest of the machine, and a gilder, obedient to a whim of Monson's was picking out the aluminium bars with gold. And looking down the long avenue between the ropes (gilded now with the sunset), one saw red signals, and two miles away an ant-hill of workmen busy altering the last falls of the run into a rising slope.

"I'll come," said Woodhouse. "I'll come right enough. But I tell you it's infernally foolhardy. If only you would give another year—"

"I tell you I won't. I tell you the thing works. I've given years enough—"

"It's not that," said Woodhouse. "We're all right with the machine. But it's the steering—"

"Haven't I been rushing, night and morning, backwards and forwards, through the squirrel's cage? If the thing steers true here, it will steer true all across England. It's just funk, I tell you, Woodhouse. We could have gone a year ago. And besides—"

"Well?" said Woodhouse.

"The money!" snapped Monson over his shoulder.

"Hang it! I never thought of the money," said Woodhouse, and then, speaking now in a very different tone to that with which he said the words before, he repeated, "I'll come. Trust me."

Monson turned suddenly, and saw all that Woodhouse had not the dexterity to say, shining on his sunset-lit face. He looked for a moment, then impulsively extended his hand. "Thanks," he said.

"All right," said Woodhouse, gripping the hand, and with a queer softening of his features. "Trust me."

Then both men turned to the big apparatus that lay with its flat wings extended upon the carrier, and stared at it meditatively. Monson, guided perhaps by a photographic study of flight of birds, and by Lilienthal's methods, had gradually drifted from Maxim's shapes towards the bird form again. The thing, however, was driven by a huge screw behind in the place of the tail; and so hovering, which needs an almost vertical adjustment of a flat tail, was rendered impossible. The body of the machine was small, almost cylindrical, and pointed. Forward and aft on the pointed ends were two small petroleum engines for the screw, and the navigators sat deep in a canoe-like recess, the foremost one steering, and being protected by a low screen, with two plate-glass windows, from the blinding rush of air. On either side a monstrous flat framework with a curved front border could be adjusted so as either to lie horizontally, or to be tilted upward or down. These wings worked rigidly together, or by releasing a pin, one could be tilted through a small angle independently of its fellow. The front edge of either wing could also be shifted back so as to diminish the wing-area about one-sixth. The machine was not only not designed to hover, but it was also incapable of fluttering. Monson's idea was to get into the air with the initial rush of the apparatus, and then to skim, much as a playing-card may be skimmed, keeping up the rush by means of the screw at the stern. Rooks and gulls fly enormous distances in that way with scarcely a perceptible movement of the wings. The bird really drives along on an aerial switchback. It glides slanting downward for a space, until it has gained considerable momentum, and then altering the inclination of its wings, glides up again almost to its original altitude. Even a Londoner who has watched the birds in the aviary in Regent's Park knows that.

But the bird is practising this art from the moment it leaves its nest. It has not only the perfect apparatus, but the perfect instinct to use it. A man off his feet has the poorest skill in balancing. Even the simple trick of the bicycle costs him some hours of labour. The instantaneous adjustments of the wings, the quick response to a passing breeze, the swift recovery of equilibrium, the giddy, eddying movements that require such absolute precision—all that he must learn, learn with infinite labour and infinite danger, if ever he is to conquer flying. The flying-machine that will start off some fine day, driven by neat "little levers," with a nice open deck like a liner, and all loaded up with bombshells and guns, is the easy dreaming of a literary man. In lives and in treasure the cost of the conquest of the empire of air may even exceed all that has been spent in man's great conquest of the sea. Certainly it will be costlier than the greatest war that has ever devastated the world.

No one knew these things better than these two practical men. And they knew they were in the front rank of the coming army. Yet there is hope even in a forlorn hope. Men are killed outright in the reserves sometimes, while others who have been left for dead in the thickest corner crawl out and survive.

"If we miss these meadows—" said Woodhouse presently in his slow way.

"My dear chap," said Monson, whose spirits had been rising fitfully during the last few days, "we mustn't miss these meadows. There's a quarter of a square mile for us to hit, fences removed, ditches levelled. We shall come down all right—rest assured. And if we don't—"

"Ah!" said Woodhouse. "If we don't!"

Before the day of the start, the newspaper people got wind of the alterations at northward end of the framework, and Monson was cheered by a decided change in the comments Romeike forwarded him. "He will be off some day," said the papers. "He will be off some day," said the South-Western season-ticket holders one to another; the seaside excursionists, the Saturday-to-Monday trippers from Sussex and Hampshire and Dorset and Devon, the eminent literary people from Haslemere, all remarked eagerly one to another, "He will be off some day," as the familiar scaffolding came in sight. And actually, one bright morning, in full view of the ten-past-ten train from Basingstoke, Monson's flying-machine started on its journey.

They saw the carrier running swiftly along its rail, and the white and gold screw spinning in the air. They heard the rapid rumble of wheels, and thud as the carrier reached the buffers at the end of its run. Then a whirr as the Flying-Machine was shot forward into the networks. All that the majority of them had seen and heard before. The thing went with a dropping flight through the framework and rose again, and then every beholder shouted, or screamed, or yelled, or shrieked after his kind. For instead of the customary concussion and stoppage, the Flying-Machine flew out of its five years' cage like a bolt from a crossbow, and drove slantingly upward into the air, curved round a little, so as to cross the line, and soared in the direction of Wimbledon Common.

It seemed to hang momentarily in the air and grow smaller, then it ducked and vanished over the clustering blue tree-tops to the east of Coombe Hill, and no one stopped staring and gasping until long after it had disappeared.

That was what the people in the train from Basingstoke saw. If you had drawn a line down the middle of that train, from engine to guard's van, you would not have found a living soul on the opposite side to the flying-machine. It was a mad rush from window to window as the thing crossed the line. And the engine-driver and stoker never took their eyes off the low hills about Wimbledon, and never noticed that they had run clean through Coombe and Malden and Raynes Park, until with returning animation, they found themselves pelting, at the most indecent pace, into Wimbledon station.

From the moment when Monson had started the carrier with a "Now!" neither he nor Woodhouse said a word. Both men sat with clenched teeth. Monson had crossed the line with a curve that was too sharp, and Woodhouse had opened and shut his white lips; but neither spoke. Woodhouse simply gripped his seat, and breathed sharply through his teeth, watching the blue country to the west rushing past, and down, and away from him. Monson knelt at his post forward, and his hands trembled on the spoked wheel that moved the wings. He could see nothing before him but a mass of white clouds in the sky.

The machine went slanting upward, travelling with an enormous speed still, but losing momentum every moment. The land ran away underneath with diminishing speed.

"Now!" said Woodhouse at last, and with a violent effort Monson wrenched over the wheel and altered the angle of the wings. The machine seemed to hang for half a minute motionless in mid-air, and then he saw the hazy blue house-covered hills of Kilburn and Hampstead jump up before his eyes and rise steadily, until the little sunlit dome of the Albert Hall appeared through his windows. For a moment he scarcely understood the meaning of this upward rush of the horizon, but as the nearer and nearer houses came into view, he realised what he had done. He had turned the wings over too far, and they were swooping steeply downward towards the Thames.

The thought, the question, the realisation were all the business of a second of time. "Too much!" gasped Woodhouse. Monson brought the wheel halfway back with a jerk, and forthwith the Kilburn and Hampstead ridge dropped again to the lower edge of his windows. They had been a thousand feet above Coombe and Malden station; fifty seconds after they whizzed, at a frightful pace, not eighty feet above the East Putney station, on the Metropolitan District line, to the screaming astonishment of a platformful of people. Monson flung up the vans against the air, and over Fulham they rushed up their atmospheric switchback again, steeply—too steeply. The 'buses went floundering across the Fulham Road, the people yelled.

Then down again, too steeply still, and the distant trees and houses about Primrose Hill leapt up across Monson's window, and then suddenly he saw straight before him the greenery of Kensington Gardens and the towers of the Imperial Institute. They were driving straight down upon South Kensington. The pinnacles of the Natural History Museum rushed up into view. There came one fatal second of swift thought, a moment of hesitation. Should he try and clear the towers, or swerve eastward?

He made a hesitating attempt to release the right wing, left the catch half released, and gave a frantic clutch at the wheel.

The nose of the machine seemed to leap up before him. The wheel pressed his hand with irresistible force, and jerked itself out of his control.

Woodhouse, sitting crouched together, gave a hoarse cry, and sprang up towards Monson. "Too far!" he cried, and then he was clinging to the gunwale for dear life, and Monson had been jerked clean overhead, and was falling backwards upon him.

So swiftly had the thing happened that barely a quarter of the people going to and fro in Hyde Park, and Brompton Road, and the Exhibition Road saw anything of the aerial catastrophe. A distant winged shape had appeared above the clustering houses to the south, had fallen and risen, growing larger as it did so; had swooped swiftly down towards the Imperial Institute, a broad spread of flying wings, had swept round in a quarter circle, dashed eastward, and then suddenly sprang vertically into the air. A black object shot out of it, and came spinning downward. A man! Two men clutching each other! They came whirling down, separated as they struck the roof of Students' Club, and bounded off into the green bushes on its southward side.

For perhaps half a minute, the pointed stem of the big machine still pierced vertically upward, the screw spinning desperately. For one brief instant, that yet seemed an age to all who watched, it had hung motionless in mid-air. Then a spout of yellow flame licked up its length from the stern engine, and swift, swifter, swifter, and flaring like a rocket, it rushed down upon the solid mass of masonry which was formerly the Royal College of Science. The big screw of white and gold touched the parapet, and crumpled up like wet linen. Then the blazing spindle-shaped body smashed and splintered, smashing and splintering in its fall, upon the north-westward angle of the building.

But the crash, the flame of blazing paraffin that shot heavenward from the shattered engines of the machine, the crushed horrors that were found in the garden beyond the Students' Club, the masses of yellow parapet and red brick that fell headlong into the roadway, the running to and fro of people like ants in a broken ant-hill, the galloping of fire-engines, the gathering of crowds—all these things do not belong to this story, which was written only to tell how the first of all successful flying-machines was launched and flew. Though he failed, and failed disastrously, the record of Monson's work remains a sufficient monument—to guide the next of that band of gallant experimentalists who will sooner or later master this great problem of flying. And between Worcester Park and Malden there still stands that portentous avenue of iron-work, rusting now, and dangerous here and there, to witness to the first desperate struggle for man's right of way through the air.

12

The Cone

The night was hot and overcast, the sky red, rimmed with the lingering sunset of mid-summer. They sat at the open window, trying to fancy the air was fresher there. The trees and shrubs of the garden stood stiff and dark; beyond in the roadway a gas-lamp burnt, bright orange against the hazy blue of the evening. Farther were the three lights of the railway signal against the lowering sky. The man and woman spoke to one another in low tones.

"He does not suspect?" said the man, a little nervously.

"Not he." She said peevishly, as though that too irritated her. "He thinks of nothing but the works and the prices of fuel. He has no imagination, no poetry."

"None of these men of iron have," he said sententiously. "They have no hearts."

"He has not," she said. She turned her discontented face towards the window. The distant sound of a roaring and rushing drew nearer and grew in volume; the house quivered; one heard the metallic rattle of the tender. As the train passed, there was a glare of light above the cutting and a driving tumult of smoke; one, two, three, four, five, six, seven, eight black oblongs—eight trucks—passed across the dim grey of the embankment, and were suddenly extinguished one by one in the throat of the tunnel, which with the last, seemed to swallow down train, smoke, and sound in one abrupt gulp.

"This country was all fresh and beautiful once," he said; "and now—it is Gehenna. Down that way—nothing but pot-banks and chimneys belching fire and dust into the face of heaven...But what does it matter? An end comes, an end to all this cruelty...To-morrow." He spoke the last word in a whisper.

"To-morrow," she said, speaking in a whisper too, and still staring out of the window.

"Dear!" he said, putting his hand on hers.

She turned with a start, and their eyes searched one another's. Hers softened to his gaze. "My dear one!" she said, and then: "It seems so strange—that you should have come into my life like this—to open—" She paused.

"To open?" he said.

"All this wonderful world—" she hesitated, and spoke still more softly—"this world of love to me."

Then suddenly the door clicked and closed. They turned their heads, and he started violently back. In the shadow of the room stood a great shadowy figure—silent. They saw the face dimly in the half-light, with unexpressive dark patches under the penthouse brows. Every muscle in Raut's body suddenly became tense. When could the door have opened? What had he heard? Had he heard all? What had he seen? A tumult of questions.

The new-comer's voice came at last, after a pause that seemed interminable. "Well?" he said.

"I was afraid I had missed you, Horrocks," said the man at the window, gripping the window-ledge with his hand. His voice was unsteady.

The clumsy figure of Horrocks came forward out of the shadow. He made no answer to Raut's remark. For a moment he stood above them.

The woman's heart was cold within her. "I told Mr. Raut it was just possible you might come back," she said, in a voice that never quivered.

Horrocks, still silent, sat down abruptly in the chair by her little work-table. His big hands were clenched; one saw now the fire of his eyes under the shadow of his brows. He was trying to get his breath. His eyes went from the woman he had trusted to the friend he had trusted, and then back to the woman.

By this time and for the moment all three half understood one another. Yet none dared say a word to ease the pent-up things that choked them.

It was the husband's voice that broke the silence at last.

"You wanted to see me?" he said to Raut.

Raut started as he spoke. "I came to see you," he said, resolved to lie to the last.

"Yes," said Horrocks.

"You promised," said Raut, "to show me some fine effects of moonlight and smoke."

"I promised to show you some fine effects of moonlight and smoke," repeated Horrocks in a colourless voice.

"And I thought I might catch you to-night before you went down to the works," proceeded Raut, "and come with you."

There was another pause. Did the man mean to take the thing coolly? Did he after all know? How long had he been in the room? Yet even at the moment when they heard the door, their attitudes... Horrocks glanced at the profile of the woman, shadowy pallid in the half-light. Then he glanced at Raut, and seemed to recover himself suddenly. "Of course," he said, "I promised to show you the works under their proper dramatic conditions. It's odd how I could have forgotten."

"If I am troubling you—" began Raut.

Horrocks started again. A new light had suddenly come into the sultry gloom of his eyes. "Not in the least," he said.

"Have you been telling Mr. Raut of all these contrasts of flame and shadow you think so splendid?" said the woman, turning now to her husband for the first time, her confidence creeping back again, her voice just one half-note too high. "That dreadful theory of yours that machinery is beautiful, and everything else in the world ugly. I thought he would not spare you, Mr. Raut. It's his great theory, his one discovery in art."

"I am slow to make discoveries," said Horrocks grimly, damping her suddenly. "But what I discover..." He stopped.

"Well?" she said.

"Nothing;" and suddenly he rose to his feet.

"I promised to show you the works," he said to Raut, and put his big, clumsy hand on his friend's shoulder. "And you are ready to go?"

"Quite," said Raut, and stood up also.

There was another pause. Each of them peered through the indistinctness of the dusk at the other two. Horrocks' hand still rested on Raut's shoulder. Raut half fancied still that the incident was trivial after all. But Mrs. Horrocks knew her husband better, knew that grim quiet in his voice, and the confusion in her mind took a vague shape of physical evil. "Very well," said Horrocks, and dropping his hand, turned towards the door.

"My hat?" Raut looked round in the half-light.

"That's my work-basket," said Mrs. Horrocks, with a gust of hysterical laughter. Their hands came together on the back of the chair. "Here it is!" he said. She had an impulse to warn him in an undertone, but she could not frame a word. "Don't go!" and "Beware of him!" struggled in her mind, and the swift moment passed.

"Got it?" said Horrocks, standing with the door half open.

Raut stepped towards him. "Better say good-bye to Mrs. Horrocks," said the ironmaster, even more grimly quiet in his tone than before.

Raut started and turned. "Good-evening, Mrs. Horrocks," he said, and their hands touched.

Horrocks held the door open with a ceremonial politeness unusual in him towards men. Raut went out, and then, after a wordless look at her, her husband followed. She stood motionless while Raut's light footfall and her husband's heavy tread, like bass and treble, passed down the passage together. The front door slammed heavily. She went to the window, moving slowly, and stood watching—leaning forward. The two men appeared for a moment at the gateway in the road, passed under the street-lamp, and were hidden by the black masses of the shrubbery. The lamplight fell for a moment on their faces, showing only unmeaning pale patches, telling nothing of what she still feared, and doubted, and craved vainly to know. Then she sank down into a crouching attitude in the big armchair, her eyes wide open and staring out at the red lights from the furnaces that flickered in the sky. An hour after she was still there, her attitude scarcely changed.

The oppressive stillness of the evening weighed heavily upon Raut. They went side by side down the road in silence, and in silence turned into the cinder-made by-way that presently opened out the prospect of the valley.

A blue haze, half dust, half mist, touched the long valley with mystery. Beyond were Hanley and Etruria, grey and dark masses, outlined thinly by the rare golden dots of the street-lamps, and here and there a gaslit window, or the yellow glare of some late-working factory or crowded public-house. Out of the masses, clear and slender against the evening sky, rose a multitude of tall chimneys, many of them reeking, a few smokeless during a season of "play." Here and there a pallid patch and ghostly stunted beehive shapes showed the position of a pot-bank, or a wheel, black and sharp against the hot lower sky, marked some colliery where they raise the iridescent coal of the place. Nearer at hand was the broad stretch of railway, and half invisible trains shunted—a steady puffing and rumbling, with every run a ringing concussion and a rhythmic series of impacts, and a passage of intermittent puffs of white steam across the further view. And to the left, between the railway and the dark mass of the low hill beyond, dominating the whole view, colossal, inky-black, and crowned with smoke and fitful flames, stood the great cylinders of the Jeddah Company Blast Furnaces, the central edifices of the big ironworks of which Horrocks was the manager. They stood heavy and threatening, full of an incessant turmoil of flames and seething molten iron, and about the feet of them rattled the rolling-mills, and the steam-hammer beat heavily and splashed the white iron sparks hither and thither. Even as they looked, a truckful of fuel was shot into one of the giants, and the red flames gleamed out, and a confusion of smoke and black dust came boiling upwards towards the sky.

"Certainly you get some fine effects of colour with your furnaces," said Raut, breaking a silence that had become apprehensive.

Horrocks grunted. He stood with his hands in his pockets, frowning down at the dim steaming railway and the busy ironworks beyond, frowning as if he were thinking out some knotty problem.

Raut glanced at him and away again. "At present your moonlight effect is hardly ripe," he continued, looking upward. "The moon is still smothered by the vestiges of daylight."

Horrocks stared at him with the expression of a man who has suddenly awakened. "Vestiges of daylight...? Of course, of course." He too looked up at the moon, pale still in the midsummer sky. "Come along," he said suddenly, and gripping Raut's arm in his hand, made a move towards the path that dropped from them to the railway.

Raut hung back. Their eyes met and saw a thousand things in a moment that their eyes came near to say. Horrocks' hand tightened and then relaxed. He let go, and before Raut was aware of it, they were arm in arm, and walking, one unwillingly enough, down the path.

"You see the fine effect of the railway signals towards Burslem," said Horrocks, suddenly breaking into loquacity, striding fast, and tightening the grip of his elbow the while. "Little green lights and red and white lights, all against the haze. You have an eye for effect, Raut. It's a fine effect. And look at those furnaces of mine, how they rise upon us as we come down the hill. That to the right is my pet—seventy feet of him. I packed him myself, and he's boiled away cheerfully with iron in his guts for five long years. I've a particular fancy for him. That line of red there—a lovely bit of warm orange you'd call it, Raut—that's the puddlers' furnaces, and there, in the hot light, three black figures—did you see the white splash of the steam-hammer then—? That's the rolling mills. Come along! Clang, clatter, how it goes rattling across the floor! Sheet tin, Raut—, amazing stuff. Glass mirrors are not in it when that stuff comes from the mill. And squelch—! There goes the hammer again. Come along!"

He had to stop talking to catch at his breath. His arm twisted into Raut's with benumbing tightness. He had come striding down the black path towards the railway as though he was possessed.

Raut had not spoken a word, had simply hung back against Horrocks' pull with all his strength.

"I say," he said now, laughing nervously, but with an undernote of snarl in his voice, "why on earth are you nipping my arm off, Horrocks, and dragging me along like this?"

At length Horrocks released him. His manner changed again. "Nipping your arm off?" he said. "Sorry. But it's you taught me the trick of walking in that friendly way."

"You haven't learnt the refinements of it yet then," said Raut, laughing artificially again. "By Jove! I'm black and blue," Horrocks offered no apology. They stood now near the bottom of the hill, close to the fence that bordered the railway. The ironworks had grown larger and spread out with their approach. They looked up to the blast furnaces now instead of down; the further view of Etruria and Hanley had dropped out of sight with their descent. Before them, by the stile rose a notice-board, bearing still dimly visible, the words, "Beware Of The Trains," half hidden by splashes of coaly mud.

"Fine effects," said Horrocks, waving his arm. "Here comes a train. The puffs of smoke, the orange glare, the round eye of light in front of it, the melodious rattle. Fine effects! But these furnaces of mine used to be finer, before we shoved cones in their throats, and saved the gas."

"How?" said Raut. "Cones?"

"Cones, my man, cones. I'll show you one nearer. The flames used to flare out of the open throats, great—what is it—? Pillars of cloud by day, red and black smoke, and pillars of fire by night. Now we run it off in pipes, and burn it to heat the blast, and the top is shut by a cone. You'll be interested in that cone."

"But every now and then," said Raut, "you get a burst of fire and smoke up there."

"The cone's not fixed, it's hung by a chain from a lever, and balanced by an equipoise. You shall see it nearer. Else of course, there'd be no way of getting fuel into the thing. Every now and then the cone dips, and out comes the flare."

"I see," said Raut. He looked over his shoulder. "The moon gets brighter," he said.

"Come along," said Horrocks abruptly, gripping his shoulder again, and moving him suddenly towards the railway crossing. And then came one of those swift incidents, vivid, but so rapid that they leave one doubtful and reeling. Halfway across, Horrocks' hand suddenly clenched upon him like a vice, and swung him backward and through a half-turn, so that he looked up the line. And there a chain of lamp-lit carriage-windows telescoped swiftly as it came towards them, and the red and yellow lights of an engine grew larger and larger, rushing down upon them. As he grasped what this meant, he turned his face to Horrocks, and pushed with all his strength against the arm that held him back between the rails. The struggle did not last a moment. Just as certain as it was that Horrocks held him there, so certain was it that he had been violently lugged out of danger.

"Out of the way," said Horrocks, with a gasp, as the train came rattling by, and they stood panting by the gate into the ironworks.

"I did not see it coming," said Raut, still even in spite of his own apprehensions, trying to keep up an appearance of ordinary intercourse.

Horrocks answered with a grunt. "The cone," he said, and then, as one who recovers himself, "I thought you did not hear."

"I didn't," said Raut.

"I wouldn't have had you run over then, for the world," said Horrocks.

"For a moment I lost my nerve," said Raut.

Horrocks stood for half a minute, then turned abruptly towards the ironworks again. "See how fine these great mounds of mine, these clinker-heaps, look in the night! That truck yonder, up above there! Up it goes, and out-tilts the slag. See the palpitating red stuff go sliding down the slope. As we get nearer, the heap rises up and cuts the blast furnaces. See the quiver up above the big one. Not that way! This way, between the heaps. That goes to the puddling furnaces, but I want to show you the canal first." He came and took Raut by the elbow, and so they went along side by side. Raut answered Horrocks vaguely. What, he asked himself, had really happened on the line? Was he deluding himself with his own fancies, or had Horrocks actually held him back in the way of the train? Had he just been within an ace of being murdered?

Suppose this slouching, scowling monster did know anything? For a minute or two then Raut was really afraid for his life, but the mood passed as he reasoned with himself. After all, Horrocks might have heard nothing. At any rate, he had pulled him out of the way in time. His odd manner might be due to the mere vague jealousy he had shown once before. He was talking now of the ash-heaps and the canal. "Eigh?" said Horrocks.

"What?" said Raut. "Rather! The haze in the moonlight. Fine!"

"Our canal," said Horrocks, stopping suddenly. "Our canal by moonlight and firelight is an immense effect. You've never seen it? Fancy that! You've spent too many of your evenings philandering up in Newcastle there. I tell you, for real florid effects—But you shall see. Boiling water..."

As they came out of the labyrinth of clinker-heaps and mounds of coal and ore, the noises of the rolling-mill sprang upon them suddenly, loud, near, and distinct. Three shadowy workmen went by and touched their caps to Horrocks. Their faces were vague in the darkness. Raut felt a futile impulse to address them, and before he could frame his words, they passed into the shadows. Horrocks pointed to the canal close before them now: a weird-looking place it seemed, in the blood-red reflections of the furnaces. The hot water that cooled the tuyeres came into it, some fifty yards up—a tumultuous, almost boiling affluent, and the steam rose up from the water in silent white wisps and streaks, wrapping damply about them, an incessant succession of ghosts coming up from the black and red eddies, a white uprising that made the head swim. The shining black tower of the larger blast-furnace rose overhead out of the mist, and its tumultuous riot filled their ears. Raut kept away from the edge of the water, and watched Horrocks.

"Here it is red," said Horrocks, "blood-red vapour as red and hot as sin; but yonder there, where the moonlight falls on it, and it drives across the clinker-heaps, it is as white as death."

Raut turned his head for a moment, and then came back hastily to his watch on Horrocks. "Come along to the rolling-mills," said Horrocks. The threatening hold was not so evident that time, and Raut felt a little reassured. But all the same, what on earth did Horrocks mean about "white as death" and "red as sin"? Coincidence, perhaps?

They went and stood behind the puddlers for a little while, and then through the rolling-mills, where amidst an incessant din the deliberate steam-hammer beat the juice out of the succulent iron, and black, half-naked Titans rushed the plastic bars, like hot sealing-wax, between the wheels. "Come on," said Horrocks in Raut's ear, and they went and peeped through the little glass hole behind the tuyeres, and saw the tumbled fire writhing in the pit of the blast-furnace. It left one eye blinded for a while. Then, with green and blue patches dancing across the dark, they went to the lift by which the trucks of ore and fuel and lime were raised to the top of the big cylinder.

And out upon the narrow rail that overhung the furnace, Raut's doubts came upon him again. Was it wise to be here? If Horrocks did know—everything! Do what he would, he could not resist a violent trembling. Right under foot was a sheer depth of seventy feet. It was a dangerous place. They pushed by a truck of fuel to get to the railing that crowned the place. The reek of the furnace, a sulphurous vapour streaked with pungent bitterness, seemed to make the distant hillside of Hanley quiver. The moon was riding out now from among a drift of clouds, halfway up the sky above the undulating wooded outlines of Newcastle. The steaming canal ran away from below them under an indistinct bridge, and vanished into the dim haze of the flat fields towards Burslem.

"That's the cone I've been telling you of," shouted Horrocks; "and, below that, sixty feet of fire and molten metal, with the air of the blast frothing through it like gas in soda-water."

Raut gripped the hand-rail tightly, and stared down at the cone. The heat was intense. The boiling of the iron and the tumult of the blast made a thunderous accompaniment to Horrocks' voice. But the thing had to be gone through now. Perhaps, after all...

"In the middle," bawled Horrocks, "temperature near a thousand degrees. If YOU were dropped into it...flash into flame like a pinch of gunpowder in a candle. Put your hand out and feel the heat of his breath. Why, even up here I've seen the rain-water boiling off the trucks. And that cone there. It's a damned sight too hot for roasting cakes. The top side of it's three hundred degrees."

"Three hundred degrees!" said Raut.

"Three hundred centigrade, mind!" said Horrocks. "It will boil the blood out of you in no time."

"Eigh?" said Raut, and turned.

"Boil the blood out of you in...No, you don't!"

"Let me go!" screamed Raut. "Let go my arm!"

With one hand he clutched at the hand-rail, then with both. For a moment the two men stood swaying. Then suddenly, with a violent jerk, Horrocks had twisted him from his hold. He clutched at Horrocks and missed, his foot went back into empty air; in mid-air he twisted himself, and then cheek and shoulder and knee struck the hot cone together.

He clutched the chain by which the cone hung, and the thing sank an infinitesimal amount as he struck it. A circle of glowing red appeared about him, and a tongue of flame, released from the chaos within, flickered up towards him. An intense pain assailed him at the knees, and he could smell the singeing of his hands. He raised himself to his feet, and tried to climb up the chain, and then something struck his head. Black and shining with the moonlight, the throat of the furnace rose about him.

Horrocks, he saw, stood above him by one of the trucks of fuel on the rail. The gesticulating figure was bright and white in the moonlight, and shouting, "Fizzle, you fool! Fizzle, you hunter of women! You hot-blooded hound! Boil! Boil! Boil!"

Suddenly he caught up a handful of coal out of the truck, and flung it deliberately, lump after lump, at Raut.

"Horrocks!" cried Raut. "Horrocks!"

He clung crying to the chain, pulling himself up from the burning of the cone. Each missile Horrocks flung hit him. His clothes charred and glowed, and as he struggled the cone dropped, and a rush of hot suffocating gas whooped out and burned round him in a swift breath of flame.

His human likeness departed from him. When the momentary red had passed, Horrocks saw a charred, blackened figure, its head streaked with blood, still clutching and fumbling with the chain, and writhing in agony—a cindery animal, an inhuman, monstrous creature that began a sobbing intermittent shriek.

Abruptly, at the sight, the ironmaster's anger passed. A deadly sickness came upon him. The heavy odour of burning flesh came drifting up to his nostrils. His sanity returned to him.

"God have mercy upon me!" he cried. "O God! What have I done?"

He knew the thing below him, save that it still moved and felt, was already a dead man—that the blood of the poor wretch must be boiling in his veins. An intense realisation of that agony came to his mind, and overcame every other feeling. For a moment he stood irresolute, and then, turning to the truck, he hastily tilted its contents upon the struggling thing that had once been a man. The mass fell with a thud, and went radiating over the cone. With the thud the shriek ended, and a boiling confusion of smoke, dust, and flame came rushing up towards him. As it passed, he saw the cone clear again.

Then he staggered back, and stood trembling, clinging to the rail with both hands. His lips moved, but no words came to them.

Down below was the sound of voices and running steps. The clangour of rolling in the shed ceased abruptly.

13

The Flying Man

The Ethnologist looked at the bhimraj feather thoughtfully. "They seemed loth to part with it," he said.

"It is sacred to the Chiefs," said the lieutenant; "just as yellow silk, you know, is sacred to the Chinese Emperor."

The Ethnologist did not answer. He hesitated. Then opening the topic abruptly, "What on earth is this cock-and-bull story they have of a flying man?"

The lieutenant smiled faintly. "What did they tell you?"

"I see," said the Ethnologist, "that you know of your fame."

The lieutenant rolled himself a cigarette. "I don't mind hearing about it once more. How does it stand at present?"

"It's so confoundedly childish," said the Ethnologist, becoming irritated. "How did you play it off upon them?"

The lieutenant made no answer, but lounged back in his folding-chair, still smiling.

"Here am I, come four hundred miles out of my way to get what is left of the folk-lore of these people, before they are utterly demoralised by missionaries and the military, and all I find are a lot of impossible legends about a sandy-haired scrub of an infantry lieutenant. How he is invulnerable—how he can jump over elephants—how he can fly. That's the toughest nut. One old gentleman described your wings, said they had black plumage and were not quite as long as a mule. Said he often saw you by moonlight hovering over the crests out towards the Shendu country. Confound it, man!"

The lieutenant laughed cheerfully. "Go on," he said. "Go on."

The Ethnologist did. At last he wearied. "To trade so," he said, "on these unsophisticated children of the mountains. How could you bring yourself to do it, man?"

"I'm sorry," said the lieutenant, "but truly the thing was forced upon me. I can assure you I was driven to it. And at the time I had not the faintest idea of how the Chin imagination would take it. Or curiosity. I can only plead it was an indiscretion and not malice that made me replace the folk-lore by a new legend. But as you seem aggrieved, I will try and explain the business to you.

"It was in the time of the last Lushai expedition but one, and Walters thought these people, you have been visiting, were friendly. So, with an airy confidence in my capacity for taking care of myself, he sent me up the gorge—fourteen miles of it—with three of the Derbyshire men and half a dozen Sepoys, two mules, and his blessing, to see what popular feeling was like at that village you visited. A force of ten—not counting the mules—fourteen miles, and during a war! You saw the road?"

"Road!" said the Ethnologist.

"It's better now than it was. When we went up, we had to wade in the river for a mile, where the valley narrows, with a smart stream frothing round our knees and the stones as slippery as ice. There it was I dropped my rifle. Afterwards the Sappers blasted the cliff with dynamite and made the convenient way you came by. Then below, where those very high cliffs come, we had to keep on dodging across the river—I should say we crossed it a dozen times in a couple of miles.

"We got in sight of the place early the next morning. You know how it lies, on a spur halfway between the big hills, and as we began to appreciate how wickedly quiet the village lay under the sunlight, we came to a stop to consider.

"At that they fired a lump of filed brass idol at us, just by way of a welcome. It came twanging down the slope to the right of us where the boulders are, missed my shoulder by an inch or so, and plugged the mule that carried all the provisions and utensils. I never heard such a death-rattle before or since. And at that we became aware of a number of gentlemen carrying matchlocks, and dressed in things like plaid dusters, dodging about along the neck between the village and the crest to the east.

"'Right about face,' I said. 'Not too close together.'

"And with that encouragement my expedition of ten men came round and set off at a smart trot down the valley again hitherward. We did not wait to save anything our dead had carried, but we kept the second mule with us—he carried my tent and some other rubbish—out of a feeling of friendship.

"So ended the battle—ingloriously. Glancing back, I saw the valley dotted with the victors, shouting and firing at us. But no one was hit. These Chins and their guns are very little good except at a sitting shot. They will sit and finick over a boulder for hours taking aim, and when they fire running it is chiefly for stage effect. Hooker, one of the Derbyshire men, fancied himself rather with the rifle, and stopped behind for half a minute to try his luck as we turned the bend. But he got nothing.

"I'm not a Xenophon to spin much of a yarn about my retreating army. We had to pull the enemy up twice in the next two miles when he became a bit pressing, by exchanging shots with him, but it was a fairly monotonous affair—hard breathing chiefly—until we got near the place where the hills run in towards the river and pinch the valley into a gorge. And there we very luckily caught a glimpse of half a dozen round black heads coming slanting-ways over the hill to the left of us—the east that is—and almost parallel with us.

"At that I called a halt. 'Look here,' says I to Hooker and the other Englishmen; 'what are we to do now?' and I pointed to the heads.

"'Headed orf, or I'm a nigger,' said one of the men."

"'We shall be,' said another. 'You know the Chin way, George?'

"'They can pot every one of us at fifty yards,' says Hooker, 'in the place where the river is narrow. It's just suicide to go on down.'

"I looked at the hill to the right of us. It grew steeper lower down the valley, but it still seemed climbable. And all the Chins we had seen hitherto had been on the other side of the stream.

"'It's that or stopping,' says one of the Sepoys.

"So we started slanting up the hill. There was something faintly suggestive of a road running obliquely up the face of it, and that we followed. Some Chins presently came into view up the valley, and I heard some shots. Then I saw one of the Sepoys was sitting down about thirty yards below us. He had simply sat down without a word, apparently not wishing to give trouble. At that I called a halt again; I told Hooker to try another shot, and went back and found the man was hit in the leg. I took him up, carried him along to put him on the mule—already pretty well laden with the tent and other things which we had no time to take off. When I got up to the rest with him, Hooker had his empty Martini in his hand, and was grinning and pointing to a motionless black spot up the valley. All the rest of the Chins were behind boulders or back round the bend. 'Five hundred yards,' says Hooker, 'if an inch. And I'll swear I hit him in the head.'

"I told him to go and do it again, and with that we went on again.

"Now the hillside kept getting steeper as we pushed on, and the road we were following more and more of a shelf. At last it was mere cliff above and below us. 'It's the best road I have seen yet in Chin Lushai land,' said I to encourage the men, though I had a fear of what was coming.

"And in a few minutes the way bent round a corner of the cliff. Then, finis! The ledge came to an end.

"As soon as he grasped the position one of the Derbyshire men fell a-swearing at the trap we had fallen into. The Sepoys halted quietly. Hooker grunted and reloaded, and went back to the bend.

"Then two of the Sepoy chaps helped their comrade down and began to unload the mule.

"Now, when I came to look about me, I began to think we had not been so very unfortunate after all. We were on a shelf perhaps ten yards across it at widest. Above it the cliff projected so that we could not be shot down upon, and below was an almost sheer precipice of perhaps two or three hundred feet. Lying down we were invisible to anyone across the ravine. The only approach was along the ledge, and on that one man was as good as a host. We were in a natural stronghold, with only one disadvantage, our sole provision against hunger and thirst was one live mule. Still we were at most eight or nine miles from the main expedition, and no doubt, after a day or so, they would send up after us if we did not return.

"After a day or so..."

The lieutenant paused. "Ever been thirsty, Graham?"

"Not that kind," said the Ethnologist.

"H'm. We had the whole of that day, the night, and the next day of it, and only a trifle of dew we wrung out of our clothes and the tent. And below us was the river going giggle, giggle, round a rock in mid stream. I never knew such a barrenness of incident, or such a quantity of sensation. The sun might have had Joshua's command still upon it for all the motion one could see; and it blazed like a near furnace. Towards the evening of the first day one of the Derbyshire men said something—nobody heard what—and went off round the bend of the cliff. We heard shots, and when Hooker looked round the corner he was gone. And in the morning the Sepoy whose leg was shot was in delirium, and jumped or fell over the cliff. Then we took the mule and shot it, and that must needs go over the cliff too in its last struggles, leaving eight of us.

"We could see the body of the Sepoy down below, with the head in the water. He was lying face downwards, and so far as I could make out was scarcely smashed at all. Badly as the Chins might covet his head, they had the sense to leave it alone until the darkness came.

"At first we talked of all the chances there were of the main body hearing the firing, and reckoned whether they would begin to miss us, and all that kind of thing, but we dried up as the evening came on. The Sepoys played games with bits of stone among themselves, and afterwards told stories. The night was rather chilly. The second day nobody spoke. Our lips were black and our throats afire, and we lay about on the ledge and glared at one another. Perhaps it's as well we kept our thoughts to ourselves. One of the British soldiers began writing some blasphemous rot on the rock with a bit of pipeclay, about his last dying will, until I stopped it. As I looked over the edge down into the valley and saw the river rippling I was nearly tempted to go after the Sepoy. It seemed a pleasant and desirable thing to go rushing down through the air with something to drink—or no more thirst at any rate—at the bottom. I remembered in time, though, that I was the officer in command, and my duty to set a good example, and that kept me from any such foolishness.

"Yet, thinking of that, put an idea into my head. I got up and looked at the tent and tent ropes, and wondered why I had not thought of it before. Then I came and peered over the cliff again. This time the height seemed greater and the pose of the Sepoy rather more painful. But it was that or nothing. And to cut it short, I parachuted.

"I got a big circle of canvas out of the tent, about three times the size of that table-cover, and plugged the hole in the centre, and I tied eight ropes round it to meet in the middle and make a parachute. The other chaps lay about and watched me as though they thought it was a new kind of delirium. Then I explained my notion to the two British soldiers and how I meant to do it, and as soon as the short dusk had darkened into night, I risked it. They held the thing high up, and I took a run the whole length of the ledge. The thing filled with air like a sail, but at the edge I will confess I funked and pulled up.

"As soon as I stopped I was ashamed of myself—as well I might be in front of privates—and went back and started again. Off I jumped this time—with a kind of sob, I remember—clean into the air, with the big white sail bellying out above me.

"I must have thought at a frightful pace. It seemed a long time before I was sure that the thing meant to keep steady. At first it heeled sideways. Then I noticed the face of the rock which seemed to be streaming up past me, and me motionless. Then I looked down and saw in the darkness the river and the dead Sepoy rushing up towards me. But in the indistinct light I also saw three Chins, seemingly aghast at the sight of me, and that the Sepoy was decapitated. At that I wanted to go back again.

"Then my boot was in the mouth of one, and in a moment he and I were in a heap with the canvas fluttering down on the top of us. I fancy I dashed out his brains with my foot. I expected nothing more than to be brained myself by the other two, but the poor heathen had never heard of Baldwin, and incontinently bolted.

"I struggled out of the tangle of dead Chin and canvas, and looked round. About ten paces off lay the head of the Sepoy staring in the moonlight. Then I saw the water and went and drank. There wasn't a sound in the world but the footsteps of the departing Chins, a faint shout from above, and the gluck of the water. So soon as I had drunk my full I started off down the river.

"That about ends the explanation of the flying man story. I never met a soul the whole eight miles of the way. I got to Walters' camp by ten o'clock, and a born idiot of a sentinel had the cheek to fire at me as I came trotting out of the darkness. So soon as I had hammered my story into Winter's thick skull, about fifty men started up the valley to clear the Chins out and get our men down. But for my own part I had too good a thirst to provoke it, by going with them.

"You have heard what kind of a yarn the Chins made of it. Wings as long as a mule, eh—? And black feathers! The gay lieutenant bird! Well, well."

The lieutenant meditated cheerfully for a moment. Then he added, "You would scarcely credit it, but when they got to the ridge at last, they found two more of the Sepoys had jumped over."

"The rest were all right?" asked the Ethnologist.

"Yes," said the lieutenant; "the rest were all right, barring a certain thirst, you know."

And at the memory he helped himself to soda and whisky again.

14

The Moth

Probably you have heard of Hapley—not W.T. Hapley, the son, but the celebrated Hapley, the Hapley of 'Periplaneta Hapliia,' Hapley the entomologist.

If so you know at least of the great feud between Hapley and Professor Pawkins, though certain of its consequences may be new to you. For those who have not, a word or two of explanation is necessary, which the idle reader may go over with a glancing eye, if his indolence so incline him.

It is amazing how very widely diffused is the ignorance of such really important matters as this Hapley-Pawkins feud. Those epoch-making controversies, again that have convulsed the Geological Society are, I verily believe, almost entirely unknown outside the fellowship of that body. I have heard men of fair general education even refer to the great scenes at these meetings as vestry-meeting squabbles. Yet the great hate of the English and Scotch geologists has lasted now half a century, and has "left deep and abundant marks upon the body of the science." And this Hapley-Pawkins business, though perhaps a more personal affair, stirred passions as profound, if not profounder. Your common man has no conception of the zeal that animates a scientific investigator, the fury of contradiction you can arouse in him. It is the odium theologicum (theological hatred) in a new form. There are men, for instance, who would gladly burn Professor Ray Lankester at Smithfield for his treatment of the

Mollusca in the Encyclopaedia. That fantastic extension of the Cephalopods to cover the Pteropods...But I wander from Hapley and Pawkins.

It began years and years ago, with a revision of the Microlepidoptera (whatever these may be) by Pawkins, in which he extinguished a new species created by Hapley. Hapley, who was always quarrelsome, replied by a stinging impeachment of the entire classification of Pawkins*. Pawkins in his "Rejoinder**" suggested that Hapley's microscope was as defective as his power of observation, and called him an "irresponsible meddler—" Hapley was not a professor at that time. Hapley in his retort***, spoke of "blundering collectors," and described, as if inadvertently, Pawkins' revision as a "miracle of ineptitude." It was war to the knife. However, it would scarcely interest the reader to detail how these two great men quarrelled, and how the split between them widened until from the Microlepidoptera they were at war upon every open question in entomology. There were memorable occasions. At times the Royal Entomological Society meetings resembled nothing so much as the Chamber of Deputies. On the whole, I fancy Pawkins was nearer the truth than Hapley. But Hapley was skilful with his rhetoric, had a turn for ridicule rare in a scientific man, was endowed with vast energy, and had a fine sense of injury in the matter of the extinguished species; while Pawkins was a man of dull presence, prosy of speech, in shape not unlike a water-barrel, over-conscientious with testimonials, and suspected of jobbing museum appointments. So the young men gathered round Hapley and applauded him. It was a long struggle, vicious from the beginning and growing at last to pitiless antagonism. The successive turns of fortune, now an advantage to one side and now to another—now Hapley tormented by some success of Pawkins, and now Pawkins outshone by Hapley, belong rather to the history of entomology than to this story.

But in 1891 Pawkins, whose health had been bad for some time, published some work upon the "mesoblast" of the Death's-Head

---

* "Remarks on a Recent Revision of Microlepidoptera," *Quarterly Journal Entomological Society*, 1863.

** "Rejoinder to Certain Remarks," etc. Ibid. 1864.

*** "Further Remarks," etc. Ibid.

Moth. What the mesoblast of the Death's-Head Moth may be does not matter a rap in this story. But the work was far below his usual standard, and gave Hapley an opening he had coveted for years. He must have worked night and day to make the most of his advantage.

In an elaborate critique he rent Pawkins to tatters—one can fancy the man's disordered black hair, and his queer dark eyes flashing as he went for his antagonist—and Pawkins made a reply, halting, ineffectual, with painful gaps of silence, and yet malignant. There was no mistaking his will to wound Hapley, nor his incapacity to do it. But few of those who heard him—I was absent from that meeting—realised how ill the man was.

Hapley got his opponent down, and meant to finish him. He followed with a simply brutal attack upon Pawkins, in the form of a paper upon the development of moths in general, a paper showing evidence of a most extraordinary amount of mental labour, and yet couched in a violently controversial tone. Violent as it was, an editorial note witnesses that it was modified. It must have covered Pawkins with shame and confusion of face. It left no loophole; it was murderous in argument, and utterly contemptuous in tone; an awful thing for the declining years of a man's career.

The world of entomologists waited breathlessly for the rejoinder from Pawkins. He would try one, for Pawkins had always been game. But when it came it surprised them. For the rejoinder of Pawkins was to catch influenza, proceed to pneumonia, and die.

It was perhaps as effectual a reply as he could make under the circumstances, and largely turned the current of feeling against Hapley. The very people who had most gleefully cheered on those gladiators became serious at the consequence. There could be no reasonable doubt the fret of the defeat had contributed to the death of Pawkins. There was a limit even to scientific controversy, said serious people. Another crushing attack was already in the press and appeared on the day before the funeral. I don't think Hapley exerted himself to stop it. People remembered how Hapley had hounded down his rival, and forgot that rival's defects. Scathing satire reads ill over fresh mould. The thing provoked comment in the daily papers. This it was that made me think that you had probably heard of Hapley and this controversy. But, as I have already remarked, scientific workers live very much in a world of their own; half the people, I dare say, who go along Piccadilly to the Academy every year, could not tell you where the learned societies abide. Many even think that research is a kind of happy-family cage in which all kinds of men lie down together in peace.

In his private thoughts Hapley could not forgive Pawkins for dying. In the first place, it was a mean dodge to escape the absolute pulverisation Hapley had in hand for him, and in the second, it left Hapley's mind with a queer gap in it. For twenty years he had worked hard, sometimes far into the night, and seven days a week, with microscope, scalpel, collecting-net, and pen, and almost entirely with reference to Pawkins. The European reputation he had won had come as an incident in that great antipathy. He had gradually worked up to a climax in this last controversy. It had killed Pawkins, but it had also thrown Hapley out of gear, so to speak, and his doctor advised him to give up work for a time, and rest. So Hapley went down into a quiet village in Kent, and thought day and night of Pawkins, and good things it was now impossible to say about him.

At last Hapley began to realise in what direction the preoccupation tended. He determined to make a fight for it, and started by trying to read novels. But he could not get his mind off Pawkins, white in the face and making his last speech—every sentence a beautiful opening for Hapley. He turned to fiction—and found it had no grip on him. He read the "Island Nights' Entertainments" until his "sense of causation" was shocked beyond endurance by the Bottle Imp. Then he went to Kipling, and found he "proved nothing," besides being irreverent and vulgar. These scientific people have their limitations. Then unhappily, he tried Besant's "Inner House," and the opening chapter set his mind upon learned societies and Pawkins at once.

So Hapley turned to chess, and found it a little more soothing. He soon mastered the moves and the chief gambits and commoner closing positions, and began to beat the Vicar. But then the cylindrical contours of the opposite king began to resemble Pawkins standing up and gasping ineffectually against checkmate, and Hapley decided to give up chess.

Perhaps the study of some new branch of science would after all be better diversion. The best rest is change of occupation. Hapley determined to plunge at diatoms, and had one of his smaller microscopes and Halibut's monograph sent down from London. He thought that perhaps if he could get up a vigorous quarrel with Halibut, he might be able to begin life afresh and forget Pawkins.

And very soon he was hard at work in his habitual strenuous fashion, at these microscopic denizens of the wayside pool.

It was on the third day of the diatoms that Hapley became aware of a novel addition to the local fauna. He was working late at the microscope, and the only light in the room was the brilliant little lamp with the special form of green shade. Like all experienced microscopists, he kept both eyes open. It is the only way to avoid excessive fatigue. One eye was over the instrument, and bright and distinct before that was the circular field of the microscope, across which a brown diatom was slowly moving. With the other eye Hapley saw, as it were, without seeing. He was only dimly conscious of the brass side of the instrument, the illuminated part of the tablecloth, a sheet of notepaper, the foot of the lamp, and the darkened room beyond.

Suddenly his attention drifted from one eye to the other. The tablecloth was of the material called tapestry by shopmen, and rather brightly coloured. The pattern was in gold, with a small amount of crimson and pale blue upon a greyish ground. At one point the pattern seemed displaced, and there was a vibrating movement of the colours at this point.

Hapley suddenly moved his head back and looked with both eyes. His mouth fell open with astonishment.

It was a large moth or butterfly; its wings spread in butterfly fashion!

It was strange it should be in the room at all, for the windows were closed. Strange that it should not have attracted his attention when fluttering to its present position. Strange that it should match the tablecloth. Stranger far that to him, Hapley, the great entomologist, it was altogether unknown. There was no delusion. It was crawling slowly towards the foot of the lamp.

"New Genus, by heavens! And in England!" said Hapley, staring.

Then he suddenly thought of Pawkins. Nothing would have maddened Pawkins more...And Pawkins was dead!

Something about the head and body of the insect became singularly suggestive of Pawkins, just as the chess king had been.

"Confound Pawkins!" said Hapley. "But I must catch this." And looking round him for some means of capturing the moth, he rose slowly out of his chair. Suddenly the insect rose, struck the edge of the lamp-shade—Hapley heard the "ping—" and vanished into the shadow.

In a moment Hapley had whipped off the shade, so that the whole room was illuminated. The thing had disappeared, but soon his practised eye detected it upon the wall-paper near the door. He went towards it poising the lamp-shade for capture. Before he was within striking distance, however, it had risen and was fluttering round the room. After the fashion of its kind, it flew with sudden starts and turns, seeming to vanish here and reappear there. Once Hapley struck, and missed; then again.

The third time he hit his microscope. The instrument swayed, struck and overturned the lamp, and fell noisily upon the floor. The lamp turned over on the table and, very luckily, went out. Hapley was left in the dark. With a start he felt the strange moth blunder into his face.

It was maddening. He had no lights. If he opened the door of the room the thing would get away. In the darkness he saw Pawkins quite distinctly laughing at him. Pawkins had ever an oily laugh. He swore furiously and stamped his foot on the floor.

There was a timid rapping at the door.

Then it opened, perhaps a foot, and very slowly. The alarmed face of the landlady appeared behind a pink candle flame; she wore a nightcap over her grey hair and had some purple garment over her shoulders. "What was that fearful smash?" she said. "Has anything—" The strange moth appeared fluttering about the chink of the door. "Shut that door!" said Hapley, and suddenly rushed at her.

The door slammed hastily. Hapley was left alone in the dark. Then in the pause he heard his landlady scuttle upstairs, lock her door, and drag something heavy across the room and put against it.

It became evident to Hapley that his conduct and appearance had been strange and alarming. Confound the moth! And Pawkins! However, it was a pity to lose the moth now. He felt his way into the hall and found the matches, after sending his hat down upon the floor with a noise like a drum. With the lighted candle he returned to the sitting-room. No moth was to be seen. Yet once for a moment it seemed that the thing was fluttering round his head. Hapley very suddenly decided to give up the moth and go to bed. But he was excited. All night long his sleep was broken by dreams of the moth, Pawkins, and his landlady. Twice in the night he turned out and soused his head in cold water.

One thing was very clear to him. His landlady could not possibly understand about the strange moth, especially as he had failed to catch it. No one but an entomologist would understand quite how he felt. She was probably frightened at his behaviour, and yet he failed to see how he could explain it. He decided to say nothing further about the events of last night. After breakfast he saw her in her garden, and decided to go out and talk, to reassure her. He talked to her about beans and potatoes, bees, caterpillars, and the price of fruit. She replied in her usual manner, but she looked at him a little suspiciously, and kept walking as he walked, so that there was always a bed of flowers, or a row of beans, or something of the sort, between them. After a while he began to feel singularly irritated at this, and to conceal his vexation went indoors and presently went out for a walk.

The moth, or butterfly, trailing an odd flavour of Pawkins with it, kept coming into that walk, though he did his best to keep his mind off it. Once he saw it quite distinctly, with its wings flattened out, upon the old stone wall that runs along the west edge of the park, but going up to it he found it was only two lumps of grey and yellow lichen. "This," said Hapley, "is the reverse of mimicry. Instead of a butterfly looking like a stone, here is a stone looking like a butterfly!" Once something hovered and fluttered round his head, but by an effort of will he drove that impression out of his mind again.

In the afternoon Hapley called upon the Vicar, and argued with him upon theological questions. They sat in the little arbour covered with briar, and smoked as they wrangled. "Look at that moth!" said Hapley, suddenly, pointing to the edge of the wooden table.

"Where?" said the Vicar.

"You don't see a moth on the edge of the table there?" said Hapley.

"Certainly not," said the Vicar.

Hapley was thunderstruck. He gasped. The Vicar was staring at him. Clearly the man saw nothing. "The eye of faith is no better than the eye of science," said Hapley awkwardly.

"I don't see your point," said the Vicar, thinking it was part of the argument.

That night Hapley found the moth crawling over his counterpane. He sat on the edge of the bed in his shirt-sleeves and reasoned with himself. Was it pure hallucination? He knew he was slipping, and he battled for his sanity with the same silent energy he had formerly displayed against Pawkins. So persistent is mental habit, that he felt as if it were still a struggle with Pawkins. He was well versed in psychology. He knew that such visual illusions do come as a result of mental strain. But the point was, he did not only see the moth, he had heard it when it touched the edge of the lamp-shade, and afterwards when it hit against the wall, and he had felt it strike his face in the dark.

He looked at it. It was not at all dream-like, but perfectly clear and solid-looking in the candle-light. He saw the hairy body, and the short feathery antennae, the jointed legs, even a place where the down was rubbed from the wing. He suddenly felt angry with himself for being afraid of a little insect.

His landlady had got the servant to sleep with her that night, because she was afraid to be alone. In addition she had locked the door, and put the chest of drawers against it. They listened and talked in whispers after they had gone to bed, but nothing occurred to alarm them. About eleven they had ventured to put the candle out, and had both dozed off to sleep. They woke up with a start, and sat up in bed, listening in the darkness.

Then they heard slippered feet going to and fro in Hapley's room. A chair was overturned, and there was a violent dab at the wall. Then a china mantel ornament smashed upon the fender. Suddenly the door of the room opened, and they heard him upon the landing. They clung to one another, listening. He seemed to be dancing upon the staircase. Now he would go down three or four steps quickly, then up again, then hurry down into the hall. They heard the umbrella-stand go over, and the fanlight break. Then the bolt shot and the chain rattled. He was opening the door.

They hurried to the window. It was a dim grey night; an almost unbroken sheet of watery cloud was sweeping across the moon, and the hedge and trees in front of the house were black against the pale roadway. They saw Hapley, looking like a ghost in his shirt and white trousers, running to and fro in the road, and beating the air. Now he would stop, now he would dart very rapidly at something invisible, now he would move upon it with stealthy strides. At last he went out of sight up the road towards the down. Then, while they argued who should go down and lock the door, he returned. He was walking very fast, and he came straight into the house, closed the door carefully, and went quietly up to his bedroom. Then everything was silent.

"Mrs. Colville," said Hapley, calling down the staircase next morning, "I hope I did not alarm you last night."

"You may well ask that!" said Mrs. Colville.

"The fact is, I am a sleep-walker, and the last two nights I have been without my sleeping mixture. There is nothing to be alarmed about, really. I am sorry I made such an ass of myself. I will go over the down to Shoreham, and get some stuff to make me sleep soundly. I ought to have done that yesterday."

But halfway over the down, by the chalk pits, the moth came upon Hapley again. He went on, trying to keep his mind upon chess problems, but it was no good. The thing fluttered into his face, and he struck at it with his hat in self-defence. Then rage, the old rage—the rage he had so often felt against Pawkins—came upon him again. He went on, leaping and striking at the eddying insect. Suddenly he trod on nothing, and fell headlong.

There was a gap in his sensations, and Hapley found himself sitting on the heap of flints in front of the opening of the chalk-pits, with a leg twisted back under him. The strange moth was still fluttering round his head. He struck at it with his hand, and turning his head saw two men approaching him. One was the village doctor. It occurred to Hapley that this was lucky. Then it came into his mind with extraordinary vividness, that no one would ever be able to see the strange moth except himself, and that it behooved him to keep silent about it.

Late that night however, after his broken leg was set, he was feverish and forgot his self-restraint. He was lying flat on his bed, and he began to run his eyes round the room to see if the moth was still about. He tried not to do this, but it was no good. He soon caught sight of the thing resting close to his hand, by the nightlight, on the green tablecloth. The wings quivered. With a sudden wave of anger he smote at it with his fist, and the nurse woke up with a shriek. He had missed it.

"That moth!" he said; and then, "It was fancy. Nothing!"

All the time he could see quite clearly the insect going round the cornice and darting across the room, and he could also see that the nurse saw nothing of it and looked at him strangely. He must keep himself in hand. He knew he was a lost man if he did not keep himself in hand. But as the night waned the fever grew upon him, and the very dread he had of seeing the moth made him see it. About five, just as the dawn was grey, he tried to get out of bed and catch it, though his leg was afire with pain. The nurse had to struggle with him.

On account of this, they tied him down to the bed. At this the moth grew bolder, and once he felt it settle in his hair. Then, because he struck out violently with his arms, they tied these also. At this the moth came and crawled over his face, and Hapley wept, swore, screamed, prayed for them to take it off him, unavailingly.

The doctor was a blockhead, a just-qualified general practitioner, and quite ignorant of mental science. He simply said there was no moth. Had he possessed the wit, he might still, perhaps, have saved Hapley from his fate by entering into his delusion, and covering his face with gauze, as he prayed might be done. But as I say, the doctor was a blockhead, and until the leg was healed Hapley was kept tied to his bed, and with the imaginary moth crawling over him. It never left him while he was awake and it grew to a monster in his dreams. While he was awake he longed for sleep, and from sleep he awoke screaming.

So now Hapley is spending the remainder of his days in a padded room, worried by a moth that no one else can see. The asylum doctor calls it hallucination; but Hapley, when he is in his easier mood, and can talk, says it is the ghost of Pawkins, and consequently a unique specimen and well worth the trouble of catching.

15

The Remarkable Case of Davidson's Eyes

The transitory mental aberration of Sidney Davidson, remarkable enough in itself, is still more remarkable if Wade's explanation is to be credited. It sets one dreaming of the oddest possibilities of intercommunication in the future, of spending an intercalary five minutes on the other side of the world, or being watched in our most secret operations by unsuspected eyes. It happened that I was the immediate witness of Davidson's seizure, and so it falls naturally to me to put the story upon paper.

When I say that I was the immediate witness of his seizure, I mean that I was the first on the scene. The thing happened at the Harlow Technical College just beyond the Highgate Archway. He was alone in the larger laboratory when the thing happened. I was in the smaller room, where the balances are, writing up some notes. The thunderstorm had completely upset my work, of course. It was just after one of the louder peals that I thought I heard some glass smash in the other room. I stopped writing, and turned round to listen. For a moment I heard nothing; the hail was playing the devil's tattoo on the corrugated zinc of the roof. Then came another sound, a smash—no doubt of it this time. Something heavy had been knocked off the bench. I jumped up at once and went and opened the door leading into the big laboratory.

I was surprised to hear a queer sort of laugh, and saw Davidson standing unsteadily in the middle of the room, with a dazzled look on his face. My first impression was that he was drunk. He did not notice me. He was clawing out at something invisible a yard in front of his face. He put out his hand slowly, rather hesitatingly, and then clutched nothing. "What's come to it?" he said. He held up his hands to his face, fingers spread out. "Great Scott!" he said. The thing happened three or four years ago, when everyone swore by that personage. Then he began raising his feet clumsily, as though he had expected to find them glued to the floor.

"Davidson!" cried I. "What's the matter with you?" He turned round in my direction and looked about for me. He looked over me and at me and on either side of me, without the slightest sign of seeing me. "Waves," he said; "and a remarkably neat schooner. I'd swear that was Bellows's voice. Hullo!" He shouted suddenly at the top of his voice.

I thought he was up to some foolery. Then I saw littered about his feet the shattered remains of the best of our electrometers. "What's up, man?" said I. "You've smashed the electrometer!"

"Bellows again!" said he. "Friends left, if my hands are gone. Something about electrometers. Which way are you, Bellows?" He suddenly came staggering towards me. "The damned stuff cuts like butter," he said. He walked straight into the bench and recoiled. "None so buttery, that!" he said, and stood swaying.

I felt scared. "Davidson," said I, "what on earth's come over you?"

He looked round him in every direction. "I could swear that was Bellows. Why don't you show yourself like a man, Bellows?"

It occurred to me that he must be suddenly struck blind. I walked round the table and laid my hand upon his arm. I never saw a man more startled in my life. He jumped away from me, and came round into an attitude of self-defense, his face fairly distorted with terror: "Good God!" he cried. "What was that?"

"It's I—Bellows. Confound it, Davidson!"

He jumped when I answered him and stared—how can I express it—? Right through me. He began talking, not to me, but to himself. "Here in broad daylight on a clear beach. Not a place to hide in." He looked about him wildly. "Here! I'm off." He suddenly turned and ran headlong into the big electromagnet—so violently that, as we found afterwards, he bruised his shoulder and jawbone cruelly. At that he stepped back a pace, and cried out with almost a whimper, "What, in Heaven's name, has come over me?" He stood, blanched with terror and trembling violently, with his right arm clutching his left, where that had collided with the magnet.

By that time I was excited, and fairly excited. "Davidson," said I, "don't be afraid."

He was startled at my voice, but not so excessively as before. I repeated my words in as clear and firm a tone as I could assume. "Bellows," he said, "is that you?"

"Can't you see it's me?"

He laughed. "I can't even see it's myself. Where the devil are we?" "Here," said I, "in the laboratory."

"The laboratory!" he answered, in a puzzled tone, and put his hand to his forehead. "I was in the laboratory—till that flash came, but I'm hanged if I'm there now. What ship is that?"

"There's no ship," said I. "Do be sensible, old chap."

"No ship!" he repeated, and seemed to forget my denial forthwith. "I suppose," said he, slowly, "we're both dead. But the rummy part is I feel just as though I still had a body. Don't get used to it all at once, I suppose. The old shop was struck by lightning, I suppose. Jolly quick thing, Bellows—eigh?"

"Don't talk nonsense. You're very much alive. You are in the laboratory, blundering about. You've just smashed a new electrometer. I don't envy you when Boyce arrives."

He stared away from me towards the diagrams of cryohydrates. "I must be deaf," said he. "They've fired a gun, for there goes the puff of smoke, and I never heard a sound."

I put my hand on his arm again, and this time he was less alarmed. "We seem to have a sort of invisible bodies," said he. "By Jove! There's a boat coming round the headland! It's very much like the old life after all—in a different climate."

I shook his arm. "Davidson," I cried, "wake up!"

It was just then that Boyce came in. So soon as he spoke Davidson exclaimed: "Old Boyce! Dead too! What a lark!" I hastened to explain that Davidson was in a kind of somnambulistic trance. Boyce was interested at once. We both did all we could to rouse the fellow out of his extraordinary state. He answered our questions, and asked us some of his own, but his attention seemed distracted by his hallucination about a beach and a ship. He kept interpolating observations concerning some boat and the davits and sails filling with the wind. It made one feel queer, in the dusky laboratory, to hear him saying such things.

He was blind and helpless. We had to walk him down the passage, one at each elbow, to Boyce's private room, and while

Boyce talked to him there, and humored him about this ship idea, I went along the corridor and asked old Wade to come and look at him. The voice of our Dean sobered him a little, but not very much. He asked where his hands were, and why he had to walk about up to his waist in the ground. Wade thought over him a long time—you know how he knits his brows—and then made him feel the couch, guiding his hands to it. "That's a couch," said Wade. "The couch in the private room of Professor Boyce. Horsehair stuffing."

Davidson felt about, and puzzled over it, and answered presently that he could feel it all right, but he couldn't see it.

"What do you see?" asked Wade. Davidson said he could see nothing but a lot of sand and broken-up shells. Wade gave him some other things to feel, telling him what they were, and watching him keenly.

"The ship is almost hull down," said Davidson, presently, apropos of nothing. "Never mind the ship," said Wade. "Listen to me, Davidson. Do you know what hallucination means?"

"Rather," said Davidson.

"Well, everything you see is hallucinatory."

"Bishop Berkeley," said Davidson.

"Don't mistake me," said Wade. "You are alive, and in this room of Boyce's. But something has happened to your eyes. You cannot see; you can feel and hear, but not see. Do you follow me?"

"It seems to me that I see too much." Davidson rubbed his knuckles into his eyes. "Well?" he said.

"That's all. Don't let it perplex you. Bellows, here, and I will take you home in a cab."

"Wait a bit." Davidson thought. "Help me to sit down," said he, presently; "and now—I'm sorry to trouble you—but will you tell me all that over again?"

Wade repeated it very patiently. Davidson shut his eyes, and pressed his hands upon his forehead. "Yes," said he. "It's quite right. Now my eyes are shut I know you're right. That's you, Bellows, sitting by me on the couch. I'm in England again. And we're in the dark."

Then he opened his eyes. "And there," said he, "is the sun just rising, and the yards of the ship, and a tumbled sea, and a couple of birds flying. I never saw anything so real. And I'm sitting up to my neck in a bank of sand."

He bent forward and covered his face with his hands. Then he opened his eyes again. "Dark sea and sunrise! And yet I'm sitting on a sofa in old Boyce's room...! God help me!"

That was the beginning. For three weeks this strange affection of Davidson's eyes continued unabated. It was far worse than being blind. He was absolutely helpless, and had to be fed like a newly hatched bird, and led about and undressed. If he attempted to move he fell over things or struck himself against walls or doors. After a day or so he got used to hearing our voices without seeing us, and willingly admitted he was at home, and that Wade was right in what he told him. My sister, to whom he was engaged, insisted on coming to see him, and would sit for hours every day while he talked about this beach of his. Holding her hand seemed to comfort him immensely. He explained that when we left the College and drove home—he lived in Hampstead Village—it appeared to him as if we drove right through a sandhill—it was perfectly black until he emerged again—and through rocks and trees and solid obstacles, and when he was taken to his own room it made him giddy and almost frantic with the fear of falling, because going upstairs seemed to lift him thirty or forty feet above the rocks of his imaginary island. He kept saying he should smash all the eggs. The end was that he had to be taken down into his father's consulting-room and laid upon a couch that stood there.

He described the island as being a bleak kind of place on the whole, with very little vegetation, except some peaty stuff, and a lot of bare rock. There were multitudes of penguins, and they made the rocks white and disagreeable to see. The sea was often rough, and once there was a thunderstorm, and he lay and shouted at the silent flashes. Once or twice seals pulled up on the beach but, only on the first two or three days. He said it was very funny the way in which the penguins used to waddle right through him, and how he seemed to lie among them without disturbing them.

I remember one odd thing, and that was when he wanted very badly to smoke. We put a pipe in his hands—he almost poked his eye out with it—and lit it. But he couldn't taste anything. I've since found it's the same with me—I don't know if it's the usual case—that I cannot enjoy tobacco at all unless I can see the smoke.

But the queerest part of his vision came when Wade sent him out in a Bath-chair to get fresh air. The Davidsons hired a chair, and got that deaf and obstinate dependent of theirs, Widgery, to attend to it. Widgery's ideas of healthy expeditions were peculiar. My sister, who had been to the Dog's Home, met them in Camden Town, towards King's Cross. Widgery trotting along complacently, and Davidson evidently most distressed, trying in his feeble, blind way to attract Widgery's attention.

He positively wept when my sister spoke to him. "Oh, get me out of this horrible darkness!" he said, feeling for her hand. "I must get out of it, or I shall die." He was quite incapable of explaining what was the matter, but my sister decided he must go home, and presently, as they went up the hill towards Hampstead, the horror seemed to drop from him. He said it was good to see the stars again, though it was then about noon and a blazing day.

"It seemed," he told me afterwards, "as if I was being carried irresistibly towards the water. I was not very much alarmed at first. Of course it was night there—a lovely night."

"Of course?" I asked, for that struck me as odd.

"Of course," said he. "It's always night there when it is day here... Well, we went right into the water, which was calm and shining under the moonlight—just a broad swell that seemed to grow broader and flatter as I came down into it. The surface glistened just like a skin—it might have been empty space underneath for all I could tell to the contrary. Very slowly, for I rode slanting into it, the water crept up to my eyes. Then I went under, and the skin seemed to break and heal again about my eyes. The moon gave a jump up in the sky and grew green and dim, and fish, faintly glowing, came darting round me—and things that seemed made of luminous glass, and I passed through a tangle of seaweeds that shone with an oily luster. And so I drove down into the sea, and the stars went out one by one, and the moon grew greener and darker, and the seaweed became a luminous purple-red. It was all very faint and mysterious, and everything seemed to quiver. And all the while I could hear the wheels of the Bath-chair creaking, and the footsteps of people going by, and a man in the distance selling the special "Pall Mall."

"I kept sinking down deeper and deeper into the water. It became inky black about me, not a ray from above came down into that darkness, and the phosphorescent things grew brighter and brighter. The snaky branches of the deeper weeds flickered like the flames of spirit-lamps; but after a time, there were no more weeds. The fishes came staring and gaping towards me, and into me and through me. I never imagined such fishes before. They had lines of fire along the sides of them as though they had been outlined with a luminous pencil. And there was a ghastly thing swimming backward with a lot of twining arms. And then I saw, coming very slowly towards me through the gloom, a hazy mass of light that resolved itself as it drew nearer into multitudes of fishes, struggling and darting round something that drifted. I drove on straight towards it, and presently I saw in the midst of the tumult, and by the light of the fish, a bit of splintered spar looming over me, and a dark hull tilting over, and some glowing phosphorescent forms that were shaken and writhed as the fish bit at them. Then it was I began to try to attract Widgery's attention. A horror came upon me. Ugh! I should have driven right into those half-eaten—things. If your sister had not come! They had great holes in them, Bellows, and...Never mind. But it was ghastly!"

For three weeks Davidson remained in this singular state, seeing what at the time we imagined was an altogether phantasmal world, and stone blind to the world around him. Then, one Tuesday, when I called, I met old Davidson in the passage. "He can see his thumb!" the old gentleman said, in a perfect transport. He was struggling into his overcoat. "He can see his thumb, Bellows!" he said, with the tears in his eyes. "The lad will be all right yet."

I rushed in to Davidson. He was holding up a little book before his face, and looking at it and laughing in a weak kind of way.

"It's amazing," said he. "There's a kind of patch come there." He pointed with his finger. "I'm on the rocks as usual, and the penguins are staggering and flapping about as usual, and there's been a whale showing every now and then, but it's got too dark now to make him out. But put something there, and I see it—I do see it. It's very dim and broken in places, but I see it all the same, like a faint specter of itself. I found it out this morning while they were dressing me. It's like a hole in this infernal phantom world. Just put your hand by mine. No—not there. Ah! Yes! I see it. The base of your thumb and a bit of cuff! It looks like the ghost of a bit of your hand sticking out of the darkening sky. Just by it there's a group of stars like a cross coming out."

From that time Davidson began to mend. His account of the change, like his account of the vision, was oddly convincing. Over patches of his field of vision the phantom world grew fainter, grew transparent, as it were, and through these translucent gaps he began to see dimly the real world about him. The patches grew in size and number, ran together and spread until only here and there were blind spots left upon his eyes. He was able to get up and steer himself about, feed himself once more, read, smoke, and behave like an ordinary citizen again. At first it was very confusing to him to have these two pictures overlapping each other like the changing views of a lantern, but in a little while he began to distinguish the real from the illusory.

At first he was unfeignedly glad, and seemed only too anxious to complete his cure by taking exercise and tonics. But as that odd island of his began to fade away from him, he became queerly interested in it. He wanted particularly to go down into the deep sea again, and would spend half his time wandering about the low-lying parts of London, trying to find the water-logged wreck he had seen drifting. The glare of real daylight very soon impressed him so vividly as to blot out everything of his shadowy world, but of a night time, in a darkened room, he could still see the white-splashed rocks of the island, and the clumsy penguins staggering to and fro. But even these grew fainter and fainter, and at last, soon after he married my sister, he saw them for the last time.

And now to tell of the queerest thing of all. About two years after his cure, I dined with the Davidsons, and after dinner a man named Atkins called in. He is a lieutenant in the Royal Navy, and a pleasant, talkative man. He was on friendly terms with my brother-in-law, and was soon on friendly terms with me. It came out that he was engaged to Davidson's cousin, and incidentally he took out a kind of pocket photograph case to show us a new rendering of his fiancée. "And, by the bye," said he, "here's the old Fulmar."

Davidson looked at it casually. Then suddenly his face lit up. "Good heavens!" said he. "I could almost swear—"

"What?" said Atkins.

"That I had seen that ship before."

"Don't see how you can have. She hasn't been out of the South Seas for six years, and before then—"

"But," began Davidson, and then, "Yes—that's the ship I dreamt of. I'm sure that's the ship I dreamt of. She was standing off an island that swarmed with penguins, and she fired a gun."

"Good Lord!" said Atkins, who had never heard the particulars of the seizure. "How the deuce could you dream that?"

And then, bit by bit, it came out that on the very day Davidson was seized, 'H.M.S. Fulmar' had actually been off a little rock to the south of Antipodes Island. A boat had landed overnight to get penguins' eggs, had been delayed, and a thunderstorm drifting up, the boat's crew had waited until the morning before rejoining the ship. Atkins had been one of them, and he corroborated, word for word, the descriptions Davidson had given of the island and the boat. There is not the slightest doubt in any of our minds that Davidson has really seen the place. In some unaccountable way, while he moved hither and thither in London, his sight moved hither and thither in a manner that corresponded, about this distant island. How is absolutely a mystery.

That completes the remarkable story of Davidson's eyes. It is perhaps the best authenticated case in existence of a real vision at a distance. Explanation, there is none forthcoming, except what Professor Wade has thrown out. But his explanation invokes the Fourth Dimension, and a dissertation on theoretical kinds of space. To talk of there being "a kink in space" seems mere nonsense to me; it may be because I am no mathematician. When I said that nothing would alter the fact that the place is eight thousand miles away, he answered that two points might be a yard away on a sheet of paper and yet be brought together by bending the paper round. The reader may grasp his argument, but I certainly do not. His idea seems to be that Davidson, stooping between the poles of the big electromagnet, had some extraordinary twist given to his retinal elements through the sudden change in the field of force due to the lightning.

He thinks, as a consequence of this, that it may be possible to live visually in one part of the world, while one lives bodily in another. He has even made some experiments in support of his views; but so far, he has simply succeeded in blinding a few dogs. I believe that is the net result of his work, though I have not seen him for some weeks. Latterly, I have been so busy with my work in connection with the 'Saint Pancras' installation that I have had little opportunity of calling to see him. But the whole of his theory seems fantastic to me. The facts concerning Davidson stand on an altogether different footing, and I can testify personally to the accuracy of every detail I have given.

16

The Sad Story of a Dramatic Critic

I was—you shall hear immediately why I am not now—Egbert Craddock Cummins. The name remains. I am still (Heaven help me!) Dramatic Critic to the 'Fiery Cross'. What I shall be in a little while I do not know. I write in great trouble and confusion of mind. I will do what I can to make myself clear in the face of terrible difficulties. You must bear with me a little. When a man is rapidly losing his own identity, he naturally finds a difficulty in expressing himself. I will make it perfectly plain in a minute, when once I get my grip upon the story. Let me see—where am I? I wish I knew. Ah, I have it! Dead self! Egbert Craddock Cummins!

In the past I should have disliked writing anything quite so full of "I" as this story must be. It is full of "I's" before and behind, like the beast in Revelation—the one with a head like a calf, I am afraid. But my tastes have changed since I became a Dramatic Critic and studied the masters—G.R.S., G.B.S., G.A.S., and others. Everything has changed since then. At least the story is about myself—so that there is some excuse for me. And it is really not egotism, because as I say, since those days my identity has undergone an entire alteration.

That past...! I was—in those days—rather a nice fellow, rather shy—taste for grey in my clothes, weedy little moustache, face "interesting," slight stutter which I had caught in early life from a schoolfellow. Engaged to a very nice girl, named Delia. Fairly new, she was—cigarettes—liked me because I was human and original. Considered I was like Lamb—on the strength of the stutter,

I believe. Father, an eminent authority on postage stamps. She read a great deal in the British Museum. (A perfect pairing ground for literary people, that British Museum—you should read George Egerton and Justin Huntly M'Carthy and Gissing and the rest of them.) We loved in our intellectual way, and shared the brightest hopes. (All gone now.) And her father liked me because I seemed honestly eager to hear about stamps. She had no mother. Indeed, I had the happiest prospects a young man could have. I never went to theatres in those days. My Aunt Charlotte before she died had told me not to.

Then Barnaby, the editor of the 'Fiery Cross', made me—in spite of my spasmodic efforts to escape—Dramatic Critic. He is a fine, healthy man, Barnaby, with an enormous head of frizzy black hair and a convincing manner, and he caught me on the staircase going to see Wembly. He had been dining, and was more than usually buoyant. "Hullo, Cummins!" he said. "The very man I want!" He caught me by the shoulder or collar or something, ran me up the little passage, and flung me over the waste-paper basket into the armchair in his office. "Pray be seated," he said, as he did so. Then he ran across the room and came back with some pink and yellow tickets and pushed them into my hand. "Opéra Comique," he said, "Thursday; Friday, the Surrey; Saturday, the Frivolity. That's all, I think."

"But—" I began.

"Glad you're free," he said, snatching some proofs off the desk and beginning to read.

"I don't quite understand," I said.

"Eigh?" he said, at the top of his voice, as though he thought I had gone, and was startled at my remark.

"Do you want me to criticise these plays?"

"Do something with 'em...Did you think it was a treat?"

"But I can't."

"Did you call me a fool?"

"Well, I've never been to a theatre in my life."

"Virgin soil."

"But I don't know anything about it, you know."

"That's just it. New view. No habits. No clichés in stock. Ours is a live paper, not a bag of tricks. None of your clockwork professional journalism in this office. And I can rely on your integrity—"

"But I've conscientious scruples—"

He caught me up suddenly and put me outside his door. "Go and talk to Wembly about that," he said. "He'll explain."

As I stood perplexed, he opened the door again, said, "I forgot this," thrust a fourth ticket into my hand (it was for that night—in twenty minutes' time) and slammed the door upon me. His expression was quite calm, but I caught his eye.

I hate arguments. I decided that I would take his hint and become (to my own destruction) a Dramatic Critic. I walked slowly down the passage to Wembly. That Barnaby has a remarkably persuasive way. He has made few suggestions during our very pleasant intercourse of four years that he has not ultimately won me round to adopting. It may be, of course, that I am of a yielding disposition; certainly I am too apt to take my colour from my circumstances. It is, indeed, to my unfortunate susceptibility to vivid impressions that all my misfortunes are due. I have already alluded to the slight stammer I had acquired from a schoolfellow in my youth. However, this is a digression...I went home in a cab to dress.

I will not trouble the reader with my thoughts about the first-night audience, strange assembly as it is—, those I reserve for my Memoirs, nor the humiliating story of how I got lost during the entr'acte in a lot of red plush passages, and saw the third act from the gallery. The only point upon which I wish to lay stress was the remarkable effect of the acting upon me. You must remember I had lived a quite and retired life, and had never been to the theatre before, and that I am extremely sensitive to vivid impressions. At the risk of repetition I must insist upon these points.

The first effect was a profound amazement, not untinctured by alarm. The phenomenal unnaturalness of acting is a thing discounted in the minds of most people by early visits to the theatre. They get used to the fantastic gestures, the flamboyant emotions, the weird mouthings, melodious snortings, agonising yelps, lip-gnawings, glaring horrors, and other emotional symbolism of the stage. It becomes at least a mere deaf-and-dumb language to them, which they read intelligently pari passu with the hearing of the dialogue. But all this was new to me. The thing was called a modern comedy, the people were supposed to be English and were dressed like fashionable Americans of the current epoch, and I fell into the natural error of supposing that the actors were trying to represent human beings. I looked round on my first-night audience with a kind of wonder, discovered—as all new Dramatic Critics do—that it rested with me to reform the Drama, and after a supper choked with emotion, went off to the office to write a column, piebald with "new paragraphs" (as all my stuff is—it fills out so) and purple with indignation. Barnaby was delighted.

But I could not sleep that night. I dreamt of actors—actors glaring, actors smiting their chests, actors flinging out a handful of extended fingers, actors smiling bitterly, laughing despairingly, falling hopelessly, dying idiotically. I got up at eleven with a slight headache, read my notice in the 'Fiery Cross', breakfasted, and went back to my room to shave. (It's my habit to do so.) Then an odd thing happened. I could not find my razor. Suddenly it occurred to me that I had not unpacked it the day before.

"Ah!" said I, in front of the looking-glass. Then "Hullo!"

Quite involuntarily, when I had thought of my portmanteau, I had flung up the left arm (fingers fully extended) and clutched at my diaphragm with my right hand. I am an acutely self-conscious man at all times. The gesture struck me as absolutely novel for me. I repeated it, for my own satisfaction. "Odd!" Then (rather puzzled) I turned to my portmanteau.

After shaving, my mind reverted to the acting I had seen, and I entertained myself before the cheval glass with some imitations of Jafferay's more exaggerated gestures. "Really, one might think it a disease." I said—, "Stage-Walkitis!" (There's many a truth spoken in jest.) Then, if I remember rightly, I went off to see Wembly, and afterwards lunched at the British Museum with Delia. We actually spoke about our prospects, in the light of my new appointment.

But that appointment was the beginning of my downfall. From that day I necessarily became a persistent theatre-goer, and almost insensibly I began to change. The next thing I noticed after the gesture about the razor, was to catch myself bowing ineffably when I met Delia, and stooping in an old-fashioned, courtly way over her hand. Directly I caught myself, I straightened myself up and became very uncomfortable. I remember she looked at me curiously. Then, in the office, I found myself doing "nervous business," fingers on teeth, when Barnaby asked me a question I could not very well answer. Then, in some trifling difference with Delia, I clasped my hand to my brow. And I pranced through my social transactions at times singularly like an actor! I tried not to—

no one could be more keenly alive to the arrant absurdity of the histrionic bearing. And I did!

It began to dawn on me what it all meant. The acting, I saw, was too much for my delicately-strung nervous system. I have always, I know, been too amenable to the suggestions of my circumstances. Night after night of concentrated attention to the conventional attitudes and intonation of the English stage was gradually affecting my speech and carriage. I was giving way to the infection of sympathetic imitation. Night after night my plastic nervous system took the print of some new amazing gesture, some new emotional exaggeration—and retained it. A kind of theatrical veneer threatened to plate over and obliterate my private individuality altogether. I saw myself in a kind of vision. Sitting by myself one night, my new self seemed to me to glide, posing and gesticulating, across the room. He clutched his throat, he opened his fingers, he opened his legs in walking like a high-class marionette. He went from attitude to attitude. He might have been clockwork. Directly after this I made an ineffectual attempt to resign my theatrical work. But Barnaby persisted in talking about the Polywhiddle Divorce all the time I was with him, and I could get no opportunity of saying what I wished.

And then Delia's manner began to change towards me. The ease of our intercourse vanished. I felt she was learning to dislike me. I grinned, and capered, and scowled, and posed at her in a thousand ways, and knew—with what a voiceless agony—! That I did it all the time. I tried to resign again, and Barnaby talked about "X" and "Z" and "Y" in the New Review, and gave me a strong cigar to smoke, and so routed me. And then I walked up the Assyrian Gallery in the manner of Irving to meet Delia, and so precipitated the crisis.

"Ah—! Dear!" I said, with more sprightliness and emotion in my voice than had ever been in all my life before I became (to my own undoing) a Dramatic Critic.

She held out her hand rather coldly, scrutinising my face as she did so. I prepared, with a new-won grace, to walk by her side.

"Egbert," she said, standing still, and thought. Then she looked at me.

I said nothing. I felt what was coming. I tried to be the old Egbert Craddock Cummins of shambling gait and stammering sincerity, whom she loved, but I felt even as I did so that I was a new thing, a thing of surging emotions and mysterious fixity—like no human being that ever lived, except upon the stage. "Egbert," she said, "you are not yourself."

"Ah!" Involuntarily I clutched my diaphragm and averted my head (as is the way with them).

"There!" she said.

"What do you mean?" I said, whispering in vocal italics—you know how they do it—turning on her, perplexity on face, right hand down, left on brow. I knew quite well what she meant. I knew quite well the dramatic unreality of my behaviour. But I struggled against it in vain. "What do you mean?" I said, and in a kind of hoarse whisper, "I don't understand!"

She really looked as though she disliked me. "What do you keep on posing for?" she said. "I don't like it. You didn't used to."

"Didn't used to!" I said slowly, repeating this twice. I glared up and down the gallery, with short, sharp glances. "We are alone," I said swiftly. "Listen!" I poked my forefinger towards her, and glared at her. "I'm under a curse."

I saw her hands tighten upon her sunshade. "You are under some bad influence or other," said Delia. "You should give it up. I never knew anyone change as you have done."

"Delia!" I said, lapsing into the pathetic. "Pity me. Augh! Delia! Pit—y me!"

She eyed me critically. "Why you keep playing the fool like this I don't know," she said. "Anyhow, I really cannot go about with a man who behaves as you do. You made us both ridiculous on Wednesday. Frankly, I dislike you, as you are now. I met you here to tell you so—as it's about the only place where we can be sure of being alone together—"

"Delia!" said I, with intensity, knuckles of clenched hands white. "You don't mean—"

"I do," said Delia. "A woman's lot is sad enough at the best of times. But with you—"

I clapped my hand on my brow.

"So, good-bye," said Delia, without emotion.

"Oh, Delia!" I said. "Not this?"

"Good-bye, Mr. Cummins," she said.

By a violent effort I controlled myself and touched her hand. I tried to say some word of explanation to her. She looked into my working face and winced. "I must do it," she said hopelessly. Then she turned from me and began walking rapidly down the gallery.

Heavens! How the human agony cried within me! I loved Delia. But nothing found expression—I was already too deeply crusted with my acquired self.

"Good-baye!" I said at last, watching her retreating figure. How I hated myself for doing it! After she had vanished, I repeated in a dreamy way, "Good-baye!" looking hopelessly round me. Then, with a kind of heart-broken cry, I shook my clenched fists in the air, staggered to the pedestal of a winged figure, buried my face in my arms, and made my shoulders heave. Something within me said "Ass!" as I did so. (I had the greatest difficulty in persuading the Museum policeman, who was attracted by my cry of agony, that I was not intoxicated, but merely suffering from a transient indisposition.)

But even this great sorrow has not availed to save me from my fate. I see it, everyone sees it; I grow more "theatrical" every day. And no one could be more painfully aware of the pungent silliness of theatrical ways. The quite, nervous, but pleasing, E.C. Cummins vanishes. I cannot save him. I am driven like a dead leaf before the winds of March. My tailor even enters into the spirit of my disorder. He has a peculiar sense of what is fitting. I tried to get a dull grey suit from him this spring, and he foisted a brilliant blue upon me, and I see he has put braid down the sides of my new dress trousers. My hairdresser insists upon giving me a "wave."

I am beginning to associate with actors. I detest them, but it is only in their company that I feel I am not glaringly conspicuous. Their talk infects me. I notice a growing tendency to dramatic brevity, to dashes and pauses in my style, to a punctuation of bows and attitudes. Barnaby has remarked it too. I offended Wembly by calling him "Dear Boy" yesterday. I dread the end, but cannot escape from it.

The fact is, I am being obliterated. Living a grey, retired life all my youth, I came to the theatre a delicate sketch of a man, a thing of tints and faint lines. Their gorgeous colouring has effaced me altogether. People forget how much mode of expression, method of movement, are a matter of contagion. I have heard of stage-struck people before, and thought it a figure of speech. I spoke of it jestingly, as a disease. It is no jest. It is a disease. And I have got it bad! Deep down within me I protest against the wrong done to my personality—unavailingly. For three hours or more a week

I have to go and concentrate my attention on some fresh play, and the suggestions of the drama strengthen their awful hold upon me. My manners grow so flamboyant, my passions so professional, that I doubt, as I said at the outset, whether it is really myself that behaves in such a manner. I feel merely the core of this dramatic casing, that grows thicker and presses upon me—me and mine. I feel like King John's abbot in his cope of lead.

I doubt, indeed, whether I should not abandon the struggle altogether—leave this sad world of ordinary life for which I am so ill-fitted, abandon the name of Cummins for some professional pseudonym, complete my self-effacement, and—a thing of tricks and tatters, of posing and pretence—go upon the stage. It seems my only resort—"to hold mirror up to Nature." For in the ordinary life, I will confess, no one now seems to regard me as both sane and sober. Only upon the stage, I feel convinced, will people take me seriously. That will be the end of it. I know that will be the end of it. And yet...I will frankly confess...all that marks off your actor from your common man...I detest. I am still largely of my Aunt Charlotte's opinion, that playacting is unworthy of a pure-minded man's attention, much more participation. Even now I would resign my dramatic criticism and try a rest. Only I can't get hold of Barnaby. Letters of resignation he never notices. He says it is against the etiquette of journalism to write to your Editor. And when I go to see him, he gives me another big cigar and some strong whisky and soda, and then something always turns up to prevent my explanation.

17

The Stolen Bacillus

"This again," said the Bacteriologist, slipping a glass slide under the microscope, "is a preparation of the celebrated Bacillus of cholera—the cholera germ."

The pale-faced man peered down the microscope. He was evidently not accustomed to that kind of thing, and held a limp white hand over his disengaged eye. "I see very little," he said.

"Touch this screw," said the Bacteriologist; "perhaps the microscope is out of focus for you. Eyes vary so much. Just the fraction of a turn this way or that."

"Ah! Now I see," said the visitor. "Not so very much to see after all. Little streaks and shreds of pink. And yet those little particles, those mere atomies, might multiply and devastate a city! Wonderful!"

He stood up, and releasing the glass slip from the microscope, held it in his hand towards the window. "Scarcely visible," he said, scrutinising the preparation. He hesitated. "Are these—alive? Are they dangerous now?"

"Those have been stained and killed," said the Bacteriologist. "I wish, for my own part, we could kill and stain every one of them in the universe."

"I suppose," the pale man said with a slight smile, "that you scarcely care to have such things about you in the living—in the active state?"

"On the contrary, we are obliged to," said the Bacteriologist. "Here, for instance—" He walked across the room and took up one of several sealed tubes. "Here is the living thing. This is a cultivation of the actual living disease bacteria." He hesitated. "Bottled cholera, so to speak."

A slight gleam of satisfaction appeared momentarily in the face of the pale man.

"It's a deadly thing to have in your possession," he said, devouring the little tube with his eyes. The Bacteriologist watched the morbid pleasure in his visitor's expression. This man, who had visited him that afternoon with a note of introduction from an old friend, interested him from the very contrast of their dispositions. The lank black hair and deep grey eyes, the haggard expression and nervous manner, the fitful yet keen interest of his visitor were a novel change from the phlegmatic deliberations of the ordinary scientific worker with whom the Bacteriologist chiefly associated. It was perhaps natural, with a hearer evidently so impressionable to the lethal nature of his topic, to take the most effective aspect of the matter.

He held the tube in his hand thoughtfully. "Yes, here is the pestilence imprisoned. Only break such a little tube as this into a supply of drinking-water, say to these minute particles of life that one must needs stain and examine with the highest powers of the microscope even to see, and that one can neither smell nor taste—say to them, 'Go forth, increase and multiply, and replenish the cisterns,' and death—mysterious, untraceable death, death swift and terrible, death full of pain and indignity—would be released upon this city, and go hither and thither seeking his victims. Here he would take the husband from the wife, here the child from its mother, here the statesman from his duty, and here the toiler from his trouble. He would follow the water-mains, creeping along streets, picking out and punishing a house here and a house there where they did not boil their drinking-water, creeping into the wells of the mineral-water makers, getting washed into salad, and lying dormant in ices. He would wait ready to be drunk in the horse-troughs, and by unwary children in the public fountains. He would soak into the soil, to reappear in springs and wells at a thousand unexpected places. Once start him at the water supply, and before we could ring him in, and catch him again, he would have decimated the metropolis."

He stopped abruptly. He had been told rhetoric was his weakness.

"But he is quite safe here, you know—quite safe."

The pale-faced man nodded. His eyes shone. He cleared his throat. "These Anarchist—rascals," said he, "are fools, blind fools—to use bombs when this kind of thing is attainable. I think—"

A gentle rap, a mere light touch of the finger-nails was heard at the door. The Bacteriologist opened it. "Just a minute, dear," whispered his wife.

When he re-entered the laboratory his visitor was looking at his watch. "I had no idea I had wasted an hour of your time," he said. "Twelve minutes to four. I ought to have left here by half-past three. But your things were really too interesting. No, positively I cannot stop a moment longer. I have an engagement at four."

He passed out of the room reiterating his thanks, and the Bacteriologist accompanied him to the door, and then returned thoughtfully along the passage to his laboratory. He was musing on the ethnology of his visitor. Certainly the man was not a Teutonic type nor a common Latin one. "A morbid product, anyhow, I am afraid," said the Bacteriologist to himself. "How he gloated on those cultivations of disease-germs!" A disturbing thought struck him. He turned to the bench by the vapour-bath, and then very quickly to his writing-table. Then he felt hastily in his pockets, and then rushed to the door. "I may have put it down on the hall table," he said.

"Minnie!" he shouted hoarsely in the hall.

"Yes, dear," came a remote voice.

"Had I anything in my hand when I spoke to you, dear, just now?"

Pause.

"Nothing, dear, because I remember—"

"Blue ruin!" cried the Bacteriologist, and incontinently ran to the front door and down the steps of his house to the street.

Minnie, hearing the door slam violently, ran in alarm to the window. Down the street a slender man was getting into a cab. The Bacteriologist, hatless, and in his carpet slippers, was running and gesticulating wildly towards this group. One slipper came off, but he did not wait for it. "He has gone mad!" said Minnie; "It's that horrid science of his"; and opening the window, would have called after him. The slender man, suddenly glancing round, seemed struck with the same idea of mental disorder. He pointed hastily to the Bacteriologist, said something to the cabman, the apron of the cab slammed, the whip swished, the horse's feet clattered, and in a moment cab, and Bacteriologist hotly in pursuit, had receded up the vista of the roadway and disappeared round the corner.

Minnie remained straining out of the window for a minute. Then she drew her head back into the room again. She was dumbfounded. "Of course he is eccentric," she meditated. "But running about London—in the height of the season, too—in his socks!" A happy thought struck her. She hastily put her bonnet on, seized his shoes, went into the hall, took down his hat and light overcoat from the pegs, emerged upon the doorstep, and hailed a cab that opportunely crawled by. "Drive me up the road and round Havelock Crescent, and see if we can find a gentleman running about in a velveteen coat and no hat."

"Velveteen coat, ma'am, and no 'at. Very good, ma'am." And the cabman whipped up at once in the most matter-of-fact way, as if he drove to this address every day in his life.

Some few minutes later the little group of cabmen and loafers that collects round the cabmen's shelter at Haverstock Hill were startled by the passing of a cab with a ginger-coloured screw of a horse, driven furiously.

They were silent as it went by, and then as it receded—"That's 'Arry 'Icks. Wot's he got?" said the stout gentleman known as old Tootles.

"He's a-using his whip, he is, to rights," said the ostler boy.

"Hullo!" said poor old Tommy Byles; "here's another bloomin' loonatic. Blowed if there ain't."

"It's old George," said old Tootles, "and he's drivin' a loonatic, as you say. Ain't he a-clawin' out of the keb? Wonder if he's after 'Arry 'Icks?"

The group round the cabmen's shelter became animated. Chorus: "Go it, George!" "It's a race." "You'll ketch 'em!" "Whip up!"

"She's a goer, she is!" said the ostler boy.

"Strike me giddy!" cried old Tootles. "Here! I'm a-goin' to begin in a minute. Here's another comin'. If all the kebs in Hampstead ain't gone mad this morning!"

"It's a fieldmale this time," said the ostler boy.

"She's a followin' him," said old Tootles. "Usually the other way about."

"What's she got in her 'and?"

"Looks like a 'igh 'at."

"What a bloomin' lark it is! Three to one on old George," said the ostler boy. "Nexst!"

Minnie went by in a perfect roar of applause. She did not like it but she felt that she was doing her duty, and whirled on down Haverstock Hill and Camden Town High Street with her eyes ever intent on the animated back view of old George, who was driving her vagrant husband so incomprehensibly away from her.

The man in the foremost cab sat crouched in the corner, his arms tightly folded, and the little tube that contained such vast possibilities of destruction gripped in his hand. His mood was a singular mixture of fear and exultation. Chiefly he was afraid of being caught before he could accomplish his purpose, but behind this was a vaguer but larger fear of the awfulness of his crime. But his exultation far exceeded his fear. No Anarchist before him had ever approached this conception of his. Ravachol, Vaillant, all those distinguished persons whose fame he had envied dwindled into insignificance beside him. He had only to make sure of the water supply, and break the little tube into a reservoir. How brilliantly he had planned it, forged the letter of introduction and got into the laboratory, and how brilliantly he had seized his opportunity! The world should hear of him at last. All those people who had sneered at him, neglected him, preferred other people to him, found his company undesirable, should consider him at last. Death, death, death! They had always treated him as a man of no importance. All the world had been in a conspiracy to keep him under. He would teach them yet, what it is to isolate a man. What was this familiar street? Great Saint Andrew's Street, of course! How fared the chase? He craned out of the cab. The Bacteriologist was scarcely fifty yards behind. That was bad. He would be caught and stopped yet. He felt in his pocket for money, and found half-a-sovereign. This he thrust up through the trap in the top of the cab into the man's face. "More," he shouted, "if only we get away."

The money was snatched out of his hand. "Right you are," said the cabman, and the trap slammed, and the lash lay along the glistening side of the horse. The cab swayed, and the Anarchist, half-standing under the trap, put the hand containing the little glass tube upon the apron to preserve his balance. He felt the brittle thing crack, and the broken half of it rang upon the floor of the cab. He fell back into the seat with a curse, and stared dismally at the two or three drops of moisture on the apron.

He shuddered.

"Well! I suppose I shall be the first. Phew! Anyhow, I shall be a Martyr. That's something. But it is a filthy death, nevertheless. I wonder if it hurts as much as they say."

Presently a thought occurred to him—he groped between his feet. A little drop was still in the broken end of the tube, and he drank that to make sure. It was better to make sure. At any rate, he would not fail.

Then it dawned upon him that there was no further need to escape the Bacteriologist. In Wellington Street he told the cabman to stop, and got out. He slipped on the step, and his head felt queer. It was rapid stuff this cholera poison. He waved his cabman out of existence, so to speak, and stood on the pavement with his arms folded upon his breast awaiting the arrival of the Bacteriologist. There was something tragic in his pose. The sense of imminent death gave him a certain dignity. He greeted his pursuer with a defiant laugh.

"Vive l'Anarchie! You are too late, my friend. I have drunk it. The cholera is abroad!"

The Bacteriologist from his cab beamed curiously at him through his spectacles. "You have drunk it! An Anarchist! I see now." He was about to say something more, and then checked himself. A smile hung in the corner of his mouth. He opened the apron of his cab as if to descend, at which the Anarchist waved him a dramatic farewell and strode off towards Waterloo Bridge, carefully jostling his infected body against as many people as possible. The Bacteriologist was so preoccupied with the vision of him that he scarcely manifested the slightest surprise at the appearance of Minnie upon the pavement with his hat and shoes and overcoat. "Very good of you to bring my things," he said, and remained lost in contemplation of the receding figure of the Anarchist.

"You had better get in," he said, still staring. Minnie felt absolutely convinced now that he was mad, and directed the cabman home on her own responsibility. "Put on my shoes? Certainly dear," said he, as the cab began to turn, and hid the strutting black figure, now small in the distance, from his eyes. Then suddenly something grotesque struck him, and he laughed. Then he remarked, "It is really very serious, though.

"You see, that man came to my house to see me, and he is an Anarchist. No—don't faint, or I cannot possibly tell you the rest. And I wanted to astonish him, not knowing he was an Anarchist, and took up a cultivation of that new species of Bacterium I was telling you of, that infest, and I think cause, the blue patches upon various monkeys; and like a fool, I said it was Asiatic cholera. And he ran away with it to poison the water of London, and he certainly might have made things look blue for this civilised city. And now he has swallowed it. Of course, I cannot say what will happen, but you know it turned that kitten blue, and the three puppies—in patches, and the sparrow—bright blue. But the bother is, I shall have all the trouble and expense of preparing some more.

"Put on my coat on this hot day! Why? Because we might meet Mrs. Jabber. My dear, Mrs. Jabber is not a draught. But why should I wear a coat on a hot day because of Mrs. ——? Oh! Very well."

18

The Temptation of Harringay

It is quite impossible to say whether this thing really happened. It depends entirely on the word of R.M. Harringay, who is an artist.

Following his version of the affair, the narrative deposes that Harringay went into his studio about ten o'clock to see what he could make of the head, that he had been working at the day before. The head in question was that of an Italian organ-grinder, and Harringay thought—but was not quite sure—that the title would be the "Vigil." So far he is frank, and his narrative bears the stamp of truth. He had seen the man expectant for pennies, and with a promptness that suggested genius, had, had him in at once.

"Kneel. Look up at that bracket," said Harringay. "As if you expected pennies.

"Don't grin!" said Harringay. "I don't want to paint your gums. Look as though you were unhappy."

Now, after a night's rest, the picture proved decidedly unsatisfactory. "It's good work," said Harringay. "That little bit in the neck...But."

He walked about the studio and looked at the thing from this point and from that. Then he said a wicked word. In the original the word is given.

"Painting," he says he said. "Just a painting of an organ-grinder—a mere portrait. If it was a live organ-grinder I wouldn't mind. But somehow I never make things alive. I wonder if my imagination is wrong." This, too, has a truthful air. His imagination is wrong.

"That creative touch! To take canvas and pigment and make a man—as Adam was made of red ochre! But this thing! If you met it walking about the streets you would know it was only a studio production. The little boys would tell it to 'Garnome and git frimed.' Some little touch...Well—it won't do as it is."

He went to the blinds and began to pull them down. They were made of blue holland with the rollers at the bottom of the window, so that you pull them down to get more light. He gathered his palette, brushes, and mahl stick from his table. Then he turned to the picture and put a speck of brown in the corner of the mouth; and shifted his attention thence to the pupil of the eye. Then he decided that the chin was a trifle too impassive for a vigil.

Presently he put down his impedimenta, and lighting a pipe surveyed the progress of his work. "I'm hanged if the thing isn't sneering at me," said Harringay, and he still believes it sneered.

The animation of the figure had certainly increased, but scarcely in the direction he wished. There was no mistake about the sneer. "Vigil of the Unbeliever," said Harringay. "Rather subtle and clever that! But the left eyebrow isn't cynical enough."

He went and dabbed at the eyebrow, and added a little to the lobe of the ear to suggest materialism. Further consideration ensued. "Vigil's off, I'm afraid," said Harringay. "Why not Mephistopheles? But that's a bit too common. 'A Friend of the Doge—' not so seedy. The armour won't do, though. Too Camelot. How about a scarlet robe and call him 'One of the Sacred College'? Humour in that, and an appreciation of Middle Italian History.

"There's always Benvenuto Cellini," said Harringay; "with a clever suggestion of a gold cup in one corner. But that would scarcely suit the complexion."

He describes himself as babbling in this way in order to keep down an unaccountably unpleasant sensation of fear. The thing was certainly acquiring anything but a pleasing expression. Yet it was as certainly becoming far more of a living thing than it had been—if a sinister one—far more alive than anything he had ever painted before. "Call it 'Portrait of a Gentleman,'" said Harringay; "'A Certain Gentleman.'

"Won't do," said Harringay, still keeping up his courage. "Kind of thing they call Bad Taste. That sneer will have to come out. That gone, and a little more fire in the eye—never noticed how warm his eye was before—and he might do for—? What price

Passionate Pilgrim? But that devilish face won't do—this, side of the Channel.

"Some little inaccuracy does it," he said; "eyebrows probably too oblique—" therewith pulling the blind lower to get a better light, and resuming palette and brushes.

The face on the canvas seemed animated by a spirit of its own. Where the expression of diablerie came in he found impossible to discover. Experiment was necessary. The eyebrows—it could scarcely be the eyebrows? But he altered them. No, that was no better; in fact, if anything, a trifle more satanic. The corner of the mouth? Pah! More than ever a leer—and now, retouched, it was ominously grim. The eye, then? Catastrophe! He had filled his brush with vermilion instead of brown, and yet he had felt sure it was brown! The eye seemed now to have rolled in its socket, and was glaring at him an eye of fire. In a flash of passion, possibly with something of the courage of panic, he struck the brush full of bright red, athwart the picture; and then a very curious thing, a very strange thing indeed, occurred—if it did occur.

The diabolified Italian before him shut both his eyes, pursed his mouth, and wiped the colour off his face with his hand.

Then the red eye opened again, with a sound like the opening of lips, and the face smiled. "That was rather hasty of you," said the picture.

Harringay states that, now that the worst had happened, his self-possession returned. He had a saving persuasion that devils were reasonable creatures.

"Why do you keep moving about then," he said, "making faces and all that—sneering and squinting, while I am painting you?"

"I don't," said the picture.

"You do," said Harringay.

"It's yourself," said the picture.

"It's not myself," said Harringay.

"It is yourself," said the picture. "No! Don't go hitting me with paint again, because it's true. You have been trying to fluke an expression on my face all the morning. Really, you haven't an idea what your picture ought to look like."

"I have," said Harringay.

"You have not," said the picture: "You never have with your pictures. You always start with the vaguest presentiment of what you are going to do; it is to be something beautiful—you are sure of that—and devout, perhaps, or tragic; but beyond that it is all experiment and chance. My dear fellow! You don't think you can paint a picture like that?"

Now it must be remembered that for what follows we have only Harringay's word.

"I shall paint a picture exactly as I like," said Harringay, calmly.

This seemed to disconcert the picture a little. "You can't paint a picture without an inspiration," it remarked.

"But I had an inspiration—for this."

"Inspiration!" sneered the sardonic figure; "A fancy that came from your seeing an organ-grinder looking up at a window! Vigil! Ha, ha! You just started painting on the chance of something coming—that's what you did. And when I saw you at it I came. I want a talk with you!

"Art, with you," said the picture—, "it's a poor business. You potter. I don't know how it is, but you don't seem able to throw your soul into it. You know too much. It hampers you. In the midst of your enthusiasms you ask yourself whether something like this has not been done before. And..."

"Look here," said Harringay, who had expected something better than criticism from the devil. "Are you going to talk studio to me?" He filled his number twelve hoghair with red paint.

"The true artist," said the picture, "is always an ignorant man. An artist who theorises about his work is no longer artist but critic. Wagner...I say—! What's that red paint for?"

"I'm going to paint you out," said Harringay. "I don't want to hear all that Tommy Rot. If you think just because I'm an artist by trade I'm going to talk studio to you, you make a precious mistake."

"One minute," said the picture, evidently alarmed. "I want to make you an offer—a genuine offer. It's right what I'm saying. You lack inspirations. Well. No doubt you've heard of the Cathedral of Cologne, and the Devil's Bridge, and—"

"Rubbish," said Harringay. "Do you think I want to go to perdition simply for the pleasure of painting a good picture, and getting it slated. Take that."

His blood was up. His danger only nerved him to action, so he says. So he planted a dab of vermilion in his creature's mouth. The Italian spluttered and tried to wipe it off—evidently horribly surprised. And then—according to Harringay—there began a very remarkable struggle, Harringay splashing away with the red paint, and the picture wriggling about and wiping it off as fast as he put it on. "Two masterpieces," said the demon. "Two indubitable masterpieces for a Chelsea artist's soul. It's a bargain?" Harringay replied with the paint brush.

For a few minutes nothing could be heard but the brush going and the spluttering and ejaculations of the Italian. A lot of the strokes he caught on his arm and hand, though Harringay got over his guard often enough. Presently the paint on the palette gave out and the two antagonists stood breathless, regarding each other. The picture was so smeared with red that it looked as if it had been rolling about a slaughterhouse, and it was painfully out of breath and very uncomfortable with the wet paint trickling down its neck. Still, the first round was in its favour on the whole. "Think," it said, sticking pluckily to its point, "two supreme masterpieces—in different styles. Each equivalent to the Cathedral..."

"I know," said Harringay, and rushed out of the studio and along the passage towards his wife's boudoir.

In another minute he was back with a large tin of enamel—Hedge Sparrow's Egg Tint, it was, and a brush. At the sight of that the artistic devil with the red eye began to scream. "Three masterpieces—culminating masterpieces."

Harringay delivered cut two across the demon, and followed with a thrust in the eye. There was an indistinct rumbling. "Four masterpieces," and a spitting sound.

But Harringay had the upper hand now and meant to keep it. With rapid, bold strokes he continued to paint over the writhing canvas, until at last it was a uniform field of shining Hedge Sparrow tint. Once the mouth reappeared and got as far as "Five master—" before he filled it with enamel; and near the end the red eye opened and glared at him indignantly. But at last nothing remained save a gleaming panel of drying enamel. For a little while a faint stirring beneath the surface puckered it slightly here and there, but presently even that died away and the thing was perfectly still.

Then Harringay—according to Harringay's account—lit his pipe and sat down and stared at the enamelled canvas, and tried to make out clearly what had happened. Then he walked round behind it, to see if the back of it was at all remarkable. Then it was he began to regret he had not photographed the Devil before he painted him out.

This is Harringay's story—not mine. He supports it by a small canvas (24 by 20) enamelled a pale green, and by violent asseverations. It is also true that he never has produced a masterpiece, and in the opinion of his intimate friends probably never will.

19

A Slip under the Microscope

Outside the laboratory windows was a watery-grey fog, and within a close warmth and the yellow light of the green-shaded gas lamps that stood two to each table down its narrow length. On each table stood a couple of glass jars containing the mangled vestiges of the crayfish, mussels, frogs, and guinea pigs upon which the students had been working, and down the side of the room, facing the windows, were shelves bearing bleached dissections in spirits, surmounted by a row of beautifully executed anatomical drawings in whitewood frames and overhanging a row of cubical lockers. All the doors of the laboratory were panelled with blackboard, and on these were the half-erased diagrams of the previous day's work. The laboratory was empty, save for the demonstrator, who sat near the preparation-room door, and silent, save for a low, continuous murmur and the clicking of the rocker microtome at which he was working. But scattered about the room were traces of numerous students: hand-bags, polished boxes of instruments, in one place a large drawing covered by newspaper, and in another a prettily bound copy of 'News from Nowhere', a book oddly at variance with its surroundings. These things had been put down hastily as the students had arrived and hurried at once to secure their seats in the adjacent lecture theatre. Deadened by the closed door, the measured accents of the professor sounded as a featureless muttering.

Presently, faint through the closed windows came the sound of the Oratory clock striking the hour of eleven. The clicking of the microtome ceased, and the demonstrator looked at his watch, rose, thrust his hands into his pockets, and walked slowly down the laboratory towards the lecture theatre door. He stood listening for a moment, and then his eye fell on the little volume by William Morris. He picked it up, glanced at the title, smiled, opened it, looked at the name on the fly-leaf, ran the leaves through with his hand, and put it down. Almost immediately the even murmur of the lecturer ceased, there was a sudden burst of pencils rattling on the desks in the lecture theatre, a stirring, a scraping of feet, and a number of voices speaking together. Then a firm footfall approached the door, which began to open, and stood ajar, as some indistinctly heard question arrested the new-comer.

The demonstrator turned, walked slowly back past the microtome, and left the laboratory by the preparation-room door. As he did so, first one, and then several students carrying notebooks entered the laboratory from the lecture theatre, and distributed themselves among the little tables, or stood in a group about the doorway. They were an exceptionally heterogeneous assembly, for while Oxford and Cambridge still recoil from the blushing prospect of mixed classes, the College of Science anticipated America in the matter years ago—mixed socially, too, for the prestige of the College is high, and its scholarships, free of any age limit, dredge deeper even than do those of the Scotch universities. The class numbered one-and-twenty, but some remained in the theatre questioning the professor, copying the blackboard diagrams before they were washed off, or examining the special specimens he had produced to illustrate the day's teaching. Of the nine who had come into the laboratory three were girls, one of whom, a little fair woman, wearing spectacles and dressed in greyish-green, was peering out of the window at the fog, while the other two, both wholesome-looking, plain-faced schoolgirls, unrolled and put on the brown holland aprons they wore while dissecting. Of the men, two went down the laboratory to their places, one a pallid, dark-bearded man, who had once been a tailor; the other a pleasant-featured, ruddy young man of twenty, dressed in a well-fitting brown suit; young Wedderburn, the son of Wedderburn, the eye specialist. The others formed a little knot near the theatre door. One of these, a dwarfed, spectacled figure, with a hunchback, sat on a bent wood stool; two others, one a short, dark youngster, and the other a flaxen-haired, reddish-complexioned young man, stood leaning side by side against the slate sink, while the fourth stood facing them, and maintained the larger share of the conversation.

This last person was named Hill. He was a sturdily built young fellow, of the same age as Wedderburn; he had a white face, dark grey eyes, hair of an indeterminate colour, and prominent, irregular features. He talked rather louder than was needful, and thrust his hands deeply into his pockets. His collar was frayed and blue with the starch of a careless laundress, his clothes were evidently ready-made, and there was a patch on the side of his boot near the toe. And as he talked or listened to the others, he glanced now and again towards the lecture theatre door. They were discussing the depressing peroration of the lecture they had just heard, the last lecture it was in the introductory course in zoology. "From ovum to ovum is the goal of the higher vertebrata," the lecturer had said in his melancholy tones, and so had neatly rounded off the sketch of comparative anatomy he had been developing. The spectacled hunchback had repeated it, with noisy appreciation, had tossed it towards the fair-haired student with an evident provocation, and had started one of these vague, rambling discussions on generalities, so unaccountably dear to the student mind all the world over.

"That is our goal, perhaps—I admit it, as far as science goes," said the fair-haired student, rising to the challenge. "But there are things above science."

"Science," said Hill confidently, "is systematic knowledge. Ideas that don't come into the system—must anyhow—be loose ideas." He was not quite sure whether that was a clever saying or a fatuity until his hearers took it seriously.

"The thing I cannot understand," said the hunchback, at large, "is whether Hill is a materialist or not."

"There is one thing above matter," said Hill promptly, feeling he had a better thing this time; aware too, of someone in the doorway behind him, and raising his voice a trifle for her benefit, "and that is, the delusion that there is something above matter."

"So we have your gospel at last," said the fair student. "It's all a delusion, is it? All our aspirations to lead something more than dogs' lives, all our work for anything beyond ourselves. But see how inconsistent you are. Your socialism, for instance. Why do you trouble about the interests of the race? Why do you concern yourself about the beggar in the gutter? Why are you bothering yourself to lend that book—" he indicated William Morris by a movement of the head—"to everyone in the lab.?"

"Girl," said the hunchback indistinctly, and glanced guiltily over his shoulder.

The girl in brown, with the brown eyes, had come into the laboratory, and stood on the other side of the table behind him, with her rolled-up apron in one hand, looking over her shoulder, listening to the discussion. She did not notice the hunchback, because she was glancing from Hill to his interlocutor. Hill's consciousness of her presence betrayed itself to her only in his studious ignorance of the fact; but she understood that, and it pleased her. "I see no reason," said he, "why a man should live like a brute because he knows of nothing beyond matter, and does not expect to exist a hundred years hence."

"Why shouldn't he?" said the fair-haired student.

"Why should he?" said Hill.

"What inducement has he?"

"That's the way with all you religious people. It's all a business of inducements. Cannot a man seek after righteousness for righteousness' sake?"

There was a pause. The fair man answered, with a kind of vocal padding, "But—you see—inducement—when I said inducement," to gain time. And then the hunchback came to his rescue and inserted a question. He was a terrible person in the debating society with his questions, and they invariably took one form—a demand for a definition, "What's your definition of righteousness?" said the hunchback at this stage.

Hill experienced a sudden loss of complacency at this question, but even as it was asked, relief came in the person of Brooks, the laboratory attendant, who entered by the preparation-room door, carrying a number of freshly killed guinea pigs by their hind legs. "This is the last batch of material this session," said the youngster who had not previously spoken.

Brooks advanced up the laboratory, smacking down a couple of guinea pigs at each table. The rest of the class, scenting the prey from afar, came crowding in by the lecture theatre door, and the discussion perished abruptly as the students who were not already in their places hurried to them to secure the choice of a specimen. There was a noise of keys rattling on split rings as lockers were opened and dissecting instruments taken out. Hill was already standing by his table, and his box of scalpels was sticking out of his pocket. The girl in brown came a step towards him, and leaning over his table, said softly, "Did you see that I returned your book, Mr. Hill?"

During the whole scene she and the book had been vividly present in his consciousness; but he made a clumsy pretence of looking at the book and seeing it for the first time. "Oh, yes," he said, taking it up. "I see. Did you like it?"

"I want to ask you some questions about it—some time."

"Certainly," said Hill. "I shall be glad." He stopped awkwardly. "You liked it?" he said.

"It's a wonderful book. Only some things I don't understand."

Then suddenly the laboratory was hushed by a curious, braying noise. It was the demonstrator. He was at the blackboard ready to begin the day's instruction, and it was his custom to demand silence by a sound midway between the "Er" of common intercourse and the blast of a trumpet. The girl in brown slipped back to her place: it was immediately in front of Hill's, and Hill, forgetting her forthwith, took a notebook out of the drawer of his table, turned over its leaves hastily, drew a stumpy pencil from his pocket, and prepared to make a copious note of the coming demonstration. For demonstrations and lectures are the sacred text of the College students. Books, saving only the Professor's own, you may—it is even expedient to—ignore.

Hill was the son of a Landport cobbler, and had been hooked by a chance blue paper the authorities had thrown out to the Landport Technical College. He kept himself in London on his allowance of a guinea a week, and found that, with proper care, this also covered his clothing allowance, an occasional waterproof collar, that is; and ink and needles and cotton, and suchlike necessaries for a man about town. This was his first year and his first session, but the brown old man in Landport had already got himself detested in many public-houses by boasting of his son, "the Professor." Hill was a vigorous youngster, with a serene contempt for the clergy of all denominations, and a fine ambition to reconstruct the world. He regarded his scholarship as a brilliant opportunity. He had begun to read at seven, and had read steadily whatever came in his way, good or bad, since then. His worldly experience had been limited to the island of Portsea, and acquired chiefly in the wholesale boot factory in which he had worked by day, after passing the seventh standard of the Board school. He had a considerable gift of speech, as the College Debating Society, which met amidst the crushing machines and mine models in the metallurgical theatre downstairs, already recognised—recognised by a violent battering of desks whenever he rose. And he was just at that fine emotional age when life opens at the end of a narrow pass like a broad valley at one's feet, full of the promise of wonderful discoveries and tremendous achievements. And his own limitations, save that he knew, that he knew, neither Latin nor French, were all unknown to him.

At first his interest had been divided pretty equally between his biological work at the College and social and theological theorising, an employment which he took in deadly earnest. Of a night, when the big museum library was not open, he would sit on the bed of his room in Chelsea with his coat and a muffler on, and write out the lecture notes and revise his dissection memoranda, until Thorpe called him out by a whistle—the landlady objected to open the door to attic visitors—and then the two would go prowling about the shadowy, shiny, gas-lit streets, talking, very much in the fashion of the sample just given, of the God idea, and Righteousness, and Carlyle, and the Reorganisation of Society. And in the midst of it all Hill, arguing not only for Thorpe, but for the casual passer-by, would lose the thread of his argument glancing at some pretty painted face that looked meaningly at him as he passed. Science and Righteousness! But once or twice lately there had been signs that a third interest was creeping into his life, and he had found his attention wandering from the fate of the mesoblastic somites or the probable meaning of the blastopore, to the thought of the girl with the brown eyes who sat at the table before him.

She was a paying student; she descended inconceivable social altitudes to speak to him. At the thought of the education she must have had, and the accomplishments she must possess, the soul of Hill became abject within him. She had spoken to him first over a difficulty about the alisphenoid of a rabbit's skull, and he had found that, in biology at least, he had no reason for self-abasement. And from that, after the manner of young people starting from any starting-point, they got to generalities, and while Hill attacked her upon the question of socialism—, some instinct told him to spare her a direct assault upon her religion—she was gathering resolution to undertake what she told herself was his aesthetic education. She was a year or two older than he, though the thought never occurred to him. The loan of 'News from Nowhere' was the beginning of a series of cross loans. Upon some absurd first principle of his, Hill had never "wasted time" upon poetry, and it seemed an appalling deficiency to her. One day in the lunch hour, when she chanced upon him alone in the little museum where the skeletons were arranged, shamefully eating the bun that constituted his midday meal, she retreated, and returned to lend him, with a slightly furtive air, a volume of Browning. He stood sideways towards her and took the book rather clumsily, because he was holding the bun in the other hand. And in the retrospect his voice lacked the cheerful clearness he could have wished.

That occurred after the examination in comparative anatomy, on the day before the College turned out its students, and was carefully locked up by the officials, for the Christmas holidays. The excitement of cramming for the first trial of strength had for a little while dominated Hill, to the exclusion of his other interests. In the forecasts of the result in which everyone indulged he was surprised to find that no one regarded him as a possible competitor for the Harvey Commemoration Medal, of which this and the two subsequent examinations disposed. It was about this time that Wedderburn, who so far had lived inconspicuously on the uttermost margin of Hill's perceptions, began to take on the appearance of an obstacle. By a mutual agreement, the nocturnal prowlings with Thorpe ceased for the three weeks before the examination, and his landlady pointed out that she really could not supply so much lamp oil at the price. He walked to and fro from the College with little slips of mnemonics in his hand, lists of crayfish appendages, rabbits' skull-bones, and vertebrate nerves, for example, and became a positive nuisance to foot passengers in the opposite direction.

But by a natural reaction, Poetry and the girl with the brown eyes ruled the Christmas holiday. The pending results of the examination became such a secondary consideration that Hill marvelled at his father's excitement. Even had he wished it, there was no comparative anatomy to read in Landport, and he was too poor to buy books, but the stock of poets in the library was extensive, and Hill's attack was magnificently sustained. He saturated himself with the fluent numbers of Longfellow and Tennyson, and fortified himself with Shakespeare; found a kindred soul in Pope, and a master in Shelley, and heard and fled the siren voices of Eliza Cook and Mrs. Hemans. But he read no more Browning, because he hoped for the loan of other volumes from Miss Haysman when he returned to London.

He walked from his lodgings to the College with that volume of Browning in his shiny black bag, and his mind teeming with the finest general propositions about poetry. Indeed, he framed first this little speech and then that with which to grace the return. The morning was an exceptionally pleasant one for London; there was a clear, hard frost and undeniable blue in the sky, a thin haze softened every outline, and warm shafts of sunlight struck between the house blocks and turned the sunny side of the street to amber and gold. In the hall of the College he pulled off his glove and signed his name with fingers so stiff with cold that the characteristic dash under the signature he cultivated became a quivering line. He imagined Miss Haysman about him everywhere. He turned at the staircase, and there, below he saw a crowd struggling at the foot of the notice-board. This possibly, was the biology list. He forgot Browning and Miss Haysman for the moment, and joined the scrimmage. And at last, with his cheek flattened against the sleeve of the man on the step above him, he read the list—

CLASS 1 H. J. Somers Wedderburn William Hill

and thereafter followed a second class that is outside our present sympathies. It was characteristic that he did not trouble to look for Thorpe on the physics list, but backed out of the struggle at once, and in a curious emotional state between pride over common second-class humanity and acute disappointment at Wedderburn's success, went on his way upstairs. At the top, as he was hanging up his coat in the passage, the zoological demonstrator, a young man from Oxford, who secretly regarded him as a blatant "mugger" of the very worst type, offered his heartiest congratulations.

At the laboratory door Hill stopped for a second to get his breath, and then entered. He looked straight up the laboratory and saw all five girl students grouped in their places, and Wedderburn, the once retiring Wedderburn, leaning rather gracefully against the window, playing with the blind tassel and talking, apparently, to the five of them. Now, Hill could talk bravely enough and even overbearingly to one girl, and he could have made a speech to a roomful of girls, but this business of standing at ease and appreciating, fencing, and returning quick remarks round a group was, he knew, altogether beyond him. Coming up the staircase his feelings for Wedderburn had been generous, a certain admiration perhaps, a willingness to shake his hand conspicuously and heartily as one who had fought but the first round. But before Christmas Wedderburn had never gone up to that end of the room to talk. In a flash Hill's mist of vague excitement condensed abruptly to a vivid dislike of Wedderburn. Possibly his expression changed. As he came up to his place, Wedderburn nodded carelessly to him, and the others glanced round. Miss Haysman looked at him and away again, the faintest touch of her eyes. "I can't agree with you, Mr. Wedderburn," she said.

"I must congratulate you on your first-class, Mr. Hill," said the spectacled girl in green, turning round and beaming at him.

"It's nothing," said Hill, staring at Wedderburn and Miss Haysman talking together, and eager to hear what they talked about.

"We poor folks in the second class don't think so," said the girl in spectacles.

What was it Wedderburn was saying? Something about William Morris! Hill did not answer the girl in spectacles, and the smile died out of his face. He could not hear, and failed to see how he could "cut in." Confound Wedderburn! He sat down, opened his bag, hesitated whether to return the volume of Browning forthwith, in the sight of all, and instead drew out his new notebooks for the short course in elementary botany that was now beginning, and which would terminate in February. As he did so, a fat, heavy man, with a white face and pale grey eyes—Bindon, the professor of botany, who came up from Kew for January and February—came in by the lecture theatre door, and passed, rubbing his hands together and smiling, in silent affability down the laboratory.

In the subsequent six weeks Hill experienced some very rapid and curiously complex emotional developments. For the most part he had Wedderburn in focus—a fact that Miss Haysman never suspected. She told Hill (for in the comparative privacy of the museum she talked a good deal to him of socialism and Browning and general propositions) that she had met Wedderburn at the house of some people she knew, and "he's inherited his cleverness; for his father, you know, is the great eye specialist."

"My father is a cobbler," said Hill, quite irrelevantly, and perceived the want of dignity even as he said it. But the gleam of jealousy did not offend her. She conceived herself the fundamental source of it. He suffered bitterly from a sense of Wedderburn's unfairness, and a realisation of his own handicap. Here was this Wedderburn had picked up a prominent man for a father, and instead of his losing so many marks on the score of that advantage, it was counted to him for righteousness! And while Hill had to introduce himself and talk to Miss Haysman clumsily over mangled guinea pigs in the laboratory, this Wedderburn, in some backstairs way, had access to her social altitudes, and could converse in a polished argot that Hill understood perhaps, but felt incapable of speaking. Not of course, that he wanted to. Then it seemed to Hill that for Wedderburn to come there day after day with cuffs unfrayed, neatly tailored, precisely barbered, quietly perfect, was in itself an ill-bred, sneering sort of proceeding. Moreover, it was a stealthy thing for Wedderburn to behave insignificantly for a space, to mock modesty, to lead Hill to fancy that he himself was beyond dispute the man of the year, and then suddenly to dart in front of him, and incontinently to swell up in this fashion. In addition to these things, Wedderburn displayed an increasing disposition to join in any conversational grouping that included Miss Haysman, and would venture, and indeed seek occasion, to pass opinions derogatory to socialism and atheism. He goaded Hill to incivilities by neat, shallow, and exceedingly effective personalities about the socialist leaders, until Hill hated Bernard Shaw's graceful egotisms, William Morris's limited editions and luxurious wall-papers, and Walter Crane's charmingly absurd ideal working men, about as much as he hated Wedderburn. The dissertations in the laboratory, that had been his glory in the previous term, became a danger, degenerated into inglorious tussles with Wedderburn, and Hill kept to them only out of an obscure perception that his honour was involved. In the debating society Hill knew quite clearly that, to a thunderous accompaniment of banged desks, he could have pulverised Wedderburn. Only Wedderburn never attended the debating society to be pulverised, because—nauseous affectation—! He "dined late."

You must not imagine that these things presented themselves in quite such a crude form to Hill's perception. Hill was a born generaliser. Wedderburn to him was not so much an individual obstacle as a type, the salient angle of a class. The economic theories that, after infinite ferment, had shaped themselves in Hill's mind, became abruptly concrete at the contact. The world became full of easy-mannered, graceful, gracefully-dressed, conversationally dexterous, finally shallow Wedderburn's, Bishops Wedderburn, Wedderburn M.P.'s, Professors Wedderburn, Wedderburn landlords, all with finger-bowl shibboleths and epigrammatic cities of refuge from a sturdy debater. And everyone ill-clothed or ill-dressed, from the cobbler to the cab-runner, was a man and a brother, a fellow-sufferer, to Hill's imagination. So that he became, as it were, a champion of the fallen and oppressed, albeit to outward seeming only a self-assertive, ill-mannered young man, and an unsuccessful champion at that. Again and again a skirmish over the afternoon tea that the girl students had inaugurated left Hill with flushed cheeks and a tattered temper, and the debating society noticed a new quality of sarcastic bitterness in his speeches.

You will understand now how it was necessary, if only in the interests of humanity, that Hill should demolish Wedderburn in the forthcoming examination and outshine him in the eyes of Miss Haysman; and you will perceive too, how Miss Haysman fell into some common feminine misconceptions. The Hill-Wedderburn quarrel, for in his unostentatious way Wedderburn reciprocated Hill's ill-veiled rivalry, became a tribute to her indefinable charm; she was the Queen of Beauty in a tournament of scalpels and stumpy pencils. To her confidential friend's secret annoyance, it even troubled her conscience, for she was a good girl, and painfully aware, from Ruskin and contemporary fiction, how entirely men's activities are determined by women's attitudes. And if Hill never by any chance mentioned the topic of love to her, she only credited him with the finer modesty for that omission.

So the time came on for the second examination, and Hill's increasing pallor confirmed the general rumour that he was working hard. In the aerated bread shop near South Kensington Station you would see him, breaking his bun and sipping his milk, with his eyes intent upon a paper of closely written notes. In his bedroom there were propositions about buds and stems round his looking-glass, a diagram to catch his eye, if soap should chance to spare it, above his washing basin. He missed several meetings of the debating society, but he found the chance encounters with Miss Haysman in the spacious ways of the adjacent art museum, or in the little museum at the top of the College, or in the College corridors, more frequent and very restful. In particular, they used to meet in a little gallery full of wrought-iron chests and gates, near the art library, and there Hill used to talk, under the gentle stimulus of her flattering attention, of Browning and his personal ambitions. A characteristic she found remarkable in him was his freedom from avarice. He contemplated quite calmly the prospect of living all his life on an income below a hundred pounds a year. But he was determined to be famous, to make, recognisably in his own proper person, the world a better place to live in. He took Bradlaugh and John Burns for his leaders and models, poor, even impecunious, great men. But Miss Haysman thought that such lives were deficient on the aesthetic side, by which, though she did not know it, she meant good wall-paper and upholstery, pretty books, tasteful clothes, concerts, and meals nicely cooked and respectfully served.

At last came the day of the second examination, and the professor of botany, a fussy, conscientious man, rearranged all the tables in a long narrow laboratory to prevent copying, and put his demonstrator on a chair on a table (where he felt, he said, like a Hindoo god), to see all the cheating, and stuck a notice outside the door, "Door closed," for no earthly reason that any human being could discover. And all the morning from ten till one the quill of Wedderburn shrieked defiance at Hill's, and the quills of the others chased their leaders in a tireless pack, and so also it was in the afternoon. Wedderburn was a little quieter than usual, and Hill's face was hot all day, and his overcoat bulged with textbooks and notebooks against the last moment's revision. And the next day, in the morning and in the afternoon, was the practical examination, when sections had to be cut and slides identified. In the morning Hill was depressed because he knew he had cut a thick section, and in the afternoon came the mysterious slip.

It was just the kind of thing that the botanical professor was always doing. Like the income tax, it offered a premium to the cheat. It was a preparation under the microscope, a little glass slip, held in its place on the stage of the instrument by light steel clips, and the inscription set forth that the slip was not to be moved. Each student was to go in turn to it, sketch it, write in his book of answers what he considered it to be, and return to his place. Now, to move such a slip is a thing one can do by a chance movement of the finger, and in a fraction of a second.

The professor's reason for decreeing that the slip should not be moved depended on the fact that the object he wanted identified was characteristic of a certain tree stem. In the position in which it was placed it was a difficult thing to recognise, but once the slip was moved so as to bring other parts of the preparation into view, its nature was obvious enough.

Hill came to this, flushed from a contest with staining reagents, sat down on the little stool before the microscope, turned the mirror to get the best light, and then, out of sheer habit, shifted the slips. At once he remembered the prohibition, and with an almost continuous motion of his hands, moved it back, and sat paralysed with astonishment at his action.

Then slowly, he turned his head. The professor was out of the room; the demonstrator sat aloft on his impromptu rostrum, reading the Quarterly Journal Microbiology Science; the rest of the examinees were busy, and with their backs to him. Should he own up to the accident now? He knew quite clearly what the thing was. It was a lenticel, a characteristic preparation from the elder-tree. His eyes roved over his intent fellow-students, and Wedderburn suddenly glanced over his shoulder at him with a queer expression in his eyes. The mental excitement that had kept Hill at an abnormal pitch of vigour these two days gave way to a curious nervous tension. His book of answers was beside him. He did not write down what the thing was, but with one eye at the microscope he began making a hasty sketch of it. His mind was full of this grotesque puzzle in ethics that had suddenly been sprung upon him. Should he identify it? Or should he leave this question unanswered? In that case Wedderburn would probably come out first in the second result. How could he tell now whether he might not have identified the thing without shifting it? It was possible that Wedderburn had failed to recognise it, of course. Suppose Wedderburn too had shifted the slide?

He looked up at the clock. There were fifteen minutes in which to make up his mind. He gathered up his book of answers and the coloured pencils he used in illustrating his replies and walked back to his seat.

He read through his manuscript, and then sat thinking and gnawing his knuckle. It would look queer now if he owned up. He must beat Wedderburn. He forgot the examples of those starry gentlemen, John Burns and Bradlaugh. Besides, he reflected, the glimpse of the rest of the slip he had, had was, after all, quite accidental, forced upon him by chance, a kind of providential revelation rather than an unfair advantage. It was not nearly so dishonest to avail himself of that as it was of Broome, who believed in the efficacy of prayer, to pray daily for a first-class. "Five minutes more," said the demonstrator, folding up his paper and becoming observant. Hill watched the clock hands until two minutes remained; then he opened the book of answers, and, with hot ears and an affectation of ease, gave his drawing of the lenticel its name.

When the second pass list appeared, the previous positions of Wedderburn and Hill were reversed, and the spectacled girl in green, who knew the demonstrator in private life (where he was practically human), said that in the result of the two examinations taken together Hill had the advantage of a mark—167 to 166 out of a possible 200. Everyone admired Hill in a way, though the suspicion of "mugging" clung to him. But Hill was to find congratulations and Miss Haysman's enhanced opinion of him, and even the decided decline in the crest of Wedderburn, tainted by an unhappy memory. He felt a remarkable access of energy at first, and the note of a democracy marching to triumph returned to his debating society speeches; he worked at his comparative anatomy with tremendous zeal and effect, and he went on with his aesthetic education. But through it all, a vivid little picture was continually coming before his mind's eye—of a sneakish person manipulating a slide.

No human being had witnessed the act, and he was cocksure that no higher power existed to see, it; but for all that it worried him. Memories are not dead things but alive; they dwindle in disuse, but they harden and develop in all sorts of queer ways if they are being continually fretted. Curiously enough, though at the time he perceived clearly that the shifting was accidental, as the days wore on, his memory became confused about it, until at last he was not sure—although he assured himself that he was sure—whether the movement had been absolutely involuntary. Then it is possible that Hill's dietary was conducive to morbid conscientiousness; a breakfast frequently eaten in a hurry, a midday bun, and at such hours after five as chanced to be convenient, such meat as his means determined, usually in a chop-house in a back street off the Brompton Road. Occasionally he treated himself to threepenny or ninepenny classics, and they usually represented a suppression of potatoes or chops. It is indisputable that outbreaks of self-abasement and emotional revival have a distinct relation to periods of scarcity. But apart from this influence on the feelings, there was in Hill a distinct aversion to falsity that the blasphemous Landport cobbler had inculcated by strap and tongue from his earliest years. Of one fact about professed atheists I am convinced; they may be—they usually are—fools, void of subtlety, revilers of holy institutions, brutal speakers, and mischievous knaves, but they lie with difficulty. If it were not so, if they had the faintest grasp of the idea of compromise, they would simply be liberal churchmen. And moreover, this memory poisoned his regard for Miss Haysman. For she now so evidently preferred him to Wedderburn that he felt sure he cared for her, and began reciprocating her attentions by timid marks of personal regard; at one time he even bought a bunch of violets, carried it about in his pocket, and produced it, with a stumbling explanation, withered and dead, in the gallery of old iron. It poisoned too, the denunciation of capitalist dishonesty that had been one of his life's pleasures. And lastly, it poisoned his triumph in Wedderburn. Previously he had been Wedderburn's superior in his own eyes, and had raged simply at a want of recognition. Now he began to fret at the darker suspicion of positive inferiority. He fancied he found justifications for his position in Browning, but they vanished on analysis. At last—moved, curiously enough, by exactly the same motive forces that had resulted in his dishonesty—he went to Professor Bindon, and made a clean breast of the whole affair. As Hill was a paid student, Professor Bindon did not ask him to sit down, and he stood before the professor's desk as he made his confession.

"It's a curious story," said Professor Bindon, slowly realising how the thing reflected on himself, and then letting his anger rise—, "a most remarkable story. I can't understand your doing it, and I can't understand this avowal. You're a type of student—Cambridge men would never dream—I suppose I ought to have thought—why did you cheat?"

"I didn't cheat," said Hill.

"But you have just been telling me you did."

"I thought I explained—"

"Either you cheated or you did not cheat—"

"I said my motion was involuntary."

"I am not a metaphysician, I am a servant of science—of fact. You were told not to move the slip. You did move the slip. If that is not cheating—"

"If I was a cheat," said Hill, with the note of hysterics in his voice, "should I come here and tell you?"

"Your repentance, of course, does you credit," said Professor Bindon, "but it does not alter the original facts."

"No, sir," said Hill, giving in, in utter self-abasement.

"Even now you cause an enormous amount of trouble. The examination list will have to be revised."

"I suppose so, sir."

"Suppose so? Of course it must be revised. And I don't see how I can conscientiously pass you."

"Not pass me?" said Hill. "Fail me?"

"It's the rule in all examinations. Or where should we be? What else did you expect? You don't want to shirk the consequences of your own acts?"

"I thought, perhaps—" said Hill. And then, "Fail me? I thought, as I told you, you would simply deduct the marks given for that slip."

"Impossible!" said Bindon. "Besides, it would still leave you above Wedderburn. Deduct only the marks! Preposterous! The Departmental Regulations distinctly say—"

"But it's my own admission, sir."

"The Regulations say nothing whatever of the manner in which the matter comes to light. They simply provide—"

"It will ruin me. If I fail this examination, they won't renew my scholarship."

"You should have thought of that before."

"But, sir, consider all my circumstances—"

"I cannot consider anything. Professors in this College are machines. The Regulations will not even let us recommend our students for appointments. I am a machine, and you have worked me. I have to do—"

"It's very hard, sir."

"Possibly it is."

"If I am to be failed this examination, I might as well go home at once."

"That is as you think proper." Bindon's voice softened a little; he perceived he had been unjust, and provided he did not contradict himself, he was disposed to amelioration. "As a private person," he said, "I think this confession of yours goes far to mitigate your offence. But you have set the machinery in motion, and now it must take its course. I—I am really sorry you gave way."

A wave of emotion prevented Hill from answering. Suddenly, very vividly, he saw the heavily-lined face of the old Landport cobbler, his father. "Good God! What a fool I have been!" he said hotly and abruptly.

"I hope," said Bindon, "that it will be a lesson to you."

But, curiously enough, they were not thinking of quite the same indiscretion.

There was a pause.

"I would like a day to think, sir, and then I will let you know—about going home, I mean," said Hill, moving towards the door.

The next day Hill's place was vacant. The spectacled girl in green was, as usual, first with the news. Wedderburn and Miss Haysman were talking of a performance of 'The Meistersingers' when she came up to them.

"Have you heard?" she said.

"Heard what?"

"There was cheating in the examination."

"Cheating!" said Wedderburn, with his face suddenly hot. "How?"

"That slide—"

"Moved? Never!"

"It was. That slide that we weren't to move—"

"Nonsense!" said Wedderburn. "Why! How could they find out? Who do they say—?"

"It was Mr. Hill."

"Hill!"

"Mr. Hill!"

"Not—surely not the immaculate Hill?" said Wedderburn, recovering.

"I don't believe it," said Miss Haysman. "How do you know?"

"I didn't," said the girl in spectacles. "But I know it now for a fact. Mr. Hill went and confessed to Professor Bindon himself."

"By Jove!" said Wedderburn. "Hill of all people. But I am always inclined to distrust these philanthropists-on-principle—"

"Are you quite sure?" said Miss Haysman, with a catch in her breath.

"Quite. It's dreadful, isn't it? But, you know, what can you expect? His father is a cobbler."

Then Miss Haysman astonished the girl in spectacles.

"I don't care. I will not believe it," she said, flushing darkly under her warm-tinted skin. "I will not believe it until he has told me so himself—face to face. I would scarcely believe it then," and abruptly she turned her back on the girl in spectacles, and walked to her own place.

"It's true, all the same," said the girl in spectacles, peering and smiling at Wedderburn.

But Wedderburn did not answer her. She was indeed one of those people who seemed destined to make unanswered remarks.

20

In the Abyss

The lieutenant stood in front of the steel sphere and gnawed a piece of pine splinter. "What do you think of it, Steevens?" he said.

"It's an idea," said Steevens, in the tone of one who keeps an open mind.

"I believe it will smash—flat," said the lieutenant.

"He seems to have calculated it all out pretty well," said Steevens, still impartial.

"But think of the pressure," said the lieutenant. "At the surface of the water it's fourteen pounds to the inch, thirty feet down it's double that; sixty, treble; ninety, four times; nine hundred, forty times; five thousand, three hundred—that's a mile—it's two hundred and forty times fourteen pounds; that's—let's see—thirty hundredweight—a ton and a half, Steevens; a ton and a half to the square inch. And the ocean where he's going is five miles deep. That's seven and a half—"

"Sounds a lot," said Steevens, "but it's jolly thick steel."

The lieutenant made no answer, but resumed his pine splinter. The object of their conversation was a huge ball of steel, having an exterior diameter of perhaps nine feet. It looked like the shot for some Titanic piece of artillery. It was elaborately nested in a monstrous scaffolding built into the framework of the vessel, and the gigantic spars that were presently to sling it overboard gave the stern of the ship an appearance that had raised the curiosity of every decent sailor who had sighted it, from the Pool of London to the Tropic of Capricorn. In two places, one above the other, the steel gave place to a couple of circular windows of enormously thick glass, and one of these, set in steel frame of great solidity, was now partially unscrewed. Both the men had seen the interior of this globe for the first time that morning. It was elaborately padded with air cushions, with little studs sunk between bulging pillows to work the simple mechanism of the affair. Everything was elaborately padded, even the Myers apparatus which was to absorb carbonic acid and replace the oxygen inspired by its tenant, when he had crept in by the glass manhole, and had been screwed in. It was so elaborately padded that a man might have been fired from a gun in it with perfect safety. And it had need to be, for presently a man was to crawl in through that glass manhole, to be screwed up tightly, and to be flung overboard, and to sink down—down—down, for five miles, even as the lieutenant said. It had taken the strongest hold of his imagination; it made him a bore at mess; and he found Steevens the new arrival aboard, a godsend to talk to about it, over and over again.

"It's my opinion," said the lieutenant, "that, that glass will simply bend in and bulge and smash, under a pressure of that sort. Daubree has made rocks run like water under big pressures—and you mark my words—"

"If the glass did break in," said Steevens, "what then?"

"The water would shoot in like a jet of iron. Have you ever felt a straight jet of high pressure water? It would hit as hard as a bullet. It would simply smash him and flatten him. It would tear down his throat, and into his lungs; it would blow in his ears—"

"What a detailed imagination you have!" protested Steevens, who saw things vividly.

"It's a simple statement of the inevitable," said the lieutenant.

"And the globe?"

"Would just give out a few little bubbles, and it would settle down comfortably against the Day of Judgment, among the oozes and the bottom clay—with poor Elstead spread over his own smashed cushions like butter over bread."

He repeated this sentence as though he liked it very much. "Like butter over bread," he said.

"Having a look at the jigger?" said a voice, and Elstead stood behind them, spick and span in white, with a cigarette between his teeth, and his eyes smiling out of the shadow of his ample hat-brim. "What's that about bread and butter, Weybridge? Grumbling as usual about the insufficient pay of naval officers? It won't be more than a day now before I start. We are to get the slings ready today. This clean sky and gentle swell is just the kind of thing for swinging off a dozen tons of lead and iron, isn't it?"

"It won't affect you much," said Weybridge.

"No. Seventy or eighty feet down, and I shall be there in a dozen seconds, there's not a particle moving, though the wind shriek itself hoarse up above, and the water lifts halfway to the clouds. No. Down there—" He moved to the side of the ship and the other two followed him. All three leant forward on their elbows and stared down into the yellow-green water.

"Peace," said Elstead, finishing his thought aloud.

"Are you dead certain that clockwork will act?" asked Weybridge presently.

"It has worked thirty-five times," said Elstead. "It's bound to work."

"But if it doesn't?"

"Why shouldn't it?"

"I wouldn't go down in that confounded thing," said Weybridge, "for twenty thousand pounds."

"Cheerful chap you are," said Elstead, and spat sociably at a bubble below.

"I don't understand yet how you mean to work the thing," said Steevens.

"In the first place, I'm screwed into the sphere," said Elstead, "and when I've turned the electric light off on three times to show I'm cheerful, I'm swung out over the stern by that crane, with all those big lead sinkers slung below me. The top lead weight has a roller carrying a hundred fathoms of strong cord rolled up, and that's all that joins the sinkers to the sphere, except the slings that will be cut when the affair is dropped. We use cord rather than wire rope because it's easier to cut and more buoyant—necessary points, as you will see.

"Through each of these lead weights you notice there is a hole, and an iron rod will be run through that and will project six feet on the lower side. If that rod is rammed up from below, it knocks up a lever and sets the clockwork in motion at the side of the cylinder on which the cord winds.

"Very well. The whole affair is lowered gently into the water, and the slings are cut. The sphere floats—, with the air in it, it's lighter than water—, but the lead weights go down straight and the cord runs out. When the cord is all paid out, the sphere will go down too, pulled down by the cord."

"But why the cord?" asked Steevens. "Why not fasten the weights directly to the sphere?"

"Because of the smash down below. The whole affair will go rushing down, mile after mile, at a headlong pace at last. It would be knocked to pieces on the bottom if it wasn't for that cord. But the weights will hit the bottom, and directly they do, the buoyancy of the sphere will come into play. It will go on sinking slower and slower; come to stop at last, and then begin to float upward again.

"That's where the clockwork comes in. Directly the weights smash against the sea bottom, the rod will be knocked through and will kick up the clockwork, and the cord will be rewound on the reel. I shall be lugged down to the sea bottom. There I shall stay for half an hour, with the electric light on, looking about me. Then the clockwork will release a spring knife, the cord will be cut, and up I shall rush again, like a soda-water bubble. The cord itself will help the flotation."

"And if you should chance to hit a ship?" said Weybridge.

"I should come up at such a pace, I should go clean through it," said Elstead, "like a cannon ball. You needn't worry about that."

"And suppose some nimble crustacean should wriggle into your clockwork—"

"It would be a pressing sort of invitation for me to stop," said Elstead, turning his back on the water and staring at the sphere.

They had swung Elstead overboard by eleven o'clock. The day was serenely bright and calm, with the horizon lost in haze. The electric glare in the little upper compartment beamed cheerfully three times. Then they let him down slowly to the surface of the water, and a sailor in the stern chains hung ready to cut the tackle that held the lead weights and the sphere together. The globe, which had looked so large on deck, looked the smallest thing conceivable under the stern of the ship. It rolled a little, and its two dark windows, which floated uppermost, seemed like eyes turned up in round wonderment at the people who crowded the rail. A voice wondered how Elstead liked the rolling. "Are you ready?" sang out the commander. "Ay, ay, sir!" "Then let her go!"

The rope of the tackle tightened against the blade and was cut, and an eddy rolled over the globe in a grotesquely helpless fashion.

Someone waved a handkerchief, someone else tried an ineffectual cheer, a middy was counting slowly, "Eight, nine, ten!" Another roll, then a jerk and a splash the thing righted itself.

It seemed to be stationary for a moment, to grow rapidly smaller, and then the water closed over it, and it became visible, enlarged by refraction and dimmer, below the surface. Before one could count three it had disappeared. There was a flicker of white light far down in the water, that diminished to a speck and vanished. Then there was nothing but a depth of water going down into blackness, through which a shark was swimming.

Then suddenly the screw of the cruiser began to rotate, the water was crickled, the shark disappeared in a wrinkled confusion, and a torrent of foam rushed across the crystalline clearness that had swallowed up Elstead. "What's the idea?" said one A.B. to another.

"We're going to lay off about a couple of miles, 'fear he should hit us when he comes up," said his mate.

The ship steamed slowly to her new position. Aboard her almost everyone who was unoccupied remained watching the breathing swell into which the sphere had sunk. For the next half-hour it is doubtful if a word was spoken that did not bear directly or indirectly on Elstead. The December sun was now high in the sky, and the heat very considerable.

"He'll be cold enough down there," said Weybridge. "They say that below a certain depth sea water's always just about freezing."

"Where'll he come up?" asked Steevens. "I've lost my bearings."

"That's the spot," said the commander, who prided himself on his omniscience. He extended a precise finger south-eastward. "And this, I reckon, is pretty nearly the moment," he said. "He's been thirty-five minutes."

"How long does it take to reach the bottom of the ocean?" asked Steevens.

"For a depth of five miles, and reckoning—as we did—an acceleration of two feet per second, both ways, is just about three-quarters of a minute."

"Then he's overdue," said Weybridge.

"Pretty nearly," said the commander. "I suppose it takes a few minutes for that cord of his to wind in."

"I forgot that," said Weybridge, evidently relieved.

And then began the suspense. A minute slowly dragged itself out, and no sphere shot out of the water. Another followed, and nothing broke the low oily swell. The sailors explained to one another that little point about the winding-in of the cord. The rigging was dotted with expectant faces. "Come up, Elstead!" called one hairy-chested salt impatiently, and the others caught it up, and shouted as though they were waiting for the curtain of a theatre to rise.

The commander glanced irritably at them.

"Of course, if the acceleration's less than two," he said, "he'll be all the longer. We aren't absolutely certain that was the proper figure. I'm no slavish believer in calculations."

Steevens agreed concisely. No one on the quarter-deck spoke for a couple of minutes. Then Steevens' watchcase clicked.

When, twenty-one minutes after the sun reached the zenith, they were still waiting for the globe to reappear, and not a man aboard had dared to whisper that hope was dead. It was Weybridge who first gave expression to that realisation. He spoke while the sound of eight bells still hung in the air. "I always distrusted that window," he said quite suddenly to Steevens.

"Good God!" said Steevens; "you don't think—?"

"Well!" said Weybridge, and left the rest to his imagination.

"I'm no great believer in calculations myself," said the commander dubiously, "so that I'm not altogether hopeless yet." And at midnight the gunboat was steaming slowly in a spiral round the spot where the globe had sunk, and the white beam of the electric light fled and halted and swept discontentedly onward again over the waste of phosphorescent waters under the little stars.

"If his window hasn't burst and smashed him," said Weybridge, "then it's a cursed sight worse, for his clockwork has gone wrong, and he's alive now, five miles under our feet, down there in the cold and dark, anchored in that little bubble of his, where never a ray of light has shone or a human being lived, since the waters were gathered together. He's there without food, feeling hungry and thirsty and scared, wondering whether he'll starve or stifle. Which will it be? The Myers apparatus is running out, I suppose. How long do they last?"

"Good heavens!" he exclaimed; "What little things we are! What daring little devils! Down there, miles and miles of water—all water, and all this empty water about us and this sky. Gulfs!"

He threw his hands out, and as he did so, a little white streak swept noiselessly up the sky, travelled more slowly, stopped, became a motionless dot, as though a new star had fallen up into the sky. Then it went sliding back again and lost itself amidst the reflections of the stars and the white haze of the sea's phosphorescence.

At the sight he stopped, arm extended and mouth open. He shut his mouth, opened it again, and waved his arms with an impatient gesture. Then he turned, shouted "Elstead ahoy!" to the first watch, and went at a run to Lindley and the search-light. "I saw him," he said "Starboard there! His light's on, and he's just shot out of the water. Bring the light round. We ought to see him drifting, when he lifts on the swell."

But they never picked up the explorer until dawn. Then they almost ran him down. The crane was swung out and a boat's crew hooked the chain to the sphere. When they had shipped the sphere, they unscrewed the manhole and peered into the darkness of the interior (for the electric light chamber was intended to illuminate the water about the sphere, and was shut off entirely from its general cavity).

The air was very hot within the cavity, and the indiarubber at the lip of the manhole was soft. There was no answer to their eager questions and no sound of movement within. Elstead seemed to be lying motionless, crumpled in the bottom of the globe. The ship's doctor crawled in and lifted him out to the men outside. For a moment or so they did not know whether Elstead was alive or dead. His face, in the yellow light of the ship's lamps, glistened with perspiration. They carried him down to his own cabin.

He was not dead, they found, but in a state of absolute nervous collapse, and besides cruelly bruised. For some days he had to lie perfectly still. It was a week before he could tell his experiences.

Almost his first words were that he was going down again. The sphere would have to be altered, he said, in order to allow him to throw off the cord if need be, and that was all. He had, had the most marvellous experience. "You thought I should find nothing but ooze," he said. "You laughed at my explorations, and I've discovered a new world!" He told his story in disconnected fragments, and chiefly from the wrong end, so that it is impossible to re-tell it in his words. But what follows is the narrative of his experience.

It began atrociously, he said. Before the cord ran out, the thing kept rolling over. He felt like a frog in a football. He could see nothing but the crane and the sky overhead, with an occasional glimpse of people on the ships rail. He couldn't tell a bit which way the thing would roll next. Suddenly he would find his footing going up, and try to step, and over he went rolling, head over heels, and just anyhow, on the padding. Any other shape would have been more comfortable, but no other shape was to be relied upon under the huge pressure of the nethermost abyss.

Suddenly the swaying ceased; the globe righted, and when he had picked himself up, he saw the water all about him greeny-blue, with an attenuated light filtering down from above, and a shoal of little floating things went rushing up past him, as it seemed to him, towards the light. And even as he looked, it grew darker and darker, until the water above was as dark as the midnight sky, albeit of greener shade, and the water below black. And little transparent things in the water developed a faint glint of luminosity, and shot past him in faint greenish streaks.

And the feeling of falling! It was just like the start of a lift, he said, only it kept on. One has to imagine what that means, that keeping on. It was then of all times that Elstead repented of his adventure. He saw the chances against him in an altogether new light. He thought of the big cuttle-fish people knew to exist in the middle waters, the kind of things they find half digested in whales at times, or floating dead and rotten and half eaten by fish. Suppose one caught hold and wouldn't let go. And had the clockwork really been sufficiently tested? But whether he wanted to go on or go back mattered not the slightest now.

In fifty seconds everything was as black as night outside, except where the beam from his light struck through the waters, and picked out every now and then some fish or scrap of sinking matter. They flashed by too fast for him to see what they were. Once he thinks he passed a shark. And then the sphere began to get hot by friction against the water. They had underestimated this, it seems.

The first thing he noticed was that he was perspiring, and then he heard a hissing growing louder under his feet, and saw a lot of little bubbles—very little bubbles they were—rushing upward like a fan through the water outside. Steam! He felt the window, and it was hot. He turned on the minute glow-lamp that lit his own cavity, looked at the padded watch by the studs, and saw he had been travelling now for two minutes. It came into his head that the window would crack through the conflict of temperatures, for he knew the bottom water is very near freezing.

Then suddenly the floor of the sphere seemed to press against his feet, the rush of bubbles outside grew slower and slower, and the hissing diminished. The sphere rolled a little. The window had not cracked, nothing had given, and he knew that the dangers of sinking, at any rate, were over.

In another minute or so he would be on the floor of the abyss. He thought, he said, of Steevens and Weybridge and the rest of them five miles overhead, higher to him than the highest clouds that ever floated over land are to us, steaming slowly and staring down and wondering what had happened to him.

He peered out of the window. There were no more bubbles now, and the hissing had stopped. Outside there was a heavy blackness—as black as black velvet—except where the electric light pierced the empty water and showed the colour of it—a yellow-green. Then three things like shapes of fire swam into sight, following each other through the water. Whether they were little and near or big and far off he could not tell.

Each was outlined in a bluish light almost as bright as the lights of a fishing smack, a light which seemed to be smoking greatly, and all along the sides of them were specks of this, like the lighter portholes of a ship. Their phosphorescence seemed to go out as they came into the radiance of his lamp, and he saw then that they were little fish of some strange sort, with huge heads, vast eyes, and dwindling bodies and tails. Their eyes were turned towards him, and he judged they were following him down. He supposed they were attracted by his glare.

Presently others of the same sort joined them. As he went on down, he noticed that the water became of a pallid colour, and that little specks twinkled in his ray like motes in a sunbeam. This was probably due to the clouds of ooze and mud that the impact of his leaden sinkers had disturbed.

By the time he was drawn down to the lead weights he was in a dense fog of white that his electric light failed altogether to pierce for more than a few yards, and many minutes elapsed before the hanging sheets of sediment subsided to any extent. Then, lit by his light and by the transient phosphorescence of a distant shoal of fishes, he was able to see under the huge blackness of the super-incumbent water an undulating expanse of greyish-white ooze, broken here and there by tangled thickets of a growth of sea lilies, waving hungry tentacles in the air.

Farther away were the graceful, translucent outlines of a group of gigantic sponges. About this floor there were scattered a number of bristling flattish tufts of rich purple and black, which he decided must be some sort of sea-urchin, and small, large-eyed or blind things having a curious resemblance, some to woodlice, and others to lobsters, crawled sluggishly across the track of the light and vanished into the obscurity again, leaving furrowed trails behind them.

Then suddenly the hovering swarm of little fishes veered about and came towards him as a flight of starlings might do. They passed over him like a phosphorescent snow, and then he saw behind them some larger creature advancing towards the sphere.

At first he could see it only dimly, a faintly moving figure remotely suggestive of a walking man, and then it came into the spray of light that the lamp shot out. As the glare struck it, it shut its eyes, dazzled. He stared in rigid astonishment.

It was a strange vertebrated animal. Its dark purple head was dimly suggestive of a chameleon, but it had such a high forehead and such a braincase as no reptile ever displayed before; the vertical pitch of its face gave it a most extraordinary resemblance to a human being.

Two large and protruding eyes projected from sockets in chameleon fashion, and it had a broad reptilian mouth with horny lips beneath its little nostrils. In the position of the ears were two huge gill-covers, and out of these floated a branching tree of coralline filaments, almost like the tree-like gills that very young rays and sharks possess.

But the humanity of the face was not the most extraordinary thing about the creature. It was a biped; its almost globular body was poised on a tripod of two frog-like legs and a long thick tail, and its fore limbs, which grotesquely caricatured the human hand, much as a frog's do, carried a long shaft of bone, tipped with copper. The colour of the creature was variegated; its head, hands and legs were purple; but its skin, which hung loosely upon it, even as clothes might do, was a phosphorescent grey. And it stood there blinded by the light.

At last this unknown creature of the abyss blinked its eyes open, and shading them with its disengaged hand, opened its mouth and gave vent to a shouting noise, articulate almost as speech might be, that penetrated even the steel case and padded jacket of the sphere. How a shouting may be accomplished without lungs Elstead does not profess to explain. It then moved sideways out of the glare into the mystery of shadow that bordered it on either side, and Elstead felt rather than saw that it was coming towards him. Fancying the light had attracted it, he turned the switch that cut off the current. In another moment something soft dabbed upon the steel, and the globe swayed.

Then the shouting was repeated, and it seemed to him that a distant echo answered it. The dabbing recurred, and the whole globe swayed and ground against the spindle over which the wire was rolled. He stood in the blackness and peered out into the everlasting night of the abyss. And presently he saw, very faint and remote, other phosphorescent quasi-human forms hurrying towards him.

Hardly knowing what he did, he felt about in his swaying prison for the stud of the exterior electric light, and came by accident against his own small glow-lamp in its padded recess. The sphere twisted, and then threw him down; he heard shouts like shouts of surprise, and when he rose to his feet, he saw two pairs of stalked eyes peering into the lower window and reflecting his light.

In another moment hands were dabbing vigorously at his steel casing, and there was a sound, horrible enough in his position, of the metal protection of the clockwork being vigorously hammered. That indeed sent his heart into his mouth, for if these strange creatures succeeded in stopping that, his release would never occur. Scarcely had he thought as much when he felt the sphere sway violently, and the floor of it press hard against his feet. He turned off the small glow-lamp that lit the interior, and sent the ray of the large light in the separate compartment, out into the water. The sea-floor and the man-like creatures had disappeared, and a couple of fish chasing each other dropped suddenly by the window.

He thought at once that these strange denizens of the deep sea had broke the rope, and that he had escaped. He drove up faster and faster, and then stopped with a jerk that sent him flying against the padded roof of his prison. For half a minute perhaps, he was too astonished to think.

Then he felt that the sphere was spinning slowly, and rocking, and it seemed to him that it was also being drawn through the water. By crouching close to the window, he managed to make his weight effective and roll that part of the sphere downward, but he could see nothing save the pale ray of his light striking down ineffectively into the darkness. It occurred to him that he would see more if he turned the lamp off, and allowed his eyes to grow accustomed to the profound obscurity.

In this he was wise. After some minutes the velvety blackness became a translucent blackness, and then, far away, and as faint as zodiacal light of an English summer evening, he saw shapes moving below. He judged these creatures had detached his cable, and were towing him along the sea bottom.

And then he saw something faint and remote across the undulations of the submarine plain, a broad horizon of pale luminosity that extended this way and that way as far as the range of his little window permitted him to see. To this he was being towed, as a balloon might be towed by men out of the open country into a town. He approached it very slowly, and very slowly the dim irradiation was gathered together into more definite shapes.

It was nearly five o'clock before he came over this luminous area, and by that time he could make out an arrangement suggestive of streets and houses grouped about a vast roofless erection that was grotesquely suggestive of a ruined abbey. It was spread out like a map below him. The houses were all roofless enclosures of walls, and their substance being, as he afterwards saw, of phosphorescent bones, gave the place an appearance as if it were built of drowned moonshine.

Among the inner caves of the place waving trees of crinoid stretched their tentacles, and tall, slender, glassy sponges shot like shining minarets and lilies of filmy light out of the general glow of the city. In the open spaces of the place he could see a stirring movement as of crowds of people, but he was too many fathoms above them to distinguish the individuals in those crowds.

Then slowly they pulled him down, and as they did so, the details of the place crept slowly upon his apprehension. He saw that the courses of the cloudy buildings were marked out with beaded lines of round objects, and then he perceived that at several points below him, in broad open spaces, were forms like the encrusted shapes of ships.

Slowly and surely he was drawn down, and the forms below him became brighter, clearer, more distinct. He was being pulled down, he perceived, towards the large building in the centre of the town, and he could catch a glimpse ever and again of the multitudinous forms that were lugging at his cord. He was astonished to see that the rigging of one of the ships, which formed such a prominent feature of the place, was crowded with a host of gesticulating figures regarding him, and then the walls of the great building rose about him silently, and hid the city from his eyes.

And such walls they were, of water-logged wood, and twisted wire-rope, and iron spars, and copper, and the bones and skulls of dead men. The skulls ran in zigzag lines and spirals and fantastic curves over the building; and in and out of their eye-sockets, and over the whole surface of the place, lurked and played a multitude of silvery little fishes.

Suddenly his ears were filled with a low shouting and a noise like the violent blowing of horns, and this gave place to a fantastic chant. Down the sphere sank, past the huge pointed windows, through which he saw vaguely a great number of these strange, ghostlike people regarding him, and at last he came to rest, as it seemed, on a kind of altar that stood in the centre of the place.

And now he was at such a level that he could see these strange people of the abyss plainly once more. To his astonishment, he perceived that they were prostrating themselves before him, all save one, dressed as it seemed in a robe of placoid scales, and crowned with a luminous diadem, who stood with his reptilian mouth opening and shutting, as though he led the chanting of the worshippers.

A curious impulse made Elstead turn on his small glow-lamp again, so that he became visible to these creatures of the abyss, albeit the glare made them disappear forthwith into night. At this sudden sight of him, the chanting gave place to a tumult of exultant shouts; and Elstead, being anxious to watch them, turned his light off again, and vanished from before their eyes. But for a time he was too blind to make out what they were doing, and when at last he could distinguish them, they were kneeling again. And thus they continued worshipping him, without rest or intermission, for a space of three hours.

Most circumstantial was Elstead's account of this astounding city and its people, these people of perpetual night, who have never seen sun or moon or stars, green vegetation, nor any living, air-breathing creatures, who know nothing of fire, nor any light but the phosphorescent light of living things.

Startling as is his story, it is yet more startling to find that scientific men, of such eminence as Adams and Jenkins, find nothing incredible in it. They tell me they see no reason why intelligent, water-breathing, vertebrated creatures, inured to a low temperature and enormous pressure, and of such a heavy structure, that neither alive nor dead would they float, might not live upon the bottom of the deep sea, and quite unsuspected by us, descendants like ourselves of the great Theriomorpha of the New Red Sandstone age.

We should be known to them however, as strange, meteoric creatures, wont to fall catastrophically dead out of the mysterious blackness of their watery sky. And not only we ourselves, but our ships, our metals, our appliances, would come raining down out of the night. Sometimes sinking things would smite down and crush them, as if it were the judgment of some unseen power above, and sometimes would come things of utmost rarity or utility, or shapes of inspiring suggestion. One can understand, perhaps, something of their behaviour at the descent of a living man, if one thinks what a barbaric people might do, to whom an enhaloed, shining creature came suddenly out of the sky.

At one time or another Elstead probably told the officers of the 'Ptarmigan' every detail of his strange twelve hours in the abyss. That he also intended to write them down is certain, but he never did, and so unhappily we have to piece together the discrepant fragments of his story from the reminiscences of Commander Simmons, Weybridge, Steevens, Lindley, and the others.

We see the thing darkly in fragmentary glimpses—the huge ghostly building, the bowing, chanting people, with their dark chameleon-like heads and faintly luminous clothing, and Elstead, with his light turned on again, vainly trying to convey to their minds that the cord by which the sphere was held was to be severed. Minute after minute slipped away, and Elstead, looking at his watch, was horrified to find that he had oxygen only for four hours more. But the chant in his honour kept on as remorselessly as if it was the marching song of his approaching death.

The manner of his release he does not understand, but to judge by the end of cord that hung from the sphere, it had been cut through by rubbing against the edge of the altar. Abruptly the sphere rolled over, and he swept up, out of their world, as an ethereal creature clothed in a vacuum would sweep through our own atmosphere back to its native ether again. He must have torn out of their sight as a hydrogen bubble hastens upwards from our air. A strange ascension it must have seemed to them.

The sphere rushed up with even greater velocity than, when weighted with the lead sinkers, it had rushed down. It became exceedingly hot. It drove up with the windows uppermost, and he remembers the torrent of bubbles frothing against the glass. Every moment he expected this to fly. Then suddenly something like a huge wheel seemed to be released in his head, the padded compartment began spinning about him, and he fainted. His next recollection was of his cabin, and of the doctor's voice.

But that is the substance of the extraordinary story that Elstead related in fragments to the officers of the 'Ptarmigan'. He promised to write it all down at a later date. His mind was chiefly occupied with the improvement of his apparatus, which was effected at Rio.

It remains only to tell that on February 2, 1896, he made his second descent into the ocean abyss, with the improvements his first experience suggested. What happened we shall probably never knew. He never returned. The 'Ptarmigan' beat about over the point of his submersion, seeking him in vain for thirteen days. Then she returned to Rio, and the news was telegraphed to his friends. So the matter remains for the present. But it is hardly probable that no further attempt will be made to verify his strange story of these hitherto unsuspected cities of the deep sea.

21

The Apple

"I must get rid of it," said the man in the corner of the carriage, abruptly breaking the silence.

Mr. Hinchcliff looked up, hearing imperfectly. He had been lost in the rapt contemplation of the college cap tied by a string to his portmanteau handles—the outward and visible sign of his newly-gained pedagogic position—in the rapt appreciation of the college cap and the pleasant anticipations it excited. For Mr. Hinchcliff had just matriculated at London University, and was going to be junior assistant at the Holmwood Grammar School—a very enviable position. He stared across the carriage at his fellow-traveller.

"Why not give it away?" said this person. "Give it away! Why not?"

He was a tall, dark sunburnt man with a pale face. His arms were folded tightly, and his feet were on the seat in front of him. He was pulling at a lank black moustache. He stared hard at his toes.

"Why not?" he said.

Mr. Hinchcliff coughed.

The stranger lifted his eyes—they were curious, dark-grey eyes—and stared blankly at Mr. Hinchcliff for the best part of a minute, perhaps. His expression grew to interest.

"Yes," he said slowly. "Why not? And end it."

"I don't quite follow you, I'm afraid," said Mr. Hinchcliff, with another cough.

"You don't quite follow me?" said the stranger quite mechanically, his singular eyes wandering from Mr. Hinchcliff to the bag with its ostentatiously displayed cap, and back to Mr. Hinchcliff's downy face.

"You're so abrupt, you know," apologised Mr. Hinchcliff.

"Why shouldn't I?" said the stranger, following his thoughts. "You are a student?" he said, addressing Mr. Hinchcliff.

"I am—by Correspondence—of the London University," said Mr. Hinchcliff, with irrepressible pride, and feeling nervously at his tie.

"In pursuit of knowledge," said the stranger, and suddenly took his feet off the seat, put his fist on his knees, and stared at Mr. Hinchcliff as though he had never seen a student before. "Yes," he said, and flung out an index finger. Then he rose, took a bag from the hat-rack, and unlocked it. Quite silently he drew out something round and wrapped in a quantity of silver-paper, and unfolded this carefully. He held it out towards Mr. Hinchcliff—a small, very smooth, golden-yellow fruit.

Mr. Hinchcliff's eyes and mouth were open. He did not offer to take this object—if he was intended to take it.

"That," said this fantastic stranger, speaking very slowly, "is the Apple of the Tree of Knowledge. Look at it—small, and bright, and wonderful—Knowledge—and I am going to give it to you."

Mr. Hinchcliff's mind worked painfully for a minute, and then the sufficient explanation, "Mad!" flashed across his brain, and illuminated the whole situation. One humoured madmen. He put his head a little on one side.

"The Apple of the Tree of Knowledge, eigh!" said Mr. Hinchcliff, regarding it with a finely assumed air of interest, and then looking at the interlocutor. "But don't you want to eat it yourself? And besides—how did you come by it?"

"It never fades. I have had it now for three months. And it is ever bright and smooth and ripe and desirable, as you see it." He laid his hand on his knee and regarded the fruit musingly. Then he began to wrap it again in the papers, as though he had abandoned his intention of giving it away.

"But how did you come by it?" said Mr. Hinchcliff, who had his argumentative side. "And how do you know that it is the Fruit of the Tree?"

"I bought this fruit," said the stranger, "three months ago—for a drink of water and a crust of bread. The man who gave it to me—because I kept the life in him—was an Armenian. Armenia!

That wonderful country, the first of all countries, where the ark of the Flood remains to this day, buried in the glaciers of Mount Ararat. This man I say, fleeing with others from Kurds who had come upon them, went up into desolate places among the mountains—places beyond the common knowledge of men. And fleeing from imminent pursuit, they came to a slope, high among the mountain-peaks, green with a grass like knife-blades, that cut and slashed most pitilessly at anyone who went into it. The Kurds were close behind, and there was nothing for it but to plunge in, and the worst of it was that the paths they made through it, at the price of their blood, served for the Kurds to follow. Every one of the fugitives was killed save this Armenian and another. He heard the screams and cries of his friends, and the swish of the grass about those who were pursuing them—it was tall grass rising overhead. And then a shouting and answers, and when presently he paused, everything was still. He pushed out again, not understanding, cut and bleeding, until he came out on a steep slope of rocks below a precipice, and then he saw the grass was all on fire, and the smoke of it rose like a veil between him and his enemies."

The stranger paused. "Yes?" said Mr. Hinchcliff. "Yes?"

"There he was, all torn and bloody from the knife-blades of the grass, the rocks blazing under the afternoon sun—the sky molten brass—and the smoke of the fire driving towards him. He dared not stay there. Death he did not mind, but torture! Far away beyond the smoke he heard shouts and cries. Women screaming. So he went clambering up a gorge in the rocks—everywhere were bushes with dry branches that stuck like thorns among the leaves—until he clambered over the brow of a ridge that hid him. And then he met his companion, a shepherd, who had also escaped. And counting cold and famine and thirst as nothing against the Kurds, they went on into the heights, and among the snow and ice. They wandered three whole days.

"The third day came the vision. I suppose hungry men often do see visions, but then there is this fruit." He lifted the wrapped globe in his hand. "And I have heard it too, from other mountaineers who have known something of the legend. It was in the evening time, when the stars were increasing, that they came down a slope of polished rock into a huge dark valley all set about with strange, contorted trees and in these hung little globes like glow-worm spheres, strange round yellow lights.

"Suddenly this valley was lit far away, many miles away, far down it, with a golden flame marching slowly athwart it, that made the stunted trees against it black as night, and turned the slopes all about them and their figures to the likeness of fiery gold. And at the vision they, knowing the legends of mountains, instantly knew that it was Eden they saw, or the sentinel of Eden, and they fell upon their faces like men struck dead.

"When they dared to look again the valley was dark for a space, and then the light came again—returning, a burning amber.

"At that the shepherd sprang to his feet, and with a shout began to run down towards the light, but the other man was too fearful to follow him. He stood stunned, amazed, and terrified, watching his companion recede towards the marching glare. And hardly had the shepherd set out when there came a noise like thunder, the beating of invisible wings hurrying up the valley, and a great and terrible fear; and at that the man who gave me the fruit turned—if he might still escape. And hurrying headlong up the slope again, with that tumult sweeping after him, he stumbled against one of these stunted bushes, and a ripe fruit came off it into his hand. This fruit. Forthwith, the wings and thunder rolled all about him. He fell and fainted, and when he came to his senses, he was back among the blackened ruins of his own village, and I and the others were attending to the wounded. A vision? But the golden fruit of the tree was still clutched in his hand. There were others there who knew the legend, knew what that strange fruit might be." He paused. "And this is it," he said.

It was a most extraordinary story to be told in a third-class carriage on a Sussex railway. It was as if the real was a mere veil to the fantastic, and here was the fantastic poking through. "Is it?" was all Mr. Hinchcliff could say.

"The legend," said the stranger, "tells that those thickets of dwarfed trees growing about the garden sprang from the apple that Adam carried in his hand when he and Eve were driven forth. He felt something in his hand, saw the half-eaten apple, and flung it petulantly aside. And there they grow, in that desolate valley, girdled round with the everlasting snows, and there the fiery swords keep ward against the Judgment Day."

"But I thought these things were—" Mr Hinchcliff paused—"fables—parables rather. Do you mean to tell me that there in Armenia—"

The stranger answered the unfinished question with the fruit in his open hand.

"But you don't know," said Mr. Hinchcliff, "that, that is the fruit of the Tree of Knowledge. The man may have had—a sort of mirage, say. Suppose—"

"Look at it," said the stranger.

It was certainly a strange-looking globe, not really an apple, Mr. Hinchcliff saw and a curious glowing golden colour, almost as though light itself was wrought into its substance. As he looked at it, he began to see more vividly the desolate valley among the mountains, the guarding swords of fire, the strange antiquities of the story he had just heard. He rubbed a knuckle into his eye. "But—" said he.

"It has kept like that, smooth and full, three months. Longer than that it is now by some days. No drying, withering, no decay."

"And you yourself," said Mr. Hinchcliff, "really believe that—"

"Is the Forbidden Fruit."

There was no mistaking the earnestness of the man's manner and his perfect sanity. "The Fruit of Knowledge," he said.

"Suppose it was?" said Mr. Hinchcliff, after a pause, still staring at it. "But after all," said Mr. Hinchcliff, "it's not my kind of knowledge—not the sort of knowledge. I mean, Adam and Eve have eaten it already."

"We inherit their sins—not their knowledge," said the stranger. "That would make it clear and bright again. We should see into everything, through everything, into the deepest meaning of everything—"

"Why don't you eat it then?" said Mr. Hinchcliff, with an inspiration.

"I took it intending to eat it," said the stranger. "Man has fallen. Merely to eat again could scarcely—"

"Knowledge is power," said Mr. Hinchcliff.

"But is it happiness? I am older than you—more than twice as old. Time after time I have held this in my hand, and my heart has failed me at the thought of all that one might know, that terrible lucidity—Suppose suddenly all the world became pitilessly clear?"

"That, I think, would be a great advantage," said Mr. Hinchcliff, "on the whole."

"Suppose you saw into the hearts and minds of everyone about you, into their most secret recesses—people you loved, whose love you valued?"

"You'd soon find out the humbugs," said Mr. Hinchcliff, greatly struck by the idea.

"And worse—to know yourself, bare of your most intimate illusions. To see yourself in your place. All that your lusts and weaknesses prevented your doing. No merciful perspective."

"That might be an excellent thing too. 'Know thyself,' you know."

"You are young," said the stranger.

"If you don't care to eat it, and it bothers you, why don't you throw it away?"

"There again, perhaps, you will not understand me. To me, how could one throw away a thing like that, glowing, wonderful? Once one has it, one is bound. But, on the other hand, to give it away! To give it away to someone who thirsted after knowledge, who found no terror in the thought of that clear perception—"

"Of course," said Mr. Hinchcliff thoughtfully, "it might be sort of poisonous fruit."

And then his eye caught something motionless, the end of a white board black-lettered outside the carriage window. "—mwood," he saw. He started convulsively. "Gracious!" said Mr. Hinchcliff. "Holmwood—!" And the practical present blotted out the mystic realisations that had been stealing upon him.

In another moment he was opening the carriage-door, portmanteau in hand. The guard was already fluttering his green flag. Mr. Hinchcliff jumped out. "Here!" said a voice behind him, and he saw the dark eyes of the stranger shining and the golden fruit, bright and bare, held out of the open carriage-door. He took it instinctively, the train was already moving.

"No!" shouted the stranger, and made a snatch at it as if to take it back.

"Stand away," cried a country porter, thrusting forward to close the door. The stranger shouted something Mr. Hinchcliff did not catch, head and arm thrust excitedly out of the window, and then the shadow of the bridge fell on him, and in a trice he was hidden. Mr. Hinchcliff stood astonished, staring at the end of the last waggon receding round the bend, and with the wonderful fruit in his hand. For the fraction of a minute his mind was confused, and then he became aware that two or three people on the platform were regarding him with interest. Was he not the new Grammar School master making his debut? It occurred to him that, so far as they could tell, the fruit might very well be the naive refreshment of an orange. He flushed at the thought, and thrust the fruit into his side pocket, where it bulged undesirably. But there was no help for it, so he went towards them, awkwardly concealing his sense of awkwardness, to ask the way to the Grammar School, and the means of getting his portmanteau and the two tin boxes which lay up the platform thither. Of all the odd and fantastic yarns to tell a fellow!

His luggage could be taken on a truck for sixpence, he found, and he could precede it on foot. He fancied an ironical note in the voices. He was painfully aware of his contour.

The curious earnestness of the man in the train, and the glamour of the story he told, had for a time, diverted the current of Mr. Hinchcliff's thoughts. It drove like a mist before his immediate concerns. Fires that went to and fro! But the preoccupation of his new position, and the impression he was to produce upon Holmwood generally, and the school people in particular, returned upon him with reinvigorating power before he left the station and cleared his mental atmosphere. But it is extraordinary what an inconvenient thing the addition of a soft and rather brightly-golden fruit, not three inches in diameter, may prove to a sensitive youth on his best appearance. In the pocket of his black jacket it bulged dreadfully, spoilt the lines altogether. He passed a little old lady in black, and he felt her eye drop upon the excrescence at once. He was wearing one glove and carrying the other, together with his stick, so that to bear the fruit openly was impossible. In one place, were the road into the town seemed suitably secluded, he took his encumbrance out of his pocket and tried it in his hat. It was just too large, the hat wobbled ludicrously, and just as he was taking it out again, a butcher's boy came driving round the corner.

"Confound it!" said Mr. Hinchcliff.

He would have eaten the thing, and attained omniscience there and then, but it would seem so silly to go into town sucking a juicy fruit—and it certainly felt juicy. If one of the boys should come by, it might do him a serious injury with his discipline so to be seen. And the juice might make his face sticky and get upon his cuffs—or it might be an acid juice as potent as lemon, and take all the colour out of his clothes.

Then round a bend in the lane came two pleasant sunlit girlish figures. They were walking slowly towards the town and chattering—at any moment they might look round and see a hot-faced young man behind them carrying a kind of phosphorescent yellow tomato! They would be sure to laugh.

"Hang!" said Mr. Hinchcliff, and with a swift jerk sent the encumbrance flying over the stone wall of an orchard that there abutted on the road. As it vanished, he felt a faint twinge of loss that lasted scarcely a moment. He adjusted the stick and glove in his hand, and walked on, erect and self-conscious, to pass the girls.

But in the darkness of the night Mr. Hinchcliff had a dream, and saw the valley, and the flaming swords, and the contorted trees, and knew that it really was the Apple of the Tree of Knowledge that he had thrown regardlessly away. And he awoke very unhappy.

In the morning his regret had passed, but afterwards it returned and troubled him; never however when he was happy or busily occupied. At last, one moonlight night about eleven, when all Holmwood was quiet, his regrets returned with redoubled force, and therewith an impulse to adventure. He slipped out of the house and over the playground wall, went through the silent town to Station Lane, and climbed into the orchard where he had thrown the fruit. But nothing was to be found of it there among the dewy grass and the faint intangible globes of dandelion down.

22

The Plattner Story

Whether the story of Gottfried Plattner is to be credited or not, is a pretty question in the value of evidence. On the one hand, we have seven witnesses—to be perfectly exact, we have six and a half pairs of eyes, and one undeniable fact; and on the other we have—what is it—? Prejudice, common sense, the inertia of opinion. Never were there seven more honest-seeming witnesses; never was there a more undeniable fact than the inversion of Gottfried Plattner's anatomical structure, and—never was there a more preposterous story than the one they have to tell! The most preposterous part of the story is the worthy Gottfried's contribution (for I count him as one of the seven). Heaven forbid that I should be led into giving countenance to superstition by a passion for impartiality, and so come to share the fate of Eusapia's patrons! Frankly, I believe there is something crooked about this business of Gottfried Plattner; but what that crooked factor is, I will admit as frankly, I do not know. I have been surprised at the credit accorded to the story in the most unexpected and authoritative quarters. The fairest way to the reader, however will be for me to tell it without further comment.

Gottfried Plattner is, in spite of his name, a free-born Englishman. His father was an Alsatian who came to England in the Sixties, married a respectable English girl of unexceptionable antecedents, and died, after a wholesome and uneventful life (devoted, I understand, chiefly to the laying of parquet flooring), in 1887. Gottfried's age is seven-and-twenty. He is, by virtue of his heritage of three languages, Modern Languages Master in a small private school in the South of England. To the casual observer he is singularly like any other Modern Languages Master in any other small private school. His costume is neither very costly nor very fashionable, but on the other hand it is not markedly cheap or shabby; his complexion, like his height and his bearing, is inconspicuous. You would notice, perhaps that, like the majority of people, his face was not absolutely symmetrical, his right eye a little larger than the left, and his jaw a trifle heavier on the right side. If you, as an ordinary careless person, were to bare his chest and feel his heart beating, you would probably find it quite like the heart of any one else. But here you and the trained observer would part company. If you found his heart quite ordinary, the trained observer would find it quite otherwise. And once the thing was pointed out to you, you too would perceive the peculiarity easily enough. It is that Gottfried's heart beats on the right side of his body.

Now, that is not the only singularity of Gottfried's structure, although it is the only one that would appeal to the untrained mind. Careful sounding of Gottfried's internal arrangements, by a well-known surgeon, seems to point to the fact that all the other unsymmetrical parts of his body are similarly misplaced. The right lobe of his liver is on the left side, the left on his right; while his lungs too, are similarly contraposed. What is still more singular, unless Gottfried is a consummate actor, we must believe that his right hand has recently become his left. Since the occurrences we are about to consider (as impartially as possible), he has found the utmost difficulty in writing, except from right to left across the paper with his left hand. He cannot throw with his right hand, he is perplexed at meal times between knife and fork, and his ideas of the rule of the road—he is a cyclist—are still a dangerous confusion. And there is not a scrap of evidence to show that before these occurrences Gottfried was at all left-handed. There is yet another wonderful fact in this preposterous business. Gottfried produces three photographs of himself. You have him at the age of five or six, thrusting fat legs at you from under a plaid frock, and scowling. In that photograph his left eye is a little larger than his right, and his jaw is a trifle heavier on the left side. This is the reverse of his present living conditions: The photograph of Gottfried at fourteen seems to contradict these facts, but that is because it is one of those cheap "Gem" photographs that were then in vogue, taken direct upon metal, and therefore reversing things just as a looking-glass would. A third photograph represents him at one-and-twenty and confirms the record of the others. There seems here evidence of the strongest confirmatory character that Gottfried has exchanged his left side for his right. Yet how a human being can be so changed, short of a fantastic and pointless miracle, it is exceedingly hard to suggest.

In one way, of course, these facts might be explicable on the supposition that Plattner has undertaken an elaborate mystification, on the strength of his heart's displacement. Photographs may be fudged, and left-handedness imitated. But the character of the man does not lend itself to any such theory. He is quiet, practical, unobtrusive and thoroughly sane, from the Nordau standpoint. He likes beer, and smokes moderately, takes walking exercise daily, and has a healthily high estimate of the value of his teaching. He has a good but untrained tenor voice, and takes a pleasure in singing airs of a popular and cheerful character. He is fond, but not morbidly fond, of reading—, chiefly fiction pervaded with a vaguely pious optimism—, sleeps well, and rarely dreams. He is in fact, the very last person to evolve a fantastic fable. Indeed, so far from forcing this story upon the world, he has been singularly reticent on the matter. He meets enquirers with a certain engaging—bashfulness is almost the word, that disarms the most suspicious. He seems genuinely ashamed that anything so unusual has occurred to him.

It is to be regretted that Plattner's aversion to the idea of post-mortem dissection may postpone, perhaps for ever, the positive proof that his entire body has had its left and right sides transposed. Upon that fact mainly the credibility of his story hangs. There is no way of taking a man and moving him about in space, as ordinary people understand space, that will result in our changing his sides. Whatever you do, his right is still his right, his left his left. You can do that with a perfectly thin and flat thing, of course. If you were to cut a figure out of paper, any figure with a right and left side, you could change its sides simply by lifting it up and turning it over. But with a solid it is different. Mathematical theorists tell us that the only way in which the right and left sides of a solid body can be changed is by taking that body clean out of space as we know it—, taking it out of ordinary existence, that is, and turning it somewhere outside space. This is a little abstruse, no doubt, but any one with any knowledge of mathematical theory will assure the reader of its truth. To put the thing in technical language, the curious inversion of Plattner's right and left sides is proof that he has moved out of our space into what is called the Fourth Dimension, and that he has returned again to our world. Unless we choose to consider ourselves the victims of an elaborate and motiveless fabrication, we are almost bound to believe that this has occurred.

So much for the tangible facts. We come now to the account of the phenomena that attended his temporary disappearance from the world. It appears that in the Sussexville Proprietary School Plattner not only discharged the duties of Modern Languages Master, but also taught chemistry, commercial geography, book-keeping, shorthand, drawing, and any other additional subject to which the changing fancies of the boys' parents might direct attention. He knew little or nothing of these various subjects, but in secondary as distinguished from Board or elementary schools, knowledge in the teacher is, very properly, by no means so necessary as high moral character and gentlemanly tone. In chemistry he was particularly deficient, knowing he says, nothing beyond the Three Gases (whatever the three gases may be). As however, his pupils began by knowing nothing, and derived all their information from him, this caused him (or any one) but little inconvenience for several terms. Then a little boy named Whibble joined the school, who had been educated (it seems) by some mischievous relative into an enquiring habit of mind. This little boy followed Plattner's lessons with marked and sustained interest, and in order to exhibit his zeal on the subject, brought at various times, substances for Plattner to analyse. Plattner, flattered by this evidence of his power of awakening interest, and trusting to the boy's ignorance, analysed these, and even made general statements as to their composition. Indeed he was so far stimulated by his pupil as to obtain a work upon analytical chemistry and study it during his supervision of the evening's preparation. He was surprised to find chemistry quite an interesting subject.

So far the story is absolutely commonplace. But now the greenish powder comes upon the scene. The source of that greenish powder seems, unfortunately lost. Master Whibble tells a tortuous story of finding it done up in a packet in a disused limekiln near the Downs. It would have been an excellent thing for Plattner, and possibly for Master Whibble's family, if a match could have been applied to that powder there and then. The young gentleman certainly did not bring it to school in a packet, but in a common eight-ounce graduated medicine bottle, plugged with masticated newspaper. He gave it to Plattner at the end of the afternoon school. Four boys had been detained after school prayers in order to complete some neglected tasks, and Plattner was supervising these in the small classroom in which the chemical teaching was conducted. The appliances for the practical teaching of chemistry in the Sussexville Proprietary School, as in most small schools in this country, are characterised by a severe simplicity. They are kept in a small cupboard standing in a recess, and having about the same capacity as a common travelling trunk. Plattner, being bored with his passive superintendence, seems to have welcomed the intervention of Whibble with his green powder as an agreeable diversion, and unlocking this cupboard, proceeded at once with his analytical experiments. Whibble sat, luckily for himself, at a safe distance, regarding him. The four malefactors, feigning a profound absorption in their work, watched him furtively with the keenest interest. For even within the limits of the Three Gases, Plattner's practical chemistry was, I understand, temerarious.

They are practically unanimous in their account of Plattner's proceedings. He poured a little of the green powder into a test-tube, and tried the substance with water, hydrochloric acid, nitric acid, and sulphuric acid in succession. Getting no result, he emptied out a little heap—nearly half the bottleful, in fact—upon a slate and tried a match. He held the medicine bottle in his left hand. The stuff began to smoke and melt, and then—exploded with deafening violence and a blinding flash.

The five boys, seeing the flash and being prepared for catastrophes, ducked below their desks, and were none of them seriously hurt. The window was blown out into the playground, and the blackboard on its easel was upset. The slate was smashed to atoms. Some plaster fell from the ceiling. No other damage was done to the school edifice or appliances, and the boys at first, seeing nothing of Plattner, fancied he was knocked down and lying out of their sight below the desks. They jumped out of their places to go to his assistance, and were amazed to find the space empty. Being still confused by the sudden violence of the report, they hurried to the open door, under the impression that he must have been hurt, and have rushed out of the room. But Carson, the foremost, nearly collided in the doorway with the principal, Mr. Lidgett.

Mr. Lidgett is a corpulent, excitable man with one eye. The boys describe him as stumbling into the room mouthing some of those tempered expletives irritable schoolmasters accustom themselves to use—lest worse befall. "Wretched mumchancer!" he said. "Where's Mr. Plattner?" The boys are agreed on the very words. ("Wobbler," "snivelling puppy," and "mumchancer" are, it seems, among the ordinary small change of Mr. Lidgett's scholastic commerce.)

Where's Mr. Plattner? That was a question that was to be repeated many times in the next few days. It really seemed as though that frantic hyperbole, "blown to atoms," had for once realise itself. There was not a visible particle of Plattner to be seen; not a drop of blood nor a stitch of clothing to be found. Apparently he had been blown clean out of existence and left not a wrack behind. Not so much as would cover a sixpenny piece, to quote a proverbial expression! The evidence of his absolute disappearance, as a consequence of that explosion, is indubitable.

It is not necessary to enlarge here upon the commotion excited in the Sussexville Proprietary School, and in Sussexville and elsewhere, by this event. It is quite possible indeed, that some of the readers of these pages may recall the hearing of some remote and dying version of that excitement during the last summer holidays. Lidgett, it would seem, did everything in his power to suppress and minimise the story. He instituted a penalty of twenty-five lines for any mention of Plattner's name among the boys, and stated in the schoolroom that he was clearly aware of his assistant's whereabouts. He was afraid, he explains, that the possibility of an explosion happening, in spite of the elaborate precautions taken to minimise the practical teaching of chemistry, might injure the reputation of the school; and so might any mysterious quality in Plattner's departure. Indeed, he did everything in his power to make the occurrence seem as ordinary as possible. In particular, he cross-examined the five eye-witnesses of the occurrence so searchingly that they began to doubt the plain evidence of their senses. But in spite of these efforts, the tale, in a magnified and distorted state, made a nine days' wonder in the district, and several parents withdrew their sons on colourable pretexts. Not the least remarkable point in the matter is the fact that a large number of people in the neighbourhood dreamed singularly vivid dreams of Plattner during the period of excitement before his return, and that these dreams had a curious uniformity. In almost all of them Plattner was seen, sometimes singly, sometimes in company, wandering about through a coruscating iridescence. In all cases his face was pale and distressed, and in some he gesticulated towards the dreamer. One or two of the boys, evidently under the influence of nightmare, fancied that Plattner approached them with remarkable swiftness, and seemed to look closely into their very eyes. Others fled with Plattner from the pursuit of vague and extraordinary creatures of a globular shape. But all these fancies were forgotten in enquiries and speculations when, on the Wednesday next, but one after the Monday of the explosion, Plattner returned.

The circumstances of his return were as singular as those of his departure. So far as Mr. Lidgett's somewhat choleric outline can be filled in from Plattner's hesitating statements, it would appear that on Wednesday evening, towards the hour of sunset, the former gentleman, having dismissed evening preparation, was engaged in his garden, picking and eating strawberries, a fruit of which he is inordinately fond. It is a large old-fashioned garden, secured from observation fortunately, by a high and ivy-covered red-brick wall. Just as he was stooping over a particularly prolific plant, there was a flash in the air and a heavy thud, and before he could look round, some heavy body struck him violently from behind. He was pitched forward, crushing the strawberries he held in his hand, and that so roughly, that his silk hat—Mr. Lidgett adheres to the older ideas of scholastic costume—was driven violently down upon his forehead, and almost over one eye. This heavy missile, which slid over him sideways and collapsed into a sitting posture among the strawberry plants, proved to be our long-lost Mr. Gottfried Plattner, in an extremely dishevelled condition. He was collarless and hatless, his linen was dirty, and there was blood upon his hands. Mr. Lidgett was so indignant and surprised that he remained on all-fours, and with his hat jammed down on his eye, while he expostulated vehemently with Plattner for his disrespectful and unaccountable conduct.

This scarcely idyllic scene completes what I may call the exterior version of the Plattner story—its exoteric aspect. It is quite unnecessary to enter here into all the details of his dismissal by Mr. Lidgett. Such details, with the full names and dates and references, will be found in the larger report of these occurrences that was laid before the Society for the Investigation of Abnormal Phenomena. The singular transposition of Plattner's right and left sides was scarcely observed for the first day or so, and then first in connection with his disposition to write from right to left across the blackboard. He concealed rather than ostended this curious confirmatory circumstance, as he considered it would unfavourably affect his prospects in a new situation. The displacement of his heart was discovered some months after, when he was having a tooth extracted under anaesthetics. He then, very unwillingly, allowed a cursory surgical examination to be made of himself, with a view to a brief account in the "Journal of Anatomy." That exhausts the statement of the material facts; and we may now go on to consider Plattner's account of the matter.

But first let us clearly differentiate between the preceding portion of this story and what is to follow. All I have told thus far is established by such evidence as even a criminal lawyer would approve. Every one of the witnesses is still alive; the reader, if he have the leisure, may hunt the lads out to-morrow, or even brave the terrors of the redoubtable Lidgett, and cross-examine and trap and test to his heart's content; Gottfried Plattner himself, and his twisted heart and his three photographs are producible. It may be taken as proved that he did disappear for nine days as the consequence of an explosion; that he returned almost as violently, under circumstances in their nature annoying to Mr. Lidgett, whatever the details of those circumstances may be; and that he returned inverted, just as a reflection returns from a mirror. From the last fact, as I have already stated, it follows almost inevitably that Plattner, during those nine days, must have been in some state of existence altogether out of space. The evidence to these statements is indeed, far stronger than that upon which most murderers are hanged. But for his own particular account of where he had been, with its confused explanations and well-nigh self-contradictory details, we have only Mr. Gottfried Plattner's word. I do not wish to discredit that, but I must point out—what so many writers upon obscure psychic phenomena fail to do—that we are passing here from the practically undeniable to that kind of matter which any reasonable man is entitled to believe or reject as he thinks proper. The previous statements render it plausible; its discordance with common experience tilts it towards the incredible. I would prefer not to sway the beam of the reader's judgment either way, but simply to tell the story as Plattner told it me. He gave me his narrative, I may state, at my house at Chislehurst, and so soon as he had left me that evening, I went into my study and wrote down everything as I remembered it. Subsequently he was good enough to read over a type-written copy, so that its substantial correctness is undeniable.

He states that at the moment of the explosion he distinctly thought he was killed. He felt lifted off his feet and driven forcibly backward. It is a curious fact for psychologists that he thought clearly during his backward flight, and wondered whether he should hit the chemistry cupboard or the blackboard easel. His heels struck ground, and he staggered and fell heavily into a sitting position on something soft and firm. For a moment the concussion stunned him. He became aware at once of a vivid scent of singed hair, and he seemed to hear the voice of Lidgett asking for him. You will understand that for a time his mind was greatly confused.

At first he was distinctly under the impression that he was still in the classroom. He perceived quite distinctly the surprise of the boys and the entry of Mr. Lidgett. He is quite positive upon that score. He did not hear their remarks; but that he ascribed to the deafening effect of the experiment. Things about him seemed curiously dark and faint, but his mind explained that on the obvious but mistaken idea that the explosion had engendered a huge volume of dark smoke.

Through the dimness the figures of Lidgett and the boys moved, as faint and silent as ghosts Plattner's face still tingled with the stinging heat of the flash. He was, he says, "all muddled." His first definite thoughts seem to have been of his personal safety. He thought he was perhaps blinded and deafened. He felt his limbs and face in a gingerly manner. Then his perceptions grew clearer, and he was astonished to miss the old familiar desks and other schoolroom furniture about him. Only dim, uncertain, grey shapes stood in the place of these. Then came a thing that made him shout aloud, and awoke his stunned faculties to instant activity. Two of the boys, gesticulating, walked one after the other clean through him! Neither manifested the slightest consciousness of his presence. It is difficult to imagine the sensation he felt. They came against him, he says, with no more force than a wisp of mist.

Plattner's first thought after that was that he was dead. Having been brought up with thoroughly sound views in these matters, however he was a little surprised to find his body still about him. His second conclusion was that he was not dead, but that the others were: that the explosion had destroyed the Sussexville Proprietary School and every soul in it except himself. But that too, was scarcely satisfactory. He was thrown back upon astonished observation.

Everything about him was extraordinarily dark: at first it seemed to have an altogether ebony blackness. Overhead was a black firmament. The only touch of light in the scene was a faint greenish glow at the edge of the sky in one direction, which threw into prominence a horizon of undulating black hills. This I say, was his impression at first. As his eye grew accustomed to the darkness, he began to distinguish a faint quality of differentiating greenish colour in the circumambient night. Against this background the furniture and occupants of the classroom, it seems, stood out like phosphorescent spectres, faint and impalpable. He extended his hand, and thrust it without an effort through the wall of the room by the fireplace.

He describes himself as making a strenuous effort to attract attention. He shouted to Lidgett, and tried to seize the boys as they went to and fro. He only desisted from these attempts when Mrs. Lidgett, whom he (as an Assistant Master) naturally disliked, entered the room. He says the sensation of being in the world, and yet not a part of it, was an extraordinarily disagreeable one. He compared his feelings, not inaptly, to those of a cat watching a mouse through a window. Whenever he made a motion to communicate with the dim, familiar world about him, he found an invisible, incomprehensible barrier preventing intercourse. He then turned his attention to his solid environment. He found the medicine bottle still unbroken in his hand, with the remainder of the green powder therein. He put this in his pocket, and began to feel about him. Apparently, he was sitting on a boulder of rock covered with a velvety moss. The dark country about him, he was unable to see, the faint, misty picture of the schoolroom blotting it out, but he had a feeling (due perhaps to a cold wind) that he was near the crest of a hill, and that a steep valley fell away beneath his feet. The green glow along the edge of the sky seemed to be growing in extent and intensity. He stood up, rubbing his eyes.

It would seem that he made a few steps, going steeply downhill, and then stumbled, nearly fell, and sat down again upon a jagged mass of rock to watch the dawn. He became aware that the world about him was absolutely silent. It was as still as it was dark, and though there was a cold wind blowing up the hill-face, the rustle of grass, the soughing of the boughs that should have accompanied it, were absent. He could hear, therefore, if he could not see, that the hillside upon which he stood was rocky and desolate. The green grew brighter every moment, and as it did so, a faint, transparent blood-red mingled with, but did not mitigate, the blackness of the sky overhead and the rocky desolations about him. Having regard to what follows, I am inclined to think that, that redness may have been an optical effect due to contrast. Something black fluttered momentarily against the livid yellow-green of the lower sky, and then the thin and penetrating voice of a bell rose out of the black gulf below him. An oppressive expectation grew with the growing light.

It is probable that an hour or more elapsed while he sat there, the strange green light growing brighter every moment, and spreading slowly, in flamboyant fingers, upward towards the zenith. As it grew, the spectral vision of our world became relatively or absolutely fainter. Probably both, for the time must have been about that of our earthly sunset. So far as his vision of our world went, Plattner, by his few steps downhill, had passed through the floor of the classroom, and was now, it seemed, sitting in mid-air in the larger schoolroom downstairs. He saw the boarders distinctly, but much more faintly than he had seen Lidgett. They were preparing their evening tasks, and he noticed with interest that several were cheating with their Euclid riders by means of a crib, a compilation whose existence he had hitherto never suspected. As the time passed, they faded steadily, as steadily as the light of the green dawn increased.

Looking down into the valley, he saw that the light had crept far down its rocky sides, and that the profound blackness of the abyss was now broken by a minute green glow, like the light of a glow-worm. And almost immediately the limb of a huge heavenly body of blazing green rose over the basaltic undulations of the distant hills, and the monstrous hill-masses about him came out gaunt and desolate, in green light and deep, ruddy black shadows. He became aware of a vast number of ball-shaped objects drifting as thistledown drifts over the high ground. There were none of these nearer to him than the opposite side of the gorge. The bell below twanged quicker and quicker, with something like impatient insistence, and several lights moved hither and thither. The boys at work at their desks were now almost imperceptibly faint.

This extinction of our world, when the green sun of this other universe rose, is a curious point upon which Plattner insists. During the Other-World night, it is difficult to move about, on account of the vividness with which the things of this world are visible. It becomes a riddle to explain why, if this is the case, we in this world catch no glimpse of the Other-World. It is due, perhaps, to the comparatively vivid illumination of this world of ours. Plattner describes the midday of the Other-World, at its brightest as not being nearly so bright as this world at full moon, while its night is profoundly black. Consequently, the amount of light, even in an ordinary dark room, is sufficient to render the things of the Other-World invisible, on the same principle that faint phosphorescence is only visible in the profoundest darkness. I have tried, since he told me his story, to see something of the Other-World by sitting for a long space in a photographer's dark room at night. I have certainly seen indistinctly the form of greenish slopes and rocks, but only, I must admit, very indistinctly indeed. The reader may possibly be more successful. Plattner tells me that since his return he has dreamt and seen and recognised places in the Other-World, but this is probably due to his memory of these scenes. It seems quite possible that people with unusually keen eyesight may occasionally catch a glimpse of this strange Other-World about us.

However, this is a digression. As the green sun rose, a long street of black buildings became perceptible, though only darkly and indistinctly, in the gorge, and after some hesitation, Plattner began to clamber down the precipitous descent towards them. The descent was long and exceedingly tedious, being so not only by the extraordinary steepness, but also by reason of the looseness of the boulders with which the whole face of the hill was strewn. The noise of his descent—now and then his heels struck fire from the rocks—seemed now the only sound in the universe, for the beating of the bell had ceased. As he drew nearer, he perceived that the various edifices had a singular resemblance to tombs and mausoleums and monuments, saving only that they were all uniformly black instead of being white, as most sepulchres are. And then he saw, crowding out of the largest building, very much as people disperse from church, a number of pallid, rounded, pale-green figures. These dispersed in several directions about the broad street of the place, some going through side alleys and reappearing upon the steepness of the hill, others entering some of the small black buildings which lined the way.

At the sight of these things drifting up towards him, Plattner stopped staring. They were not walking, they were indeed limbless, and they had the appearance of human heads, beneath which a tadpole-like body swung. He was too astonished at their strangeness, too full, indeed of strangeness, to be seriously alarmed by them. They drove towards him, in front of the chill wind that was blowing uphill, much as soap-bubbles drive before a draught. And as he looked at the nearest of those approaching, he saw it was indeed a human head, albeit with singularly large eyes, and wearing such an expression of distress and anguish as he had never seen before upon mortal countenance. He was surprised to find that it did not turn to regard him, but seemed to be watching and following some unseen moving thing. For a moment he was puzzled, and then it occurred to him that this creature was watching with its enormous eyes something that was happening in the world he had just left. Nearer it came, and nearer, and he was too astonished to cry out. It made a very faint fretting sound as it came close to him. Then it struck his face with a gentle pat—, its touch was very cold—, and drove past him, and upward towards the crest of the hill.

An extraordinary conviction flashed across Plattner's mind that this head had a strong likeness to Lidgett. Then he turned his attention to the other heads that were now swarming thickly up the hillside. None made the slightest sign of recognition. One or two, indeed, came close to his head and almost followed the example of the first, but he dodged convulsively out of the way. Upon most of them he saw the same expression of unavailing regret he had seen upon the first, and heard the same faint sounds of wretchedness from them. One or two wept, and one rolling swiftly uphill wore an expression of diabolical rage. But others were cold, and several had a look of gratified interest in their eyes. One at least, was almost in an ecstasy of happiness. Plattner does not remember that he recognised any more likenesses in those he saw at this time.

For several hours, perhaps Plattner watched these strange things dispersing themselves over the hills, and not till long after they had ceased to issue from the clustering black buildings in the gorge, did he resume his downward climb. The darkness about him increased so much that he had a difficulty in stepping true. Overhead the sky was now a bright, pale green. He felt neither hunger nor thirst. Later, when he did, he found a chilly stream running down the centre of the gorge, and the rare moss upon the boulders, when he tried it at last in desperation, was good to eat.

He groped about among the tombs that ran down the gorge, seeking vaguely for some clue to these inexplicable things. After a long time he came to the entrance of the big mausoleum-like building from which the heads had issued. In this he found a group of green lights burning upon a kind of basaltic altar, and a bell-rope from a belfry overhead hanging down into the centre of the place. Round the wall ran a lettering of fire in a character unknown to him. While he was still wondering at the purport of these things, he heard the receding tramp of heavy feet echoing far down the street. He ran out into the darkness again, but he could see nothing. He had a mind to pull the bell-rope, and finally decided to follow the footsteps. But, although he ran far, he never overtook them; and his shouting was of no avail. The gorge seemed to extend an interminable distance. It was as dark as earthly starlight throughout its length, while the ghastly green day lay along the upper edge of its precipices. There were none of the heads, now, below. They were all, it seemed, busily occupied along the upper slopes. Looking up, he saw them drifting hither and thither, some hovering stationary, some flying swiftly through the air. It reminded him, he said, of "big snowflakes"; only these were black and pale green.

In pursuing the firm, undeviating footsteps that he never overtook, in groping into new regions of this endless devil's dyke, in clambering up and down the pitiless heights, in wandering about the summits, and in watching the drifting faces, Plattner states that he spent the better part of seven or eight days. He did not keep count, he says. Though once or twice he found eyes watching him, he had word with no living soul. He slept among the rocks on the hillside. In the gorge things earthly were invisible, because from the earthly standpoint, it was far underground. On the altitudes, so soon as the earthly day began, the world became visible to him. He found himself sometimes stumbling over the dark green rocks, or arresting himself on a precipitous brink, while all about him the green branches of the Sussexville lanes were swaying; or again, he seemed to be walking through the Sussexville streets, or watching unseen the private business of some household. And then it was he discovered, that to almost every human being in our world there pertained some of these drifting heads: that every one in the world is watched intermittently by these helpless disembodiments.

What are they—these Watchers of the Living? Plattner never learned. But two, that presently found and followed him, were like his childhood's memory of his father and mother. Now and then other faces turned their eyes upon him: eyes like those of dead people who had swayed him, or injured him, or helped him in his youth and manhood. Whenever they looked at him, Plattner was overcome with a strange sense of responsibility. To his mother he ventured to speak; but she made no answer. She looked sadly, steadfastly, and tenderly—a little reproachfully too, it seemed—into his eyes.

He simply tells this story: he does not endeavour to explain. We are left to surmise who these Watchers of the Living may be, or if they are indeed the Dead, why they should so closely and passionately watch a world they have left for ever. It may be—indeed to my mind it seems just—that, when our life has closed, when evil or good is no longer a choice for us, we may still have to witness the working out of the train of consequences we have laid. If human souls continue after death, then surely human interests continue after death. But that is merely my own guess at the meaning of the things seen. Plattner offers no interpretation, for none was given him. It is well the reader should understand this clearly. Day after day, with his head reeling, he wandered about this green-lit world outside the world, weary and, towards the end, weak and hungry. By day—by our earthly day, that is—the ghostly vision of the old familiar scenery of Sussexville, all about him, irked and worried him. He could not see where to put his feet, and ever and again with a chilly touch one of these Watching Souls would come against his face. And after dark the multitude of these Watchers about him, and their intent distress, confused his mind beyond describing. A great longing to return to the earthly life that was so near and yet so remote consume him. The unearthliness of things about him produced a positively painful mental distress. He was worried beyond describing by his own particular followers. He would shout at them to desist from staring at him, scold at them, hurry away from them. They were always mute and intent. Run as he might over the uneven ground, they followed his destinies.

On the ninth day, towards evening, Plattner heard the invisible footsteps approaching, far away down the gorge. He was then wandering over the broad crest of the same hill upon which he had fallen in his entry into this strange Other-World of his. He turned to hurry down into the gorge, feeling his way hastily, and was arrested by the sight of the thing that was happening in a room in a back street near the school. Both of the people in the room he knew by sight. The windows were open, the blinds up, and the setting sun shone clearly into it, so that it came out quite brightly at first, a vivid oblong of room, lying like a magic-lantern picture upon the black landscape and the livid green dawn. In addition to the sunlight, a candle had just been lit in the room.

On the bed lay a lank man, his ghastly white face terrible upon the tumbled pillow. His clenched hands were raised above his head. A little table beside the bed carried a few medicine bottles, some toast and water, and an empty glass. Every now and then the lank man's lips fell apart, to indicate a word he could not articulate. But the woman did not notice that he wanted anything, because she was busy turning out papers from an old-fashioned bureau in the opposite corner of the room. At first the picture was very vivid indeed, but as the green dawn behind it grew brighter and brighter, so it became fainter and more and more transparent.

As the echoing footsteps paced nearer and nearer, those footsteps that sound so loud in that Other-World and come so silently in this, Plattner perceived about him a great multitude of dim faces gathering together out of the darkness and watching the two people in the room. Never before had he seen so many of the Watchers of the Living. A multitude had eyes only for the sufferer in the room, another multitude, in infinite anguish, watched the woman as she hunted with greedy eyes for something she could not find. They crowded about Plattner, they came across his sight and buffeted his face, the noise of their unavailing regrets was all about him. He saw clearly only now and then. At other times the picture quivered dimly, through the veil of green reflections upon their movements. In the room it must have been very still, and Plattner says the candle flame streamed up into a perfectly vertical line of smoke, but in his ears each footfall and its echoes beat like a clap of thunder. And the faces! Two, more particularly near the woman's: one a woman's also, white and clear-featured, a face which might have once been cold and hard, but which was now softened by the touch of a wisdom strange to earth. The other might have been the woman's father. Both were evidently absorbed in the contemplation of some act of hateful meanness, so it seemed, which they could no longer guard against and prevent. Behind were others, teachers, it may be, who had taught ill, friends whose influence had failed. And over the man, too—a multitude, but none that seemed to be parents or teachers! Faces that might once have been coarse, now purged to strength by sorrow! And in the forefront one face, a girlish one, neither angry nor remorseful, but merely patient and weary, and as it seemed to Plattner, waiting for relief. His powers of description fail him at the memory of this multitude of ghastly countenances. They gathered on the stroke of the bell He saw them all in the space of a second. It would seem that he was so worked on by his excitement that, quite involuntarily, his restless fingers took the bottle of green powder out of his pocket and held it before him. But he does not remember that.

Abruptly the footsteps ceased. He waited for the next, and there was silence, and then suddenly cutting through the unexpected stillness like a keen, thin blade, came the first stroke of the bell. At that the multitudinous faces swayed to and fro and a louder crying began all about him. The woman did not hear; she was burning something now in the candle flame. At the second stroke everything grew dim, and a breath of wind, icy cold, blew through the host of watchers. They swirled about him like an eddy of dead leaves in the spring, and at the third stroke something was extended through them to the bed. You have heard of a beam of light. This was like a beam of darkness, and looking again at it, Plattner saw that it was a shadowy arm and hand.

The green sun was now topping the black desolations of the horizon, and the vision of the room was very faint. Plattner could see that the white of the bed struggled, and was convulsed; and that the woman looked round over her shoulder at it, startled.

The cloud of watchers lifted high like a puff of green dust before the wind, and swept swiftly downward towards the temple in the gorge. Then suddenly Plattner understood the meaning of the shadowy black arm that stretched across his shoulder and clutched its prey. He did not dare turn his head to see the Shadow behind the arm. With a violent effort, and covering his eyes, he set himself to run, made perhaps twenty strides, then slipped on a boulder, and fell. He fell forward on his hands; and the bottle smashed and exploded as he touched the ground.

In another moment he found himself, stunned and bleeding, sitting face to face with Lidgett in the old walled garden behind the school.

There the story of Plattner's experiences ends. I have resisted, I believe successfully, the natural disposition of a writer of fiction to dress up incidents of this sort. I have told the thing as far as possible in the order in which Plattner told it to me. I have carefully avoided any attempt at style, effect, or construction. It would have been easy, for instance, to have worked the scene of the death-bed into a kind of plot in which Plattner might have been involved. But, quite apart from the objectionableness of falsifying a most extraordinary true story, any such trite devices would spoil to my mind, the peculiar effect of this dark world, with its livid green illumination and its drifting Watchers of the Living, which, unseen and unapproachable to us, is yet lying all about us.

It remains to add, that a death did actually occur in Vincent Terrace, just beyond the school garden, and so far as can be proved, at the moment of Plattner's return. Deceased was a rate-collector and insurance agent. His widow, who was much younger than himself, married last month a Mr. Whymper, a veterinary surgeon of Allbeeding. As the portion of this story given here has in various forms circulated orally in Sussexville, she has consented to my use of her name, on condition that I make it distinctly known that she emphatically contradicts every detail of Plattner's account of her husband's last moments. She burnt no will, she says, although Plattner never accused her of doing so; her husband made but one will, and that just after their marriage. Certainly, from a man who had never seen it, Plattner's account of the furniture of the room was curiously accurate.

One other thing, even at the risk of an irksome repetition, I must insist upon, lest I seem to favour the credulous, superstitious view. Plattner's absence from the world for nine days is, I think, proved. But that does not prove his story. It is quite conceivable that even outside space hallucinations may be possible. That at least, the reader must bear distinctly in mind.

23

The Purple Pileus

Mr. Coombes was sick of life. He walked away from his unhappy home, and sick not only of his own existence but of everybody else's, turned aside down Gaswork Lane to avoid the town, and, crossing the wooden bridge that goes over the canal to Starling's Cottages, was presently alone in the damp pine woods and out of sight and sound of human habitation. He would stand it no longer. He repeated aloud with blasphemies unusual to him that he would stand it no longer.

He was a pale-faced little man, with dark eyes and a fine and very black moustache. He had a very stiff, upright collar slightly frayed, that gave him an illusory double chin, and his overcoat (albeit shabby) was trimmed with astrachan. His gloves were a bright brown with black stripes over the knuckles, and split at the finger ends. His appearance, his wife had said once in the dear, dead days beyond recall—, before he married her, that is—, was military. But now she called him—It seems a dreadful thing to tell of between husband and wife, but she called him "a little grub." It wasn't the only thing she had called him, either.

The row had arisen about that beastly Jennie again. Jennie was his wife's friend, and by no invitation of Mr. Coombes, she came in every blessed Sunday to dinner, and made a shindy all the afternoon. She was a big, noisy girl, with a taste for loud colours and a strident laugh; and this Sunday she had outdone all her previous intrusions by bringing in a fellow with her, a chap as showy as herself. And Mr. Coombes, in a starchy, clean collar and his Sunday frock-coat, had sat dumb and wrathful at his own table, while his wife and her guests talked foolishly and undesirably, and laughed aloud. Well, he stood that, and after dinner (which, "as usual," was late), what must Miss Jennie do but go to the piano and play banjo tunes, for all the world as if it were a week-day! Flesh and blood could not endure such goings on. They would hear next door, they would hear in the road, it was a public announcement of their disrepute. He had to speak.

He had felt himself go pale, and a kind of rigour had affected his respiration as he delivered himself. He had been sitting on one of the chairs by the window—the new guest had taken possession of the armchair. He turned his head. "Sun Day!" he said over the collar, in the voice of one who warns. "Sun Day!" What people call a "nasty" tone, it was.

Jennie had kept on playing, but his wife, who was looking through some music that was piled on the top of the piano, had stared at him. "What's wrong now?" she said; "Can't people enjoy themselves?"

"I don't mind rational 'njoyment, at all," said little Coombes, "but I ain't a-going to have week-day tunes playing on a Sunday in this house."

"What's wrong with my playing now?" said Jennie, stopping and twirling round on the music-stool with a monstrous rustle of flounces.

Coombes saw it was going to be a row, and opened too vigorously, as is common with your timid, nervous men all the world over. "Steady on with that music-stool!" said he; "It ain't made for 'eavy-weights."

"Never you mind about weights," said Jennie, incensed. "What was you saying behind my back about my playing?"

"Surely you don't 'old with not having a bit of music on a Sunday, Mr. Coombes?" said the new guest, leaning back in the armchair, blowing a cloud of cigarette smoke and smiling in a kind of pitying way. And simultaneously his wife said something to Jennie about "Never mind 'im. You go on, Jinny."

"I do," said Mr. Coombes, addressing the new guest.

"May I arst why?" said the new guest, evidently enjoying both his cigarette and the prospect of an argument. He was, by the bye, a lank young man, very stylishly dressed in bright drab, with a white cravat and a pearl and silver pin. It had been better taste to come in a black coat, Mr. Coombes thought.

"Because," began Mr. Coombes, "it don't suit me. I'm a business man. I 'ave to study my connection. Rational 'njoyment—"

"His connection!" said Mrs. Coombes scornfully. "That's what he's always a-saying. We got to do this, and we got to do that—"

"If you don't mean to study my connection," said Mr. Coombes, "what did you marry me for?"

"I wonder," said Jennie, and turned back to the piano.

"I never saw such a man as you," said Mrs. Coombes.

"You've altered all round since we were married. Before—"

Then Jennie began at the tum, tum, tum again.

"Look here!" said Mr. Coombes, driven at last to revolt, standing up and raising his voice. "I tell you I won't have that." The frock-coat heaved with his indignation.

"No vi'lence, now," said the long young man in drab, sitting up.

"Who the juice are you?" said Mr. Coombes fiercely.

Whereupon they all began talking at once. The new guest said he was Jennie's "intended," and meant to protect her, and Mr. Coombes said he was welcome to do so anywhere but in his (Mr. Coombes') house; and Mrs. Coombes said he ought to be ashamed of insulting his guests, and (as I have already mentioned) that he was getting a regular little grub; and the end was, that Mr. Coombes ordered his visitors out of the house, and they wouldn't go, and so he said he would go himself. With his face burning and tears of excitement in his eyes, he went into the passage, and as he struggled with his overcoat—his frock-coat sleeves got concertinaed up his arm—and gave a brush at his silk hat, Jennie began again at the piano, and strummed him insultingly out of the house. Tum, tum, tum. He slammed the shop door so that the house quivered. That briefly, was the immediate making of his mood. You will perhaps begin to understand his disgust with existence.

As he walked along the muddy path under the firs—, it was late October, and the ditches and heaps of fir needles were gorgeous with clumps of fungi—, he recapitulated the melancholy history of his marriage. It was brief and commonplace enough. He now perceived with sufficient clearness that his wife had married him out of a natural curiosity and in order to escape from her worrying, laborious, and uncertain life in the workroom; and, like the majority of her class, she was far too stupid to realise that it was her duty to co-operate with him in his business. She was greedy of enjoyment, loquacious, and socially-minded, and evidently disappointed to find the restraints of poverty still hanging about her. His worries exasperated her, and the slightest attempt to control her proceedings resulted in a charge of "grumbling." Why couldn't he be nice—as he used to be? And Coombes was such a harmless little man too, nourished mentally on Self-Help, and with a meagre ambition of self-denial and competition, that was to end in a "sufficiency." Then Jennie came in as a female Mephistopheles, a gabbling chronicle of "fellers," and was always wanting his wife to go to theatres, and "all that." And in addition were aunts of his wife, and cousins (male and female) to eat up capital, insult him personally, upset business arrangements, annoy good customers, and generally blight his life. It was not the first occasion by many that Mr. Coombes had fled his home in wrath and indignation, and something like fear, vowing furiously and even aloud that he wouldn't stand it, and so frothing away his energy along the line of least resistance. But never before had he been quite so sick of life as on this particular Sunday afternoon. The Sunday dinner may have had its share in his despair—and the greyness of the sky. Perhaps too, he was beginning to realise his unendurable frustration as a business man as the consequence of his marriage. Presently bankruptcy, and after that—Perhaps she might have reason to repent when it was too late. And destiny, as I have already intimated, had planted the path through the wood with evil-smelling fungi, thickly and variously planted it, not only on the right side, but on the left.

A small shopman is in such a melancholy position, if his wife turns out a disloyal partner. His capital is all tied up in his business, and to leave her means to join the unemployed in some strange part of the earth. The luxuries of divorce are beyond him altogether. So that the good old tradition of marriage for better or worse holds inexorably for him, and things work up to tragic culminations. Bricklayers kick their wives to death, and dukes betray theirs; but it is among the small clerks and shopkeepers nowadays that it comes most often to a cutting of throats. Under the circumstances it is not so very remarkable—and you must take it as charitably as you can—that the mind of Mr. Coombes ran for a while on some such glorious close to his disappointed hopes, and that he thought of razors, pistols, bread-knives, and touching letters to the coroner denouncing his enemies by name, and praying piously for forgiveness. After a time his fierceness gave way to melancholia.

He had been married in this very overcoat, in his first and only frock-coat that was buttoned up beneath it. He began to recall their courting along this very walk, his years of penurious saving to get capital, and the bright hopefulness of his marrying days. For it all to work out like this! Was there no sympathetic ruler anywhere in the world? He reverted to death as a topic.

He thought of the canal he had just crossed, and doubted whether he shouldn't stand with his head out, even in the middle, and it was while drowning, was in his mind that the purple pileus caught his eye. He looked at it mechanically for a moment, and stopped and stooped towards it to pick it up, under the impression that it was some such small leather object as a purse. Then he saw that it was the purple top of a fungus, a peculiarly poisonous-looking purple: slimy, shiny, and emitting a sour odour. He hesitated with his hand an inch or so from it, and the thought of poison crossed his mind. With that he picked the thing, and stood up again with it in his hand.

The odour was certainly strong—acrid, but by no means disgusting. He broke off a piece, and the fresh surface was a creamy white, that changed like magic in the space of ten seconds to a yellowish-green colour. It was even an inviting-looking change. He broke off two other pieces to see it repeated. They were wonderful things these fungi, thought Mr. Coombes, and all of them the deadliest poisons, as his father had often told him. Deadly poisons!

There is no time like the present for a rash resolve. Why not here and now? Thought Mr. Coombes. He tasted a little piece, a very little piece indeed—a mere crumb. It was so pungent that he almost spat it out again, then merely hot and full-flavoured. A kind of German mustard with a touch of horse-radish and—well, mushroom. He swallowed it in the excitement of the moment. Did he like it or did he not? His mind was curiously careless. He would try another bit. It really wasn't bad—it was good. He forgot his troubles in the interest of the immediate moment. Playing with death it was. He took another bite, and then deliberately finished a mouthful. A curious, tingling sensation began in his finger-tips and toes. His pulse began to move faster. The blood in his ears sounded like a mill-race. "Try bi' more," said Mr. Coombes. He turned and looked about him, and found his feet unsteady. He saw, and struggled towards, a little patch of purple a dozen yards away. "Jol' goo' stuff," said Mr. Coombes. "E—lomore ye'."

He pitched forward and fell on his face, his hands outstretched towards the cluster of pilei. But he did not eat any more of them. He forgot forthwith.

He rolled over and sat up with a look of astonishment on his face. His carefully brushed silk hat had rolled away towards the ditch. He pressed his hand to his brow. Something had happened, but he could not rightly determine what it was. Anyhow, he was no longer dull—he felt bright, cheerful. And his throat was afire. He laughed in the sudden gaiety of his heart. Had he been dull? He did not know; but at any rate he would be dull no longer. He got up and stood unsteadily, regarding the universe with an agreeable smile. He began to remember. He could not remember very well, because of a steam roundabout that was beginning in his head. And he knew he had been disagreeable at home, just because they wanted to be happy. They were quite right; life should be as gay as possible. He would go home and make it up, and reassure them. And why not take some of this delightful toadstool with him, for them to eat? A hatful, no less. Some of those red ones with white spots as well, and a few yellow. He had been a dull dog, an enemy to merriment; he would make up for it. It would be gay to turn his coat-sleeves inside out, and stick some yellow gorse into his waistcoat pockets. Then home—singing—for a jolly evening.

After the departure of Mr. Coombes, Jennie discontinued playing, and turned round on the music-stool again. "What a fuss about nothing!" said Jennie.

"You see, Mr. Clarence, what I've got to put up with," said Mrs. Coombes.

"He is a bit hasty," said Mr. Clarence judicially.

"He ain't got the slightest sense of our position," said Mrs. Coombes; "that's what I complain of. He cares for nothing but his old shop; and if I have a bit of company, or buy anything to keep myself decent, or get any little thing I want out of the housekeeping money, there's disagreeables. 'Economy' he says; 'struggle for life,' and all that. He lies awake of nights about it, worrying how he can screw me out of a shilling. He wanted us to eat Dorset butter once. If once I was to give in to him—there!"

"Of course," said Jennie.

"If a man values a woman," said Mr. Clarence, lounging back in the armchair, "he must be prepared to make sacrifices for her.

For my own part," said Mr. Clarence, with his eye on Jennie, "I shouldn't think of marrying till I was in a position to do the thing in style. It's downright selfishness. A man ought to go through the rough-and-tumble by himself, and not drag her—"

"I don't agree altogether with that," said Jennie. "I don't see why a man shouldn't have a woman's help, provided he doesn't treat her meanly, you know. It's meanness—"

"You wouldn't believe," said Mrs. Coombes. "But I was a fool to 'ave 'im. I might 'ave known. If it 'adn't been for my father, we shouldn't 'ave 'ad not a carriage to our wedding."

"Lord! He didn't stick out at that?" said Mr. Clarence, quite shocked.

"Said he wanted the money for his stock, or some such rubbish. Why, he wouldn't have a woman in to help me once a week if it wasn't for my standing out plucky. And the fusses he makes about money—comes to me well, pretty near crying, with sheets of paper and figgers. 'If only we can tide over this year,' he says, 'the business is bound to go.' 'If only we can tide over this year,' I says; 'then it'll be, if only we can tide over next year. I know you,' I says. 'And you don't catch me screwing myself lean and ugly. Why didn't you marry a slavey?' I says, 'if you wanted one—instead of a respectable girl,' I says."

So Mrs. Coombes. But we will not follow this unedifying conversation further. Suffice it that Mr. Coombes was very satisfactorily disposed of, and they had a snug little time round the fire. Then Mrs. Coombes went to get the tea, and Jennie sat coquettishly on the arm of Mr. Clarence's chair until the tea-things clattered outside. "What was that I heard?" asked Mrs. Coombes playfully, as she entered, and there was badinage about kissing. They were just sitting down to the little circular table when the first intimation of Mr. Coombes' return was heard.

This was a fumbling at the latch of the front door.

"'Ere's my lord," said Mrs. Coombes. "Went out like a lion and comes back like a lamb, I'll lay."

Something fell over in the shop: a chair, it sounded like. Then there was a sound as of some complicated step exercise in the passage. Then the door opened and Coombes appeared. But it was Coombes transfigured. The immaculate collar had been torn carelessly from his throat. His carefully-brushed silk hat, half-full of a crush of fungi, was under one arm; his coat was inside out, and his waistcoat adorned with bunches of yellow-blossomed furze. These little eccentricities of Sunday costume however, were quite overshadowed by the change in his face; it was livid white, his eyes were unnaturally large and bright, and his pale blue lips were drawn back in a cheerless grin. "Merry!" he said. He had stopped dancing to open the door. "Rational 'njoyment. Dance." He made three fantastic steps into the room, and stood bowing.

"Jim!" shrieked Mrs. Coombes, and Mr. Clarence sat petrified, with a dropping lower jaw.

"Tea," said Mr. Coombes. "Jol' thing, tea. Tose-stools, too. Brosher."

"He's drunk," said Jennie in a weak voice. Never before had she seen this intense pallor in a drunken man, or such shining, dilated eyes.

Mr. Coombes held out a handful of scarlet agaric to Mr. Clarence. "Jo' stuff," said he; "ta' some."

At that moment he was genial. Then at the sight of their startled faces he changed, with the swift transition of insanity, into overbearing fury. And it seemed as if he had suddenly recalled the quarrel of his departure. In such a huge voice as Mrs. Coombes had never heard before, he shouted, "My house. I'm master 'ere. Eat what I give yer!" He bawled this, as it seemed, without an effort, without a violent gesture, standing there as motionless as one who whispers, holding out a handful of fungus.

Clarence approved himself a coward. He could not meet the mad fury in Coombes' eyes; he rose to his feet, pushing back his chair, and turned, stooping. At that Coombes rushed at him. Jennie saw her opportunity and, with the ghost of a shriek, made for the door.

Mrs. Coombes followed her. Clarence tried to dodge. Over went the tea-table with a smash as Coombes clutched him by the collar and tried to thrust the fungus into his mouth. Clarence was content to leave his collar behind him, and shot out into the passage with red patches of fly agaric still adherent to his face. "Shut 'im in!" cried Mrs. Coombes, and would have closed the door, but her supports deserted her; Jennie saw the shop door open, and vanished thereby, locking it behind her, while Clarence went on hastily into the kitchen. Mr. Coombes came heavily against the door, and Mrs. Coombes, finding the key was inside, fled upstairs and locked herself in the spare bedroom.

So the new convert to joie de vivre emerged upon the passage, his decorations a little scattered, but that respectable hatful of fungi still under his arm. He hesitated at the three ways, and decided on the kitchen. Whereupon Clarence, who was fumbling with the key, gave up the attempt to imprison his host, and fled into the scullery, only to be captured before he could open the door into the yard. Mr. Clarence is singularly reticent of the details of what occurred. It seems that Mr. Coombes' transitory irritation had vanished again, and he was once more a genial playfellow. And as there were knives and meat choppers about, Clarence very generously resolved to humour him and so avoid anything tragic. It is beyond dispute that Mr. Coombes played with Mr. Clarence to his heart's content; they could not have been more playful and familiar if they had known each other for years. He insisted gaily on Clarence trying the fungi and, after a friendly tussle, was smitten with remorse at the mess he was making of his guest's face. It also appears that Clarence was dragged under the sink and his face scrubbed with the blacking brush—, he being still resolved to humour the lunatic at any cost—, and that finally, in a somewhat dishevelled, chipped, and discoloured condition, he was assisted to his coat and shown out by the back door, the shopway being barred by Jennie. Mr. Coombes' wandering thoughts then turned to Jennie. Jennie had been unable to unfasten the shop door, but she shot the bolts against Mr. Coombes' latchkey, and remained in possession of the shop for the rest of the evening.

It would appear that Mr. Coombes then returned to the kitchen, still in pursuit of gaiety, and, albeit a strict Good Templar, drank (or spilt down the front of the first and only frock-coat) no less than five bottles of the stout Mrs. Coombes insisted upon having for her health's sake. He made cheerful noises by breaking off the necks of the bottles with several of his wife's wedding-present dinner-plates, and during the earlier part of this great drunk he sang divers merry ballads. He cut his finger rather badly with one of the bottles—, the only bloodshed in this story—, and what with that, and the systematic convulsion of his inexperienced physiology by the liquorish brand of Mrs. Coombes' stout, it may be the evil of the fungus poison was somehow allayed. But we prefer to draw a veil over the concluding incidents of this Sunday afternoon. They ended in the coal cellar, in a deep and healing sleep.

An interval of five years elapsed. Again it was a Sunday afternoon in October, and again Mr. Coombes walked through the pine wood beyond the canal. He was still the same dark-eyed, black-moustached little man that he was at the outset of the story, but his double chin was now scarcely so illusory as it had been. His overcoat was new, with a velvet lapel, and a stylish collar with turn-down corners, free of any coarse starchiness, had replaced the original all-round article. His hat was glossy, his gloves newish—though one finger had split and been carefully mended. And a casual observer would have noticed about him a certain rectitude of bearing, a certain erectness of head that marks the man who thinks well of himself. He was a master now, with three assistants. Beside him walked a larger sunburnt parody of himself, his brother Tom, just back from Australia. They were recapitulating their early struggles, and Mr. Coombes had just been making a financial statement.

"It's a very nice little business, Jim," said brother Tom. "In these days of competition you're jolly lucky to have worked it up so. And you're jolly lucky too, to have a wife who's willing to help like yours does."

"Between ourselves," said Mr. Coombes, "it wasn't always so. It wasn't always like this. To begin with, the missus was a bit giddy. Girls are funny creatures."

"Dear me!

"Yes. You'd hardly think it, but she was downright extravagant, and always having slaps at me. I was a bit too easy and loving, and all that, and she thought the whole blessed show was run for her. Turned the 'ouse into a regular caravansery, always having her relations and girls from business in, and their chaps. Comic songs a' Sunday, it was getting to, and driving trade away. And she was making eyes at the chaps, too! I tell you Tom, the place wasn't my own."

"Shouldn't 'a' thought it."

"It was so. Well—I reasoned with her. I said, 'I ain't a duke, to keep a wife like a pet animal. I married you for 'elp and company.' I said, 'You got to 'elp and pull the business through.' She wouldn't 'ear of it. 'Very well,' I says; 'I'm a mild man till I'm roused,' I says, 'and it's getting to that.' But she wouldn't 'ear of no warnings."

"Well?"

"It's the way with women. She didn't think I 'ad it in me to be roused. Women of her sort (between ourselves, Tom) don't respect a man until they're a bit afraid of him. So I just broke out to show her. In comes a girl named Jennie, that used to work with her, and her chap. We 'ad a bit of a row, and I came out 'ere—it was just such another day as this—and I thought it all out. Then I went back and pitched into them."

"You did?"

"I did. I was mad, I can tell you. I wasn't going to 'it 'er if I could 'elp it, so I went back and licked into this chap, just to show 'er what I could do. 'E was a big chap, too. Well, I chucked him, and smashed things about, and gave 'er a scaring, and she ran up and locked 'erself into the spare room."

"Well?"

"That's all. I says to 'er the next morning, 'Now you know,' I says, 'what I'm like when I'm roused.' And I didn't have to say anything more."

"And you've been happy ever after, eh?"

"So to speak. There's nothing like putting your foot down with them. If it 'adn't been for that afternoon I should 'a' been tramping the roads now, and she'd 'a' been grumbling at me, and all her family grumbling for bringing her to poverty—I know their little ways. But we're all right now. And it's a very decent little business, as you say."

They proceeded on their way meditatively. "Women are funny creatures," said Brother Tom. "They want a firm hand," says Coombes.

"What a lot of these funguses there are about here!" remarked Brother Tom presently. "I can't see what use they are in the world."

Mr. Coombes looked. "I dessay they're sent for some wise purpose," said Mr. Coombes.

And that was as much thanks as the purple pileus ever got for maddening this absurd little man to the pitch of decisive action, and so altering the whole course of his life.

24

The Red Room

"I can assure you," said I, "that it will take a very tangible ghost to frighten me." And I stood up before the fire with my glass in my hand.

"It is your own choosing," said the man with the withered arm, and glanced at me askance.

"Eight-and-twenty years," said I, "I have lived, and never a ghost have I seen as yet."

The old woman sat staring hard into the fire, her pale ayes wide open. "Ay," she broke in; "and eight-and-twenty years you have lived and never seen the likes of this house, I reckon. There's a many things to see, when one's still but eight-and-twenty." She swayed her head slowly from side to side. "A many things to see and sorrow for."

I half suspected the old people were trying to enhance the spiritual terrors of their house by their droning insistence. I put down my empty glass on the table and looked about the room, and caught a glimpse of myself, abbreviated and broadened to an impossible sturdiness, in the queer old mirror at the end of the room. "Well," I said, "if I see anything tonight, I shall be so much the wiser. For I come to the business with an open mind."

"It's your own choosing," said the man, with the withered arm, once more.

I heard the sound of a stick and a shambling step on the flags in the passage outside, and the door creaked on its hinges as a second old man entered, more bent, more wrinkled, more aged even than the first. He supported himself by a single crutch, his eyes were covered by a shade, and his lower lip, half averted, hung pale and pink from his decaying yellow teeth. He made straight for an armchair on the opposite side of the table, sat down clumsily, and began to cough. The man with the withered arm gave this new-comer a short glance of positive dislike; the old woman took no notice of his arrival, but remained with her eyes fixed steadily on the fire.

"I said—it's your own choosing," said the man with the withered arm, when the coughing had ceased for a while.

"It's my own choosing," I answered.

The man with the shade became aware of my presence for the first time, and threw his head back for a moment and sideways, to see me. I caught a momentary glimpse of his eyes, small and bright and inflamed. Then he began to cough and splutter again.

"Why don't you drink?" said the man with the withered arm, pushing the beer towards him. The man with the shade, poured out a glassful with a shaky arm that splashed half as much again on the deal table. A monstrous shadow of him crouched upon the wall and mocked his action as he poured and drank. I must confess I had scarce expected these grotesque custodians. There is to my mind something inhuman in senility, something crouching and atavistic; the human qualities seem to drop from old people insensibly day by day. The three of them made me feel uncomfortable, with their gaunt silences, their bent carriage, their evident unfriendliness to me and to one another.

"If," said I, "you will show me to this haunted room of yours, I will make myself comfortable there."

The old man with the cough jerked his head back so suddenly that it startled me, and shot another glance of his red eyes at me from under the shade; but no one answered me. I waited a minute, glancing from one to the other.

"If," I said a little louder, "if you will show me to this haunted room of yours, I will relieve you from the task of entertaining me."

"There's a candle on the slab outside the door," said the man with the withered arm, looking at my feet as he addressed me. "But if you go to the red room to-night—"

("This night of all nights!" said the old woman.)

"You go alone."

"Very well," I answered. "And which way do I go?"

"You go along the passage for a bit," said he, "until you come to a door, and through that is a spiral staircase, and halfway up that is a landing and another door covered with baize. Go through that and down the long corridor to the end, and the red room is on your left up the steps."

"Have I got that right?" I said, and repeated his directions. He corrected me in one particular.

"And are you really going?" said the man with the shade, looking at me again for the third time, with that queer, unnatural tilting of the face.

("This night of all nights!" said the old woman.)

"It is what I came for," I said, and moved towards the door. As I did so, the old man with the shade rose and staggered round the table, so as to be closer to the others and to the fire. At the door I turned and looked at them, and saw they were all close together, dark against the firelight, staring at me over their shoulders, with an intent expression on their ancient faces.

"Good-night," I said, setting the door open.

"It's your own choosing," said the man with the withered arm.

I left the door wide open until the candle was well alight, and then I shut them in and walked down the chilly, echoing passage.

I must confess that the oddness of these three old pensioners in whose charge her ladyship had left the castle, and the deep-toned, old-fashioned furniture of the housekeeper's room in which they foregathered, affected me in spite of my efforts to keep myself at a matter-of-fact phase. They seemed to belong to another age, an older age, an age when things spiritual were different from this of ours, less certain; an age when omens and witches were credible, and ghosts beyond denying. Their very existence was spectral; the cut of their clothing, fashions born in dead brains. The ornaments and conveniences of the room about them were ghostly—the thoughts of vanished men, which still haunted, rather than participated in the world of to-day. But with an effort I sent such thoughts to the right-about. The long, draughty subterranean passage was chilly and dusty, and my candle flared and made the shadows cower and quiver. The echoes rang up and down the spiral staircase, and a shadow came sweeping up after me, and one fled before me into the darkness overhead. I came to the landing and stopped there for a moment, listening to a rustling that I fancied I heard; then, satisfied of the absolute silence, I pushed open the baize-covered door and stood in the corridor.

The effect was scarcely what I expected, for the moonlight, coming in by the great window on the grand staircase, picked out everything in vivid black shadow or silvery illumination. Everything was in its place: the house might have been deserted on the yesterday instead of eighteen months ago. There were candles in the sockets of the sconces, and whatever dust had gathered on the carpets or upon the polished flooring was distributed so evenly as to be invisible in the moonlight. I was about to advance, and stopped abruptly. A bronze group stood upon the landing, hidden from me by the corner of the wall, but its shadow fell with marvellous distinctness upon the white panelling, and gave me the impression of someone crouching to waylay me. I stood rigid for half a minute perhaps. Then, with my hand in the pocket that held my revolver, I advanced, only to discover a Ganymede and Eagle glistening in the moonlight. That incident for at time restored my nerve, and a porcelain Chinaman on a buhl table, whose head rocked silently as I passed him, scarcely startled me.

The door to the red room and the steps up to it were in a shadowy corner. I moved my candle from side to side, in order to see clearly the nature of the recess in which I stood before opening the door. Here it was, thought I, that my predecessor was found, and the memory of that story gave me a sudden twinge of apprehension. I glanced over my shoulder at the Ganymede in the moonlight, and opened the door of the red room rather hastily, with my face half turned to the pallid silence of the landing.

I entered, closed the door behind me at once, turned the key I found in the lock within, and stood with the candle held aloft, surveying the scene of my vigil, the great red room of Lorraine Castle, in which the young duke had died. Or rather, in which he had begun his dying, for he had opened the door and fallen headlong down the steps I had just ascended. That had been the end of his vigil, of his gallant attempt to conquer the ghostly tradition of the place; and never, I thought, had apoplexy better served the ends of superstition. And there were other and older stories that clung to the room, back to the half-credible beginning of it all, the tale of a timid wife and the tragic end that came to her husband's jest of frightening her. And looking around that large shadowy room, with its shadowy window bays, its recesses and alcoves, one could well understand the legends that had sprouted in its black corners, its germinating darkness. My candle was a little tongue of flame in its vastness, that failed to pierce the opposite end of the room, and left an ocean of mystery and suggestion beyond its island of light.

I resolved to make a systematic examination of the place at once, and dispel the fanciful suggestions of its obscurity before they obtained a hold upon me. After satisfying myself of the fastening of the door, I began to walk about the room, peering round each article of furniture, tucking up the valances of the bed, and opening its curtains wide. I pulled up the blinds and examined the fastenings of the several windows before closing the shutters, leant forward and looked up the blackness of the wide chimney, and tapped the dark oak panelling for any secret opening. There were two big mirrors in the room, each with a pair of sconces bearing candles, and on the mantelshelf too, were more candles in china candlesticks. All these I lit one after the other. The fire was laid—, an unexpected consideration from the old housekeeper—, and I lit it, to keep down any disposition to shiver, and when it was burning well, I stood round with my back to it and regarded the room again. I had pulled up a chintz-covered armchair and a table, to form a kind of barricade before me, and on this lay my revolver ready to hand. My precise examination had done me good, but I still found the remoter darkness of the place, and its perfect stillness, too stimulating for the imagination. The echoing of the stir and crackling of the fire was no sort of comfort to me. The shadow in the alcove at the end in particular had that undefinable quality of a presence, that odd suggestion of a lurking, living thing, that comes so easily in silence and solitude. At last, to reassure myself, I walked with a candle into it, and satisfied myself that there was nothing tangible there. I stood that candle upon the floor of the alcove, and left it in that position.

By this time I was in a state of considerable nervous tension, although to my reason there was no adequate cause for the condition. My mind, however, was perfectly clear. I postulated quite unreservedly that nothing supernatural could happen, and to pass the time I began to string some rhymes together, Ingoldsby fashion, of the original legend of the place. A few I spoke aloud, but the echoes were not pleasant. For the same reason I also abandoned, after a time, a conversation with myself upon the impossibility of ghosts and haunting. My mind reverted to the three old and distorted people downstairs, and I tried to keep it upon that topic. The sombre reds and blacks of the room troubled me; even with seven candles the place was merely dim. The one in the alcove flared in a draught, and the fire-flickering kept the shadows and penumbra perpetually shifting and stirring. Casting about for a remedy, I recalled the candles I had seen in the passage, and, with a slight effort, walked out into the moonlight, carrying a candle and leaving the door open, and presently returned with as many as ten. These I put in various knick-knacks of china with which the room was sparsely adorned, lit and placed where the shadows had lain deepest, some on the floor, some in the window recesses, until at last my seventeen candles were so arranged that not an inch of the room darkened, but had the direct light of at least one of them. It occurred to me that when the ghost came, I could warn him not to trip over them. The room was now quite brightly illuminated. There was something very cheery and reassuring in these little streaming flames, and snuffing them gave me an occupation, and afforded a helpful sense of the passage of time. Even with that however, the brooding expectation of the vigil weighed heavily upon me. It was after midnight that the candle in the alcove suddenly went out, and the black shadow sprang back to its place. I did not see the candle go out; I simply turned and saw that the darkness was there, as one might start and see the unexpected presence of a stranger. "By Jove!" said I aloud; "That draught's a strong one!" and taking the matches from the table, I walked across the room in a leisurely manner to relight the corner again. My first match would not strike, and as I succeeded with the second, something seemed to blink on the wall before me. I turned my head involuntarily, and saw that the two candles on the little table by the fireplace were extinguished. I rose at once to my feet.

"Odd!" I said. "Did I do that myself in a flash of absent-mindedness?"

I walked back, relit one, and as I did so, I saw the candle in the right sconce of one of the mirrors wink and go right out, and almost immediately its companion followed it. There was no mistake about it. The flame vanished, as if the wicks had been suddenly nipped between a finger and thumb, leaving the wick neither glowing nor smoking, but black. While I stood gaping, the candle at the foot of the bed went out, and the shadows seemed to take another step towards me.

"This won't do!" said I, and first one and then another candle on the mantelshelf followed. "What's up?" I cried, with a queer high note getting into my voice somehow. At that the candle on the wardrobe went out, and the one I had relit in the alcove followed.

"Steady on!" I said. "These candles are wanted," speaking with a half-hysterical facetiousness, and scratching away at a match, all the while, for the mantel candlesticks. My hands trembled so much that twice I missed the rough paper of the matchbox. As the mantel emerged from darkness again, two candles in the remoter end of the window were eclipsed. But with the same match I also relit the larger mirror candles, and those on the floor near the doorway, so that for the moment I seemed to gain on the extinctions. But then in a volley there vanished four lights at once in different corners of the room, and I struck another match in quivering haste, and stood hesitating whither to take it.

As I stood undecided, an invisible hand seemed to sweep out the two candles on the table. With a cry of terror, I dashed at the alcove, then into the corner, and then into the window, relighting three, as two more vanished by the fireplace; then, perceiving a better way, I dropped the matches on the iron-bound deed-box in the corner, and caught up the bedroom candlestick. With this I avoided the delay of striking matches; but for all that the steady process of extinction went on, and the shadows I feared and fought against returned, and crept in upon me, first a step gained on this side of me and then on that. It was like a ragged storm-cloud sweeping out of the stars. Now and then one returned for a minute, and was lost again. I was now almost frantic with the horror of the coming darkness, and my self-possession deserted me. I leaped panting and dishevelled from candle to candle in a vain struggle against that remorseless advance.

I bruised myself on the thigh against the table, I sent a chair headlong, I stumbled and fell and whisked the cloth from the table in my fall. My candle rolled away from me, and I snatched another as I rose. Abruptly this was blown out, as I swung it off the table, by the wind of my sudden movement, and immediately the two remaining candles followed. But there was light still in the room, a red light that stayed off the shadows from me. The fire! Of course I could still thrust my candle between the bars and relight it!

I turned to where the flames were still dancing between the glowing coals, and splashing red reflections upon the furniture, made two steps towards the grate, and incontinently the flames dwindled and vanished, the glow vanished, the reflections rushed together and vanished, and as I thrust the candle between the bars darkness closed upon me like the shutting of an eye, wrapped about me in a stifling embrace, sealed my vision, and crushed the last vestiges of reason from my brain. The candle fell from my hand. I flung out my arms in a vain effort to thrust that ponderous blackness away from me, and, lifting up my voice, screamed with all my might—once, twice, thrice. Then I think I must have staggered to my feet. I know I thought suddenly of the moonlit corridor and, with my head bowed and my arms over my face, made a run for the door.

But I had forgotten the exact position of the door, and struck myself heavily against the corner of the bed. I staggered back, turned, and was either struck or struck myself against some other bulky furniture. I have a vague memory of battering myself thus, to and fro in the darkness, of a cramped struggle, and of my own wild crying as I darted to and fro, of a heavy blow at last upon my forehead, a horrible sensation of falling that lasted an age, of my last frantic effort to keep my footing, and then I remember no more.

I opened my eyes in daylight. My head was roughly bandaged, and the man with the withered arm was watching my face. I looked about me, trying to remember what had happened, and for a space I could not recollect. I turned to the corner, and saw the old woman, no longer abstracted, pouring out some drops of medicine from a little blue phial into a glass. "Where am I?" I asked; "I seem to remember you, and yet I cannot remember who you are."

They told me then, and I heard of the haunted red room as one who hears a tale. "We found you at dawn," said he, "and there was blood on your forehead and lips."

It was very slowly I recovered my memory of my experience. "You believe now," said the old man, "that the room is haunted?" He spoke no longer as one who greets an intruder, but as one who grieves for a broken friend.

"Yes," said I; "the room is haunted."

"And you have seen it. And we, who have lived here all our lives, have never set eyes upon it. Because we have never dared... Tell us, is it truly the old earl who—"

"No," said I; "it is not."

"I told you so," said the old lady, with the glass in her hand. "It is his poor young countess who was frightened—"

"It is not," I said. "There is neither ghost of earl nor ghost of countess in that room, there is no ghost there at all; but worse, far worse—"

"Well?" they said.

"The worst of all the things that haunt poor mortal man," said I; "and that is, in all its nakedness—Fear! Fear that will not have light nor sound, that will not bear with reason, that deafens and darkens and overwhelms. It followed me through the corridor, it fought against me in the room—"

I stopped abruptly. There was an interval of silence. My hand went up to my bandages.

Then the man with the shade sighed and spoke. "That is it," said he. "I knew that was it. A power of darkness. To put such a curse upon a woman! It lurks there always. You can feel it even in the daytime, even of a bright summer's day, in the hangings, in the curtains, keeping behind you however you face about. In the dusk it creeps along the corridor and follows you, so that you dare not turn. There is Fear in that room of hers—black Fear, and there will be—so long as this house of sin endures."

25

The Sea Raiders

1.

Until the extraordinary affair at Sidmouth, the peculiar species Haploteuthis ferox was known to science only generically, on the strength of a half-digested tentacle obtained near the Azores, and a decaying body pecked by birds and nibbled by fish, found early in 1896 by Mr. Jennings, near Land's End.

In no department of zoological science, indeed are we quite so much in the dark as with regard to the deep-sea cephalopods. A mere accident, for instance, it was that led to the Prince of Monaco's discovery of nearly a dozen new forms in the summer of 1895, a discovery in which the before-mentioned tentacle was included. It chanced that a cachalot was killed off Terceira by some sperm whalers, and in its last struggles charged almost to the Prince's yacht, missed it, rolled under, and died within twenty yards of his rudder. And in its agony it threw up a number of large objects, which the Prince, dimly perceiving they were strange and important, was by a happy expedient, able to secure before they sank. He set his screws in motion, and kept them circling in the vortices thus created until a boat could be lowered. And these specimens were whole cephalopods and fragments of cephalopods, some of gigantic proportions, and almost all of them unknown to science!

It would seem, indeed, that these large and agile creatures, living in the middle depths of the sea, must to a large extent, for ever remain unknown to us, since under water they are too nimble for nets, and it is only by such rare, unlooked-for accidents that specimens can be obtained. In the case of Haploteuthis ferox, for instance, we are still altogether ignorant of its habitat, as ignorant as we are of the breeding-ground of the herring or the sea-ways of the salmon. And zoologists are altogether at a loss to account for its sudden appearance on our coast. Possibly it was the stress of a hunger migration that drove it hither out of the deep. But it will be, perhaps, better to avoid necessarily inconclusive discussion, and to proceed at once with our narrative.

The first human being to set eyes upon a living Haploteuthis—the first human being to survive, that is, for there can be little doubt now that the wave of bathing fatalities and boating accidents that travelled along the coast of Cornwall and Devon in early May was due to this cause—was a retired tea-dealer of the name of Fison, who was stopping at a Sidmouth boarding-house. It was in the afternoon, and he was walking along the cliff path between Sidmouth and Ladram Bay. The cliffs in this direction are very high, but down the red face of them in one place a kind of ladder staircase has been made. He was near this when his attention was attracted by what at first he thought to be a cluster of birds struggling over a fragment of food that caught the sunlight, and glistened pinkish-white. The tide was right out, and this object was not only far below him, but remote across a broad waste of rock reefs covered with dark seaweed and interspersed with silvery shining tidal pools. And he was, moreover dazzled by the brightness of the further water.

In a minute, regarding this again, he perceived that his judgment was in fault, for over this struggle circled a number of birds, jackdaws and gulls for the most part, the latter gleaming blindingly when the sunlight smote their wings, and they seemed minute in comparison with it. And his curiosity was, perhaps aroused all the more strongly because of his first insufficient explanations.

As he had nothing better to do than amuse himself, he decided to make this object, whatever it was, the goal of his afternoon walk, instead of Ladram Bay, conceiving it might perhaps be a great fish of some sort, stranded by some chance, and flapping about in its distress. And so he hurried down the long steep ladder, stopping at intervals of thirty feet or so to take breath and scan the mysterious movement.

At the foot of the cliff he was, of course, nearer his object than he had been; but, on the other hand, it now came up against the incandescent sky, beneath the sun, so as to seem dark and indistinct. Whatever was pinkish of it was now hidden by a skerry of weedy boulders. But he perceived that it was made up of seven rounded bodies distinct or connected, and that the birds kept up a constant croaking and screaming, but seemed afraid to approach it too closely.

Mr. Fison, torn by curiosity, began picking his way across the wave-worn rocks, and finding the wet seaweed that covered them thickly rendered them extremely slippery, he stopped, removed his shoes and socks, and rolled his trousers above his knees. His object was, of course, merely to avoid stumbling into the rocky pools about him, and perhaps he was rather glad, as all men are, of an excuse to resume, even for a moment, the sensations of his boyhood. At any rate, it is to this, no doubt, that he owes his life.

He approached his mark with all the assurance which the absolute security of this country against all forms of animal life gives its inhabitants. The round bodies moved to and fro, but it was only when he surmounted the skerry of boulders, I have mentioned, that he realised the horrible nature of the discovery. It came upon him with some suddenness.

The rounded bodies fell apart as he came into sight over the ridge, and displayed the pinkish object to be the partially devoured body of a human being, but whether of a man or woman he was unable to say. And the rounded bodies were new and ghastly-looking creatures, in shape somewhat resembling an octopus, with huge and very long and flexible tentacles, coiled copiously on the ground. The skin had a glistening texture, unpleasant to see, like shiny leather. The downward bend of the tentacle-surrounded mouth, the curious excrescence at the bend, the tentacles, and the large intelligent eyes, gave the creatures a grotesque suggestion of a face. They were the size of a fair-sized swine about the body, and the tentacles seemed to him to be many feet in length. There were, he thinks, seven or eight at least of the creatures. Twenty yards beyond them, amid the surf of the now returning tide, two others were emerging from the sea.

Their bodies lay flatly on the rocks, and their eyes regarded him with evil interest; but it does not appear that Mr. Fison was afraid, or that he realised that he was in any danger. Possibly his confidence is to be ascribed to the limpness of their attitudes. But he was horrified, of course, and intensely excited and indignant, at such revolting creatures preying upon human flesh. He thought they had chanced upon a drowned body. He shouted to them, with the idea of driving them off, and finding they did not budge, cast about him, picked up a big rounded lump of rock, and flung it at one.

And then, slowly uncoiling their tentacles, they all began moving towards him—creeping at first deliberately, and making a soft purring sound to each other.

In a moment Mr. Fison realised that he was in danger. He shouted again, threw both his boots, and started off, with a leap, forthwith. Twenty yards off he stopped and faced about, judging them slow, and behold! The tentacles of their leader were already pouring over the rocky ridge on which he had just been standing!

At that he shouted again, but this time not threatening, but a cry of dismay, and began jumping, striding, slipping, wading across the uneven expanse between him and the beach. The tall red cliffs seemed suddenly at a vast distance, and he saw, as though they were creatures in another world, two minute workmen engaged in the repair of the ladder-way, and little suspecting the race for life that was beginning below them. At one time he could hear the creatures splashing in the pools not a dozen feet behind him, and once he slipped and almost fell.

They chased him to the very foot of the cliffs, and desisted only when he had been joined by the workmen at the foot of the ladder-way up the cliff. All three of the men pelted them with stones for a time, and then hurried to the cliff top and along the path towards Sidmouth, to secure assistance and a boat, and to rescue the desecrated body from the clutches of these abominable creatures.

2.

And as if he had not already been in sufficient peril that day, Mr. Fison went with the boat to point out the exact spot of his adventure.

As the tide was down, it required a considerable detour to reach the spot, and when at last they came off the ladder-way, the mangled body had disappeared. The water was now running in, submerging first one slab of slimy rock and then another, and the four men in the boat—the workmen, that is, the boatman, and Mr. Fison—now turned their attention from the bearings off shore to the water beneath the keel.

At first they could see little below them, save a dark jungle of laminaria, with an occasional darting fish. Their minds were set on adventure, and they expressed their disappointment freely. But presently they saw one of the monsters swimming through the water seaward, with a curious rolling motion that suggested to Mr. Fison the spinning roll of a captive balloon. Almost immediately after, the waving streamers of laminaria were extraordinarily perturbed, parted for a moment, and three of these beasts became darkly visible, struggling for what was probably some fragment of the drowned man. In a moment the copious olive-green ribbons had poured again over this writhing group.

At that all four men, greatly excited, began beating the water with oars and shouting, and immediately they saw a tumultuous movement among the weeds. They desisted to see more clearly, and as soon as the water was smooth, they saw, as it seemed to them, the whole sea bottom among the weeds set with eyes.

"Ugly swine!" cried one of the men. "Why, there's dozens!"

And forthwith the things began to rise through the water about them. Mr. Fison has since described to the writer this startling eruption out of the waving laminaria meadows. To him it seemed to occupy a considerable time, but it is probable that really it was an affair of a few seconds only. For a time nothing but eyes, and then he speaks of tentacles streaming out and parting the weed fronds this way and that. Then these things, growing larger, until at last the bottom was hidden by their intercoiling forms, and the tips of tentacles rose darkly here and there into the air above the swell of the waters.

One came up boldly to the side of the boat, and clinging to this with three of its sucker-set tentacles, threw four others over the gunwale, as if with an intention either of oversetting the boat or of clambering into it. Mr. Fison at once caught up the boathook, and jabbing furiously at the soft tentacles, forced it to desist. He was struck in the back and almost pitched overboard by the boatman, who was using his oar to resist a similar attack on the other side of the boat. But the tentacles on either side at once relaxed their hold, slid out of sight, and splashed into the water.

"We'd better get out of this," said Mr. Fison, who was trembling violently. He went to the tiller, while the boatman and one of the workmen seated themselves and began rowing. The other workman stood up in the fore part of the boat, with the boathook, ready to strike any more tentacles that might appear. Nothing else seems to have been said. Mr. Fison had expressed the common feeling beyond amendment. In a hushed, scared mood, with faces white and drawn, they set about escaping from the position into which they had so recklessly blundered.

But the oars had scarcely dropped into the water before dark, tapering, serpentine ropes had bound them, and were about the rudder; and creeping up the sides of the boat with a looping motion came the suckers again. The men gripped their oars and pulled, but it was like trying to move a boat in a floating raft of weeds. "Help here!" cried the boatman, and Mr. Fison and the second workman rushed to help lug at the oar.

Then the man with the boathook—his name was Ewan, or Ewen—sprang up with a curse and began striking downward over the side, as far as he could reach, at the bank of tentacles that now clustered along the boat's bottom. And, at the same time, the two rowers stood up to get a better purchase for the recovery of their oars. The boatman handed his to Mr. Fison, who lugged desperately, and meanwhile, the boatman opened a big clasp-knife, and leaning over the side of the boat, began hacking at the spiralling arms upon the oar shaft.

Mr. Fison, staggering with the quivering rocking of the boat, his teeth set, his breath coming short, and the veins starting on his hands as he pulled at his oar, suddenly cast his eyes seaward. And there, not fifty yards off, across the long rollers of the incoming tide, was a large boat standing in towards them, with three women and a little child in it. A boatman was rowing, and a little man in a pink-ribboned straw hat and whites stood in the stern hailing them. For a moment, of course, Mr. Fison thought of help, and then he thought of the child. He abandoned his oar forthwith, threw up his arms in a frantic gesture, and screamed to the party in the boat to keep away "for God's sake!" It says much for the modesty and courage of Mr. Fison that he does not seem to be aware that there was any quality of heroism in his action at this juncture. The oar he had abandoned was at once drawn under, and presently reappeared floating about twenty yards away.

At the same moment Mr. Fison felt the boat under him lurch violently, and a hoarse scream, a prolonged cry of terror from Hill, the boatman, caused him to forget the party of excursionists altogether. He turned, and saw Hill crouching by the forward rowlock, his face convulsed with terror, and his right arm over the side and drawn tightly down. He gave now a succession of short, sharp cries, "Oh! Oh! Oh—! Oh!" Mr. Fison believes that he must have been hacking at the tentacles below the water-line, and have been grasped by them, but of course, it is quite impossible to say now certainly what had happened. The boat was heeling over, so that the gunwale was within ten inches of the water, and both Ewan and the other labourer were striking down into the water, with oar and boathook, on either side of Hill's arm. Mr. Fison instinctively placed himself to counterpoise them.

Then Hill, who was a burly, powerful man, made a strenuous effort, and rose almost to a standing position. He lifted his arm, indeed, clean out of the water. Hanging to it was a complicated tangle of brown ropes, and the eyes of one of the brutes that had hold of him, glaring straight and resolute, showed momentarily above the surface. The boat heeled more and more, and the green-brown water came pouring in a cascade over the side. Then Hill slipped and fell with his ribs across the side, and his arm and the mass of tentacles about it splashed back into the water. He rolled over; his boot kicked Mr. Fison's knee as that gentleman rushed forward to seize him, and in another moment fresh tentacles had whipped about his waist and neck, and after a brief, convulsive struggle, in which the boat was nearly capsized, Hill was lugged overboard. The boat righted with a violent jerk that all but sent Mr. Fison over the other side, and hid the struggle in the water from his eyes.

He stood staggering to recover his balance for a moment, and as he did so he became aware that the struggle and the inflowing tide had carried them close upon the weedy rocks again. Not four yards off a table of rock still rose in rhythmic movements above the in-wash of the tide. In a moment Mr. Fison seized the oar from Ewan, gave one vigorous stroke, then dropping it, ran to the bows and leapt. He felt his feet slide over the rock, and by a frantic effort, leapt again towards a further mass. He stumbled over this, came to his knees, and rose again.

"Look out!" cried someone, and a large drab body struck him. He was knocked flat into a tidal pool by one of the workmen, and as he went down he heard smothered, choking cries, that he believed at the time came from Hill. Then he found himself marvelling at the shrillness and variety of Hill's voice. Someone jumped over him, and a curving rush of foamy water poured over him, and passed. He scrambled to his feet dripping, and without looking seaward, ran as fast as his terror would let him shoreward. Before him, over the flat space of scattered rocks, stumbled the two workmen—one a dozen yards in front of the other.

He looked over his shoulder at last, and seeing that he was not pursued, faced about. He was astonished. From the moment of the rising of the cephalopods out of the water he had been acting too swiftly to fully comprehend his actions. Now it seemed to him as if he had suddenly jumped out of an evil dream.

For there were the sky, cloudless and blazing with the afternoon sun, the sea weltering under its pitiless brightness, the soft creamy foam of the breaking water, and the low, long, dark ridges of rock. The righted boat floated, rising and falling gently on the swell about a dozen yards from shore. Hill and the monsters, all the stress and tumult of that fierce fight for life, had vanished as though they had never been.

Mr. Fison's heart was beating violently; he was throbbing to the finger-tips, and his breath came deep.

There was something missing. For some seconds he could not think clearly enough what this might be. Sun, sky, sea, rocks—what was it? Then he remembered the boatload of excursionists. It had vanished. He wondered whether he had imagined it. He turned, and saw the two workmen standing side by side under the projecting masses of the tall pink cliffs. He hesitated whether he should make one last attempt to save the man Hill. His physical excitement seemed to desert him suddenly, and leave him aimless and helpless. He turned shoreward, stumbling and wading towards his two companions.

He looked back again, and there were now two boats floating, and the one farthest out at sea pitched clumsily, bottom upward.

3.

So it was Haploteuthis ferox made its appearance upon the Devonshire coast. So far, this has been its most serious aggression.

Mr. Fison's account, taken together with the wave of boating and bathing casualties to which I have already alluded, and the absence of fish from the Cornish coasts that year, points clearly to a shoal of these voracious deep-sea monsters prowling slowly along the sub-tidal coastline. Hunger migration has, I know, been suggested as the force that drove them hither; but, for my own part, I prefer to believe the alternative theory of Hemsley. Hemsley holds that a pack or shoal of these creatures may have become enamoured of human flesh by the accident of a foundered ship sinking among them, and have wandered in search of it out of their accustomed zone; first way-laying and following ships, and so coming to our shores in the wake of the Atlantic traffic. But to discuss Hemsley's cogent and admirably-stated arguments would be out of place here.

It would seem that the appetites of the shoal were satisfied by the catch of eleven people—for, so far as can be ascertained, there were ten people in the second boat, and certainly these creatures gave no further signs of their presence off Sidmouth that day. The coast between Seaton and Budleigh Salterton was patrolled all that evening and night by four Preventive Service boats, the men in which were armed with harpoons and cutlasses, and as the evening advanced, a number of more or less similarly equipped expeditions, organised by private individuals, joined them. Mr. Fison took no part in any of these expeditions.

About midnight excited hails were heard from a boat about a couple of miles out at sea to the south-east of Sidmouth, and a lantern was seen waving in a strange manner to and fro and up and down. The nearer boats at once hurried towards the alarm. The venturesome occupants of the boat, a seaman, a curate, and two schoolboys, had actually seen the monsters passing under their boat. The creatures, it seems, like most deep-sea organisms, were phosphorescent, and they had been floating, five fathoms deep or so, like creatures of moonshine through the blackness of the water, their tentacles retracted and as if asleep, rolling over and over, and moving slowly in a wedge-like formation towards the south-east.

These people told their story in gesticulated fragments, as first one boat drew alongside and then another. At last there was a little fleet of eight or nine boats collected together, and from them a tumult, like the chatter of a marketplace, rose into the stillness of the night. There was little or no disposition to pursue the shoal, the people had neither weapons nor experience for such a dubious chase, and presently—even with a certain relief, it may be—the boats turned shoreward.

And now to tell what is perhaps the most astonishing fact in this whole astonishing raid. We have not the slightest knowledge of the subsequent movements of the shoal, although the whole south-west coast was now alert for it. But it may, perhaps, be significant that a cachalot was stranded off Sark on June 3. Two weeks and three days after this Sidmouth affair, a living Haploteuthis came ashore on Calais sands. It was alive, because several witnesses saw its tentacles moving in a convulsive way. But it is probable that it was dying. A gentleman named Pouchet obtained a rifle and shot it.

That was the last appearance of a living Haploteuthis. No others were seen on the French coast. On the 15th of June a dead carcass, almost complete, was washed ashore near Torquay, and a few days later a boat from the Marine Biological station, engaged in dredging off Plymouth, picked up a rotting specimen, slashed deeply with a cutlass wound. How the former had come by its death it is impossible to say. And on the last day of June, Mr. Egbert Caine, an artist, bathing near Newlyn, threw up his arms, shrieked, and was drawn under. A friend bathing with him made no attempt to save him, but swam at once for the shore. This is the last fact to tell of this extraordinary raid from the deeper sea. Whether it is really the last of these horrible creatures it is, as yet, premature to say. But it is believed, and certainly it is to be hoped, that they have returned now, and returned for good, to the sunless depths of the middle seas, out of which they have so strangely and so mysteriously arisen.

26

The Story of the Late Mr. Elvesham

I set this story down, not expecting it will be believed, but if possible, to prepare a way of escape for the next victim. He perhaps, may profit by my misfortune. My own case, I know is hopeless, and I am now in some measure prepared to meet my fate.

My name is Edward George Eden. I was born at Trentham, in Staffordshire, my father being employed in the gardens there. I lost my mother when I was three years old, and my father when I was five, my uncle, George Eden, then adopting me as his own son. He was a single man, self-educated, and well-known in Birmingham as an enterprising journalist; he educated me generously, fired my ambition to succeed in the world, and at his death, which happened four years ago, left me his entire fortune, a matter of about five hundred pounds after all outgoing charges were paid. I was then eighteen. He advised me in his will to expend the money in completing my education. I had already chosen the profession of medicine, and through his posthumous generosity and my good fortune in a scholarship competition, I became a medical student at University College, London. At the time of the beginning of my story I lodged at 11A University Street in a little upper room, very shabbily furnished and draughty, overlooking the back of Shoolbred's premises. I used this little room both to live in and sleep in, because I was anxious to eke out my means to the very last shillingsworth.

I was taking a pair of shoes to be mended at a shop in the Tottenham Court Road when I first encountered the little old man with the yellow face, with whom my life has now become so inextricably entangled. He was standing on the kerb, and staring at the number on the door in a doubtful way, as I opened it. His eyes—they were dull grey eyes, and reddish under the rims—fell to my face, and his countenance immediately assumed an expression of corrugated amiability.

"You come," he said, "apt to the moment. I had forgotten the number of your house. How do you do, Mr. Eden?"

I was a little astonished at his familiar address, for I had never set eyes on the man before. I was a little annoyed too, at his catching me with my boots under my arm. He noticed my lack of cordiality.

"Wonder who the deuce I am, eh? A friend, let me assure you. I have seen you before, though you haven't seen me. Is there anywhere where I can talk to you?"

I hesitated. The shabbiness of my room upstairs was not a matter for every stranger. "Perhaps," said I, "we might walk down the street. I'm unfortunately prevented—" My gesture explained the sentence before I had spoken it.

"The very thing," he said, and faced this way, and then that. "The street? Which way shall we go?" I slipped my boots down in the passage. "Look here!" he said abruptly; "this business of mine is a rigmarole. Come and lunch with me, Mr. Eden. I'm an old man, a very old man, and not good at explanations, and what with my piping voice and the clatter of the traffic—"

He laid a persuasive skinny hand that trembled a little upon my arm.

I was not so old that an old man might not treat me to a lunch. Yet at the same time I was not altogether pleased by this abrupt invitation. "I had rather—" I began. "But I had rather," he said, catching me up, "and a certain civility is surely due to my grey hairs."

And so I consented, and went with him.

He took me to Blavitiski's; I had to walk slowly to accommodate myself to his paces; and over such a lunch as I had never tasted before, he fended off my leading question, and I took a better note of his appearance. His clean-shaven face was lean and wrinkled, his shrivelled, lips fell over a set of false teeth, and his white hair was thin and rather long; he seemed small to me—though, indeed, most people seemed small to me—and his shoulders were rounded and bent. And watching him, I could not help but observe that he too was taking note of me, running his eyes, with a curious touch of greed in them, over me, from my broad shoulders to my sun-tanned hands, and up to my freckled face again. "And now," said he, as we lit our cigarettes, "I must tell you of the business in hand.

"I must tell you then, that I am an old man, a very old man." He paused momentarily. "And it happens that I have money that I must presently be leaving, and never a child have I to leave it to." I thought of the confidence trick, and resolved I would be on the alert for the vestiges of my five hundred pounds. He proceeded to enlarge on his loneliness, and the trouble he had to find a proper disposition of his money. "I have weighed this plan and that plan, charities, institutions, and scholarships, and libraries, and I have come to this conclusion at last—," he fixed his eyes on my face—, "that I will find some young fellow, ambitious, pure-minded, and poor, healthy in body and healthy in mind, and in short, make him my heir, give him all that I have." He repeated, "Give him all that I have. So that he will suddenly be lifted out of all the trouble and struggle in which his sympathies have been educated, to freedom and influence."

I tried to seem disinterested. With a transparent hypocrisy I said, "And you want my help, my professional services maybe, to find that person."

He smiled, and looked at me over his cigarette, and I laughed at his quiet exposure of my modest pretence.

"What a career such a man might have!" he said. "It fills me with envy to think how I have accumulated that another man may spend—

"But there are conditions, of course, burdens to be imposed. He must, for instance, take my name. You cannot expect everything without some return. And I must go into all the circumstances of his life before I can accept him. He must be sound. I must know his heredity, how his parents and grandparents died, have the strictest inquiries made into his private morals—"

This modified my secret congratulations a little.

"And do I understand," said I, "that I—?"

"Yes," he said, almost fiercely. "You. You."

I answered never a word. My imagination was dancing wildly, my innate scepticism was useless to modify its transports. There was not a particle of gratitude in my mind—I did not know what to say nor how to say it. "But why me in particular?" I said at last.

He had chanced to hear of me from Professor Haslar, he said, as a typically sound and sane young man, and he wished, as far as possible, to leave his money where health and integrity were assured.

That was my first meeting with the little old man. He was mysterious about himself; he would not give his name yet, he said, and after I had answered some questions of his, he left me at the Blavitski portal. I noticed that he drew a handful of gold coins from his pocket when it came to paying for the lunch. His insistence upon bodily health was curious. In accordance with an arrangement we had made I applied that day for a life policy in the Loyal Insurance Company for a large sum, and I was exhaustively overhauled by the medical advisers of that company in the subsequent week. Even that did not satisfy him, and he insisted I must be re-examined by the great Doctor Henderson. It was Friday in Whitsun week before he came to a decision. He called me down, quite late in the evening—, nearly nine it was—, from cramming chemical equations for my Preliminary Scientific examination. He was standing in the passage under the feeble gas-lamp, and his face was a grotesque interplay of shadows. He seemed more bowed than when I had first seen him, and his cheeks had sunk in a little.

His voice shook with emotion. "Everything is satisfactory, Mr. Eden," he said. "Everything is quite, quite satisfactory. And this night of all nights, you must dine with me and celebrate your—accession." He was interrupted by a cough. "You won't have long to wait, either," he said, wiping his handkerchief across his lips, and gripping my hand with his long bony claw that was disengaged. "Certainly not very long to wait."

We went into the street and called a cab. I remember every incident of that drive vividly, the swift, easy motion, the vivid contrast of gas and oil and electric light, the crowds of people in the streets, the place in Regent Street to which we went, and the sumptuous dinner we were served with there. I was disconcerted at first by the well-dressed waiter's glances at my rough clothes, bothered by the stones of the olives, but as the champagne warmed my blood, my confidence revived. At first the old man talked of himself. He had already told me his name in the cab; he was Egbert Elvesham, the great philosopher, whose name I had known since I was a lad at school. It seemed incredible to me that this man, whose intelligence had so early dominated mine, this great abstraction, should suddenly realise itself as this decrepit, familiar figure. I dare say every young fellow who has suddenly fallen among celebrities has felt something of my disappointment. He told me now of the future that the feeble streams of his life would presently leave dry for me, houses, copyrights, investments; I had never suspected that philosophers were so rich. He watched me drink and eat with a touch of envy. "What a capacity for living you have!" he said; and then with a sigh, a sigh of relief I could have thought it, "It will not be long."

"Ay," said I, my head swimming now with champagne; "I have a future perhaps—of a fairly agreeable sort, thanks to you. I shall now have the honour of your name. But you have a past. Such a past as is worth all my future."

He shook his head and smiled, as I thought, with half-sad appreciation of my flattering admiration. "That future," he said, "would you in truth change it?" The waiter came with liqueurs. "You will not perhaps mind taking my name, taking my position, but would you indeed—willingly—take my years?"

"With your achievements," said I gallantly.

He smiled again. "Kummel—both," he said to the waiter, and turned his attention to a little paper packet he had taken from his pocket. "This hour," said he, "this after-dinner hour is the hour of small things. Here is a scrap of my unpublished wisdom." He opened the packet with his shaking yellow fingers, and showed a little pinkish powder on the paper. "This," said he—"well, you must guess what it is. But Kummel—put but a dash of this powder in it—is Himmel." His large greyish eyes watched mine with an inscrutable expression.

It was a bit of a shock to me to find this great teacher gave his mind to the flavour of liqueurs. However, I feigned an interest in his weakness, for I was drunk enough for such small sycophancy.

He parted the powder between the little glasses, and rising suddenly, with a strange unexpected dignity, held out his hand towards me. I imitated his action, and the glasses rang. "To a quick succession," said he, and raised his glass towards his lips.

"Not that," I said hastily. "Not that."

He paused with the liqueur at the level of his chin, and his eyes blazing into mine.

"To a long life," said I.

He hesitated. "To a long life," said he, with a sudden bark of laughter, and with eyes fixed on one another we tilted the little glasses. His eyes looked straight into mine, and as I drained the stuff off, I felt a curiously intense sensation. The first touch of it set my brain in a furious tumult; I seemed to feel an actual physical stirring in my skull, and a seething humming filled my ears. I did not notice the flavour in my mouth, the aroma that filled my throat; I saw only the grey intensity of his gaze that burnt into mine. The draught, the mental confusion, the noise and stirring in my head, seemed to last an interminable time. Curious vague impressions of half-forgotten things danced and vanished on the edge of my consciousness. At last he broke the spell. With a sudden explosive sigh he put down his glass.

"Well?" he said.

"It's glorious," said I, though I had not tasted the stuff.

My head was spinning. I sat down. My brain was chaos. Then my perception grew clear and minute as though I saw things in a concave mirror. His manner seemed to have changed into something nervous and hasty. He pulled out his watch and grimaced at it. "Eleven-seven! And to-night I must—Seven-twenty-five. Waterloo! I must go at once." He called for the bill, and struggled with his coat. Officious waiters came to our assistance. In another moment I was wishing him good-bye, over the apron of a cab, and still with an absurd feeling of minute distinctness, as though—how can I express it—? I not only saw but felt through an inverted opera-glass.

"That stuff," he said. He put his hand to his forehead. "I ought not to have given it to you. It will make your head split to-morrow. Wait a minute. Here." He handed me out a little flat thing like a seidlitz-powder. "Take that in water as you are going to bed. The other thing was a drug. Not till you're ready to go to bed, mind. It will clear your head. That's all. One more shake—Futurus!"

I gripped his shrivelled claw. "Good-bye," he said, and by the droop of his eyelids I judged he too was a little under the influence of that brain-twisting cordial.

He recollected something else with a start, felt in his breast-pocket, and produced another packet, this time a cylinder the size and shape of a shaving-stick. "Here," said he. "I'd almost forgotten. Don't open this until I come to-morrow—but take it now."

It was so heavy that I well-nigh dropped it. "All ri'!" said I, and he grinned at me through the cab window as the cabman flicked his horse into wakefulness. It was a white packet he had given me, with red seals at either end and along its edge. "If this isn't money," said I, "it's platinum or lead."

I stuck it with elaborate care into my pocket, and with a whirling brain walked home through the Regent Street loiterers and the dark back streets beyond Portland Road. I remember the sensations of that walk very vividly, strange as they were. I was still so far myself that I could notice my strange mental state, and wonder whether this stuff I had, had was opium—a drug beyond my experience. It is hard now to describe the peculiarity of my mental strangeness—mental doubling vaguely expresses it. As I was walking up Regent Street I found in my mind a queer persuasion that it was Waterloo Station, and had an odd impulse to get into the Polytechnic as a man might get into a train. I put a knuckle in my eye, and it was Regent Street. How can I express it? You see a skilful actor looking quietly at you, he pulls a grimace, and lo—! Another person. Is it too extravagant if I tell you that it seemed to me as if Regent Street had, for the moment, done that? Then, being persuaded it was Regent Street again, I was oddly muddled about some fantastic reminiscences that cropped up. "Thirty years ago," thought I, "it was here that I quarrelled with my brother." Then I burst out laughing, to the astonishment and encouragement of a group of night prowlers. Thirty years ago I did not exist, and never in my life had I boasted a brother. The stuff was surely liquid folly, for the poignant regret for that lost brother still clung to me. Along Portland Road the madness took another turn. I began to recall vanished shops, and to compare the street with what it used to be. Confused, troubled thinking is comprehensible enough after the drink I had taken, but what puzzled me were these curiously vivid phantasm memories that had crept into my mind, and not only the memories that had crept in, but also the memories that had slipped out. I stopped opposite Stevens', the natural history dealer's, and cudgelled my brains to think what he had to do with me. A 'bus went by, and sounded exactly like the rumbling of a train. I seemed to be dipping into some dark, remote pit for the recollection. "Of course," said I, at last, "he has promised me three frogs to-morrow. Odd I should have forgotten."

Do they still show children dissolving views? In those I remember one view would begin like a faint ghost, and grow and oust another. In just that way it seemed to me that a ghostly set of new sensations was struggling with those of my ordinary self.

I went on through Euston Road to Tottenham Court Road, puzzled, and a little frightened, and scarcely noticed the unusual way I was taking, for commonly I used to cut through the intervening network of back streets. I turned into University Street, to discover that I had forgotten my number. Only by a strong effort did I recall 11A, and even then it seemed to me that it was a thing some forgotten person had told me. I tried to steady my mind by recalling the incidents of the dinner, and for the life of me I could conjure up no picture of my host's face; I saw him only as a shadowy outline, as one might see oneself reflected in a window through which one was looking. In his place however, I had a curious exterior vision of myself, sitting at a table, flushed, bright-eyed, and talkative.

"I must take this other powder," said I. "This is getting impossible."

I tried the wrong side of the hall for my candle and the matches, and had a doubt of which landing my room might be on. "I'm drunk," I said, "that's certain," and blundered needlessly on the staircase to sustain the proposition.

At the first glance my room seemed unfamiliar. "What rot!" I said, and stared about me. I seemed to bring myself back by the effort, and the odd phantasmal quality passed into the concrete familiar. There was the old looking-glass, with my notes on the albumens stuck in the corner of the frame, my old everyday suit of clothes pitched about the floor. And yet it was not so real after all. I felt an idiotic persuasion trying to creep into my mind, as it were, that I was in a railway carriage in a train just stopping, that I was peering out of the window at some unknown station. I gripped the bed-rail firmly to reassure myself. "It's clairvoyance, perhaps," I said. "I must write to the Psychical Research Society."

I put the rouleau on my dressing-table, sat on my bed, and began to take off my boots. It was as if the picture of my present sensations was painted over some other picture that was trying to show through. "Curse it!" Said I; "My wits are going, or am I in two places at once?" Half-undressed, I tossed the powder into a glass and drank it off. It effervesced, and became a fluorescent amber colour. Before I was in bed my mind was already tranquillised. I felt the pillow at my cheek, and thereupon I must have fallen asleep.

I awoke abruptly out of a dream of strange beasts, and found myself lying on my back. Probably every one knows that dismal, emotional dream from which one escapes, awake indeed, but strangely cowed. There was a curious taste in my mouth, a tired feeling in my limbs, a sense of cutaneous discomfort. I lay with my head motionless on my pillow, expecting that my feeling of strangeness and terror would pass away, and that I should then doze off again to sleep. But instead of that, my uncanny sensations increased. At first I could perceive nothing wrong about me. There was a faint light in the room, so faint that it was the very next thing to darkness, and the furniture stood out in it as vague blots of absolute darkness. I stared with my eyes just over the bedclothes.

It came into my mind that some one had entered the room to rob me of my rouleau of money, but after lying for some moments, breathing regularly to simulate sleep, I realised this was mere fancy. Nevertheless, the uneasy assurance of something wrong kept fast hold of me. With an effort I raised my head from the pillow, and peered about me at the dark. What it was I could not conceive. I looked at the dim shapes around me, the greater and lesser darknesses that indicated curtains, table, fireplace, bookshelves, and so forth. Then I began to perceive something unfamiliar in the forms of the darkness. Had the bed turned round? Yonder should be the bookshelves, and something shrouded and pallid rose there, something that would not answer to the bookshelves, however I looked at it. It was far too big to be my shirt thrown on a chair.

Overcoming a childish terror, I threw back the bedclothes and thrust my leg out of bed. Instead of coming out of my truckle-bed upon the floor, I found my foot scarcely reached the edge of the mattress. I made another step, as it were, and sat up on the edge of the bed. By the side of my bed should be the candle, and the matches upon the broken chair. I put out my hand and touched—nothing. I waved my hand in the darkness, and it came against some heavy hanging, soft and thick in texture, which gave a rustling noise at my touch. I grasped this and pulled it; it appeared to be a curtain suspended over the head of my bed.

I was now thoroughly awake, and beginning to realise that I was in a strange room. I was puzzled. I tried to recall the overnight circumstances, and I found them now, curiously enough, vivid in my memory: the supper, my reception of the little packages, my wonder whether I was intoxicated, my slow undressing, the coolness to my flushed face of my pillow. I felt a sudden distrust. Was that last night, or the night before? At any rate, this room was strange to me, and I could not imagine how I had got into it. The dim, pallid outline was growing paler, and I perceived it was a window, with the dark shape of an oval toilet-glass against the weak intimation of the dawn that filtered through the blind. I stood up, and was surprised by a curious feeling of weakness and unsteadiness. With trembling hands outstretched, I walked slowly towards the window, getting, nevertheless, a bruise on the knee from a chair by the way. I fumbled round the glass, which was large, with handsome brass sconces, to find the blind-cord. I could not find any. By chance I took hold of the tassel, and with the click of a spring the blind ran up.

I found myself looking out upon a scene that was altogether strange to me. The night was overcast, and through the flocculent grey of the heaped clouds there filtered a faint half-light of dawn. Just at the edge of the sky the cloud-canopy had a blood-red rim. Below everything was dark and indistinct, dim hills in the distance, a vague mass of buildings running up into pinnacles, trees like spilt ink, and below the window a tracery of black bushes and pale grey paths. It was so unfamiliar that for the moment I thought myself still dreaming. I felt the toilet-table; it appeared to be made of some polished wood, and was rather elaborately furnished—there were little cut-glass bottles and a brush upon it. There was also a queer little object, horse-shoe-shaped it felt, with smooth, hard projections, lying in a saucer. I could find no matches nor candlestick.

I turned my eyes to the room again. Now the blind was up, faint spectres of its furnishing came out of the darkness. There was a huge curtained bed, and the fireplace at its foot had a large white mantel with something of the shimmer of marble.

I leant against the toilet-table, shut my eyes and opened them again, and tried to think. The whole thing was far too real for dreaming. I was inclined to imagine there was still some hiatus in my memory, as a consequence of my draught of that strange liqueur; that I had come into my inheritance perhaps, and suddenly lost my recollection of everything since my good fortune had been announced. Perhaps if I waited a little, things would be clearer to me again. Yet my dinner with old Elvesham was now singularly vivid and recent. The champagne, the observant waiters, the powder, and the liqueurs—I could have staked my soul it all happened a few hours ago.

And then occurred a thing so trivial and yet so terrible to me that I shiver now to think of that moment. I spoke aloud. I said, "How the devil did I get here...?" And the voice was not my own.

It was not my own, it was thin, the articulation was slurred, the resonance of my facial bones was different. Then to reassure myself, I ran one hand over the other, and felt loose folds of skin, the bony laxity of age. "Surely," I said, in that horrible voice that had somehow established itself in my throat, "surely this thing is a dream!" Almost as quickly as if I did it involuntarily, I thrust my fingers into my mouth. My teeth had gone. My finger-tips ran on the flaccid surface of an even row of shrivelled gums. I was sick with dismay and disgust.

I felt then a passionate desire to see myself, to realise at once in its full horror the ghastly change that had come upon me. I tottered to the mantel, and felt along it for matches. As I did so, a barking cough sprang up in my throat, and I clutched the thick flannel nightdress I found about me. There were no matches there, and I suddenly realised that my extremities were cold. Sniffing and coughing, whimpering a little, perhaps, I fumbled back to bed. "It is surely a dream," I whispered to myself as I clambered back, "surely a dream." It was a senile repetition. I pulled the bedclothes over my shoulders, over my ears, I thrust my withered hand under the pillow, and determined to compose myself to sleep. Of course it was a dream. In the morning the dream would be over, and I should wake up strong and vigorous again to my youth and studies. I shut my eyes, breathed regularly, and finding myself wakeful, began to count slowly through the powers of three.

But the thing I desired would not come. I could not get to sleep. And the persuasion of the inexorable reality of the change that had happened to me grew steadily. Presently I found myself with my eyes wide open, the powers of three forgotten, and my skinny fingers upon my shrivelled gums, I was indeed, suddenly and abruptly, an old man. I had in some unaccountable manner fallen through my life and come to old age, in some way I had been cheated of all the best of my life, of love, of struggle, of strength, and hope. I grovelled into the pillow and tried to persuade myself that such hallucination was possible. Imperceptibly, steadily, the dawn grew clearer.

At last, despairing of further sleep, I sat up in bed and looked about me. A chill twilight rendered the whole chamber visible. It was spacious and well-furnished, better furnished than any room I had ever slept in before. A candle and matches became dimly visible upon a little pedestal in a recess. I threw back the bedclothes, and shivering with the rawness of the early morning, albeit it was summer-time, I got out and lit the candle. Then trembling horribly, so that the extinguisher rattled on its spike, I tottered to the glass and saw—Elvesham's face! It was none the less horrible because I had already dimly feared as much. He had already seemed physically weak and pitiful to me, but seen now, dressed only in a coarse flannel nightdress, that fell apart and showed the stringy neck, seen now as my own body, I cannot describe its desolate decrepitude. The hollow cheeks, the straggling tail of dirty grey hair, the rheumy bleared eyes, the quivering, shrivelled lips, the lower displaying a gleam of the pink interior lining, and those horrible dark gums showing. You who are mind and body together, at your natural years, cannot imagine what this fiendish imprisonment meant to me. To be young and full of the desire and energy of youth, and to be caught, and presently to be crushed in this tottering ruin of a body...

But I wander from the course of my story. For some time I must have been stunned at this change that had come upon me. It was daylight when I did so far gather myself together as to think. In some inexplicable way I had been changed, though how short of magic, the thing had been done, I could not say. And as I thought, the diabolical ingenuity of Elvesham came home to me. It seemed plain to me that as I found myself in his, so he must be in possession of my body, of my strength, that is, and my future. But how to prove it? Then, as I thought, the thing became so incredible, even to me, that my mind reeled, and I had to pinch myself, to feel my toothless gums, to see myself in the glass, and touch the things about me, before I could steady myself to face the facts again. Was all life hallucination? Was I indeed Elvesham, and he me? Had I been dreaming of Eden overnight? Was there any Eden? But if I was Elvesham, I should remember where I was on the previous morning, the name of the town in which I lived, what happened before the dream began. I struggled with my thoughts. I recalled the queer doubleness of my memories overnight. But now my mind was clear. Not the ghost of any memories but those proper to Eden could I raise.

"This way lies insanity!" I cried in my piping voice. I staggered to my feet, dragged my feeble, heavy limbs to the washhand-stand, and plunged my grey head into a basin of cold water. Then, towelling myself, I tried again. It was no good. I felt beyond all question that I was indeed Eden, not Elvesham. But Eden in Elvesham's body!

Had I been a man of any other age, I might have given myself up to my fate as one enchanted. But in these sceptical days miracles do not pass current. Here was some trick of psychology. What a drug and a steady stare could do, a drug and a steady stare, or some similar treatment, could surely undo. Men have lost their memories before. But to exchange memories as one does umbrellas! I laughed. Alas! Not a healthy laugh, but a wheezing, senile titter. I could have fancied old Elvesham laughing at my plight, and a gust of petulant anger, unusual to me, swept across my feelings. I began dressing eagerly in the clothes I found lying about on the floor, and only realised when I was dressed that it was an evening suit I had assumed. I opened the wardrobe and found some more ordinary clothes, a pair of plaid trousers, and an old-fashioned dressing-gown. I put a venerable smoking-cap on my venerable head, and coughing a little from my exertions, tottered out upon the landing.

It was then, perhaps a quarter to six, and the blinds were closely drawn and the house quite silent. The landing was a spacious one, a broad, richly-carpeted staircase went down into the darkness of the hall below, and before me a door ajar showed me a writing-desk, a revolving bookcase, the back of a study chair, and a fine array of bound books, shelf upon shelf.

"My study," I mumbled, and walked across the landing. Then at the sound of my voice a thought struck me, and I went back to the bedroom and put in the set of false teeth. They slipped in with the ease of old, habit. "That's better," said I, gnashing them, and so returned to the study.

The drawers of the writing-desk were locked. Its revolving top was also locked. I could see no indications of the keys, and there were none in the pockets of my trousers. I shuffled back at once to the bedroom, and went through the dress suit, and afterwards the pockets of all the garments I could find. I was very eager, and one might have imagined that burglars had been at work, to see my room when I had done. Not only were there no keys to be found, but not a coin, nor a scrap of paper—save only the receipted bill of the overnight dinner.

A curious weariness asserted itself. I sat down and stared at the garments flung here and there, their pockets turned inside out. My first frenzy had already flickered out. Every moment I was beginning to realise the immense intelligence of the plans of my enemy, to see more and more clearly the hopelessness of my position. With an effort I rose and hurried hobbling into the study again. On the staircase was a housemaid pulling up the blinds. She stared, I think, at the expression of my face. I shut the door of the study behind me, and seizing a poker, began an attack upon the desk. That is how they found me. The cover of the desk was split, the lock smashed, the letters torn out of the pigeon-holes, and tossed about the room. In my senile rage I had flung about the pens and other such light stationery, and overturned the ink. Moreover, a large vase upon the mantel had got broken—I do not know how. I could find no cheque-book, no money, no indications of the slightest use for the recovery of my body. I was battering madly at the drawers, when the butler, backed by two women-servants, intruded upon me.

That simply is the story of my change. No one will believe my frantic assertions. I am treated as one demented, and even at this moment I am under restraint. But I am sane, absolutely sane, and to prove it I have sat down to write this story minutely as the things happened to me. I appeal to the reader, whether there is any trace of insanity in the style or method, of the story he has been reading. I am a young man locked away in an old man's body. But the clear fact is incredible to everyone. Naturally I appear demented to those who will not believe this, naturally I do not know the names of my secretaries, of the doctors who come to see me, of my servants and neighbours, of this town (wherever it is) where I find myself. Naturally I lose myself in my own house, and suffer inconveniences of every sort. Naturally I ask the oddest questions. Naturally I weep and cry out, and have paroxysms of despair. I have no money and no cheque-book. The bank will not recognise my signature, for I suppose that, allowing for the feeble muscles I now have, my handwriting is still Eden's. These people about me will not let me go to the bank personally. It seems, indeed, that there is no bank in this town, and that I have an account in some part of London. It seems that Elvesham kept the name of his solicitor secret from all his household—I can ascertain nothing. Elvesham was, of course, a profound student of mental science, and all my declarations of the facts of the case merely confirm the theory that my insanity is the outcome of overmuch brooding upon psychology. Dreams of the personal identity indeed! Two days ago I was a healthy youngster, with all life before me; now I am a furious old man, unkempt, and desperate, and miserable, prowling about a great, luxurious, strange house, watched, feared, and avoided as a lunatic by everyone about me. And in London, there is Elvesham beginning life again in a vigorous body, and with all the accumulated knowledge and wisdom of threescore and ten. He has stolen my life.

What has happened I do not clearly know. In the study are volumes of manuscript notes referring chiefly to the psychology of memory, and parts of what may be either calculations or ciphers in symbols absolutely strange to me. In some passages there are indications that he was also occupied with the philosophy of mathematics. I take it he has transferred the whole of his memories, the accumulation that makes up his personality, from this old withered brain of his to mine, and similarly, that he has transferred mine to his discarded tenement. Practically, that is, he has changed bodies. But how such a change may be possible is without the range of my philosophy. I have been a materialist for all my thinking life, but here suddenly, is a clear case of man's detachability from matter.

One desperate experiment I am about to try. I sit writing here before putting the matter to issue. This morning, with the help of a table-knife that I had secreted at breakfast, I succeeded in breaking open a fairly obvious secret drawer in this wrecked writing-desk. I discovered nothing save a little green glass phial containing a white powder. Round the neck of the phial was a label, and thereon was written this one word, "Release." This may be—is most probably, poison. I can understand Elvesham placing poison in my way, and I should be sure that it was his intention so to get rid of the only living witness against him, were it not for this careful concealment. The man has practically solved the problem of immortality. Save for the spite of chance, he will live in my body until it has aged, and then, again throwing that aside, he will assume some other victim's youth and strength. When one remembers his heartlessness, it is terrible to think of the ever-growing experience that...How long has he been leaping from body to body...? But I tire of writing. The powder appears to be soluble in water. The taste is not unpleasant.

There the narrative found upon Mr. Elvesham's desk ends. His dead body lay between the desk and the chair. The latter had been pushed back, probably by his last convulsions. The story was written in pencil and in a crazy hand, quite unlike his usual minute characters. There remain only two curious facts to record. Indisputably there was some connection between Eden and Elvesham, since the whole of Elvesham's property was bequeathed to the young man. But he never inherited. When Elvesham committed suicide, Eden was, strangely enough, already dead. Twenty-four hours before, he had been knocked down by a cab and killed instantly, at the crowded crossing at the intersection of Gower Street and Euston Road. So that the only human being who could have thrown light upon this fantastic narrative is beyond the reach of questions.

27

Under the Knife

"What if I die under it?" The thought recurred again and again, as I walked home from Haddon's. It was a purely personal question. I was spared the deep anxieties of a married man, and I knew there were few of my intimate friends but would find my death troublesome chiefly on account of their duty of regret. I was surprised indeed, and perhaps a little humiliated, as I turned the matter over, to think how few could possibly exceed the conventional requirement. Things came before me stripped of glamour, in a clear dry light, during that walk from Haddon's house over Primrose Hill. There were the friends of my youth: I perceived now that our affection was a tradition, which we foregathered rather laboriously to maintain. There were the rivals and helpers of my later career: I suppose I had been cold-blooded or undemonstrative—one perhaps implies the other. It may be that even the capacity for friendship is a question of physique. There had been a time in my own life when I had grieved bitterly enough at the loss of a friend; but as I walked home that afternoon the emotional side of my imagination was dormant. I could not pity myself, nor feel sorry for my friends, nor conceive of them as grieving for me.

I was interested in this deadness of my emotional nature—no doubt a concomitant of my stagnating physiology; and my thoughts wandered off along the line it suggested. Once before, in my hot youth, I had suffered a sudden loss of blood, and had been within an ace of death. I remembered now that my affections as well as my passions had drained out of me, leaving scarce anything but a tranquil resignation, a dreg of self-pity. It had been weeks before the old ambitions and tendernesses, and all the complex moral interplay of a man had reasserted themselves. It occurred to me that the real meaning of this numbness might be a gradual slipping away from the pleasure-pain guidance of the animal man. It has been proven, I take it, as thoroughly as anything can be proven in this world, that the higher emotions, the moral feelings, even the subtle unselfishness of love, are evolved from the elemental desires and fears of the simple animal: they are the harness in which man's mental freedom goes. And it may be that as death overshadows us, as our possibility of acting diminishes, this complex growth of balanced impulse, propensity and aversion, whose interplay inspires our acts, goes with it. Leaving what?

I was suddenly brought back to reality by an imminent collision with the butcher-boy's tray. I found that I was crossing the bridge over the Regent's Park Canal, which runs parallel with that in the Zoological Gardens. The boy in blue had been looking over his shoulder at a black barge advancing slowly, towed by a gaunt white horse. In the Gardens a nurse was leading three happy little children over the bridge. The trees were bright green; the spring hopefulness was still unstained by the dusts of summer; the sky in the water was bright and clear, but broken by long waves, by quivering bands of black, as the barge drove through. The breeze was stirring; but it did not stir me as the spring breeze used to do.

Was this dullness of feeling in itself an anticipation? It was curious that I could reason and follow out a network of suggestion as clearly as ever: so at least, it seemed to me. It was calmness rather than dullness that was coming upon me. Was there any ground for the relief in the presentiment of death? Did a man near to death begin instinctively to withdraw himself from the meshes of matter and sense, even before the cold hand was laid upon his? I felt strangely isolated—isolated without regret—from the life and existence about me. The children playing in the sun and gathering strength and experience for the business of life, the park-keeper gossiping with a nursemaid, the nursing mother, the young couple intent upon each other as they passed me, the trees by the wayside spreading new pleading leaves to the sunlight, the stir in their branches—I had been part of it all, but I had nearly done with it now.

Some way down the Broad Walk I perceived that I was tired, and that my feet were heavy. It was hot that afternoon, and I turned aside and sat down on one of the green chairs that line the way. In a minute I had dozed into a dream, and the tide of my thoughts washed up a vision of the resurrection. I was still sitting in the chair, but I thought myself actually dead, withered, tattered, dried, one eye (I saw) pecked out by birds. "Awake!" cried a voice; and incontinently the dust of the path and the mould under the grass became insurgent. I had never before thought of Regent's Park as a cemetery, but now, through the trees, stretching as far as eye could see, I beheld a flat plain of writhing graves and heeling tombstones. There seemed to be some trouble: the rising dead appeared to stifle as they struggled upward, they bled in their struggles, the red flesh was torn away from the white bones. "Awake!" cried a voice; but I determined I would not rise to such horrors. "Awake!" They would not let me alone. "Wake up!" said an angry voice. A cockney angel! The man who sells the tickets was shaking me, demanding my penny.

I paid my penny, pocketed my ticket, yawned, stretched my legs, and feeling now rather less torpid, got up and walked on towards Langham Place. I speedily lost myself again in a shifting maze of thoughts about death. Going across Marylebone Road into that crescent at the end of Langham Place, I had the narrowest escape from the shaft of a cab, and went on my way with a palpitating heart and a bruised shoulder. It struck me that it would have been curious if my meditations on my death on the morrow had led to my death that day.

But I will not weary you with more of my experiences that day and the next. I knew more and more certainly that I should die under the operation; at times I think I was inclined to pose to myself. At home I found everything prepared; my room cleared of needless objects and hung with white sheets; a nurse installed and already at loggerheads with my housekeeper. They wanted me to go to bed early, and after a little resistance I obeyed.

In the morning I was very indolent, and though I read my newspapers and the letters that came by the first post, I did not find them very interesting. There was a friendly note from Addison, my old school friend, calling my attention to two discrepancies and a printer's error in my new book, with one from Langridge venting some vexation over Minton. The rest were business communications. I breakfasted in bed. The glow of pain at my side seemed more massive. I knew it was pain, and yet, if you can understand, I did not find it very painful. I had been awake and hot and thirsty in the night, but in the morning bed felt comfortable. In the night-time I had lain thinking of things that were past; in the morning I dozed over the question of immortality. Haddon came, punctual to the minute, with a neat black bag; and Mowbray soon followed. Their arrival stirred me up a little. I began to take a more personal interest in the proceedings. Haddon moved the little octagonal table close to the bedside, and with his broad back to me, began taking things out of his bag. I heard the light click of steel upon steel. My imagination, I found, was not altogether stagnant. "Will you hurt me much?" I said in an off-hand tone.

"Not a bit," Haddon answered over his shoulder. "We shall chloroform you. Your heart's as sound as a bell." And as he spoke, I had a whiff of the pungent sweetness of the anaesthetic.

They stretched me out, with a convenient exposure of my side, and, almost before I realised what was happening, the chloroform was being administered. It stings the nostrils, and there is a suffocating sensation at first. I knew I should die—that this was the end of consciousness for me. And suddenly I felt that I was not prepared for death: I had a vague sense of a duty overlooked—I knew not what. What was it I had not done? I could think of nothing more to do, nothing desirable left in life; and yet I had the strangest disinclination to death. And the physical sensation was painfully oppressive. Of course the doctors did not know they were going to kill me. Possibly I struggled. Then I fell motionless, and a great silence, a monstrous silence, and an impenetrable blackness came upon me.

There must have been an interval of absolute unconsciousness, seconds or minutes. Then with a chilly, unemotional clearness, I perceived that I was not yet dead. I was still in my body; but all the multitudinous sensations that come sweeping from it to make up the background of consciousness had gone, leaving me free of it all. No, not free of it all; for as yet something still held me to the poor stark flesh upon the bed—held me, yet not so closely that I did not feel myself external to it, independent of it, straining away from it. I do not think I saw, I do not think I heard; but I perceived all that was going on, and it was as if I both heard and saw. Haddon was bending over me, Mowbray behind me; the scalpel—it was a large scalpel—was cutting my flesh at the side under the flying ribs. It was interesting to see myself cut like cheese, without a pang, without even a qualm. The interest was much of a quality with that one might feel in a game of chess between strangers. Haddon's face was firm and his hand steady; but I was surprised to perceive (how I know not) that he was feeling the gravest doubt as to his own wisdom in the conduct of the operation.

Mowbray's thoughts too, I could see. He was thinking that Haddon's manner showed too much of the specialist. New suggestions came up like bubbles through a stream of frothing meditation, and burst one after another in the little bright spot of his consciousness. He could not help noticing and admiring Haddon's swift dexterity, in spite of his envious quality and his disposition to detract. I saw my liver exposed. I was puzzled at my own condition. I did not feel that I was dead, but I was different in some way from my living self. The grey depression, that had weighed on me for a year or more and coloured all my thoughts, was gone. I perceived and thought without any emotional tint at all. I wondered if everyone perceived things in this way under chloroform, and forgot it again when he came out of it. It would be inconvenient to look into some heads, and not forget.

Although I did not think that I was dead, I still perceived quite clearly that I was soon to die. This brought me back to the consideration of Haddon's proceedings. I looked into his mind, and saw that he was afraid of cutting a branch of the portal vein. My attention was distracted from details by the curious changes going on in his mind. His consciousness was like the quivering little spot of light which is thrown by the mirror of a galvanometer. His thoughts ran under it like a stream, some through the focus bright and distinct, some shadowy in the half-light of the edge. Just now the little glow was steady; but the least movement on Mowbray's part, the slightest sound from outside, even a faint difference in the slow movement of the living flesh he was cutting, set the light-spot shivering and spinning. A new sense-impression came rushing up through the flow of thoughts; and lo! The light-spot jerked away towards it, swifter than a frightened fish. It was wonderful to think that upon that unstable, fitful thing depended all the complex motions of the man; that for the next five minutes, therefore, my life hung upon its movements. And he was growing more and more nervous in his work. It was as if a little picture of a cut vein grew brighter, and struggled to oust from his brain another picture of a cut falling short of the mark. He was afraid: his dread of cutting too little was battling with his dread of cutting too far.

Then, suddenly, like an escape of water from under a lock-gate, a great uprush of horrible realisation set all his thoughts swirling, and simultaneously I perceived that the vein was cut. He started back with a hoarse exclamation, and I saw the brown-purple blood gather in a swift bead, and run trickling. He was horrified. He pitched the red-stained scalpel on to the octagonal table; and instantly both doctors flung themselves upon me, making hasty and ill-conceived efforts to remedy the disaster. "Ice!" said Mowbray, gasping. But I knew that I was killed, though my body still clung to me.

I will not describe their belated endeavours to save me, though I perceived every detail. My perceptions were sharper and swifter than they had ever been in life; my thoughts rushed through my mind with incredible swiftness, but with perfect definition. I can only compare their crowded clarity to the effects of a reasonable dose of opium. In a moment it would all be over, and I should be free. I knew I was immortal, but what would happen I did not know. Should I drift off presently, like a puff of smoke from a gun, in some kind of half-material body, an attenuated version of my material self? Should I find myself suddenly among the innumerable hosts of the dead, and know the world about me for the phantasmagoria it had always seemed? Should I drift to some spiritualistic seance, and there make foolish, incomprehensible attempts to affect a purblind medium? It was a state of unemotional curiosity, of colourless expectation. And then I realised a growing stress upon me, a feeling as though some huge human magnet was drawing me upward out of my body. The stress grew and grew. I seemed an atom for which monstrous forces were fighting. For one brief, terrible moment sensation came back to me. That feeling of falling headlong which comes in nightmares, that feeling a thousand times intensified, that and a black horror swept across my thoughts in a torrent. Then the two doctors, the naked body with its cut side, the little room, swept away from under me and vanished, as a speck of foam vanishes down an eddy.

I was in mid-air. Far below was the West End of London, receding rapidly—, for I seemed to be flying swiftly upward—, and as it receded, passing westward like a panorama. I could see, through the faint haze of smoke, the innumerable roofs chimney-set, the narrow roadways, stippled with people and conveyances, the little specks of squares, and the church steeples like thorns sticking out of the fabric. But it spun away as the earth rotated on its axis, and in a few seconds (as it seemed) I was over the scattered clumps of town about Ealing, the little Thames a thread of blue to the south, and the Chiltern Hills and the North Downs coming up like the rim of a basin, far away and faint with haze. Up I rushed. And at first I had not the faintest conception what this headlong rush upward could mean.

Every moment the circle of scenery beneath me grew wider and wider, and the details of town and field, of hill and valley, got more and more hazy and pale and indistinct, a luminous grey was mingled more and more with the blue of the hills and the green of the open meadows; and a little patch of cloud, low and far to the west, shone ever more dazzlingly white. Above, as the veil of atmosphere between myself and outer space grew thinner, the sky, which had been a fair springtime blue at first, grew deeper and richer in colour, passing steadily through the intervening shades, until presently it was as dark as the blue sky of midnight, and presently as black as the blackness of a frosty starlight, and at last as black as no blackness I had ever beheld. And first one star, and then many, and at last an innumerable host broke out upon the sky: more stars than anyone has ever seen from the face of the earth. For the blueness of the sky in the light of the sun and stars sifted and spread abroad blindingly: there is diffused light even in the darkest skies of winter, and we do not see the stars by day only because of the dazzling irradiation of the sun. But now I saw things—I know not how; assuredly with no mortal eyes—and that defect of bedazzlement blinded me no longer. The sun was incredibly strange and wonderful. The body of it was a disc of blinding white light: not yellowish, as it seems to those who live upon the earth, but livid white, all streaked with scarlet streaks and rimmed about with a fringe of writhing tongues of red fire. And shooting halfway across the heavens from either side of it and brighter than the Milky Way, were two pinions of silver-white, making it look more like those winged globes I have seen in Egyptian sculpture than anything else I can remember upon earth. These I knew for the solar corona, though I had never seen anything of it but a picture during the days of my earthly life.

When my attention came back to the earth again, I saw that it had fallen very far away from me. Field and town were long since indistinguishable, and all the varied hues of the country were merging into a uniform bright grey, broken only by the brilliant white of the clouds that lay scattered in flocculent masses over Ireland and the west of England. For now I could see the outlines of the north of France and Ireland, and all this Island of Britain, save where Scotland passed over the horizon to the north, or where the coast was blurred or obliterated by cloud. The sea was a dull grey, and darker than the land; and the whole panorama was rotating slowly towards the east.

All this had happened so swiftly that until I was some thousand miles or so from the earth I had no thought for myself. But now I perceived I had neither hands nor feet, neither parts nor organs, and that I felt neither alarm nor pain. All about me I perceived that the vacancy (for I had already left the air behind) was cold beyond the imagination of man; but it troubled me not. The sun's rays shot through the void, powerless to light or heat until they should strike on matter in their course. I saw things with a serene self-forgetfulness, even as if I were God. And down below there, rushing away from me—, countless miles in a second—, where a little dark spot on the grey marked the position of London, two doctors were struggling to restore life to the poor hacked and outworn shell I had abandoned. I felt then such release, such serenity as I can compare to no mortal delight I have ever known.

It was only after I had perceived all these things that the meaning of that headlong rush of the earth grew into comprehension. Yet it was so simple, so obvious, that I was amazed at my never anticipating the thing that was happening to me. I had suddenly been cut adrift from matter: all that was material of me was there upon earth, whirling away through space, held to the earth by gravitation, partaking of the earth's inertia, moving in its wreath of epicycles round the sun, and with the sun and the planets on their vast march through space. But the immaterial has no inertia, feels nothing of the pull of matter for matter: where it parts from its garment of flesh, there it remains (so far as space concerns it any longer) immovable in space. I was not leaving the earth: the earth was leaving me, and not only the earth but the whole solar system was streaming past. And about me in space, invisible to me, scattered in the wake of the earth upon its journey, there must be an innumerable multitude of souls, stripped like myself of the material, stripped like myself of the passions of the individual and the generous emotions of the gregarious brute, naked intelligences, things of newborn wonder and thought, marvelling at the strange release that had suddenly come on them!

As I receded faster and faster from the strange white sun in the black heavens, and from the broad and shining earth upon which my being had begun, I seemed to grow in some incredible manner vast: vast as regards this world I had left, vast as regards the moments and periods of a human life. Very soon I saw the full circle of the earth, slightly gibbous, like the moon when she nears her full, but very large; and the silvery shape of America was now in the noonday blaze wherein (as it seemed) little England had been basking but a few minutes ago. At first the earth was large, and shone in the heavens, filling a great part of them; but every moment she grew smaller and more distant. As she shrank, the broad moon in its third quarter crept into view over the rim of her disc. I looked for the constellations. Only that part of Aries directly behind the sun and the Lion, which the earth covered, were hidden. I recognised the tortuous, tattered band of the Milky Way with Vega very bright between sun and earth; and Sirius and Orion shone splendid against the unfathomable blackness in the opposite quarter of the heavens. The Pole Star was overhead, and the Great Bear hung over the circle of the earth. And away beneath and beyond the shining corona of the sun were strange groupings of stars I had never seen in my life—notably a dagger-shaped group that I knew for the Southern Cross. All these were no larger than when they had shone on earth, but the little stars that one scarce sees shone now against the setting of black vacancy as brightly as the first-magnitudes had done, while the larger worlds were points of indescribable glory and colour. Aldebaran was a spot of blood-red fire, and Sirius condensed to one point the light of innumerable sapphires. And they shone steadily: they did not scintillate, they were calmly glorious. My impressions had an adamantine hardness and brightness: there was no blurring softness, no atmosphere, nothing but infinite darkness set with the myriads of these acute and brilliant points and specks of light. Presently, when I looked again, the little earth seemed no bigger than the sun, and it dwindled and turned as I looked, until in a second's space (as it seemed to me), it was halved; and so it went on swiftly dwindling. Far away in the opposite direction, a little pinkish pin's head of light, shining steadily, was the planet Mars. I swam motionless in vacancy, and without a trace of terror or astonishment, watched the speck of cosmic dust, we call the world fall away from me.

Presently it dawned upon me that my sense of duration had changed; that my mind was moving not faster but infinitely slower, that between each separate impression there was a period of many days. The moon spun once round the earth as I noted this; and I perceived clearly the motion of Mars in his orbit. Moreover, it appeared as if the time between thought and thought grew steadily greater, until at last a thousand years was but a moment in my perception.

At first the constellations had shone motionless against the black background of infinite space; but presently it seemed as though the group of stars about Hercules and the Scorpion was contracting, while Orion and Aldebaran and their neighbours were scattering apart. Flashing suddenly out of the darkness there came a flying multitude of particles of rock, glittering like dust-specks in a sunbeam, and encompassed in a faintly luminous cloud. They swirled all about me, and vanished again in a twinkling far behind. And then I saw that a bright spot of light, that shone a little to one side of my path, was growing very rapidly larger, and perceived that it was the planet Saturn rushing towards me. Larger and larger it grew, swallowing up the heavens behind it, and hiding every moment a fresh multitude of stars. I perceived its flattened, whirling body, its disc-like belt, and seven of its little satellites. It grew and grew, till it towered enormous; and then I plunged amid a streaming multitude of clashing stones and dancing dust-particles and gas-eddies, and saw for a moment the mighty triple belt like three concentric arches of moonlight above me, its shadow black on the boiling tumult below. These things happened in one-tenth of the time it takes to tell them. The planet went by like a flash of lightning; for a few seconds it blotted out the sun, and there and then became a mere black, dwindling, winged patch against the light. The earth, the mother mote of my being, I could no longer see.

So with a stately swiftness, in the profoundest silence, the solar system fell from me as it had been a garment, until the sun was a mere star amid the multitude of stars, with its eddy of planet-specks lost in the confused glittering of the remoter light. I was no longer a denizen of the solar system: I had come to the outer Universe, I seemed to grasp and comprehend the whole world of matter. Ever more swiftly the stars closed in about the spot where Antares and Vega had vanished in a phosphorescent haze, until that part of the sky had the semblance of a whirling mass of nebulae, and ever before me yawned vaster gaps of vacant blackness, and the stars shone fewer and fewer. It seemed as if I moved towards a point between Orion's belt and sword; and the void about that region opened vaster and vaster every second, an incredible gulf of nothingness into which I was falling. Faster and ever faster the universe rushed by, a hurry of whirling motes at last, speeding silently into the void. Stars glowing brighter and brighter, with their circling planets catching the light in a ghostly fashion as I neared them, shone out and vanished again into inexistence; faint comets, clusters of meteorites, winking specks of matter, eddying light-points, whizzed past, some perhaps a hundred millions of miles or so from me at most, few nearer, travelling with unimaginable rapidity, shooting constellations, momentary darts of fire, through that black, enormous night. More than anything else it was like a dusty draught, sunbeam-lit. Broader and wider and deeper grew the starless space, the vacant Beyond, into which I was being drawn. At last a quarter of the heavens was black and blank, and the whole headlong rush of stellar universe closed in behind me like a veil of light that is gathered together. It drove away from me like a monstrous jack-o'-lantern driven by the wind. I had come out into the wilderness of space. Ever the vacant blackness grew broader, until the hosts of the stars seemed only like a swarm of fiery specks hurrying away from me, inconceivably remote, and the darkness, the nothingness and emptiness, was about me on every side. Soon the little universe of matter, the cage of points in which I had begun to be, was dwindling, now to a whirling disc of luminous glittering, and now to one minute disc of hazy light. In a little while it would shrink to a point, and at last would vanish altogether.

Suddenly feeling came back to me—feeling in the shape of overwhelming terror; such a dread of those dark vastitudes as no words can describe, a passionate resurgence of sympathy and social desire. Were there other souls, invisible to me as I to them, about me in the blackness? Or was I indeed, even as I felt, alone?

Had I passed out of being into something that was neither being nor not-being? The covering of the body, the covering of matter, had been torn from me, and the hallucinations of companionship and security. Everything was black and silent. I had ceased to be. I was nothing. There was nothing, save only that infinitesimal dot of light that dwindled in the gulf. I strained myself to hear and see, and for a while there was naught but infinite silence, intolerable darkness, horror, and despair.

Then I saw that about the spot of light into which the whole world of matter had shrunk there was a faint glow. And in a band on either side of that the darkness was not absolute. I watched it for ages, as it seemed to me, and through the long waiting the haze grew imperceptibly more distinct. And then about the band appeared an irregular cloud of the faintest, palest brown. I felt a passionate impatience; but the things grew brighter so slowly that they scarce seemed to change. What was unfolding itself? What was this strange reddish dawn in the interminable night of space?

The cloud's shape was grotesque. It seemed to be looped along its lower side into four projecting masses, and above, it ended in a straight line. What phantom was it? I felt assured I had seen that figure before; but I could not think what, nor where, nor when it was. Then the realisation rushed upon me. It was a clenched Hand. I was alone in space, alone with this huge, shadowy Hand, upon which the whole Universe of Matter lay like an unconsidered speck of dust. It seemed as though I watched it through vast periods of time. On the forefinger glittered a ring; and the universe from which I had come was but a spot of light upon the ring's curvature. And the thing that the hand gripped had the likeness of a black rod. Through a long eternity I watched this Hand, with the ring and the rod, marvelling and fearing and waiting helplessly on what might follow. It seemed as though nothing could follow: that I should watch for ever, seeing only the Hand and the thing it held, and understanding nothing of its import. Was the whole universe but a refracting speck upon some greater Being? Were our worlds but the atoms of another universe, and those again of another, and so on through an endless progression? And what was I? Was I indeed immaterial? A vague persuasion of a body gathering about me came into my suspense. The abysmal darkness about the Hand filled with impalpable suggestions, with uncertain, fluctuating shapes.

Came a sound, like the sound of a tolling bell: faint, as if infinitely far; muffled, as though heard through thick swathings of darkness: a deep, vibrating resonance, with vast gulfs of silence between each stroke. And the Hand appeared to tighten on the rod. And I saw far above the Hand, towards the apex of the darkness, a circle of dim phosphorescence, a ghostly sphere whence these sounds came throbbing; and at the last stroke the Hand vanished, for the hour had come, and I heard a noise of many waters. But the black rod remained as a great band across the sky. And then a voice, which seemed to run to the uttermost parts of space, spoke, saying, "There will be no more pain."

At that an almost intolerable gladness and radiance rushed in upon me, and I saw the circle shining white and bright, and the rod black and shining, and many things else distinct and clear. And the circle was the face of the clock, and the rod the rail of my bed. Haddon was standing at the foot, against the rail, with a small pair of scissors on his fingers; and the hands of my clock on the mantel over his shoulder were clasped together over the hour of twelve. Mowbray was washing something in a basin at the octagonal table, and at my side I felt a subdued feeling that could scarce be spoken of as pain.

The operation had not killed me. And I perceived, suddenly, that the dull melancholy of half a year was lifted from my mind.

28

A Story of the Stone Age

1. Ugh-lomi and Uya

This story is of a time beyond the memory of man, before the beginning of history, a time when one might have walked dryshod from France (as we call it now) to England, and when a broad and sluggish Thames flowed through its marshes to meet its father Rhine, flowing through a wide and level country that is under water in these latter days, and which we know by the name of the North Sea. In that remote age the valley which runs along the foot of the Downs did not exist, and the south of Surrey was a range of hills, fir-clad on the middle slopes, and snow-capped the better part of the year. The cores its summits still remain as Leith Hill, and Pitch Hill, and Hindhead. On the lower slopes of the range below the grassy spaces where the wild horses grazed were forests of yew and sweet-chestnut and elm, and the thickets and dark places hid the grizzly bear and the hyaena, and the grey apes clambered through the branches. And still lower amidst the woodland and marsh and open grass along the Wey did this little drama play itself out to the end that I have to tell. Fifty thousand years ago it was, fifty thousand years—if the estimates of the geologists are correct.

And in those days the spring-time was as joyful as it is now, and sent the blood coursing in just the same fashion. The afternoon sky was blue with piled white clouds sailing through it, and the south-west wind came like a soft caress. The new-come swallows drove to and fro. The reaches of the river were spangled with white ranunculus, the marshy places were starred with lady's-smock and lit with marshmallow wherever the regiments of the sedges lowered their swords, and the northward moving hippopotami, shiny black monsters, sporting clumsily, came floundering and blundering through it all, rejoicing dimly and possessed with one clear idea, to splash the river muddy.

Up the river and well in sight of the hippopotami, a number of little buff-coloured animals dabbled in the water. There was no fear, no rivalry, and no enmity between them and the hippopotami. As the great bulks came crashing through the reeds and smashed the mirror of the water into silvery splashes, these little creatures shouted and gesticulated with glee. It was the surest sign of high spring. "Boloo!" they cried. "Baayah. Boloo!" They were the children of the men folk, the smoke of whose encampment rose from the knoll at the river's bend. Wild-eyed youngsters they were, with matted hair and little broad-nosed impish faces, covered (as some children are covered even nowadays) with a delicate down of hair. They were narrow in the loins and long in the arms. And their ears had no lobes, and had little pointed tips, a thing that still, in rare instances, survives. Stark-naked vivid little gipsies, as active as monkeys and as full of chatter, though a little wanting in words.

Their elders were hidden from the wallowing hippopotami by the crest of the knoll. The human squatting-place was a trampled area among the dead brown fronds of Royal Fern, through which the crosiers of this year's growth were unrolling to tie light and warmth. The fire was a smouldering heap of char, light grey and black, replenished by the old women from time to time with brown leaves. Most of the men were asleep—they slept sitting with their foreheads on their knees. They had killed that morning a good quarry, enough for all, a deer that had been wounded in a rutting fight; so that there had been no quarrelling among them, and some of the women were still gnawing the bones that lay scattered about. Others were making a heap of leaves and sticks to feed Brother Fire when the darkness came again, that he might grow strong and tall therewith, and guard them against the beasts. And two were piling flints that they brought, an armful at a time, from the bend of the river where the children were at play.

None of these buff-skinned savages were clothed, but some wore about their hips rude girdles of adder-skin or crackling undressed hide, from which depended little bags, not made, but torn from the paws of beasts, and carrying the rudely-dressed flints that were men's chief weapons and tools. And one woman, the mate of Uya the Cunning Man, wore a wonderful necklace of perforated fossils—that others had worn before her. Beside some of the sleeping men lay the big antlers of the elk, with the tines chipped to sharp edges, and long sticks, hacked at the ends with flints into sharp points. There was little else save these things and the smouldering fire to mark these human beings off from the wild animals that ranged the country. But Uya the Cunning did not sleep, but sat with a bone in his hand and scraped busily thereon with a flint, a thing no animal would do. He was the oldest man in the tribe, beetle-browed, prognathous, lank-armed; he had a beard and his cheeks were hairy, and his chest and arms were black with thick hair. And by virtue both of his strength and cunning he was master of the tribe, and his share was always the most and the best.

Eudena had hidden herself among the alders, because she was afraid of Uya. She was still a girl, and her eyes were bright and her smile pleasant to see. He had given her a piece of the liver, a man's piece, and a wonderful treat for a girl to get; but as she took it the other woman with the necklace had looked at her, an evil glance, and Ugh-lomi had made a noise in his throat. At that, Uya had looked at him long and steadfastly, and Ugh-lomi's face had fallen. And then Uya had looked at her. She was frightened and she had stolen away, while the feeding was still going on, and Uya was busy with the marrow of a bone. Afterwards he had wandered about as if looking for her. And now she crouched among the alders, wondering mightily what Uya might be doing with the flint and the bone. And Ugh-lomi was not to be seen.

Presently a squirrel came leaping through the alders, and she lay so quiet the little man was within six feet of her before he saw her. Whereupon he dashed up a stem in a hurry and began to chatter and scold her. "What are you doing here," he asked, "away from the other men beasts?" "Peace," said Eudena, but he only chattered more, and then she began to break off the little black cones to throw at him. He dodged and defied her, and she grew excited and rose up to throw better, and then she saw Uya coming down the knoll. He had seen the movement of her pale arm amidst the thicket—he was very keen-eyed.

At that she forgot the squirrel and set off through the alders and reeds as fast as she could go. She did not care where she went so long as she escaped Uya. She splashed nearly knee-deep through a swampy place, and saw in front of her a slope of ferns—growing more slender and greener as they passed up out of the light into the shade of the young chestnut trees. She was soon amidst the trees—she was very fleet of foot, and she ran on and on, until the forest was old and the trees great, and the vines about their stems where the light came were thick as young trees, and the ropes of ivy stout and tight. On she went, and she doubled and doubled again, and then at last lay down amidst some ferns in a hollow place near a thicket, and listened with her heart beating in her ears.

She heard footsteps presently rustling among the dead leaves, far off, and they died away and everything was still again, except the scandalising of the midges—for the evening was drawing on—and the incessant whisper of the leaves. She laughed silently to think the cunning Uya should go by her. She was not frightened. Sometimes, playing with the other girls and lads, she had fled into the wood, though never so far as this. It was pleasant to be hidden and alone.

She lay a long time there, glad of her escape, and then she sat up listening.

It was a rapid pattering growing louder and coming towards her, and in a little while she could hear grunting noises and the snapping of twigs. It was a drove of the lean grisly wild swine. She turned about her, for a boar is an ill fellow to pass too closely, on account of the sideway slash of his tusks, and she made off slantingly through the trees. But the patter came nearer, they were not feeding as they wandered, but going fast—or else they would not overtake her—and she caught the limb of a tree, swung on to it, and ran up the stem with something of the agility of a monkey.

Down below the sharp bristling backs of the swine were already passing when she looked down. And she knew the short, sharp grunts they made meant fear. What were they afraid of? A man? They were in a great hurry for just a man.

And then, so suddenly it made her grip on the branch tighten involuntarily, a fawn started in the brake and rushed after the swine. Something else went by, low and grey, with a long body; she did not know what it was, indeed she saw it only momentarily through the interstices of the young leaves; and then there came a pause.

She remained stiff and expectant, rigid almost as though she was a part of the tree she clung to, peering down.

Then far away among the trees, clear for a moment, then hidden, then visible knee-deep in ferns, then gone again, ran a man. She knew it was young Ugh-lomi by the fair colour of his hair, and there was red upon his face. Somehow his frantic flight and that scarlet mark made her feel sick. And then nearer, running heavily and breathing hard, came another man also running. At first she could not see, and then she saw, foreshortened and clear to her Uya, running with great strides and his eyes staring. He was not going after Ugh-lomi. His face was white. It was Uya—afraid! He passed, and was still loud hearing, when something else, something large and with grizzled fur, swinging along with soft swift strides, came rushing in pursuit of him.

Eudena suddenly became rigid, ceased to breathe, her clutch convulsive, and her eyes starting.

She had never seen the thing before she did not even see him clearly now, but she knew at once it was the Terror of the Woodshade. His name was a legend, the children would frighten one another, frighten even themselves with his name and run screaming to the squatting-place. No man had ever killed any of his kind. Even the mighty mammoth feared his Anger. It was the grizzly bear, the lord of world as the world went then.

As he ran he made a continuous growling rumble. "Men in my very lair! Fighting and blood. At the very mouth of my lair. Men, men, men. Fighting and blood." For he was the lord of the wood and of the caves.

Long after he had passed she remained, a girl of stone, staring down through the branches. All her power of action had gone from her. She gripped by instinct with hands and knees and feet. It was some time before she could think, and then only one thing was clear in her mind, that the Terror was between her and the tribe—that it would be impossible to descend.

Presently when her fear was a little abated she clambered into a more comfortable position, where a great branch forked. The trees rose about her, so that she could see nothing of Brother Fire, who is black by day. Birds began to stir about her, and things that had gone into hiding for fear of her movements crept out...

After a time the blue overhead deepened, and the taller branches flamed out at the touch of the sunset. High overhead the rooks, who were wiser than men, went cawing home to their squatting-places among the elms. Looking down, things were clearer and darker. Eudena thought of going back to the squatting-place; she let herself down some way, and then the fear of the Terror of the Woodshade came again. While she hesitated a rabbit squealed dismally, and she dared not descend farther.

The shadows gathered, and the deeps of the forest began stirring. Eudena went up the tree again to be nearer the light. Down below the shadows came out of their hiding-places and walked abroad. Overhead the blue deepened. A dreadful stillness came, and then the leaves began whispering.

Eudena shivered and thought of Brother Fire.

The shadows now were gathering in the trees, they sat on the branches and watched her. Branches and leaves were turned to ominous, quiet black shapes that would spring on her if she stirred. Then the white owl, flitting silently, came ghostly through the shades. Darker grew the world and darker, until the leaves and twigs against the sky were black, and the ground was hidden.

She remained there all night, an age-long vigil, straining her ears for the things that went on below in the darkness, and keeping motionless lest some stealthy beast should discover her. Man in those days was never alone in the dark, save for such rare accidents as this. Age after age he had learnt the lesson of its terror—a lesson we poor children of his have nowadays painfully to unlearn. Eudena, though in age a woman, was in heart like a little child. She kept as still, poor little animal, as a hare before it is started.

The stars gathered and watched her—her one grain of comfort. In one bright one she fancied there was something like Ugh-lomi. Then she fancied it was Ugh-lomi. And near him, red and duller, was Uya, and as the night passed Ugh-lomi fled before him up the sky.

She tried to see Brother Fire, who guarded the squatting-place from beasts, but he was not in sight. And far away she heard the mammoths trumpeting as they went down to the drinking-place, and once some huge bulk with heavy paces hurried along, making a noise like a calf, but what it was she could not see. But she thought from the voice it was Yaaa the rhinoceros, who stabs with his nose, goes always alone, and rages without cause.

At last the little stars began to hide, and then the larger ones. It was like all the animals vanishing before the Terror. The Sun was coming, lord of the sky, as the grizzly was lord of the forest. Eudena wondered what would happen if one star stayed behind. And then the sky paled to the dawn.

When the daylight came the fear of lurking things passed, and she could descend. She was stiff, but not so stiff as you would have been, dear young lady (by virtue of your upbringing), and as she had not been trained to eat at least once in three hours, but instead had often fasted three days, she did not feel uncomfortably hungry. She crept down the tree very cautiously, and went her way stealthily through the wood, and not a squirrel sprang or deer started but the terror of the grizzly bear froze her marrow.

Her desire was now to find her people again. Her dread of Uya the Cunning was consumed by a greater dread of loneliness. But she had lost her direction. She had run heedlessly overnight, and she could not tell whether the squatting-place was sunward or where it lay. Ever and again she stopped and listened, and at last, very far away, she heard a measured chinking. It was so faint even in the morning stillness that she could tell it must be far away. But she knew the sound was that of a man sharpening a flint.

Presently the trees began to thin out, and then came a regiment of nettles barring the way. She turned aside, and then she came to a fallen tree that she knew, with a noise of bees about it. And so presently she was in sight of the knoll, very far off, and the river under it, and the children and the hippopotami just as they had been yesterday, and the thin spire of smoke swaying in the morning breeze. Far away by the river was the cluster of alders where she had hidden. And at the sight of that the fear of Uya returned, and she crept into a thicket of bracken, out of which a rabbit scuttled, and lay awhile to watch the squatting-place.

The men were mostly out of sight, saving Wau, the flint-chopper; and at that she felt safer. They were away hunting food, no doubt. Some of the women too, were down in the stream, stooping intent, seeking mussels, crayfish, and water-snails, and at the sight of their occupation Eudena felt hungry. She rose, and ran through the fern, designing to join them. As she went she heard a voice among the bracken calling softly. She stopped. Then suddenly she heard a rustle behind her, and turning, saw Ugh-lomi rising out of the fern. There were streaks of brown blood and dirt on his face, and his eyes were fierce, and the white stone of Uya, the white Fire Stone, that none but Uya dared to touch, was in his hand. In a stride he was beside her and gripped her arm. He swung her about, and thrust her before him towards the woods. "Uya," he said, and waved his arms about. She heard a cry, looked back, and saw all the women standing up, and two wading out of the stream. Then came a nearer howling, and the old woman with the beard, who watched the fire on the knoll, was waving her arms, and Wau, the man who had been chipping the flint, was getting to his feet. The little children too, were hurrying and shouting.

"Come!" said Ugh-lomi, and dragged her by the arm.

She still did not understand.

"Uya," said Ugh-lomi, and she glanced back again at the screaming curve of figures, and dimly understood.

Wau and all the women and children were coming towards them, a scattered array of buff shock-headed figures, howling, leaping, and crying. Over the knoll two youths hurried. Down among the ferns to the right came a man, heading them off from the wood. Ugh-lomi left her arm, and the two began running side by side, leaping the bracken and stepping clear and wide. Eudena, knowing her fleetness and the fleetness of Ugh-lomi, laughed aloud at the unequal chase. They were an exceptionally straight-limbed couple for those days.

They soon cleared the open, and drew near the wood of chestnut-trees again—neither afraid now because neither was alone. They slackened their pace, already not excessive. And suddenly Eudena cried and swerved aside, pointing, and looking up through the tree-stems. Ugh-lomi saw the feet and legs of men running towards him. Eudena was already running off at a tangent. And as he too turned to follow her they heard the voice of Uya coming through the trees, and roaring out his rage at them.

Then terror came in their hearts, not the terror that numbs, but the terror that makes one silent and swift. They were cut off now on two sides. They were in a sort of corner of pursuit. On the right hand, and near by them, came the men swift and heavy, with bearded Uya, antler in hand, leading them; and on the left, scattered as one scatters corn, yellow dashes among the fern and grass, ran Wau and the women; and even the little children from the shallow had joined the chase. The two parties converged upon them. Off they went, with Eudena ahead.

They knew there was no mercy for them. There was no hunting so sweet to these ancient men as the hunting of men. Once the fierce passion of the chase was lit, the feeble beginnings of humanity in them were thrown to the winds. And Uya in the night had marked Ugh-lomi with the death word. Ugh-lomi was the day's quarry.

They ran straight—it was their only chance—taking whatever ground came in the way—a spread of stinging nettles, an open glade, a clump of grass out of which a hyaena fled snarling. Then woods again, long stretches of shady leaf-mould and moss under the green trunks. Then a stiff slope, tree-clad, and long vistas of trees, a glade, a succulent green area of black mud, a wide open space again, and then a clump of lacerating brambles, with beast tracks through it. Behind them the chase trailed out and scattered, with Uya ever at their heels. Eudena kept the first place, running light and with her breath easy, for Ugh-lomi carried the Fire Stone in his hand.

It told on his pace—not at first, but after a time. His footsteps behind her suddenly grew remote. Glancing over her shoulder as they crossed another open space, Eudena saw that Ugh-lomi was many yards behind her, and Uya close upon him, with antler already raised in the air to strike him down. Wau and the others were but just emerging from the shadow of the woods.

Seeing Ugh-lomi in peril, Eudena ran sideways, looking back, threw up her arms and cried aloud, just as the antler flew. And young Ugh-lomi, expecting this and understanding her cry, ducked his head, so that the missile merely struck his scalp lightly, making but a trivial wound, and flew over him. He turned forthwith, the quartzite Fire Stone in both hands, and hurled it straight at Uya's body as he ran loose from the throw. Uya shouted, but could not dodge it. It took him under the ribs, heavy and flat, and he reeled and went down without a cry. Ugh-lomi caught up the antler—one tine of it was tipped with his own blood—and came running on again with a red trickle just coming out of his hair.

Uya rolled over twice, and lay a moment before he got up, and then he did not run fast. The colour of his face was changed. Wau overtook him, and then others, and he coughed and laboured in his breath. But he kept on.

At last the two fugitives gained the bank of the river, where the stream ran deep and narrow, and they still had fifty yards in hand of Wau, the foremost pursuer, the man who made the smiting stones. He carried one, a large flint, the shape of an oyster and double the size, chipped to a chisel edge, in either hand.

They sprang down the steep bank into the stream, rushed through the water, swam the deep current in two or three strokes, and came out wading again, dripping and refreshed, to clamber up the farther bank. It was undermined, and with willows growing thickly therefrom, so that it needed clambering. And while Eudena was still among the silvery branches and Ugh-lomi still in the water—for the antler had encumbered him—Wau came up against the sky on the opposite bank, and the smiting stone, thrown cunningly, took the side of Eudena's knee. She struggled to the top and fell.

They heard the pursuers shout to one another, and Ugh-lomi, climbing to her and moving jerkily to mar Wau's aim, felt the second smiting stone graze his ear, and heard the water splashing below him.

Then it was Ugh-lomi, the stripling, proved himself to have come to man's estate. For running on, he found Eudena fell behind, limping, and at that he turned, and crying savagely and with a face terrible with sudden wrath and trickling blood, ran swiftly past her back to the bank, whirling the antler round his head. And Eudena kept on, running stoutly still, though she must needs limp at every step, and the pain was already sharp.

So that Wau, rising over the edge and clutching the straight willow branches, saw Ugh-lomi towering over him, gigantic against the blue; saw his whole body swing round, and the grip of his hands upon the antler. The edge of the antler came sweeping through the air, and he saw no more. The water under the osiers whirled and eddied and went crimson six feet down the stream. Uya following, stopped knee-high across the stream, and the man who was swimming turned about.

The other men who trailed after—they were none of them very mighty men (for Uya was more cunning than strong, brooking no sturdy rivals—) slackened momentarily at the sight of Ugh-lomi standing there above the willows, bloody and terrible, between them and the halting girl, with the huge antler waving in his hand. It seemed as though he had gone into the water a youth, and come out of it a man full grown.

He knew what there was behind him. A broad stretch of grass, and then a thicket, and in that Eudena could hide. That was clear in his mind, though his thinking powers were too feeble to see what should happen thereafter. Uya stood knee-deep, undecided and unarmed. His heavy mouth hung open, showing his canine teeth, and he panted heavily. His side was flushed and bruised under the hair. The other man beside him carried a sharpened stick. The rest of the hunters came up one by one to the top of the bank, hairy, long-armed men clutching flints and sticks. Two ran off along the bank down stream, and then clambered down to the water, where Wau had come to the surface struggling weakly. They gibbered at him without any sane attempt to help, and presently he went under again. Two others threatened Ugh-lomi from the bank.

He answered back, shouts, vague insults, gestures. Then Uya, who had been standing hesitating, roared with rage, and whirling his fists came plunging through the water. His followers came splashing after him.

Ugh-lomi glanced over his shoulder and found Eudena already vanished into the thicket. He would perhaps have waited for Uya, but Uya preferred to spar in the water below him until the others were beside him. Human tactics in those days, in all serious fighting, were the tactics of the pack. Prey that turned at bay they gathered around and rushed. Ugh-lomi felt the rush coming, and hurling the antler at Uya, turned about and fled.

When he halted to look back from the shadow of the thicket, he found only three of his pursuers had followed him across the river, and they were going back again. Uya, with a bleeding mouth, was on the farther side of the stream again, but lower down, and he held his hand to his side. The others were in the river dragging something to shore. For a time at least the chase was intermitted.

Ugh-lomi stood watching for a space, and snarled at the sight of Uya. Then he turned and plunged into the thicket.

In a minute, Eudena came hastening to join him, and they went on hand in hand. He dimly perceived the pain she suffered from the cut and bruised knee, and chose the easier ways. But they went on all that day, mile after mile, through wood and thicket, until at last they came to the chalk land, open grass with rare woods of beech, and the birch growing near water, and they saw the Wealden mountains nearer, and groups of horses grazing together. They went circumspectly, keeping always near thicket and cover, for this was a strange region—even its ways were strange. Steadily the ground rose, until the chestnut forests spread wide and blue below them, and the Thames marshes shone silvery, high and far. They saw no men, for in those days men were still only just come into this part of the world, and were moving but slowly along the river-ways. Towards evening they came on the river again, but now it ran in a gorge, between high cliffs of white chalk that sometimes overhung it. Down the cliffs was a scrub of birches and there were many birds there. And high up the cliff was a little shelf by a tree, whereon they clambered to pass the night.

They had had scarcely any food; it was not the time of year for berries, and they had no time to go aside to snare or waylay. They tramped in a hungry weary silence, gnawing at twigs and leaves. But over the surface of the cliffs were a multitude of snails, and in a bush were the freshly laid eggs of a little bird, and then Ugh-lomi threw at and killed a squirrel in a beech-tree, so that at last they fed well. Ugh-lomi watched during the night, his chin on his knees; and he heard young foxes crying hard by, and the noise of mammoths down the gorge, and the hyaenas yelling and laughing far away. It was chilly, but they dared not light a fire. Whenever he dozed, his spirit went abroad, and straightway met with the spirit of Uya, and they fought. And always Ugh-lomi was paralysed so that he could not smite nor run, and then he would awake suddenly. Eudena too, dreamt evil things of Uya, so that they both awoke with the fear of him in their hearts, and by the light of the dawn they saw a woolly rhinoceros go blundering down the valley.

During the day they caressed one another and were glad of the sunshine, and Eudena's leg was so stiff she sat on the ledge all day. Ugh-lomi found great flints sticking out of the cliff face, greater than any he had seen, and he dragged some to the ledge and began chipping, so as to be armed against Uya when he came again. And at one he laughed heartily, and Eudena laughed, and they threw it about in derision. It had a hole in it. They stuck their fingers through it, it was very funny indeed. Then they peeped at one another through it. Afterwards, Ugh-lomi got himself a stick, and thrusting by chance at this foolish flint, the stick went in and stuck there. He had rammed it in too tightly to withdraw it. That was still stranger—scarcely funny, terrible almost, and for a time Ugh-lomi did not greatly care to touch the thing. It was as if the flint had bit and held with its teeth. But then he got familiar with the odd combination. He swung it about, and perceived dimly that the stick with the heavy stone on the end struck a better blow than anything he knew. He went to and fro swinging it, and striking with it; but later he tired of it and threw it aside. In the afternoon he went up over the brow of the white cliff, and lay watching by a rabbit-warren until the rabbits came out to play. There were no men thereabouts, and the rabbits were heedless. He threw a smiting stone he had made and got a kill.

That night they made a fire from flint sparks and bracken fronds, and talked and caressed by it. And in their sleep Uya's spirit came again, and suddenly, while Ugh-lomi was trying to fight vainly, the foolish flint on the stick came into his hand, and struck Uya with it, and behold! It killed him. But afterwards came other dreams of Uya—for spirits take a lot of killing, and he had to be killed again. Then after that the stone would not keep on the stick. He awoke tired and rather gloomy, and was sulky all the forenoon, in spite of Eudena's kindliness, and instead of hunting he sat chipping a sharp edge to the singular flint, and looking strangely at her. Then he bound the perforated flint on to the stick with strips of rabbit. And afterwards he walked up and down the ledge, striking with it, and muttering to himself, and thinking of Uya. It felt very fine and heavy in the hand.

Several days, more than there was any counting in those days, five days, it may be, or six, did Ugh-lomi and Eudena stay on that shelf in the gorge of the river, and they lost all fear of men, and their fire burnt redly of a night. And they were very merry together; there was food every day, sweet water, and no enemies. Eudena's knee was well in a couple of days, for those ancient savages had quick-healing flesh. Indeed, they were very happy.

On one of those days, although it has little to do with this story, Ugh-lomi dropped a chunk of flint on the cliff. He saw it fall, and go bounding across the river bank into the river, and after laughing and thinking it over a little he tried another. This smashed a bush of hazel in the most interesting way. They spent all the morning dropping stones from the ledge and in the afternoon they discovered this new and interesting pastime was also possible from the cliff brow. The next day they had forgotten this delight. Or at least, it seemed they had forgotten.

But Uya came in dreams to spoil the paradise. Three nights he came fighting Ugh-lomi. In the morning after these dreams Ugh-lomi would walk up and down, threatening him and swinging the axe, and at last came the night after Ugh-lomi brained the otter, and they had feasted. Uya went too far. Ugh-lomi awoke, scowling under his heavy brows, and he took his axe, and extending his hand towards Eudena he bade her wait for him upon the ledge. Then he clambered down the white declivity, glanced up once from the foot of it and flourished his axe, and without looking back again went striding along the river bank until the overhanging cliff at the bend hid him.

Two days and nights did Eudena sit alone by the fire on the ledge waiting, and in the night the beasts howled over the cliffs and down the valley, and on the cliff over against her the hunched hyaenas prowled black against the sky. But no evil thing came near her save fear. Once far away, she heard the roaring of a lion, following the horses as they came northward over the grass lands with the spring. All that time she waited—the waiting that is pain.

And the third day Ugh-lomi came back, up the river. The plumes of a raven were in his hair. The axe was red-stained, and had long dark hairs upon it, and he carried the necklace that had marked the favourite of Uya in his hand. He walked in the soft places, giving no heed to his trail. Save a raw cut below his jaw there was not a wound upon him. "Uya!" cried Ugh-lomi exultant, and Eudena saw it was well. He put the necklace on Eudena, and they ate and drank together. And after eating he began to rehearse the whole story from the beginning, when Uya had cast his eyes on Eudena, and Uya and Ugh-lomi, fighting in the forest, had been chased by the bear, eking out his scanty words with abundant pantomime, springing to his feet and whirling the stone axe round when it came to the fighting. The last fight was a mighty one, stamping and shouting, and once a blow at the fire that sent a torrent of sparks up into the night. And Eudena sat red in the light of the fire, gloating on him, her face flushed and her eyes shining, and the necklace Uya had made about her neck. It was a splendid time, and the stars that look down on us looked down on her, our ancestor—who has been dead now these fifty thousand years.

2. The Cave Bear

In the days when Eudena and Ugh-lomi fled from the people of Uya towards the fir-clad mountains of the Weald, across the forests of sweet chestnut and the grass-clad chalkland, and hid themselves at last in the gorge of the river between the chalk cliffs, men were few and their squatting-places far between. The nearest men to them were those of the tribe, a full day's journey down the river, and up the mountains there were none. Man was indeed a newcomer to this part of the world in that ancient time, coming slowly along the rivers, generation after generation, from one squatting-place to another, from the south-westward. And the animals that held the land, the hippopotami and rhinoceros of the river valleys, the horses of the grass plains, the deer and swine of the woods, the grey apes in the branches, the cattle of the uplands, feared him but little—let alone the mammoths in the mountains and the elephants that came through the land in the summer-time out of the south. For why should they fear him, with but the rough, chipped flints that he had not learnt to haft and which he threw but ill, and the poor spear of sharpened wood, as all his weapons against hoof and horn, tooth and claw?

Andoo, the huge cave bear, who lived in the cave up the gorge, had never even seen a man in all his wise and respectable life, until midway through one night, as he was prowling down the gorge along the cliff edge, he saw the glare of Eudena's fire upon the ledge, and Eudena red and shining, and Ugh-lomi, with a gigantic shadow mocking him upon the white cliff, going to and fro, shaking his mane of hair, and waving the axe of stone—the first axe of stone—while he chanted of the killing of Uya. The cave bear was far up the gorge, and he saw the thing slanting-ways and far off. He was so surprised he stood quite still upon the edge, sniffing the novel odour of burning bracken, and wondering whether the dawn was coming up in the wrong place.

He was the lord of the rocks and caves, was the cave bear, as his slighter brother, the grizzly, was lord of the thick woods below, and as the dappled lion—the lion of those days was dappled—was lord of the thorn-thickets, reed-beds, and open plains. He was the greatest of all meat-eaters; he knew no fear, none preyed on him, and none gave him battle; only the rhinoceros was beyond his strength. Even the mammoth shunned his country. This invasion perplexed him. He noticed these new beasts were shaped like monkeys, and sparsely hairy like young pigs. "Monkey and young pig," said the cave bear. "It might not be so bad. But that red thing that jumps, and the black thing jumping with it yonder! Never in my life have I seen such things before."

He came slowly along the brow of the cliff towards them, stopping thrice to sniff and peer, and the reek of the fire grew stronger. A couple of hyaenas also were so intent upon the thing below that Andoo, coming soft and easy, was close upon them before they knew of him or he of them. They started guiltily and went lurching off. Coming round in a wheel, a hundred yards off, they began yelling and calling him names for the start they had had. "Ya-ha!" they cried. "Who can't grub his own burrow? Who eats roots like a pig...? Ya-ha!" For even in those days the hyaena's manners were just as offensive as they are now.

"Who answers the hyaena?" growled Andoo, peering through the midnight dimness at them, and then going to look at the cliff edge.

There was Ugh-lomi still telling his story, and the fire getting low, and the scent of the burning hot and strong.

Andoo stood on the edge of the chalk cliff for some time, shifting his vast weight from foot to foot, and swaying his head to and fro, with his mouth open, his ears erect and twitching, and the nostrils of his big, black muzzle sniffing. He was very curious, was the cave bear, more curious than any of the bears that live now, and the flickering fire and the incomprehensible movements of the man, let alone the intrusion into his indisputable province, stirred him with a sense of strange new happenings. He had been after red deer fawn that night, for the cave bear was a miscellaneous hunter, but this quite turned him from that enterprise.

"Ya-ha!" yelled the hyaenas behind. "Ya-ha-ha!"

Peering through the starlight, Andoo saw there were now three or four going to and fro against the grey hillside. "They will hang about me now all the night until I kill," said Andoo. "Filth of the world!" And mainly to annoy them, he resolved to watch the red flicker in the gorge until the dawn came to drive the hyaena scum home. And after a time they vanished, and he heard their voices, like a party of Cockney bean-feasters, away in the beech-woods. Then they came slinking near again. Andoo yawned and went on along the cliff, and they followed. Then he stopped and went back.

It was a splendid night, beset with shining constellations, the same stars, but not the same constellations we know, for since those days all the stars have had time to move into new places. Far away across the open space beyond where the heavy-shouldered, lean-bodied hyaenas blundered and howled, was a beech-wood, and the mountain slopes rose beyond, a dim mystery, until their snow-capped summits came out white and cold and clear, touched by the first rays of the yet unseen moon. It was a vast silence, save when the yell of the hyaenas flung a vanishing discordance across its peace, or when from down the hills the trumpeting of the new-come elephants came faintly on the faint breeze. And below now, the red flicker had dwindled and was steady, and shone a deeper red, and Ugh-lomi had finished his story and was preparing to sleep, and Eudena sat and listened to the strange voices of unknown beasts, and watched the dark eastern sky growing deeply luminous at the advent of the moon. Down below, the river talked to itself, and things unseen went to and fro.

After a time the bear went away, but in an hour he was back again. Then, as if struck by a thought, he turned, and went up the gorge...

The night passed, and Ugh-lomi slept on. The waning moon rose and lit the gaunt white cliff overhead with a light that was pale and vague. The gorge remained in a deeper shadow, and seemed all the darker. Then by imperceptible degrees the day came stealing in the wake of the moonlight. Eudena's eyes wandered to the cliff brow overhead once, and then again. Each time the line was sharp and clear against the sky, and yet she had a dim perception of something lurking there. The red of the fire grew deeper and deeper, grey scales spread upon it, its vertical column of smoke became more and more visible, and up and down the gorge, things that had been unseen grew clear in a colourless illumination. She may have dozed.

Suddenly she started up from her squatting position, erect and alert, scrutinising the cliff up and down.

She made the faintest sound, and Ugh-lomi too, light sleeping like an animal, was instantly awake. He caught up his axe and came noiselessly to her side.

The light was still dim, the world now all in black and dark grey, and one sickly star still lingered overhead. The ledge they were on was a little grassy space, six feet wide perhaps, and twenty feet long, sloping outwardly, and with a handful of St. John's wort growing near the edge. Below it, the soft white rock fell away in a steep slope of nearly fifty feet to the thick bush of hazel that fringed the river. Down the river this slope increased, until some way off a thin grass held its own right up to the crest of the cliff. Overhead, forty or fifty feet of rock bulged into the great masses characteristic of chalk, but at the end of the ledge a gully, a precipitous groove of discoloured chalk, slashed the face of the cliff, and gave a footing to a scrubby growth, by which Eudena and Ugh-lomi went up and down.

They stood as noiseless as startled deer, with every sense expectant. For a minute they heard nothing, and then came a faint rattling of dust down the gully, and the creaking of twigs.

Ugh-lomi gripped his axe, and went to the edge of the ledge, for the bulge of the chalk overhead had hidden the upper part of the gully. And forthwith, with a sudden contraction of the heart, he saw the cave bear halfway down from the brow, and making a gingerly backward step with his flat hind-foot. His hind-quarters were towards Ugh-lomi, and he clawed at the rocks and bushes so that he seemed flattened against the cliff. He looked none the less for that. From his shining snout to his stumpy tail he was a lion and a half, the length of two tall men. He looked over his shoulder, and his huge mouth was open with the exertion of holding up his great carcase, and his tongue lay out...

He got his footing, and came down slowly, a yard nearer.

"Bear," said Ugh-lomi, looking round with his face white.

But Eudena, with terror in her eyes, was pointing down the cliff.

Ugh-lomi's mouth fell open. For down below, with her big fore-feet against the rock, stood another big brown-grey bulk—the she-bear. She was not so big as Andoo, but she was big enough for all that.

Then suddenly Ugh-lomi gave a cry, and catching up a handful of the litter of ferns that lay scattered on the ledge, he thrust it into the pallid ash of the fire. "Brother Fire!" he cried, "Brother Fire!" And Eudena, starting into activity, did likewise. "Brother Fire! Help, help! Brother Fire!"

Brother Fire was still red in his heart, but he turned to grey as they scattered him. "Brother Fire!" They screamed. But he whispered and passed, and there was nothing but ashes. Then Ugh-lomi danced with anger and struck the ashes with his fist. But Eudena began to hammer the firestone against a flint. And the eyes of each were turning ever and again towards the gully by which Andoo was climbing down. Brother Fire!

Suddenly the huge furry hind-quarters of the bear came into view, beneath the bulge of the chalk that had hidden him. He was still clambering gingerly down the nearly vertical surface. His head was yet out of sight, but they could hear him talking to himself. "Pig and monkey," said the cave bear. "It ought to be good."

Eudena struck a spark and blew at it; it twinkled brighter and then—went out. At that she cast down flint and firestone and began wringing her hands. Her face was wet with tears. Then she sprang to her feet and scrambled a dozen feet up the cliff above the ledge. How she hung on even for a moment I do not know, for the chalk was vertical and without grip for a monkey. In a couple of seconds she had slid back to the ledge again with bleeding hands.

Ugh-lomi was making frantic rushes about the ledge—now he would go to the edge, now to the gully. He did not know what to do, he could not think. The she-bear looked smaller than her mate—much. If they rushed down on her together, one might live. "Eigh?" said the cave bear, and Ugh-lomi turned again and saw his little eyes peering under the bulge of the chalk. "Stand away!" said the bear; "I'm going to jump down."

Eudena, cowering at the end of the ledge, began to scream like a gripped rabbit.

At that a sort of madness came upon Ugh-lomi. With a mighty cry, he caught up his axe and began to clamber up the gully to the bear. He uttered neither word nor cry. The monster gave a grunt of surprise. In a moment Ugh-lomi was clinging to a bush right underneath the bear, and in another he was hanging to its back half buried in fur, with one fist clutched in the hair under its jaw. The bear was too astonished at this fantastic attack to do more than cling passive. And then the axe, the first of all axes, rang in its skull.

The bear's head twisted from side to side, and he began a petulant scolding growl. The axe bit within an inch of the left eye, and the hot blood blinded that side. At that the brute roared with surprise and anger, and his teeth gnashed six inches from Ugh-lomi's face. Then the axe, clubbed close, came down heavily on the corner of the jaw.

The next blow blinded the right side and called forth a roar, this time of pain. Eudena saw the huge, flat feet slipping and sliding, and suddenly the bear gave a clumsy leap sideways, as if for the ledge. Then everything vanished, and the hazels smashed, and a roar of pain and a tumult of shouts and growls came up from far below.

Eudena screamed and ran to the edge and peered over. For a moment, man and bears were a heap together, Ugh-lomi uppermost; and then he had sprung clear and was scaling the gully again, with the bears rolling and striking at one another among the hazels. But he had left his axe below, and three knob-ended streaks of carmine were shooting down his thigh. "Up!" he cried, and in a moment Eudena was preceding him to the top of the cliff.

In half a minute they were at the crest, their hearts pumping noisily, with Andoo and his wife far and safe below them. Andoo was sitting on his haunches, both paws at work, trying with quick exasperated movements to wipe the blindness out of his eyes, and the she-bear stood on all-fours a little way off, ruffled in appearance and growling angrily. Ugh-lomi flung himself flat on the grass, and lay panting and bleeding with his face on his arms.

For a second Eudena regarded the bears, then she came and sat beside him, looking at him...

Presently she put forth her hand timidly and touched him, and made the guttural sound that was his name. He turned over and raised himself on his arm. His face was pale, like the face of one who is afraid. He looked at her steadfastly for a moment, and then suddenly he laughed. "Waugh!" he said exultantly.

"Waugh!" said she—a simple but expressive conversation.

Then Ugh-lomi came and knelt beside her, and on hands and knees peered over the brow and examined the gorge. His breath was steady now, and the blood on his leg had ceased to flow, though the scratches the she-bear had made were open and wide. He squatted up and sat staring at the footmarks of the great bear as they came to the gully—they were as wide as his head and twice as long. Then he jumped up and went along the cliff face until the ledge was visible. Here he sat down for some time thinking, while Eudena watched him.

At last Ugh-lomi rose, as one whose mind is made up. He returned towards the gully, Eudena keeping close by him, and together they clambered to the ledge. They took the firestone and a flint, and then Ugh-lomi went down to the foot of the cliff very cautiously, and found his axe. They returned to the cliff now as quietly as they could, and turning their faces resolutely up-stream set off at a brisk walk. The ledge was a home no longer, with such callers in the neighbourhood. Ugh-lomi carried the axe and Eudena the firestone. So simple was a Palaeolithic removal.

They went up-stream, although it might lead to the very lair of the cave bear, because there was no other way to go. Down the stream was the tribe, and had not Ugh-lomi killed Uya and Wau? By the stream they had to keep—because of drinking.

So they marched, through beech trees, with the gorge deepening until the river flowed, a frothing rapid, five hundred feet below them. And of all the changeful things in this world of change, the courses of rivers, in deep valleys change least. It was the river Wey, the river we know to-day, and they marched over the very spots where nowadays stand little Guildford and Godalming—the first human beings to come into the land. Once a grey ape chattered and vanished, and all along the cliff edge, vast and even, ran the spoor of the great cave bear.

And then the spoor of the bear fell away from the cliff, showing, Ugh-lomi thought, that he came from some place to the left, and keeping to the cliff's edge, they presently came to an end. They found themselves looking down on a great semi-circular space caused by the collapse of the cliff. It had smashed right across the gorge, banking the up-stream water back in a pool which overflowed in a rapid. The slip had happened long ago. It was grassed over, but the face of the cliffs that stood about the semi-circle was still almost fresh-looking and white as on the day when the rock must have broken and slid down. Starkly exposed and black under the foot of these cliffs were the mouths of several caves. And as they stood there, looking at the space, and disinclined to skirt it, because they thought the bears' lair lay somewhere on the left in the direction they must needs take, they saw suddenly first one bear and then two coming up the grass slope to the right and going across the amphitheatre towards the caves. Andoo was first, and he dropped a little on his fore-foot, and his mien was despondent, and the she-bear came shuffling behind.

Eudena and Ugh-lomi stepped quite noiselessly back from the cliff until they could just see the bears over the verge. Then Ugh-lomi stopped. Eudena pulled his arm, but he turned with a forbidding gesture, and her hand dropped. Ugh-lomi stood watching the bears, with his axe in his hand, until they had vanished into the cave. He growled softly, and shook the axe at the she-bear's receding quarters. Then to Eudena's terror, instead of creeping off with her, he lay flat down and crawled forward into such a position that he could just see the cave. It was bears—and he did it as calmly as if it had been rabbits he was watching!

He lay still, like a barked log, sun-dappled, in the shadow of the trees. He was thinking. And Eudena had learnt, even when a little girl, that when Ugh-lomi became still like that, jaw-bone on fist, novel things presently began to happen.

It was an hour before the thinking was over; it was noon when the two little savages had found their way to the cliff brow that overhung the bears' cave. And all the long afternoon they fought desperately with a great boulder of chalk; trundling it, with nothing but their unaided sturdy muscles, from the gully where it had hung like a loose tooth, towards the cliff top. It was full two yards about, it stood as high as Eudena's waist, it was obtuse-angled and toothed with flints. And when the sun set it was poised, three inches from the edge, above the cave of the great cave bear.

In the cave, conversation languished during the afternoon. The she-bear snoozed sulkily in her corner—for she was fond of pig and monkey—and Andoo was busy licking the side of his paw and smearing his face to cool the smart and inflammation of his wounds. Afterwards he went and sat just within the mouth of the cave, blinking out at the afternoon sun with his uninjured eye, and thinking.

"I never was so startled in my life," he said at last. "They are the most extraordinary beasts. Attacking me!"

"I don't like them," said the she-bear, out of the darkness behind.

"A feebler sort of beast I never saw. I can't think what the world is coming to. Scraggy, weedy legs... Wonder how they keep warm in winter?"

"Very likely they don't," said the she-bear.

"I suppose it's a sort of monkey gone wrong."

"It's a change," said the she-bear.

A pause.

"The advantage he had was merely accidental," said Andoo. "These things will happen at times."

"I can't understand why you let go," said the she-bear.

That matter had been discussed before, and settled. So Andoo, being a bear of experience, remained silent for a space. Then he resumed upon a different aspect of the matter. "He has a sort of claw—a long claw that he seemed to have first on one paw and then on the other. Just one claw. They're very odd things. The bright thing too, they seemed to have—like that glare that comes in the sky in daytime—only it jumps about—it's really worth seeing. It's a thing with a root, too—like grass when it is windy."

"Does it bite?" asked the she-bear. "If it bites it can't be a plant."

"No—I don't know," said Andoo. "But it's curious, anyhow."

"I wonder if they are good eating?" said the she-bear.

"They look it," said Andoo, with appetite—for the cave bear, like the polar bear, was an incurable carnivore—no roots or honey for him.

The two bears fell into a meditation for a space. Then Andoo resumed his simple attentions to his eye. The sunlight up the green slope before the cave mouth grew warmer in tone and warmer, until it was a ruddy amber.

"Curious sort of thing—day," said the cave bear. "Lot too much of it, I think. Quite unsuitable for hunting. Dazzles me always. I can't smell nearly so well by day."

The she-bear did not answer, but there came a measured crunching sound out of the darkness. She had turned up a bone. Andoo yawned. "Well," he said. He strolled to the cave mouth and stood with his head projecting, surveying the amphitheatre. He found he had to turn his head completely round to see objects on his right-hand side. No doubt that eye would be all right to-morrow.

He yawned again. There was a tap overhead, and a big mass of chalk flew out from the cliff face, dropped a yard in front of his nose, and starred into a dozen unequal fragments. It startled him extremely.

When he had recovered a little from his shock, he went and sniffed curiously at the representative pieces of the fallen projectile. They had a distinctive flavour, oddly reminiscent of the two drab animals of the ledge. He sat up and pawed the larger lump, and walked round it several times trying to find a man about it somewhere...

When night had come he went off down the river gorge to see if he could cut off either of the ledge's occupants. The ledge was empty, there were no signs of the red thing, but as he was rather hungry he did not loiter long that night, but pushed on to pick up a red deer fawn. He forgot about the drab animals. He found a fawn, but the doe was close by and made an ugly fight for her young. Andoo had to leave the fawn, but as her blood was up she stuck to the attack, and at last he got in a blow of his paw at her nose, and so got hold of her. More meat but less delicacy, and the she-bear, following, had her share. The next afternoon, curiously enough, the very fellow of the first white rock fell, and smashed precisely according to precedent.

The aim of the third, that fell the night after however, was better. It hit Andoo's unspeculative skull with a crack that echoed up the cliff, and the white fragments went dancing to all the points of the compass. The she-bear coming after him and sniffing curiously at him, found him lying in an odd sort of attitude, with his head wet and all out of shape. She was a young she-bear, and inexperienced, and having sniffed about him for some time and licked him a little, and so forth, she decided to leave him until the odd mood had passed, and went on her hunting alone.

She looked up the fawn of the red doe they had killed two nights ago, and found it. But it was lonely hunting without Andoo, and she returned caveward before dawn. The sky was grey and overcast, the trees up the gorge were black and unfamiliar, and into her ursine mind came a dim sense of strange and dreary happenings. She lifted up her voice and called Andoo by name. The sides of the gorge re-echoed her.

As she approached the caves she saw in the half light, and heard, a couple of jackals scuttle off, and immediately after a hyaena howled and a dozen clumsy bulks went lumbering up the slope, and stopped and yelled derision. "Lord of the rocks and caves—ya-ha!" Came down the wind. The dismal feeling in the she-bear's mind became suddenly acute. She shuffled across the amphitheatre.

"Ya-ha!" said the hyaenas, retreating. "Ya-ha!"

The cave bear was not lying quite in the same attitude, because the hyaenas had been busy, and in one place his ribs showed white. Dotted over the turf about him lay the smashed fragments of the three great lumps of chalk. And the air was full of the scent of death.

The she-bear stopped dead. Even now, that the great and wonderful Andoo was killed was beyond her believing. Then she heard far overhead a sound, a queer sound, a little like the shout of a hyaena but fuller and lower in pitch. She looked up, with her little dawn-blinded eyes, seeing little, her nostrils quivering. And there, on the cliff edge, far above her against the bright pink of dawn, were two little shaggy round dark things, the heads of Eudena and Ugh-lomi, as they shouted derision at her. But though she could not see them very distinctly she could hear, and dimly she began to apprehend. A novel feeling as of imminent strange evils came into her heart.

She began to examine the smashed fragments of chalk that lay about Andoo. For a space she stood still, looking about her and making a low continuous sound that was almost a moan. Then she went back incredulously to Andoo to make one last effort to rouse him.

3. The First Horseman

In the days before Ugh-lomi killed the great cave bear there was little trouble between the horses and men. Indeed they lived apart—the men in the river swamps and thickets, the horses on the wide grassy uplands between the chestnuts and the pines. Sometimes a pony would come straying into the clogging marshes to make a flint-hacked meal, and sometimes the tribe would find one, the kill of a lion, and drive off the jackals, and feast heartily while the sun was high. These horses of the old time were clumsy at the fetlock and dun-coloured, with a rough tail and big head. They came every spring-time north-westward into the country, after the swallows and before the hippopotami, as the grass on the wide downland stretches grew long. They came only in small bodies thus far, each herd, a stallion and two or three mares and a foal or so, having its own stretch of country, and they went again when the chestnut-trees were yellow and the wolves came down the Wealden mountains.

It was their custom to graze right out in the open, going into cover only in the heat of the day. They avoided the long stretches of thorn and beechwood, preferring an isolated group of trees, void of ambuscade, so that it was hard to come upon them. They were never fighters; their heels and teeth were for one another, but in the clear country, once they were started, no living thing came near them, though perhaps the elephant might have done so, had he felt the need. And in those days man seemed a harmless thing enough. No whisper of prophetic intelligence told the species of the terrible slavery that was to come, of the whip and spur and bearing-rein, the clumsy load and the slippery street, the insufficient food, and the knacker's yard, that was to replace the wide grass-land and the freedom of the earth.

Down in the Wey marshes Ugh-lomi and Eudena had never seen the horses closely, but now they saw them every day as the two of them raided out from their lair on the ledge in the gorge, raiding together in search of food. They had returned to the ledge after the killing of Andoo; for of the she-bear they were not afraid. The she-bear had become afraid of them, and when she winded them she went aside. The two went together everywhere; for since they had left the tribe Eudena was not so much Ugh-lomi's woman as his mate; she learnt to hunt even—as much that is, as any woman could. She was indeed a marvellous woman. He would lie for hours watching a beast, or planning catches in that shock head of his, and she would stay beside him, with her bright eyes upon him, offering no irritating suggestions—as still as any man. A wonderful woman!

At the top of the cliff was an open grassy lawn and then beechwoods, and going through the beechwoods one came to the edge of the rolling grassy expanse, and in sight of the horses. Here on the edge of the wood and bracken, were the rabbit-burrows, and here among the fronds Eudena and Ugh-lomi would lie with their throwing-stones ready, until the little people came out to nibble and play in the sunset. And while Eudena would sit, a silent figure of watchfulness, regarding the burrows, Ugh-lomi's eyes were ever away across the greensward at those wonderful grazing strangers.

In a dim way he appreciated their grace and their supple nimbleness. As the sun declined in the evening-time, and the heat of the day passed, they would become active, would start chasing one another, neighing, dodging, shaking their manes, coming round in great curves, sometimes so close that the pounding of the turf sounded like hurried thunder. It looked so fine that Ugh-lomi wanted to join in badly. And sometimes one would roll over on the turf, kicking four hoofs heavenward, which seemed formidable and was certainly much less alluring.

Dim imaginings ran through Ugh-lomi's mind as he watched—by virtue of which two rabbits lived the longer. And sleeping, his brains were clearer and bolder—for that was the way in those days. He came near the horses, he dreamt, and fought, smiting-stone against hoof, but then the horses changed to men or, at least, to men with horses' heads, and he awoke in a cold sweat of terror.

Yet the next day in the morning, as the horses were grazing, one of the mares whinnied, and they saw Ugh-lomi coming up the wind. They all stopped their eating and watched him. Ugh-lomi was not coming towards them, but strolling obliquely across the open, looking at anything in the world but horses. He had stuck three fern-fronds into the mat of his hair, giving him a remarkable appearance, and he walked very slowly. "What's up now?" said the Master Horse, who was capable, but inexperienced.

"It looks more like the first half of an animal than anything else in the world," he said. "Fore-legs and no hind."

"It's only one of those pink monkey things," said the Eldest Mare. "They're a sort of river monkey. They're quite common on the plains."

Ugh-lomi continued his oblique advance. The Eldest Mare was struck with the want of motive in his proceedings.

"Fool!" said the Eldest Mare, in a quick conclusive way she had. She resumed her grazing. The Master Horse and the Second Mare followed suit.

"Look! He's nearer," said the Foal with a stripe.

One of the younger foals made uneasy movements. Ugh-lomi squatted down and sat regarding the horses fixedly. In a little while he was satisfied that they meant neither flight nor hostilities. He began to consider his next procedure. He did not feel anxious to kill, but he had his axe with him, and the spirit of sport was upon him. How would one kill one of these creatures—? These great beautiful creatures!

Eudena, watching him with a fearful admiration from the cover of the bracken, saw him presently go on all fours, and so proceed again. But the horses preferred him a biped to a quadruped, and the Master Horse threw up his head and gave the word to move. Ugh-lomi thought they were off for good, but after a minute's gallop they came round in a wide curve, and stood winding him. Then as a rise in the ground hid him they tailed out, the Master Horse leading and approached him spirally.

He was as ignorant of the possibilities of a horse as they were of his. And at this stage it would seem he funked. He knew this kind of stalking would make red deer or buffalo charge, if it was persisted in. At any rate Eudena saw him jump up and come walking towards her with the fern plumes held in his hand.

She stood up, and he grinned to show that the whole thing was an immense lark, and that what he had done was just what he had planned to do from the very beginning. So that incident ended. But he was very thoughtful all that day.

The next day this foolish drab creature with the leonine mane, instead of going about the grazing or hunting he was made for, was prowling round the horses again. The Eldest Mare was all for silent contempt. "I suppose he wants to learn something from us," she said, and "Let him." The next day he was at it again. The Master Horse decided he meant absolutely nothing. But as a matter of fact, Ugh-lomi, the first of men to feel that curious spell of the horse that binds us even to this day, meant a great deal. He admired them unreservedly. There was a rudiment of the snob in him, I am afraid, and he wanted to be near these beautifully-curved animals. Then here were vague conceptions of a kill. If only they would let him come near them! But they drew the line, he found, at fifty yards. If he came nearer than that they moved off—with dignity. I suppose it was the way he had blinded Andoo that made him think of leaping on the back of one of them. But though Eudena after a time came out in the open too, and they did some unobtrusive stalking, things stopped there.

Then one memorable day a new idea came to Ugh-lomi. The horse looks down and level, but he does not look up. No animals look up—they have too much common-sense. It was only that fantastic creature man, could waste his wits skyward. Ugh-lomi made no philosophical deductions, but he perceived the thing was so. So he spent a weary day in a beech that stood in the open, while Eudena stalked. Usually the horses went into the shade in the heat of the afternoon, but that day the sky was overcast, and they would not, in spite of Eudena's solicitude.

It was two days after that, that Ugh-lomi had his desire. The day was blazing hot, and the multiplying flies asserted themselves. The horses stopped grazing before midday, and came into the shadow below him, and stood in couples nose to tail, flapping.

The Master Horse, by virtue of his heels, came closest to the tree. And suddenly there was a rustle and a creak, a thud...Then a sharp chipped flint bit him on the cheek. The Master Horse stumbled, came on one knee, rose to his feet, and was off like the wind. The air was full of the whirl of limbs, the prance of hoofs, and snorts of alarm. Ugh-lomi was pitched a foot in the air, came down again, up again, his stomach was hit violently, and then his knees got a grip of something between them. He found himself clutching with knees, feet, and hands, careering violently with extraordinary oscillation through the air—his axe gone heaven knows whither. "Hold tight," said Mother Instinct, and he did.

He was aware of a lot of coarse hair in his face, some of it between his teeth, and of green turf streaming past in front of his eyes. He saw the shoulder of the Master Horse, vast and sleek, with the muscles flowing swiftly under the skin. He perceived that his arms were round the neck, and that the violent jerkings he experienced had a sort of rhythm.

Then he was in the midst of a wild rush of tree-stems, and then there were fronds of bracken about, and then more open turf. Then a stream of pebbles rushing past, little pebbles flying sideways athwart the stream from the blow of the swift hoofs. Ugh-lomi began to feel frightfully sick and giddy, but he was not the stuff to leave go simply because he was uncomfortable.

He dared not leave his grip, but he tried to make himself more comfortable. He released his hug on the neck, gripping the mane instead. He slipped his knees forward, and pushing back, came into a sitting position where the quarters broaden.

It was nervous work, but he managed it, and at last he was fairly seated astride, breathless indeed, and uncertain, but with that frightful pounding of his body at any rate relieved.

Slowly the fragments of Ugh-lomi's mind got into order again. The pace seemed to him terrific, but a kind of exultation was beginning to oust his first frantic terror. The air rushed by, sweet and wonderful, the rhythm of the hoofs changed and broke up and returned into itself again. They were on turf now, a wide glade—the beech-trees a hundred yards away on either side, and a succulent band of green starred with pink blossom and shot with silver water here and there, meandered down the middle. Far off was a glimpse of blue valley—far away. The exultation grew. It was man's first taste of pace.

Then came a wide space dappled with flying fallow deer scattering this way and that, and then a couple of jackals, mistaking Ugh-lomi for a lion, came hurrying after him. And when they saw it was not a lion they still came on out of curiosity. On galloped the horse, with his one idea of escape, and after him the jackals, with pricked ears and quickly-barked remarks. "Which kills which?" said the first jackal. "It's the horse being killed," said the second. They gave the howl of following, and the horse answered to it as a horse answers nowadays to the spur.

On they rushed, a little tornado through the quiet day, putting up startled birds, sending a dozen unexpected things darting to cover, raising a myriad of indignant dung-flies, smashing little blossoms, flowering complacently, back into their parental turf. Trees again, and then splash, splash across a torrent; then a hare shot out of a tuft of grass under the very hoofs of the Master Horse, and the jackals left them incontinently. So presently they broke into the open again, a wide expanse of turfy hillside—the very fellow of the grassy downs that fall northward nowadays from the Epsom Stand.

The first hot bolt of the Master Horse was long since over. He was falling into a measured trot, and Ugh-lomi, albeit bruised exceedingly and quite uncertain of the future, was in a state of glorious enjoyment. And now came a new development. The pace broke again, the Master Horse came round on a short curve, and stopped dead...

Ugh-lomi became alert. He wished he had a flint, but the throwing flint he had carried in a thong about his waist was—like the axe—heaven knows where. The Master Horse turned his head, and Ugh-lomi became aware of an eye and teeth. He whipped his leg into a position of security, and hit at the cheek with his fist. Then the head went down somewhere out of existence apparently, and the back he was sitting on flew up into a dome. Ugh-lomi became a thing of instinct again—strictly prehensile; he held by knees and feet, and his head seemed sliding towards the turf. His fingers were twisted into the shock of mane, and the rough hair of the horse saved him. The gradient he was on lowered again, and then—, "Whup!" said Ugh-lomi astonished, and the slant was the other way up. But Ugh-lomi was a thousand generations nearer the primordial than man: no monkey could have held on better. And the lion had been training the horse for countless generations against the tactics of rolling and rearing back. But he kicked like a master, and buck-jumped rather neatly. In five minutes Ugh-lomi lived a lifetime. If he came off, the horse would kill him, he felt assured.

Then the Master Horse decided to stick to his old tactics again, and suddenly went off at a gallop. He headed down the slope, taking the steep places at a rush, swerving neither to the right nor to the left, and as they rode down, the wide expanse of valley sank out of sight behind the approaching skirmishers of oak and

Hawthorn. They skirted a sudden hollow with the pool of a spring, rank weeds and silver bushes. The ground grew softer and the grass taller, and on the right-hand side and the left came scattered bushes of May—still splashed with belated blossom. Presently the bushes thickened until they lashed the passing rider, and little flashes and gouts of blood came out on horse and man. Then the way opened again.

And then came a wonderful adventure. A sudden squeal of unreasonable anger rose amidst the bushes, the squeal of some creature bitterly wronged. And crashing after them appeared a big, grey-blue shape. It was Yaaa the big-horned rhinoceros, in one of those fits of fury of his, charging full tilt, after the manner of his kind. He had been startled at his feeding, and someone, it did not matter who, was to be ripped and trampled therefore. He was bearing down on them from the left, with his wicked little eye red, and his great horn down, and his little tail like a jury-mast behind him. For a minute Ugh-lomi was minded to slip off and dodge, and then behold! The staccato of the hoofs grew swifter, and the rhinoceros and his stumpy hurrying little legs seemed to slide out at the back corner of Ugh-lomi's eye. In two minutes they were through the bushes of May, and out in the open, going fast. For a space he could hear the ponderous paces in pursuit receding behind him, and then it was just as if Yaaa had not lost his temper, as if Yaaa had never existed.

The pace never faltered, on they rode land on.

Ugh-lomi was now all exultation. To exult in those days was to insult. "Ya-ha! Big nose," he said, trying to crane back and see some remote speck of a pursuer. "Why don't you carry your smiting-stone in your fist?" He ended with a frantic whoop.

But that whoop was unfortunate, for coming close to the ear of the horse, and being quite unexpected, it startled the stallion extremely. He shied violently. Ugh-lomi suddenly found himself uncomfortable again. He was hanging on to the horse, he found, by one arm and one knee.

The rest of the ride was honourable but unpleasant. The view was chiefly of blue sky, and that was combined with the most unpleasant physical sensations. Finally a bush of thorn lashed him and he let go.

He hit the ground with his cheek and shoulder, and then, after a complicated and extraordinarily rapid movement, hit it again with the end of his backbone. He saw splashes and sparks of light and colour. The ground seemed bouncing about just like the horse had done. Then he found he was sitting on turf, six yards beyond the bush. In front of him was a space of grass, growing greener and greener, and a number of human beings in the distance, and the horse was going round at a smart gallop quite a long way off to the right.

The human beings were on the opposite side of the river, some still in the water, but they were all running away as hard as they could go. The advent of a monster that took to pieces was not the sort of novelty they cared for. For quite a minute Ugh-lomi sat regarding them in a purely spectacular spirit. The bend of the river, the knoll among the reeds and royal ferns, the thin streams of smoke going up to Heaven, were all perfectly familiar to him. It was the squatting-place of the Sons of Uya, of Uya from whom he had fled with Eudena, and whom he had waylaid in the chestnut woods and killed with the First Axe.

He rose to his feet, still dazed from his fall, and as he did so the scattering fugitives turned and regarded him. Some pointed to the receding horse and chattered. He walked slowly towards them, staring. He forgot the horse, he forgot his own bruises, in the growing interest of this encounter. There were fewer of them than there had been—he supposed the others must have hid—the heap of fern or the night fire was not so high. By the flint heaps should have sat Wau—but then he remembered he had killed Wau. Suddenly brought back to this familiar scene, the gorge and the bears and Eudena seemed things remote, things dreamt of.

He stopped at the bank and stood regarding the tribe. His mathematical abilities were of the slightest, but it was certain there were fewer. The men might be away, but there were fewer women and children. He gave the shout of home-coming. His quarrel had been with Uya and Wau—not with the others. "Children of Uya!" he cried. They answered with his name, a little fearfully because of the strange way he had come.

For a space they spoke together. Then an old woman lifted a shrill voice and answered him. "Our Lord is a Lion."

Ugh-lomi did not understand that saying. They answered him again several together, "Uya comes again. He comes as a Lion. Our Lord is a Lion. He comes at night. He slays whom he will. But none other may slay us, Ugh-lomi. None other may slay us."

Still Ugh-lomi did not understand.

"Our Lord is a Lion. He speaks no more to men."

Ugh-lomi stood regarding them. He had had dreams—he knew that though he had killed Uya, Uya still existed. And now they told him Uya was a Lion.

The shrivelled old woman, the mistress of the fire-minders, suddenly turned and spoke softly to those next to her. She was a very old woman indeed, she had been the first of Uya's wives, and he had let her live beyond the age to which it is seemly a woman should live. She had been cunning from the first, cunning to please Uya and to get food. And now she was great in counsel. She spoke softly, and Ugh-lomi watched her shrivelled form across the river with a curious distaste. Then she called aloud, "Come over to us, Ugh-lomi."

A girl suddenly lifted up her voice. "Come over to us, Ugh-lomi," she said. And they all began crying, "Come over to us, Ugh-lomi."

It was strange how their manner changed after the old woman called.

He stood quite still watching them all. It was pleasant to be called, and the girl who had called first was a pretty one. But she made him think of Eudena.

"Come over to us, Ugh-lomi," they cried, and the voice of the shrivelled old woman rose above them all. At the sound of her voice his hesitation returned.

He stood on the river bank, Ugh-lomi—Ugh the Thinker—with his thoughts slowly taking shape. Presently one and then another paused to see what he would do. He was minded to go back, he was minded not to. Suddenly his fear or his caution got the upper hand. Without answering them he turned, and walked back towards the distant thorn-trees, the way he had come. Forthwith the whole tribe started crying to him again very eagerly. He hesitated and turned, then he went on, then he turned again, and then once again, regarding them with troubled eyes as they called. The last time he took two paces back, before his fear stopped him. They saw him stop once more, and suddenly shake his head and vanish among the hawthorn-trees.

Then all the women and children lifted up their voices together, and called to him in one last vain effort.

Far down the river the reeds were stirring in the breeze, where convenient for his new sort of feeding, the old lion, who had taken to man-eating, had made his lair.

The old woman turned her face that way, and pointed to the hawthorn thickets. "Uya," she screamed, "there goes thine enemy! There goes thine enemy, Uya! Why do you devour us nightly? We have tried to snare him! There goes thine enemy, Uya!"

But the lion who preyed upon the tribe was taking his siesta. The cry went unheard. That day he had dined on one of the plumper girls, and his mood was a comfortable placidity. He really did not understand that he was Uya or that Ugh-lomi was his enemy.

So it was that Ugh-lomi rode the horse, and heard first of Uya the lion, who had taken the place of Uya the Master, and was eating up the tribe. And as he hurried back to the gorge, his mind was no longer full of the horse, but of the thought that Uya was still alive, to slay or be slain. Over and over again he saw the shrunken band of women and children crying that Uya was a lion. Uya was a lion!

And presently, fearing the twilight might come upon him, Ugh-lomi began running.

4. Uya the Lion

The old lion was in luck. The tribe had a certain pride in their ruler, but that was all the satisfaction they got out of it. He came the very night that Ugh-lomi killed Uya the Cunning, and so it was they named him Uya. It was the old woman, the fire-minder, who first named him Uya. A shower had lowered the fires to a glow, and made the night dark. And as they conversed together, and peered at one another in the darkness, and wondered fearfully what Uya would do to them in their dreams now that he was dead, they heard the mounting reverberations of the lion's roar close at hand. Then everything was still.

They held their breath, so that almost the only sounds were the patter of the rain and the hiss of the raindrops in the ashes. And then, after an interminable time, a crash, and a shriek of fear, and a growling. They sprang to their feet, shouting, screaming, running this way and that, but brands would not burn, and in a minute the victim was being dragged away through the ferns. It was Irk, the brother of Wau.

So the lion came.

The ferns were still wet from the rain the next night, and he came and took Click with the red hair. That sufficed for two nights.

And then in the dark, between the moons he came three nights, night after night, and that, though they had good fires. He was an old lion with stumpy teeth, but very silent and very cool; he knew of fires before; these were not the first of mankind that had ministered to his old age. The third night he came between the outer fire and the inner, and he leapt the flint heap, and pulled down Irm the son of Irk, who had seemed like to be the leader. That was a dreadful night, because they lit great flares of fern and ran screaming, and the lion missed his hold of Irm. By the glare of the fire they saw Irm struggle up, and run a little way towards them, and then the lion in two bounds had him down again. That was the last of Irm.

So fear came, and all the delight of spring passed out of their lives. Already there were five gone out of the tribe, and four nights added three more to the number. Food-seeking became spiritless, none knew who might go next, and all day the women toiled, even the favourite women, gathering litter and sticks for the night fires. And the hunters hunted ill: in the warm spring-time hunger came again as though it was still winter. The tribe might have moved, had they had a leader, but they had no leader, and none knew where to go that the lion could not follow them. So the old lion waxed fat and thanked heaven for the race of men. Two of the children and a youth died while the moon was still new, and then it was the shrivelled old fire-minder first bethought herself in a dream of Eudena and Ugh-lomi, and of the way Uya, had been slain. She had lived in fear of Uya all her days, and now she lived in fear of the lion. That Ugh-lomi could kill Uya for good—Ugh-lomi whom she had seen born—was impossible. It was Uya still seeking his enemy!

And then came the strange return of Ugh-lomi, a wonderful animal seen galloping far across the river, that suddenly changed into two animals, a horse and a man. Following this portent, the vision of Ugh-lomi on the farther bank of the river...Yes, it was all plain to her. Uya was punishing them, because they had not hunted down Ugh-lomi and Eudena.

The men came straggling back to the chances of the night while the sun was still golden in the sky. They were received with the story of Ugh-lomi. She went across the river with them and showed them his spoor hesitating on the farther bank. Siss the Tracker knew the feet for Ugh-lomi's. "Uya needs Ugh-lomi," cried the old woman, standing on the left of the bend, a gesticulating figure of flaring bronze in the sunset. Her cries were strange sounds, flitting to and fro on the borderland of speech, but this was the sense they carried: "The lion needs Eudena. He comes night after night seeking Eudena and Ugh-lomi. When he cannot find Eudena and Ugh-lomi, he grows angry and he kills. Hunt Eudena and Ugh-lomi, Eudena whom he pursued, and Ugh-lomi for whom he gave the death-word! Hunt Eudena and Ugh-lomi!"

She turned to the distant reed-bed, as sometimes she had turned to Uya in his life. "Is it not so, my lord?" she cried. And as if in answer, the tall reeds bowed before a breath of wind.

Far into the twilight the sound of hacking was heard from the squatting-places. It was the men sharpening their ashen spears against the hunting of the morrow. And in the night, early before the moon rose, the lion came and took the girl of Siss the Tracker.

In the morning before the sun had risen, Siss the Tracker, and the lad Wau-hau, who now chipped flints, and One Eye, and Bo, and the snail-eater, the two red-haired men, and Cat's-skin and Snake, all the men that were left alive of the Sons of Uya, taking their ash spears and their smiting-stones, and with throwing stones in the beast-paw bags, started forth upon the trail of Ugh-lomi through the hawthorn thickets where Yaaa the Rhinoceros and his brothers were feeding, and up the bare downland towards the beechwoods.

That night the fires burnt high and fierce, as the waxing moon set, and the lion left the crouching women and children in peace.

And the next day, while the sun was still high, the hunters returned—all save One Eye, who lay dead with a smashed skull at the foot of the ledge. (When Ugh-lomi came back that evening from stalking the horses, he found the vultures already busy over him.) And with them the hunters brought Eudena bruised and wounded, but alive. That had been the strange order of the shrivelled old woman, that she was to be brought alive—, "She is no kill for us. She is for Uya the Lion." Her hands were tied with thongs, as though she had been a man, and she came weary and drooping—her hair over her eyes and matted with blood. They walked about her, and ever and again the Snail-Eater, whose name she had given, would laugh and strike her with his ashen spear. And after he had struck her with his spear, he would look over his shoulder like one who had done an over-bold deed. The others too, looked over their shoulders ever and again, and all were in a hurry save Eudena. When the old woman saw them coming, she cried aloud with joy.

They made Eudena cross the river with her hands tied, although the current was strong, and when she slipped the old woman screamed, first with joy and then for fear she might be drowned. And when they had dragged Eudena to shore, she could not stand for a time, albeit they beat her sore. So they let her sit with her feet touching the water, and her eyes staring before her, and her face set, whatever they might do or say. All the tribe came down to the squatting-place, even curly little Haha, who as yet could scarcely toddle, and stood staring at Eudena and the old woman, as now we should stare at some strange wounded beast and its captor.

The old woman tore off the necklace of Uya that was about Eudena's neck, and put it on herself—she had been the first to wear it. Then she tore at Eudena's hair, and took a spear from Siss and beat her with all her might. And when she had vented the warmth of her heart on the girl she looked closely into her face. Eudena's eyes were closed and her features were set, and she lay so still that for a moment the old woman feared she was dead until her nostrils quivered. At that the old woman slapped her face and laughed and gave the spear to Siss again, and went a little way off from her and began to talk and jeer at her after her manner.

The old woman had more words than any in the tribe. And her talk was a terrible thing to hear. Sometimes she screamed and moaned incoherently, and sometimes the shape of her guttural cries was the mere phantom of thoughts. But she conveyed to Eudena, nevertheless, much of the things that were yet to come, of the Lion and of the torment he would do her. "And Ugh-lomi! Ha, ha! Ugh-lomi was slain?"

And suddenly Eudena's eyes opened and she sat up again, and her look met the old woman's fair and level. "No," she said slowly, like one trying to remember, "I did not see my Ugh-lomi slain. I did not see my Ugh-lomi slain."

"Tell her," cried the old woman. "Tell her—he that killed him. Tell her how Ugh-lomi was slain."

She looked, and all the women and children there looked, from man to man.

None answered her. They stood shamefaced.

"Tell her," said the old woman. The men looked at one another.

Eudena's face suddenly lit.

"Tell her," she said. "Tell her, mighty men! Tell her the killing of Ugh-lomi."

The old woman rose and struck her sharply across her mouth.

"We could not find Ugh-lomi," said Siss the Tracker, slowly. "Who hunts two, kills none."

Then Eudena's heart leapt, but she kept her face hard. It was well, for the old woman looked at her sharply, with murder in her eyes.

Then the old woman turned her tongue upon the men because they had feared to go on after Ugh-lomi. She dreaded no one now Uya was slain. She scolded them as one scolds children. And they scowled at her, and began to accuse one another. Until suddenly Siss the Tracker raised his voice and bade her hold her peace.

And so when the sun was setting they took Eudena and went—though their hearts sank within them—along the trail the old lion had made in the reeds. All the men went together. At one place was a group of alders, and here they hastily bound Eudena where the lion might find her when he came abroad in the twilight, and having done so they hurried back until they were near the squatting-place. Then they stopped. Siss stopped first and looked back again at the alders. They could see her head even from the squatting-place, a little black shock under the limb of the larger tree. That was as well.

All the women and children stood watching upon the crest of the mound. And the old woman stood and screamed for the lion to take her whom he sought, and counselled him on the torments he might do her.

Eudena was very weary now, stunned by beatings and fatigue and sorrow, and only the fear of the thing that was still to come upheld her. The sun was broad and blood-red between the stems of the distant chestnuts, and the west was all on fire; the evening breeze had died to a warm tranquillity. The air was full of midge swarms, the fish in the river hard by would leap at times, and now and again a cockchafer would drone through the air. Out of the corner of her eye Eudena could see a part of the squatting-knoll, and little figures standing and staring at her. And—a very little sound but very clear—she could hear the beating of the firestone. Dark and near to her and very still was the reed-fringed thicket of the lair.

Presently the firestone ceased. She looked for the sun and found he had gone, and overhead and growing brighter was the waxing moon. She looked towards the thicket of the lair, seeking shapes in the reeds, and then suddenly she began to wriggle and wriggle, weeping and calling upon Ugh-lomi.

But Ugh-lomi was far away. When they saw her head moving with her struggles, they shouted together on the knoll, and then she desisted and was still. And then came the bats, and the star that was like Ugh-lomi crept out of its blue hiding-place in the west. She called to it, but softly, because she feared the lion. And all through the coming of the twilight the thicket was still.

So the dark crept upon Eudena, and the moon grew bright, and the shadows of things that had fled up the hillside and vanished with the evening came back to them short and black, And the dark shapes in the thicket of reeds and alders where the lion lay, gathered, and a faint stir began there. But nothing came out therefrom all through the gathering of the darkness.

She looked at the squatting-place and saw the fires glowing smoky-red, and the men and women going to and fro. The other way, over the river, a white mist was rising. Then far away came the whimpering of young foxes and the yell of a hyaena.

There were long gaps of aching waiting. After a long time some animal splashed in the water, and seemed to cross the river at the ford beyond the lair, but what animal it was she could not see. From the distant drinking-pools she could hear the sound of splashing, and the noise of elephants—so still was the night.

The earth was now a colourless arrangement of white reflections and impenetrable shadows, under the blue sky. The silvery moon was already spotted with the filigree crests of the chestnut woods, and over the shadowy eastward bills the stars were multiplying. The knoll fires were bright red now, and black figures stood waiting against them. They were waiting for a scream...Surely it would be soon.

The night suddenly seemed full of movement. She held her breath. Things were passing—one, two, three—subtly sneaking shadows...Jackals.

Then a long waiting again.

Then, asserting itself as real at once over all the sounds her mind had imagined, came a stir in the thicket, then a vigorous movement. There was a snap. The reeds crashed heavily, once, twice, thrice, and then everything was still save a measured swishing. She heard a low tremulous growl, and then everything was still again. The stillness lengthened—would it never end? She held her breath; she bit her lips to stop screaming. Then something scuttled through the undergrowth. Her scream was involuntary. She did not hear the answering yell from the mound.

Immediately the thicket woke up to vigorous movement again. She saw the grass stems waving in the light of the setting moon, the alders swaying. She struggled violently—her last struggle. But nothing came towards her. A dozen monsters seemed rushing about in that little place for a couple of minutes, and then again came silence. The moon sank behind the distant chestnuts and the night was dark.

Then an odd sound, a sobbing panting, that grew faster and fainter. Yet another silence, and then dim sounds and the grunting of some animal.

Everything was still again. Far away eastwards an elephant trumpeted, and from the woods came a snarling and yelping that died away.

In the long interval the moon shone out again, between the stems of the trees on the ridge, sending two great bars of light, and a bar of darkness across the reedy waste. Then came a steady rustling, a splash, and the reeds swayed wider and wider apart. And at last they broke open, cleft from root to crest... The end had come.

She looked to see the thing that had come out of the reeds. For a moment it seemed certainly the great head and jaw she expected, and then it dwindled and changed. It was a dark low thing, that remained silent, but it was not the lion. It became still—everything became still. She peered. It was like some gigantic frog, two limbs and a slanting body. Its head moved about searching the shadows...

A rustle, and it moved clumsily, with a sort of hopping. And as it moved it gave a low groan.

The blood rushing through her veins was suddenly joy. "Ugh-lomi!" she whispered.

The thing stopped. "Eudena," he answered softly with pain in his voice, and peering into the alders.

He moved again, and came out of the shadow beyond the reeds into the moonlight. All his body was covered with dark smears. She saw he was dragging his legs, and that he gripped his axe, the first axe, in one hand. In another moment he had struggled into the position of all fours, and had staggered over to her. "The lion," he said in a strange mingling of exultation and anguish. "Wau—!

I have slain a lion. With my own hand. Even as I slew the great bear." He moved to emphasise his words, and suddenly broke off with a faint cry. For a space he did not move.

"Let me free," whispered Eudena...

He answered her no words but pulled himself up from his crawling attitude by means of the alder stem, and hacked at her thongs with the sharp edge of his axe. She heard him sob at each blow. He cut away the thongs about her chest and arms, and then his hand dropped. His chest struck against her shoulder and he slipped down beside her and lay still.

But the rest of her release was easy. Very hastily she freed herself. She made one step from the tree, and her head was spinning, Her last conscious movement was towards him. She reeled, and suddenly fell headlong beside him. Her hand fell upon his thigh. It was soft and wet, and gave way under her pressure; he cried out at her touch, and writhed and lay still again, with her hand upon him.

Presently a dark dog-like shape came very softly through the reeds. This stopped dead and stood sniffing, hesitated, and at last turned and slunk back into the shadows.

Long was the time they remained there motionless, with the light of the setting moon shining on their limbs. Very slowly, as slowly as the setting of the moon, did the shadow of the reeds towards the mound flow over them. Presently their legs were hidden, and Ugh-lomi was but a bust of silver. The shadow crept to his neck, crept over his face, and so at last the darkness of the night swallowed them up.

The shadow became full of instinctive stirrings. There was a patter of feet, and a faint snarling—the sound of a blow.

There was little sleep that night for the women and children at the squatting-place until they heard Eudena scream. But the men were weary and sat dozing. When Eudena screamed they felt assured of their safety, and hurried to get the nearest places to the fires. The old woman laughed at the scream, and laughed again because Si, the little sister of Eudena, whimpered. Directly the dawn came, they were all alert and looking towards the alders. They could see that Eudena had been taken. They could not help feeling glad to think that Uya was appeased. But across the minds of the men the thought of Ugh-lomi fell like a shadow. They could understand revenge, for the world was old in revenge, but they did not think of rescue. Suddenly a hyaena fled out of the thicket, and came galloping across the reed space. His muzzle and paws were dark-stained. At that sight all the men shouted and clutched at throwing-stones and ran towards him, for no animal is so pitiful a coward as the hyaena by day. All men hated the hyaena because he preyed on children, and would come and bite when one was sleeping on the edge of the squatting-place. And Cat's-skin, throwing fair and straight, hit the brute shrewdly on the flank, whereat the whole tribe yelled with delight.

At the noise they made there came a flapping of wings from the lair of the lion, and three white-headed vultures rose slowly and circled and came to rest amidst the branches of an alder, overlooking the lair. "Our lord is abroad," said the old woman, pointing. "The vultures have their share of Eudena." For a space they remained there, and then first one and then another dropped back into the thicket.

Then over the eastern woods, and touching the whole world to life and colour, poured, with the exaltation of a trumpet blast, the light of the rising sun. At the sight of him the children shouted together, and clapped their hands and began to race off towards the water. Only little Si lagged behind and looked wonderingly at the alders where she had seen the head of Eudena overnight.

But Uya, the old lion, was not abroad but at home, and he lay very still, and a little on one side. He was not in his lair, but a little way from it in a place of trampled grass. Under one eye was a little wound, the feeble little bite of the first axe. But all the ground beneath his chest was ruddy brown with a vivid streak, and in his chest was a little hole that had been made by Ugh-lomi's stabbing-spear. Along his side and at his neck the vultures had marked their claims. For so Ugh-lomi had slain him, lying stricken under his paw and thrusting haphazard at his chest. He had driven the spear in with all his strength and stabbed the giant to the heart. So it was the reign of the lion, of the second incarnation of Uya the Master, came to an end.

From the knoll the bustle of preparation grew, the hacking of spears and throwing-stones. None spake the name of Ugh-lomi for fear that it might bring him. The men were going to keep together, close together, in the hunting for a day or so. And their hunting was to be Ugh-lomi, lest instead he should come a-hunting them.

But Ugh-lomi was lying very still and silent, outside the lion's lair, and Eudena squatted beside him, with the ash spear, all smeared with lion's blood, gripped in her hand.

5. The Fight in the Lion's Thicket

Ugh-lomi lay still, his back against an alder, and his thigh was a red mass terrible to see. No civilised man could have lived who had been so sorely wounded, but Eudena got him thorns to close his wounds, and squatted beside him day and night, smiting the flies from him with a fan of reeds by day, and in the night threatening the hyaenas who came too near with the first axe in her hand; and in a little while he began to heal. It was high summer, and there was no rain. Little food they had, during the first two days his wounds were open. In the low place where they hid were no roots nor little beasts, and the stream, with its water-snails and fish, was in the open, a hundred yards away. She could not go abroad by day for fear of the tribe, her brothers and sisters, nor by night for fear of the beasts, both on his account and hers. So they shared the lion with the vultures. But there was a trickle of water near by, and Eudena brought him plenty in her hands.

Where Ugh-lomi lay was well hidden from the tribe by a thicket of alders, and all fenced about with bulrushes and tall reeds. The dead lion he had killed lay near his old lair on a place of trampled reeds fifty yards away, in sight through the reed-stems, and the vultures fought each other for the choicest pieces and kept the jackals off him. Very soon a cloud of flies that looked like bees hung over him, and Ugh-lomi could hear their humming. And when Ugh-lomi's flesh was already healing—and it was not many days before that began—only a few bones of the lion remained scattered and shining white.

For the most part Ugh-lomi sat still during the day, looking before him at nothing, sometimes he would mutter of the horses and bears and lions, and sometimes he would beat the ground with the first axe and say the names of the tribe—he seemed to have no fear of bringing the tribe—for hours together. But chiefly he slept, dreaming little because of his loss of blood and the slightness of his food. During the short summer night both kept awake. All the while the darkness lasted things moved about them, things they never saw by day. For some nights the hyaenas did not come, and then one moonless night near a dozen came and fought for what was left of the lion. The night was a tumult of growling, and Ugh-lomi and Eudena could hear the bones snap in their teeth. But they knew the hyaena dare not attack any creature alive and awake, and so they were not greatly afraid.

Of a daytime Eudena would go along the narrow path, the old lion had made in the reeds until she was beyond the bend, and then she would creep into the thicket and watch the tribe. She would lie close by the alders, where they had bound her to offer her up to the lion, and thence she could see them on the knoll by the fire, little and clear, as she had seen them that night. But she told Ugh-lomi little of what she saw, because she feared to bring them by their names. For so they believed in those days, that naming called.

She saw the men prepare stabbing-spears and throwing-stones on the morning after Ugh-lomi had slain the lion, and go out to hunt him, leaving the women and children on the knoll. Little they knew how near he was as they tracked off in single file towards the hills, with Siss the Tracker leading them. And she watched the women and children, after the men had gone, gathering fern-fronds and twigs for the night fire, and the boys and girls running and playing together. But the very old woman made her feel afraid. After a long space towards noon, when most of the others were down at the stream by the bend, she came and stood on the hither side of the knoll, a gnarled brown figure, and gesticulated so that Eudena could scarce believe she was not seen. Eudena lay like a hare in its form, with shining eyes fixed on the bent witch away there, and presently she dimly understood it was the lion the old woman was worshipping—the lion Ugh-lomi had slain.

And the next day the hunters came back weary, carrying a fawn, and Eudena watched the feast enviously. And then came a strange thing. She saw—distinctly she heard—the old woman shrieking and gesticulating and pointing towards her. She was afraid, and crept like a snake out of sight again. But presently curiosity overcame her and she was back at her spying-place, and as she peered her heart stopped, for there were all the men, with their weapons in their hands, walking together towards her from the knoll.

She dared not move lest her movement should be seen, but she pressed herself close to the ground. The sun was low and the golden light was in the faces of the men. She saw they carried a piece of rich red meat thrust through by an ashen stake. Presently they stopped. "Go on!" screamed the old woman. Cat's-skin grumbled, and they came on, searching the thicket with sun-dazzled eyes. "Here!" said Siss. And they took the ashen stake with the meat upon it and thrust it into the ground. "Uya!" cried Siss, "Behold thy portion. And Ugh-lomi we have slain. Of a truth we have slain Ugh-lomi. This day we slew Ugh-lomi, and to-morrow we will bring his body to you." And the others repeated the words.

They looked at each other and behind them, and partly turned and began going back. At first they walked half turned to the thicket, then facing the mound they walked faster, looking over their shoulders, then faster; soon they ran, it was a race at last, until they were near the knoll. Then Siss who was hindmost was first to slacken his pace.

The sunset passed and the twilight came, the fires glowed red against the hazy blue of the distant chestnut trees, and the voices over the mound were merry. Eudena lay scarcely stirring, looking from the mound to the meat and then to the mound. She was hungry, but she was afraid. At last she crept back to Ugh-lomi.

He looked round at the little rustle of her approach. His face was in shadow. "Have you got me some food?" he said.

She said she could find nothing, but that she would seek further, and went back along the lion's path until she could see the mound again, but she could not bring herself to take the meat; she had the brute's instinct of a snare. She felt very miserable.

She crept back at last towards Ugh-lomi and heard him stirring and moaning. She turned back to the mound again; then she saw something in the darkness near the stake, and peering distinguished a jackal. In a flash she was brave and angry; she sprang up, cried out, and ran towards the offering. She stumbled and fell, and heard the growling of the jackal going off.

When she arose only the ashen stake lay on the ground, the meat was gone. So she went back, to fast through the night with Ugh-lomi; and Ugh-lomi was angry with her, because she had no food for him; but she told him nothing of the things she had seen.

Two days passed and they were near starving, when the tribe slew a horse. Then came the same ceremony, and a haunch was left on the ashen stake; but this time Eudena did not hesitate.

By acting and words she made Ugh-lomi understand, but he ate most of the food before he understood; and then he grew merry with his food. "I am Uya," he said; "I am the Lion. I am the Great Cave Bear, I who was only Ugh-lomi. I am Wau the Cunning. It is well that they should feed me, for presently I will kill them all."

Then Eudena's heart was light, and she laughed with him; and afterwards she ate what he had left of the horseflesh with gladness.

After that it was he had a dream, and the next day he made Eudena bring him the lion's teeth and claws—so much of them as she could find—and hack him a club of alder, and he put the teeth and claws very cunningly into the wood so that the points were outward. Very long it took him, and he blunted two of the teeth hammering them in, and was very angry and threw the thing away; but afterwards he dragged himself to where he had thrown it and finished it—a club of a new sort set with teeth. That day there was more meat for them both, an offering to the lion from the tribe.

It was one day—more than a hand's fingers of days, more than anyone has skill to count—after Ugh-lomi had made the club, that Eudena (while he was asleep) was lying in the thicket watching the squatting-place. There had been no meat for three days. And the old woman came and worshipped after her manner. Now while she worshipped, Eudena's little sister Si and another, the child of the first girl Siss had loved, came over the knoll and stood regarding her skinny figure, and presently they began to mock her. Eudena found this entertaining, but suddenly the old woman turned on them quickly and saw them. For a moment she stood and they stood motionless, and then with a shriek of rage she rushed towards them, and all three disappeared over the crest of the knoll.

Presently the children reappeared among the ferns over the shoulder of the hill. Little Si ran first, for she was an active girl, and the other child ran squealing with the old woman close upon her. And over the knoll came Siss with a bone in his hand, and Bo and Cat's-skin obsequiously behind him, each holding a piece of food, and they laughed aloud and shouted to see the old woman so angry. And with a shriek the child was caught and the old woman set to work slapping and the child screaming, and it was very good after-dinner fun for them. Little Si ran on a little way and stopped at last between fear and curiosity.

And suddenly came the mother of the child, with hair streaming, panting, and with a stone in her hand, and the old woman turned about like a wild cat. She was the equal of any woman, was the old chief of the fire-minders, in spite of her years; but before she could do anything Siss shouted to her and the clamour rose loud. Other shock heads came into sight. It seemed the whole tribe was at home and feasting. But the old woman dared not go on wreaking herself on the child Siss befriended. Nevertheless it was a fine row.

Everyone made noises and called names, even little Si. Abruptly the old woman let go of the child she had caught and made a swift run at Si who had no friends; and Si, realising her danger when it was almost upon her, with a faint cry of terror made off headlong, not heeding whither she ran, straight to the lair of the lion. She swerved aside into the reeds presently, not realising whither she went.

But the old woman was a wonderful old woman, as active as she was spiteful, and she caught Si by the streaming hair within thirty yards of Eudena. All the tribe now was running down the knoll and shouting, ready to see the fun.

Then something stirred in Eudena and, thinking all of little Si and nothing of her fear, she sprang up from her ambush and ran swiftly forward. The old woman did not see her, for she was busy beating little Si's face with her hand, beating with all her heart, and suddenly something hard and heavy struck her cheek. She went reeling, and saw Eudena with flaming eyes and cheeks between her and little Si. She shrieked with astonishment and terror, and little Si, not understanding, set off towards the gaping tribe. They were quite close now, for the sight of Eudena had driven their fading fear of the lion out of their heads.

In a moment Eudena had turned from the cowering old woman and overtaken Si. "Si!" she cried, "Si!" She caught the child up in her arms as it stopped, pressed the nail-lined face to hers, and turned about to run towards her lair, the lair of the old lion. The old woman stood waist-high in the reeds, and screamed foul things and inarticulate rage, but did not dare to intercept her; and at the bend of the path Eudena looked back and saw all the men of the tribe crying to one another and Siss coming at a trot along the lion's trail.

She ran straight along the narrow way through the reeds to the shady place where Ugh-lomi sat with his healing thigh, just awakened by the shouting and rubbing his eyes. She came to him, a woman, with little Si in her arms. Her heart throbbed in her throat. "Ugh-lomi!" she cried, "Ugh-lomi, the tribe comes!"

Ugh-lomi sat staring in stupid astonishment at her and Si.

She pointed with Si in one arm. She sought among her feeble store of words to explain. She could hear the men calling. Apparently they had stopped outside. She put down Si and caught up the new club with the lion's teeth, and put it into Ugh-lomi's hand, and ran three yards and picked up the first axe.

"Ah!" said Ugh-lomi, waving the new club, and suddenly he perceived the occasion and, rolling over, began to struggle to his feet.

He stood, but clumsily. He supported himself by one hand against the tree, and just touched the ground gingerly with the toe of his wounded leg. In the other hand he gripped the new club. He looked at his healing thigh; and suddenly the reeds began whispering, and ceased and whispered again, and coming cautiously along the track among the reeds, bending down and holding his fire-hardened stabbing-stick of ash in his hand, appeared Siss. He stopped dead, and his eyes met Ugh-lomi's.

Ugh-lomi forgot he had a wounded leg. He stood firmly on both feet. Something trickled. He glanced down and saw a little gout of blood had oozed out along the edge of the healing wound. He rubbed his hand there to give him the grip of his club, and fixed his eyes again on Siss. The fighting spirit now swiftly and suddenly overflowed.

"Wau!" he cried, and sprang forward, and Siss, still stooping and watchful, drove his stabbing-stick up very quickly in an ugly thrust. It ripped Ugh-lomi's guarding arm and the club came down in a counter that Siss was never to understand. He fell, as an ox falls to the pole-axe, at Ugh-lomi's feet.

To Bo it seemed the strangest thing. He had a comforting sense of tall reeds on either side, and an impregnable rampart, Siss, between him and any danger. Snail-eater was close behind and there was no danger there. He was prepared to shove behind and send Siss to death or victory. That was his place as second man. He saw the blunt of the spear Siss carried leap away from him, and suddenly a dull whack and the broad back fell away forward, and he looked Ugh-lomi in the face over his prostrate leader. It felt to Bo as if his heart had fallen down a well. He had a throwing-stone in one hand and an ashen stabbing-stick in the other. He did not live to the end of his momentary hesitation which to use.

Snail-eater was a readier man, and besides Bo did not fall forward as Siss had done, but gave at his knees and hips, crumpling up with the toothed club upon his head, smiting him down. The Snail-eater drove his spear forward swift and straight, and took Ugh-lomi in the muscle of the shoulder, and then he drove him hard with the smiting-stone in his other and, shouting out as he did so. The new club swished ineffectually through the reeds. Eudena saw Ugh-lomi come staggering back from the narrow path into the open space, tripping over Siss and with a foot of ashen stake sticking out of him over his arm, and then the Snail-eater, whose name she had given, had his final injury from her, as his exultant face came out of the reeds after his spear. For she swung the first axe swift and high, and hit him fair and square on the temple; and down he went on Siss at prostrate Ugh-lomi's feet.

But before Ugh-lomi could get to his feet, the two red-haired men were tumbling out of the reeds, spears and smiting-stones ready, and Snake hard behind them. One she struck on the neck, but not to fell him, and he blundered aside and spoilt his brother's blow at Ugh-lomi's head. In a moment Ugh-lomi dropped his club and had his assailant by the waist, and had pitched him sideways sprawling. He snatched at his club again and recovered it. The man Eudena had hit stabbed at her with his spear as he stumbled from her blow, and involuntarily she gave ground to avoid him. He hesitated between her and Ugh-lomi, half turned, gave a vague cry at finding Ugh-lomi so near, and in a moment Ugh-lomi had him by the throat, and the club had its third victim. As he went down Ugh-lomi shouted—no words, but an exultant cry.

The other red-haired man was six feet from her with his back to her, and a darker red streaking his head. He was struggling to his feet. She had an irrational impulse to stop his rising. She flung the axe at him, missed, saw his face in profile, and he had swerved beyond little Si, and was running through the reeds. She had a transitory vision of Snake standing in the throat of the path, half turned away from her, and then she saw his back. She saw the club whirling through the air, and the shock head of Ugh-lomi, with blood in the hair and blood upon the shoulder, vanishing below the reeds in pursuit. Then she heard Snake scream like a woman.

She ran past Si to where the handle of the axe stuck out of a clump of fern, and turning, found herself panting and alone with three motionless bodies. The air was full of shouts and screams. For a space she was sick and giddy, and then it came into her head that Ugh-lomi was being killed along the reed-path, and with an inarticulate cry she leapt over the body of Bo and hurried after him. Snake's feet lay across the path, and his head was among the reeds. She followed the path until it bent round and opened out by the alders, and thence she saw all that was left of the tribe in the open, scattering like dead leaves before a gale, and going back over the knoll. Ugh-lomi was hard upon Cat's-skin.

But Cat's-skin was fleet of foot and got away, and so did young Wau-Hau when Ugh-lomi turned upon him, and Ugh-lomi pursued Wau-Hau far beyond the knoll before he desisted. He had the rage of battle on him now, and the wood thrust through his shoulder stung him like a spear. When she saw he was in no danger she stopped running and stood panting, watching the distant active figures run up and vanish one by one over the knoll. In a little time she was alone again. Everything had happened very swiftly. The smoke of Brother Fire rose straight and steady from the squatting-place, just as it had done ten minutes ago, when the old woman had stood yonder worshipping the lion.

And after a long time, as it seemed, Ugh-lomi reappeared over the knoll, and came back to Eudena, triumphant and breathing heavily. She stood, her hair about her eyes and hot-faced, with the blood-stained axe in her hand, at the place where the tribe had offered her as a sacrifice to the lion. "Wau!" cried Ugh-lomi at the sight of her, his face alight with the fellowship of battle, and he waved his new club, red now and hairy; and at the sight of his glowing face her tense pose relaxed somewhat, and she stood weeping and rejoicing.

Ugh-lomi had a queer unaccountable pang at the sight of her tears; but he only shouted "Wau!" the louder and shook the axe east and west. He called to her to follow him and turned back, striding, with the club swinging in his hand, towards the squatting-place, as if he had never left the tribe; and she stopped weeping and followed as a woman should.

So Ugh-lomi and Eudena came back to the squatting-place from which they had fled many days before from the face of Uya; and by the squatting-place lay a deer half eaten, just as there had been before Ugh-lomi was man or Eudena woman. So Ugh-lomi sat down to eat, and Eudena beside him like a man, and the rest of the tribe watched them from safe hiding-places. And after a time one of the elder girls came back timorously and carrying little Si in her arms, and Eudena called to them by name, and offered them food. But the elder girl was afraid and would not come, though Si struggled to come to Eudena. Afterwards, when Ugh-lomi had eaten, he sat dozing, and at last he slept, and slowly the others came out of the hiding-places and drew near. And when Ugh-lomi woke, save that there were no men to be seen, it seemed as though he had never left the tribe.

Now there is a thing strange but true: that all through this fight Ugh-lomi forgot that he was lame, and was not lame, and after he had rested behold! He was a lame man; and he remained a lame man to the end of his days.

Cat's-skin and the second red-haired man and Wau-Hau, who chipped flints cunningly, as his father had done before him, fled from the face of Ugh-lomi, and none knew where they hid. But two days after they came and squatted among the bracken under the chestnuts a good way off from the knoll and watched. Ugh-lomi's rage had gone, he moved to go against them and did not, and at sundown they went away. That day too, they found the old woman among the ferns, where Ugh-lomi had blundered upon her when he had pursued Wau-Hau. She was dead and more ugly than ever, but whole. The jackals and vultures had tried her and left her—; she was ever a wonderful old woman.

The next day the three men came again and squatted nearer, and Wau-Hau had two rabbits to hold up, and the red-haired man a wood-pigeon, and Ugh-Lomi stood before their women and mocked them.

The next day they sat again nearer—without stones or sticks, and with the same offerings, and Cat's-skin had a trout. It was rare men caught fish in those days but Cat's-skin would stand silently in the water for hours and catch them with his hand. And the fourth day Ugh-lomi suffered these three to come to the squatting-place in peace, with the food they had with them. Ugh-lomi ate the trout. Thereafter for many moons Ugh-lomi was master, and had his will in peace. And on the fulness of time he was killed and eaten as Uya had been slain.

29

The Crystal Egg

There was, until a year ago, a little and very grimy-looking shop near Seven Dials over which, in weather-worn yellow lettering, the name of "C. Cave, Naturalist and Dealer in Antiquities," was inscribed. The contents of its window were curiously variegated. They comprised some elephant tusks and an imperfect set of chessmen, beads and weapons, a box of eyes, two skulls of tigers and one human, several moth-eaten stuffed monkeys (one holding a lamp), an old-fashioned cabinet, a fly-blown ostrich egg or so, some fishing-tackle, and an extraordinarily dirty, empty glass fish-tank. There was also, at the moment the story begins, a mass of crystal, worked into the shape of an egg and brilliantly polished. And at that two people, who stood outside the window, were looking, one of them a tall, thin clergyman, the other a black-bearded young man of dusky complexion and unobtrusive costume. The dusky young man spoke with eager gesticulation, and seemed anxious for his companion to purchase the article.

While they were there, Mr. Cave came into his shop, his beard still wagging with the bread and butter of his tea. When he saw these men and the object of their regard, his countenance fell. He glanced guiltily over his shoulder, and softly shut the door. He was a little old man, with pale face and peculiar watery blue eyes; his hair was a dirty grey, and he wore a shabby blue frock-coat, an ancient silk hat, and carpet slippers very much down at heel. He remained watching the two men as they talked. The clergyman went deep into his trouser pocket, examined a handful of money, and showed his teeth in an agreeable smile. Mr. Cave seemed still more depressed when they came into the shop.

The clergyman, without any ceremony, asked the price of the crystal egg. Mr. Cave glanced nervously towards the door leading into the parlour, and said five pounds. The clergyman protested that the price was high, to his companion as well as to Mr. Cave—it was, indeed, very much more than Mr. Cave had intended to ask, when he had stocked the article—and an attempt at bargaining ensued. Mr. Cave stepped to the shop-door, and held it open. "Five pounds is my price," he said, as though he wished to save himself the trouble of unprofitable discussion. As he did so, the upper portion of a woman's face appeared above the blind in the glass upper panel of the door leading into the parlour, and stared curiously at the two customers. "Five pounds is my price," said Mr. Cave, with a quiver in his voice.

The swarthy young man had so far remained a spectator, watching Cave keenly. Now he spoke. "Give him five pounds," he said. The clergyman glanced at him to see if he were in earnest, and, when he looked at Mr. Cave again, he saw that the latter's face was white. "It's a lot of money," said the clergyman, and diving into his pocket, began counting his resources. He had little more than thirty shillings, and he appealed to his companion, with whom he seemed to be on terms of considerable intimacy. This gave Mr. Cave an opportunity of collecting his thoughts, and he began to explain in an agitated manner that the crystal was not, as a matter of fact, entirely free for sale. His two customers were naturally surprised at this, and inquired why he had not thought of that before he began to bargain. Mr. Cave became confused, but he stuck to his story, that the crystal was not in the market that afternoon, that a probable purchaser of it had already appeared. The two, treating this as an attempt to raise the price still further, made as if they would leave the shop. But at this point the parlour door opened, and the owner of the dark fringe and the little eyes appeared.

She was a coarse-featured, corpulent woman, younger and very much larger than Mr. Cave; she walked heavily, and her face was flushed. "That crystal is for sale," she said. "And five pounds is a good enough price for it. I can't think what you're about Cave, not to take the gentleman's offer!"

Mr. Cave, greatly perturbed by the irruption, looked angrily at her over the rims of his spectacles, and without excessive assurance, asserted his right to manage his business in his own way. An altercation began. The two customers watched the scene with interest and some amusement, occasionally assisting Mrs. Cave with suggestions. Mr. Cave, hard driven, persisted in a confused and impossible story of an enquiry for the crystal that morning, and his agitation became painful. But he stuck to his point with extraordinary persistence. It was the young Oriental who ended this curious controversy. He proposed that they should call again in the course of two days—so as to give the alleged enquirer a fair chance. "And then we must insist," said the clergyman. "Five pounds." Mrs. Cave took it on herself to apologise for her husband, explaining that he was sometimes "a little odd," and as the two customers left, the couple prepared for a free discussion of the incident in all its bearings.

Mrs. Cave talked to her husband with singular directness. The poor little man, quivering with emotion, muddled himself between his stories, maintaining on the one hand that he had another customer in view, and on the other asserting that the crystal was honestly worth ten guineas. "Why did you ask five pounds?" said his wife. "Do let me manage my business my own way!" said Mr. Cave.

Mr. Cave had living with him a step-daughter and a step-son, and at supper that night the transaction was re-discussed. None of them had a high opinion of Mr. Cave's business methods, and this action seemed a culminating folly.

"It's my opinion he's refused that crystal before," said the step-son, a loose-limbed lout of eighteen.

"But Five Pounds!" said the step-daughter, an argumentative young woman of six-and-twenty.

Mr. Cave's answers were wretched; he could only mumble weak assertions that he knew his own business best. They drove him from his half-eaten supper into the shop, to close it for the night, his ears aflame and tears of vexation behind his spectacles. "Why had he left the crystal in the window so long? The folly of it!" That was the trouble closest in his mind. For a time he could see no way of evading sale.

After supper his step-daughter and step-son smartened themselves up and went out and his wife retired upstairs to reflect upon the business aspects of the crystal, over a little sugar and lemon and so forth in hot water. Mr. Cave went into the shop, and stayed there until late, ostensibly to make ornamental rockeries for gold-fish cases but really for a private purpose that will be better explained later. The next day Mrs. Cave found that the crystal had been removed from the window, and was lying behind some second-hand books on angling. She replaced it in a conspicuous position. But she did not argue further about it, as a nervous headache disinclined her from debate. Mr. Cave was always disinclined. The day passed disagreeably. Mr. Cave was, if anything, more absent-minded than usual, and uncommonly irritable withal. In the afternoon, when his wife was taking her customary sleep, he removed the crystal from the window again.

The next day Mr. Cave had to deliver a consignment of dog-fish at one of the hospital schools, where they were needed for dissection. In his absence Mrs. Cave's mind reverted to the topic of the crystal, and the methods of expenditure suitable to a windfall of five pounds. She had already devised some very agreeable expedients, among others a dress of green silk for herself and a trip to Richmond, when a jangling of the front door bell summoned her into the shop. The customer was an examination coach who came to complain of the non-delivery of certain frogs asked for the previous day. Mrs. Cave did not approve of this particular branch of Mr. Cave's business, and the gentleman, who had called in a somewhat aggressive mood, retired after a brief exchange of words—entirely civil so far as he was concerned. Mrs. Cave's eye then naturally turned to the window; for the sight of the crystal was an assurance of the five pounds and of her dreams. What was her surprise to find it gone!

She went to the place behind the locker on the counter, where she had discovered it the day before. It was not there; and she immediately began an eager search about the shop.

When Mr. Cave returned from his business with the dog-fish, about a quarter to, two in the afternoon, he found the shop in some confusion, and his wife, extremely exasperated and on her knees behind the counter, routing among his taxidermic material. Her face came up hot and angry over the counter, as the jangling bell announced his return, and she forthwith accused him of "hiding it."

"Hid what?" asked Mr. Cave.

"The crystal!"

At that Mr. Cave, apparently much surprised, rushed to the window. "Isn't it here?" he said. "Great Heavens! What has become of it?"

Just then, Mr. Cave's step-son re-entered the shop from the inner room—he had come home a minute or so before Mr. Cave—and he was blaspheming freely. He was apprenticed to a second-hand furniture dealer down the road, but he had his meals at home, and he was naturally annoyed to find no dinner ready.

But when he heard of the loss of the crystal, he forgot his meal, and his anger was diverted from his mother to his step-father. Their first idea, of course, was that he had hidden it. But Mr. Cave stoutly denied all knowledge of its fate—freely offering his bedabbled affidavit in the matter—and at last was worked up to the point of accusing, first, his wife and then his step-son of having taken it with a view to a private sale. So began an exceedingly acrimonious and emotional discussion, which ended for Mrs. Cave in a peculiar nervous condition midway between hysterics and amuck, and caused the step-son to be half-an-hour late at the furniture establishment in the afternoon. Mr. Cave took refuge from his wife's emotions in the shop.

In the evening the matter was resumed, with less passion and in a judicial spirit, under the presidency of the step-daughter. The supper passed unhappily and culminated in a painful scene. Mr. Cave gave way at last to extreme exasperation, and went out banging the front door violently. The rest of the family, having discussed him with the freedom his absence warranted, hunted the house from garret to cellar, hoping to light upon the crystal.

The next day the two customers called again. They were received by Mrs. Cave almost in tears. It transpired that no one could imagine all that she had stood from Cave at various times in her married pilgrimage... She also gave a garbled account of the disappearance. The clergyman and the Oriental laughed silently at one another, and said it was very extraordinary. As Mrs. Cave seemed disposed to give them the complete history of her life they made to leave the shop. Thereupon Mrs. Cave, still clinging to hope, asked for the clergyman's address, so that, if she could get anything out of Cave, she might communicate it. The address was duly given, but apparently was afterwards mislaid. Mrs. Cave can remember nothing about it.

In the evening of that day, the Caves seem to have exhausted their emotions, and Mr. Cave, who had been out in the afternoon, supped in a gloomy isolation that contrasted pleasantly with the impassioned controversy of the previous days. For some time matters were very badly strained in the Cave household, but neither crystal nor customer reappeared.

Now without mincing the matter, we must admit that Mr. Cave was a liar. He knew perfectly well where the crystal was. It was in the rooms of Mr. Jacoby Wace, Assistant Demonstrator at St. Catherine's Hospital, Westbourne Street. It stood on the sideboard partially covered by a black velvet cloth, and beside a decanter of American whisky. It is from Mr. Wace, indeed, that the particulars upon which this narrative is based were derived. Cave had taken off the thing to the hospital hidden in the dog-fish sack, and there had pressed the young investigator to keep it for him. Mr. Wace was a little dubious at first. His relationship to Cave was peculiar. He had a taste for singular characters, and he had more than once invited the old man to smoke and drink in his rooms, and to unfold his rather amusing views of life in general and of his wife in particular. Mr. Wace had encountered Mrs. Cave too, on occasions when Mr. Cave was not at home to attend to him. He knew the constant interference to which Cave was subjected, and having weighed the story judicially, he decided to give the crystal a refuge. Mr. Cave promised to explain the reasons for his remarkable affection for the crystal more fully on a later occasion, but he spoke distinctly of seeing visions therein. He called on Mr. Wace the same evening.

He told a complicated story. The crystal he said had come into his possession with other oddments at the forced sale of another curiosity dealer's effects, and not knowing what its value might be, he had ticketed it at ten shillings. It had hung upon his hands at that price for some months, and he was thinking of "reducing the figure," when he made a singular discovery.

At that time his health was very bad—and it must be borne in mind that, throughout all this experience, his physical condition was one of ebb—and he was in considerable distress by reason of the negligence, the positive ill-treatment even, he received from his wife and step-children. His wife was vain, extravagant, unfeeling and had a growing taste for private drinking; his step-daughter was mean and over-reaching; and his step-son had conceived a violent dislike for him, and lost no chance of showing it. The requirements of his business pressed heavily upon him, and Mr. Wace does not think that he was altogether free from occasional intemperance. He had begun life in a comfortable position, he was a man of fair education, and he suffered, for weeks at a stretch, from melancholia and insomnia. Afraid to disturb his family, he would slip quietly from his wife's side, when his thoughts became intolerable, and wander about the house. And about three o'clock one morning, late in August, chance directed him into the shop.

The dirty little place was impenetrably black except in one spot, where he perceived an unusual glow of light. Approaching this, he discovered it to be the crystal egg, which was standing on the corner of the counter towards the window. A thin ray smote through a crack in the shutters, impinged upon the object, and seemed as it were to fill its entire interior.

It occurred to Mr. Cave that this was not in accordance with the laws of optics as he had known them in his younger days. He could understand the rays being refracted by the crystal and coming to a focus in its interior, but this diffusion jarred with his physical conceptions. He approached the crystal nearly, peering into it and round it, with a transient revival of the scientific curiosity that in his youth had determined his choice of a calling. He was surprised to find the light not steady, but writhing within the substance of the egg, as though that object was a hollow sphere of some luminous vapour. In moving about to get different points of view, he suddenly found that he had come between it and the ray, and that the crystal none the less remained luminous. Greatly astonished, he lifted it out of the light ray and carried it to the darkest part of the shop. It remained bright for some four or five minutes, when it slowly faded and went out. He placed it in the thin streak of daylight, and its luminousness was almost immediately restored.

So far, at least, Mr. Wace was able to verify the remarkable story of Mr. Cave. He has himself repeatedly held this crystal in a ray of light (which had to be of a less diameter than one millimetre). And in a perfect darkness, such as could be produced by velvet wrapping, the crystal did undoubtedly appear very faintly phosphorescent. It would seem, however, that the luminousness was of some exceptional sort, and not equally visible to all eyes; for Mr. Harbinger—whose name will be familiar to the scientific reader in connection with the Pasteur Institute—was quite unable to see any light whatever. And Mr. Wace's own capacity for its appreciation was out of comparison inferior to that of Mr. Cave's. Even with Mr. Cave the power varied very considerably: his vision was most vivid during states of extreme weakness and fatigue.

Now, from the outset this light in the crystal exercised a curious fascination upon Mr. Cave. And it says more for his loneliness of soul than a volume of pathetic writing could do, that he told no human being of his curious observations. He seems to have been living in such an atmosphere of petty spite that to admit the existence of a pleasure would have been to risk the loss of it. He found that as the dawn advanced, and the amount of diffused light increased, the crystal became to all appearance non-luminous. And for some time he was unable to see anything in it, except at night-time, in dark corners of the shop.

But the use of an old velvet cloth, which he used as a background for a collection of minerals, occurred to him, and by doubling this, and putting it over his head and hands, he was able to get a sight of the luminous movement within the crystal even in the day-time. He was very cautious lest he should be thus discovered by his wife, and he practised this occupation only in the afternoons, while she was asleep upstairs, and then circumspectly in a hollow under the counter. And one day, turning the crystal about in his hands, he saw something. It came and went like a flash, but it gave him the impression that the object had for a moment opened to him the view of a wide and spacious and strange country; and turning it about, he did, just as the light faded, see the same vision again.

Now, it would be tedious and unnecessary to state all the phases of Mr. Cave's discovery from this point. Suffice that the effect was this: the crystal, being peered into at an angle of about 137 degrees from the direction of the illuminating ray, gave a clear and consistent picture of a wide and peculiar countryside. It was not dream-like at all: it produced a definite impression of reality, and the better the light the more real and solid it seemed. It was a moving picture: that is to say, certain objects moved in it, but slowly in an orderly manner like real things, and according as the direction of the lighting and vision changed, the picture changed also. It must, indeed, have been like looking through an oval glass at a view, and turning the glass about to get at different aspects.

Mr. Cave's statements, Mr. Wace assures me, were extremely circumstantial, and entirely free from any of that emotional quality that taints hallucinatory impressions. But it must be remembered that all the efforts of Mr. Wace to see any similar clarity in the faint opalescence of the crystal were wholly unsuccessful, try as he would. The difference in intensity of the impressions received by the two men was very great, and it is quite conceivable that what was a view to Mr. Cave was a mere blurred nebulosity to Mr. Wace.

The view, as Mr. Cave described it, was invariably of an extensive plain, and he seemed always to be looking at it from a considerable height, as if from a tower or a mast. To the east and to the west the plain was bounded at a remote distance by vast reddish cliffs, which reminded him of those he had seen in some picture; but what the picture was Mr. Wace was unable to ascertain. These cliffs passed north and south—he could tell the points of the compass by the stars that were visible of a night—receding in an almost illimitable perspective and fading into the mists of the distance before they met. He was nearer the eastern set of cliffs, on the occasion of his first vision the sun was rising over them, and black against the sunlight and pale against their shadow appeared a multitude of soaring forms that Mr. Cave regarded as birds. A vast range of buildings spread below him; he seemed to be looking down upon them; and as they approached the blurred and refracted edge of the picture, they became indistinct. There were also trees curious in shape, and in colouring, a deep mossy green and an exquisite grey, beside a wide and shining canal. And something great and brilliantly coloured flew across the picture. But the first time Mr. Cave saw these pictures he saw only in flashes, his hands shook, his head moved, the vision came and went, and grew foggy and indistinct. And at first he had the greatest difficulty in finding the picture again once the direction of it was lost.

His next clear vision, which came about a week after the first, the interval having yielded nothing but tantalising glimpses and some useful experience, showed him the view down the length of the valley. The view was different, but he had a curious persuasion, which his subsequent observations abundantly confirmed, that he was regarding this strange world from exactly the same spot, although he was looking in a different direction. The long facade of the great building, whose roof he had looked down upon before, was now receding in perspective. He recognised the roof. In the front of the facade was a terrace of massive proportions and extraordinary length, and down the middle of the terrace, at certain intervals, stood huge but very graceful masts, bearing small shiny objects which reflected the setting sun. The import of these small objects did not occur to Mr. Cave until some time after, as he was describing the scene to Mr. Wace. The terrace overhung a thicket of the most luxuriant and graceful vegetation, and beyond this was a wide grassy lawn on which certain broad creatures, in form like beetles but enormously larger, reposed. Beyond this again was a richly decorated causeway of pinkish stone; and beyond that, and lined with dense red weeds, and passing up the valley exactly parallel with the distant cliffs, was a broad and mirror-like expanse of water. The air seemed full of squadrons of great birds, manoeuvring in stately curves; and across the river was a multitude of splendid buildings, richly coloured and glittering with metallic tracery and facets, among a forest of moss-like and lichenous trees. And suddenly something flapped repeatedly across the vision, like the fluttering of a jewelled fan or the beating of a wing, and a face, or rather the upper part of a face with very large eyes, came as it were close to his own and as if on the other side of the crystal. Mr. Cave was so startled and so impressed by the absolute reality of these eyes, that he drew his head back from the crystal to look behind it. He had become so absorbed in watching that he was quite surprised to find himself in the cool darkness of his little shop, with its familiar odour of methyl, mustiness, and decay. And as he blinked about him, the glowing crystal faded, and went out.

Such were the first general impressions of Mr. Cave. The story is curiously direct and circumstantial. From the outset, when the valley first flashed momentarily on his senses, his imagination was strangely affected, and as he began to appreciate the details of the scene he saw, his wonder rose to the point of a passion. He went about his business listless and distraught, thinking only of the time when he should be able to return to his watching. And then a few weeks after his first sight of the valley came the two customers, the stress and excitement of their offer, and the narrow escape of the crystal from sale, as I have already told.

Now, while the thing was Mr. Cave's secret, it remained a mere wonder, a thing to creep to covertly and peep at, as a child might peep upon a forbidden garden. But Mr. Wace has, for a young scientific investigator, a particularly lucid and consecutive habit of mind. Directly the crystal and its story came to him, and he had satisfied himself, by seeing the phosphorescence with his own eyes, that there really was a certain evidence for Mr. Cave's statements, he proceeded to develop the matter systematically. Mr. Cave was only too eager to come and feast his eyes on this wonderland he saw, and he came every night from half-past eight until half-past ten, and sometimes, in Mr. Wace's absence, during the day. On Sunday afternoons, also he came. From the outset Mr. Wace made copious notes, and it was due to his scientific method that the relation between the direction from which the initiating ray entered the crystal and the orientation of the picture were proved. And by covering the crystal in a box perforated only with a small aperture to admit the exciting ray, and by substituting black holland for his buff blinds, he greatly improved the conditions of the observations; so that in a little while they were able to survey the valley in any direction they desired.

So having cleared the way, we may give a brief account of this visionary world within the crystal. The things were in all cases seen by Mr. Cave, and the method of working was invariably for him to watch the crystal and report what he saw, while Mr. Wace (who as a science student had learnt the trick of writing in the dark) wrote a brief note of his report. When the crystal faded, it was put into its box in the proper position and the electric light turned on. Mr. Wace asked questions, and suggested observations to clear up difficult points. Nothing, indeed, could have been less visionary and more matter-of-fact.

The attention of Mr. Cave had been speedily directed to the bird-like creatures he had seen so abundantly present in each of his earlier visions. His first impression was soon corrected, and he considered for a time that they might represent a diurnal species of bat. Then he thought, grotesquely enough, that they might be cherubs. Their heads were round, and curiously human, and it was the eyes of one of them that had so startled him on his second observation. They had broad, silvery wings, not feathered, but glistening almost as brilliantly as new-killed fish and with the same subtle play of colour, and these wings were not built on the plan of a bird-wing or bat, Mr. Wace learned, but supported by curved ribs radiating from the body. (A sort of butterfly wing with curved ribs seems best to express their appearance.) The body was small, but fitted with two bunches of prehensile organs, like long tentacles, immediately under the mouth. Incredible as it appeared to Mr. Wace, the persuasion at last became irresistible, that it was these creatures which owned the great quasi-human buildings and the magnificent garden that made the broad valley so splendid. And Mr. Cave perceived that the buildings, with other peculiarities, had no doors, but that the great circular windows, which opened freely, gave the creatures egress and entrance. They would alight upon their tentacles, fold their wings to a smallness almost rod-like, and hop into the interior. But among them was a multitude of smaller-winged creatures, like great dragon-flies and moths and flying beetles, and across the greensward brilliantly-coloured gigantic ground-beetles crawled lazily to and fro. Moreover, on the causeways and terraces, large-headed creatures similar to the greater winged flies, but wingless, were visible, hopping busily upon their hand-like tangle of tentacles.

Allusion has already been made to the glittering objects upon masts that stood upon the terrace of the nearer building. It dawned upon Mr. Cave, after regarding one of these masts very fixedly on one particularly vivid day, that the glittering object there was a crystal exactly like that into which he peered. And a still more careful scrutiny convinced him that each one in a vista of nearly twenty carried a similar object.

Occasionally one of the large flying creatures would flutter up to one, and folding its wings and coiling a number of its tentacles about the mast, would regard the crystal fixedly for a space—, sometimes for as long as fifteen minutes. And a series of observations, made at the suggestion of Mr. Wace, convinced both watchers that, so far as this visionary world was concerned, the crystal into which they peered actually stood at the summit of the end-most mast on the terrace, and that on one occasion at least one of these inhabitants of this other world had looked into Mr. Cave's face while he was making these observations.

So much for the essential facts of this very singular story. Unless we dismiss it all as the ingenious fabrication of Mr. Wace, we have to believe one of two things: either that Mr. Cave's crystal was in two worlds at once, and that, while it was carried about in one, it remained stationary in the other, which seems altogether absurd; or else that it had some peculiar relation of sympathy with another and exactly similar crystal in this other world, so that what was seen in the interior of the one in this world, was under suitable conditions, visible to an observer in the corresponding crystal in the other world; and vice versa. At present indeed, we do not know of any way in which two crystals could so come en rapport, but nowadays we know enough to understand that the thing is not altogether impossible. This view of the crystals as en rapport was the supposition that occurred to Mr. Wace, and to me at least it seems extremely plausible...

And where was this other world? On this also, the alert intelligence of Mr. Wace speedily threw light. After sunset, the sky darkened rapidly—there was a very brief twilight interval indeed—and the stars shone out. They were recognisably the same as those we see, arranged in the same constellations. Mr. Cave recognised the Bear, the Pleiades, Aldebaran, and Sirius: so that the other world must be somewhere in the solar system, and at the utmost, only a few hundreds of millions of miles from our own. Following up this clue, Mr. Wace learned that the midnight sky was a darker blue even than our midwinter sky, and that the sun seemed a little smaller. And there were two small moons! "Like our moon but smaller, and quite differently marked" one of which moved so rapidly that its motion was clearly visible as one regarded it. These moons were never high in the sky, but vanished as they rose: that is, every time they revolved they were eclipsed because they were so near their primary planet. And all this answers quite completely although, Mr. Cave did not know it, to what must be the condition of things on Mars.

Indeed, it seems an exceedingly plausible conclusion that peering into this crystal Mr. Cave did actually see the planet Mars and its inhabitants. And if that be the case, then the evening star that shone so brilliantly in the sky of that distant vision, was neither more nor less than our own familiar earth.

For a time the Martians—if they were Martians—do not seem to have known of Mr. Cave's inspection. Once or twice one would come to peer, and go away very shortly to some other mast, as though the vision was unsatisfactory. During this time Mr. Cave was able to watch the proceedings of these winged people without being disturbed by their attentions, and although his report is necessarily vague and fragmentary, it is nevertheless very suggestive. Imagine the impression of humanity a Martian observer would get who, after a difficult process of preparation and with considerable fatigue to the eyes, was able to peer at London from the steeple of St. Martin's Church for stretches, at longest, of four minutes at a time. Mr. Cave was unable to ascertain if the winged Martians were the same as the Martians who hopped about the causeways and terraces, and if the latter could put on wings at will. He several times saw certain clumsy bipeds, dimly suggestive of apes, white and partially translucent, feeding among certain of the lichenous trees, and once some of these fled before one of the hopping, round-headed Martians. The latter caught one in its tentacles, and then the picture faded suddenly and left Mr. Cave most tantalisingly in the dark. On another occasion a vast thing, that Mr. Cave thought at first was some gigantic insect, appeared advancing along the causeway beside the canal with extraordinary rapidity. As this drew nearer Mr. Cave perceived that it was a mechanism of shining metals and of extraordinary complexity. And then, when he looked again, it had passed out of sight.

After a time Mr. Wace aspired to attract the attention of the Martians, and the next time that the strange eyes of one of them appeared close to the crystal Mr. Cave cried out and sprang away, and they immediately turned on the light and began to gesticulate in a manner suggestive of signalling. But when at last Mr. Cave examined the crystal again the Martian had departed.

Thus far these observations had progressed in early November, and then Mr. Cave, feeling that the suspicions of his family about the crystal were allayed, began to take it to and fro with him in order that, as occasion arose in the daytime or night, he might comfort himself with what was fast becoming the most real thing in his existence.

In December Mr. Wace's work in connection with a forthcoming examination became heavy, the sittings were reluctantly suspended for a week, and for ten or eleven days—he is not quite sure which—he saw nothing of Cave. He then grew anxious to resume these investigations, and the stress of his seasonal labours being abated, he went down to Seven Dials. At the corner he noticed a shutter before a bird fancier's window, and then another at a cobbler's. Mr. Cave's shop was closed.

He rapped and the door was opened by the step-son in black. He at once called Mrs. Cave, who was, Mr. Wace could not but observe, in cheap but ample widow's weeds of the most imposing pattern. Without any very great surprise Mr. Wace learnt that Cave was dead and already buried. She was in tears, and her voice was a little thick. She had just returned from Highgate. Her mind seemed occupied with her own prospects and the honourable details of the obsequies, but Mr. Wace was at last able to learn the particulars of Cave's death. He had been found dead in his shop in the early morning, the day after his last visit to Mr. Wace, and the crystal had been clasped in his stone-cold hands. His face was smiling, said Mrs. Cave, and the velvet cloth from the minerals lay on the floor at his feet. He must have been dead five or six hours when he was found.

This came as a great shock to Wace, and he began to reproach himself bitterly for having neglected the plain symptoms of the old man's ill-health. But his chief thought was of the crystal. He approached that topic in a gingerly manner, because he knew Mrs. Cave's peculiarities. He was dumbfounded to learn that it was sold.

Mrs. Cave's first impulse, directly Cave's body had been taken upstairs, had been to write to the mad clergyman who had offered five pounds for the crystal, informing him of its recovery; but after a violent hunt in which her daughter joined her, they were convinced of the loss of his address. As they were without the means required to mourn and bury Cave in the elaborate style the dignity of an old Seven Dials inhabitant demands, they had appealed to a friendly fellow-tradesman in Great Portland Street. He had very kindly taken over a portion of the stock at a valuation. The valuation was his own and the crystal egg was included in one of the lots. Mr. Wace, after a few suitable consolatory observations, a little off-handedly proffered perhaps, hurried at once to Great Portland Street. But there he learned that the crystal egg had already been sold to a tall, dark man in grey. And there the material facts in this curious, and to me at least very suggestive, story come abruptly to an end. The Great Portland Street dealer did not know who the tall dark man in grey was, nor had he observed him with sufficient attention to describe him minutely. He did not even know which way this person had gone after leaving the shop. For a time Mr. Wace remained in the shop, trying the dealer's patience with hopeless questions, venting his own exasperation. And at last, realising abruptly that the whole thing had passed out of his hands, had vanished like a vision of the night, he returned to his own rooms, a little astonished to find the notes he had made still tangible and visible upon his untidy table.

His annoyance and disappointment were naturally very great. He made a second call (equally ineffectual) upon the Great Portland Street dealer, and he resorted to advertisements in such periodicals as were likely to come into the hands of a bric-à-brac collector. He also wrote letters to 'The Daily Chronicle' and 'Nature', but both those periodicals, suspecting a hoax, asked him to reconsider his action before they printed, and he was advised that such a strange story, unfortunately so bare of supporting evidence, might imperil his reputation as an investigator. Moreover, the calls of his proper work were urgent. So that after a month or so, save for an occasional reminder to certain dealers, he had reluctantly to abandon the quest for the crystal egg, and from that day to this it remains undiscovered. Occasionally however, he tells me, and I can quite believe him, he has bursts of zeal, in which he abandons his more urgent occupation and resumes the search.

Whether or not it will remain lost for ever, with the material and origin of it, are things equally speculative at the present time. If the present purchaser is a collector, one would have expected the enquiries of Mr. Wace to have readied him through the dealers. He has been able to discover Mr. Cave's clergyman and "Oriental—" no other than the Rev. James Parker and the young Prince of Bosso-Kuni in Java. I am obliged to them for certain particulars. The object of the Prince was simply curiosity—and extravagance. He was so eager to buy, because Cave was so oddly reluctant to sell. It is just as possible that the buyer in the second instance was simply a casual purchaser and not a collector at all, and the crystal egg, for all I know, may at the present moment be within a mile of me, decorating a drawing-room or serving as a paper-weight—its remarkable functions all unknown. Indeed, it is partly with the idea of such a possibility that I have thrown this narrative into a form that will give it a chance of being read by the ordinary consumer of fiction.

My own ideas in the matter are practically identical with those of Mr. Wace. I believe the crystal on the mast in Mars and the crystal egg of Mr. Cave's to be in some physical, but at present quite inexplicable, way en rapport, and we both believe further that the terrestrial crystal must have been—possibly at some remote date—sent hither from that planet, in order to give the Martians a near view of our affairs. Possibly the fellows to the crystals in the other masts are also on our globe. No theory of hallucination suffices for the facts.

30

The Lost Inheritance

"My uncle," said the man with the glass eye, "was what you might call a hemi-semi-demi millionaire. He was worth about a hundred and twenty thousand. Quite. And he left me all his money."

I glanced at the shiny sleeve of his coat, and my eye travelled up to the frayed collar.

"Every penny," said the man with the glass eye, and I caught the active pupil looking at me with a touch of offence.

"I've never had any windfalls like that," I said, trying to speak enviously and propitiate him.

"Even a legacy isn't always a blessing," he remarked with a sigh, and with an air of philosophical resignation he put the red nose and the wiry moustache into his tankard for a space.

"Perhaps not," I said.

"He was an author, you see, and he wrote a lot of books."

"Indeed!"

"That was the trouble of it all." He stared at me with the available eye to see if I grasped his statement, then averted his face a little and produced a toothpick.

"You see," he said, smacking his lips after a pause, "it was like this. He was my uncle—my maternal uncle. And he had—what shall I call it—? A weakness for writing, edifying literature. Weakness is hardly the word—downright mania is nearer the mark. He's been librarian in a Polytechnic, and as soon as the money came to him he began to indulge his ambition. It's a simply extraordinary and incomprehensible thing to me. Here was a man of thirty-seven suddenly dropped into a perfect pile of gold, and he didn't go—not a day's bust on it. One would think a chap would go and get himself dressed a bit decent—say a couple of dozen pair of trousers at a West End tailor's; but he never did. You'd hardly believe it, but when he died he hadn't even a gold watch. It seems wrong for people like that to have money. All he did was just to take a house, and order in pretty nearly five tons of books and ink and paper, and set to writing, edifying literature as hard as ever he could write. I can't understand it! But he did. The money came to him, curiously enough, through a maternal uncle of his, unexpected like, when he was seven-and-thirty. My mother, it happened, was his only relation in the wide, wide world, except some second cousins of his. And I was her only son. You follow all that? The second cousins had one only son too, but they brought him to see the old man too soon. He was rather a spoilt youngster, was this son of theirs, and directly he set eyes on my uncle, he began bawling out as hard as he could. 'Take 'im away—er,' he says, 'take 'im away,' and so did for himself entirely. It was pretty straight sailing, you'd think, for me, eh? And my mother, being a sensible, careful woman, settled the business in her own mind long before he did.

"He was a curious little chap, was my uncle, as I remember him. I don't wonder at the kid being scared. Hair just like these Japanese dolls they sell, black and straight and stiff all round the brim and none in the middle, and below, a whitish kind of face and rather large dark grey eyes moving about behind his spectacles. He used to attach a great deal of importance to dress, and always wore a flapping overcoat and a big-brimmed felt hat of a most extraordinary size. He looked a rummy little beggar, I can tell you. Indoors it was, as a rule, a dirty red flannel dressing-gown and a black skull-cap he had. That black skull-cap made him look like the portraits of all kinds of celebrated people. He was always moving about from house to house, was my uncle, with his chair which had belonged to Savage Landor, and his two writing-tables, one of Carlyle's and the other of Shelley's, so the dealer told him, and the completest portable reference library in England, he said he had—and he lugged the whole caravan, now to a house at Down, near Darwin's old place, then to Reigate, near Meredith, then off to Haslemere, then back to Chelsea for a bit, and then up to Hampstead. He knew there was something wrong with his stuff, but he never knew there was anything wrong with his brains. It was always the air, or the water, or the altitude, or some tommy-rot like that. 'So much depends on environment,' he used to say, and stare at you hard, as if he half suspected you were hiding a grin at him somewhere under your face. 'So much depends on environment to a sensitive mind like mine.'

"What was his name? You wouldn't know it if I told you. He wrote nothing that anyone has ever read—nothing. No one could read it. He wanted to be a great teacher, he said, and he didn't know what he wanted to teach any more than a child. So he just blethered at large about Truth and Righteousness, and the Spirit of History, and all that. Book after book he wrote and published at his own expense. He wasn't quite right in his head, you know really; and to hear him go on at the critics—not because they slated him, mind you—he liked that—but because they didn't take any notice of him at all. 'What do the nations want?' he would ask, holding out his brown old claw. 'Why, teaching—guidance! They are scattered upon the hills like sheep without a shepherd. There is War and Rumours of War, the unlaid Spirit of Discord abroad in the land, Nihilism, Vivisection, Vaccination, Drunkenness, Penury, Want, Socialistic Error, Selfish Capital! Do you see the clouds, Ted—?' My name, you know—'Do you see the clouds lowering over the land? and behind it all—the Mongol waits!' He was always very great on Mongols, and the Spectre of Socialism, and suchlike things.

"Then out would come his finger at me, and with his eyes all afire and his skull-cap askew, he would whisper: 'And here am I. What did I want? Nations to teach. Nations! I say it with all modesty, Ted, I could. I would guide them; nay! But I will guide them to a safe haven, to the land of Righteousness, flowing with milk and honey.'

"That's how he used to go on. Ramble, rave about the nations, and righteousness, and that kind of thing. Kind of mincemeat of Bible and blethers. From fourteen up to three-and-twenty, when I might have been improving my mind, my mother used to wash me and brush my hair (at least in the earlier years of it), with a nice parting down the middle, and take me, once or twice a week, to hear this old lunatic jabber about things he had read of in the morning papers, trying to do it as much like Carlyle as he could, and I used to sit according to instructions, and look intelligent and nice, and pretend to be taking it all in. Afterwards I used to go of my own free will, out of a regard for the legacy. I was the only person that used to go see him. He wrote, I believe, to every man who made the slightest stir in the world, sending him a copy or so of his books, and inviting him to come and talk about the nations to him; but half of them didn't answer, and none ever came. And when the girl let you in—she was an artful bit of goods, that girl—there were heaps of letters on the hall-seat waiting to go off, addressed to Prince Bismarck, the President of the United States, and such-like people. And one went up the staircase and along the cobwebby passage—, the housekeeper drank like fury, and his passages were always cobwebby—, and found him at last, with books turned down all over the room, and heaps of torn paper on the floor, and telegrams and newspapers littered about, and empty coffee-cups and half-eaten bits of toast on the desk and the mantel. You'd see his back humped up, and his hair would be sticking out quite straight between the collar of that dressing-gown thing and the edge of his skull-cap.

"'A moment!' he would say. 'A moment!' over his shoulder. 'The mot juste, you know, Ted, le mot juste. Righteous thought righteously expressed—Aah—! Concatenation. And now, Ted,' he'd say, spinning round in his study chair, 'how's Young England?' That was his silly name for me.

"Well, that was my uncle, and that was how he talked—to me, at any rate. With others about he seemed a bit shy. And he not only talked to me, but he gave me his books, books of six hundred pages or so, with cock-eyed headings, 'The Shrieking Sisterhood,' 'The Behemoth of Bigotry,' 'Crucibles and Cullenders,' and so on. All very strong, and none of them original. The very last time, but one that I saw him, he gave me a book. He was feeling ill even then, and his hand shook and he was despondent. I noticed it because I was naturally on the look-out for those little symptoms. 'My last book, Ted,' he said. 'My last book, my boy; my last word to the deaf and hardened nations;' and I'm hanged if a tear didn't go rolling down his yellow old cheek. He was regular crying because it was so nearly over, and he hadn't only written about fifty-three books of rubbish. 'I've sometimes thought, Ted—' he said, and stopped.

"'Perhaps I've been a bit hasty and angry with this stiff-necked generation. A little more sweetness, perhaps, and a little less blinding light. I've sometimes thought—I might have swayed them. But I've done my best, Ted.'

"And then, with a burst, for the first and last time in his life he owned himself a failure. It showed he was really ill. He seemed to think for a minute, and then he spoke quietly and low, as sane and sober as I am now. 'I've been a fool, Ted,' he said. 'I've been flapping nonsense all my life. Only He who readeth the heart knows whether this is anything more than vanity. Ted, I don't. But He knows, He knows, and if I have done foolishly and vainly, in my heart—in my heart—'

"Just like that he spoke, repeating himself, and he stopped quite short and handed the book to me, trembling. Then the old shine came back into his eye. I remember it all fairly well, because I repeated it and acted it to my old mother when I got home, to cheer her up a bit. 'Take this book and read it,' he said. 'It's my last word, my very last word. I've left all my property to you, Ted, and may you use it better than I have done.' And then he fell a-coughing.

"I remember that quite well even now, and how I went home cock-a-hoop, and how he was in bed the next time I called. The housekeeper was downstairs drunk, and I fooled about—as a young man will—with the girl in the passage before I went to him. He was sinking fast. But even then his vanity clung to him.

"'Have you read it?' he whispered.

"'Sat, up all night reading it,' I said in his ear to cheer him. 'It's the last,' said I, and then, with a memory of some poetry or other in my head, 'but it's the bravest and best.'

"He smiled a little and tried to squeeze my hand as a woman might do, and left off squeezing in the middle, and lay still. 'The bravest and the best,' said I again, seeing it pleased him. But he didn't answer. I heard the girl giggle outside the door, for occasionally we'd had just a bit of innocent laughter, you know, at his ways. I looked at his face, and his eyes were closed, and it was just as if somebody had punched in his nose on either side. But he was still smiling. It's queer to think of—he lay dead, lay dead there, an utter failure, with the smile of success on his face.

"That was the end of my uncle. You can imagine me and my mother saw that he had a decent funeral. Then, of course, came the hunt for the will. We began decent and respectful at first, and before the day was out we were ripping chairs, and smashing bureau panels, and sounding walls. Every hour we expected those others to come in. We asked the housekeeper, and found she'd actually witnessed a will—on an ordinary half-sheet of notepaper it was written, and very short, she said—not a month ago. The other witness was the gardener, and he bore her out word for word. But I'm hanged if there was that or any other will to be found. The way my mother talked must have made him turn in his grave. At last a lawyer at Reigate sprang one on us that had been made years ago during some temporary quarrel with my mother. I'm blest if that wasn't the only will to be discovered anywhere, and it left every penny he possessed to that 'Take 'im away' youngster of his second cousin's—a chap who'd never had to stand his talking, not for one afternoon of his life."

The man with the glass eye stopped.

"I thought you said—" I began.

"Half a minute," said the man with the glass eye. "I had to wait for the end of the story till this very morning, and I was a blessed sight more interested than you are. You just wait a bit too. They executed the will, and the other chap inherited, and directly he was one-and-twenty he began to blew it. How he did blew it, to be sure! He bet, he drank, he got in the papers for this and that. I tell you, it makes me wiggle to think of the times he had. He blewed every ha'penny of it before he was thirty, and the last I heard of him was—Holloway! Three years ago.

"Well, I naturally fell on hard times, because as you see, the only trade I knew was legacy-cadging. All my plans were waiting over to begin, so to speak, when the old chap died. I've had my ups and downs since then. Just now it's a period of depression. I tell you frankly, I'm on the look-out for help. I was hunting round my room to find something to raise a bit on for immediate necessities, and the sight of all those presentation volumes—no one will buy them, not to wrap butter in, even—well, they annoyed me. I promised him not to part with them, and I never kept a promise easier. I let out at them with my boot, and sent them shooting across the room. One lifted at the kick, and spun through the air. And out of it flapped—You guess?

"It was the will. He'd given it to me himself in that very last volume of all."

He folded his arms on the table, and looked sadly with the active eye at his empty tankard. He shook his head slowly, and said softly, "I'd never opened the book, much more cut a page!" Then he looked up, with a bitter laugh, for sympathy. "Fancy hiding it there! Eigh? Of all places."

He began to fish absently for a dead fly with a finger. "It just shows you the vanity of authors," he said, looking up at me. "It wasn't no trick of his. He'd meant perfectly fair. He'd really thought I was really going home to read that blessed book of his through. But it shows you, don't it—?" his eye went down to the tankard again—, "It shows you too, how we poor human beings fail to understand one another."

But there was no misunderstanding the eloquent thirst of his eye. He accepted with ill-feigned surprise. He said, in the usual subtle formula, that he didn't mind if he did.

31

The Star

It was on the first day of the New Year that the announcement was made, almost simultaneously from three observatories, that the motion of the planet Neptune, the outermost of all the planets that wheel about the sun, had become very erratic. Ogilvy had already called attention to a suspected retardation in its velocity in December. Such a piece of news was scarcely calculated to interest a world the greater portion of whose inhabitants were unaware of the existence of the planet Neptune, nor outside the astronomical profession did the subsequent discovery of a faint remote speck of light in the region of the perturbed planet cause any very great excitement. Scientific people, however, found the intelligence remarkable enough, even before it became known that the new body was rapidly growing larger and brighter, that its motion was quite different from the orderly progress of the planets, and that the deflection of Neptune and its satellite was becoming now of an unprecedented kind.

Few people without a training in science can realise the huge isolation of the solar system. The sun with its specks of planets, its dust of planetoids, and its impalpable comets, swims in a vacant immensity that almost defeats the imagination. Beyond the orbit of Neptune there is space, vacant so far as human observation has penetrated, without warmth or light or sound, blank emptiness, for twenty million times a million miles. That is the smallest estimate of the distance to be traversed before the very nearest of the stars is attained. And saving a few comets more unsubstantial than the thinnest flame, no matter had ever to human knowledge crossed this gulf of space, until early in the twentieth century this strange wanderer appeared. A vast mass of matter it was, bulky, heavy, rushing without warning out of the black mystery of the sky into the radiance of the sun. By the second day it was clearly visible to any decent instrument, as a speck with a barely sensible diameter, in the constellation Leo near Regulus. In a little while an opera glass could attain it.

On the third day of the new year the newspaper readers of two hemispheres were made aware for the first time of the real importance of this unusual apparition in the heavens. "A Planetary Collision," one London paper headed the news, and proclaimed Duchaine's opinion that this strange new planet would probably collide with Neptune. The leader writers enlarged upon the topic; so that in most of the capitals of the world, on January 3rd, there was an expectation, however vague of some imminent phenomenon in the sky; and as the night followed the sunset round the globe, thousands of men turned their eyes skyward to see—the old familiar stars just as they had always been.

Until it was dawn in London and Pollux setting and the stars overhead grown pale. The Winter's dawn it was, a sickly filtering accumulation of daylight, and the light of gas and candles shone yellow in the windows to show where people were astir. But the yawning policeman saw the thing, the busy crowds in the markets stopped agape, workmen going to their work betimes, milkmen, the drivers of news-carts, dissipation going home jaded and pale, homeless wanderers, sentinels on their beats, and in the country, labourers trudging afield, poachers slinking home, all over the dusky quickening country it could be seen—and out at sea by seamen watching for the day—a great white star, come suddenly into the westward sky!

Brighter it was than any star in our skies; brighter than the evening star at its brightest. It still glowed out white and large, no mere twinkling spot of light, but a small round clear shining disc, an hour after the day had come. And where science has not reached, men stared and feared, telling one another of the wars and pestilences that are foreshadowed by these fiery signs in the Heavens. Sturdy Boers, dusky Hottentots, Gold Coast negroes, Frenchmen, Spaniards, Portuguese, stood in the warmth of the sunrise watching the setting of this strange new star.

And in a hundred observatories there had been suppressed excitement, rising almost to shouting pitch, as the two remote bodies had rushed together; and a hurrying to and fro, to gather photographic apparatus and spectroscope, and this appliance and that, to record this novel astonishing sight, the destruction of a world. For it was a world, a sister planet of our earth, far greater than our earth indeed, that had so suddenly flashed into flaming death. Neptune it was, had been struck, fairly and squarely, by the strange planet from outer space and the heat of the concussion had incontinently turned two solid globes into one vast mass of incandescence. Round the world that day, two hours before the dawn, went the pallid great white star, fading only as it sank westward and the sun mounted above it. Everywhere men marvelled at it, but of all those who saw it none could have marvelled more than those sailors, habitual watchers of the stars, who far away at sea had heard nothing of its advent and saw it now rise like a pigmy moon and climb zenithward and hang overhead and sink westward with the passing of the night.

And when next it rose over Europe everywhere were crowds of watchers on hilly slopes, on house-roofs, in open spaces, staring eastward for the rising of the great new star. It rose with a white glow in front of it, like the glare of a white fire, and those who had seen it come into existence the night before cried out at the sight of it. "It is larger," they cried. "It is brighter!" And, indeed the moon a quarter full and sinking in the west was in its apparent size beyond comparison, but scarcely in all its breadth had it as much brightness now as the little circle of the strange new star.

"It is brighter!" cried the people clustering in the streets. But in the dim observatories the watchers held their breath and peered at one another. "It is nearer." They said. "Nearer!"

And voice after voice repeated, "It is nearer," and the clicking telegraph took that up, and it trembled along telephone wires, and in a thousand cities grimy compositors fingered the type. "It is nearer." Men writing in offices, struck with a strange realisation, flung down their pens, men talking in a thousand places suddenly came upon a grotesque possibility in those words, "It is nearer." It hurried along wakening streets, it was shouted down the frost-stilled ways of quiet villages; men who had read these things from the throbbing tape stood in yellow-lit doorways shouting the news to the passers-by. "It is nearer." Pretty women, flushed and glittering, heard the news told jestingly between the dances, and feigned an intelligent interest they did not feel. "Nearer! Indeed. How curious! How very, very clever people must be to find out things like that!"

Lonely tramps faring through the wintry night murmured those words to comfort themselves—looking skyward. "It has need to be nearer, for the night's as cold as charity. Don't seem much warmth from it, if it is nearer, all the same."

"What is a new star to me?" cried the weeping woman kneeling beside her dead.

The schoolboy, rising early for his examination work, puzzled it out for himself—with the great white star shining broad and bright through the frost-flowers of his window. "Centrifugal, centripetal." He said, with his chin on his fist. "Stop a planet in its flight, rob it of its centrifugal force, what then? Centripetal has it, and down it falls into the sun! And this—!

"Do we come in the way? I wonder—"

The light of that day went the way of its brethren, and with the later watches of the frosty darkness rose the strange star again. And it was now so bright that the waxing moon seemed but a pale yellow ghost of itself, hanging huge in the sunset. In a South African city a great man had married, and the streets were alight to welcome his return with his bride. "Even the skies have illuminated." Said the flatterer. Under Capricorn, two negro lovers, daring the wild beasts and evil spirits, for love of one another, crouched together in a cane brake where the fire-flies hovered. "That is our star." They whispered, and felt strangely comforted by the sweet brilliance of its light.

The master mathematician sat in his private room and pushed the papers from him. His calculations were already finished. In a small white phial there still remained a little of the drug that had kept him awake and active for four long nights. Each day, serene, explicit, patient as ever, he had given his lecture to his students, and then had come back at once to this momentous calculation. His face was grave, a little drawn and hectic from his drugged activity. For some time he seemed lost in thought. Then he went to the window, and the blind went up with a click. Half way up the sky, over the clustering roofs, chimneys and steeples of the city, hung the star.

He looked at it as one might look into the eyes of a brave enemy. "You may kill me," he said after a silence. "But I can hold you—

and all the universe for that matter—in the grip of this little brain. I would not change. Even now."

He looked at the little phial. "There will be no need of sleep again," he said. The next day at noon, punctual to the minute, he entered his lecture theatre, put his hat on the end of the table as his habit was, and carefully selected a large piece of chalk. It was a joke among his students that he could not lecture without that piece of chalk to fumble in his fingers, and once he had been stricken to impotence by their hiding his supply. He came and looked under his grey eyebrows at the rising tiers of young fresh faces, and spoke with his accustomed studied commonness of phrasing. "Circumstances have arisen—circumstances beyond my control," he said and paused, "which will debar me from completing the course I had designed. It would seem, gentlemen, if I may put the thing clearly and briefly, that—Man has lived in vain."

The students glanced at one another. Had they heard aright? Mad? Raised eyebrows and grinning lips there were, but one or two faces remained intent upon his calm grey-fringed face. "It will be interesting," he was saying, "to devote this morning to an exposition, so far as I can make it clear to you, of the calculations that have led me to this conclusion. Let us assume—"

He turned towards the blackboard, meditating a diagram in the way that was usual to him. "What was that about 'lived in vain'?" whispered one student to another. "Listen," said the other, nodding towards the lecturer.

And presently they began to understand.

That night the star rose later, for its proper eastward motion had carried it some way across Leo towards Virgo, and its brightness was so great that the sky became a luminous blue as it rose, and every star was hidden in its turn, save only Jupiter near the zenith, Capella, Aldebaran, Sirius and the pointers of the Bear. It was very white and beautiful. In many parts of the world that night a pallid halo encircled it about. It was perceptibly larger; in the clear refractive sky of the tropics it seemed as if it were nearly a quarter the size of the moon. The frost was still on the ground in England, but the world was as brightly lit as if it were midsummer moonlight. One could see to read quite ordinary print by that cold clear light, and in the cities the lamps burnt yellow and wan.

And everywhere the world was awake that night, and throughout Christendom a sombre murmur hung in the keen air over the country side like the belling of bees in the heather, and this murmurous tumult grew to a clangour in the cities. It was the tolling of the bells in a million belfry towers and steeples, summoning the people to sleep no more, to sin no more, but to gather in their churches and pray. And overhead, growing larger and brighter as the earth rolled on its way and the night passed, rose the dazzling star.

And the streets and houses were alight in all the cities, the shipyards glared, and whatever roads led to high country were lit and crowded all night long. And in all the seas about the civilised lands, ships with throbbing engines, and ships with bellying sails, crowded with men and living creatures, were standing out to ocean and the north. For already the warning of the master mathematician had been telegraphed all over the world, and translated into a hundred tongues. The new planet and Neptune, locked in a fiery embrace, were whirling headlong, ever faster and faster towards the sun. Already every second this blazing mass flew a hundred miles, and every second its terrific velocity increased. As it flew now, indeed, it must pass a hundred million of miles wide of the earth and scarcely affect it. But near its destined path, as yet only slightly perturbed, spun the mighty planet Jupiter and his moons sweeping splendid round the sun. Every moment now the attraction between the fiery star and the greatest of the planets grew stronger. And the result of that attraction? Inevitably Jupiter would be deflected from its orbit into an elliptical path, and the burning star, swung by his attraction wide of its sunward rush, would "describe a curved path" and perhaps collide with, and certainly pass very close to, our earth. "Earthquakes, volcanic outbreaks, cyclones, sea waves, floods, and a steady rise in temperature to I know not what limit—" so prophesied the master mathematician.

And overhead, to carry out his words, lonely and cold and livid, blazed the star of the coming doom.

To many who stared at it that night until their eyes ached, it seemed that it was visibly approaching. And that night, too the weather changed, and the frost that had gripped all Central Europe and France and England softened towards a thaw.

But you must not imagine because I have spoken of people praying through the night and people going aboard ships and people fleeing toward mountainous country that the whole world was already in a terror because of the star. As a matter of fact, use and wont still ruled the world, and save for the talk of idle moments and the splendour of the night, nine human beings out of ten were still busy at their common occupations. In all the cities the shops, save one here and there, opened and closed at their proper hours, the doctor and the undertaker plied their trades, the workers gathered in the factories, soldiers drilled, scholars studied, lovers sought one another, thieves lurked and fled, politicians planned their schemes. The presses of the newspapers roared through the night, and many a priest of this church and that would not open his holy building to further what he considered a foolish panic. The newspapers insisted on the lesson of the year 1000—for then too, people had anticipated the end. The star was no star—mere gas—a comet; and were it a star it could not possibly strike the earth. There was no precedent for such a thing. Common sense was sturdy everywhere, scornful, jesting, a little inclined to persecute the obdurate fearful. That night, at seven-fifteen by Greenwich time, the star would be at its nearest to Jupiter. Then the world would see the turn things would take. The master mathematician's grim warnings were treated by many as so much mere elaborate self-advertisement. Common sense at last, a little heated by argument, signified its unalterable convictions by going to bed. So too, barbarism and savagery, already tired of the novelty, went about their nightly business, and save for a howling dog here and there, the beast world left the star unheeded.

And yet, when at last the watchers in the European States saw the star rise, an hour later it is true, but no larger than it had been the night before, there were still plenty awake to laugh at the master mathematician—to take the danger as if it had passed.

But hereafter the laughter ceased. The star grew—it grew with a terrible steadiness hour after hour, a little larger each hour, a little nearer the midnight zenith, and brighter and brighter, until it had turned night into a second day. Had it come straight to the earth instead of in a curved path, had it lost no velocity to Jupiter, it must have leapt the intervening gulf in a day, but as it was it took five days altogether to come by our planet. The next night it had become a third the size of the moon before it set to English eyes, and the thaw was assured. It rose over America near the size of the moon, but blinding white to look at, and hot; and a breath of hot wind blew now with its rising and gathering strength, and in Virginia, and Brazil, and down the St. Lawrence valley, it shone intermittently through a driving reek of thunder-clouds, flickering violet lightning, and hail unprecedented. In Manitoba was a thaw and devastating floods. And upon all the mountains of the earth the snow and ice began to melt that night, and all the rivers coming out of high country flowed thick and turbid, and soon—in their upper reaches—with swirling trees and the bodies of beasts and men. They rose steadily, steadily in the ghostly brilliance, and came trickling over their banks at last, behind the fleeing population of their valleys.

And along the coast of Argentina and up the South Atlantic the tides were higher than had ever been in the memory of man, and the storms drove the waters in many cases scores of miles inland, drowning whole cities. And so great grew the heat during the night that the rising of the sun was like the coming of a shadow. The earthquakes began and grew until all down America from the Arctic Circle to Cape Horn, hillsides were sliding, fissures were opening, and houses and walls crumbling to destruction. The whole side of Cotopaxi slipped out in one vast convulsion, and a tumult of lava poured out so high and broad and swift and liquid that in one day it reached the sea.

So the star, with the wan moon in its wake, marched across the Pacific, trailed the thunderstorms like the hem of a robe, and the growing tidal wave that toiled behind it, frothing and eager, poured over island and island and swept them clear of men. Until that wave came at last—in a blinding light and with the breath of a furnace, swift and terrible it came—a wall of water, fifty feet high, roaring hungrily, upon the long coasts of Asia, and swept inland across the plains of China. For a space the star, hotter now and larger and brighter than the sun in its strength, showed with pitiless brilliance the wide and populous country; towns and villages with their pagodas and trees, roads, wide cultivated fields, millions of sleepless people staring in helpless terror at the incandescent sky; and then, low and growing, came the murmur of the flood. And thus it was with millions of men that night—a flight no-whither, with limbs heavy with heat and breath fierce and scant, and the flood like a wall swift and white behind. And then death.

China was lit glowing white, but over Japan and Java and all the islands of Eastern Asia the great star was a ball of dull red fire because of the steam and smoke and ashes the volcanoes were spouting forth to salute its coming. Above was the lava, hot gases and ash, and below the seething floods, and the whole earth swayed and rumbled with the earthquake shocks. Soon the immemorial snows of Thibet and the Himalaya were melting and pouring down by ten million deepening converging channels upon the plains of Burmah and Hindostan. The tangled summits of the Indian jungles were aflame in a thousand places, and below the hurrying waters around the stems were dark objects that still struggled feebly and reflected the blood-red tongues of fire. And in a rudderless confusion a multitude of men and women fled down the broad river-ways to that one last hope of men—the open sea.

Larger grew the star, and larger, hotter, and brighter with a terrible swiftness now. The tropical ocean had lost its phosphorescence, and the whirling steam rose in ghostly wreaths from the black waves that plunged incessantly, speckled with storm-tossed ships.

And then came a wonder. It seemed to those who in Europe watched for the rising of the star that the world must have ceased its rotation. In a thousand open spaces of down and upland the people who had fled thither from the floods and the falling houses and sliding slopes of hill watched for that rising in vain. Hour followed hour through a terrible suspense, and the star rose not. Once again men set their eyes upon the old constellations they had counted lost to them forever. In England it was hot and clear overhead, though the ground quivered perpetually, but in the tropics, Sirius and Capella and Aldebaran showed through a veil of steam. And when at last the great star rose near ten hours late, the sun rose close upon it, and in the centre of its white heart was a disc of black.

Over Asia it was the star had begun to fall behind the movement of the sky, and then suddenly, as it hung over India, its light had been veiled. All the plain of India from the mouth of the Indus to the mouths of the Ganges was a shallow waste of shining water that night, out of which rose temples and palaces, mounds and hills, black with people. Every minaret was a clustering mass of people, who fell one by one into the turbid waters, as heat and terror overcame them. The whole land seemed a-wailing and suddenly there swept a shadow across that furnace of despair, and a breath of cold wind, and a gathering of clouds, out of the cooling air. Men looking up, near blinded, at the star, saw that a black disc was creeping across the light. It was the moon, coming between the star and the earth. And even as men cried to God at this respite, out of the East with a strange inexplicable swiftness sprang the sun. And then star, sun and moon rushed together across the heavens.

So it was that presently, to the European watchers, star and sun rose close upon each other, drove headlong for a space and then slower, and at last came to rest, star and sun merged into one glare of flame at the zenith of the sky. The moon no longer eclipsed the star but was lost to sight in the brilliance of the sky. And though those who were still alive regarded it for the most part with that dull stupidity that hunger, fatigue, heat and despair engender, there were still men who could perceive the meaning of these signs. Star and earth had been at their nearest, had swung about one another, and the star had passed. Already it was receding, swifter and swifter, in the last stage of its headlong journey downward into the sun.

And then the clouds gathered, blotting out the vision of the sky, the thunder and lightning wove a garment round the world; all over the earth was such a downpour of rain as men had never before seen, and where the volcanoes flared red against the cloud canopy there descended torrents of mud. Everywhere the waters were pouring off the land, leaving mud-silted ruins, and the earth littered like a storm-worn beach with all that had floated, and the dead bodies of the men and brutes, its children. For days the water streamed off the land, sweeping away soil and trees and houses in the way, and piling huge dykes and scooping out Titanic gullies over the country side. Those were the days of darkness that followed the star and the heat. All through them, and for many weeks and months, the earthquakes continued.

But the star had passed, and men, hunger-driven and gathering courage only slowly, might creep back to their ruined cities, buried granaries, and sodden fields. Such few ships as had escaped the storms of that time came stunned and shattered and sounding their way cautiously through the new marks and shoals of once familiar ports. And as the storms subsided men perceived that everywhere the days were hotter than of yore, and the sun larger, and the moon, shrunk to a third of its former size, took now fourscore days between its new, and next new moon.

But of the new brotherhood that grew presently among men, of the saving of laws and books and machines, of the strange change that had come over Iceland and Greenland and the shores of Baffin's Bay, so that the sailors coming there presently found them green and gracious, and could scarce believe their eyes, this story does not tell. Nor of the movement of mankind now that the earth was hotter, northward and southward towards the poles of the earth. It concerns itself only with the coming and the passing of the Star.

The Martian astronomers—for there are astronomers on Mars, although they are very different beings from men—were naturally profoundly interested by these things. They saw them from their own standpoint of course. "Considering the mass and temperature of the missile that was flung through our solar system into the sun," one wrote, "it is astonishing what a little damage the Earth, which it missed so narrowly, has sustained. All the familiar continental markings and the masses of the seas remain intact, and indeed the only difference seems to be a shrinkage of the white discoloration (supposed to be frozen water) round either pole." Which only shows how small the vastest of human catastrophes may seem, at a distance of a few million miles.

32

Miss Winchelsea's Heart

Miss Winchelsea was going to Rome. The matter had filled her mind for a month or more, and had overflowed so abundantly into her conversation that quite a number of people who were not going to Rome, and who were not likely to go to Rome, had made it a personal grievance against her. Some indeed had attempted quite unavailingly to convince her that Rome was not nearly such a desirable place as it was reported to be, and others had gone so far as to suggest behind her back that she was dreadfully "stuck up" about "that Rome of hers." And little Lily Hardhurst had told her friend Mr. Binns that so far as she was concerned Miss Winchelsea might "go to her old Rome and stop there; she (Miss Lily Hardhurst) wouldn't grieve." And the way in which Miss Winchelsea put herself upon terms of personal tenderness with Horace and Benvenuto Cellini and Raphael and Shelley and Keats—if she had been Shelley's widow she could not have professed a keener interest in his grave—was a matter of universal astonishment. Her dress was a triumph of tactful discretion, sensible, but not too "touristy—" Miss Winchelsea, had a great dread of being "touristy—" and her Baedeker was carried in a cover of grey to hide its glaring red. She made a prim and pleasant little figure on the Charing Cross platform, in spite of her swelling pride, when at last the great day dawned, and she could start for Rome. The day was bright, the Channel passage would be pleasant, and all the omens promised well. There was the gayest sense of adventure in this unprecedented departure.

She was going with two friends who had been fellow-students with her at the training college, nice honest girls both, though not so good at history and literature as Miss Winchelsea. They both looked up to her immensely, though physically they had to look down, and she anticipated some pleasant times to be spent in "stirring them up" to her own pitch of aesthetic and historical enthusiasm. They had secured seats already, and welcomed her effusively at the carriage door. In the instant criticism of the encounter she noted that Fanny had a slightly "touristy" leather strap, and that Helen had succumbed to a serge jacket with side pockets, into which her hands were thrust. But they were much too happy with themselves and the expedition for their friend to attempt any hint at the moment about these things. As soon as the first ecstasies were over—Fanny's enthusiasm was a little noisy and crude, and consisted mainly in emphatic repetitions of "Just fancy! We're going to Rome, my dear—! Rome—!" They gave their attention to their fellow-travellers. Helen was anxious to secure a compartment to themselves, and in order to discourage intruders, got out and planted herself firmly on the step. Miss Winchelsea peeped out over her shoulder, and made sly little remarks about the accumulating people on the platform, at which Fanny laughed gleefully.

They were travelling with one of Mr. Thomas Gunn's parties—fourteen days in Rome for fourteen pounds. They did not belong to the personally conducted party of course—Miss Winchelsea had seen to that—but they travelled with it because of the convenience of that arrangement. The people were the oddest mixture, and wonderfully amusing. There was a vociferous red-faced polyglot personal conductor in a pepper and salt suit, very long in the arms and legs and very active. He shouted proclamations. When he wanted to speak to people he stretched out an arm and held them until his purpose was accomplished. One hand was full of papers, tickets, counterfoils of tourists. The people of the personally conducted party were, it seemed, of two sorts; people the conductor wanted and could not find, and people he did not want and who followed him in a steadily growing tail up and down the platform. These people seemed, indeed to think that their one chance of reaching Rome lay in keeping close to him. Three little old ladies were particularly energetic in his pursuit, and at last maddened him to the pitch of clapping them into a carriage and daring them to emerge again. For the rest of the time, one, two, or three of their heads protruded from the window wailing enquiries about "a little wickerwork box" whenever he drew near. There was a very stout man with a very stout wife in shiny black; there was a little old man like an aged hostler.

"What can such people want in Rome?" asked Miss Winchelsea. "What can it mean to them?" There was a very tall curate in a very small straw hat, and a very short curate encumbered by a long camera stand. The contrast amused Fanny very much. Once they heard some one calling for "Snooks." "I always thought that name was invented by novelists," said Miss Winchelsea. "Fancy! Snooks. I wonder which is Mr. Snooks." Finally they picked out a very stout and resolute little man in a large check suit. "If he isn't Snooks, he ought to be," said Miss Winchelsea.

Presently the conductor discovered Helen's attempt at a corner in carriages. "Room for five," he bawled with a parallel translation on his fingers. A party of four together—mother, father, and two daughters—blundered in, all greatly excited. "It's all right, Ma—you let me," said one of the daughters, hitting her mother's bonnet with a handbag she struggled to put in the rack. Miss Winchelsea detested people who banged about and called their mother "Ma." A young man travelling alone followed. He was not at all "touristy" in his costume, Miss Winchelsea observed; his Gladstone bag was of good pleasant leather with labels reminiscent of Luxembourg and Ostend, and his boots, though brown, were not vulgar. He carried an overcoat on his arm. Before these people had properly settled in their places, came an inspection of tickets and a slamming of doors, and behold! They were gliding out of Charing Cross station on their way to Rome.

"Fancy!" cried Fanny, "We are going to Rome, my dear! Rome! I don't seem to believe it, even now."

Miss Winchelsea suppressed Fanny's emotions with a little smile, and the lady who was called "Ma" explained to people in general why they had "cut it so close" at the station. The two daughters called her "Ma" several times, toned her down in a tactless effective way, and drove her at last to the muttered inventory of a basket of travelling requisites. Presently she looked up. "Lor'!" she said, "I didn't bring them!" Both the daughters said "Oh, Ma!" but what "them" was did not appear. Presently Fanny produced "Hare's Walks in Rome," a sort of mitigated guide-book very popular among Roman visitors; and the father of the two daughters began to examine his books of tickets minutely, apparently in a search after English words. When he had looked at the tickets for a long time right way up, he turned them upside down. Then he produced a fountain pen and dated them with considerable care. The young man, having completed an unostentatious survey of his fellow travellers, produced a book and fell to reading. When Helen and Fanny were looking out of the window at Chislehurst—the place interested Fanny because the poor dear Empress of the French used to live there—Miss Winchelsea took the opportunity to observe the book the young man held. It was not a guide-book, but a little thin volume of poetry—bound. She glanced at his face—it seemed a refined pleasant face to her hasty glance. He wore a little gilt pince-nez. "Do you think she lives there now?" said Fanny, and Miss Winchelsea's inspection came to an end.

For the rest of the journey Miss Winchelsea talked little, and what she said was as pleasant and as stamped with refinement as she could make it. Her voice was always low and clear and pleasant, and she took care that on this occasion it was particularly low and clear and pleasant. As they came under the white cliffs the young man put his book of poetry away, and when at last the train stopped beside the boat, he displayed a graceful alacrity with the impedimenta of Miss Winchelsea and her friends. Miss Winchelsea hated nonsense, but she was pleased to see the young man perceived at once that they were ladies, and helped them without any violent geniality; and how nicely he showed that his civilities were to be no excuse for further intrusions. None of her little party had been out of England before, and they were all excited and a little nervous at the Channel passage. They stood in a little group in a good place near the middle of the boat—the young man had taken Miss Winchelsea's hold-all there and had told her it was a good place—and they watched the white shores of Albion recede and quoted Shakespeare and made quiet fun of their fellow travellers in the English way.

They were particularly amused at the precautions the bigger-sized people had taken against the little waves—cut lemons and flasks prevailed, one lady lay full length in a deck chair with a handkerchief over her face, and a very broad resolute man in a bright brown "touristy" suit walked all the way from England to France along the deck, with his legs as widely apart as Providence permitted. These were all excellent precautions, and nobody was ill. The personally conducted party pursued the conductor about the deck with enquiries in a manner that suggested to Helen's mind the rather vulgar image of hens with a piece of bacon peel, until at last he went into hiding below. And the young man with the thin volume of poetry stood at the stern watching England receding, looking rather lonely and sad to Miss Winchelsea's eye.

And then came Calais and tumultuous novelties, and the young man had not forgotten Miss Winchelsea's hold-all and the other little things. All three girls, though they had passed government examinations in French to any extent, were stricken with a dumb shame of their accents, and the young man was very useful. And he did not intrude. He put them in a comfortable carriage and raised his hat and went away. Miss Winchelsea thanked him in her best manner—a pleasing, cultivated manner—and Fanny said he was "nice" almost before he was out of earshot. "I wonder what he can be," said Helen. "He's going to Italy, because I noticed green tickets in his book." Miss Winchelsea almost told them of the poetry, and decided not to do so. And presently the carriage windows seized hold upon them and the young man was forgotten. It made them feel that they were doing an educated sort of thing to travel through a country whose commonest advertisements were in idiomatic French, and Miss Winchelsea made unpatriotic comparisons because there were weedy little sign-board advertisements by the rail side instead of the broad hoardings that deface the landscape in our land. But the north of France is really uninteresting country, and after a time Fanny reverted to "Hare's Walks" and Helen initiated lunch. Miss Winchelsea awoke out of a happy reverie; she had been trying to realise, she said, that she was actually going to Rome, but she perceived at Helen's suggestion that she was hungry, and they lunched out of their baskets very cheerfully. In the afternoon they were tired and silent until Helen made tea. Miss Winchelsea might have dozed, only she knew Fanny slept with her mouth open; and as their fellow passengers were two rather nice critical-looking ladies of uncertain age—who knew French well enough to talk it—she employed herself in keeping Fanny awake. The rhythm of the train became insistent, and the streaming landscape outside became at last quite painful to the eye. They were already dreadfully tired of travelling before their night's stoppage came.

The stoppage for the night was brightened by the appearance of the young man, and his manners were all that could be desired and his French quite serviceable. His coupons availed for the same hotel as theirs, and by chance as it seemed he sat next Miss Winchelsea at the table d'hote. In spite of her enthusiasm for Rome, she had thought out some such possibility very thoroughly, and when he ventured to make a remark upon the tediousness of travelling—he let the soup and fish go by before he did this—she did not simply assent to his proposition, but responded with another. They were soon comparing their journeys, and Helen and Fanny were cruelly overlooked in the conversation. It was to be the same journey, they found; one day for the galleries at Florence—"from what I hear," said the young man, "it is barely enough—," and the rest at Rome. He talked of Rome very pleasantly; he was evidently quite well read, and he quoted Horace about Soracte. Miss Winchelsea had "done" that book of Horace for her matriculation, and was delighted to cap his quotation. It gave a sort of tone to things, this incident—a touch of refinement to mere chatting. Fanny expressed a few emotions, and Helen interpolated a few sensible remarks, but the bulk of the talk on the girls' side naturally fell to Miss Winchelsea.

Before they reached Rome this young man was tacitly of their party. They did not know his name nor what he was, but it seemed he taught, and Miss Winchelsea had a shrewd idea he was an extension lecturer. At any rate he was something of that sort, something gentlemanly and refined without being opulent and impossible. She tried once or twice to ascertain whether he came from Oxford or Cambridge, but he missed her timid importunities. She tried to get him to make remarks about those places to see if he would say "come up" to them instead of "go down—" she knew that was how you told a 'Varsity man. He used the word "'Varsity—" not university—in quite the proper way.

They saw as much of Mr. Ruskin's Florence as the brief time permitted; he met them in the Pitti Gallery and went round with them, chatting brightly, and evidently very grateful for their recognition. He knew a great deal about art, and all four enjoyed the morning immensely. It was fine to go round recognising old favourites and finding new beauties, especially while so many people fumbled helplessly with Baedeker. Nor was he a bit of a prig, Miss Winchelsea said, and indeed she detested prigs. He had a distinct undertone of humour, and was funny, for example, without being vulgar, at the expense of the quaint work of Beato Angelico. He had a grave seriousness beneath it all, and was quick to seize the moral lessons of the pictures. Fanny went softly among these masterpieces; she admitted "she knew so little about them," and she confessed that to her they were "all beautiful." Fanny's "beautiful" inclined to be a little monotonous, Miss Winchelsea thought. She had been quite glad when the last sunny Alp had vanished, because of the staccato of Fanny's admiration. Helen said little, but Miss Winchelsea had found her a little wanting on the aesthetic side in the old days and was not surprised; sometimes she laughed at the young man's hesitating delicate little jests and sometimes she didn't, and sometimes she seemed quite lost to the art about them in the contemplation of the dresses of the other visitors.

At Rome the young man was with them intermittently. A rather "touristy" friend of his took him away at times. He complained comically to Miss Winchelsea. "I have only two short weeks in Rome," he said, "and my friend Leonard wants to spend a whole day at Tivoli, looking at a waterfall."

"What is your friend Leonard?" asked Miss Winchelsea abruptly.

"He's the most enthusiastic pedestrian I ever met," the young man replied—amusingly, but a little unsatisfactorily, Miss Winchelsea thought.

They had some glorious times, and Fanny could not think what they would have done without him. Miss Winchelsea's interest and Fanny's enormous capacity for admiration were insatiable. They never flagged—through pictures and sculpture galleries, immense crowded churches, ruins and museums, Judas trees and prickly pears, wine carts and palaces, they admired their way unflinchingly. They never saw a stone pine or a eucalyptus but they named and admired it; they never glimpsed Soracte but they exclaimed. Their common ways were made wonderful by imaginative play. "Here Caesar may have walked," they would say. "Raphael may have seen Soracte from this very point." They happened on the tomb of Bibulus. "Old Bibulus," said the young man. "The oldest monument of Republican Rome!" said Miss Winchelsea.

"I'm dreadfully stupid," said Fanny, "but who was Bibulus?"

There was a curious little pause.

"Wasn't he the person who built the wall?" said Helen.

The young man glanced quickly at her and laughed. "That was Balbus," he said. Helen reddened, but neither he nor Miss Winchelsea threw any light upon Fanny's ignorance about Bibulus.

Helen was more taciturn than the other three, but then she was always taciturn, and usually she took care of the tram tickets and things like that, or kept her eye on them if the young man took them, and told him where they were when he wanted them. Glorious times they had, these young people, in that pale brown cleanly city of memories that was once the world. Their only sorrow was the shortness of the time. They said indeed that the electric trams and the '70 buildings, and that criminal advertisement that glares upon the Forum, outraged their aesthetic feelings unspeakably; but that was only part of the fun. And indeed Rome is such a wonderful place that it made Miss Winchelsea forget some of her most carefully prepared enthusiasms at times, and Helen, taken unawares, would suddenly admit the beauty of unexpected things. Yet Fanny and Helen would have liked a shop window or so in the English quarter if Miss Winchelsea's uncompromising hostility to all other English visitors had not rendered that district impossible.

The intellectual and aesthetic fellowship of Miss Winchelsea and the scholarly young man passed insensibly towards a deeper feeling. The exuberant Fanny did her best to keep pace with their recondite admiration by playing her "beautiful," with vigour, and saying "Oh! Let's go," with enormous appetite whenever a new place of interest was mentioned. But Helen developed a certain want of sympathy towards the end, that disappointed Miss Winchelsea a little. She refused to "see anything" in the face of Beatrice Cenci—Shelley's Beatrice Cenci—! In the Barberini gallery; and one day, when they were deploring the electric trams, she said rather snappishly that "people must get about somehow, and it's better than torturing horses up these horrid little hills." She spoke of the Seven Hills of Rome as "horrid little hills!"

And the day they went on the Palatine—though Miss Winchelsea did not know of this—she remarked suddenly to Fanny, "Don't hurry like that, my dear; they don't want us to overtake them. And we don't say the right things for them when we do get near."

"I wasn't trying to overtake them," said Fanny, slackening her excessive pace; "I wasn't indeed." And for a minute she was short of breath.

But Miss Winchelsea had come upon happiness. It was only when she came to look back across an intervening tragedy that she quite realised how happy she had been, pacing among the cypress-shadowed ruins, and exchanging the very highest class of information the human mind can possess, the most refined impressions it is possible to convey. Insensibly emotion crept into their intercourse, sunning itself openly and pleasantly at last when Helen's modernity was not too near. Insensibly their interest drifted from the wonderful associations about them to their more intimate and personal feelings. In a tentative way information was supplied; she spoke allusively of her school, of her examination successes, of her gladness that the days of "Cram" were over. He made it quite clear that he also was a teacher. They spoke of the greatness of their calling, of the necessity of sympathy to face its irksome details, of a certain loneliness they sometimes felt.

That was in the Colosseum, and it was as far as they got that day, because Helen returned with Fanny—she had taken her into the upper galleries. Yet the private dreams of Miss Winchelsea, already vivid and concrete enough, became now realistic in the highest degree. She figured that pleasant young man, lecturing in the most edifying way to his students, herself modestly prominent as his intellectual mate and helper; she figured a refined little home, with two bureaus, with white shelves of high-class books, and autotypes of the pictures of Rossetti and Burne-Jones, with Morris's wall papers and flowers in pots of beaten copper. Indeed she figured many things. On the Pincio the two had a few precious moments together, while Helen marched Fanny off to see the muro Torto, and he spoke at once plainly. He said he hoped their friendship was only beginning, that he already found her company very precious to him, that indeed it was more than that.

He became nervous, thrusting at his glasses with trembling fingers as though he fancied his emotions made them unstable. "I should of course," he said, "tell you things about myself. I know it is rather unusual my speaking to you like this. Only our meeting has been so accidental—or providential—and I am snatching at things. I came to Rome expecting a lonely tour...and I have been so very happy, so very happy. Quite recently I found myself in a position—I have dared to think—And—"

He glanced over his shoulder and stopped. He said "Damn!" quite distinctly—and she did not condemn him for that manly lapse into profanity. She looked and saw his friend Leonard advancing. He drew nearer; he raised his hat to Miss Winchelsea, and his smile was almost a grin. "I've been looking for you everywhere, Snooks," he said. "You promised to be on the Piazza steps half an hour ago."

Snooks! The name struck Miss Winchelsea like a blow in the face. She did not hear his reply. She thought afterwards that Leonard must have considered her the vaguest-minded person. To this day she is not sure whether she was introduced to Leonard or not, nor what she said to him. A sort of mental paralysis was upon her. Of all offensive surnames—Snooks!

Helen and Fanny were returning, there were civilities, and the young men were receding. By a great effort she controlled herself to face the enquiring eyes of her friends. All that afternoon she lived the life of a heroine under the indescribable outrage of that name, chatting, observing, with "Snooks" gnawing at her heart. From the moment that it first rang upon her ears, the dream of her happiness was prostrate in the dust. All the refinement she had figured was ruined and defaced by that cognomen's unavoidable vulgarity.

What was that refined little home to her now, spite of autotypes, Morris papers, and bureaus? Athwart it in letters of fire ran an incredible inscription: "Mrs. Snooks." That may seem a little thing to the reader, but consider the delicate refinement of Miss Winchelsea's mind. Be as refined as you can and then think of writing yourself down: "Snooks." She conceived herself being addressed as Mrs. Snooks by all the people she liked least, conceived the patronymic touched with a vague quality of insult. She figured a card of grey and silver bearing "Winchelsea," triumphantly effaced by an arrow, Cupid's arrow, in favour of "Snooks." Degrading confession of feminine weakness! She imagined the terrible rejoicings of certain girl friends, of certain grocer cousins from whom her growing refinement had long since estranged her. How they would make it sprawl across the envelope that would bring their sarcastic congratulations. Would even his pleasant company compensate her for that? "It is impossible," she muttered; "impossible! Snooks!"

She was sorry for him, but not so sorry as she was for herself. For him she had a touch of indignation. To be so nice, so refined, while all the time he was "Snooks," to hide under a pretentious gentility of demeanour the badge sinister of his surname seemed a sort of treachery. To put it in the language of sentimental science she felt he had "led her on."

There were of course moments of terrible vacillation, a period even when something almost like passion bid her throw refinement to the winds. And there was something in her, an unexpurgated vestige of vulgarity, that made a strenuous attempt at proving that Snooks was not so very bad a name after all. Any hovering hesitation flew before Fanny's manner, when Fanny came with an air of catastrophe to tell that she also knew the horror. Fanny's voice fell to a whisper when she said Snooks. Miss Winchelsea would not give him any answer when at last, in the Borghese, she could have a minute with him; but she promised him a note.

She handed him that note in the little book of poetry he had lent her, the little book that had first drawn them together. Her refusal was ambiguous, allusive. She could no more tell him why she rejected him than she could have told a cripple of his hump. He too must feel something of the unspeakable quality of his name. Indeed he had avoided a dozen chances of telling it, she now perceived. So she spoke of "obstacles she could not reveal—" "reasons why the thing he spoke of was impossible." She addressed the note with a shiver, "E. K. Snooks."

Things were worse than she had dreaded; he asked her to explain. How could she explain? Those last two days in Rome were dreadful. She was haunted by his air of astonished perplexity. She knew she had given him intimate hopes, she had not the courage to examine her mind thoroughly for the extent of her encouragement. She knew he must think her the most changeable of beings. Now that she was in full retreat, she would not even perceive his hints of a possible correspondence. But in that matter he did a thing that seemed to her at once delicate and romantic. He made a go-between of Fanny. Fanny could not keep the secret, and came and told her that night under a transparent pretext of needed advice. "Mr. Snooks," said Fanny, "wants to write to me. Fancy! I had no idea. But should I let him?" They talked it over long and earnestly, and Miss Winchelsea was careful to keep the veil over her heart. She was already repenting his disregarded hints. Why should she not hear of him sometimes—painful though his name must be to her? Miss Winchelsea decided it might be permitted, and Fanny kissed her good-night with unusual emotion. After she had gone Miss Winchelsea sat for a long time at the window of her little room. It was moonlight, and down the street a man sang "Santa Lucia" with almost heart-dissolving tenderness...She sat very still.

She breathed a word very softly to herself. The word was "Snooks." Then she got up with a profound sigh, and went to bed. The next morning he said to her meaningly, "I shall hear of you through your friend."

Mr. Snooks saw them off from Rome with that pathetic interrogative perplexity still on his face, and if it had not been for Helen he would have retained Miss Winchelsea's hold-all in his hand as a sort of encyclopaedic keepsake. On their way back to England Miss Winchelsea on six separate occasions made Fanny promise to write to her the longest of long letters. Fanny, it seemed, would be quite near Mr. Snooks. Her new school—she was always going to new schools—would be only five miles from Steely Bank, and it was in the Steely Bank Polytechnic, and one or two first-class schools, that Mr. Snooks did his teaching. He might even see her at times. They could not talk much of him—she and Fanny always spoke of "him," never of Mr. Snooks—because Helen was apt to say unsympathetic things about him. Her nature had coarsened very much, Miss Winchelsea perceived, since the old Training College days; she had become hard and cynical. She thought he had a weak face, mistaking refinement for weakness as people of her stamp are apt to do, and when she heard his name was Snooks, she said she had expected something of the sort. Miss Winchelsea was careful to spare her own feelings after that, but Fanny was less circumspect.

The girls parted in London, and Miss Winchelsea returned, with a new interest in life, to the Girls' High School in which she had been an increasingly valuable assistant for the last three years. Her new interest in life was Fanny as a correspondent, and to give her a lead she wrote her a lengthy descriptive letter within a fortnight of her return. Fanny answered, very disappointingly. Fanny indeed had no literary gift, but it was new to Miss Winchelsea to find herself deploring the want of gifts in a friend. That letter was even criticised aloud in the safe solitude of Miss Winchelsea's study, and her criticism, spoken with great bitterness, was "Twaddle!" It was full of just the things Miss Winchelsea's letter had been full of, particulars of the school. And of Mr. Snooks, only this much: "I have had a letter from Mr. Snooks, and he has been over to see me on two Saturday afternoons running. He talked about Rome and you; we both talked about you. Your ears must have burnt, my dear..."

Miss Winchelsea repressed a desire to demand more explicit information, and wrote the sweetest long letter again. "Tell me all about yourself, dear. That journey has quite refreshed our ancient friendship, and I do so want to keep in touch with you." About Mr. Snooks she simply wrote on the fifth page that she was glad Fanny had seen him, and that if he should ask after her, she was to be remembered to him very kindly (underlined). And Fanny replied most obtusely in the key of that "ancient friendship," reminding Miss Winchelsea of a dozen foolish things of those old schoolgirl days at the training college, and saying not a word about Mr. Snooks!

For nearly a week Miss Winchelsea was so angry at the failure of Fanny as a go-between that she could not write to her. And then she wrote less effusively, and in her letter she asked point blank, "Have you seen Mr. Snooks?" Fanny's letter was unexpectedly satisfactory. "I have seen Mr. Snooks," she wrote, and having once named him she kept on about him; it was all Snooks—Snooks this and Snooks that. He was to give a public lecture, said Fanny, among other things. Yet Miss Winchelsea, after the first glow of gratification, still found this letter a little unsatisfactory. Fanny did not report Mr. Snooks as saying anything about Miss Winchelsea, nor as looking a little white and worn, as he ought to have been doing. And behold! Before she had replied, came a second letter from Fanny on the same theme, quite a gushing letter, and covering six sheets with her loose feminine hand.

And about this second letter was a rather odd little thing that Miss Winchelsea only noticed as she re-read it the third time. Fanny's natural femininity had prevailed even against the round and clear traditions of the training college; she was one of those she-creatures born to make all her m's and n's and u's and r's and e's alike, and to leave her o's and a's open and her i's undotted. So that it was only after an elaborate comparison of word with word that Miss Winchelsea felt assured Mr. Snooks was not really "Mr. Snooks" at all! In Fanny's first letter of gush he was Mr. "Snooks," in her second the spelling was changed to Mr. "Senoks." Miss Winchelsea's hand positively trembled as she turned the sheet over—it meant so much to her. For it had already begun to seem to her that even the name of Mrs. Snooks might be avoided at too great a price, and suddenly—this possibility! She turned over the six sheets, all dappled with that critical name, and everywhere the first letter had the form of an E! For a time she walked the room with a hand pressed upon her heart.

She spent a whole day pondering this change, weighing a letter of inquiry that should be at once discreet and effectual, weighing too what action she should take after the answer came. She was resolved that if this altered spelling was anything more than a quaint fancy of Fanny's, she would write forthwith to Mr. Snooks. She had now reached a stage when the minor refinements of behaviour disappear. Her excuse remained uninvented, but she had the subject of her letter clear in her mind, even to the hint that "circumstances in my life have changed very greatly since we talked together." But she never gave that hint. There came a third letter from that fitful correspondent Fanny. The first line proclaimed her "the happiest girl alive."

Miss Winchelsea crushed the letter in her hand—the rest unread—and sat with her face suddenly very still. She had received it just before morning school, and had opened it when the junior mathematicians were well under way. Presently she resumed reading with an appearance of great calm. But after the first sheet she went on reading the third without discovering the error: "told him frankly I did not like his name," the third sheet began. "He told me he did not like it himself—you know that sort of sudden frank way he has—" Miss Winchelsea did know. "So I said 'Couldn't you change it?' He didn't see it at first. Well, you know dear, he had told me what it really meant; it means Sevenoaks, only it has got down to Snooks—both Snooks and Noaks, dreadfully vulgar surnames though they be, are really worn forms of Sevenoaks. So I said—even I have my bright ideas at times—'if it got down from Sevenoaks to Snooks, why not get it back from Snooks to Sevenoaks?' And the long and the short of it is dear, he couldn't refuse me, and he changed his spelling there and then to Senoks for the bills of the new lecture. And afterwards, when we are married, we shall put in the apostrophe and make it Se'noks. Wasn't it kind of him to mind that fancy of mine, when many men would have taken offence? But it is just like him all over; he is as kind as he is clever. Because he knew as well as I did that I would have had him in spite of it, had he been ten times Snooks. But he did it all the same."

The class was startled by the sound of paper being viciously torn, and looked up to see Miss Winchelsea white in the face, and with some very small pieces of paper clenched in one hand. For a few seconds they stared at her stare, and then her expression changed back to a more familiar one. "Has any one finished number three?" she asked in an even tone. She remained calm after that. But impositions ruled high that day. And she spent two laborious evenings writing letters of various sorts to Fanny, before she found a decent congratulatory vein. Her reason struggled hopelessly against the persuasion that Fanny had behaved in an exceedingly treacherous manner.

One may be extremely refined and still capable of a very sore heart. Certainly Miss Winchelsea's heart was very sore. She had moods of sexual hostility, in which she generalised uncharitably about mankind. "He forgot himself with me," she said. "But Fanny is pink and pretty and soft and a fool—a very excellent match for a Man." And by way of a wedding present she sent Fanny a gracefully bound volume of poetry by George Meredith, and Fanny wrote back a grossly happy letter to say that it was "All beautiful." Miss Winchelsea hoped that some day Mr. Senoks might take up that slim book and think for a moment of the donor. Fanny wrote several times before and about her marriage, pursuing that fond legend of their "ancient friendship," and giving her happiness in the fullest detail. And Miss Winchelsea wrote to Helen for the first time after the Roman journey, saying nothing about the marriage, but expressing very cordial feelings.

They had been in Rome at Easter, and Fanny was married in the August vacation. She wrote a garrulous letter to Miss Winchelsea, describing her home-coming, and the astonishing arrangements of their "teeny weeny" little house. Mr. Se'noks was now beginning to assume a refinement in Miss Winchelsea's memory out of all proportion to the facts of the case, and she tried in vain to imagine his cultured greatness in a "teeny weeny" little house. "Am busy enamelling a cosey corner," said Fanny, sprawling to the end of her third sheet, "so excuse more." Miss Winchelsea answered in her best style, gently poking fun at Fanny's arrangements and hoping intensely that Mr. Se'noks might see the letter. Only this hope enabled her to write at all, answering not only that letter but one in November and one at Christmas.

The two latter communications contained urgent invitations for her to come to Steely Bank on a Visit during the Christmas holidays. She tried to think that he had told her to ask that, but it was too much like Fanny's opulent good-nature. She could not but believe that he must be sick of his blunder by this time; and she had more than a hope that he would presently write her a letter beginning "Dear Friend." Something subtly tragic in the separation was a great support to her, a sad misunderstanding. To have been jilted would have been intolerable. But he never wrote that letter beginning "Dear Friend."

For two years Miss Winchelsea could not go to see her friends, in spite of the reiterated invitations of Mrs. Sevenoaks—it became full Sevenoaks in the second year. Then one day near the Easter rest she felt lonely and without a soul to understand her in the world, and her mind ran once more on what is called Platonic friendship. Fanny was clearly happy and busy in her new sphere of domesticity, but no doubt he had his lonely hours. Did he ever think of those days in Rome—gone now beyond recalling? No one had understood her as he had done; no one in all the world. It would be a sort of melancholy pleasure to talk to him again, and what harm could it do? Why should she deny herself? That night she wrote a sonnet, all but the last two lines of the octave—which would not come, and the next day she composed a graceful little note to tell Fanny she was coming down.

And so she saw him again.

Even at the first encounter it was evident he had changed; he seemed stouter and less nervous, and it speedily appeared that his conversation had already lost much of its old delicacy. There even seemed a justification for Helen's description of weakness in his face—in certain lights it was weak. He seemed busy and preoccupied about his affairs, and almost under the impression that Miss Winchelsea had come for the sake of Fanny. He discussed his dinner with Fanny in an intelligent way. They only had one good long talk together, and that came to nothing. He did not refer to Rome, and spent some time abusing a man who had stolen an idea he had had for a text-book. It did not seem a very wonderful idea to Miss Winchelsea. She discovered he had forgotten the names of more than half the painters whose work they had rejoiced over in Florence.

It was a sadly disappointing week, and Miss Winchelsea was glad when it came to an end. Under various excuses she avoided visiting them again. After a time the visitor's room was occupied by their two little boys, and Fanny's invitations ceased. The intimacy of her letters had long since faded away.

33

Mr. Ledbetter's Vacation

My friend, Mr. Ledbetter, is a round-faced little man, whose natural mildness of eye is gigantically exaggerated when you catch the beam through his glasses, and whose deep, deliberate voice irritates, irritable people. A certain elaborate clearness of enunciation has come with him to his present vicarage from his scholastic days, an elaborate clearness of enunciation and a certain nervous determination to be firm and correct upon all issues, important and unimportant alike. He is a sacerdotalist and a chess player, and suspected by many of the secret practice of the higher mathematics—creditable rather than interesting things. His conversation is copious and given much to needless detail. By many indeed, his intercourse is condemned, to put it plainly, as "boring," and such have even done me the compliment to wonder why I countenance him. But, on the other hand, there is a large faction who marvel at his countenancing such a dishevelled, discreditable acquaintance as myself. Few appear to regard our friendship with equanimity. But that is because they do not know of the link that binds us, of my amiable connection via Jamaica with Mr. Ledbetter's past.

About that past he displays an anxious modesty. "I do not know what I should do if it became known," he says; and repeats, impressively, "I do not know what I should do." As a matter of fact, I doubt if he would do anything except get very red about the ears. But that will appear later; nor will I tell here of our first encounter, since, as a general rule—though I am prone to break it—the end of a story should come after, rather than before, the beginning. And the beginning of the story goes a long way back; indeed it is now nearly twenty years since Fate, by a series of complicated and startling manoeuvres, brought Mr. Ledbetter, so to speak, into my hands.

In those days I was living in Jamaica, and Mr. Ledbetter was a schoolmaster in England. He was in orders, and already recognisably the same man that he is to-day: the same rotundity of visage, the same or similar glasses, and the same faint shadow of surprise in his resting expression. He was of course, dishevelled when I saw him, and his collar less of a collar than a wet bandage, and that may have helped to bridge the natural gulf between us—but of that, as I say, later.

The business began at Hithergate-on-Sea, and simultaneously with Mr. Ledbetter's summer vacation. Thither he came for a greatly needed rest, with a bright brown portmanteau marked "F. W. L.", a new white and black straw hat, and two pairs of white flannel trousers. He was naturally exhilarated at his release from school—for he was not very fond of the boys he taught. After dinner he fell into a discussion with a talkative person established in the boarding-house to which, acting on the advice of his aunt, he had resorted. This talkative person was the only other man in the house. Their discussion concerned the melancholy disappearance of wonder and adventure in these latter days, the prevalence of globe-trotting, the abolition of distance by steam and electricity, the vulgarity of advertisement, the degradation of men by civilisation, and many such things. Particularly was the talkative person eloquent on the decay of human courage through security, a security Mr. Ledbetter rather thoughtlessly joined him in deploring. Mr. Ledbetter, in the first delight of emancipation from "duty," and being anxious, perhaps, to establish a reputation for manly conviviality, partook, rather more freely than was advisable, of the excellent whisky the talkative person produced. But he did not become intoxicated, he insists.

He was simply eloquent beyond his sober wont, and with the finer edge gone from his judgment. And after that long talk of the brave old days that were past forever, he went out into moonlit Hithergate alone and up the cliff road where the villas cluster together.

He had bewailed, and now as he walked up the silent road he still bewailed, the fate that had called him to such an uneventful life as a pedagogue's. What a prosaic existence he led, so stagnant, so colourless! Secure, methodical, year in year out, what call was there for bravery? He thought enviously of those roving, mediaeval days, so near and so remote, of quests and spies and condottieri and many a risky blade-drawing business. And suddenly came a doubt, a strange doubt, springing out of some chance thought of tortures, and destructive altogether of the position he had assumed that evening.

Was he—Mr. Ledbetter—really, after all, so brave as he assumed? Would he really be so pleased to have railways, policemen, and security vanish suddenly from the earth?

The talkative man had spoken enviously of crime. "The burglar," he said, "is the only true adventurer left on earth. Think of his single-handed fight—against the whole civilised world!" And Mr. Ledbetter had echoed his envy. "They do have some fun out of life." Mr. Ledbetter had said. "And about the only people who do. Just think how it must feel to wire a lawn!" And he had laughed wickedly. Now, in this franker intimacy of self-communion he found himself instituting a comparison between his own brand of courage and that of the habitual criminal. He tried to meet these insidious questionings with blank assertion. "I could do all that," said Mr. Ledbetter. "I long to do all that. Only I do not give way to my criminal impulses. My moral courage restrains me." But he doubted even while he told himself these things.

Mr. Ledbetter passed a large villa standing by itself. Conveniently situated above a quiet, practicable balcony was a window, gaping black, wide open. At the time he scarcely marked it, but the picture of it came with him, wove into his thoughts. He figured himself climbing up that balcony, crouching—plunging into that dark, mysterious interior. "Bah! You would not dare," said the Spirit of Doubt. "My duty to my fellow-men forbids," said Mr. Ledbetter's self-respect.

It was nearly eleven, and the little seaside town was already very still. The whole world slumbered under the moonlight. Only one warm oblong of window-blind far down the road spoke of waking life. He turned and came back slowly towards the villa of the open window. He stood for a time outside the gate, a battlefield of motives. "Let us put things to the test," said Doubt. "For the satisfaction of these intolerable doubts, show that you dare go into that house. Commit a burglary in blank. That, at any rate, is no crime." Very softly he opened and shut the gate and slipped into the shadow of the shrubbery. "This is foolish," said Mr. Ledbetter's caution. "I expected that," said Doubt. His heart was beating fast, but he was certainly not afraid. He was not afraid. He remained in that shadow for some considerable time.

The ascent of the balcony, it was evident, would have to be done in a rush, for it was all in clear moonlight, and visible from the gate into the avenue. A trellis thinly set with young, ambitious climbing roses made the ascent ridiculously easy. There in that black shadow by the stone vase of flowers, one might crouch and take a closer view of this gaping breach in the domestic defences, the open window. For a while Mr. Ledbetter was as still as the night, and then that insidious whisky tipped the balance. He dashed forward. He went up the trellis with quick, convulsive movements, swung his legs over the parapet of the balcony, and dropped panting in the shadow even as he had designed. He was trembling violently, short of breath, and his heart pumped noisily, but his mood was exultation. He could have shouted to find he was so little afraid.

A happy line that he had learnt from Wills's "Mephistopheles" came into his mind as he crouched there. "I feel like a cat on the tiles," he whispered to himself. It was far better than he had expected—this adventurous exhilaration. He was sorry for all poor men to whom burglary was unknown. Nothing happened. He was quite safe. And he was acting in the bravest manner!

And now for the window, to make the burglary complete! Must he dare do that? Its position above the front door defined it as a landing or passage, and there were no looking-glasses or any bedroom signs about it, or any other window on the first floor, to suggest the possibility of a sleeper within. For a time he listened under the ledge, then raised his eyes above the sill and peered in. Close at hand, on a pedestal, and a little startling at first, was a nearly life-size gesticulating bronze. He ducked, and after some time he peered again. Beyond was a broad landing, faintly gleaming; a flimsy fabric of bead curtain, very black and sharp, against a further window; a broad staircase, plunging into a gulf of darkness below; and another ascending to the second floor. He glanced behind him, but the stillness of the night was unbroken. "Crime," he whispered, "crime," and scrambled softly and swiftly over the sill into the house. His feet fell noiselessly on a mat of skin. He was a burglar indeed!

He crouched for a time, all ears and peering eyes. Outside was a scampering and rustling, and for a moment he repented of his enterprise. A short "miaow," a spitting, and a rush into silence, spoke reassuringly of cats. His courage grew. He stood up. Every one was abed, it seemed. So easy is it to commit a burglary, if one is so minded. He was glad he had put it to the test. He determined to take some petty trophy, just to prove his freedom from any abject fear of the law, and depart the way he had come.

He peered about him, and suddenly the critical spirit arose again. Burglars did far more than such mere elementary entrance as this: they went into rooms, they forced safes. Well—he was not afraid. He could not force safes, because that would be a stupid want of consideration for his hosts. But he would go into rooms—he would go upstairs. More: he told himself that he was perfectly secure; an empty house could not be more reassuringly still. He had to clench his hands, nevertheless, and summon all his resolution before he began very softly to ascend the dim staircase, pausing for several seconds between each step. Above was a square landing with one open and several closed doors; and all the house was still. For a moment he stood wondering what would happen if some sleeper woke suddenly and emerged. The open door showed a moonlit bedroom, the coverlet white and undisturbed. Into this room he crept in three interminable minutes and took a piece of soap for his plunder—his trophy. He turned to descend even more softly than he had ascended. It was as easy as—Hist...!

Footsteps! On the gravel outside the house—and then the noise of a latchkey, the yawn and bang of a door, and the spitting of a match in the hall below. Mr. Ledbetter stood petrified by the sudden discovery of the folly upon which he had come. "How on earth am I to get out of this?" said Mr. Ledbetter.

The hall grew bright with a candle flame, some heavy object bumped against the umbrella-stand, and feet were ascending the staircase. In a flash Mr. Ledbetter realised that his retreat was closed. He stood for a moment, a pitiful figure of penitent confusion. "My goodness! What a fool I have been!" he whispered, and then darted swiftly across the shadowy landing into the empty bedroom from which he had just come. He stood listening—quivering. The footsteps reached the first-floor landing.

Horrible thought! This was possibly the late-comer's room! Not a moment was to be lost! Mr. Ledbetter stooped beside the bed, thanked Heaven for a valance, and crawled within its protection not ten seconds too soon. He became motionless on hands and knees. The advancing candle-light appeared through the thinner stitches of the fabric, the shadows ran wildly about, and became rigid as the candle was put down.

"Lord, what a day!" said the newcomer, blowing noisily, and it seemed he deposited some heavy burthen on what Mr. Ledbetter, judging by the feet, decided to be a writing-table. The unseen then went to the door and locked it, examined the fastenings of the windows carefully and pulled down the blinds, and returning sat down upon the bed with startling ponderosity.

"What a day!" he said. "Good Lord!" and blew again, and Mr. Ledbetter inclined to believe that the person was mopping his face. His boots were good stout boots; the shadows of his legs upon the valance suggested a formidable stoutness of aspect. After a time he removed some upper garments—a coat and waistcoat, Mr. Ledbetter inferred—and casting them over the rail of the bed remained breathing less noisily, and as it seemed cooling from a considerable temperature. At intervals he muttered to himself, and once he laughed softly. And Mr. Ledbetter muttered to himself, but he did not laugh. "Of all the foolish things," said Mr. Ledbetter. "What on earth am I to do now?"

His outlook was necessarily limited. The minute apertures between the stitches of the fabric of the valance admitted a certain amount of light, but permitted no peeping. The shadows upon this curtain, save for those sharply defined legs, were enigmatical, and intermingled confusingly with the florid patterning of the chintz. Beneath the edge of the valance a strip of carpet was visible, and by cautiously depressing his eye, Mr. Ledbetter found that this strip broadened until the whole area of the floor came into view. The carpet was a luxurious one, the room spacious, and to judge by the castors and so forth of the furniture, well equipped.

What he should do he found it difficult to imagine. To wait until this person had gone to bed, and then, when he seemed to be sleeping, to creep to the door, unlock it, and bolt headlong for that balcony seemed the only possible thing to do. Would it be possible to jump from the balcony? The danger of it! When he thought of the chances against him, Mr. Ledbetter despaired.

He was within an ace of thrusting forth his head beside the gentleman's legs, coughing if necessary to attract his attention, and then, smiling, apologising and explaining his unfortunate intrusion by a few well-chosen sentences. But he found these sentences hard to choose. "No doubt, sir, my appearance is peculiar," or, "I trust, sir, you will pardon my somewhat ambiguous appearance from beneath you," was about as much as he could get.

Grave possibilities forced themselves on his attention. Suppose they did not believe him, what would they do to him? Would his unblemished high character count for nothing? Technically he was a burglar, beyond dispute. Following out this train of thought, he was composing a lucid apology for "this technical crime I have committed," to be delivered before sentence in the dock, when the stout gentleman got up and began walking about the room. He locked and unlocked drawers, and Mr. Ledbetter had a transient hope that he might be undressing. But, no! He seated himself at the writing-table, and began to write and then tear up documents. Presently the smell of burning cream-laid paper mingled with the odour of cigars in Mr. Ledbetter's nostrils.

"The position I had assumed," said Mr. Ledbetter when he told me of these things, "was in many respects an ill-advised one. A transverse bar beneath the bed depressed my head unduly, and threw a disproportionate share of my weight upon my hands. After a time, I experienced what is called, I believe, a crick in the neck. The pressure of my hands on the coarsely-stitched carpet speedily became painful. My knees too, were painful, my trousers being drawn tightly over them. At that time I wore rather higher collars than I do now—two and a half inches, in fact—and I discovered what I had not remarked before, that the edge of the one I wore was frayed slightly under the chin. But much worse than these things was an itching of my face, which I could only relieve by violent grimacing—I tried to raise my hand, but the rustle of the sleeve alarmed me. After a time I had to desist from this relief also, because—happily in time—I discovered that my facial contortions were shifting my glasses down my nose. Their fall would, of course, have exposed me, and as it was they came to rest in an oblique position of by no means stable equilibrium. In addition I had a slight cold, and an intermittent desire to sneeze or sniff caused me inconvenience. In fact, quite apart from the extreme anxiety of my position, my physical discomfort became in a short time very considerable indeed. But I had to stay there motionless, nevertheless."

After an interminable time, there began a chinking sound. This deepened into a rhythm: chink, chink, chink—twenty-five chinks—a rap on the writing-table, and a grunt from the owner of the stout legs. It dawned upon Mr. Ledbetter that this chinking was the chinking of gold. He became incredulously curious as it went on. His curiosity grew. Already, if that was the case, this extraordinary man must have counted some hundreds of pounds. At last Mr. Ledbetter could resist it no longer, and he began very cautiously to fold his arms and lower his head to the level of the floor, in the hope of peeping under the valance. He moved his feet, and one made a slight scraping on the floor. Suddenly the chinking ceased. Mr. Ledbetter became rigid. After a while the chinking was resumed. Then it ceased again, and everything was still, except Mr. Ledbetter's heart—that organ seemed to him to be beating like a drum.

The stillness continued. Mr. Ledbetter's head was now on the floor, and he could see the stout legs as far as the shins. They were quite still. The feet were resting on the toes and drawn back, as it seemed, under the chair of the owner. Everything was quite still, everything continued still. A wild hope came to Mr. Ledbetter that the unknown was in a fit or suddenly dead, with his head upon the writing-table...

The stillness continued. What had happened? The desire to peep became irresistible. Very cautiously Mr. Ledbetter shifted his hand forward, projected a pioneer finger, and began to lift the valance immediately next his eye. Nothing broke the stillness. He saw now the stranger's knees, saw the back of the writing-table, and then—he was staring at the barrel of a heavy revolver pointed over the writing-table at his head.

"Come out of that, you scoundrel!" said the voice of the stout gentleman in a tone of quiet concentration. "Come out. This side, and now. None of your hanky-panky—come right out, now."

Mr. Ledbetter came right out, a little reluctantly perhaps, but without any hanky-panky, and at once, even as he was told.

"Kneel," said the stout gentleman, "and hold up your hands."

The valance dropped again behind Mr. Ledbetter, and he rose from all fours and held up his hands. "Dressed like a parson," said the stout gentleman. "I'm blest if he isn't! A little chap, too! You scoundrel! What the deuce possessed you to come here to-night? What the deuce possessed you to get under my bed?"

He did not appear to require an answer, but proceeded at once to several very objectionable remarks upon Mr. Ledbetter's personal appearance. He was not a very big man, but he looked strong to Mr. Ledbetter: he was as stout as his legs had promised, he had rather delicately-chiselled small features distributed over a considerable area of whitish face, and quite a number of chins. And the note of his voice had a sort of whispering undertone.

"What the deuce, I say, possessed you to get under my bed?"

Mr. Ledbetter, by an effort, smiled a wan propitiatory smile. He coughed. "I can quite understand—" he said.

"Why! What on earth? It's soap! No—! You scoundrel. Don't you move that hand."

"It's soap," said Mr. Ledbetter. "From your washstand. No doubt if—"

"Don't talk," said the stout man. "I see it's soap. Of all incredible things."

"If I might explain—"

"Don't explain. It's sure to be a lie, and there's no time for explanations. What was I going to ask you? Ah! Have you any mates?"

"In a few minutes, if you—"

"Have you any mates? Curse you. If you start any soapy palaver I'll shoot. Have you any mates?"

"No," said Mr. Ledbetter.

"I suppose it's a lie," said the stout man. "But you'll pay for it if it is. Why the deuce didn't you floor me when I came upstairs? You won't get a chance to now, anyhow. Fancy getting under the bed! I reckon it's a fair cop, anyhow, so far as you are concerned."

"I don't see how I could prove an alibi," remarked Mr. Ledbetter, trying to show by his conversation that he was an educated man. There was a pause. Mr. Ledbetter perceived that on a chair beside his captor was a large black bag on a heap of crumpled papers, and that there were torn and burnt papers on the table. And in front of these, and arranged methodically along the edge were rows and rows of little yellow rouleaux—a hundred times more gold than Mr. Ledbetter had seen in all his life before. The light of two candles, in silver candlesticks, fell upon these.

The pause continued. "It is rather fatiguing holding up my hands like this," said Mr. Ledbetter, with a deprecatory smile.

"That's all right," said the fat man. "But what to do with you I don't exactly know."

"I know my position is ambiguous."

"Lord!" said the fat man, "Ambiguous! And goes about with his own soap, and wears a thundering great clerical collar. You are a blooming burglar, you are—if ever there was one!"

"To be strictly accurate," said Mr. Ledbetter, and suddenly his glasses slipped off and clattered against his vest buttons.

The fat man changed countenance, a flash of savage resolution crossed his face, and something in the revolver clicked. He put his other hand to the weapon. And then he looked at Mr. Ledbetter, and his eye went down to the dropped pince-nez.

"Full-cock now anyhow," said the fat man, after a pause, and his breath seemed to catch. "But I'll tell you, you've never been so near death before. Lord! I'm almost glad. If it hadn't been, that the revolver wasn't cocked you'd be lying dead there now."

Mr. Ledbetter said nothing, but he felt that the room was swaying.

"A miss is as good as a mile. It's lucky for both of us it wasn't. Lord!" He blew noisily. "There's no need for you to go pale-green for a little thing like that."

"If I can assure you, sir—" said Mr. Ledbetter, with an effort.

"There's only one thing to do. If I call in the police, I'm bust—a little game I've got on is bust. That won't do. If I tie you up and leave you—again, the thing may be out to-morrow. To-morrow's Sunday, and Monday's Bank Holiday—I've counted on three clear days. Shooting you's murder—and hanging; and besides, it will bust the whole blooming kernooze. I'm hanged if I can think what to do—I'm hanged if I can."

"Will you permit me—"

"You gas as much as if you were a real parson, I'm blessed if you don't. Of all the burglars you are the—Well! No—I won't permit you. There isn't time. If you start off jawing again, I'll shoot right in your stomach. See? But I know now—I know now! What we're going to do first, my man, is an examination for concealed arms—an examination for concealed arms. And look here! When I tell you to do a thing, don't start off at a gabble—do it brisk."

And with many elaborate precautions, and always pointing the pistol at Mr. Ledbetter's head, the stout man stood him up and searched him for weapons. "Why, you are a burglar!" he said "You're a perfect amateur. You haven't even a pistol-pocket in the back of your breeches. No, you don't! Shut up, now."

So soon as the issue was decided, the stout man made Mr. Ledbetter take off his coat and roll up his shirt-sleeves, and with the revolver at one ear, proceed with the packing his appearance had interrupted. From the stout man's point of view that was evidently the only possible arrangement, for if he had packed, he would have had to put down the revolver. So that even the gold on the table was handled by Mr. Ledbetter. This nocturnal packing was peculiar. The stout man's idea was evidently to distribute the weight of the gold as unostentatiously as possible through his luggage. It was by no means an inconsiderable weight. There was, Mr. Ledbetter says, altogether nearly L18,000 in gold in the black bag and on the table. There were also many little rolls of L5 bank-notes. Each rouleau of L25 was wrapped by Mr. Ledbetter in paper. These rouleaux were then put neatly in cigar-boxes and distributed between a travelling trunk, a Gladstone bag, and a hat-box. About L600 went in a tobacco tin in a dressing-bag. L10 in gold and a number of L5 notes the stout man pocketed. Occasionally he objurgated Mr. Ledbetter's clumsiness, and urged him to hurry, and several times he appealed to Mr. Ledbetter's watch for information.

Mr. Ledbetter strapped the trunk and bag, and returned the stout man the keys. It was then ten minutes to twelve, and until the stroke of midnight the stout man made him sit on the Gladstone bag, while he sat at a reasonably safe distance on the trunk and held the revolver handy and waited. He appeared to be now in a less aggressive mood, and having watched Mr. Ledbetter for some time, he offered a few remarks.

"From your accent I judge you are a man of some education," he said, lighting a cigar. "No—don't begin that explanation of yours. I know it will be longwinded from your face, and I am much too old a liar to be interested in other men's lying. You are, I say a person of education. You do well to dress as a curate. Even among educated people you might pass as a curate."

"I am a curate," said Mr. Ledbetter, "or, at least—"

"You are trying to be. I know. But you didn't ought to burgle. You are not the man to burgle. You are, if I may say it—the thing will have been pointed out to you before—a coward."

"Do you know," said Mr. Ledbetter, trying to get a final opening, "it was that very question—"

The stout man waved him into silence.

"You waste your education in burglary. You should do one of two things. Either you should forge or you should embezzle. For my own part, I embezzle. Yes; I embezzle. What do you think a man could be doing with all this gold but that? Ah! Listen! Midnight...! Ten. Eleven. Twelve. There is something very impressive to me in that slow beating of the hours. Time—space; what mysteries they are! What mysteries...It's time for us to be moving. Stand up!"

And then kindly, but firmly, he induced Mr. Ledbetter to sling the dressing bag over his back by a string across his chest, to shoulder the trunk, and over-ruling a gasping protest, to take the Gladstone bag in his disengaged hand. So encumbered, Mr. Ledbetter struggled perilously downstairs. The stout gentleman followed with an overcoat, the hat-box, and the revolver, making derogatory remarks about Mr. Ledbetter's strength, and assisting him at the turnings of the stairs.

"The back door," he directed, and Mr. Ledbetter staggered through a conservatory, leaving a wake of smashed flower-pots behind him. "Never mind the crockery," said the stout man; "it's good for trade. We wait here until a quarter past. You can put those things down. You have!"

Mr. Ledbetter collapsed panting on the trunk. "Last night," he gasped, "I was asleep in my little room, and I no more dreamt—"

"There's no need for you to incriminate yourself," said the stout gentleman, looking at the lock of the revolver. He began to hum. Mr. Ledbetter made to speak, and thought better of it.

There presently came the sound of a bell, and Mr. Ledbetter was taken to the back door and instructed to open it. A fair-haired man in yachting costume entered. At the sight of Mr. Ledbetter he started violently and clapped his hand behind him. Then he saw the stout man. "Bingham!" he cried, "who's this?"

"Only a little philanthropic do of mine—burglar I'm trying to reform. Caught him under my bed just now. He's all right. He's a frightful ass. He'll be useful to carry some of our things."

The newcomer seemed inclined to resent Mr. Ledbetter's presence at first, but the stout man reassured him.

"He's quite alone. There's not a gang in the world would own him. No—! Don't start talking, for goodness' sake."

They went out into the darkness of the garden with the trunk still bowing Mr. Ledbetter's shoulders. The man in the yachting costume walked in front with the Gladstone bag and a pistol; then came Mr. Ledbetter like Atlas; Mr. Bingham followed with the hat-box, coat, and revolver as before. The house was one of those that have their gardens right up to the cliff. At the cliff was a steep wooden stairway, descending to a bathing tent dimly visible on the beach. Below was a boat pulled up, and a silent little man with a black face stood beside it. "A few moments' explanation," said Mr. Ledbetter; "I can assure you—" Somebody kicked him, and he said no more.

They made him wade to the boat, carrying the trunk, they pulled him aboard by the shoulders and hair, they called him no better name than "scoundrel" and "burglar" all that night. But they spoke in undertones so that the general public was happily unaware of his ignominy. They hauled him aboard a yacht manned by strange, unsympathetic Orientals, and partly they thrust him and partly he fell down a gangway into a noisome, dark place, where he was to remain many days—how many he does not know, because he lost count among other things when he was sea-sick. They fed him on biscuits and incomprehensible words; they gave him water to drink mixed with unwished-for rum. And there were cockroaches, where they put him—night and day there were cockroaches, and in the night-time there were rats. The Orientals emptied his pockets and took his watch—but Mr. Bingham, being appealed to, took that himself. And five or six times the five Lascars—if they were Lascars—and the Chinaman and the negro who constituted the crew, fished him out and took him aft to Bingham and his friend to play cribbage and euchre and three-handed whist, and to listen to their stories and boastings in an interested manner.

Then these principals would talk to him as men talk to those who have lived a life of crime. Explanations they would never permit, though they made it abundantly clear to him that he was the rummiest burglar they had ever set eyes on. They said as much again and again. The fair man was of a taciturn disposition and irascible at play; but Mr. Bingham, now that the evident anxiety of his departure from England was assuaged, displayed a vein of genial philosophy. He enlarged upon the mystery of space and time, and quoted Kant and Hegel—or at least, he said he did. Several times Mr. Ledbetter got as far as: "My position under your bed, you know—" but then he always had to cut, or pass the whisky, or do some such intervening thing. After his third failure, the fair man got quite to look for this opening, and whenever Mr. Ledbetter began after that, he would roar with laughter and hit him violently on the back. "Same old start, same old story; good old burglar!" the fair-haired man would say.

So Mr. Ledbetter suffered for many days, twenty perhaps; and one evening he was taken, together with some tinned provisions, over the side and put ashore on a rocky little island with a spring. Mr. Bingham came in the boat with him, giving him good advice all the way, and waving his last attempts at an explanation aside.

"I am really not a burglar," said Mr. Ledbetter.

"You never will be," said Mr. Bingham. "You'll never make a burglar. I'm glad you are beginning to see it. In choosing a profession a man must study his temperament. If you don't, sooner or later you will fail. Compare myself, for example. All my life I have been in banks—I have got on in banks. I have even been a bank manager. But was I happy? No, Why wasn't I happy? Because it did not suit my temperament. I am too adventurous—too versatile. Practically I have thrown it over. I do not suppose I shall ever manage a bank again. They would be glad to get me, no doubt; but I have learnt the lesson of my temperament—at last... No! I shall never manage a bank again.

"Now, your temperament unfits you for crime—just as mine unfits me for respectability. I know you better than I did, and now I do not even recommend forgery. Go back to respectable courses, my man. Your lay is the philanthropic lay—that is your lay. With that voice—the Association for the Promotion of Snivelling among the Young—something in that line. You think it over.

"The island we are approaching has no name apparently—at least, there is none on the chart. You might think out a name for it while you are there—while you are thinking about all these things. It has quite drinkable water, I understand. It is one of the Grenadines—one of the Windward Islands. Yonder, dim and blue, are others of the Grenadines. There are quantities of Grenadines, but the majority are out of sight. I have often wondered what these islands are for—now, you see, I am wiser. This one at least is for you. Sooner or later some simple native will come along and take you off. Say what you like about us then—abuse us, if you like—we shan't care a solitary Grenadine! And here—here is half a sovereign's worth of silver. Do not waste that in foolish dissipation when you return to civilisation. Properly used, it may give you a fresh start in life. And do not—Don't beach her, you beggars, he can wade—! Do not waste the precious solitude before you in foolish thoughts. Properly used, it may be a turning-point in your career. Waste neither money nor time. You will die rich. I'm sorry, but I must ask you to carry your tucker to land in your arms. No; it's not deep. Curse that explanation of yours! There's not time. No, no, no! I won't listen. Overboard you go!"

And the falling night found Mr. Ledbetter—the Mr. Ledbetter who had complained that adventure was dead—sitting beside his cans of food, his chin resting upon his drawn-up knees, staring through his glasses in dismal mildness over the shining, vacant sea.

He was picked up in the course of three days by a negro fisherman and taken to St. Vincent's, and from St. Vincent's he got, by the expenditure of his last coins, to Kingston, in Jamaica. And there he might have foundered. Even nowadays he is not a man of affairs, and then he was a singularly helpless person. He had not the remotest idea what he ought to do. The only thing he seems to have done was to visit all the ministers of religion he could find in the place to borrow a passage home. But he was much too dirty and incoherent—and his story far too incredible for them. I met him quite by chance. It was close upon sunset, and I was walking out after my siesta on the road to Dunn's Battery, when I met him—I was rather bored, and with a whole evening on my hands—luckily for him. He was trudging dismally towards the town. His woebegone face and the quasi-clerical cut of his dust-stained, filthy costume caught my humour. Our eyes met. He hesitated. "Sir," he said, with a catching of the breath, "could you spare a few minutes for what I fear will seem an incredible story?"

"Incredible!" I said.

"Quite," he answered eagerly. "No one will believe it, alter it though I may. Yet I can assure you, sir—"

He stopped hopelessly. The man's tone tickled me. He seemed an odd character. "I am," he said, "one of the most unfortunate beings alive."

"Among other things, you haven't dined?" I said, struck with an idea.

"I have not," he said solemnly, "for many days."

"You'll tell it better after that," I said; and without more ado led the way to a low place I knew, where such a costume as his was unlikely to give offence. And there—with certain omissions which he subsequently supplied, I got his story. At first I was incredulous, but as the wine warmed him, and the faint suggestion of cringing which his misfortunes had added to his manner disappeared, I began to believe. At last, I was so far convinced of his sincerity that I got him a bed for the night, and next day verified the banker's reference he gave me through my Jamaica banker. And that done, I took him shopping for underwear and such like equipments of a gentleman at large. Presently came the verified reference. His astonishing story was true. I will not amplify our subsequent proceedings. He started for England in three days' time.

"I do not know how I can possibly thank you enough," began the letter he wrote me from England, "for all your kindness to a total stranger," and proceeded for some time in a similar strain. "Had it not been for your generous assistance, I could certainly never have returned in time for the resumption of my scholastic duties, and my few minutes of reckless folly would, perhaps, have proved my ruin. As it is, I am entangled in a tissue of lies and evasions, of the most complicated sort, to account for my sunburnt appearance and my whereabouts. I have rather carelessly told two or three different stories, not realising the trouble this would mean for me in the end. The truth I dare not tell. I have consulted a number of law books in the British Museum, and there is not the slightest doubt that I have connived at and abetted and aided a felony. That scoundrel Bingham was the Hithergate bank manager, I find and guilty of the most flagrant embezzlement. Please, please burn this letter when read—I trust you implicitly. The worst of it is, neither my aunt nor her friend who kept the boarding-house at which I was staying seem altogether to believe a guarded statement I have made them—practically of what actually happened. They suspect me of some discreditable adventure, but what sort of discreditable adventure they suspect me of, I do not know. My aunt says she would forgive me if I told her everything. I have—I have told her more than everything, and still she is not satisfied. It would never do to let them know the truth of the case, of course, and so I represent myself as having been waylaid and gagged upon the beach. My aunt wants to know why they waylaid and gagged me, why they took me away in their yacht. I do not know. Can you suggest any reason? I can think of nothing. If when you wrote, you could write on two sheets so that I could show her one, and on that one if you could show clearly that I really was in Jamaica this summer, and had come there by being removed from a ship, it would be of great service to me. It would certainly add to the load of my obligation to you—a load that I fear I can never fully repay. Although if gratitude..." And so forth. At the end he repeated his request for me to burn the letter.

So the remarkable story of Mr. Ledbetter's Vacation ends. That breach with his aunt was not of long duration. The old lady had forgiven him before she died.

34

THE MAN WHO COULD WORK MIRACLES

It is doubtful whether the gift was innate. For my own part, I think it came to him suddenly. Indeed, until he was thirty he was a sceptic, and did not believe in miraculous powers. And here, since it is the most convenient place, I must mention that he was a little man, and had eyes of a hot brown, very erect red hair, a moustache with ends that he twisted up, and freckles. His name was George McWhirter Fotheringay—not the sort of name by any means to lead to any expectation of miracles—and he was clerk at Gomshott's. He was greatly addicted to assertive argument. It was while he was asserting the impossibility of miracles that he had his first intimation of his extraordinary powers. This particular argument was being held in the bar of the Long Dragon, and Toddy Beamish was conducting the opposition by a monotonous but effective "So you say," that drove Mr. Fotheringay to the very limit of his patience.

There were present, besides these two, a very dusty cyclist, landlord Cox, and Miss Maybridge, the perfectly respectable and rather portly barmaid of the Dragon. Miss Maybridge was standing with her back to Mr. Fotheringay, washing glasses; the others were watching him, more or less amused by the present ineffectiveness of the assertive method. Goaded by the Torres Vedras tactics of Mr. Beamish, Mr. Fotheringay determined to make an unusual rhetorical effort. "Looky here, Mr. Beamish," said Mr. Fotheringay. "Let us clearly understand what a miracle is. It's something contrariwise to the course of nature, done by power of Will, something what couldn't happen without being specially willed."

"So you say," said Mr. Beamish, repulsing him.

Mr. Fotheringay appealed to the cyclist, who had hitherto been a silent auditor, and received his assent—given with a hesitating cough and a glance at Mr. Beamish. The landlord would express no opinion, and Mr. Fotheringay, returning to Mr. Beamish, received the unexpected concession of a qualified assent to his definition of a miracle.

"For instance," said Mr. Fotheringay, greatly encouraged. "Here would be a miracle. That lamp, in the natural course of nature, couldn't burn like that upsy-down, could it, Beamish?"

"You say it couldn't," said Beamish.

"And you?" said Fotheringay. "You don't mean to say—eh?"

"No," said Beamish reluctantly. "No, it couldn't."

"Very well," said Mr. Fotheringay. "Then here comes someone, as it might be me, along here, and stands as it might be here, and says to that lamp, as I might do, collecting all my will—'Turn upsy-down without breaking, and go on burning steady', and—Hullo!"

It was enough to make anyone say "Hullo!" The impossible, the incredible, was visible to them all. The lamp hung inverted in the air, burning quietly with its flame pointing down. It was as solid, as indisputable as ever a lamp was, the prosaic common lamp of the Long Dragon bar.

Mr. Fotheringay stood with an extended forefinger and the knitted brows of one anticipating a catastrophic smash. The cyclist, who was sitting next the lamp, ducked and jumped across the bar. Everybody jumped, more or less. Miss Maybridge turned and screamed. For nearly three seconds the lamp remained still. A faint cry of mental distress came from Mr. Fotheringay. "I can't keep it up," he said, "any longer." He staggered back, and the inverted lamp suddenly flared, fell against the corner of the bar, bounced aside, smashed upon the floor, and went out.

It was lucky it had a metal receiver, or the whole place would have been in a blaze. Mr. Cox was the first to speak, and his remark, shorn of needless excrescences, was to the effect that Fotheringay was a fool. Fotheringay was beyond disputing even so fundamental a proposition as that! He was astonished beyond measure at the thing that had occurred. The subsequent conversation threw absolutely no light on the matter so far as Fotheringay was concerned; the general opinion not only followed Mr. Cox very closely but very vehemently. Everyone accused Fotheringay of a silly trick, and presented him, to himself, as a foolish destroyer of comfort and security. His mind was in a tornado of perplexity, he was himself inclined to agree with them, and he made a remarkably ineffectual opposition to the proposal of his departure.

He went home flushed and heated, coat-collar crumpled, eyes smarting and ears red. He watched each of the ten street lamps nervously as he passed it. It was only when he found himself alone in his little bedroom in Church Row that he was able to grapple seriously with his memories of the occurrence, and ask, "What on earth happened?"

He had removed his coat and boots, and was sitting on the bed with his hands in his pockets repeating the text of his defence for the seventeenth time, "I didn't want the confounded thing to upset," when it occurred to him that at the precise moment he had said the commanding words he had inadvertently willed the thing he said, and that when he had seen the lamp in the air he had felt it depended on him to maintain it there without being clear how this was to be done. He had not a particularly complex mind, or he might have stuck for a time at that "inadvertently willed," embracing, as it does, the abstrusest problems of voluntary action; but as it was, the idea came to him with a quite acceptable haziness. And from that, following, as I must admit, no clear logical path, he came to the test of experiment.

He pointed resolutely to his candle and collected his mind, though he felt he did a foolish thing. "Be raised up," he said. But in a second that feeling vanished. The candle was raised, hung in the air one giddy moment, and as Mr. Fotheringay gasped, fell with a smash on his toilet-table, leaving him in darkness save for the expiring glow of its wick.

For a time Mr. Fotheringay sat in the darkness, perfectly still. "It did happen, after all," he said. "And 'ow I'm to explain it I don't know." He sighed heavily, and began feeling in his pockets for a match. He could find none, and he rose and groped about the toilet-table. "I wish I had a match," he said. He resorted to his coat, and there was none there, and then it dawned upon him that miracles were possible even with matches. He extended a hand and scowled at it in the dark. "Let there be a match in that hand," he said. He felt some light object fall across his palm, and his fingers closed upon a match.

After several ineffectual attempts to light this, he discovered it was a safety-match. He threw it down, and then it occurred to him that he might have willed it lit. He did, and perceived it burning in the midst of his toilet-table mat. He caught it up hastily, and it went out. His perception of possibilities enlarged, and he felt for and replaced the candle in its candlestick. "Here! You be lit," said Mr. Fotheringay, and forthwith the candle was flaring, and he saw a little black hole in the toilet-cover, with a wisp of smoke rising from it. For a time he stared from this to the little flame and back, and then looked up and met his own gaze in the looking glass. By this help he communed with himself in silence for a time.

"How about miracles now?" said Mr. Fotheringay at last, addressing his reflection.

The subsequent meditations of Mr. Fotheringay were of a severe but confused description. So far, he could see it was a case of pure willing with him. The nature of his experiences so far disinclined him for any further experiments, at least until he had reconsidered them. But he lifted a sheet of paper, and turned a glass of water pink and then green, and he created a snail, which he miraculously annihilated, and got himself a miraculous new tooth-brush. Somewhen in the small hours he had reached the fact that his will-power must be of a particularly rare and pungent quality, a fact of which he had certainly had inklings before, but no certain assurance. The scare and perplexity of his first discovery was now qualified by pride in this evidence of singularity and by vague intimations of advantage. He became aware that the church clock was striking one, and as it did not occur to him that his daily duties at Gomshott's might be miraculously dispensed with, he resumed undressing, in order to get to bed without further delay. As he struggled to get his shirt over his head, he was struck with a brilliant idea. "Let me be in bed," he said, and found himself so. "Undressed," he stipulated; and finding the sheets cold, added hastily, "and in my nightshirt—no, in a nice soft woollen nightshirt. Ah!" he said with immense enjoyment. "And now let me be comfortably asleep..."

He awoke at his usual hour and was pensive all through breakfast-time, wondering whether his overnight experience might not be a particularly vivid dream. At length his mind turned again to cautious experiments. For instance, he had three eggs for breakfast; two his landlady had supplied, good but shoppy, and one was a delicious fresh goose-egg, laid, cooked, and served by his extraordinary will. He hurried off to Gomshott's in a state of profound but carefully concealed excitement, and only remembered the shell of the third egg when his landlady spoke of it that night. All day he could do no work because of this astonishingly new self-knowledge, but this caused him no inconvenience, because he made up for it miraculously in his last ten minutes.

As the day wore on his state of mind passed from wonder to elation, albeit the circumstances of his dismissal from the Long Dragon were still disagreeable to recall, and a garbled account of the matter that had reached his colleagues led to some badinage. It was evident he must be careful how he lifted frangible articles, but in other ways his gift promised more and more as he turned it over in his mind. He intended among other things to increase his personal property by unostentatious acts of creation. He called into existence a pair of very splendid diamond studs, and hastily annihilated them again as young Gomshott came across the counting-house to his desk. He was afraid young Gomshott might wonder how he had come by them. He saw quite clearly the gift required caution and watchfulness in its exercise, but so far as he could judge the difficulties attending its mastery would be no greater than those he had already faced in the study of cycling. It was that analogy, perhaps, quite as much as the feeling that he would be unwelcome in the Long Dragon, that drove him out after supper into the lane beyond the gas-works, to rehearse a few miracles in private.

There was possibly a certain want of originality in his attempts, for apart from his will-power Mr. Fotheringay was not a very exceptional man. The miracle of Moses' rod came to his mind, but the night was dark and unfavourable to the proper control of large miraculous snakes. Then he recollected the story of "Tannhauser" that he had read on the back of the Philharmonic programme. That seemed to him singularly attractive and harmless. He stuck his walking-stick—a very nice Poona-Penang lawyer—into the turf that edged the footpath, and commanded the dry wood to blossom. The air was immediately full of the scent of roses, and by means of a match he saw for himself that this beautiful miracle was indeed accomplished. His satisfaction was ended by advancing footsteps. Afraid of a premature discovery of his powers, he addressed the blossoming stick hastily: "Go back." What he meant was "Change back;" but of course he was confused. The stick receded at a considerable velocity, and incontinently came a cry of anger and a bad word from the approaching person. "Who are you throwing brambles at, you fool?" cried a voice. "That got me on the shin."

"I'm sorry, old chap," said Mr. Fotheringay, and then realising the awkward nature of the explanation, caught nervously at his moustache. He saw Winch, one of the three Immering constables, advancing.

"What d'yer mean by it?" asked the constable. "Hullo! It's you, is it? The gent that broke the lamp at the Long Dragon!"

"I don't mean anything by it," said Mr. Fotheringay. "Nothing at all."

"What d'yer do it for then?"

"Oh, bother!" said Mr. Fotheringay.

"Bother indeed! D'yer know that stick hurt? What d'yer do it for, eh?"

For the moment Mr. Fotheringay could not think what he had done it for. His silence seemed to irritate Mr. Winch. "You've been assaulting the police, young man, this time. That's what you done."

"Look here, Mr. Winch," said Mr. Fotheringay, annoyed and confused, "I'm very sorry. The fact is—"

"Well?"

He could think of no way but the truth. "I was working a miracle." He tried to speak in an off-hand way, but try as he would he couldn't.

"Working a—! 'Ere, don't you talk rot. Working a miracle, indeed! Miracle! Well, that's downright funny! Why, you's the chap that don't believe in miracles...Fact is, this is another of your silly conjuring tricks—that's what this is. Now, I tell you—"

But Mr. Fotheringay never heard what Mr. Winch was going to tell him. He realised he had given himself away, flung his valuable secret to all the winds of heaven. A violent gust of irritation swept him to action. He turned on the constable swiftly and fiercely. "Here," he said, "I've had enough of this, I have! I'll show you a silly conjuring trick, I will! Go to Hades! Go, now!"

He was alone!

Mr. Fotheringay performed no more miracles that night nor did he trouble to see what had become of his flowering stick. He returned to the town, scared and very quiet, and went to his bedroom. "Lord!" he said, "It's a powerful gift—an extremely powerful gift. I didn't hardly mean as much as that. Not really... I wonder what Hades is like!"

He sat on the bed taking off his boots. Struck by a happy thought he transferred the constable to San Francisco, and without any more interference with normal causation went soberly to bed. In the night he dreamt of the anger of Winch.

The next day Mr. Fotheringay heard two interesting items of news. Someone had planted a most beautiful climbing rose against the elder Mr. Gomshott's private house in the Lullaborough Road, and the river as far as Rawling's Mill was to be dragged for Constable Winch.

Mr. Fotheringay was abstracted and thoughtful all that day, and performed no miracles except certain provisions for Winch, and the miracle of completing his day's work with punctual perfection in spite of all the bee-swarm of thoughts that hummed through his mind. And the extraordinary abstraction and meekness of his manner was remarked by several people, and made a matter for jesting. For the most part he was thinking of Winch.

On Sunday evening he went to chapel and oddly enough, Mr. Maydig, who took a certain interest in occult matters, preached about "things that are not lawful." Mr. Fotheringay was not a regular chapel goer, but the system of assertive scepticism, to which I have already alluded, was now very much shaken. The tenor of the sermon threw an entirely new light on these novel gifts, and he suddenly decided to consult Mr. Maydig immediately after the service. So soon as that was determined, he found himself wondering why he had not done so before.

Mr. Maydig, a lean, excitable man with quite remarkably long wrists and neck, was gratified at a request for a private conversation from a young man whose carelessness in religious matters was a subject for general remark in the town. After a few necessary delays, he conducted him to the study of the Manse, which was contiguous to the dispel, seated him comfortably, and standing in front of a cheerful fire—his legs threw a Rhodian arch of shadow on the opposite wall—requested Mr. Fotheringay to state his business.

At first Mr. Fotheringay was a little abashed, and found some difficulty in opening the matter. "You will scarcely believe me, Mr. Maydig, I am afraid—" and so forth for some time. He tried a question at last, and asked Mr. Maydig his opinion of miracles.

Mr. Maydig was still saying "Well" in an extremely judicial tone, when Mr. Fotheringay interrupted again: "You don't believe, I suppose, that some common sort of person—like myself, for instance—as it might be sitting here now, might have some sort of twist inside him that made him able to do things by his will."

"It's possible," said Mr. Maydig. "Something of the sort, perhaps, is possible."

"If I might make free with something here, I think I might show you by a sort of experiment," said Mr. Fotheringay. "Now, take that tobacco-jar on the table, for instance. What I want to know is whether what I am going to do with it is a miracle or not. Just half a minute, Mr. Maydig, please."

He knitted his brows, pointed to the tobacco-jar and said: "Be a bowl of violets."

The tobacco-jar did as it was ordered.

Mr. Maydig started violently at the change, and stood looking from the thaumaturgist to the bowl of flowers. He said nothing. Presently he ventured to lean over the table and smell the violets; they were fresh-picked and very fine ones. Then he stared at Mr. Fotheringay again.

"How did you do that?" he asked.

Mr. Fotheringay pulled his moustache. "Just told it—and there you are. Is that a miracle, or is it black art, or what is it? And what do you think's the matter with me? That's what I want to ask."

"It's a most extraordinary occurrence."

"And this day last week I knew no more that I could do things like that than you did. It came quite sudden. It's something odd about my will, I suppose, and that's as far as I can see."

"Is that—the only thing? Could you do other things besides that?"

"Lord, yes!" said Mr. Fotheringay. "Just anything." He thought, and suddenly recalled a conjuring entertainment he had seen. "Here!" He pointed. "Change into a bowl of fish—no, not that—change into a glass bowl full of water with goldfish swimming in it. That's better! You see that, Mr. Maydig?"

"It's astonishing. It's incredible. You are either a most extraordinary...But no—"

"I could change it into anything," said Mr. Fotheringay. "Just anything. Here! Be a pigeon, will you?"

In another moment a blue pigeon was fluttering round the room and making Mr. Maydig duck every time it came near him. "Stop there, will you," said Mr. Fotheringay; and the pigeon hung motionless in the air. "I could change it back to a bowl of flowers," he said, and after replacing the pigeon on the table worked that miracle. "I expect you will want your pipe in a bit," he said, and restored the tobacco-jar.

Mr. Maydig had followed all these later changes in a sort of ejaculatory silence. He stared at Mr. Fotheringay and, in a very gingerly manner, picked up the tobacco-jar, examined it, replaced it on the table. "Well!" was the only expression of his feelings.

"Now, after that it's easier to explain what I came about," said Mr. Fotheringay; and proceeded to a lengthy and involved narrative of his strange experiences, beginning with the affair of the lamp in the Long Dragon and complicated by persistent allusions to Winch. As he went on, the transient pride Mr. Maydig's consternation had caused passed away; he became the very ordinary Mr. Fotheringay of everyday intercourse again. Mr. Maydig listened intently, the tobacco-jar in his hand, and his bearing changed also with the course of the narrative. Presently, while Mr. Fotheringay was dealing with the miracle of the third egg, the minister interrupted with a fluttering extended hand—

"It is possible," he said. "It is credible. It is amazing, of course, but it reconciles a number of amazing difficulties. The power to work miracles is a gift—a peculiar quality like genius or second sight—hitherto it has come very rarely and to exceptional people. But in this case...I have always wondered at the miracles of Mahomet, and at Yogi's miracles, and the miracles of Madame Blavatsky. But, of course! Yes, it is simply a gift! It carries out so beautifully the arguments of that great thinker—" Mr. Maydig's voice sank—"his Grace the Duke of Argyll. Here we plumb some profounder law—deeper than the ordinary laws of nature. Yes—yes. Go on. Go on!"

Mr. Fotheringay proceeded to tell of his misadventure with Winch, and Mr. Maydig, no longer overawed or scared, began to jerk his limbs about and interject astonishment. "It's this what troubled me most," proceeded Mr. Fotheringay; "it's this I'm most mijitly in want of advice for; of course he's at San Francisco—wherever San Francisco may be—but of course it's awkward for both of us, as you'll see, Mr. Maydig. I don't see how he can understand what has happened, and I daresay he's scared and exasperated something tremendous, and trying to get at me. I daresay he keeps on starting off to come here. I send him back, by a miracle, every few hours, when I think of it. And of course, that's a thing he won't be able to understand, and it's bound to annoy him; and of course, if he takes a ticket every time it will cost him a lot of money. I done the best I could for him, but of course it's difficult for him to put himself in my place. I thought afterwards that his clothes might have got scorched, you know—if Hades is all it's supposed to be—before I shifted him. In that case I suppose they'd have locked him up in San Francisco. Of course I willed him a new suit of clothes on him directly I thought of it. But you see, I'm already in a deuce of a tangle—"

Mr. Maydig looked serious. "I see you are in a tangle. Yes, it's a difficult position. How you are to end it..." He became diffuse and inconclusive.

"However, we'll leave Winch for a little and discuss the larger question. I don't think this is a case of the black art or anything of the sort. I don't think there is any taint of criminality about it at all, Mr. Fotheringay—none whatever, unless you are suppressing material facts. No, it's miracles—pure miracles—miracles, if I may say so, of the very highest class."

He began to pace the hearthrug and gesticulate, while Mr. Fotheringay sat with his arm on the table and his head on his arm, looking worried. "I don't see how I'm to manage about Winch," he said.

"A gift of working miracles—apparently a very powerful gift," said Mr. Maydig, "will find a way about Winch—never fear. My dear Sir, you are a most important man—a man of the most astonishing possibilities. As evidence, for example! And in other ways, the things you may do..."

"Yes, I've thought of a thing or two," said Mr. Fotheringay. "But—some of the things came a bit twisty. You saw that fish at first? Wrong sort of bowl and wrong sort of fish. And I thought I'd ask someone."

"A proper course," said Mr. Maydig, "a very proper course—altogether the proper course." He stopped and looked at Mr. Fotheringay. "It's practically an unlimited gift. Let us test your powers, for instance. If they really are...If they really are all they seem to be."

And so, incredible as it may seem, in the study of the little house behind the Congregational Chapel, on the evening of Sunday, Nov. 10, 1896, Mr. Fotheringay, egged on and inspired by Mr. Maydig, began to work miracles. The reader's attention is specially and definitely called to the date. He will object, probably has already objected, that certain points in this story are improbable, that if any things of the sort already described had indeed occurred, they would have been in all the papers a year ago. The details immediately following he will find particularly hard to accept, because among other things they involve the conclusion that he or she, the reader in question, must have been killed in a violent and unprecedented manner more than a year ago. Now a miracle is nothing if not improbable, and as a matter of fact the reader was killed in a violent and unprecedented manner a year ago. In the subsequent course of this story that will become perfectly clear and credible, as every right-minded and reasonable reader will admit. But this is not the place for the end of the story, being but little beyond the hither side of the middle. And at first the miracles worked by Mr. Fotheringay were timid little miracles—little things with the cups and parlour fitments, as feeble as the miracles of Theosophists, and feeble as they were, they were received with awe by his collaborator. He would have preferred to settle the Winch business out of hand, but Mr. Maydig would not let him. But after they had worked a dozen of these domestic trivialities, their sense of power grew, their imagination began to show signs of stimulation, and their ambition enlarged. Their first larger enterprise was due to hunger and the negligence of Mrs. Minchin, Mr. Maydig's housekeeper. The meal to which the minister conducted Mr. Fotheringay was certainly ill-laid and uninviting as refreshment for two industrious miracle-workers; but they were seated, and Mr. Maydig was descanting in sorrow rather than in anger upon his housekeeper's shortcomings, before it occurred to Mr. Fotheringay that an opportunity lay before him. "Don't you think, Mr. Maydig," he said; "if it isn't a liberty, I—"

"My dear Mr. Fotheringay! Of course! No—I didn't think."

Mr. Fotheringay waved his hand. "What shall we have?" he said, in a large, inclusive spirit, and at Mr. Maydig's order, revised the supper very thoroughly. "As for me," he said, eyeing Mr. Maydig's selection, "I am always particularly fond of a tankard of stout and a nice Welsh rarebit, and I'll order that. I ain't much given to Burgundy," and forthwith stout and Welsh rarebit promptly appeared at his command. They sat long at their supper, talking like equals, as Mr. Fotheringay presently perceived, with a glow of surprise and gratification, of all the miracles they would presently do. "And by the bye, Mr. Maydig," said Mr. Fotheringay, "I might perhaps be able to help you—in a domestic way."

"Don't quite follow," said Mr. Maydig pouring out a glass of miraculous old Burgundy.

Mr. Fotheringay helped himself to a second Welsh rarebit out of vacancy, and took a mouthful. "I was thinking," he said, "I might be able (chum, chum) to work (chum, chum) a miracle with Mrs. Minchin (chum, chum)—make her a better woman."

Mr. Maydig put down the glass and looked doubtful. "She's—She strongly objects to interference, you know, Mr. Fotheringay. And—as a matter of fact—it's well past eleven and she's probably in bed and asleep. Do you think, on the whole—"

Mr. Fotheringay considered these objections. "I don't see that it shouldn't be done in her sleep."

For a time Mr. Maydig opposed the idea, and then he yielded. Mr. Fotheringay issued his orders, and a little less at their ease perhaps, the two gentlemen proceeded with their repast. Mr. Maydig was enlarging on the changes he might expect in his housekeeper next day, with an optimism that seemed even to Mr. Fotheringay's super senses a little forced and hectic, when a series of confused noises from upstairs began. Their eyes exchanged interrogations, and Mr. Maydig left the room hastily. Mr. Fotheringay heard him calling up to his housekeeper and then his footsteps going softly up to her.

In a minute or so the minister returned, his step light, his face radiant. "Wonderful!" he said, "and touching! Most touching!"

He began pacing the hearthrug. "A repentance—a most touching repentance—through the crack of the door. Poor woman! A most wonderful change! She had got up. She must have got up at once. She had got up out of her sleep to smash a private bottle of brandy in her box. And to confess it too!...But this gives us—it opens—a most amazing vista of possibilities. If we can work this miraculous change in her..."

"The thing's unlimited seemingly," said Mr. Fotheringay. "And about Mr. Winch—"

"Altogether unlimited." And from the hearthrug Mr. Maydig, waving the Winch difficulty aside, unfolded a series of wonderful proposals—proposals he invented as he went along.

Now what those proposals were does not concern the essentials of this story. Suffice it that they were designed in a spirit of infinite benevolence, the sort of benevolence that used to be called post-prandial. Suffice it too, that the problem of Winch remained unsolved. Nor is it necessary to describe how far that series got to its fulfilment. There were astonishing changes. The small hours found Mr. Maydig and Mr. Fotheringay careering across the chilly market-square under the still moon, in a sort of ecstasy of thaumaturgy, Mr. Maydig all flap and gesture, Mr. Fotheringay short and bristling, and no longer abashed at his greatness. They had reformed every drunkard in the Parliamentary division, changed all the beer and alcohol to water (Mr. Maydig had overruled Mr. Fotheringay on this point); they had, further, greatly improved the railway communication of the place, drained Flinder's swamp, improved the soil of One Tree Hill, and cured the Vicar's wart. And they were going to see what could be done with the injured pier at South Bridge. "The place," gasped Mr. Maydig, "won't be the same place to-morrow. How surprised and thankful everyone will be!" And just at that moment the church clock struck three.

"I say," said Mr. Fotheringay, "that's three o'clock! I must be getting back. I've got to be at business by eight. And besides, Mrs. Wimms—"

"We're only beginning," said Mr. Maydig, full of the sweetness of unlimited power. "We're only beginning. Think of all the good we're doing. When people wake—"

"But—," said Mr. Fotheringay.

Mr. Maydig gripped his arm suddenly. His eyes were bright and wild. "My dear chap," he said, "there's no hurry. Look"—he pointed to the moon at the zenith—"Joshua!"

"Joshua?" said Mr. Fotheringay.

"Joshua," said Mr. Maydig. "Why not? Stop it."

Mr. Fotheringay looked at the moon.

"That's a bit tall," he said after a pause.

"Why not?" said Mr. Maydig. "Of course it doesn't stop. You stop the rotation of the earth, you know. Time stops. It isn't as if we were doing harm."

"H'm!" said Mr. Fotheringay. "Well." He sighed. "I'll try. Here—"

He buttoned up his jacket and addressed himself to the habitable globe, with as good an assumption of confidence as lay in his power. "Jest stop rotating, will you," said Mr. Fotheringay.

Incontinently he was flying head over heels through the air at the rate of dozens of miles a minute. In spite of the innumerable circles he was describing per second, he thought; for thought is wonderful—sometimes as sluggish as flowing pitch, sometimes as instantaneous as light. He thought in a second, and willed. "Let me come down safe and sound. Whatever else happens, let me down safe and sound."

He willed it only just in time, for his clothes, heated by his rapid flight through the air, were already beginning to singe. He came down with a forcible, but by no means injurious bump in what appeared to be a mound of fresh-turned earth. A large mass of metal and masonry, extraordinarily like the clock-tower in the middle of the market-square, hit the earth near him, ricochetted over him, and flew into stonework, bricks, and masonry, like a bursting bomb. A hurtling cow hit one of the larger blocks and smashed like an egg. There was a crash that made all the most violent crashes of his past life seem like the sound of falling dust, and this was followed by a descending series of lesser crashes. A vast wind roared throughout earth and heaven' so that he could scarcely lift his head to look. For a while he was too breathless and astonished even to see where he was or what had happened. And his first movement was to feel his head and reassure himself that his streaming hair was still his own.

"Lord!" gasped Mr. Fotheringay, scarce able to speak for the gale, "I've had a squeak! What's gone wrong? Storms and thunder. And only a minute ago a fine night. It's Maydig set me on to this sort of thing. What a wind! If I go on fooling in this way I'm bound to have a thundering accident...!

"Where's Maydig?

"What a confounded mess everything's in!"

He looked about him so far as his flapping jacket would permit. The appearance of things was really extremely strange. "The sky's all right anyhow," said Mr. Fotheringay. "And that's about all that is all right. And even there it looks like a terrific gale coming up. But there's the moon overhead, just as it was just now. Bright as midday. But as for the rest—Where's the village? Where's—where's anything? And what on earth set this wind a-blowing? I didn't order no wind."

Mr. Fotheringay struggled to get to his feet in vain, and after one failure, remained on all fours, holding on. He surveyed the moonlit world to leeward, with the tails of his jacket streaming over his head. "There's something seriously wrong," said Mr. Fotheringay. "And what it is—goodness knows."

Far and wide nothing was visible in the white glare through the haze of dust that drove before a screaming gale but tumbled masses of earth and heaps of inchoate ruins, no trees, no houses, no familiar shapes, only a wilderness of disorder vanishing at last into the darkness beneath the whirling columns and streamers, the lightnings and thunderings of a swiftly rising storm. Near him in the livid glare was something that might once have been an elm-tree, a smashed mass of splinters, shivered from boughs to base, and further a twisted mass of iron girders—only too evidently the viaduct—rose out of the piled confusion.

You see when Mr. Fotheringay had arrested the rotation of the solid globe, he had made no stipulation concerning the trifling movables upon its surface. And the earth spins so fast that the surface at its equator is travelling at rather more than a thousand miles an hour, and in these latitudes at more than half that pace. So that the village, and Mr. Maydig, and Mr. Fotheringay, and everybody and everything had been jerked violently forward at about nine miles per second—that is to say, much more violently than if they had been fired out of a cannon. And every human being, every living creature, every house, and every tree—all the world as we know it—had been so jerked and smashed and utterly destroyed. That was all.

These things Mr. Fotheringay did not, of course, fully appreciate. But he perceived that his miracle had miscarried, and with that a great disgust of miracles came upon him. He was in darkness now, for the clouds had swept together and blotted out his momentary glimpse of the moon, and the air was full of fitful struggling tortured wraiths of hail. A great roaring of wind and waters filled earth and sky, and peering under his hand through the dust and sleet to windward, he saw by the play of the lightnings a vast wall of water pouring towards him.

"Maydig!" screamed Mr. Fotheringay's feeble voice amid the elemental uproar. "Here!—Maydig!"

"Stop!" cried Mr. Fotheringay to the advancing water. "Oh, for goodness' sake, stop!"

"Just a moment," said Mr. Fotheringay to the lightnings and thunder. "Stop jest a moment while I collect my thoughts...And now what shall I do?" he said. "What shall I do? Lord! I wish Maydig was about.

"I know," said Mr. Fotheringay. "And for goodness' sake let's have it right this time."

He remained on all fours, leaning against the wind, very intent to have everything right.

"Ah!" he said. "Let nothing what I'm going to order happen until I say 'Off...!' Lord! I wish I'd thought of that before!"

He lifted his little voice against the whirlwind, shouting louder and louder in the vain desire to hear himself speak. "Now then!—Here goes! Mind about that what I said just now. In the first place, when all I've got to say is done, let me lose my miraculous power, let my will become just like anybody else's will, and all these dangerous miracles be stopped. I don't like them. I'd rather, I didn't work 'em. Ever so much. That's the first thing. And the second is—let me be back just before the miracles begin; let everything be just as it was before that blessed lamp turned up. It's a big job, but it's the last. Have you got it? No more miracles, everything as it was—me back in the Long Dragon just before I drank my half-pint. That's it! Yes."

He dug his fingers into the mould, closed his eyes, and said "Off!"

Everything became perfectly still. He perceived that he was standing erect.

"So you say," said a voice.

He opened his eyes. He was in the bar of the Long Dragon, arguing about miracles with Toddy Beamish. He had a vague sense of some great thing forgotten that instantaneously passed. You see, except for the loss of his miraculous powers, everything was back as it had been; his mind and memory therefore were now just as they had been at the time when this story began. So that he knew absolutely nothing of all that is told here, knows nothing of all that is told here to this day. And among other things, of course, he still did not believe in miracles.

"I tell you that miracles, properly speaking, can't possibly happen," he said, "whatever you like to hold. And I'm prepared to prove it up to the hilt."

"That's what you think," said Toddy Beamish, and "Prove it if you can."

"Looky here, Mr. Beamish," said Mr. Fotheringay. "Let us clearly understand what a miracle is. It's something contrariwise to the course of nature done by power of Will..."

35

The Stolen Body

Mr. Bessel was the senior partner in the firm of Bessel, Hart, and Brown, of St. Paul's Churchyard, and for many years he was well known among those interested in psychical research as a liberal-minded and conscientious investigator. He was an unmarried man, and instead of living in the suburbs, after the fashion of his class, he occupied rooms in the Albany, near Piccadilly. He was particularly interested in the questions of thought transference and of apparitions of the living, and in November, 1896, he commenced a series of experiments in conjunction with Mr. Vincey, of Staple Inn, in order to test the alleged possibility of projecting an apparition of one's self by force of will through space.

Their experiments were conducted in the following manner: At a pre-arranged hour Mr. Bessel shut himself in one of his rooms in the Albany and Mr. Vincey in his sitting-room in Staple Inn, and each then fixed his mind as resolutely as possible on the other. Mr. Bessel had acquired the art of self-hypnotism, and so far as he could, he attempted first to hypnotise himself and then to project himself as a "phantom of the living" across the intervening space of nearly two miles into Mr. Vincey's apartment. On several evenings this was tried without any satisfactory result, but on the fifth or sixth occasion Mr. Vincey did actually see or imagine he saw an apparition of Mr. Bessel standing in his room. He states that the appearance, although brief, was very vivid and real. He noticed that Mr. Bessel's face was white and his expression anxious, and moreover, that his hair was disordered. For a moment Mr. Vincey, in spite of his state of expectation, was too surprised to speak or move, and in that moment it seemed to him as though the figure glanced over its shoulder and incontinently vanished.

It had been arranged that an attempt should be made to photograph any phantasm seen, but Mr. Vincey had not the instant presence of mind to snap the camera that lay ready on the table beside him, and when he did so he was too late. Greatly elated, however even by this partial success, he made a note of the exact time, and at once took a cab to the Albany to inform Mr. Bessel of this result.

He was surprised to find Mr. Bessel's outer door standing open to the night, and the inner apartments lit and in an extraordinary disorder. An empty champagne magnum lay smashed upon the floor; its neck had been broken off against the inkpot on the bureau and lay beside it. An octagonal occasional table, which carried a bronze statuette and a number of choice books, had been rudely overturned, and down the primrose paper of the wall inky fingers had been drawn, as it seemed for the mere pleasure of defilement. One of the delicate chintz curtains had been violently torn from its rings and thrust upon the fire, so that the smell of its smouldering filled the room. Indeed the whole place was disarranged in the strangest fashion. For a few minutes Mr. Vincey, who had entered sure of finding Mr. Bessel in his easy chair awaiting him, could scarcely believe his eyes, and stood staring helplessly at these unanticipated things.

Then, full of a vague sense of calamity, he sought the porter at the entrance lodge. "Where is Mr. Bessel?" he asked. "Do you know that all the furniture is broken in Mr. Bessel's room?" The porter said nothing, but obeying his gestures, came at once to Mr. Bessel's apartment to see the state of affairs. "This settles it," he said, surveying the lunatic confusion. "I didn't know of this. Mr. Bessel's gone off. He's mad!"

He then proceeded to tell Mr. Vincey that about half an hour previously, that is to say, at about the time of Mr. Bessel's apparition in Mr. Vincey's rooms, the missing gentleman had rushed out of the gates of the Albany into Vigo Street, hatless and with disordered hair, and had vanished into the direction of Bond Street. "And as he went past me," said the porter, "he laughed—a sort of gasping laugh, with his mouth open and his eyes glaring—I tell you, sir he fair scared me—! Like this."

According to his imitation it was anything but a pleasant laugh. "He waved his hand, with all his fingers crooked and clawing—like that. And he said, in a sort of fierce whisper, 'Life!' Just that one word, 'Life!'"

"Dear me," said Mr. Vincey. "Tut, tut," and "Dear me!" He could think of nothing else to say. He was naturally very much surprised. He turned from the room to the porter and from the porter to the room in the gravest perplexity. Beyond his suggestion that probably Mr. Bessel would come back presently and explain what had happened, their conversation was unable to proceed. "It might be a sudden tooth-ache," said the porter, "a very sudden and violent tooth-ache, jumping on him suddenly-like and driving him wild. I've broken things myself before now in such a case..." He thought. "If it was, why should he say 'Life' to me as he went past?"

Mr. Vincey did not know. Mr. Bessel did not return, and at last Mr. Vincey, having done some more helpless staring, and having addressed a note of brief inquiry and left it in a conspicuous position on the bureau, returned in a very perplexed frame of mind to his own premises in Staple Inn. This affair had given him a shock. He was at a loss to account for Mr. Bessel's conduct on any sane hypothesis. He tried to read, but he could not do so; he went for a short walk, and was so preoccupied that he narrowly escaped a cab at the top of Chancery Lane; and at last—a full hour before his usual time—he went to bed. For a considerable time he could not sleep because of his memory of the silent confusion of Mr. Bessel's apartment, and when at length he did attain an uneasy slumber it was at once disturbed by a very vivid and distressing dream of Mr. Bessel.

He saw Mr. Bessel gesticulating wildly, and with his face white and contorted. And inexplicably mingled with his appearance, suggested perhaps by his gestures, was an intense fear, an urgency to act. He even believes that he heard the voice of his fellow experimenter calling distressfully to him, though at the time he considered this to be an illusion. The vivid impression remained though Mr. Vincey awoke. For a space he lay awake and trembling in the darkness, possessed with that vague, unaccountable terror of unknown possibilities that comes out of dreams upon even the bravest men. But at last he roused himself, and turned over and went to sleep again, only for the dream to return with enhanced vividness.

He awoke with such a strong conviction that Mr. Bessel was in overwhelming distress and need of help that sleep was no longer possible. He was persuaded that his friend had rushed out to some dire calamity. For a time he lay reasoning vainly against this belief, but at last he gave way to it. He arose, against all reason, lit his gas, and dressed, and set out through the deserted streets—deserted, save for a noiseless policeman or so and the early news carts—towards Vigo Street to inquire if Mr. Bessel had returned.

But he never got there. As he was going down Long Acre some unaccountable impulse turned him aside out of that street towards Covent Garden, which was just waking to its nocturnal activities. He saw the market in front of him—a queer effect of glowing yellow lights and busy black figures. He became aware of a shouting, and perceived a figure turn the corner by the hotel and run swiftly towards him. He knew at once that it was Mr. Bessel. But it was Mr. Bessel transfigured. He was hatless and dishevelled, his collar was torn open, he grasped a bone-handled walking-cane near the ferrule end, and his mouth was pulled awry. And he ran, with agile strides, very rapidly. Their encounter was the affair of an instant. "Bessel!" cried Vincey.

The running man gave no sign of recognition either of Mr. Vincey or of his own name. Instead he cut at his friend savagely with the stick, hitting him in the face within an inch of the eye. Mr. Vincey, stunned and astonished, staggered back, lost his footing, and fell heavily on the pavement. It seemed to him that Mr. Bessel leapt over him as he fell. When he looked again Mr. Bessel had vanished, and a policeman and a number of garden porters and salesmen were rushing past towards Long Acre in hot pursuit.

With the assistance of several passers-by—for the whole street was speedily alive with running people—Mr. Vincey struggled to his feet. He at once became the centre of a crowd greedy to see his injury. A multitude of voices competed to reassure him of his safety, and then to tell him of the behaviour of the madman, as they regarded Mr. Bessel. He had suddenly appeared in the middle of the market screaming "Life! Life!" striking left and right with a blood-stained walking-stick, and dancing and shouting with laughter at each successful blow. A lad and two women had broken heads, and he had smashed a man's wrist; a little child had been knocked insensible, and for a time he had driven every one before him, so furious and resolute had his behaviour been. Then he made a raid upon a coffee stall, hurled its paraffin flare through the window of the post office, and fled laughing, after stunning the foremost of the two policemen who had the pluck to charge him.

Mr. Vincey's first impulse was naturally to join in the pursuit of his friend, in order if possible to save him from the violence of the indignant people. But his action was slow, the blow had half stunned him, and while this was still no more than a resolution came the news, shouted through the crowd, that Mr. Bessel had eluded his pursuers. At first Mr. Vincey could scarcely credit this, but the universality of the report, and presently the dignified return of two futile policemen, convinced him. After some aimless inquiries he returned towards Staple Inn, padding a handkerchief to a now very painful nose.

He was angry and astonished and perplexed. It appeared to him indisputable that Mr. Bessel must have gone violently mad in the midst of his experiment in thought transference, but why that should make him appear with a sad white face in Mr. Vincey's dreams seemed a problem beyond solution. He racked his brains in vain to explain this. It seemed to him at last that not simply Mr. Bessel, but the order of things must be insane. But he could think of nothing to do. He shut himself carefully into his room, lit his fire—it was a gas fire with asbestos bricks—and fearing fresh dreams if he went to bed, remained bathing his injured face, or holding up books in a vain attempt to read, until dawn. Throughout that vigil he had a curious persuasion that Mr. Bessel was endeavouring to speak to him, but he would not let himself attend to any such belief.

About dawn, his physical fatigue asserted itself, and he went to bed and slept at last in spite of dreaming. He rose late, unrested and anxious, and in considerable facial pain. The morning papers had no news of Mr. Bessel's aberration—it had come too late for them. Mr. Vincey's perplexities, to which the fever of his bruise added fresh irritation, became at last intolerable, and after a fruitless visit to the Albany, he went down to St. Paul's Churchyard to Mr. Hart, Mr. Bessel's partner, and so far as Mr. Vincey knew, his nearest friend.

He was surprised to learn that Mr. Hart, although he knew nothing of the outbreak, had also been disturbed by a vision, the very vision that Mr. Vincey had seen—Mr. Bessel, white and dishevelled, pleading earnestly by his gestures for help. That was his impression of the import of his signs. "I was just going to look him up in the Albany when you arrived," said Mr. Hart. "I was so sure of something being wrong with him."

As the outcome of their consultation the two gentlemen decided to inquire at Scotland Yard for news of their missing friend. "He is bound to be laid by the heels," said Mr. Hart. "He can't go on at that pace for long." But the police authorities had not laid Mr. Bessel by the heels. They confirmed Mr. Vincey's overnight experiences and added fresh circumstances, some of an even graver character than those he knew—a list of smashed glass along the upper half of Tottenham Court Road, an attack upon a policeman in Hampstead Road, and an atrocious assault upon a woman. All these outrages were committed between half-past twelve and a quarter to two in the morning, and between those hours—and indeed, from the very moment of Mr. Bessel's first rush from his rooms at half-past nine in the evening—they could trace the deepening violence of his fantastic career. For the last hour, at least from before one, that is, until a quarter to two, he had run amuck through London, eluding with amazing agility every effort to stop or capture him.

But after a quarter to two he had vanished. Up to that hour witnesses were multitudinous. Dozens of people had seen him, fled from him or pursued him, and then things suddenly came to an end. At a quarter to two he had been seen running down the Euston Road towards Baker Street, flourishing a can of burning colza oil and jerking splashes of flame therefrom at the windows of the houses he passed. But none of the policemen on Euston Road beyond the Waxwork Exhibition, nor any of those in the side streets down which he must have passed had he left the Euston Road, had seen anything of him. Abruptly he disappeared. Nothing of his subsequent doings came to light in spite of the keenest inquiry.

Here was a fresh astonishment for Mr. Vincey. He had found considerable comfort in Mr. Hart's conviction: "He is bound to be laid by the heels before long," and in that assurance he had been able to suspend his mental perplexities. But any fresh development seemed destined to add new impossibilities to a pile already heaped beyond the powers of his acceptance. He found himself doubting whether his memory might not have played him some grotesque trick, debating whether any of these things could possibly have happened; and in the afternoon he hunted up Mr. Hart again to share the intolerable weight on his mind. He found Mr. Hart engaged with a well-known private detective, but as that gentleman accomplished nothing in this case, we need not enlarge upon his proceedings.

All that day Mr. Bessel's whereabouts eluded an unceasingly active inquiry, and all that night. And all that day there was a persuasion in the back of Vincey's mind that Mr. Bessel sought his attention, and all through the night Mr. Bessel with a tear-stained face of anguish pursued him through his dreams. And whenever he saw Mr. Bessel in his dreams he also saw a number of other faces, vague but malignant, that seemed to be pursuing Mr. Bessel.

It was on the following day Sunday, that Mr. Vincey recalled certain remarkable stories of Mrs. Bullock, the medium, who was then attracting attention for the first time in London. He determined to consult her. She was staying at the house of that well-known inquirer, Dr. Wilson Paget, and Mr. Vincey, although he had never met that gentleman before, repaired to him forthwith with the intention of invoking her help. But scarcely had he mentioned the name of Bessel when Doctor Paget interrupted him. "Last night—just at the end," he said, "we had a communication."

He left the room, and returned with a slate on which were certain words written in a handwriting, shaky indeed, but indisputably the handwriting of Mr. Bessel!

"How did you get this?" said Mr. Vincey. "Do you mean—?"

"We got it last night," said Doctor Paget. With numerous interruptions from Mr. Vincey, he proceeded to explain how the writing had been obtained. It appears that in her seances, Mrs. Bullock passes into a condition of trance, her eyes rolling up in a strange way under her eyelids, and her body becoming rigid. She then begins to talk very rapidly, usually in voices other than her own. At the same time one or both of her hands may become active, and if slates and pencils are provided they will then write messages simultaneously with and quite independently of the flow of words from her mouth. By many she is considered an even more remarkable medium than the celebrated Mrs. Piper. It was one of these messages, the one written by her left hand, that Mr. Vincey now had before him. It consisted of eight words written disconnectedly: "George Bessel...trial excavn...Baker Street... help...starvation." Curiously enough, neither Doctor Paget nor the two other inquirers who were present had heard of the disappearance of Mr. Bessel—the news of it appeared only in the evening papers of Saturday—and they had put the message aside with many others of a vague and enigmatical sort that Mrs. Bullock has from time to time delivered.

When Doctor Paget heard Mr. Vincey's story, he gave himself at once with great energy to the pursuit of this clue to the discovery of Mr. Bessel. It would serve no useful purpose here to describe the inquiries of Mr. Vincey and himself; suffice it that the clue was a genuine one, and that Mr. Bessel was actually discovered by its aid.

He was found at the bottom of a detached shaft which had been sunk and abandoned at the commencement of the work for the new electric railway near Baker Street Station. His arm and leg and two ribs were broken. The shaft is protected by a hoarding nearly 20 feet high, and over this, incredible as it seems, Mr. Bessel, a stout, middle-aged gentleman, must have scrambled in order to fall down the shaft. He was saturated in colza oil, and the smashed tin lay beside him, but luckily the flame had been extinguished by his fall. And his madness had passed from him altogether. But he was, of course, terribly enfeebled, and at the sight of his rescuers he gave way to hysterical weeping.

In view of the deplorable state of his flat, he was taken to the house of Dr. Hatton in Upper Baker Street. Here he was subjected to a sedative treatment, and anything that might recall the violent crisis through which he had passed was carefully avoided. But on the second day he volunteered a statement.

Since that occasion Mr. Bessel has several times repeated this statement—to myself among other people—varying the details as the narrator of real experiences always does, but never by any chance contradicting himself in any particular. And the statement he makes is in substance as follows.

In order to understand it clearly it is necessary to go back to his experiments with Mr. Vincey before his remarkable attack. Mr. Bessel's first attempts at self-projection, in his experiments with Mr. Vincey, were as the reader will remember, unsuccessful. But through all of them he was concentrating all his power and will upon getting out of the body—"willing it with all my might," he says. At last, almost against expectation, came success. And Mr. Bessel asserts that he, being alive, did actually, by an effort of will, leave his body and pass into some place or state outside this world.

The release was, he asserts, instantaneous. "At one moment I was seated in my chair, with my eyes tightly shut, my hands gripping the arms of the chair, doing all I could to concentrate my mind on Vincey, and then I perceived myself outside my body—saw my body near me, but certainly not containing me, with the hands relaxing and the head drooping forward on the breast."

Nothing shakes him in his assurance of that release. He describes in a quiet, matter-of-fact way the new sensation he experienced. He felt he had become impalpable—so much he had expected, but he had not expected to find himself enormously large. So however, it would seem he became. "I was a great cloud—if I may express it that way—anchored to my body. It appeared to me, at first, as if I had discovered a greater self of which the conscious being in my brain was only a little part. I saw the Albany and Piccadilly and Regent Street and all the rooms and places in the houses, very minute and very bright and distinct, spread out below me like a little city seen from a balloon. Every now and then vague shapes like drifting wreaths of smoke made the vision a little indistinct, but at first I paid little heed to them. The thing that astonished me most, and which astonishes me still, is that I saw quite distinctly the insides of the houses as well as the streets, saw little people dining and talking in the private houses, men and women dining, playing billiards, and drinking in restaurants and hotels, and several places of entertainment crammed with people. It was like watching the affairs of a glass hive."

Such were Mr. Bessel's exact words as I took them down when he told me the story. Quite forgetful of Mr. Vincey, he remained for a space observing these things. Impelled by curiosity, he says, he stooped down, and with the shadowy arm he found himself possessed of, attempted to touch a man walking along Vigo Street. But he could not do so, though his finger seemed to pass through the man. Something prevented his doing this, but what it was he finds it hard to describe. He compares the obstacle to a sheet of glass.

"I felt as a kitten may feel," he said, "when it goes for the first time to pat its reflection in a mirror." Again and again, on the occasion when I heard him tell this story, Mr. Bessel returned to that comparison of the sheet of glass. Yet it was not altogether a precise comparison, because as the reader will speedily see, there were interruptions of this generally impermeable resistance, means of getting through the barrier to the material world again. But naturally, there is a very great difficulty in expressing these unprecedented impressions in the language of everyday experience.

A thing that impressed him instantly, and which weighed upon him throughout all this experience, was the stillness of this place—he was in a world without sound.

At first Mr. Bessel's mental state was an unemotional wonder. His thought chiefly concerned itself with where he might be. He was out of the body—out of his material body, at any rate—but that was not all. He believes, and I for one believe also, that he was somewhere out of space, as we understand it, altogether. By a strenuous effort of will he had passed out of his body into a world beyond this world, a world undreamt of, yet lying so close to it and so strangely situated with regard to it that all things on this earth are clearly visible both from without and from within, in this other world about us. For a long time, as it seemed to him, this realisation occupied his mind to the exclusion of all other matters, and then he recalled the engagement with Mr. Vincey, to which this astonishing experience was, after all, but a prelude.

He turned his mind to locomotion in this new body in which he found himself. For a time he was unable to shift himself from his attachment to his earthly carcass. For a time this new strange cloud body of his simply swayed, contracted, expanded, coiled, and writhed with his efforts to free himself, and then quite suddenly the link that bound him snapped. For a moment everything was hidden by what appeared to be whirling spheres of dark vapour, and then through a momentary gap he saw his drooping body collapse limply, saw his lifeless head drop sideways, and found he was driving along like a huge cloud in a strange place of shadowy clouds that had the luminous intricacy of London spread like a model below.

But now he was aware that the fluctuating vapour about him was something more than vapour, and the temerarious excitement of his first essay was shot with fear. For he perceived, at first indistinctly, and then suddenly very clearly, that he was surrounded by faces! That each roll and coil of the seeming cloud-stuff was a face. And such faces! Faces of thin shadow, faces of gaseous tenuity. Faces like those faces that glare with intolerable strangeness upon the sleeper in the evil hours of his dreams. Evil, greedy eyes that were full of a covetous curiosity, faces with knit brows and snarling, smiling lips; their vague hands clutched at Mr. Bessel as he passed, and the rest of their bodies was but an elusive streak of trailing darkness. Never a word they said, never a sound from the mouths that seemed to gibber. All about him they pressed in that dreamy silence, passing freely through the dim mistiness that was his body, gathering ever more numerously about him. And the shadowy Mr. Bessel, now suddenly fear-stricken, drove through the silent, active multitude of eyes and clutching hands.

So inhuman were these faces, so malignant their staring eyes, and shadowy, clawing gestures, that it did not occur to Mr. Bessel to attempt intercourse with these drifting creatures. Idiot phantoms, they seemed, children of vain desire, beings unborn and forbidden the boon of being, whose only expressions and gestures told of the envy and craving for life that was their one link with existence.

It says much for his resolution that, amidst the swarming cloud of these noiseless spirits of evil, he could still think of Mr. Vincey. He made a violent effort of will and found himself, he knew not how, stooping towards Staple Inn, saw Vincey sitting attentive and alert in his armchair by the fire.

And clustering also about him, as they clustered ever about all that lives and breathes, was another multitude of these vain voiceless shadows, longing, desiring, seeking some loophole into life.

For a space Mr. Bessel sought ineffectually to attract his friend's attention. He tried to get in front of his eyes, to move the objects in his room, to touch him. But Mr. Vincey remained unaffected, ignorant of the being that was so close to his own. The strange something that Mr. Bessel has compared to a sheet of glass separated them impermeably.

And at last Mr. Bessel did a desperate thing. I have told how that in some strange way he could see not only the outside of a man as we see him, but within. He extended his shadowy hand and thrust his vague black fingers, as it seemed, through the heedless brain.

Then suddenly, Mr. Vincey started like a man who recalls his attention from wandering thoughts, and it seemed to Mr. Bessel that a little dark-red body situated in the middle of Mr. Vincey's brain swelled and glowed as he did so. Since that experience he has been shown anatomical figures of the brain, and he knows now that this is that useless structure, as doctors call it, the pineal eye. For strange as it will seem to many, we have, deep in our brains—where it cannot possibly see any earthly light—an eye! At the time this, with the rest of the internal anatomy of the brain, was quite new to him. At the sight of its changed appearance, however, he thrust forth his finger, and rather fearful still of the consequences, touched this little spot. And instantly Mr. Vincey started, and Mr. Bessel knew that he was seen.

And at that instant it came to Mr. Bessel that evil had happened to his body, and behold! A great wind blew through all that world of shadows and tore him away. So strong was this persuasion that he thought no more of Mr. Vincey, but turned about forthwith, and all the countless faces drove back with him like leaves before a gale. But he returned too late. In an instant he saw the body that he had left inert and collapsed—lying, indeed, like the body of a man just dead—had arisen, had arisen by virtue of some strength and will beyond his own. It stood with staring eyes, stretching its limbs in dubious fashion.

For a moment he watched it in wild dismay, and then he stooped towards it. But the pane of glass had closed against him again, and he was foiled. He beat himself passionately against this, and all about him the spirits of evil grinned and pointed and mocked. He gave way to furious anger. He compares himself to a bird that has fluttered heedlessly into a room and is beating at the window-pane that holds it back from freedom.

And behold! The little body that had once been his was now dancing with delight. He saw it shouting, though he could not hear its shouts; he saw the violence of its movements grow. He watched it fling his cherished furniture about in the mad delight of existence, rend his books apart, smash bottles, drink heedlessly from the jagged fragments, leap and smite in a passionate acceptance of living. He watched these actions in paralysed astonishment. Then once more he hurled himself against the impassable barrier, and then with all that crew of mocking ghosts about him, hurried back in dire confusion to Vincey to tell him of the outrage that had come upon him.

But the brain of Vincey was now closed against apparitions, and the disembodied Mr. Bessel pursued him in vain as he hurried out into Holborn to call a cab. Foiled and terror-stricken, Mr. Bessel swept back again, to find his desecrated body whooping in a glorious frenzy down the Burlington Arcade...

And now the attentive reader begins to understand Mr. Bessel's interpretation of the first part of this strange story. The being whose frantic rush through London had inflicted so much injury and disaster had indeed Mr. Bessel's body, but it was not Mr. Bessel. It was an evil spirit out of that strange world beyond existence, into which Mr. Bessel had so rashly ventured. For twenty hours it held possession of him, and for all those twenty hours the dispossessed spirit-body of Mr. Bessel was going to and fro in that unheard-of middle world of shadows seeking help in vain. He spent many hours beating at the minds of Mr. Vincey and of his friend Mr. Hart. Each, as we know, he roused by his efforts. But the language that might convey his situation to these helpers across the gulf he did not know; his feeble fingers groped vainly and powerlessly in their brains. Once indeed, as we have already told, he was able to turn Mr. Vincey aside from his path so that he encountered the stolen body in its career, but he could not make him understand the thing that had happened: he was unable to draw any help from that encounter...

All through those hours the persuasion was overwhelming in Mr. Bessel's mind that presently his body would be killed by its furious tenant, and he would have to remain in this shadow-land for evermore. So that those long hours were a growing agony of fear. And ever as he hurried to and fro in his ineffectual excitement, innumerable spirits of that world about him mobbed him and confused his mind. And ever an envious applauding multitude poured after their successful fellow as he went upon his glorious career.

For that, it would seem, must be the life of these bodiless things of this world that is the shadow of our world. Ever they watch, coveting a way into a mortal body, in order that they may descend, as furies and frenzies, as violent lusts and mad, strange impulses, rejoicing in the body they have won. For Mr. Bessel was not the only human soul in that place. Witness the fact that he met first one, and afterwards several shadows of men, men like himself, it seemed, who had lost their bodies even it may be as he had lost his, and wandered, despairingly, in that lost world that is neither life nor death. They could not speak because that world is silent, yet he knew them for men because of their dim human bodies, and because of the sadness of their faces.

But how they had come into that world he could not tell, nor where the bodies they had lost might be, whether they still raved about the earth, or whether they were closed forever in death against return. That they were the spirits of the dead neither he nor I believe. But Doctor Wilson Paget thinks they are the rational souls of men who are lost in madness on the earth.

At last Mr. Bessel chanced upon a place where a little crowd of such disembodied silent creatures was gathered, and thrusting through them he saw below a brightly-lit room, and four or five quiet gentlemen and a woman, a stoutish woman dressed in black bombazine and sitting awkwardly in a chair with her head thrown back. He knew her from her portraits to be Mrs. Bullock, the medium. And he perceived that tracts and structures in her brain glowed and stirred as he had seen the pineal eye in the brain of Mr. Vincey glow. The light was very fitful; sometimes it was a broad illumination, and sometimes merely a faint twilight spot, and it shifted slowly about her brain. She kept on talking and writing with one hand. And Mr. Bessel saw that the crowding shadows of men about him, and a great multitude of the shadow spirits of that shadow land, were all striving and thrusting to touch the lighted regions of her brain. As one gained her brain or another was thrust away, her voice and the writing of her hand changed. So that what she said was disorderly and confused for the most part; now a fragment of one soul's message, and now a fragment of another's, and now she babbled the insane fancies of the spirits of vain desire. Then Mr. Bessel understood that she spoke for the spirit that had touch of her, and he began to struggle very furiously towards her. But he was on the outside of the crowd and at that time he could not reach her, and at last, growing anxious, he went away to find what had happened meanwhile to his body. For a long time he went to and fro seeking it in vain and fearing that it must have been killed, and then he found it at the bottom of the shaft in Baker Street, writhing furiously and cursing with pain. Its leg and an arm and two ribs had been broken by its fall. Moreover, the evil spirit was angry because his time had been so short and because of the pain—making violent movements and casting his body about.

And at that Mr. Bessel returned with redoubled earnestness to the room where the seance was going on, and so soon as he had thrust himself within sight of the place he saw one of the men who stood about the medium looking at his watch as if he meant that the seance should presently end. At that a great number of the shadows who had been striving turned away with gestures of despair. But the thought that the seance was almost over only made Mr. Bessel the more earnest, and he struggled so stoutly with his will against the others that presently he gained the woman's brain. It chanced that just at that moment it glowed very brightly, and in that instant she wrote the message that Doctor Wilson Paget preserved. And then the other shadows and the cloud of evil spirits about him had thrust Mr. Bessel away from her, and for all the rest of the seance he could regain her no more.

So he went back and watched through the long hours at the bottom of the shaft where the evil spirit lay in the stolen body it had maimed, writhing and cursing, and weeping and groaning, and learning the lesson of pain. And towards dawn the thing he had waited for happened, the brain glowed brightly and the evil spirit came out, and Mr. Bessel entered the body he had feared he should never enter again. As he did so, the silence—the brooding silence—ended; he heard the tumult of traffic and the voices of people overhead, and that strange world that is the shadow of our world—the dark and silent shadows of ineffectual desire and the shadows of lost men—vanished clean away.

He lay there for the space of about three hours before he was found. And in spite of the pain and suffering of his wounds, and of the dim damp place in which he lay; in spite of the tears—wrung from him by his physical distress—his heart was full of gladness to know that he was nevertheless back once more in the kindly world of men.

36

A Vision of Judgment

1.

Bru-a-a-a.

I listened, not understanding. Wa-ra-ra-ra.

"Good Lord!" said I, still only half awake. "What an infernal shindy!" Ra-ra-ra-ra-ra-ra-ra-ra-ra Ta-ra-rra-ra.

"It's enough," said I, "to wake—" and stopped short. Were was I? Ta-rra-rara—louder and louder.

"It's either some new invention—" Toora-toora-toora! Deafening!

"No," said I, speaking loud in order to hear myself. "That's the Last Trump." Tooo-rraa!

2.

The last note jerked me out of my grave like a hooked minnow.

I saw my monument (rather a mean little affair, and I wished I knew who'd done it), and the old elm tree and the sea view vanished like a puff of steam, and then all about me—a multitude no man could number, nations, tongues, kingdoms, peoples—children of all ages, in an amphitheatral space as vast as the sky. And over against us, seated on a throne of dazzling white cloud, the Lord God and all the host of his angels. I recognised Azreal by his darkness and Michael by his sword, and the great angel who had blown the trumpet stood with the trumpet still half raised.

3.

"Prompt," said the little man beside me. "Very prompt. Do you see the angel with the book?"

He was ducking and craning his head about to see over and under and between the souls that crowded round us. "Everybody's here," he said. "Everybody. And now we shall know—"

"There's Darwin," he said, going off at a tangent. "He'll catch it! And there—you see—? That tall, important-looking man trying to catch the eye of the Lord God, that's the Duke. But there's a lot of people one doesn't know.

"Oh! There's Priggles, the publisher. I have always wondered about printers' overs. Priggles was a clever man...But we shall know now—even about him.

"I shall hear all that. I shall get most of the fun before...My letter's S."

He drew the air in between his teeth.

"Historical characters, too. See? That's Henry the Eighth. There'll be a good bit of evidence. Oh, damn! He's Tudor."

He lowered his voice. "Notice this chap, just in front of us, all covered with hair. Paleolithic, you know. And there again—"

But I did not heed him, because I was looking at the Lord God.

4.

"Is this all?" asked the Lord God.

The angel at the book—it was one of countless volumes, like the British Museum Reading-room Catalogue, glanced at us and seemed to count us in the instant.

"That's all," he said, and added: "It was, O God, a very little planet."

The eyes of God surveyed us.

"Let us begin," said the Lord God.

5.

The angel opened the book and read a name. It was a name full of A's, and the echoes of it came back out of the uttermost parts of space. I did not catch it clearly, because the little man beside me said, in a sharp jerk, "What's that?" It sounded like "Ahab" to me; but it could not have been the Ahab of Scripture.

Instantly a small black figure was lifted up to a puffy cloud at the very feet of God. It was a stiff little figure, dressed in rich outlandish robes and crowned, and it folded its arms and scowled.

"Well?" said God, looking down at him.

We were privileged to hear the reply, and indeed the acoustic properties of the place were marvellous.

"I plead guilty," said the little figure.

"Tell them what you have done," said the Lord God.

"I was a king," said the little figure, "a great king, and I was lustful and proud and cruel. I made wars, I devastated countries, I built palaces, and the mortar was the blood of men. Hear, O God, the witnesses against me, calling to you for vengeance. Hundreds and thousands of witnesses." He waved his hands towards us. "And worse! I took a prophet—one of your prophets—"

"One of my prophets," said the Lord God.

"And because he would not bow to me, I tortured him for four days and nights, and in the end he died. I did more, O God, I blasphemed. I robbed you of your honours—"

"Robbed me of my honours," said the Lord God.

"And caused myself to be worshipped in your stead. No evil was there, but I practised it; no cruelty wherewith I did not stain my soul. And at last you smote me, O God!"

God raised his eyebrows slightly.

"And I was slain in battle. And so I stand before you, meet for your nethermost Hell! Out of your greatness daring no lies, daring no pleas, but telling the truth of my iniquities before all mankind."

He ceased. His face I saw distinctly, and it seemed to me white and terrible and proud and strangely noble. I thought of Milton's Satan.

"Most of that is from the Obelisk," said the recording Angel, finger on page.

"It is," said the Tyrannous Man, with a faint touch of surprise.

Then suddenly God bent forward and took this man in his hand, and held him up on his palm as if to see him better. He was just a little dark stroke in the middle of God's palm.

"Did he do all this?" said the Lord God.

The recording angel flattened his book with his hand.

"In a way," said the recording angel, carelessly.

Now when I looked again at the little man his face had changed in a very curious manner. He was looking at the recording angel with strange apprehension in his eyes, and one hand fluttered to his mouth. Just the movement of a muscle or so, and all that dignity of defiance was gone.

"Read," said the Lord God.

And the angel read, explaining very carefully and fully all the wickedness of the Wicked Man. It was quite a intellectual treat—A little "daring" in places, I thought, but of course Heaven has its privileges...

6.

Everybody was laughing. Even the prophet of the Lord whom the Wicked Man had tortured had a smile on his face. The Wicked Man was really such a preposterous little fellow.

"And then," reading the recording angel, with a smile that set us all agog, "one day, when he was a little irascible from over-eating, he—"

"Oh, not that," cried the Wicked Man, "nobody knew of that."

"It didn't happen," screamed the Wicked Man. "I was bad—I was really bad. Frequently bad, but there was nothing so silly—so absolutely silly—"

The angel went on reading.

"O God!" cried the Wicked Man. "Don't let them know that! I'll repent! I'll apologise..."

The Wicked Man on God's hand began to dance and weep. Suddenly shame overcame him. He made a wild rush to jump off the ball of God's little finger, but God stopped him by a dexterous turn of the wrist. Then he made a rush for a gap between hand and thumb, but thumb closed. And all the while the angel went on reading—reading. The Wicked Man rushed to and fro across God's palm, and then suddenly turned about and fled up the sleeve of God.

I expected God would turn him out, but the mercy of God is infinite.

The recording angel paused.

"Eh?" said the recording angel.

"Next," said God, and before the recording angel could call upon the name, a hairy creature in filthy rags stood upon God's palm.

7.

"Has God got Hell up his sleeve then?" said the little man beside me.

"Is there a Hell?" I asked.

"If you notice," he said—he peered between the feet of the great angels—"there's no particular indication of the Celestial City."

"Ssh!" said a little woman near us, scowling. "Hear this blessed Saint!"

8.

"He was Lord of the Earth, but I was the prophet of the God of Heaven," cried the Saint, "and all the people marvelled at the sign. For I, O God, knew of the glories of thy Paradise. No pain, no hardship, gashing with knives, splinters thrust under my nails, strips of flesh flayed off, all for the glory and honour of God."

God smiled.

"And at last I went, I in my rags and sores, smelling of my holy discomforts—"

Gabriel laughed abruptly.

"And lay outside his gates, as a sign, as a wonder—"

"As a perfect nuisance," said the recording angel, and began to read, heedless of the fact that the Saint was still speaking of gloriously unpleasant things he had done that Paradise might be his.

And behold, in that book the record of the Saint also was a revelation, a marvel.

It seemed not ten seconds before the Saint, also, was rushing to and fro over the great palm of God. Not ten seconds! And at last he also shrieked beneath that pitiless and cynical exposition, and fled also, even as the Wicked Man had fled, into the shadow of the sleeve. And it was permitted us to see into the shadow of the sleeve. And the two sat side by side, stark of all delusions, in the shadow of the robe of God's charity, like brothers.

And thither also I fled in my turn.

9.

"And now," said God, as he shook us out of his sleeve upon the planet he had given us to live upon, the planet that whirled about green Sirius for a sun, "now that you understand me and each other a little better...try again."

Then he and his great angels turned themselves about and suddenly had vanished.

The Throne had vanished.

All about me was a beautiful land, more beautiful than any I had ever seen before—waste, austere, and wonderful; and all about me were the enlightened souls of men in new clean bodies...

37

A Dream of Armageddon

The man with the white face entered the carriage at Rugby. He moved slowly in spite of the urgency of his porter, and even while he was still on the platform I noted how ill he seemed. He dropped into the corner over against me with a sigh, made an incomplete attempt to arrange his travelling shawl, and became motionless, with his eyes staring vacantly. Presently he was moved by a sense of my observation, looked up at me, and put out a spiritless hand for his newspaper. Then he glanced again in my direction.

I feigned to read. I feared I had unwittingly embarrassed him, and in a moment I was surprised to find him speaking.

"I beg your pardon?" said I.

"That book," he repeated, pointing a lean finger, "is about dreams."

"Obviously," I answered, for it was Fortnum-Roscoe's 'Dream States,' and the title was on the cover. He hung silent for a space as if he sought words. "Yes," he said at last, "but they tell you nothing." I did not catch his meaning for a second.

"They don't know," he added.

I looked a little more attentively at his face.

"There are dreams," he said, "and dreams."

That sort of proposition I never dispute.

"I suppose—" he hesitated. "Do you ever dream? I mean vividly."

"I dream very little," I answered. "I doubt if I have three vivid dreams in a year."

"Ah!" he said, and seemed for a moment to collect his thoughts.

"Your dreams don't mix with your memories?" he asked abruptly. "You don't find yourself in doubt; did this happen or did it not?"

"Hardly ever. Except just for a momentary hesitation now and then. I suppose few people do."

"Does he say—" he indicated the book.

"Says it happens at times and gives the usual explanation about intensity of impression and the like to account for its not happening as a rule. I suppose you know something of these theories—"

"Very little—except that they are wrong."

His emaciated hand played with the strap of the window for a time. I prepared to resume reading, and that seemed to precipitate his next remark. He leant forward almost as though he would touch me.

"Isn't there something called consecutive dreaming—that goes on night after night?"

"I believe there is. There are cases given in most books on mental trouble."

"Mental trouble! Yes. I dare say there are. It's the right place for them. But what I mean—" He looked at his bony knuckles. "Is that sort of thing always dreaming? Is it dreaming? Or is it something else? Mightn't it be something else?"

I should have snubbed his persistent conversation but for the drawn anxiety of his face. I remember now the look of his faded eyes and the lids red-stained—perhaps you know that look.

"I'm not just arguing about a matter of opinion," he said. "The thing's killing me."

"Dreams?"

"If you call them dreams. Night after night. Vivid—! So vivid... This—" (he indicated the landscape that went streaming by the window) "seems unreal in comparison! I can scarcely remember who I am, what business I am on..."

He paused. "Even now—"

"The dream is always the same—do you mean?" I asked.

"It's over."

"You mean?"

"I died."

"Died?"

"Smashed and killed, and now, so much of me as that dream was, is dead. Dead for ever. I dreamt I was another man, you know, living in a different part of the world and in a different time. I dreamt that night after night. Night after night I woke into that other life. Fresh scenes and fresh happenings—until I came upon the last—"

"When you died?"

"When I died."

"And since then—"

"No," he said. "Thank God! That was the end of the dream..."

It was clear I was in for this dream. And after all, I had an hour before me, the light was fading fast, and Fortnum-Roscoe has a dreary way with him. "Living in a different time," I said: "do you mean in some different age?"

"Yes."

"Past?"

"No—to come—to come."

"The year three thousand, for example?"

"I don't know what year it was. I did when I was asleep, when I was dreaming that is, but not now—not now that I am awake. There's a lot of things I have forgotten since I woke out of these dreams, though I knew them at the time when I was—I suppose it was dreaming. They called the year differently from our way of calling the year...What did they call it?" He put his hand to his forehead. "No," said he, "I forget."

He sat smiling weakly. For a moment I feared he did not mean to tell me his dream. As a rule I hate people who tell their dreams, but this struck me differently. I proffered assistance even. "It began—" I suggested.

"It was vivid from the first. I seemed to wake up in it suddenly. And it's curious that in these dreams I am speaking of I never remembered this life I am living now. It seemed as if the dream life was enough while it lasted. Perhaps—But I will tell you how I find myself when I do my best to recall it all. I don't remember anything dearly until I found myself sitting in a sort of loggia looking out over the sea. I had been dozing, and suddenly I woke up—fresh and vivid—not a bit dreamlike—because the girl had stopped fanning me."

"The girl?"

"Yes, the girl. You must not interrupt or you will put me out."

He stopped abruptly. "You won't think I'm mad?" he said.

"No," I answered; "you've been dreaming. Tell me your dream."

"I woke up, I say, because the girl had stopped fanning me. I was not surprised to find myself there or anything of that sort, you understand. I did not feel I had fallen into it suddenly. I simply took it up at that point. Whatever memory I had of this life, this nineteenth-century life, faded as I woke, vanished like a dream. I knew all about myself, knew that my name was no longer Cooper but Hedon, and all about my position in the world. I've forgotten a lot since I woke—there's a want of connection—but it was all quite clear and matter of fact then."

He hesitated again, gripping the window strap, putting his face forward and looking up at me appealingly.

"This seems bosh to you?"

"No, no!" I cried. "Go on. Tell me what this loggia was like."

"It was not really a loggia—I don't know what to call it. It faced south. It was small. It was all in shadow except the semicircle above the balcony that showed the sky and sea and the corner where the girl stood. I was on a couch—it was a metal couch with light striped cushions—and the girl was leaning over the balcony with her back to me. The light of the sunrise fell on her ear and cheek. Her pretty white neck and the little curls that nestled there, and her white shoulder were in the sun, and all the grace of her body was in the cool blue shadow. She was dressed—how can I describe it? It was easy and flowing. And altogether there she stood, so that it came to me how beautiful and desirable she was, as though I had never seen her before. And when at last I sighed and raised myself upon my arm she turned her face to me—"

He stopped.

"I have lived three-and-fifty years in this world. I have had mother, sisters, friends, wife, and daughters—all their faces, the play of their faces, I know. But the face of this girl—it is much more real to me. I can bring it back into memory so that I see it again—I could draw it or paint it. And after all—"

He stopped—but I said nothing.

"The face of a dream—the face of a dream. She was beautiful. Not that beauty which is terrible, cold, and worshipful, like the beauty of a saint; nor that beauty that stirs fierce passions; but a sort of radiation, sweet lips that softened into smiles, and grave grey eyes. And she moved gracefully, she seemed to have part with all pleasant and gracious things—"

He stopped, and his face was downcast and hidden. Then he looked up at me and went on, making no further attempt to disguise his absolute belief in the reality of his story.

"You see, I had thrown up my plans and ambitions, thrown up all I had ever worked for or desired for her sake. I had been a master man away there in the north, with influence and property and a great reputation, but none of it had seemed worth having beside her. I had come to the place, this city of sunny pleasures, with her, and left all those things to wreck and ruin just to save a remnant at least of my life. While I had been in love with her before I knew that she had any care for me, before I had imagined that she would dare—that we should dare, all my life had seemed vain and hollow, dust and ashes. It was dust and ashes. Night after night and through the long days I had longed and desired—my soul had beaten against the thing forbidden!

"But it is impossible for one man to tell another just these things. It's emotion, it's a tint, a light that comes and goes. Only while it's there, everything changes, everything. The thing is I came away and left them in their Crisis to do what they could."

"Left whom?" I asked, puzzled.

"The people up in the north there. You see—in this dream, anyhow—I had been a big man, the sort of man men come to trust in, to group themselves about. Millions of men who had never seen me were ready to do things and risk things because of their confidence in me. I had been playing that game for years, that big laborious game, that vague, monstrous political game amidst intrigues and betrayals, speech and agitation. It was a vast weltering world, and at last I had a sort of leadership against the Gang—you know it was called the Gang—a sort of compromise of scoundrelly projects and base ambitions and vast public emotional stupidities and catch-words—the Gang that kept the world noisy and blind year by year, and all the while that it was drifting, drifting towards infinite disaster. But I can't expect you to understand the shades and complications of the year—the year something or other ahead. I had it all—down to the smallest details—in my dream. I suppose I had been dreaming of it before I awoke, and the fading outline of some queer new development I had imagined still hung about me as I rubbed my eyes. It was some grubby affair that made me thank God for the sunlight. I sat up on the couch and remained looking at the woman and rejoicing—rejoicing that I had come away out of all that tumult and folly and violence before it was too late. After all, I thought, this is life—love and beauty, desire and delight, are they not worth all those dismal struggles for vague, gigantic ends? And I blamed myself for having ever sought to be a leader when I might have given my days to love. But then, thought I, if I had not spent my early days sternly and austerely, I might have wasted myself upon vain and worthless women, and at the thought all my being went out in love and tenderness to my dear mistress, my dear lady, who had come at last and compelled me—compelled me by her invincible charm for me—to lay that life aside.

"'You are worth it,' I said, speaking without intending her to hear; 'you are worth it, my dearest one; worth pride and praise and all things. Love! To have you is worth them all together.' And at the murmur of my voice she turned about."

"'Come and see,' she cried—I can hear her now—'come and see the sunrise upon Monte Solaro.'"

"I remember how I sprang to my feet and joined her at the balcony. She put a white hand upon my shoulder and pointed towards great masses of limestone, flushing, as it were, into life. I looked. But first I noted the sunlight on her face caressing the lines of her cheeks and neck. How can I describe to you the scene we had before us? We were at Capri—"

"I have been there," I said. "I have clambered up Monte Solaro and drunk vero Capri—muddy stuff like cider—at the summit."

"Ah!" said the man with the white face; "Then perhaps you can tell me—you will know if this was indeed Capri. For in this life I have never been there. Let me describe it. We were in a little room, one of a vast multitude of little rooms, very cool and sunny, hollowed out of the limestone of a sort of cape, very high above the sea. The whole island, you know, was one enormous hotel, complex beyond explaining, and on the other side there were miles of floating hotels, and huge floating stages to which the flying machines came. They called it a pleasure city. Of course, there was none of that in your time—rather, I should say, is none of that now. Of course. Now—! Yes.

"Well, this room of ours was at the extremity of the cape, so that one could see east and west. Eastward was a great cliff—a thousand feet high perhaps—coldly grey except for one bright edge of gold, and beyond it the Isle of the Sirens, and a falling coast that faded and passed into the hot sunrise. And when one turned to the west, distinct and near was a little bay, a little beach still in shadow. And out of that shadow rose Solaro straight and tall, flushed and golden crested, like a beauty throned, and the white moon was floating behind her in the sky. And before us from east to west stretched the many-tinted sea all dotted with little sailing boats.

"To the eastward, of course, these little boats were grey and very minute and clear, but to the westward they were little boats of gold—shining gold—almost like little flames. And just below us was a rock with an arch worn through it. The blue sea-water broke to green and foam all round the rock, and a galley came gliding out of the arch."

"I know that rock," I said. "I was nearly drowned there. It is called the Faraglioni."

"I Faraglioni? Yes, she called it that," answered the man with the white face. "There was some story—but that—"

He put his hand to his forehead again. "No," he said, "I forget that story.

"Well, that is the first thing I remember, the first dream I had, that little shaded room and the beautiful air and sky and that dear lady of mine, with her shining arms and her graceful robe, and how we sat and talked in half whispers to one another. We talked in whispers not because there was any one to hear, but because there was still such a freshness of mind between us that our thoughts were a little frightened I think, to find themselves at last in words. And so they went softly.

"Presently we were hungry and we went from our apartment, going by a strange passage with a moving floor, until we came to the great breakfast room—there was a fountain and music. A pleasant and joyful place it was, with its sunlight and splashing, and the murmur of plucked strings. And we sat and ate and smiled at one another, and I would not heed a man who was watching me from a table near by.

"And afterwards we went on to the dancing-hall. But I cannot describe that hall. The place was enormous—larger than any building you have ever seen—and in one place there was the old gate of Capri, caught into the wall of a gallery high overhead. Light girders, stems and threads of gold, burst from the pillars like fountains, streamed like an Aurora across the roof and interlaced, like—like conjuring tricks. All about the great circle for the dancers there were beautiful figures, strange dragons, and intricate and wonderful grotesques bearing lights. The place was inundated with artificial light that shamed the newborn day. And as we went through the throng the people turned about and looked at us, for all through the world my name and face were known, and how I had suddenly thrown up pride and struggle to come to this place. And they looked also at the lady beside me, though half the story of how at last she had come to me was unknown or mistold. And few of the men who were there, I know, but judged me a happy man, in spite of all the shame and dishonour that had come upon my name.

"The air was full of music, full of harmonious scents, full of the rhythm of beautiful motions. Thousands of beautiful people swarmed about the hall, crowded the galleries, sat in a myriad recesses; they were dressed in splendid colours and crowned with flowers; thousands danced about the great circle beneath the white images of the ancient gods, and glorious processions of youths and maidens came and went. We two danced, not the dreary monotonies of your days—of this time, I mean—but dances that were beautiful, intoxicating. And even now I can see my lady dancing—dancing joyously. She danced, you know, with a serious face; she danced with a serious dignity, and yet she was smiling at me and caressing me—smiling and caressing with her eyes.

"The music was different," he murmured. "It went—I cannot describe it; but it was infinitely richer and more varied than any music that has ever come to me awake.

"And then—it was when we had done dancing—a man came to speak to me. He was a lean, resolute man, very soberly clad for that place, and already I had marked his face watching me in the breakfasting hall, and afterwards as we went along the passage I had avoided his eye. But now, as we sat in a little alcove, smiling at the pleasure of all the people who went to and fro across the shining floor, he came and touched me, and spoke to me so that I was forced to listen. And he asked that he might speak to me for a little time apart.

"'No,' I said. 'I have no secrets from this lady. What do you want to tell me?'

"He said it was a trivial matter, or at least a dry matter, for a lady to hear.

"'Perhaps for me to hear,' said I.

"He glanced at her, as though almost he would appeal to her. Then he asked me suddenly if I had heard of a great and avenging declaration that Evesham had made. Now Evesham had always before been the man next to myself in the leadership of that great party in the north. He was a forcible, hard and tactless man, and only I had been able to control and soften him. It was on his account even more than my own, I think that the others had been so dismayed at my retreat. So this question about what he had done reawakened my old interest in the life I had put aside just for a moment.

"'I have taken no heed of any news for many days,' I said. 'What has Evesham been saying?'

"And with that the man began, nothing loath, and I must confess even I was struck by Evesham's reckless folly in the wild and threatening words he had used. And this messenger they had sent to me not only told me of Evesham's speech, but went on to ask counsel and to point out what need they had of me. While he talked, my lady sat a little forward and watched his face and mine.

"My old habits of scheming and organising reasserted themselves. I could even see myself suddenly returning to the north, and all the dramatic effect of it. All that this man said witnessed to the disorder of the party indeed, but not to its damage. I should go back stronger than I had come. And then I thought of my lady. You see—how can I tell you? There were certain peculiarities of our relationship—as things are I need not tell you about that—which would render her presence with me impossible. I should have had to leave her; indeed I should have had to renounce her clearly and openly, if I was to do all that I could do in the north. And the man knew that, even as he talked to her and me, knew it as well as she did, that my steps to duty were—first, separation, then abandonment. At the touch of that thought my dream of a return was shattered. I turned on the man suddenly, as he was imagining his eloquence was gaining ground with me.

"'What have I to do with these things now?' I said. 'I have done with them. Do you think I am coquetting with your people in coming here?'

"'No,' he said; 'but—'

"'Why cannot you leave me alone? I have done with these things. I have ceased to be anything but a private man.'

"'Yes,' he answered. 'But have you thought—? This talk of war, these reckless challenges, these wild aggressions—'

"I stood up.

"'No,' I cried. 'I won't hear you. I took count of all those things, I weighed them—and I have come away.'

"He seemed to consider the possibility of persistence. He looked from me to where the lady sat regarding us.

"'War,' he said, as if he were speaking to himself, and then turned slowly from me and walked away. I stood, caught in the whirl of thoughts his appeal had set going.

"I heard my lady's voice.

"'Dear,' she said; 'but if they have need of you—'

"She did not finish her sentence, she let it rest there. I turned to her sweet face, and the balance of my mood swayed and reeled.

"'They want me only to do the thing they dare not do themselves,' I said. 'If they distrust Evesham they must settle with him themselves.'

"She looked at me doubtfully.

"'But war—' she said.

"I saw a doubt on her face that I had seen before, a doubt of herself and me, the first shadow of the discovery that, seen strongly and completely, must drive us apart for ever.

"Now, I was an older mind than hers, and I could sway her to this belief or that.

"'My dear one,' I said, 'you must not trouble over these things. There will be no war. Certainly there will be no war. The age of wars is past. Trust me to know the justice of this case. They have no right upon me, dearest, and no one has a right upon me. I have been free to choose my life, and I have chosen this.'

"'But war—,' she said.

"I sat down beside her. I put an arm behind her and took her hand in mine. I set myself to drive that doubt away—I set myself to fill her mind with pleasant things again. I lied to her, and in lying to her I lied also to myself. And she was only too ready to believe me, only too ready to forget.

"Very soon the shadow had gone again, and we were hastening to our bathing-place in the Grotta del Bove Marino, where it was our custom to bathe every day. We swam and splashed one another, and in that buoyant water I seemed to become something lighter and stronger than a man. And at last we came out dripping and rejoicing and raced among the rocks. And then I put on a dry bathing-dress, and we sat to bask in the sun, and presently I nodded, resting my head against her knee, and she put her hand upon my hair and stroked it softly and I dozed. And behold! As it were with the snapping of the string of a violin, I was awakening, and I was in my own bed in Liverpool, in the life of to-day.

"Only for a time I could not believe that all these vivid moments had been no more than the substance of a dream.

"In truth, I could not believe it a dream for all the sobering reality of things about me. I bathed and dressed as it were by habit, and as I shaved, I argued why I of all men should leave the woman I loved to go back to fantastic politics in the hard and strenuous north. Even if Evesham did force the world back to war, what was that to me? I was a man, with the heart of a man, and why should I feel the responsibility of a deity for the way the world might go?

"You know that is not quite the way I think about affairs, about my real affairs. I am a solicitor, you know, with a point of view.

"The vision was so real, you must understand, so utterly unlike a dream that I kept perpetually recalling little irrelevant details; even the ornament of a book-cover that lay on my wife's sewing-machine in the breakfast-room recalled with the utmost vividness the gilt line that ran about the seat in the alcove where I had talked with the messenger from my deserted party. Have you ever heard of a dream that had a quality like that?"

"Like—?"

"So that afterwards you remembered little details you had forgotten."

I thought. I had never noticed the point before, but he was right.

"Never," I said. "That is what you never seem to do with dreams."

"No," he answered. "But that is just what I did. I am a solicitor, you must understand, in Liverpool, and I could not help wondering what the clients and business people I found myself talking to in my office would think if I told them suddenly I was in love with a girl who would be born a couple of hundred years or so hence, and worried about the politics of my great-great-great-grandchildren. I was chiefly busy that day negotiating a ninety-nine-year building lease. It was a private builder in a hurry, and we wanted to tie him in every possible way. I had an interview with him, and he showed a certain want of temper that sent me to bed still irritated. That night I had no dream. Nor did I dream the next night, at least, to remember.

"Something of that intense reality of conviction vanished. I began to feel sure it was a dream. And then it came again.

"When the dream came again, nearly four days later, it was very different. I think it certain that four days had also elapsed in the dream. Many things had happened in the north, and the shadow of them was back again between us, and this time it was not so easily dispelled. I began, I know with moody musings. Why in spite of all, should I go back, go back for all the rest of my days to toil and stress, insults and perpetual dissatisfaction, simply to save hundreds of millions of common people, whom I did not love, whom too often I could do no other than despise, from the stress and anguish of war and infinite misrule? And after all I might fail. They all sought their own narrow ends, and why should not I—why should not I also live as a man? And out of such thoughts her voice summoned me, and I lifted my eyes.

"I found myself awake and walking. We had come out above the Pleasure City, we were near the summit of Monte Solaro and looking towards the bay. It was the late afternoon and very clear. Far away to the left Ischia hung in a golden haze between sea and sky, and Naples was coldly white against the hills, and before us was Vesuvius with a tall and slender streamer feathering at last towards the south, and the ruins of Torre Annunziata and Castellamare glittering and near."

I interrupted suddenly: "You have been to Capri, of course?"

"Only in this dream," he said, "only in this dream. All across the bay beyond Sorrento were the floating palaces of the Pleasure City moored and chained. And northward were the broad floating stages that received the aeroplanes. Aeroplanes fell out of the sky every afternoon, each bringing its thousands of pleasure-seekers from the uttermost parts of the earth to Capri and its delights. All these things, I say, stretched below.

"But we noticed them only incidentally because of an unusual sight that evening had to show. Five war aeroplanes that had long slumbered useless in the distant arsenals of the Rhinemouth were manoeuvring now in the eastward sky. Evesham had astonished the world by producing them and others, and sending them to circle here and there. It was the threat material in the great game of bluff he was playing, and it had taken even me by surprise. He was one of those incredibly stupid energetic people who seem sent by Heaven to create disasters. His energy to the first glance seemed so wonderfully like capacity! But he had no imagination, no invention, only a stupid, vast, driving force of will, and a mad faith in his stupid idiot 'luck' to pull him through. I remember how we stood out upon the headland watching the squadron circling far away, and how I weighed the full meaning of the sight, seeing clearly the way things must go. And then even it was not too late. I might have gone back, I think, and saved the world. The people of the north would follow me I knew, granted only that in one thing I respected their moral standards. The east and south would trust me as they would trust no other northern man. And I knew I had only to put it to her and she would have let me go...Not because she did not love me!

"Only I did not want to go; my will was all the other way about. I had so newly thrown off the incubus of responsibility: I was still so fresh a renegade from duty that the daylight clearness of what I ought to do had no power at all to touch my will. My will was to live, to gather pleasures and make my dear lady happy. But though this sense of vast neglected duties had no power to draw me, it could make me silent and preoccupied, it robbed the days I had spent of half their brightness and roused me into dark meditations in the silence of the night. And as I stood and watched Evesham's aeroplanes sweep to and fro—those birds of infinite ill omen—she stood beside me watching me, perceiving the trouble indeed, but not perceiving it clearly—her eyes questioning my face, her expression shaded with perplexity. Her face was grey because the sunset was fading out of the sky. It was no fault of hers that she held me. She had asked me to go from her, and again in the night time and with tears she had asked me to go.

"At last it was the sense of her that roused me from my mood. I turned upon her suddenly and challenged her to race down the mountain slopes. 'No,' she said, as if I jarred with her gravity, but I was resolved to end that gravity, and made her run—no one can be very grey and sad who is out of breath—and when she stumbled I ran with my hand beneath her arm. We ran down past a couple of men, who turned back staring in astonishment at my behaviour—they must have recognised my face. And halfway down the slope came a tumult in the air, clang-clank, clang-clank, and we stopped, and presently over the hill-crest those war things came flying one behind the other."

The man seemed hesitating on the verge of a description.

"What were they like?" I asked.

"They had never fought," he said. "They were just like our ironclads are nowadays; they had never fought. No one knew what they might do, with excited men inside them; few even cared to speculate. They were great driving things shaped like spear-heads without a shaft, with a propeller in the place of the shaft."

"Steel?"

"Not steel."

"Aluminium?"

"No, no, nothing of that sort. An alloy that was very common—as common as brass, for example. It was called—let me see—" He squeezed his forehead with the fingers of one hand. "I am forgetting everything," he said.

"And they carried guns?"

"Little guns, firing high explosive shells. They fired the guns backwards, out of the base of the leaf, so to speak, and rammed with the beak. That was the theory, you know, but they had never been fought. No one could tell exactly what was going to happen. And meanwhile I suppose it was very fine to go whirling through the air like a flight of young swallows, swift and easy. I guess the captains tried not to think too clearly what the real thing would be like. And these flying war machines, you know, were only one sort of the endless war contrivances that had been invented and had fallen into abeyance during the long peace. There were all sorts of these things that people were routing out and furbishing up; infernal things, silly things; things that had never been tried; big engines, terrible explosives, great guns. You know the silly way of these ingenious sort of men who make these things; they turn 'em out as beavers build dams, and with no more sense of the rivers they're going to divert and the lands they're going to flood!

"As we went down the winding stepway to our hotel again, in the twilight, I foresaw it all: I saw how clearly and inevitably things were driving for war in Evesham's silly, violent hands, and I had some inkling of what war was bound to be under these new conditions. And even then, though I knew it was drawing near the limit of my opportunity, I could find no will to go back."

He sighed.

"That was my last chance.

"We didn't go into the city until the sky was full of stars, so we walked out upon the high terrace, to and fro, and—she counselled me to go back.

"'My dearest,' she said, and her sweet face looked up to me, 'this is Death. This life you lead is Death. Go back to them, go back to your duty—'

"She began to weep, saying, between her sobs, and clinging to my arm as she said it, 'Go back—Go back.'

"Then suddenly she fell mute, and glancing down at her face, I read in an instant the thing she had thought to do. It was one of those moments when one sees.

"'No!' I said.

"'No?' she asked, in surprise, and I think a little fearful at the answer to her thought.

"'Nothing,' I said, 'shall send me back. Nothing! I have chosen. Love, I have chosen, and the world must go. Whatever happens I will live this life—I will live for you! It—nothing shall turn me aside; nothing, my dear one. Even if you died—even if you died—'

"'Yes,' she murmured, softly.

"'Then—I also would die.'

"And before she could speak again I began to talk, talking eloquently—as I could do in that life—talking to exalt love, to make the life we were living seem heroic and glorious; and the thing I was deserting something hard and enormously ignoble that it was a fine thing to set aside. I bent all my mind to throw that glamour upon it, seeking not only to convert her but myself to that. We talked, and she clung to me, torn too between all that she deemed noble and all that she knew was sweet. And at last I did make it heroic, made all the thickening disaster of the world only a sort of glorious setting to our unparalleled love, and we two poor foolish souls strutted there at last, clad in that splendid delusion, drunken rather with that glorious delusion, under the still stars.

"And so my moment passed.

"It was my last chance. Even as we went to and fro there, the leaders of the south and east were gathering their resolve, and the hot answer that shattered Evesham's bluffing for ever, took shape and waited. And all over Asia, and the ocean, and the south, the air and the wires were throbbing with their warnings to prepare—prepare.

"No one living, you know, knew what war was; no one could imagine, with all these new inventions, what horror war might bring. I believe most people still believed it would be a matter of bright uniforms and shouting charges and triumphs and flags and bands—in a time when half the world drew its food supply from regions ten thousand miles away—"

The man with the white face paused. I glanced at him, and his face was intent on the floor of the carriage. A little railway station, a string of loaded trucks, a signal-box, and the back of a cottage, shot by the carriage window, and a bridge passed with a clap of noise, echoing the tumult of the train.

"After that," he said, "I dreamt often. For three weeks of nights that dream was my life. And the worst of it was there were nights when I could not dream, when I lay tossing on a bed in this accursed life; and there—somewhere lost to me—things were happening—momentous, terrible things...I lived at nights—my days, my waking days, this life I am living now, became a faded, far-away dream, a drab setting, the cover of the book."

He thought.

"I could tell you all, tell you every little thing in the dream, but as to what I did in the daytime—no, I could not tell—I do not remember. My memory—my memory has gone. The business of life slips from me—"

He leant forward, and pressed his hands upon his eyes. For a long time he said nothing.

"And then?" said I.

"The war burst like a hurricane."

He stared before him at unspeakable things.

"And then?" I urged again.

"One touch of unreality," he said, in the low tone of a man who speaks to himself, "and they would have been nightmares. But they were not nightmares—they were not nightmares. No!"

He was silent for so long that it dawned upon me that there was a danger of losing the rest of the story. But he went on talking again in the same tone of questioning self-communion."

"What was there to do but flight? I had not thought the war would touch Capri—I had seemed to see Capri as being out of it all, as the contrast to it all; but two nights after the whole place was shouting and bawling, every woman almost and every other man wore a badge—Evesham's badge—and there was no music but a jangling war-song over and over again, and everywhere men enlisting, and in the dancing halls they were drilling. The whole island was awhirl with rumours; it was said, again and again, that fighting had begun. I had not expected this. I had seen so little of the life of pleasure that I had failed to reckon with this violence of the amateurs. And as for me, I was out of it. I was like a man who might have prevented the firing of a magazine. The time had gone. I was no one; the vainest stripling with a badge counted for more than I. The crowd jostled us and bawled in our ears; that accursed song deafened us; a woman shrieked at my lady because no badge was on her, and we two went back to our own place again, ruffled and insulted—my lady white and silent, and I aquiver with rage. So furious was I, I could have quarrelled with her if I could have found one shade of accusation in her eyes.

"All my magnificence had gone from me. I walked up and down our rock cell, and outside was the darkling sea and a light to the southward that flared and passed and came again.

"'We must get out of this place,' I said over and over. 'I have made my choice, and I will have no hand in these troubles. I will have nothing of this war. We have taken our lives out of all these things. This is no refuge for us. Let us go.'

"And the next day we were already in flight from the war that covered the world.

"And all the rest was Flight—all the rest was Flight."

He mused darkly.

"How much was there of it?"

He made no answer.

"How many days?"

His face was white and drawn and his hands were clenched. He took no heed of my curiosity.

I tried to draw him back to his story with questions.

"Where did you go?" I said.

"When?"

"When you left Capri."

"Southwest," he said, and glanced at me for a second. "We went in a boat."

"But I should have thought an aeroplane?"

"They had been seized."

I questioned him no more. Presently I thought he was beginning again. He broke out in an argumentative monotone:

"But why should it be? If, indeed, this battle, this slaughter and stress is life, why have we this craving for pleasure and beauty? If there is no refuge, if there is no place of peace, and if all our dreams of quiet places are a folly and a snare, why have we such dreams? Surely it was no ignoble cravings, no base intentions, had brought us to this; it was Love had isolated us. Love had come to me with her eyes and robed in her beauty, more glorious than all else in life, in the very shape and colour of life, and summoned me away. I had silenced all the voices, I had answered all the questions—I had come to her. And suddenly there was nothing but War and Death!"

I had an inspiration. "After all," I said, "it could have been only a dream."

"A dream!" he cried, flaming upon me, "A dream—when even now—"

For the first time he became animated. A faint flush crept into his cheek. He raised his open hand and clenched it, and dropped it to his knee. He spoke, looking away from me, and for all the rest of the time he looked away. "We are but phantoms," he said, "and the phantoms of phantoms, desires like cloud shadows and wills of straw that eddy in the wind; the days pass, use and wont carry us through as a train carries the shadow of its lights—so be it! But one thing is real and certain, one thing is no dream-stuff, but eternal and enduring. It is the centre of my life, and all other things about it are subordinate or altogether vain. I loved her, that woman of a dream. And she and I are dead together!

"A dream! How can it be a dream, when it drenched a living life with unappeasable sorrow, when it makes all that I have lived for and cared for, worthless and unmeaning?

"Until that very moment when she was killed I believed we had still a chance of getting away," he said. "All through the night and morning that we sailed across the sea from Capri to Salerno, we talked of escape. We were full of hope, and it clung about us to the end, hope for the life together we should lead, out of it all, out of the battle and struggle, the wild and empty passions, the empty arbitrary 'thou shalt' and 'thou shalt not' of the world. We were uplifted, as though our quest was a holy thing, as though love for one another was a mission...

"Even when from our boat we saw the fair face of that great rock Capri—already scarred and gashed by the gun emplacements and hiding-places that were to make it a fastness—we reckoned nothing of the imminent slaughter, though the fury of preparation hung about in puffs and clouds of dust at a hundred points amidst the grey; but indeed, I made a text of that and talked. There, you know, was the rock, still beautiful, for all its scars, with its countless windows and arches and ways, tier upon tier, for a thousand feet, a vast carving of grey, broken by vine-clad terraces, and lemon and orange groves, and masses of agave and prickly pear, and puffs of almond blossom. And out under the archway that is built over the Marina Piccola other boats were coming; and as we came round the cape and within sight of the mainland, another little string of boats came into view, driving before the wind towards the south-west. In a little while a multitude had come out, the remoter just little specks of ultramarine in the shadow of the eastward cliff.

"'It is love and reason,' I said, 'fleeing from all this madness, of war.'

"And though we presently saw a squadron of aeroplanes flying across the southern sky we did not heed it. There it was—a line of little dots in the sky—and then more, dotting the south-eastern horizon, and then still more, until all that quarter of the sky was stippled with blue specks. Now they were all thin little strokes of blue, and now one and now a multitude would heel and catch the sun and become short flashes of light. They came rising and falling and growing larger, like some huge flight of gulls or rooks, or such-like birds moving with a marvellous uniformity, and ever as they drew nearer they spread over a greater width of sky. The southward wing flung itself in an arrow-headed cloud athwart the sun. And then suddenly they swept round to the eastward and streamed eastward, growing smaller and smaller and clearer and clearer again until they vanished from the sky. And after that we noted to the northward and very high Evesham's fighting machines hanging high over Naples like an evening swarm of gnats.

"It seemed to have no more to do with us than a flight of birds.

"Even the mutter of guns far away in the south-east seemed to us to signify nothing...

"Each day, each dream after that, we were still exalted, still seeking that refuge where we might live and love. Fatigue had come upon us, pain and many distresses. For though we were dusty and stained by our toilsome tramping, and half starved and with the horror of the dead men we had seen and the flight of the peasants—for very soon a gust of fighting swept up the peninsula—with these things haunting our minds it still resulted only in a deepening resolution to escape. Oh, but she was brave and patient! She who had never faced hardship and exposure had courage for herself—and me. We went to and fro seeking an outlet, over a country all commandeered and ransacked by the gathering hosts of war. Always we went on foot. At first there were other fugitives, but we did not mingle with them. Some escaped northward, some were caught in the torrent of peasantry that swept along the main roads; many gave themselves into the hands of the soldiery and were sent northward. Many of the men were impressed. But we kept away from these things; we had brought no money to bribe a passage north, and I feared for my lady at the hands of these conscript crowds. We had landed at Salerno, and we had been turned back from Cava, and we had tried to cross towards Taranto by a pass over Mount Alburno, but we had been driven back for want of food, and so we had come down among the marshes by Paestum, where those great temples stand alone. I had some vague idea that by Paestum it might be possible to find a boat or something, and take once more to sea. And there it was the battle overtook us.

"A sort of soul-blindness had me. Plainly I could see that we were being hemmed in; that the great net of that giant Warfare had us in its toils. Many times we had seen the levies that had come down from the north going to and fro, and had come upon them in the distance amidst the mountains making ways for the ammunition and preparing the mounting of the guns. Once we fancied they had fired at us, taking us for spies—at any rate a shot had gone shuddering over us. Several times we had hidden in woods from hovering aeroplanes.

"But all these things do not matter now, these nights of flight and pain...We were in an open place near those great temples at Paestum, at last, on a blank stony place dotted with spiky bushes, empty and desolate and so flat that a grove of eucalyptus far away showed to the feet of its stems. How I can see it! My lady was sitting down under a bush, resting a little, for she was very weak and weary, and I was standing up watching to see if I could tell the distance of the firing that came and went. They were still, you know, fighting far from each other, with those terrible new weapons that had never before been used: guns that would carry beyond sight, and aeroplanes that would do—What they would do no man could foretell.

"I knew that we were between the two armies, and that they drew together. I knew we were in danger, and that we could not stop there and rest!

"Though all these things were in my mind, they were in the background. They seemed to be affairs beyond our concern. Chiefly, I was thinking of my lady. An aching distress filled me. For the first time she had owned herself beaten and had fallen a-weeping. Behind me I could hear her sobbing, but I would not turn round to her because I knew she had need of weeping, and had held herself so far and so long for me. It was well, I thought, that she would weep and rest and then we would toil on again, for I had no inkling of the thing that hung so near. Even now I can see her as she sat there, her lovely hair upon her shoulder, can mark again the deepening hollow of her cheek.

"'If we had parted,' she said, 'if I had let you go.'

"'No,' said I. 'Even now, I do not repent. I will not repent; I made my choice, and I will hold on to the end."

"And then—"

"Overhead in the sky something flashed and burst, and all about us I heard the bullets making a noise like a handful of peas suddenly thrown. They chipped the stones about us, and whirled fragments from the bricks and passed..."

He put his hand to his mouth, and then moistened his lips.

"At the flash I had turned about..."

"You know—she stood up—

"She stood up, you know, and moved a step towards me—

"As though she wanted to reach me—

"And she had been shot through the heart."

He stopped and stared at me. I felt all that foolish incapacity an Englishman feels on such occasions. I met his eyes for a moment, and then stared out of the window. For a long space we kept silence. When at last I looked at him he was sitting back in his corner, his arms folded, and his teeth gnawing at his knuckles.

He bit his nail suddenly, and stared at it.

"I carried her," he said, "towards the temples, in my arms—as though it mattered. I don't know why. They seemed a sort of sanctuary, you know, they had lasted so long, I suppose.

"She must have died almost instantly. Only—I talked to her—all the way."

Silence again.

"I have seen those temples," I said abruptly, and indeed he had brought those still, sunlit arcades of worn sandstone very vividly before me.

"It was the brown one, the big brown one. I sat down on a fallen pillar and held her in my arms...Silent after the first babble was over. And after a little while the lizards came out and ran about again, as though nothing unusual was going on, as though nothing had changed...It was tremendously still there, the sun high, and the shadows still; even the shadows of the weeds upon the entablature were still—in spite of the thudding and banging that went all about the sky.

"I seem to remember that the aeroplanes came up out of the south, and that the battle went away to the west. One aeroplane was struck, and overset and fell. I remember that—though it didn't interest me in the least. It didn't seem to signify. It was like a wounded gull, you know—flapping for a time in the water. I could see it down the aisle of the temple—a black thing in the bright blue water.

"Three or four times shells burst about the beach, and then that ceased. Each time that happened all the lizards scuttled in and hid for a space. That was all the mischief done, except that once a stray bullet gashed the stone hard by—made just a fresh bright surface.

"As the shadows grew longer, the stillness seemed greater.

"The curious thing," he remarked, with the manner of a man who makes a trivial conversation, "is that I didn't think—I didn't think at all. I sat with her in my arms amidst the stones—in a sort of lethargy—stagnant.

"And I don't remember waking up. I don't remember dressing that day. I know I found myself in my office, with my letters all slit open in front of me, and how I was struck by the absurdity of being there, seeing that in reality I was sitting, stunned, in that Paestum temple with a dead woman in my arms. I read my letters like a machine. I have forgotten what they were about."

He stopped, and there was a long silence.

Suddenly I perceived that we were running down the incline from Chalk Farm to Euston. I started at this passing of time. I turned on him with a brutal question, with the tone of "Now or never."

"And did you dream again?"

"Yes."

He seemed to force himself to finish. His voice was very low.

"Once more, and as it were only for a few instants. I seemed to have suddenly awakened out of a great apathy, to have risen into a sitting position, and the body lay there on the stones beside me. A gaunt body. Not her, you know. So soon—it was not her...

"I may have heard voices. I do not know. Only I knew clearly that men were coming into the solitude and that, that was a last outrage.

"I stood up and walked through the temple, and then there came into sight—first one man with a yellow face, dressed in a uniform of dirty white, trimmed with blue, and then several, climbing to the crest of the old wall of the vanished city, and crouching there. They were little bright figures in the sunlight, and there they hung, weapon in hand, peering cautiously before them.

"And further away I saw others and then more at another point in the wall. It was a long lax line of men in open order.

"Presently the man I had first seen stood up and shouted a command, and his men came tumbling down the wall and into the high weeds towards the temple. He scrambled down with them and led them. He came facing towards me, and when he saw me he stopped.

"At first I had watched these men with a mere curiosity, but when I had seen they meant to come to the temple I was moved to forbid them. I shouted to the officer.

"'You must not come here,' I cried, 'I am here. I am here with my dead.'

"He stared, and then shouted a question back to me in some unknown tongue.

"I repeated what I had said.

"He shouted again, and I folded my arms and stood still. Presently he spoke to his men and came forward. He carried a drawn sword.

"I signed to him to keep away, but he continued to advance. I told him again very patiently and clearly: 'You must not come here. These are old temples and I am here with my dead.'

"Presently he was so close I could see his face clearly. It was a narrow face, with dull grey eyes, and a black moustache. He had a scar on his upper lip, and he was dirty and unshaven. He kept shouting unintelligible things, questions perhaps, at me.

"I know now that he was afraid of me, but at the time that did not occur to me. As I tried to explain to him he interrupted me in imperious tones, bidding me, I suppose, stand aside.

"He made to go past me, and I caught hold of him.

"I saw his face change at my grip.

"'You fool,' I cried. 'Don't you know? She is dead!'

"He started back. He looked at me with cruel eyes. I saw a sort of exultant resolve leap into them—delight. Then suddenly, with a scowl, he swept his sword back—so—and thrust."

He stopped abruptly. I became aware of a change in the rhythm of the train. The brakes lifted their voices and the carriage jarred and jerked. This present world insisted upon itself, became clamorous. I saw through the steamy window huge electric lights glaring down from tall masts upon a fog, saw rows of stationary empty carriages passing by; and then a signal-box, hoisting its constellation of green and red into the murky London twilight marched after them. I looked again at his drawn features.

"He ran me through the heart. It was with a sort of astonishment—no fear, no pain—but just amazement, that I felt it pierce me, felt the sword drive home into my body. It didn't hurt, you know. It didn't hurt at all."

The yellow platform lights came into the field of view, passing first rapidly, then slowly, and at last stopping with a jerk. Dim shapes of men passed to and fro without.

"Euston!" cried a voice.

"Do you mean—?"

"There was no pain, no sting or smart. Amazement and then darkness sweeping over everything. The hot, brutal face before me, the face of the man who had killed me, seemed to recede. It swept out of existence—"

"Euston!" clamoured the voices outside; "Euston!"

The carriage door opened, admitting a flood of sound, and a porter stood regarding us. The sounds of doors slamming, and the hoof-clatter of cab-horses, and behind these things the featureless remote roar of the London cobble-stones, came to my ears. A truckload of lighted lamps blazed along the platform.

"A darkness, a flood of darkness that opened and spread and blotted out all things."

"Any luggage, sir?" said the porter.

"And that was the end?" I asked.

He seemed to hesitate. Then, almost inaudibly, he answered "No."

"You mean?"

"I couldn't get to her. She was there on the other side of the Temple— And then—"

"Yes," I insisted. "Yes?"

"Nightmares," he cried; "nightmares indeed! My God! Great birds that fought and tore."

38

THE NEW ACCELERATOR

Certainly, if ever a man found a guinea, when he was looking for a pin it is my good friend Professor Gibberne. I have heard before of investigators overshooting the mark, but never quite to the extent that he has done. He has really, this time at any rate, without any touch of exaggeration in the phrase, found something to revolutionise human life. And that when he was simply seeking an all-round nervous stimulant to bring languid people up to the stresses of these pushful days. I have tasted the stuff now several times, and I cannot do better than describe the effect the thing had on me. That there are astonishing experiences in store for all in search of new sensations will become apparent enough.

Professor Gibberne, as many people know, is my neighbour in Folkestone. Unless my memory plays me a trick, his portrait at various ages has already appeared in 'The Strand Magazine'—I think late in 1899; but I am unable to look it up because I have lent that volume to some one who has never sent it back. The reader may, perhaps, recall the high forehead and the singularly long black eyebrows that give such a Mephistophelian touch to his face. He occupies one of those pleasant little detached houses in the mixed style that make the western end of the Upper Sandgate Road so interesting. His is the one with the Flemish gables and the Moorish portico, and it is in the little room with the mullioned bay window that he works when he is down here, and in which of an evening we have so often smoked and talked together. He is a mighty jester, but besides, he likes to talk to me about his work; he is one of those men who find a help and stimulus in talking, and so I have been able to follow the conception of the New Accelerator right up from a very early stage. Of course, the greater portion of his experimental work is not done in Folkestone, but in Gower Street, in the fine new laboratory next to the hospital that he has been the first to use.

As every one knows, or at least as all intelligent people know, the special department in which Gibberne has gained so great and deserved a reputation among physiologists is the action of drugs upon the nervous system. Upon soporifics, sedatives, and anaesthetics he is, I am told, unequalled. He is also a chemist of considerable eminence, and I suppose in the subtle and complex jungle of riddles that centres about the ganglion cell and the axis fibre there are little cleared places of his making, little glades of illumination, that until he sees fit to publish his results, are still inaccessible to every other living man. And in the last few years he has been particularly assiduous upon this question of nervous stimulants, and already, before the discovery of the New Accelerator, very successful with them. Medical science has to thank him for at least three distinct and absolutely safe invigorators of unrivalled value to practising men. In cases of exhaustion the preparation known as Gibberne's B Syrup has, I suppose, saved more lives already than any lifeboat round the coast.

"But none of these little things begin to satisfy me yet," he told me nearly a year ago. "Either they increase the central energy without affecting the nerves or they simply increase the available energy by lowering the nervous conductivity; and all of them are unequal and local in their operation. One wakes up the heart and viscera and leaves the brain stupefied, one gets at the brain champagne fashion and does nothing good for the solar plexus, and what I want—and what, if it's an earthly possibility, I mean to have—is a stimulant that stimulates all round, that wakes you up for a time from the crown of your head to the tip of your great toe, and makes you go two—or even three to everybody else's one. Eh? That's the thing I'm after."

"It would tire a man," I said.

"Not a doubt of it. And you'd eat double or treble—and all that. But just think what the thing would mean. Imagine yourself with a little phial like this—" he held up a little bottle of green glass and marked his points with it—"and in this precious phial is the power to think twice as fast, move twice as quickly, do twice as much work in a given time as you could otherwise do."

"But is such a thing possible?"

"I believe so. If it isn't, I've wasted my time for a year. These various preparations of the hypophosphites, for example, seem to show that something of the sort...Even if it was only one and a half times as fast it would do."

"It would do," I said.

"If you were a statesman in a corner, for example, time rushing up against you, something urgent to be done, eh?"

"He could dose his private secretary," I said.

"And gain—double time. And think if you, for example, wanted to finish a book."

"Usually," I said, "I wish I'd never begun 'em."

"Or a doctor, driven to death, wants to sit down and think out a case. Or a barrister—or a man cramming for an examination."

"Worth a guinea a drop," said I, "and more—to men like that."

"And in a duel, again," said Gibberne, "Where it all depends on your quickness in pulling the trigger."

"Or in fencing," I echoed.

"You see," said Gibberne, "if I get it as an all-round thing it will really do you no harm at all—except perhaps to an infinitesimal degree it brings you nearer old age. You will just have lived twice to other people's once—"

"I suppose," I meditated, "in a duel—it would be fair?"

"That's a question for the seconds," said Gibberne.

I harked back further. "And you really think such a thing Is possible?" I said.

"As possible," said Gibberne, and glanced at something that went throbbing by the window, "as a motor-bus. As a matter of fact—"

He paused and smiled at me deeply, and tapped slowly on the edge of his desk with the green phial. "I think I know the stuff... Already I've got something coming." The nervous smile upon his face betrayed the gravity of his revelation. He rarely talked of his actual experimental work unless things were very near the end. "And it may be, it may be—I shouldn't be surprised—it may even do the thing at a greater rate than twice."

"It will be rather a big thing," I hazarded.

"It will be, I think, rather a big thing."

But I don't think he quite knew what a big thing it was to be, for all that.

I remember we had several talks about the stuff after that. "The New Accelerator" he called it, and his tone about it grew more confident on each occasion. Sometimes he talked nervously of unexpected physiological results its use might have, and then he would get a little unhappy; at others he was frankly mercenary, and we debated long and anxiously how the preparation might be turned to commercial account. "It's a good thing," said Gibberne, "a tremendous thing. I know I'm giving the world something, and I think it only reasonable we should expect the world to pay. The dignity of science is all very well, but I think somehow I must have the monopoly of the stuff for, say ten years. I don't see why all the fun in life should go to the dealers in ham."

My own interest in the coming drug certainly did not wane in the time. I have always had a queer little twist towards metaphysics in my mind. I have always been given to paradoxes about space and time, and it seemed to me that Gibberne was really preparing no less than the absolute acceleration of life. Suppose a man repeatedly dosed with such a preparation: he would live an active and record life indeed, but he would be an adult at eleven, middle-aged at twenty-five, and by thirty well on the road to senile decay. It seemed to me that so far Gibberne was only going to do for any one who took his drug exactly what Nature has done for the Jews and Orientals, who are men in their teens and aged by fifty, and quicker in thought and act than we are all the time. The marvel of drugs has always been great to my mind; you can madden a man, calm a man, make him incredibly strong and alert or a helpless log, quicken this passion and allay that, all by means of drugs, and here was a new miracle to be added to this strange armoury of phials the doctors use! But Gibberne was far too eager upon his technical points to enter very keenly into my aspect of the question.

It was the 7th or 8th of August when he told me the distillation that would decide his failure or success for a time was going forward as we talked, and it was on the 10th that he told me the thing was done and the New Accelerator a tangible reality in the world. I met him as I was going up the Sandgate Hill towards Folkestone—I think I was going to get my hair cut, and he came hurrying down to meet me—I suppose he was coming to my house to tell me at once of his success. I remember that his eyes were unusually bright and his face flushed, and I noted even then the swift alacrity of his step.

"It's done," he cried, and gripped my hand, speaking very fast; "it's more than done. Come up to my house and see."

"Really?"

"Really!" he shouted. "Incredibly! Come up and see."

"And it does—twice?

"It does more, much more. It scares me. Come up and see the stuff. Taste it! Try it! It's the most amazing stuff on earth." He gripped my arm and, walking at such a pace that he forced me into a trot, went shouting with me up the hill. A whole charabancful of people turned and stared at us in unison after the manner of people in charabancs. It was one of those hot, clear days that Folkestone sees so much of, every colour incredibly bright and every outline hard. There was a breeze, of course, but not so much breeze as sufficed under these conditions to keep me cool and dry. I panted for mercy.

"I'm not walking fast, am I?" cried Gibberne, and slackened his pace to a quick march.

"You've been taking some of this stuff," I puffed.

"No," he said. "At the utmost a drop of water that stood in a beaker from which I had washed out the last traces of the stuff. I took some last night, you know. But that is ancient history, now."

"And it goes twice?" I said, nearing his doorway in a grateful perspiration.

"It goes a thousand times, many thousand times!" cried Gibberne, with a dramatic gesture, flinging open his Early English carved oak gate.

"Phew!" said I, and followed him to the door.

"I don't know how many times it goes," he said, with his latchkey in his hand.

"And you—"

"It throws all sorts of light on nervous physiology, it kicks the theory of vision into a perfectly new shape...! Heaven knows how many thousand times. We'll try all that after—The thing is to try the stuff now."

"Try the stuff?" I said, as we went along the passage.

"Rather," said Gibberne, turning on me in his study. "There it is in that little green phial there! Unless you happen to be afraid?"

I am a careful man by nature, and only theoretically adventurous. I was afraid. But on the other hand, there is pride.

"Well," I haggled. "You say you've tried it?"

"I've tried it," he said, "and I don't look hurt by it, do I? I don't even look livery and I feel—"

I sat down. "Give me the potion," I said. "If the worst comes to the worst it will save having my hair cut, and that I think is one of the most hateful duties of a civilised man. How do you take the mixture?"

"With water," said Gibberne, whacking down a carafe.

He stood up in front of his desk and regarded me in his easy chair; his manner was suddenly affected by a touch of the Harley Street specialist. "It's rum stuff, you know," he said.

I made a gesture with my hand.

"I must warn you in the first place as soon as you've got it down to shut your eyes, and open them very cautiously in a minute or so's time. One still sees. The sense of vision is a question of length of vibration, and not of multitude of impacts; but there's a kind of shock to the retina, a nasty giddy confusion just at the time, if the eyes are open. Keep 'em shut."

"Shut," I said. "Good!"

"And the next thing is, keep still. Don't begin to whack about. You may fetch something a nasty rap if you do. Remember you will be going several thousand times faster than you ever did before, heart, lungs, muscles, brain—everything—and you will hit hard without knowing it. You won't know it, you know. You'll feel just as you do now. Only everything in the world will seem to be going ever so many thousand times slower than it ever went before. That's what makes it so deuced queer."

"Lor'," I said. "And you mean—"

"You'll see," said he, and took up a little measure. He glanced at the material on his desk. "Glasses," he said, "water. All here. Mustn't take too much for the first attempt."

The little phial glucked out its precious contents.

"Don't forget what I told you," he said, turning the contents of the measure into a glass in the manner of an Italian waiter measuring whisky. "Sit with the eyes tightly shut and in absolute stillness for two minutes," he said. "Then you will hear me speak."

He added an inch or so of water to the little dose in each glass.

"By-the-bye," he said, "don't put your glass down. Keep it in your hand and rest your hand on your knee. Yes—so. And now—"

He raised his glass.

"The New Accelerator," I said.

"The New Accelerator," he answered, and we touched glasses and drank, and instantly I closed my eyes.

You know that blank non-existence into which one drops when one has taken "gas." For an indefinite interval it was like that. Then I heard Gibberne telling me to wake up, and I stirred and opened my eyes. There he stood as he had been standing, glass still in hand. It was empty, that was all the difference.

"Well?" said I.

"Nothing out of the way?"

"Nothing. A slight feeling of exhilaration, perhaps. Nothing more."

"Sounds?"

"Things are still," I said. "By Jove! Yes! They are still. Except the sort of faint pat, patter, like rain falling on different things. What is it?"

"Analysed sounds," I think he said, but I am not sure. He glanced at the window. "Have you ever seen a curtain before a window fixed in that way before?"

I followed his eyes, and there was the end of the curtain, frozen as it were, corner high, in the act of flapping briskly in the breeze.

"No," said I; "that's odd."

"And here," he said, and opened the hand that held the glass. Naturally I winced, expecting the glass to smash. But so far from smashing it did not even seem to stir; it hung in mid-air—motionless.

"Roughly speaking," said Gibberne, "an object in these latitudes falls 16 feet in the first second. This glass is falling 16 feet in a second now. Only you see, it hasn't been falling yet for the hundredth part of a second. That gives you some idea of the pace of my Accelerator." And he waved his hand round and round, over and under the slowly sinking glass. Finally, he took it by the bottom, pulled it down, and placed it very carefully on the table. "Eh?" he said to me, and laughed.

"That seems all right," I said, and began very gingerly to raise myself from my chair. I felt perfectly well, very light and comfortable, and quite confident in my mind. I was going fast all over. My heart, for example, was beating a thousand times a second, but that caused me no discomfort at all. I looked out of the window. An immovable cyclist, head down and with a frozen puff of dust behind his driving-wheel, scorched to overtake a galloping charabanc that did not stir. I gaped in amazement at this incredible spectacle. "Gibberne," I cried, "how long will this confounded stuff last?"

"Heaven knows!" he answered. "Last time I took it I went to bed and slept it off. I tell you, I was frightened. It must have lasted some minutes, I think—it seemed like hours. But after a bit it slows down rather suddenly, I believe."

I was proud to observe that I did not feel frightened—I suppose because there were two of us. "Why shouldn't we go out?" I asked.

"Why not?"

"They'll see us."

"Not they. Goodness, no! Why, we shall be going a thousand times faster than the quickest conjuring trick that was ever done. Come along! Which way shall we go? Window, or door?"

And out by the window we went.

Assuredly of all the strange experiences that I have ever had, or imagined, or read of other people having or imagining, that little raid I made with Gibberne on the Folkestone Leas, under the influence of the New Accelerator, was the strangest and maddest of all. We went out by his gate into the road, and there we made a minute examination of the statuesque passing traffic. The tops of the wheels and some of the legs of the horses of this charabanc, the end of the whip-lash and the lower jaw of the conductor—who was just beginning to yawn—were perceptibly in motion, but all the rest of the lumbering conveyance seemed still. And quite noiseless except for a faint rattling that came from one man's throat! And as parts of this frozen edifice there were a driver, you know, and a conductor, and eleven people! The effect as we walked about the thing began by being madly queer, and ended by being—disagreeable. There they were, people like ourselves and yet not like ourselves, frozen in careless attitudes, caught in mid-gesture. A girl and a man smiled at one another, a leering smile that threatened to last for evermore; a woman in a floppy capelline rested her arm on the rail and stared at Gibberne's house with the unwinking stare of eternity; a man stroked his moustache like a figure of wax, and another stretched a tiresome stiff hand with extended fingers towards his loosened hat. We stared at them, we laughed at them, we made faces at them, and then a sort of disgust of them came upon us, and we turned away and walked round in front of the cyclist towards the Leas.

"Goodness!" cried Gibberne, suddenly; "Look there!"

He pointed, and there at the tip of his finger and sliding down the air with wings flapping slowly and at the speed of an exceptionally languid snail—was a bee.

And so we came out upon the Leas. There the thing seemed madder than ever. The band was playing in the upper stand, though all the sound it made for us was a low-pitched, wheezy rattle, a sort of prolonged last sigh that passed at times into a sound like the slow, muffled ticking of some monstrous clock. Frozen people stood erect, strange, silent, self-conscious-looking dummies hung unstably in mid-stride, promenading upon the grass. I passed close to a little poodle dog suspended in the act of leaping, and watched the slow movement of his legs as he sank to earth. "Lord, look here!" cried Gibberne, and we halted for a moment before a magnificent person in white faint-striped flannels, white shoes, and a Panama hat, who turned back to wink at two gaily dressed ladies he had passed. A wink, studied with such leisurely deliberation as we could afford, is an unattractive thing. It loses any quality of alert gaiety, and one remarks that the winking eye does not completely close, that under its drooping lid appears the lower edge of an eyeball and a little line of white. "Heaven give me memory," said I, "and I will never wink again."

"Or smile," said Gibberne, with his eye on the lady's answering teeth.

"It's infernally hot somehow," said I. "Let's go slower."

"Oh, come along!" said Gibberne.

We picked our way among the bath-chairs in the path. Many of the people sitting in the chairs seemed almost natural in their passive poses, but the contorted scarlet of the bandsmen was not a restful thing to see. A purple-faced little gentleman was frozen in the midst of a violent struggle to refold his newspaper against the wind; there were many evidences that all these people in their sluggish way were exposed to a considerable breeze, a breeze that had no existence so far as our sensations went. We came out and walked a little way from the crowd, and turned and regarded it. To see all that multitude changed, to a picture, smitten rigid, as it were, into the semblance of realistic wax, was impossibly wonderful. It was absurd, of course; but it filled me with an irrational, an exultant sense of superior advantage. Consider the wonder of it! All that I had said, and thought, and done since the stuff had begun to work in my veins had happened, so far as those people, so far as the world in general went, in the twinkling of an eye. "The New Accelerator—" I began, but Gibberne interrupted me.

"There's that infernal old woman!" he said.

"What old woman?"

"Lives next door to me," said Gibberne. "Has a lapdog that yaps. Gods! The temptation is strong!"

There is something very boyish and impulsive about Gibberne at times. Before I could expostulate with him he had dashed forward, snatched the unfortunate animal out of visible existence, and was running violently with it towards the cliff of the Leas. It was most extraordinary. The little brute, you know, didn't bark or wriggle or make the slightest sign of vitality. It kept quite stiffly in an attitude of somnolent repose, and Gibberne held it by the neck. It was like running about with a dog of wood. "Gibberne," I cried, "put it down!" Then I said something else. "If you run like that, Gibberne," I cried, "you'll set your clothes on fire. Your linen trousers are going brown as it is!"

He clapped his hand on his thigh and stood hesitating on the verge. "Gibberne," I cried, coming up, "put it down. This heat is too much! It's our running so! Two or three miles a second! Friction of the air!"

"What?" he said, glancing at the dog.

"Friction of the air," I shouted. "Friction of the air. Going too fast. Like meteorites and things. Too hot. And, Gibberne! Gibberne! I'm all over pricking and a sort of perspiration. You can see people stirring slightly. I believe the stuff's working off! Put that dog down."

"Eh?" he said.

"It's working off," I repeated. "We're too hot and the stuff's working off! I'm wet through."

He stared at me. Then at the band, the wheezy rattle of whose performance was certainly going faster. Then with a tremendous sweep of the arm he hurled the dog away from him and it went spinning upward, still inanimate, and hung at last over the grouped parasols of a knot of chattering people. Gibberne was gripping my elbow. "By Jove!" he cried. "I believe it is! A sort of hot pricking and—yes. That man's moving his pocket-handkerchief! Perceptibly. We must get out of this sharp."

But we could not get out of it sharply enough. Luckily, perhaps! For we might have run, and if we had run we should, I believe, have burst into flames. Almost certainly we should have burst into flames! You know we had neither of us thought of that...But before we could even begin to run the action of the drug had ceased. It was the business of a minute fraction of a second. The effect of the New Accelerator passed like the drawing of a curtain, vanished in the movement of a hand. I heard Gibberne's voice in infinite alarm. "Sit down," he said, and flop, down upon the turf at the edge of the Leas I sat—scorching as I sat. There is a patch of burnt grass there still where I sat down. The whole stagnation seemed to wake up as I did so, the disarticulated vibration of the band rushed together into a blast of music, the promenaders put their feet down and walked their ways, the papers and flags began flapping, smiles passed into words, the winker finished his wink and went on his way complacently, and all the seated people moved and spoke.

The whole world had come alive again, was going as fast as we were, or rather we were going no faster than the rest of the world. It was like slowing down as one comes into a railway station. Everything seemed to spin round for a second or two, I had the most transient feeling of nausea, and that was all. And the little dog which had seemed to hang for a moment when the force of Gibberne's arm was expended fell with a swift acceleration clean through a lady's parasol!

That was the saving of us. Unless it was for one corpulent old gentleman in a bath-chair, who certainly did start at the sight of us and afterwards regarded us at intervals with a darkly suspicious eye, and finally, I believe, said something to his nurse about us, I doubt if a solitary person remarked our sudden appearance among them. Plop! We must have appeared abruptly. We ceased to smoulder almost at once, though the turf beneath me was uncomfortably hot. The attention of everyone—including even the Amusements' Association band, which on this occasion, for the only time in its history, got out of tune—was arrested by the amazing fact, and the still more amazing yapping and uproar caused by the fact that a respectable, over-fed lapdog sleeping quietly to the east of the bandstand should suddenly fall through the parasol of a lady on the west—in a slightly singed condition due to the extreme velocity of its movements through the air. In these absurd days, too, when we are all trying to be as psychic, and silly, and superstitious as possible! People got up and trod on other people, chairs were overturned, the Leas policeman ran. How the matter settled itself I do not know—we were much too anxious to disentangle ourselves from the affair and get out of range of the eye of the old gentleman in the bath-chair to make minute inquiries. As soon as we were sufficiently cool and sufficiently recovered from our giddiness and nausea and confusion of mind to do so we stood up and, skirting the crowd, directed our steps back along the road below the Metropole towards Gibberne's house. But amidst the din I heard very distinctly the gentleman who had been sitting beside the lady of the ruptured sunshade using quite unjustifiable threats and language to one of those chair-attendants who have "Inspector" written on their caps. "If you didn't throw the dog," he said, "who did?"

The sudden return of movement and familiar noises, and our natural anxiety about ourselves (our clothes were still dreadfully hot, and the fronts of the thighs of Gibberne's white trousers were scorched a drabbish brown), prevented the minute observations I should have liked to make on all these things. Indeed, I really made no observations of any scientific value on that return. The bee, of course, had gone. I looked for that cyclist, but he was already out of sight as we came into the Upper Sandgate Road or hidden from us by traffic; the charabanc, however, with its people now all alive and stirring, was clattering along at a spanking pace almost abreast of the nearer church.

We noted however, that the window-sill on which we had stepped through, getting out of the house was slightly singed, and that the impressions of our feet on the gravel of the path were unusually deep.

So it was, I had my first experience of the New Accelerator. Practically we had been running about and saying and doing all sorts of things in the space of a second or so of time. We had lived half an hour while the band had played, perhaps two bars. But the effect it had upon us was that the whole world had stopped for our convenient inspection. Considering all things, and particularly considering our rashness in venturing out of the house, the experience might certainly have been much more disagreeable than it was. It showed, no doubt, that Gibberne has still much to learn before his preparation is a manageable convenience, but its practicability it certainly demonstrated beyond all cavil.

Since that adventure he has been steadily bringing its use under control, and I have several times, and without the slightest bad result, taken measured doses under his direction; though I must confess I have not yet ventured abroad again while under its influence. I may mention, for example, that this story has been written at one sitting and without interruption, except for the nibbling of some chocolate, by its means. I began at 6.25, and my watch is now very nearly at the minute past the half-hour. The convenience of securing a long, uninterrupted spell of work in the midst of a day full of engagements cannot be exaggerated. Gibberne is now working at the quantitative handling of his preparation, with especial reference to its distinctive effects upon different types of constitution. He then hopes to find a Retarder with which to dilute its present rather excessive potency. The Retarder will, of course, have the reverse effect to the Accelerator; used alone it should enable the patient to spread a few seconds over many hours of ordinary time, and so to maintain an apathetic inaction, a glacier-like absence of alacrity, amidst the most animated or irritating surroundings. The two things together must necessarily work an entire revolution in civilised existence. It is the beginning of our escape from that Time Garment of which Carlyle speaks. While this Accelerator will enable us to concentrate ourselves with tremendous impact upon any moment or occasion that demands our utmost sense and vigour, the Retarder will enable us to pass in passive tranquillity through infinite hardship and tedium. Perhaps I am a little optimistic about the Retarder, which has indeed still to be discovered, but about the Accelerator there is no possible sort of doubt whatever. Its appearance upon the market in a convenient, controllable, and assimilable form is a matter of the next few months. It will be obtainable of all chemists and druggists, in small green bottles, at a high but, considering its extraordinary qualities, by no means excessive price. Gibberne's Nervous Accelerator it will be called, and he hopes to be able to supply it in three strengths: one in 200, one in 900, and one in 2000, distinguished by yellow, pink, and white labels respectively.

No doubt its use renders a great number of very extraordinary things possible; for of course, the most remarkable, and possibly, even criminal proceedings may be effected with impunity by thus dodging, as it were, into the interstices of time. Like all potent preparations it will be liable to abuse. We have however, discussed this aspect of the question very thoroughly, and we have decided that this is purely a matter of medical jurisprudence and altogether outside our province. We shall manufacture and sell the Accelerator, and as for the consequences—we shall see.

39

The Inexperienced Ghost

The scene amidst which Clayton told his last story comes back very vividly to my mind. There he sat, for the greater part of the time, in the corner of the authentic settle by the spacious open fire, and Sanderson sat beside him smoking the Broseley clay that bore his name. There was Evans, and that marvel among actors, Wish, who is also a modest man. We had all come down to the Mermaid Club that Saturday morning, except Clayton, who had slept there overnight—which indeed gave him the opening of his story. We had golfed until golfing was invisible; we had dined, and we were in that mood of tranquil kindliness when men will suffer a story. When Clayton began to tell one, we naturally supposed he was lying. It may be that indeed he was lying—of that the reader will speedily be able to judge as well as I. He began, it is true, with an air of matter-of-fact anecdote, but that we thought was only the incurable artifice of the man.

"I say!" he remarked, after a long consideration of the upward rain of sparks from the log that Sanderson had thumped. "You know I was alone here last night?"

"Except for the domestics," said Wish.

"Who sleep in the other wing," said Clayton. "Yes. Well—" He pulled at his cigar for some little time as though he still hesitated about his confidence. Then he said, quite quietly, "I caught a ghost!"

"Caught a ghost, did you?" said Sanderson. "Where is it?"

And Evans, who admires Clayton immensely and has been four weeks in America, shouted, "Caught a ghost, did you, Clayton? I'm glad of it! Tell us all about it right now."

Clayton said he would in a minute, and asked him to shut the door.

He looked apologetically at me. "There's no eavesdropping of course, but we don't want to upset our very excellent service with any rumours of ghosts in the place. There's too much shadow and oak panelling to trifle with that. And this, you know, wasn't a regular ghost. I don't think it will come again—ever."

"You mean to say you didn't keep it?" said Sanderson.

"I hadn't the heart to," said Clayton.

And Sanderson said he was surprised.

We laughed, and Clayton looked aggrieved. "I know," he said, with the flicker of a smile, "but the fact is it really was a ghost, and I'm as sure of it as I am that I am talking to you now. I'm not joking. I mean what I say."

Sanderson drew deeply at his pipe, with one reddish eye on Clayton, and then emitted a thin jet of smoke more eloquent than many words.

Clayton ignored the comment. "It is the strangest thing that has ever happened in my life. You know, I never believed in ghosts or anything of the sort, before, ever; and then you know, I bag one in a corner; and the whole business is in my hands."

He meditated still more profoundly, and produced and began to pierce a second cigar with a curious little stabber he affected.

"You talked to it?" asked Wish.

"For the space, probably, of an hour."

"Chatty?" I said, joining the party of the sceptics.

"The poor devil was in trouble," said Clayton, bowed over his cigar-end and with the very faintest note of reproof.

"Sobbing?" some one asked.

Clayton heaved a realistic sigh at the memory. "Good Lord!" he said; "Yes." And then, "Poor fellow! Yes."

"Where did you strike it?" asked Evans, in his best American accent.

"I never realised," said Clayton, ignoring him, "the poor sort of thing a ghost might be," and he hung us up again for a time, while he sought for matches in his pocket and lit and warmed to his cigar.

"I took an advantage," he reflected at last.

We were none of us in a hurry. "A character," he said, "remains just the same character for all that it's been disembodied. That's a thing we too often forget. People with a certain strength or fixity of purpose may have ghosts of a certain strength and fixity of purpose—most haunting ghosts, you know, must be as one-idea'd as monomaniacs and as obstinate as mules to come back again and again. This poor creature wasn't." He suddenly looked up rather queerly, and his eye went round the room. "I say it," he said, "in all kindliness, but that is the plain truth of the case. Even at the first glance he struck me as weak."

He punctuated with the help of his cigar.

"I came upon him, you know, in the long passage. His back was towards me and I saw him first. Right off I knew him for a ghost. He was transparent and whitish; clean through his chest I could see the glimmer of the little window at the end. And not only his physique but his attitude struck me as being weak. He looked, you know, as though he didn't know in the slightest whatever he meant to do. One hand was on the panelling and the other fluttered to his mouth. Like—so!"

"What sort of physique?" said Sanderson.

"Lean. You know that sort of young man's neck that has two great flutings down the back, here and here—so! And a little, meanish head with scrubby hair and rather bad ears. Shoulders bad, narrower than the hips; turndown collar, ready-made short jacket, trousers baggy and a little frayed at the heels. That's how he took me. I came very quietly up the staircase. I did not carry a light, you know—the candles are on the landing table and there is that lamp—and I was in my list slippers, and I saw him as I came up. I stopped dead at that—taking him in. I wasn't a bit afraid. I think that in most of these affairs one is never nearly so afraid or excited as one imagines one would be. I was surprised and interested. I thought, 'Good Lord! Here's a ghost at last! And I haven't believed for a moment in ghosts during the last five-and-twenty years.'"

"Um," said Wish.

"I suppose I wasn't on the landing a moment before he found out I was there. He turned on me sharply, and I saw the face of an immature young man, a weak nose, a scrubby little moustache, a feeble chin. So for an instant we stood—he looking over his shoulder at me—and regarded one another. Then he seemed to remember his high calling. He turned round, drew himself up, projected his face, raised his arms, spread his hands in approved ghost fashion—came towards me. As he did so his little jaw dropped, and he emitted a faint, drawn-out 'Boo.' No, it wasn't—not a bit dreadful. I'd dined. I'd had a bottle of champagne, and being all alone, perhaps two or three—perhaps even four or five—whiskies, so I was as solid as rocks and no more frightened than if I'd been assailed by a frog. 'Boo!' I said. 'Nonsense. You don't belong to this place. What are you doing here?'

"I could see him wince. 'Boo-oo,' he said.

"'Boo—be hanged! Are you a member?' I said; and just to show I didn't care a pin for him I stepped through a corner of him and made to light my candle. 'Are you a member?' I repeated, looking at him sideways.

"He moved a little so as to stand clear of me, and his bearing became crestfallen. 'No,' he said, in answer to the persistent interrogation of my eye; 'I'm not a member—I'm a ghost.'

"'Well, that doesn't give you the run of the Mermaid Club. Is there any one you want to see, or anything of that sort?' And doing it as steadily as possible for fear that he should mistake the carelessness of whisky for the distraction of fear, I got my candle alight. I turned on him, holding it. 'What are you doing here?' I said.

"He had dropped his hands and stopped his booing, and there he stood, abashed and awkward, the ghost of a weak, silly, aimless young man. 'I'm haunting,' he said.

"'You haven't any business to,' I said in a quiet voice.

"'I'm a ghost,' he said, as if in defence.

"'That may be, but you haven't any business to haunt here. This is a respectable private club; people often stop here with nursemaids and children, and going about in the careless way you do, some poor little mite could easily come upon you and be scared out of her wits. I suppose you didn't think of that?'

"'No, sir,' he said, 'I didn't.'

"'You should have done. You haven't any claim on the place, have you? Weren't murdered here, or anything of that sort?'

"'None, sir; but I thought as it was old and oak-panelled—'

"'That's no excuse.' I regarded him firmly. 'Your coming here is a mistake,' I said, in a tone of friendly superiority. I feigned to see if I had my matches, and then looked up at him frankly. 'If I were you I wouldn't wait for cock-crow—I'd vanish right away.'

"He looked embarrassed. 'The fact is, sir—' he began.

"'I'd vanish,' I said, driving it home.

"'The fact is, sir, that—somehow—I can't.'

"'You can't?'

"'No, sir. There's something I've forgotten. I've been hanging about here since midnight last night, hiding in the cupboards of the empty bedrooms and things like that. I'm flurried. I've never come haunting before, and it seems to put me out.'

"'Put you out?'

"'Yes, sir. I've tried to do it several times, and it doesn't come off. There's some little thing has slipped me, and I can't get back.'

"That, you know, rather bowled me over. He looked at me in such an abject way that for the life of me I couldn't keep up quite the high, hectoring vein I had adopted. 'That's queer,' I said, and as I spoke I fancied I heard some one moving about down below. 'Come into my room and tell me more about it,' I said. 'I didn't, of course, understand this.' And I tried to take him by the arm. But, of course, you might as well have tried to take hold of a puff of smoke! I had forgotten my number, I think; anyhow, I remember going into several bedrooms—it was lucky I was the only soul in that wing—until I saw my traps. 'Here we are,' I said, and sat down in the armchair; 'sit down and tell me all about it. It seems to me you have got yourself into a jolly awkward position, old chap.'

"Well, he said he wouldn't sit down! He'd prefer to flit up and down the room if it was all the same to me. And so he did, and in a little while we were deep in a long and serious talk. And presently, you know, something of those whiskies and sodas evaporated out of me, and I began to realise just a little what a thundering rum and weird business it was that I was in. There he was, semi-transparent—the proper conventional phantom, and noiseless except for his ghost of a voice—flitting to and fro in that nice, clean, chintz-hung old bedroom. You could see the gleam of the copper candlesticks through him, and the lights on the brass fender, and the corners of the framed engravings on the wall, and there he was telling me all about this wretched little life of his that had recently ended on earth. He hadn't a particularly honest face, you know, but being transparent, of course, he couldn't avoid telling the truth."

"Eh?" said Wish, suddenly sitting up in his chair.

"What?" said Clayton.

"Being transparent—couldn't avoid telling the truth—I don't see it," said Wish.

"I don't see it," said Clayton, with inimitable assurance. "But it is so, I can assure you nevertheless. I don't believe he got once a nail's breadth off the Bible truth. He told me how he had been killed—he went down into a London basement with a candle to look for a leakage of gas—and described himself as a senior English master in a London private school when that release occurred."

"Poor wretch!" said I.

"That's what I thought, and the more he talked the more I thought it. There he was, purposeless in life and purposeless out of it. He talked of his father and mother and his schoolmaster, and all who had ever been anything to him in the world, meanly. He had been too sensitive, too nervous; none of them had ever valued him properly or understood him, he said. He had never had a real friend in the world, I think; he had never, had a success. He had shirked games and failed examinations. 'It's like that with some people,' he said; 'whenever I got into the examination-room or anywhere everything seemed to go.' Engaged to be married of course—to another oversensitive person, I suppose—when the indiscretion with the gas escape ended his affairs. 'And where are you now?' I asked. 'Not in—?'

"He wasn't clear on that point at all. The impression he gave me was of a sort of vague, intermediate state, a special reserve for souls too non-existent for anything so positive as either sin or virtue. I don't know. He was much too egotistical and unobservant to give me any clear idea of the kind of place, kind of country, there is on the Other Side of Things. Wherever he was, he seems to have fallen in with a set of kindred spirits: ghosts of weak Cockney young men, who were on a footing of Christian names, and among these there was certainly a lot of talk about 'going haunting' and things like that. Yes—going haunting! They seemed to think 'haunting' a tremendous adventure, and most of them funked it all the time. And so primed, you know, he had come."

"But really!" said Wish to the fire.

"These are the impressions he gave me, anyhow," said Clayton, modestly. "I may, of course, have been in a rather uncritical state, but that was the sort of background he gave to himself. He kept flitting up and down, with his thin voice going—talking, talking about his wretched self, and never a word of clear, firm statement from first to last. He was thinner and sillier and more pointless than if he had been real and alive. Only then, you know, he would not have been in my bedroom here—if he had been alive. I should have kicked him out."

"Of course," said Evans, "there ARE poor mortals like that."

"And there's just as much chance of their having ghosts as the rest of us," I admitted.

"What gave a sort of point to him, you know, was the fact that he did seem within limits to have found himself out. The mess he had made of haunting had depressed him terribly. He had been told it would be a 'lark'; he had come expecting it to be a 'lark,' and here it was, nothing but another failure added to his record! He proclaimed himself an utter out-and-out failure. He said, and I can quite believe it, that he had never tried to do anything all his life that he hadn't made a perfect mess of—and through all the wastes of eternity he never would. If he had had sympathy, perhaps—He paused at that, and stood regarding me. He remarked that, strange as it might seem to me, nobody, not any one, ever had given him the amount of sympathy I was doing now. I could see what he wanted straight away, and I determined to head him off at once. I may be a brute, you know, but being the Only Real Friend, the recipient of the confidences of one of these egotistical weaklings, ghost or body, is beyond my physical endurance. I got up briskly. 'Don't you brood on these things too much,' I said. 'The thing you've got to do is to get out of this—get out of this sharp. You pull yourself together and try.' 'I can't,' he said. 'You try,' I said, and try he did."

"Try!" said Sanderson. "How?"

"Passes," said Clayton.

"Passes?"

"Complicated series of gestures and passes with the hands. That's how he had come in and that's how he had to get out again. Lord! What a business I had!"

"But how could any series of passes—" I began.

"My dear man," said Clayton, turning on me and putting a great emphasis on certain words, "you want everything clear. I don't know how. All I know is that you do—that he did anyhow, at least. After a fearful time, you know, he got his passes right and suddenly disappeared."

"Did you," said Sanderson, slowly, "observe the passes?"

"Yes," said Clayton, and seemed to think. "It was tremendously queer," he said. "There we were, I and this thin vague ghost, in that silent room, in this silent, empty inn, in this silent little Friday-night town. Not a sound except our voices and a faint panting he made when he swung. There was the bedroom candle, and one candle on the dressing-table alight, that was all—sometimes one or other would flare up into a tall, lean, astonished flame for a space. And queer things happened. 'I can't,' he said; 'I shall never—!' And suddenly he sat down on a little chair at the foot of the bed and began to sob and sob. Lord! What a harrowing, whimpering thing he seemed!

"'You pull yourself together,' I said, and tried to pat him on the back, and...my confounded hand went through him! By that time, you know, I wasn't nearly so—massive as I had been on the landing. I got the queerness of it full. I remember snatching back my hand out of him, as it were, with a little thrill, and walking over to the dressing-table. 'You pull yourself together,' I said to him, 'and try.' And in order to encourage and help him I began to try as well."

"What!" said Sanderson, "The passes?"

"Yes, the passes."

"But—" I said, moved by an idea that eluded me for a space.

"This is interesting," said Sanderson, with his finger in his pipe-bowl. "You mean to say this ghost of yours gave away—"

"Did his level best to give away the whole confounded barrier? Yes."

"He didn't," said Wish; "he couldn't. Or you'd have gone there too."

"That's precisely it," I said, finding my elusive idea put into words for me.

"That is precisely it," said Clayton, with thoughtful eyes upon the fire.

For just a little while there was silence.

"And at last he did it?" said Sanderson.

"At last he did it. I had to keep him up to it hard, but he did it at last—rather suddenly. He despaired, we had a scene, and then he got up abruptly and asked me to go through the whole performance, slowly, so that he might see. 'I believe,' he said, 'if I could see I should spot what was wrong at once.' And he did. 'I know,' he said. 'What do you know?' said I. 'I know,' he repeated.

Then he said, peevishly, 'I can't do it if you look at me—I really can't; it's been that, partly, all along. I'm such a nervous fellow that you put me out.' Well, we had a bit of an argument. Naturally I wanted to see; but he was as obstinate as a mule, and suddenly I had come over as tired as a dog—he tired me out. 'All right,' I said, 'I won't look at you,' and turned towards the mirror, on the wardrobe, by the bed.

"He started off very fast. I tried to follow him by looking in the looking-glass, to see just what it was had hung. Round went his arms and his hands, so, and so, and so, and then with a rush came to the last gesture of all—you stand erect and open out your arms—and so, don't you know, he stood. And then he didn't! He didn't! He wasn't! I wheeled round from the looking-glass to him. There was nothing! I was alone, with the flaring candles and a staggering mind. What had happened? Had anything happened? Had I been dreaming...? And then, with an absurd note of finality about it, the clock upon the landing discovered the moment was ripe for striking one. So—! Ping! And I was as grave and sober as a judge, with all my champagne and whisky gone into the vast serene. Feeling queer, you know—confoundedly queer! Queer! Good Lord!"

He regarded his cigar-ash for a moment. "That's all that happened," he said.

"And then you went to bed?" asked Evans.

"What else was there to do?"

I looked Wish in the eye. We wanted to scoff, and there was something, something perhaps in Clayton's voice and manner, that hampered our desire.

"And about these passes?" said Sanderson.

"I believe I could do them now."

"Oh!" said Sanderson, and produced a pen-knife and set himself to grub the dottel out of the bowl of his clay.

"Why don't you do them now?" said Sanderson, shutting his pen-knife with a click.

"That's what I'm going to do," said Clayton.

"They won't work," said Evans.

"If they do—" I suggested.

"You know, I'd rather you didn't," said Wish, stretching out his legs.

"Why?" asked Evans.

"I'd rather he didn't," said Wish.

"But he hasn't got 'em right," said Sanderson, plugging too much tobacco in his pipe.

"All the same, I'd rather he didn't," said Wish.

We argued with Wish. He said that for Clayton to go through those gestures was like mocking a serious matter. "But you don't believe—?" I said. Wish glanced at Clayton, who was staring into the fire, weighing something in his mind. "I do—more than half anyhow, I do," said Wish.

"Clayton," said I, "you're too good a liar for us. Most of it was all right. But that disappearance...happened to be convincing. Tell us, it's a tale of cock and bull."

He stood up without heeding me, took the middle of the hearthrug, and faced me. For a moment he regarded his feet thoughtfully, and then for all the rest of the time his eyes were on the opposite wall, with an intent expression. He raised his two hands slowly to the level of his eyes and so began...

Now, Sanderson is a Freemason, a member of the lodge of the Four Kings, which devotes itself so ably to the study and elucidation of all the mysteries of Masonry past and present, and among the students of this lodge Sanderson is by no means the least. He followed Clayton's motions with a singular interest in his reddish eye. "That's not bad," he said, when it was done. "You really do, you know, put things together Clayton, in a most amazing fashion. But there's one little detail out."

"I know," said Clayton. "I believe I could tell you which."

"Well?"

"This," said Clayton, and did a queer little twist and writhing and thrust of the hands.

"Yes."

"That, you know, was what he couldn't get right," said Clayton. "But how do you—?"

"Most of this business, and particularly how you invented it, I don't understand at all," said Sanderson, "but just that phase—I do." He reflected. "These happen to be a series of gestures—connected with a certain branch of esoteric Masonry—Probably you know. Or else—how?" He reflected still further. "I do not see I can do any harm in telling you just the proper twist. After all, if you know, you know; if you don't, you don't."

"I know nothing," said Clayton, "except what the poor devil let out last night."

"Well, anyhow," said Sanderson, and placed his churchwarden very carefully upon the shelf over the fireplace. Then very rapidly he gesticulated with his hands.

"So?" said Clayton, repeating.

"So," said Sanderson, and took his pipe in hand again.

"Ah, now," said Clayton, "I can do the whole thing—right."

He stood up before the waning fire and smiled at us all. But I think there was just a little hesitation in his smile. "If I begin—" he said.

"I wouldn't begin," said Wish.

"It's all right!" said Evans. "Matter is indestructible. You don't think any jiggery-pokery of this sort is going to snatch Clayton into the world of shades. Not it! You may try, Clayton, so far as I'm concerned, until your arms drop off at the wrists."

"I don't believe that," said Wish, and stood up and put his arm on Clayton's shoulder. "You've made me half believe in that story somehow, and I don't want to see the thing done!"

"Goodness!" said I, "Here's Wish frightened!"

"I am," said Wish, with real or admirably feigned intensity. "I believe that if he goes through these motions right he'll go."

"He'll not do anything of the sort," I cried. "There's only one way out of this world for men, and Clayton is thirty years from that. Besides... And such a ghost! Do you think—?"

Wish interrupted me by moving. He walked out from among our chairs and stopped beside the tole and stood there. "Clayton," he said, "you're a fool."

Clayton, with a humorous light in his eyes, smiled back at him. "Wish," he said, "is right and all you others are wrong. I shall go. I shall get to the end of these passes, and as the last swish whistles through the air, Presto—! This hearthrug will be vacant, the room will be blank amazement, and a respectably dressed gentleman of fifteen stone will plump into the world of shades. I'm certain. So will you be. I decline to argue further. Let the thing be tried."

"No," said Wish, and made a step and ceased, and Clayton raised his hands once more to repeat the spirit's passing.

By that time, you know, we were all in a state of tension—largely because of the behaviour of Wish. We sat all of us with our eyes on Clayton—I at least, with a sort of tight, stiff feeling about me as though from the back of my skull to the middle of my thighs my body had been changed to steel. And there, with a gravity that was imperturbably serene, Clayton bowed and swayed and waved his hands and arms before us. As he drew towards the end one piled up, one tingled in one's teeth. The last gesture, I have said, was to swing the arms out wide open, with the face held up. And when at last he swung out to this closing gesture I ceased even to breathe. It was ridiculous, of course, but you know that ghost-story feeling. It was after dinner, in a queer, old shadowy house. Would he, after all—?

There he stood for one stupendous moment, with his arms open and his upturned face, assured and bright, in the glare of the hanging lamp. We hung through that moment as if it were an age, and then came from all of us something that was half a sigh of infinite relief and half a reassuring "No!" For visibly—he wasn't going. It was all nonsense. He had told an idle story, and carried it almost to conviction, that was all...! And then in that moment the face of Clayton, changed.

It changed. It changed as a lit house changes when its lights are suddenly extinguished. His eyes were suddenly eyes that were fixed, his smile was frozen on his lips, and he stood there still. He stood there, very gently swaying.

That moment, too was an age. And then, you know, chairs were scraping, things were falling, and we were all moving. His knees seemed to give, and he fell forward, and Evans rose and caught him in his arms...

It stunned us all. For a minute I suppose no one said a coherent thing. We believed it, yet could not believe it...I came out of a muddled stupefaction to find myself kneeling beside him, and his vest and shirt were torn open, and Sanderson's hand lay on his heart...

Well—the simple fact before us could very well wait our convenience; there was no hurry for us to comprehend. It lay there for an hour; it lies athwart my memory, black and amazing still, to this day. Clayton had, indeed, passed into the world that lies so near to and so far from our own, and he had gone thither by the only road that mortal man may take. But whether he did indeed pass there by that poor ghost's incantation, or whether he was stricken suddenly by apoplexy in the midst of an idle tale—as the coroner's jury would have us believe—is no matter for my judging; it is just one of those inexplicable riddles that must remain unsolved until the final solution of all things shall come. All I certainly know is that, in the very moment, in the very instant, of concluding those passes, he changed, and staggered, and fell down before us—dead!

40

The Land Ironclads

1.

The young lieutenant lay beside the war correspondent and admired the idyllic calm of the enemy's lines through his field-glass.

"So far as I can see," he said at last, "one man."

"What's he doing?" asked the war correspondent.

"Field-glass at us," said the young lieutenant.

"And this is War!"

"No," said the young lieutenant; "it's Bloch."

"The game's a draw."

"No! They've got to win or else they lose. A draw's a win for our side."

They had discussed the political situation fifty times or so, and the war correspondent was weary of it. He stretched out his limbs. "Aaai s'pose it is!" he yawned.

Flut!

"What was that?"

"Shot at us."

The war correspondent shifted to a slightly lower position. "No one shot at him," he complained.

"I wonder if they think we shall get so bored we shall go home?"

The war correspondent made no reply.

"There's the harvest, of course..."

They had been there a month. Since the first brisk movements after the declaration of war things had gone slower and slower, until it seemed as though the whole machine of events must have run down. To begin with, they had, had almost a scampering time; the invader had come across the frontier on the very dawn of the war in half-a-dozen parallel columns behind a cloud of cyclists and cavalry, with a general air of coming straight on the capital, and the defender horsemen had held him up, and peppered him and forced him to open out to outflank, and had then bolted to the next position in the most approved style, for a couple of days, until in the afternoon, bump! They had the invader against their prepared lines of defence. He did not suffer so much as had been hoped and expected: he was coming on, it seemed, with his eyes open, his scouts winded the guns, and down he sat at once without the shadow of an attack and began grubbing trenches for himself, as though he meant to sit down there to the very end of time. He was slow, but much more wary than the world had been led to expect, and he kept convoys tucked in and shielded his slow-marching infantry sufficiently well to prevent any heavy adverse scoring.

"But he ought to attack," the young lieutenant had insisted.

"He'll attack us at dawn, somewhere along the lines. You'll get the bayonets coming into the trenches just about when you see," the war correspondent had held until a week ago.

The young lieutenant winked when he said that.

When one early morning the men the defenders sent to lie out five hundred yards before the trenches, with a view to the unexpected emptying of magazines into any night attack, gave way to causeless panic and blazed away at nothing for ten minutes, the war correspondent understood the meaning of that wink.

"What would you do if you were the enemy?" said the war correspondent, suddenly.

"If I had men like I've got now?"

"Yes."

"Take those trenches."

"How?"

"Oh—dodges! Crawl out halfway at night before moonrise and get into touch with the chaps we send out. Blaze at 'em if they tried to shift, and so bag some of 'em in the daylight. Learn that patch of ground by heart, lie all day in squatty holes, and come on nearer next night. There's a bit over there, lumpy ground, where they could get across to rushing distance—easy. In a night or so. It would be a mere game for our fellows; it's what they're made for...Guns? Shrapnel and stuff wouldn't stop good men who meant business."

"Why don't they do that?

"Their men aren't brutes enough; that's the trouble. They're a crowd of devitalised townsmen, and that's the truth of the matter. They're clerks, they're factory hands, they're students, they're civilised men. They can write, they can talk, they can make and do all sorts of things, but they're poor amateurs at war. They've got no physical staying power, and that's the whole thing. They've never slept in the open one night in their lives; they've never drunk anything but the purest water-company water; they've never gone short of three meals a day since they left their feeding-bottles. Half their cavalry never cocked leg over horse till it enlisted six months ago. They ride their horses as though they were bicycles—you watch 'em! They're fools at the game, and they know it. Our boys of fourteen can give their grown men points...Very well—"

The war correspondent mused on his face with his nose between his knuckles.

"If a decent civilisation," he said, "cannot produce better men for war than—"

He stopped with belated politeness. "I mean—"

"Than our open-air life," said the young lieutenant.

"Exactly," said the war correspondent. "The civilisation has to stop."

"It looks like it," the young lieutenant admitted.

"Civilisation has science, you know," said the war correspondent. "It invented and it makes the rifles and guns and things you use."

"Which our nice healthy hunters and stockmen and so on, rowdy-dowdy cowpunchers and nigger-whackers, can use ten times better than—What's that?"

"What?" said the war correspondent, and then seeing his companion busy with his field-glass he produced his own: "Where?" said the war correspondent, sweeping the enemy's lines.

"It's nothing," said the young lieutenant, still looking.

"What's nothing?"

The young lieutenant put down his glass and pointed. "I thought I saw something there, behind the stems of those trees. Something black. What it was I don't know."

The war correspondent tried to get even by intense scrutiny.

"It wasn't anything," said the young lieutenant, rolling over to regard the darkling evening sky, and generalised: "There never will be anything any more for ever. Unless—"

The war correspondent looked inquiry.

"They may get their stomachs wrong, or something—living without proper drains."

A sound of bugles came from the tents behind. The war correspondent slid backward down the sand and stood up. "Boom!" came from somewhere far away to the left. "Halloa!" he said, hesitated, and crawled back to peer again. "Firing at this time is jolly bad manners."

The young lieutenant was uncommunicative for a space.

Then he pointed to the distant clump of trees again. "One of our big guns. They were firing at that," he said.

"The thing that wasn't anything?"

"Something over there, anyhow."

Both men were silent, peering through their glasses for a space. "Just when it's twilight," the lieutenant complained. He stood up.

"I might stay here a bit," said the war correspondent.

The lieutenant shook his head. "There's nothing to see," he apologised, and then went down to where his little squad of sun-brown, loose-limbed men had been yarning in the trench. The war correspondent stood up also, glanced for a moment at the businesslike bustle below him, gave perhaps twenty seconds to those enigmatical trees again, then turned his face toward the camp.

He found himself wondering whether his editor would consider the story of how somebody thought he saw something black behind a clump of trees, and how a gun was fired at this illusion by somebody else, too trivial for public consumption.

"It's the only gleam of a shadow of interest," said the war correspondent, "for ten whole days."

"No," he said presently; "I'll write that other article, 'Is War Played Out?'"

He surveyed the darkling lines in perspective, the tangle of trenches one behind another, one commanding another, which the defender had made ready. The shadows and mists swallowed up their receding contours, and here and there a lantern gleamed, and here and there knots of men were busy about small fires. "No troops on earth could do it," he said...

He was depressed. He believed that there were other things in life better worth having than proficiency in war; he believed that in the heart of civilisation, for all its stresses, its crushing concentrations of forces, its injustice and suffering, there lay something that might be the hope of the world; and the idea that any people, by living in the open air, hunting perpetually, losing touch with books and art and all the things that intensify life, might hope to resist and break that great development to the end of time, jarred on his civilised soul.

Apt to his thought came a file of the defender soldiers, and passed him in the gleam of a swinging lamp that marked the way.

He glanced at their red-lit faces, and one shone out for a moment, a common type of face in the defender's ranks: ill-shaped nose, sensuous lips, bright clear eyes full of alert cunning, slouch hat cocked on one side and adorned with the peacock's plume of the rustic Don Juan turned soldier, a hard brown skin, a sinewy frame, an open, tireless stride, and a master's grip on his rifle.

The war correspondent returned their salutations and went on his way.

"Louts," he whispered. "Cunning, elementary louts. And they are going to beat the townsmen at the game of war!"

From the red glow among the nearer tents came first one and then half-a-dozen hearty voices, bawling in a drawling unison the words of a particularly slab and sentimental patriotic song.

"Oh, go it!" muttered the war correspondent, bitterly.

2.

It was opposite the trenches called after Hackbone's Hut that the battle began. There the ground stretched broad and level between the lines, with scarcely shelter for a lizard, and it seemed to the startled, just-awakened men who came crowding into the trenches that this was one more proof of that inexperience of the enemy of which they had heard so much. The war correspondent would not believe his ears at first, and swore that he and the war artist, who, still imperfectly roused, was trying to put on his boots by the light of a match held in his hand, were the victims of a common illusion. Then, after putting his head in a bucket of cold water, his intelligence came back as he towelled. He listened. "Gollys!" he said; "that's something more than scare firing this time. It's like ten thousand carts on a bridge of tin."

There came a sort of enrichment to that steady uproar. "Machine-guns!"

Then, "Guns!"

The artist, with one boot on, thought to look at his watch, and went to it hopping.

"Half an hour from dawn," he said. "You were right about their attacking, after all..."

The war correspondent came out of the tent, verifying the presence of chocolate in his pocket as he did so. He had to halt for a moment or so until his eyes were toned down to the night a little. "Pitch!" he said. He stood for a space to season his eyes before he felt justified in striking out for a black gap among the adjacent tents. The artist coming out behind him fell over a tent-rope. It was half-past two o'clock in the morning of the darkest night in time, and against a sky of dull black silk the enemy was talking search-lights, a wild jabber of search-lights. "He's trying to blind our riflemen," said the war correspondent with a flash, and waited for the artist and then set off with a sort of discreet haste again. "Whoa!" he said, presently. "Ditches!"

They stopped.

"It's the confounded search-lights," said the war correspondent.

They saw lanterns going to and fro, near by, and men falling in to march down to the trenches. They were for following them, and then the artist began to get his night eyes. "If we scramble this," he said, "and it's only a drain, there's a clear run up to the ridge." And that way they took. Lights came and went in the tents behind, as the men turned out, and ever and again they came to broken ground and staggered and stumbled. But in a little while they drew near the crest. Something that sounded like the impact of a tremendous railway accident happened in the air above them, and the shrapnel bullets seethed about them like a sudden handful of hail. "Right-ho!" said the war correspondent, and soon they judged they had come to the crest and stood in the midst of a world of great darkness and frantic glares, whose principal fact was sound.

Right and left of them and all about them was the uproar, an army-full of magazine fire, at first chaotic and monstrous, and then, eked out by little flashes and gleams and suggestions, taking the beginnings of a shape. It looked to the war correspondent as though the enemy must have attacked in line and with his whole force—in which case he was either being or was already annihilated.

"Dawn and the dead," he said, with his instinct for headlines. He said this to himself, but afterwards by means of shouting he conveyed an idea to the artist, "They must have meant it for a surprise," he said.

It was remarkable how the firing kept on. After a time he began to perceive a sort of rhythm in this inferno of noise. It would decline—decline perceptibly, droop towards something that was comparatively a pause—a pause of inquiry. "Aren't you all dead yet?" this pause seemed to say. The flickering fringe of rifle-flashes would become attenuated and broken, and the whack-bang of enemy's big guns two miles away there would come up out of the deeps. Then suddenly, east or west of them, something would startle the rifles to a frantic outbreak again.

The war correspondent taxed his brain for some theory of conflict that would account for this, and was suddenly aware that the artist and he were vividly illuminated. He could see the ridge on which they stood, and before them in black outline a file of riflemen hurrying down towards the nearer trenches. It became visible that a light rain was falling, and farther away towards the enemy was a clear space with men—"our men—?" Running across it in disorder. He saw one of those men throw up his hands and drop. And something else black and shining loomed up on the edge of the beam-coruscating flashes; and behind it and far away a calm, white eye regarded the world. "Whit, whit, whit," sang something in the air, and then the artist was running for cover, with the war correspondent behind him. Bang came shrapnel, bursting close at hand as it seemed, and our two men were lying flat in a dip in the ground, and the light and everything had gone again, leaving a vast note of interrogation upon the light.

The war correspondent came within brawling range. "What the deuce was it? Shooting our men down!"

"Black," said the artist, "and like a fort. Not two hundred yards from the first trench."

He sought for comparison in his mind. "Something between a big blockhouse and a giant's dish-cover," he said.

"And they were running!" said the war correspondent.

"You'd run if a thing like that, with a search-light to help it, turned up like a prowling nightmare in the middle of the night."

They crawled to what they judged the edge of the dip and lay regarding the unfathomable dark. For a space they could distinguish nothing, and then a sudden convergence of the search-lights of both sides brought the strange thing out again.

In that flickering pallor it had the effect of a large and clumsy black insect, an insect the size of an iron-clad cruiser, crawling obliquely to the first line of trenches and firing shots out port-holes in its side. And on its carcass the bullets must have been battering with more than the passionate violence of hail on a roof of tin.

Then in the twinkling of an eye the curtain of the dark had fallen again and the monster had vanished, but the crescendo of musketry marked its approach to the trenches.

They were beginning to talk about the thing to each other, when a flying bullet kicked dirt into the artist's face, and they decided abruptly to crawl down into the cover of the trenches. They had got down with an unobtrusive persistence into the second line, before the dawn had grown clear enough for anything to be seen. They found themselves in a crowd of expectant riflemen, all noisily arguing about what would happen next. The enemy's contrivance had done execution upon the outlying men, it seemed, but they did not believe it would do any more. "Come the day and we'll capture the lot of them," said a burly soldier.

"Them?" said the war correspondent.

"They say there's a regular string of 'em, crawling along the front of our lines... Who cares?"

The darkness filtered away so imperceptibly that at no moment could one declare decisively that one could see. The search-lights ceased to sweep hither and thither. The enemy's monsters were dubious patches of darkness upon the dark, and then no longer dubious, and so they crept out into distinctness. The war correspondent, munching chocolate absentmindedly, beheld at last a spacious picture of battle under the cheerless sky, whose central focus was an array of fourteen or fifteen huge clumsy shapes lying in perspective on the very edge of the first line trenches, at intervals of perhaps three hundred yards, and evidently firing down upon the crowded riflemen. They were so close in that the defender's guns had ceased, and only the first line of trenches was in action.

The second line commanded the first, and as the light grew, the war correspondent could make out the riflemen who were fighting these monsters, crouched in knots and crowds behind the transverse banks that crossed the trenches against the eventuality of an enfilade. The trenches close to the big machines were empty save for the crumpled suggestions of dead and wounded men; the defenders had been driven right and left as soon as the prow of land ironclad had loomed up over the front of the trench. The war correspondent produced his field-glass, and was immediately a centre of inquiry from the soldiers about him.

They wanted to look, they asked questions, and after he had announced that the men across the traverses seemed unable to advance or retreat, and were crouching under cover rather than fighting, he found it advisable to loan his glasses to a burly and incredulous corporal. He heard a strident voice, and found a lean and sallow soldier at his back talking to the artist.

"There's chaps down there caught" the men was saying. "If they retreat they got to expose themselves, and the fire's too straight..."

"They aren't firing much, but every shot's a hit."

"Who?"

"The chaps in that thing. The men who're coming up—"

"Coming up where?"

"We're evacuating them trenches where we can. Our chaps are coming back up the zigzags...No end of 'em hit...But when we get clear our turn'll come. Rather! Those things won't be able to cross a trench or get into it; and before they can get back our guns'll smash 'em up. Smash 'em right up. See?" A brightness came into his eyes. "Then we'll have a go at the beggars inside," he said.

The war correspondent thought for a moment, trying to realise the idea. Then he set himself to recover his field-glasses from the burly corporal.

The daylight was getting clearer now. The clouds were lifting, and a gleam of lemon-yellow amidst the level masses to the east portended sunrise. He looked again at the land ironclad. As he saw it in the bleak, grey dawn, lying obliquely upon the slope and on the very lip of the foremost trench, the suggestion of a stranded vessel was very strong indeed. It might have been from eighty to a hundred feet long—it was about two hundred and fifty yards away—its vertical side was ten feet high or so, smooth for that height, and then with a complex patterning under the eaves of its flattish turtle cover. This patterning was a close interlacing of port-holes, rifle barrels, and telescope tubes—sham and real—indistinguishable one from the other. The thing had come into such a position as to enfilade the trench, which was empty now, so far as he could see, except for two or three crouching knots of men and the tumbled dead. Behind it, across the plain, it had scored the grass with a train of linked impressions, like the dotted tracings sea-things leave in sand. Left and right of that track dead men and wounded men were scattered—men it had picked off as they fled back from their advanced positions in the search-light glare from the invader's lines. And now it lay with its head projecting a little over the trench it had won, as if it were a single sentient thing planning the next phase of its attack...

He lowered his glasses and took a more comprehensive view of the situation. These creatures of night had evidently won the first line of trenches and the fight had come to a pause. In the increasing light he could make out by a stray shot or a chance exposure that the defender's marksmen were lying thick in the second and third line of trenches up towards the low crest of the position, and in such of the zigzags as gave them a chance of a converging fire. The men about him were talking of guns. "We're in the line of big guns at the crest, but they'll soon shift one to pepper them" the lean man said, reassuringly.

"Whup," said the corporal.

"Bang! Bang! Bang! Whir-r-r-r-r!" it was a sort of nervous jump, and all the rifles were going off by themselves. The war correspondent found himself and artist, two idle men crouching behind a line of preoccupied backs, of industrious men discharging magazines. The monster had moved. It continued to move regardless of the hail that splashed its skin with bright new specks of lead. It was singing a mechanical little ditty to itself, "Tuf-tuf, tuf-tuf, tuf-tuf," and squirting out little jets of steam behind. It had humped itself up, as a limpet does before it crawls; it had its skirt and displayed along the length of it—feet! They were thick, stumpy feet, between knobs and buttons in shape—flat, broad things, reminding one of the feet of elephants or the legs of caterpillars; and then, as the skirt rose higher, the war correspondent, scrutinising the thing through his glasses again, saw that these feet hung, as it were, on the rims of wheels. His thoughts whirled back to Victoria Street, Westminster, and he saw himself in the piping times of peace, seeking matter for an interview.

"Mr.—Mr. Diplock," he said; "and he called them Pedrails... Fancy meeting them here!"

The marksman beside him raised his head and shoulders in a speculative mood to fire more certainly—it seemed so natural to assume the attention of the monster must be distracted by this trench before it—and was suddenly knocked backwards by a bullet through his neck. His feet flew up, and he vanished out of the margin of the watcher's field of vision. The war correspondent grovelled tighter, but after a glance behind him at a painful little confusion, he resumed his field-glass, for the thing was putting down its feet one after the other, and hoisting itself farther and farther over the trench. Only a bullet in the head could have stopped him looking just then.

The lean man with the strident voice ceased firing to turn and reiterate his point. "They can't possibly cross," he bawled. "They—"

"Bang! Bang! Bang! Bang—!" Drowned everything.

The lean man continued speaking for a word or so, then gave it up, shook his head to enforce the impossibility of anything crossing a trench like the one below, and resumed business once more.

And all the while that great bulk was crossing. When the war correspondent turned his glass on it again it had bridged the trench, and its queer feet were rasping away at the farther bank, in the attempt to get a hold there. It got its hold. It continued to crawl until the greater bulk of it was over the trench—until it was all over. Then it paused for a moment, adjusted its skirt a little nearer the ground, gave an unnerving "toot, toot," and came on abruptly at a pace of, perhaps, six miles an hour straight up the gentle slope towards our observer.

The war correspondent raised himself on his elbow and looked a natural inquiry at the artist.

For a moment the men about him stuck to their position and fired furiously. Then the lean man in a mood of precipitancy slid backwards, and the war correspondent said "Come along," to the artist, and led the movement along the trench.

As they dropped down, the vision of a hillside of trench being rushed by a dozen vast cockroaches disappeared for a space, and instead was one of a narrow passage, crowded with men, for the most part receding, through one or two turned or halted. He never turned back to see the nose of the monster creep over the brow of the trench; he never even troubled to keep in touch with the artist. He heard the "whit" of bullets about him soon enough, and saw a man before him stumble and drop, and then he was one of a furious crowd fighting to get into a transverse zigzag ditch that enabled the defenders to get under cover up and down the hill. It was like a theatre panic. He gathered from signs and fragmentary words that on ahead another of these monsters had also won to the second trench.

He lost his interest in the general course of the battle for a space altogether; he became simply a modest egotist, in a mood of hasty circumspection, seeking the farthest rear, amidst a dispersed multitude of disconcerted riflemen similarly employed. He scrambled down through trenches, he took his courage in both hands and sprinted across the open, he had moments of panic when it seemed madness not to be quadrupedal, and moments of shame when he stood up and faced about to see how the fight was going. And he was one of many thousand very similar men that morning. On the ridge he halted in a knot of scrub, and was for a few minutes almost minded to stop and see things out.

The day was now fully come. The grey sky had changed to blue, and of all the cloudy masses of dawn there remained only a few patches of dissolving fleeciness. The world below was bright and singularly clear. The ridge was not, perhaps, more than a hundred feet or so above the general plain, but in this flat region it sufficed to give the effect of extensive view. Away on the north side of the ridge, little and far, were the camps, the ordered wagons, all the gear of a big army; with officers galloping about and men doing aimless things. Here and there men were falling in, however, and the cavalry was forming up on the plain beyond the tents. The bulk of men who had been in the trenches were still on the move to the rear, scattered like sheep without a shepherd over the farther slopes. Here and there were little rallies and attempts to wait and do—something vague; but the general drift was away from any concentration. There on the southern side was the elaborate lacework of trenches and defences, across which these iron turtles, fourteen of them spread out over a line of perhaps three miles, were now advancing as fast as a man could trot, and methodically shooting down and breaking up any persistent knots of resistance. Here and there stood little clumps of men, outflanked and unable to get away, showing the white flag, and the invader's cyclist infantry was advancing now across the open, in open order, but unmolested, to complete the work of the machines. Surveyed at large, the defenders already looked a beaten army. A mechanism that was effectually ironclad against bullets, that could at a pinch cross a thirty-foot trench, and that seemed able to shoot out rifle-bullets with unerring precision, was clearly an inevitable victor against anything but rivers, precipices, and guns.

He looked at his watch. "Half-past four! Lord! What thing can happen in two hours. Here's the whole blesses army being walked over, and at half-past two—"

"And even now our blessed louts haven't done a thing with their guns!"

He scanned the ridge right and left of him with his glasses. He turned again to the nearest land ironclad, advancing now obliquely to him and not three hundred yards away, and then scanned the ground over which he must retreat if he was not to be captured.

"They'll do nothing," he said, and glanced at the enemy.

And then from far away to the left came the thud of a gun, followed very rapidly by a rolling gun-fire.

He hesitated and decided to stay.

3.

The defender had relied chiefly upon his rifles in the event of an assault. His guns he kept concealed at various points upon and behind the ridge ready to bring them into action against any artillery preparations for an attack on the part of his antagonist. The situation had rushed upon him with the dawn, and by the time the gunners had their guns ready for motion, the land ironclads were already in among the foremost trenches. There is a natural reluctance to fire into one's own broken men, and many of the guns, being intended simply to fight an advance of the enemy's artillery, were not in positions to hit anything in the second line of trenches. After that the advance of the land ironclads was swift. The defender-general found himself suddenly called upon to invent a new sort of warfare, in which guns were to fight alone amidst broken and retreating infantry. He had scarcely thirty minutes in which to think it out. He did not respond to call, and what happened that morning was that the advance of the land ironclads forced the fight, and each gun and battery made what play its circumstance dictated. For the most part it was poor play.

Some of the guns got in two or three shots, some one or two, and the percentage of misses was unusually high. The howitzers, of course, did nothing. The land ironclads in each case followed much the same tactics. As soon as a gun came into play the monster turned itself almost end-on, so as to minimise the chances of a square hit, and made not for the gun, but for the nearest point on its flank from which the gunners could be shot down. Few of the hits scored were very effectual; only one of the things was disabled, and that was the one that fought the three batteries attached to the brigade on the left wing. Three that were hit when close upon the guns were clean shot through without being put out of action. Our war correspondent did not see that one momentary arrest of the tide of victory on the left; he saw only the very ineffectual fight of half-battery 96B close at hand upon his right. This he watched some time beyond the margin of safety.

Just after he heard the three batteries opening up upon his left he became aware of the thud of horses' hoofs from the sheltered side of the slope, and presently saw first one and then two other guns galloping into position along the north side of the ridge, well out of sight of the great bulk that was now creeping obliquely towards the crest and cutting up the lingering infantry beside it and below, as it came.

The half-battery swung round into line—each gun describing its curve—halted, unlimbered, and prepared for action...

"Bang!"

The land ironclad had become visible over the brow of the hill, and just visible as a long black back to the gunners. It halted, as though it hesitated.

The two remaining guns fired, and then their big antagonist had swung round and was in full view, end-on, against the sky, coming at a rush.

The gunners became frantic in their haste to fire again. They were so near the war correspondent could see the expression of their excited faces through his field-glass. As he looked he saw a man drop, and realised for the first time that the ironclad was shooting.

For a moment the big black monster crawled with an accelerated pace towards the furiously active gunners. Then, as if moved by a generous impulse, it turned its full broadside to their attack, and scarcely forty yards away from them. The war correspondent turned his field-glass back to the gunners and perceived it was now shooting down the men about the guns with the most deadly rapidity.

Just for a moment it seemed splendid, and then it seemed horrible. The gunners were dropping in heaps about their guns. To lay a hand on a gun was death. "Bang!" went the gun on the left, a hopeless miss, and that was the only second shot the half-battery fired. In another moment half-a-dozen surviving artillerymen were holding up their hands amidst a scattered muddle of dead and wounded men, and the fight was done.

The war correspondent hesitated between stopping in his scrub and waiting for an opportunity to surrender decently, or taking to an adjacent gully he had discovered. If he surrendered it was certain he would get no copy off; while, he escaped, there were all sorts of chances. He decided to follow the gully, and take the first offer in the confusion beyond the camp of picking up a horse.

4.

Subsequent authorities have found fault with the first land ironclads in many particulars, but assuredly they served their purpose on the day of their appearance. They were essentially long, narrow, and very strong steel frameworks carrying the engines, and borne upon eight pairs of big pedrail wheels, each about ten feet in diameter, each a driving wheel and set upon long axles free to swivel round a common axis. This arrangement gave them the maximum of adaptability to the contours of the ground. They crawled level along the ground with one foot high upon a hillock and another deep in a depression, and they could hold themselves erect and steady sideways upon even a steep hillside. The engineers directed the engines under the command of the captain, who had lookout points at small ports all round the upper edge of the adjustable skirt of twelve-inch iron-plating which protected the whole affair, and who could also raise or depress a conning-tower set about the port-holes through the centre of the iron top cover. The riflemen each occupied a small cabin of peculiar construction, and these cabins were slung along the sides of and before and behind the great main framework, in a manner suggestive of the slinging of the seats of an Irish jaunting-car. Their rifles, however, were very different pieces of apparatus from the simple mechanisms in the hands of their adversaries.

These were in the first place automatic, ejected their cartridges and loaded again from a magazine each time they fired, until the ammunition store was at an end, and they had the most remarkable sights imaginable, sights which threw a bright little camera-obscura picture into the light-tight box in which the riflemen sat below. This camera-obscura picture was marked with two crossed lines, and whatever was covered by the intersection of these two lines, that the rifle hit. The sighting was ingeniously contrived. The rifleman stood at the table with a like an elaboration of a draughtsman's dividers in his hand, and he opened and closed these dividers, so that they were always at the apparent height—if it was an ordinary-sized man—of the man he wanted to kill. A little twisted strand of wire like an electric-light wire ran from this implement up to the gun, and as the dividers opened and shut the sights went up or down. Changes in the clearness of the atmosphere, due to changes of moisture, were met by an ingenious use of that meteorologically sensitive substance, catgut, and when the land ironclad moved forward the sights got a compensatory deflection in the direction of its motion. The rifleman stood up in his pitch-dark chamber and watched the little picture before him. One hand held the dividers for judging distance, and the other grasped a big knob like a door-handle. As he pushed this knob about the rifle above swung to correspond, and the picture passed to and fro like an agitated panorama. When he saw a man he wanted to shoot he brought him up to the cross-lines, and then pressed a finger upon a little push like an electric bell-push, conveniently placed in the centre of the knob. Then the man was shot. If by any chance the rifleman missed his target he moved the knob a trifle, or readjusted his dividers, pressed the push, and got him the second time.

This rifle and its sights protruded from a port-hole, exactly like a great number of other port-holes that ran in a triple row under the eaves of the cover of the land ironclad. Each port-hole displayed a rifle and sight in dummy, so that the real ones could only be hit by a chance shot, and if one was, then the young man below said "Pshaw!" turned on an electric light, lowered the injured instrument into his camera, replaced the injured part, or put up a new rifle if the injury was considerable.

You must conceive these cabins as hung clear above the swing of the axles, and inside the big wheels upon which the great elephant-like feet were hung, and behind these cabins along the centre of the monster ran a central gallery into which they opened, and along which worked the big compact engines. It was like a long passage into which this throbbing machinery had been packed, and the captain stood about the middle, close to the ladder that led to his conning-tower, and directed the silent, alert engineers—for the most part by signs. The throb and noise of the engines mingled with the reports of the rifles and the intermittent clangour of the bullet hail upon the armour. Ever and again he would touch the wheel that raised his conning-tower, step up his ladder until his engineers could see nothing of him above the waist, and then come down again with orders. Two small electric lights were all the illumination of this space—they were placed to make him most clearly visible to his subordinates; the air was thick with the smell of oil and petrol, and had the war correspondent been suddenly transferred from the spacious dawn outside to the bowels of this apparatus he would have thought himself fallen into another world.

The captain, of course, saw both sides of the battle. When he raised his head into his conning-tower there were the dewy sunrise, the amazed and disordered trenches, the flying and falling soldiers, the depressed-looking groups of prisoners, the beaten guns; when he bent down again to signal "half speed," "quarter speed," "half circle, round toward the right," or what not, he was in the oil-smelling twilight of the ill-lit engine-room. Close beside him on either side was the mouth-piece of a speaking-tube, and ever and again he would direct one side or other of his strange craft to "concentrate fire forward on gunners," or to "clear out trench about a hundred yards on our right front."

He was a young man, healthy enough but by no means sun-tanned, and of a type of feature and expression that prevails in

His Majesty's Navy: alert, intelligent, quiet. He and his engineers and riflemen all went about their work, calm and reasonable men. They had none of that flapping strenuousness of the half-wit in a hurry, that excessive strain upon the blood-vessels, that hysteria of effort which is so frequently regarded as the proper state of mind for heroic deeds.

For the enemy these young engineers were defeating they felt a certain qualified pity and a quite unqualified contempt. They regarded these big, healthy men they were shooting down precisely as these same big, healthy men might regard some inferior kind of nigger. They despised them for making war; despised their brawling patriotisms and their emotionality profoundly; despised them, above all, for the petty cunning and the almost brutish want of imagination their method of fighting displayed. "If they must make war," these young men thought, "Why in thunder don't they do it like sensible men?" They resented the assumption that their own side was too stupid to do anything more than play their enemy's game, that they were going to play this costly folly according to the rules of unimaginative men. They resented being forced to the trouble of making man-killing machinery; resented the alternative of having to massacre these people or endure their truculent yappings; resented the whole unfathomable imbecility of war.

Meanwhile, with something of the mechanical precision of a good clerk posting a ledger, the rifleman moved their knobs and pressed their buttons...

The captain of Land Ironclad Number Three had halted on the crest close to his captured half-battery. His lined up prisoners stood hard by and waited for the cyclists behind to come for them. He surveyed the victorious morning through his conning-tower.

He read the general's signals. "Five and Four are to keep among the guns to the left and prevent any attempt to recover them. Seven and Eleven and Twelve, stick to the guns you have got; Seven, got into position to command the guns taken by Three. Then we're to do something else, are we? Six and One, quicken up to about ten miles an hour and walk round behind that camp to the levels near the river—we shall bag the whole crowd of them," interjected the young man. "Ah, here we are! Two and Three, Eight and Nine, Thirteen and Fourteen, space out to a thousand yards, wait for the word, and then go slowly to cover the advance of the cyclist infantry against any change of mounted troops. That's all right. But where's Ten? Halloa! Ten to repair and get movable as soon as possible. They've broken up Ten!"

The discipline of the new war machines was business-like rather than pedantic, and the head of the captain came down out of the conning-tower to tell his men: "I say, you chaps there. They've broken up Ten. Not badly, I think; but anyhow, he's stuck."

But that still left thirteen of the monsters in action to finish up the broken army.

The war correspondent stealing down his gully looked back and saw them all lying along the crest and talking fluttering congratulatory flags to one another. Their iron sides were shining golden in the light of the rising sun.

5.

The private adventures of the war correspondent terminated in surrender about one o'clock in the afternoon, and by that time he had stolen a horse, pitched off it, and narrowly escaped being rolled upon; found the brute had broken its leg, and shot it with his revolver. He had spent some hours in the company of a squad of dispirited riflemen, had quarrelled with them about topography at last, and gone off by himself in a direction that should have brought him to the banks of the river and didn't. Moreover, he had eaten all his chocolate and found nothing in the whole world to drink. Also, it had become extremely hot. From behind a broken, but attractive, stone wall he had seen far away in the distance the defender-horsemen trying to charge cyclists in open order, with land ironclads outflanking them on either side. He had discovered that cyclists could retreat over open turf before horsemen with a sufficient margin of speed to allow of frequent dismounts and much terribly effective sharp-shooting, and he had a sufficient persuasion that those horsemen, having charged their hearts out, had halted just beyond his range of vision and surrendered. He had been urged to sudden activity by a forward movement of one of those machines that had threatened to enfilade his wall. He had discovered a fearful blister on his heel.

He was now in a scrubby gravelly place, sitting down and meditating on his pocket-handkerchief, which had in some extraordinary way become in the last twenty-four hours extremely ambiguous in hue. "It's the whitest thing I've got," he said.

He had known all along that the enemy was east, west and south of him, but when he heard land ironclads Number One and Six talking in their measured, deadly way not half a mile to the north he decided to make his own little unconditional peace without any further risks. He was for hoisting his white flag to a brush and taking up a position of modest obscurity near it until some one came along. He became aware of voices, clatter, and the distinctive noises of a body of horses, quite near, and he put his handkerchief in his pocket again and went to see what was going forward.

The sound of firing ceased, and then as he drew near he heard the deep sounds of many simple, coarse, but hearty and noble-hearted soldiers of the old school swearing with vigour.

He emerged from his scrub upon a big level plain, and far away a fringe of trees marked the banks of the river.

In the centre of the picture was a still intact road bridge, and big railway bridge a little to the right. Two land ironclads rested, with a general air of being long, harmless sheds, in a pose of anticipatory peacefulness right and left of the picture, completely commanding two miles and more of the river levels. Emerged and halted a few yards from the scrub was the remainder of the defender's cavalry, dusty, a little disordered and obviously annoyed, but still a very fine show of men. In the middle distance three or four men and horses were receiving medical attendance, and nearer a knot of officers regarded the distant novelties in mechanism with profound distaste. Every one was very distinctly aware of the twelve other ironclads, and of the multitude of townsmen soldiers, on bicycles or afoot, encumbered now by prisoners and captured war-gear, but otherwise thoroughly effective, who were sweeping like a great net in their rear.

"Checkmate," said the war correspondent, walking out into the open. "But I surrender in the best of company. Twenty-four hours ago I thought war was impossible—and these beggars have captured the whole blessed army! Well! Well!" He thought of his talk with the young lieutenant. "If there's no end to the surprises of science, the civilised people have it, of course. As long as their science keeps going they will necessarily be ahead of open-country men. Still..." He wondered for a space what might have happened to the young lieutenant.

The war correspondent was one of those inconsistent people who always want the beaten side to win. When he saw all these burly, sun-tanned horsemen, disarmed and dismounted and lined up; when he saw their horses unskilfully led away by the singularly not equestrian cyclists to whom they had surrendered; when he saw these truncated Paladins watching this scandalous sight, he forgot altogether that he had called these men "cunning louts" and wished them beaten not four-and-twenty hours ago. A month ago he had seen that regiment in its pride going forth to war, and had told of its terrible prowess, how it could charge in open order with each man firing from his saddle, and sweep before it anything else that ever came out to battle in any sort of order, foot or horse. And it had, had to fight a few score of young men in atrociously unfair machines!

"Manhood versus Machinery" occurred to him as a suitable headline. Journalism curdles all one's mind to phrases.

He strolled as near the lined-up prisoners as the sentinels seemed disposed to permit, and surveyed them and compared their sturdy proportions with those of their lightly built captors.

"Smart degenerates," he muttered. "Anaemic cockneydom."

The surrendered officers came quite close to him presently, and he could hear the colonel's high-pitched tenor. The poor gentleman had spent three years of arduous toil upon the best material in the world perfecting that shooting from the saddle charge, and he was inquiring with phrases of blasphemy, natural in the circumstances, what one could be expected to do against this suitably consigned ironmongery.

"Guns," said some one.

"Big guns they can walk around. You can't shift big guns to keep pace with them, and little guns in the open they rush. I saw 'em rushed. You might do a surprised now and then—assassinate the brutes, perhaps—"

"You might make things like 'em."

"What? More ironmongery? Us...?"

"I'll call my article," meditated the war correspondent, "'Mankind versus Ironmongery,' and quote the old boy at the beginning."

And he was much too good a journalist to spoil his contrast by remarking that the half-dozen comparatively slender young men in blue pyjamas who were standing about their victorious land ironclad, drinking coffee and eating biscuits, had also in their eyes and carriage something not altogether degraded below the level of a man.

41

The Magic Shop

I had seen the Magic Shop from afar several times; I had passed it once or twice, a shop window of alluring little objects, magic balls, magic hens, wonderful cones, ventriloquist dolls, the material of the basket trick, packs of cards that looked all right, and all that sort of thing, but never had I thought of going in until one day, almost without warning, Gip hauled me by my finger right up to the window, and so conducted himself that there was nothing for it but to take him in. I had not thought the place was there, to tell the truth—a modest-sized frontage in Regent Street, between the picture shop and the place where the chicks run about just out of patent incubators—but there it was sure enough. I had fancied it was down nearer the Circus, or round the corner in Oxford Street, or even in Holborn; always over the way and a little inaccessible it had been, with something of the mirage in its position; but here it was now quite indisputably, and the fat end of Gip's pointing finger made a noise upon the glass.

"If I was rich," said Gip, dabbing a finger at the Disappearing Egg, "I'd buy myself that. And that"—which was The Crying Baby, Very Human—"and that," which was a mystery, and called, so a neat card asserted, "Buy One and Astonish Your Friends.

"Anything," said Gip, "will disappear under one of those cones. I have read about it in a book. And there, dadda, is the Vanishing Halfpenny—, only they've put it this way up so's we can't see how it's done."

Gip, dear boy, inherits his mother's breeding, and he did not propose to enter the shop or worry in any way; only you know, quite unconsciously he lugged my finger doorward, and he made his interest clear.

"That," he said, and pointed to the Magic Bottle.

"If you had that?" I said; at which promising inquiry he looked up with a sudden radiance.

"I could show it to Jessie," he said, thoughtful as ever of others.

"It's less than a hundred days to your birthday, Gibbles," I said, and laid my hand on the door-handle.

Gip made no answer, but his grip tightened on my finger, and so we came into the shop.

It was no common shop this; it was a magic shop, and all the prancing precedence Gip would have taken in the matter of mere toys was wanting. He left the burthen of the conversation to me.

It was a little, narrow shop, not very well lit, and the door-bell pinged again with a plaintive note as we closed it behind us. For a moment or so we were alone and could glance about us. There was a tiger in papier-mâché on the glass case that covered the low counter—a grave, kind-eyed tiger that waggled his head in a methodical manner; there were several crystal spheres, a china hand holding magic cards, a stock of magic fish-bowls in various sizes, and an immodest magic hat that shamelessly displayed its springs. On the floor were magic mirrors; one to draw you out long and thin, one to swell your head and vanish your legs, and one to make you short and fat like a draught; and while we were laughing at these the shopman, as I suppose, came in.

At any rate, there he was behind the counter—a curious, sallow, dark man, with one ear larger than the other and a chin like the toe-cap of a boot.

"What can we have the pleasure?" he said, spreading his long, magic fingers on the glass case; and so with a start we were aware of him.

"I want," I said, "to buy my little boy a few simple tricks."

"Legerdemain?" he asked. "Mechanical? Domestic?"

"Anything amusing?" said I.

"Um!" said the shopman, and scratched his head for a moment as if thinking. Then, quite distinctly, he drew from his head a glass ball. "Something in this way?" he said, and held it out.

The action was unexpected. I had seen the trick done at entertainments endless times before—it's part of the common stock of conjurers—but I had not expected it here.

"That's good," I said, with a laugh.

"Isn't it?" said the shopman.

Gip stretched out his disengaged hand to take this object and found merely a blank palm.

"It's in your pocket," said the shopman, and there it was!

"How much will that be?" I asked.

"We make no charge for glass balls," said the shopman politely. "We get them"—he picked one out of his elbow as he spoke—"free." He produced another from the back of his neck, and laid it beside its predecessor on the counter. Gip regarded his glass ball sagely, then directed a look of inquiry at the two on the counter, and finally brought his round-eyed scrutiny to the shopman, who smiled.

"You may have those too," said the shopman, "and, if you don't mind, one from my mouth. So!"

Gip counselled me mutely for a moment, and then in a profound silence put away the four balls, resumed my reassuring finger, and nerved himself for the next event.

"We get all our smaller tricks in that way," the shopman remarked.

I laughed in the manner of one who subscribes to a jest. "Instead of going to the wholesale shop," I said. "Of course, it's cheaper."

"In a way," the shopman said. "Though we pay in the end. But not so heavily—as people suppose...Our larger tricks, and our daily provisions and all the other things we want, we get out of that hat... And you know sir, if you'll excuse my saying it, there isn't a wholesale shop, not for Genuine Magic goods, sir. I don't know if you noticed our inscription—the Genuine Magic shop." He drew a business-card from his cheek and handed it to me. "Genuine," he said, with his finger on the word, and added, "There is absolutely no deception, sir."

He seemed to be carrying out the joke pretty thoroughly, I thought.

He turned to Gip with a smile of remarkable affability. "You, you know, are the Right Sort of Boy."

I was surprised at his knowing that, because, in the interests of discipline, we keep it rather a secret even at home; but Gip received it in unflinching silence, keeping a steadfast eye on him.

"It's only the Right Sort of Boy gets through that doorway."

And, as if by way of illustration, there came a rattling at the door, and a squeaking little voice could be faintly heard. "Nyar! I warn a' go in there, dadda, I warn a' go in there. Ny-a-a-ah!" And then the accents of a down-trodden parent, urging consolations and propitiations. "It's locked, Edward," he said.

"But it isn't," said I.

"It is, sir," said the shopman, "always—for that sort of child," and as he spoke we had a glimpse of the other youngster, a little, white face, pallid from sweet-eating and over-sapid food, and distorted by evil passions, a ruthless little egotist, pawing at the enchanted pane. "It's no good sir," said the shopman, as I moved, with my natural helpfulness, doorward, and presently the spoilt child was carried off howling.

"How do you manage that?" I said, breathing a little more freely.

"Magic!" said the shopman, with a careless wave of the hand, and behold! Sparks of coloured fire flew out of his fingers and vanished into the shadows of the shop.

"You were saying," he said, addressing himself to Gip, "before you came in, that you would like one of our 'Buy One and Astonish your Friends' boxes?"

Gip, after a gallant effort, said "Yes."

"It's in your pocket."

And leaning over the counter—he really had an extraordinarily long body—this amazing person produced the article in the customary conjurer's manner. "Paper," he said, and took a sheet out of the empty hat with the springs; "string," and behold his mouth was a string-box, from which he drew an unending thread, which when he had tied his parcel he bit off—and, it seemed to me, swallowed the ball of string. And then he lit a candle at the nose of one of the ventriloquist's dummies, stuck one of his fingers (which had become sealing-wax red) into the flame, and so sealed the parcel. "Then there was the Disappearing Egg," he remarked, and produced one from within my coat-breast and packed it, and also The Crying Baby, Very Human. I handed each parcel to Gip as it was ready, and he clasped them to his chest.

He said very little, but his eyes were eloquent; the clutch of his arms was eloquent. He was the play-ground of unspeakable emotions. These you know, were real magics. Then, with a start,

I discovered something moving about in my hat—something soft and jumpy. I whipped it off, and a ruffled pigeon—no doubt a confederate—dropped out and ran on the counter, and went, I fancy, into a cardboard box behind the papier-mâché tiger.

"Tut, tut!" said the shopman, dexterously relieving me of my headdress; "careless bird, and—as I live—nesting!"

He shook my hat, and shook out into his extended hand two or three eggs, a large marble, a watch, about half-a-dozen of the inevitable glass balls, and then crumpled, crinkled paper, more and more and more, talking all the time of the way in which people neglect to brush their hats inside as well as out, politely of course, but with a certain personal application. "All sorts of things accumulate, sir...Not you, of course, in particular...Nearly every customer... Astonishing what they carry about with them..." The crumpled paper rose and billowed on the counter more and more and more, until he was nearly hidden from us, until he was altogether hidden, and still his voice went on and on. "We none of us know what the fair semblance of a human being may conceal, sir. Are we all then no better than brushed exteriors, whited sepulchres—"

His voice stopped—exactly like when you hit a neighbour's gramophone with a well-aimed brick, the same instant silence, and the rustle of the paper stopped, and everything was still...

"Have you done with my hat?" I said, after an interval.

There was no answer.

I stared at Gip, and Gip stared at me, and there were our distortions in the magic mirrors, looking very rum, and grave, and quiet...

"I think we'll go now," I said. "Will you tell me how much all this comes to...?

"I say," I said, on a rather louder note, "I want the bill; and my hat, please."

It might have been a sniff from behind the paper pile...

"Let's look behind the counter, Gip," I said. "He's making fun of us."

I led Gip round the head-wagging tiger, and what do you think there was behind the counter? No one at all! Only my hat on the floor, and a common conjurer's lop-eared white rabbit lost in meditation, and looking as stupid and crumpled as only a conjurer's rabbit can do. I resumed my hat, and the rabbit lolloped a lollop or so out of my way.

"Dadda!" said Gip, in a guilty whisper.

"What is it, Gip?" said I.

"I do like this shop, dadda."

"So should I," I said to myself, "if the counter wouldn't suddenly extend itself to shut one off from the door." But I didn't call Gip's attention to that. "Pussy!" he said, with a hand out to the rabbit as it came lolloping past us; "Pussy, do Gip a magic!" And his eyes followed it as it squeezed through a door I had certainly not remarked a moment before. Then this door opened wider, and the man with one ear larger than the other appeared again. He was smiling still, but his eye met mine with something between amusement and defiance. "You'd like to see our show-room, sir," he said, with an innocent suavity. Gip tugged my finger forward. I glanced at the counter and met the shopman's eye again. I was beginning to think the magic just a little too genuine. "We haven't very much time," I said. But somehow we were inside the show-room before I could finish that.

"All goods of the same quality," said the shopman, rubbing his flexible hands together, "and that is the Best. Nothing in the place that isn't genuine Magic, and warranted thoroughly rum. Excuse me, sir!"

I felt him pull at something that clung to my coat-sleeve, and then I saw he held a little, wriggling red demon by the tail—the little creature bit and fought and tried to get at his hand—and in a moment he tossed it carelessly behind a counter. No doubt the thing was only an image of twisted indiarubber, but for the moment—! And his gesture was exactly that of a man who handles some petty biting bit of vermin. I glanced at Gip, but Gip was looking at a magic rocking-horse. I was glad he hadn't seen the thing. "I say," I said, in an undertone, and indicating Gip and the red demon with my eyes, "you haven't many things like that about, have you?"

"None of ours! Probably brought it with you," said the shopman—also in an undertone, and with a more dazzling smile than ever. "Astonishing what people will carry about with them unawares!" And then to Gip, "Do you see anything you fancy here?"

There were many things that Gip fancied there.

He turned to this astonishing tradesman with mingled confidence and respect. "Is that a Magic Sword?" he said.

"A Magic Toy Sword. It neither bends, breaks, nor cuts the fingers. It renders the bearer invincible in battle against any one under eighteen. Half-a-crown to seven and sixpence, according to size. These panoplies on cards are for juvenile knights-errant and very useful—shield of safety, sandals of swiftness, helmet of invisibility."

"Oh, daddy!" gasped Gip.

I tried to find out what they cost, but the shopman did not heed me. He had got Gip now; he had got him away from my finger; he had embarked upon the exposition of all his confounded stock, and nothing was going to stop him. Presently I saw with a qualm of distrust and something very like jealousy that Gip had hold of this person's finger, as usually he has hold of mine. No doubt the fellow was interesting, I thought, and had an interestingly faked lot of stuff, really good faked stuff, still—

I wandered after them, saying very little, but keeping an eye on this prestidigital fellow. After all, Gip was enjoying it. And no doubt when the time came to go we should be able to go quite easily.

It was a long, rambling place, that show-room, a gallery broken up by stands and stalls and pillars, with archways leading off to other departments, in which the queerest-looking assistants loafed and stared at one, and with perplexing mirrors and curtains. So perplexing, indeed, were these that I was presently unable to make out the door by which we had come.

The shopman showed Gip magic trains that ran without steam or clockwork, just as you set the signals, and then some very, very valuable boxes of soldiers that all came alive directly you took off the lid and said—I myself haven't a very quick ear and it was a tongue-twisting sound, but Gip—he has his mother's ear—got it in no time. "Bravo!" said the shopman, putting the men back into the box unceremoniously and handing it to Gip. "Now," said the shopman, and in a moment Gip had made them all alive again.

"You'll take that box?" asked the shopman.

"We'll take that box," said I, "unless you charge its full value. In which case it would need a Trust Magnate—"

"Dear heart! No!" And the shopman swept the little men back again, shut the lid, waved the box in the air, and there it was, in brown paper, tied up and—with Gip's full name and address on the paper!

The shopman laughed at my amazement.

"This is the genuine magic," he said. "The real thing."

"It's a little too genuine for my taste," I said again.

After that he fell to showing Gip tricks, odd tricks, and still odder the way they were done. He explained them, he turned them inside out, and there was the dear little chap nodding his busy bit of a head in the sagest manner.

I did not attend as well as I might. "Hey, presto!" Said the Magic Shopman, and then would come the clear, small "Hey, presto!" Of the boy. But I was distracted by other things. It was being borne in upon me just how tremendously rum this place was; it was, so to speak, inundated by a sense of rumness. There was something a little rum about the fixtures even, about the ceiling, about the floor, about the casually distributed chairs. I had a queer feeling that whenever I wasn't looking at them straight they went askew, and moved about, and played a noiseless puss-in-the-corner behind my back. And the cornice had a serpentine design with masks—masks altogether too expressive for proper plaster.

Then abruptly my attention was caught by one of the odd-looking assistants. He was some way off and evidently unaware of my presence—I saw a sort of three-quarter length of him over a pile of toys and through an arch—and you know, he was leaning against a pillar in an idle sort of way doing the most horrid things with his features! The particular horrid thing he did was with his nose. He did it just as though he was idle and wanted to amuse himself. First of all it was a short, blobby nose, and then suddenly he shot it out like a telescope, and then out it flew and became thinner and thinner until it was like a long, red, flexible whip. Like a thing in a nightmare it was! He flourished it about and flung it forth as a fly-fisher flings his line.

My instant thought was that Gip mustn't see him. I turned about, and there was Gip quite preoccupied with the shopman, and thinking no evil. They were whispering together and looking at me. Gip was standing on a little stool, and the shopman was holding a sort of big drum in his hand.

"Hide and seek, dadda!" cried Gip. "You're He!"

And before I could do anything to prevent it, the shopman had clapped the big drum over him. I saw what was up directly. "Take that off," I cried, "this instant! You'll frighten the boy. Take it off!"

The shopman with the unequal ears did so without a word, and held the big cylinder towards me to show its emptiness. And the little stool was vacant! In that instant my boy had utterly disappeared...?

You know, perhaps, that sinister something that comes like a hand out of the unseen and grips your heart about. You know it takes your common self away and leaves you tense and deliberate, neither slow nor hasty, neither angry nor afraid. So it was with me.

I came up to this grinning shopman and kicked his stool aside.

"Stop this folly!" I said. "Where is my boy?"

"You see," he said, still displaying the drum's interior, "there is no deception—"

I put out my hand to grip him, and he eluded me by a dexterous movement. I snatched again, and he turned from me and pushed open a door to escape. "Stop!" I said, and he laughed, receding. I leapt after him—into utter darkness.

Thud!

"Lor' bless my 'eart! I didn't see you coming, sir!"

I was in Regent Street, and I had collided with a decent-looking working man; and a yard away, perhaps, and looking a little perplexed with himself, was Gip. There was some sort of apology, and then Gip had turned and come to me with a bright little smile, as though for a moment he had missed me.

And he was carrying four parcels in his arm!

He secured immediate possession of my finger.

For the second I was rather at a loss. I stared round to see the door of the magic shop, and behold, it was not there! There was no door, no shop, nothing, only the common pilaster between the shop where they sell pictures and the window with the chicks...!

I did the only thing possible in that mental tumult; I walked straight to the kerbstone and held up my umbrella for a cab.

"'Ansoms," said Gip, in a note of culminating exultation.

I helped him in, recalled my address with an effort, and got in also. Something unusual proclaimed itself in my tail-coat pocket, and I felt and discovered a glass ball. With a petulant expression I flung it into the street.

Gip said nothing.

For a space neither of us spoke.

"Dada!" said Gip, at last. "That was a proper shop!"

I came round with that to the problem of just how the whole thing had seemed to him. He looked completely undamaged—so far, good; he was neither scared nor unhinged, he was simply tremendously satisfied with the afternoon's entertainment, and there in his arms were the four parcels.

Confound it! What could be in them?

"Um!" I said. "Little boys can't go to shops like that every day."

He received this with his usual stoicism, and for a moment I was sorry I was his father and not his mother, and so couldn't suddenly there, coram publico, in our hansom, kiss him. After all, I thought, the thing wasn't so very bad.

But it was only when we opened the parcels that I really began to be reassured. Three of them contained boxes of soldiers, quite ordinary lead soldiers, but of so good a quality as to make Gip altogether forget that originally these parcels had been Magic Tricks of the only genuine sort, and the fourth contained a kitten, a little living white kitten, in excellent health and appetite and temper.

I saw this unpacking with a sort of provisional relief. I hung about in the nursery for quite an unconscionable time...

That happened six months ago. And now I am beginning to believe it is all right. The kitten had only the magic natural to all kittens, and the soldiers seem as steady a company as any colonel could desire. And Gip—?

The intelligent parent will understand that I have to go cautiously with Gip.

But I went so far as this one day. I said, "How would you like your soldiers to come alive, Gip, and march about by themselves?"

"Mine do," said Gip. "I just have to say a word I know before I open the lid."

"Then they march about alone?"

"Oh, quite, dadda. I shouldn't like them if they didn't do that."

I displayed no unbecoming surprise, and since then I have taken occasion to drop in upon him once or twice, unannounced, when the soldiers were about, but so far I have never discovered them performing in anything like a magical manner.

It's so difficult to tell.

There's also a question of finance. I have an incurable habit of paying bills. I have been up and down Regent Street several times, looking for that shop. I am inclined to think, indeed that in that matter honour is satisfied, and that since Gip's name and address are known to them, I may very well leave it to these people, whoever they may be, to send in their bill in their own time.

42

THE TRUTH ABOUT PYECRAFT

He sits not a dozen yards away. If I glance over my shoulder I can see him. And if I catch his eye—and usually I catch his eye—it meets me with an expression—

It is mainly an imploring look—and yet with suspicion in it.

Confound his suspicion! If I wanted to tell on him I should have told long ago. I don't tell and I don't tell, and he ought to feel at his ease. As if anything so gross and fat as he, could feel at ease! Who would believe me if I did tell?

Poor old Pyecraft! Great, uneasy jelly of substance! The fattest clubman in London.

He sits at one of the little club tables in the huge bay by the fire, stuffing. What is he stuffing? I glance judiciously and catch him biting at a round of hot buttered teacake, with his eyes on me. Confound him—! With his eyes on me!

That settles it, Pyecraft! Since you will be abject, since you will behave as though I was not a man of honour, here right under your embedded eyes, I write the thing down—the plain truth about Pyecraft. The man I helped, the man I shielded, and who has requited me by making my club unendurable, absolutely unendurable, with his liquid appeal, with the perpetual "don't tell" of his looks.

And, besides, why does he keep on eternally eating?

Well, here goes for the truth, the whole truth, and nothing but the truth!

Pyecraft—I made the acquaintance of Pyecraft in this very smoking-room. I was a young, nervous new member, and he saw it. I was sitting all alone, wishing I knew more of the members, and suddenly he came, a great rolling front of chins and abdomina, towards me and grunted and sat down in a chair close by me and wheezed for a space, and scraped for a space with a match and lit a cigar, and then addressed me. I forget what he said—something about the matches not lighting properly, and afterwards as he talked he kept stopping the waiters one by one as they went by, and telling them about the matches in that thin, fluty voice he has. But, anyhow, it was in some such way we began our talking.

He talked about various things and came round to games. And thence to my figure and complexion. "You ought to be a good cricketer," he said. I suppose I am slender, slender to what some people would call lean, and I suppose I am rather dark, still—I am not ashamed of having a Hindu great-grandmother, but for all that, I don't want casual strangers to see through me at a glance to her. So that I was set against Pyecraft from the beginning.

But he only talked about me in order to get to himself.

"I expect," he said, "you take no more exercise than I do, and probably you eat no less." (Like all excessively obese people he fancied he ate nothing.) "Yet—," and he smiled an oblique smile—"we differ."

And then he began to talk about his fatness and his fatness; all he did for his fatness and all he was going to do for his fatness; what people had advised him to do for his fatness and what he had heard of people doing for fatness similar to his. "A priori," he said, "one would think a question of nutrition could be answered by dietary and a question of assimilation by drugs." It was stifling. It was dumpling talk. It made me feel swelled to hear him.

One stands that sort of thing once in a way at a club, but a time came when I fancied I was standing too much. He took to me altogether too conspicuously. I could never go into the smoking-room or he would come wallowing towards me, and sometimes he came and gormandised round and about me while I had my lunch. He seemed at times almost to be clinging to me. He was a bore, but not so fearful a bore as to be limited to me; and from the first there was something in his manner—almost as though he knew, almost as though he penetrated to the fact that I might—that there was a remote, exceptional chance in me that no one else presented.

"I'd give anything to get it down," he would say—"anything," and peer at me over his vast cheeks and pant.

Poor old Pyecraft! He has just gonged, no doubt to order another buttered teacake!

He came to the actual thing one day. "Our Pharmacopoeia," he said, "our Western Pharmacopoeia, is anything but the last word of medical science. In the East, I've been told—"

He stopped and stared at me. It was like being at an aquarium.

I was quite suddenly angry with him. "Look here," I said, "who told you about my great-grandmother's recipes?"

"Well," he fenced.

"Every time we've met for a week," I said—"and we've met pretty often—you've given me a broad hint or so about that little secret of mine."

"Well," he said, "now the cat's out of the bag, I'll admit, yes, it is so. I had it—"

"From Pattison?"

"Indirectly," he said, which I believe was lying, "yes."

"Pattison," I said, "took that stuff at his own risk."

He pursed his mouth and bowed.

"My great-grandmother's recipes," I said, "are queer things to handle. My father was near making me promise—"

"He didn't?"

"No. But he warned me. He himself used one—once."

"Ah...! But do you think—? Suppose—suppose there did happen to be one—"

"The things are curious documents," I said.

"Even the smell of 'em...No!"

But after going so far Pyecraft was resolved I should go farther. I was always a little afraid if I tried his patience too much he would fall on me suddenly and smother me. I own I was weak. But I was also annoyed with Pyecraft. I had got to that state of feeling for him that disposed me to say, "Well, take the risk!" The little affair of Pattison to which I have alluded was a different matter altogether. What it was doesn't concern us now, but I knew anyhow, that the particular recipe I used then was safe. The rest I didn't know so much about, and on the whole, I was inclined to doubt their safety pretty completely.

Yet even if Pyecraft got poisoned—

I must confess the poisoning of Pyecraft struck me as an immense undertaking.

That evening I took that queer, odd-scented sandal-wood box out of my safe and turned the rustling skins over. The gentleman who wrote the recipes for my great-grandmother evidently had a weakness for skins of a miscellaneous origin, and his handwriting was cramped to the last degree. Some of the things are quite unreadable to me—though my family, with its Indian Civil Service associations, has kept up a knowledge of Hindustani from generation to generation—and none are absolutely plain sailing. But I found the one that I knew was there, soon enough, and sat on the floor by my safe for some time looking at it.

"Look here," said I to Pyecraft next day, and snatched the slip away from his eager grasp.

"So far as I can make it out, this is a recipe for Loss of Weight. ("Ah!" said Pyecraft.) I'm not absolutely sure, but I think it's that. And if you take my advice you'll leave it alone. Because, you know—I blacken my blood in your interest, Pyecraft—my ancestors on that side were, so far as I can gather, a jolly queer lot. See?"

"Let me try it," said Pyecraft.

I leant back in my chair. My imagination made one mighty effort and fell flat within me. "What in Heaven's name, Pyecraft," I asked, "do you think you'll look like when you get thin?"

He was impervious to reason. I made him promise never to say a word to me about his disgusting fatness again whatever happened—never, and then I handed him that little piece of skin.

"It's nasty stuff," I said.

"No matter," he said, and took it.

He goggled at it. "But—but—" he said.

He had just discovered that it wasn't English.

"To the best of my ability," I said, "I will do you a translation."

I did my best. After that we didn't speak for a fortnight. Whenever he approached me I frowned and motioned him away, and he respected our compact, but at the end of a fortnight he was as fat as ever. And then he got a word in.

"I must speak," he said. "It isn't fair. There's something wrong. It's done me no good. You're not doing your great-grandmother justice."

"Where's the recipe?"

He produced it gingerly from his pocket-book.

I ran my eye over the items. "Was the egg addled?" I asked.

"No, ought it to have been?"

"That," I said, "goes without saying in all my poor dear great-grandmother's recipes. When condition or quality is not specified you must get the worst. She was drastic or nothing...And there's one or two possible alternatives to some of these other things. You got fresh rattlesnake venom."

"I got a rattlesnake from Jamrach's. It cost—it cost—"

"That's your affair, anyhow. This last item—"

"I know a man who—"

"Yes. H'm. Well, I'll write the alternatives down. So far as I know the language, the spelling of this recipe is particularly atrocious. By-the-bye, dog here probably means pariah dog."

For a month after that I saw Pyecraft constantly at the club and as fat and anxious as ever. He kept our treaty, but at times he broke the spirit of it by shaking his head despondently. Then one day in the cloak-room he said, "Your great-grandmother—"

"Not a word against her," I said; and he held his peace.

I could have fancied he had desisted, and I saw him one day talking to three new members about his fatness as though he was in search of other recipes. And then, quite unexpectedly, his telegram came.

"Mr. Formalyn!" bawled a page-boy under my nose, and I took the telegram and opened it at once.

"For Heaven's sake come—Pyecraft."

"H'm," said I, and to tell the truth I was so pleased at the rehabilitation of my great-grandmother's reputation this evidently promised that I made a most excellent lunch.

I got Pyecraft's address from the hall porter. Pyecraft inhabited the upper half of a house in Bloomsbury, and I went there so soon as I had done my coffee and Trappistine. I did not wait to finish my cigar.

"Mr. Pyecraft?" said I, at the front door.

They believed he was ill; he hadn't been out for two days.

"He expects me," said I, and they sent me up.

I rang the bell at the lattice-door upon the landing.

"He shouldn't have tried it, anyhow," I said to myself. "A man who eats like a pig ought to look like a pig."

An obviously worthy woman, with an anxious face and a carelessly placed cap, came and surveyed me through the lattice.

I gave my name and she let me in a dubious fashion.

"Well?" said I, as we stood together inside Pyecraft's piece of the landing.

"'E said you was to come in if you came," she said, and regarded me, making no motion to show me anywhere. And then, confidentially, "'E's locked in, sir."

"Locked in?"

"Locked himself in yesterday morning and 'asn't let any one in since, sir. And ever and again swearing. Oh, my!"

I stared at the door she indicated by her glances.

"In there?" I said.

"Yes, sir."

"What's up?"

She shook her head sadly, "'E keeps on calling for vittles, sir. 'Eavy vittles 'e wants. I get 'im what I can. Pork 'e's 'ad, sooit puddin', sossiges, noo bread. Everythink like that. Left outside, if you please, and me go away. 'E's eatin', sir, somethink Awful."

There came a piping bawl from inside the door: "That Formalyn?"

"That you, Pyecraft?" I shouted, and went and banged the door.

"Tell her to go away."

I did.

Then I could hear a curious pattering upon the door, almost like someone feeling for the handle in the dark, and Pyecraft's familiar grunts.

"It's all right," I said, "she's gone."

But for a long time the door didn't open.

I heard the key turn. Then Pyecraft's voice said, "Come in."

I turned the handle and opened the door. Naturally I expected to see Pyecraft.

Well, you know, he wasn't there!

I never had such a shock in my life. There was his sitting-room in a state of untidy disorder, plates and dishes among the books and writing things, and several chairs overturned, but Pyecraft—

"It's all right, o' man; shut the door," he said, and then I discovered him.

There he was right up close to the cornice in the corner by the door, as though some one had glued him to the ceiling. His face was anxious and angry. He panted and gesticulated. "Shut the door," he said. "If that woman gets hold of it—"

I shut the door, and went and stood away from him and stared.

"If anything gives way and you tumble down," I said, "you'll break your neck, Pyecraft."

"I wish I could," he wheezed.

"A man of your age and weight getting up to kiddish gymnastics—"

"Don't," he said, and looked agonized. "Your damned great-grandmother—"

"No!" I cried.

"Be careful," I warned him.

"I'll tell you," he said, and gesticulated.

"How the deuce," said I, "are you holding on up there?"

And then abruptly I realized that he was not holding on at all, that he was floating up there—just as a gas-filled bladder might have floated in the same position. He began a struggle to thrust himself away from the ceiling and to clamber down the wall to me. "It's that prescription," he panted, as he did so. "Your great-gran—"

He took hold of a framed engraving rather carelessly as he spoke and it gave way, and he flew back to the ceiling again, while the picture smashed onto the sofa. Bump he went against the ceiling, and I knew then why he was all over white on the more salient curves and angles of his person. He tried again more carefully, coming down by way of the mantel.

It was really a most extraordinary spectacle, that great, fat, apoplectic-looking man upside down and trying to get from the ceiling to the floor. "That prescription," he said. "Too successful."

"How?"

"Loss of weight—almost complete."

And then, of course, I understood.

"By Jove, Pyecraft," said I, "what you wanted was a cure for fatness! But you always called it weight. You would call it weight."

Somehow I was extremely delighted. I quite liked Pyecraft for the time. "Let me help you!" I said, and took his hand and pulled him down. He kicked about, trying to get a foothold somewhere. It was very like holding a flag on a windy day.

"That table," he said, pointing, "is solid mahogany and very heavy. If you can put me under that—"

I did, and there he wallowed about like a captive balloon, while I stood on his hearthrug and talked to him.

I lit a cigar. "Tell me," I said, "what happened?"

"I took it," he said.

"How did it taste?"

"Oh, beastly!"

I should fancy they all did. Whether one regards the ingredients or the probable compound or the possible results, almost all of my great-grandmother's remedies appear to me at least to be extraordinarily uninviting. For my own part—

"I took a little sip first."

"Yes?"

"And as I felt lighter and better after an hour, I decided to take the draught."

"My dear Pyecraft!"

"I held my nose," he explained. "And then I kept on getting lighter and lighter—and helpless, you know."

He gave way to a sudden burst of passion. "What the goodness am I to do?" he said.

"There's one thing pretty evident," I said, "that you mustn't do. If you go out of doors, you'll go up and up." I waved an arm upward. "They'd have to send Santos-Dumont after you to bring you down again."

"I suppose it will wear off?"

I shook my head. "I don't think you can count on that," I said.

And then there was another burst of passion, and he kicked out at adjacent chairs and banged the floor. He behaved just as I should have expected a great, fat, self-indulgent man to behave under trying circumstances—that is to say, very badly. He spoke of me and my great-grandmother with an utter want of discretion.

"I never asked you to take the stuff," I said.

And generously disregarding the insults he was putting upon me, I sat down in his armchair and began to talk to him in a sober, friendly fashion.

I pointed out to him that this was a trouble he had brought upon himself, and that it had almost an air of poetical justice. He had eaten too much. This he disputed, and for a time we argued the point.

He became noisy and violent, so I desisted from this aspect of his lesson. "And then," said I, "you committed the sin of euphuism. You called it not Fat, which is just and inglorious, but Weight. You—"

He interrupted to say he recognised all that. What was he to do?

I suggested he should adapt himself to his new conditions. So we came to the really sensible part of the business. I suggested that it would not be difficult for him to learn to walk about on the ceiling with his hands—

"I can't sleep," he said.

But that was no great difficulty. It was quite possible, I pointed out, to make a shake-up under a wire mattress, fasten the under things on with tapes, and have a blanket, sheet, and coverlet to button at the side. He would have to confide in his housekeeper, I said; and after some squabbling he agreed to that. (Afterwards it was quite delightful to see the beautifully matter-of-fact way with which the good lady took all these amazing inversions.) He could have a library ladder in his room, and all his meals could be laid on the top of his bookcase. We also hit on an ingenious device by which he could get to the floor whenever he wanted, which was simply to put the *British Encyclopaedia* (tenth edition) on the top of his open shelves. He just pulled out a couple of volumes and held on, and down he came. And we agreed there must be iron staples along the skirting, so that he could cling to those whenever he wanted to get about the room on the lower level.

As we got on with the thing I found myself almost keenly interested. It was I who called in the housekeeper and broke matters to her, and it was I chiefly who fixed up the inverted bed. In fact, I spent two whole days at his flat. I am a handy, interfering sort of man with a screw-driver, and I made all sorts of ingenious adaptations for him—ran a wire to bring his bells within reach, turned all his electric lights up instead of down, and so on. The whole affair was extremely curious and interesting to me, and it was delightful to think of Pyecraft like some great, fat blow-fly, crawling about on his ceiling and clambering round the lintels of his doors from one room to another, and never, never, never coming to the club any more...

Then, you know, my fatal ingenuity got the better of me. I was sitting by his fire drinking his whisky, and he was up in his favourite corner by the cornice, tacking a Turkey carpet to the ceiling, when the idea struck me. "By Jove, Pyecraft!" I said, "all this is totally unnecessary."

And before I could calculate the complete consequences of my notion I blurted it out. "Lead underclothing," said I, and the mischief was done.

Pyecraft received the thing almost in tears. "To be right ways up again—" he said.

I gave him the whole secret before I saw where it would take me. "Buy sheet lead," I said, "stamp it into discs. Sew 'em all over your underclothes until you have enough. Have lead-soled boots, carry a bag of solid lead, and the thing is done! Instead of being a prisoner here you may go abroad again, Pyecraft; you may travel—"

A still happier idea came to me. "You need never fear a shipwreck. All you need do is just slip off some or all of your clothes, take the necessary amount of luggage in your hand, and float up in the air—"

In his emotion he dropped the tack-hammer within an ace of my head. "By Jove!" he said, "I shall be able to come back to the club again."

The thing pulled me up short. "By Jove!" I said faintly. "Yes. Of course—you will."

He did. He does. There he sits behind me now, stuffing—as I live—! A third go of buttered tea-cake. And no one in the whole world knows—except his housekeeper and me—that he weighs practically nothing; that he is a mere boring mass of assimilatory matter, mere clouds in clothing, niente, nefas, the most inconsiderable of men. There he sits watching until I have done this writing. Then, if he can, he will waylay me. He will come billowing up to me...

He will tell me over again all about it, how it feels, how it doesn't feel, how he sometimes hopes it is passing off a little. And always somewhere in that fat, abundant discourse he will say, "The secret's keeping, eh? If any one knew of it—I should be so ashamed...Makes a fellow look such a fool, you know. Crawling about on a ceiling and all that..."

And now to elude Pyecraft, occupying, as he does, an admirable strategic position between me and the door.

43

The Valley of Spiders

Towards midday the three pursuers came abruptly round a bend in the torrent bed upon the sight of a very broad and spacious valley. The difficult and winding trench of pebbles along which they had tracked the fugitives for so long, expanded to a broad slope, and with a common impulse the three men left the trail, and rode to a little eminence set with olive-dun trees, and there halted, the two others, as became them, a little behind the man with the silver-studded bridle.

For a space they scanned the great expanse below them with eager eyes. It spread remoter and remoter, with only a few clusters of sere thorn bushes here and there, and the dim suggestions of some now waterless ravine, to break its desolation of yellow grass. Its purple distances melted at last into the bluish slopes of the further hills—hills it might be of a greener kind—and above them invisibly supported, and seeming indeed to hang in the blue, were the snow-clad summits of mountains—that grew larger and bolder to the north-westward as the sides of the valley drew together. And westward the valley opened until a distant darkness under the sky told where the forests began. But the three men looked neither east nor west, but only steadfastly across the valley.

The gaunt man with the scarred lip was the first to speak. "Nowhere," he said, with a sigh of disappointment in his voice. "But after all, they had a full day's start."

"They don't know we are after them," said the little man on the white horse.

"She would know," said the leader bitterly, as if speaking to himself.

"Even then they can't go fast. They've got no beast but the mule, and all to-day the girl's foot has been bleeding—"

The man with the silver bridle flashed a quick intensity of rage on him. "Do you think I haven't seen that?" he snarled.

"It helps, anyhow," whispered the little man to himself.

The gaunt man with the scarred lip stared impassively. "They can't be over the valley," he said. "If we ride hard—"

He glanced at the white horse and paused.

"Curse all white horses!" said the man with the silver bridle, and turned to scan the beast his curse included.

The little man looked down between the melancholy ears of his steed.

"I did my best," he said.

The two others stared again across the valley for a space. The gaunt man passed the back of his hand across the scarred lip.

"Come up!" said the man who owned the silver bridle, suddenly. The little man started and jerked his rein, and the horse hoofs of the three made a multitudinous faint pattering upon the withered grass as they turned back towards the trail...

They rode cautiously down the long slope before them, and so came through a waste of prickly, twisted bushes and strange dry shapes of horny branches that grew amongst the rocks, into the levels below. And there the trail grew faint, for the soil was scanty, and the only herbage was this scorched dead straw that lay upon the ground. Still, by hard scanning, by leaning beside the horses' necks and pausing ever and again, even these white men could contrive to follow after their prey.

There were trodden places, bent and broken blades of the coarse grass, and ever and again the sufficient intimation of a footmark. And once the leader saw a brown smear of blood where the half-caste girl may have trod. And at that under his breath he cursed her for a fool.

The gaunt man checked his leader's tracking, and the little man on the white horse rode behind, a man lost in a dream. They rode one after another, the man with the silver bridle led the way, and they spoke never a word. After a time it came to the little man on the white horse that the world was very still. He started out of his dream. Besides the little noises of their horses and equipment, the whole great valley kept the brooding quiet of a painted scene.

Before him went his master and his fellow, each intently leaning forward to the left, each impassively moving with the paces of his horse; their shadows went before them—still, noiseless, tapering attendants; and nearer a crouched cool shape was his own. He looked about him. What was it had gone? Then he remembered the reverberation from the banks of the gorge and the perpetual accompaniment of shifting, jostling pebbles. And, moreover—? There was no breeze. That was it! What a vast, still place it was, a monotonous afternoon slumber. And the sky open and blank, except for a sombre veil of haze that had gathered in the upper valley.

He straightened his back, fretted with his bridle, puckered his lips to whistle, and simply sighed. He turned in his saddle for a time, and stared at the throat of the mountain gorge out of which they had come. Blank! Blank slopes on either side, with never a sign of a decent beast or tree—much less a man. What a land it was! What a wilderness! He dropped again into his former pose.

It filled him with a momentary pleasure to see a wry stick of purple black flash out into the form of a snake, and vanish amidst the brown. After all, the infernal valley was alive. And then, to rejoice him still more, came a little breath across his face, a whisper that came and went, the faintest inclination of a stiff black-antlered bush upon a little crest, the first intimations of a possible breeze. Idly he wetted his finger, and held it up.

He pulled up sharply to avoid a collision with the gaunt man, who had stopped at fault upon the trail. Just at that guilty moment he caught his master's eye looking towards him.

For a time he forced an interest in the tracking. Then, as they rode on again, he studied his master's shadow and hat and shoulder, appearing and disappearing behind the gaunt man's nearer contours. They had ridden four days out of the very limits of the world into this desolate place, short of water, with nothing but a strip of dried meat under their saddles, over rocks and mountains, where surely none but these fugitives had ever been before—for that!

And all this was for a girl, a mere wilful child! And the man had whole cityfuls of people to do his basest bidding—girls, women! Why in the name of passionate folly this one in particular? Asked the little man, and scowled at the world, and licked his parched lips with a blackened tongue. It was the way of the master, and that was all he knew. Just because she sought to evade him...

His eye caught a whole row of high plumed canes bending in unison, and then the tails of silk that hung before his neck flapped and fell. The breeze was growing stronger. Somehow it took the stiff stillness out of things—and that was well.

"Hullo!" said the gaunt man.

All three stopped abruptly.

"What?" asked the master. "What?"

"Over there," said the gaunt man, pointing up the valley.

"What?"

"Something coming towards us."

And as he spoke a yellow animal crested a rise and came bearing down upon them. It was a big wild dog, coming before the wind, tongue out, at a steady pace, and running with such an intensity of purpose that he did not seem to see the horsemen he approached. He ran with his nose up, following, it was plain, neither scent nor quarry. As he drew nearer the little man felt for his sword. "He's mad," said the gaunt rider.

"Shout!" said the little man, and shouted.

The dog came on. Then when the little man's blade was already out, it swerved aside and went panting by them and past. The eyes of the little man followed its flight. "There was no foam," he said. For a space the man with the silver-studded bridle stared up the valley. "Oh, come on!" he cried at last. "What does it matter?" And jerked his horse into movement again.

The little man left the insoluble mystery of a dog that fled from nothing but the wind, and lapsed into profound musings on human character. "Come on!" he whispered to himself. "Why should it be given to one man to say 'Come on!' with that stupendous violence of effect. Always, all his life, the man with the silver bridle has been saying that. If I said it—!" Thought the little man. But people marvelled when the master was disobeyed even in the wildest things. This half-caste girl seemed to him, seemed to every one, mad—blasphemous almost. The little man, by way of comparison, reflected on the gaunt rider with the scarred lip, as stalwart as his master, as brave and, indeed perhaps braver, and yet for him there was obedience, nothing but to give obedience duly and stoutly...

Certain sensations of the hands and knees called the little man back to more immediate things. He became aware of something. He rode up beside his gaunt fellow. "Do you notice the horses?" he said in an undertone.

The gaunt face looked interrogation.

"They don't like this wind," said the little man, and dropped behind as the man with the silver bridle turned upon him.

"It's all right," said the gaunt-faced man.

They rode on again for a space in silence. The foremost two rode downcast upon the trail, the hindmost man watched the haze that crept down the vastness of the valley, nearer and nearer, and noted how the wind grew in strength moment by moment. Far away on the left he saw a line of dark bulks—wild hog perhaps, galloping down the valley, but of that he said nothing, nor did he remark again upon the uneasiness of the horses.

And then he saw first one and then a second great white ball, a great shining white ball like a gigantic head of thistledown, that drove before the wind athwart the path. These balls soared high in the air, and dropped and rose again and caught for a moment, and hurried on and passed, but at the sight of them the restlessness of the horses increased.

Then presently he saw that more of these drifting globes—and then soon very many more—were hurrying towards him down the valley.

They became aware of a squealing. Athwart the path a huge boar rushed, turning his head but for one instant to glance at them, and then hurling on down the valley again. And at that, all three stopped and sat in their saddles, staring into the thickening haze that was coming upon them.

"If it were not for this thistledown—" began the leader.

But now a big globe came drifting past within a score of yards of them. It was really not an even sphere at all, but a vast, soft, ragged, filmy thing, a sheet gathered by the corners, an aerial jelly-fish, as it were, but rolling over and over as it advanced, and trailing long, cobwebby threads and streamers that floated in its wake.

"It isn't thistledown," said the little man.

"I don't like the stuff," said the gaunt man.

And they looked at one another.

"Curse it!" cried the leader. "The air's full of it up there. If it keeps on at this pace long, it will stop us altogether."

An instinctive feeling, such as lines out a herd of deer at the approach of some ambiguous thing, prompted them to turn their horses to the wind, ride forward for a few paces, and stare at that advancing multitude of floating masses. They came on before the wind with a sort of smooth swiftness, rising and falling noiselessly, sinking to earth, rebounding high, soaring—all with a perfect unanimity, with a still, deliberate assurance.

Right and left of the horsemen the pioneers of this strange army passed. At one that rolled along the ground, breaking shapelessly and trailing out reluctantly into long grappling ribbons and bands, all three horses began to shy and dance. The master was seized with a sudden unreasonable impatience. He cursed the drifting globes roundly. "Get on!" he cried; "Get on! What do these things matter? How can they matter? Back to the trail!" He fell swearing at his horse and sawed the bit across its mouth.

He shouted aloud with rage. "I will follow that trail, I tell you!" he cried. "Where is the trail?"

He gripped the bridle of his prancing horse and searched amidst the grass. A long and clinging thread fell across his face, a grey streamer dropped about his bridle arm, some big, active thing with many legs ran down the back of his head. He looked up to discover one of those grey masses anchored as it were above him by these things and flapping out ends as a sail flaps when a boat comes, about—but noiselessly.

He had an impression of many eyes, of a dense crew of squat bodies, of long, many-jointed limbs hauling at their mooring ropes to bring the thing down upon him. For a space he stared up, reining in his prancing horse with the instinct born of years of horsemanship. Then the flat of a sword smote his back, and a blade flashed overhead and cut the drifting balloon of spider-web free, and the whole mass lifted softly and drove clear and away.

"Spiders!" cried the voice of the gaunt man. "The things are full of big spiders! Look, my lord!"

The man with the silver bridle still followed the mass that drove away.

"Look, my lord!"

The master found himself staring down at a red, smashed thing on the ground that, in spite of partial obliteration, could still wriggle unavailing legs. Then when the gaunt man pointed to another mass that bore down upon them, he drew his sword hastily. Up the valley now it was like a fog bank torn to rags. He tried to grasp the situation.

"Ride for it!" the little man was shouting. "Ride for it down the valley."

What happened then was like the confusion of a battle. The man with the silver bridle saw the little man go past him slashing furiously at imaginary cobwebs, saw him cannon into the horse of the gaunt man and hurl it and its rider to earth. His own horse went a dozen paces before he could rein it in. Then he looked up to avoid imaginary dangers, and then back again to see a horse rolling on the ground, the gaunt man standing and slashing over it at a rent and fluttering mass of grey that streamed and wrapped about them both. And thick and fast as thistledown on waste land on a windy day in July, the cobweb masses were coming on.

The little man had dismounted, but he dared not release his horse. He was endeavouring to lug the struggling brute back with the strength of one arm, while with the other he slashed aimlessly, The tentacles of a second grey mass had entangled themselves with the struggle, and this second grey mass came to its moorings, and slowly sank.

The master set his teeth, gripped his bridle, lowered his head, and spurred his horse forward. The horse on the ground rolled over, there were blood and moving shapes upon the flanks, and the gaunt man, suddenly leaving it, ran forward towards his master, perhaps ten paces. His legs were swathed and encumbered with grey; he made ineffectual movements with his sword. Grey streamers waved from him; there was a thin veil of grey across his face. With his left hand he beat at something on his body, and suddenly he stumbled and fell. He struggled to rise, and fell again, and suddenly, horribly, began to howl, "Oh—ohoo, ohooh!"

The master could see the great spiders upon him, and others upon the ground.

As he strove to force his horse nearer to this gesticulating, screaming grey object that struggled up and down, there came a clatter of hoofs, and the little man, in act of mounting, swordless, balanced on his belly athwart the white horse, and clutching its mane, whirled past. And again a clinging thread of grey gossamer swept across the master's face. All about him, and over him, it seemed this drifting, noiseless cobweb circled and drew nearer him...

To the day of his death he never knew just how the event of that moment happened. Did he, indeed, turn his horse, or did it really of its own accord stampede after its fellow? Suffice it that in another second he was galloping full tilt down the valley with his sword whirling furiously overhead. And all about him on the quickening breeze, the spiders' air-ships, their air bundles and air sheets, seemed to him to hurry in a conscious pursuit.

Clatter, clatter, thud, thud—the man with the silver bridle rode, heedless of his direction, with his fearful face looking up now right, now left, and his sword arm ready to slash. And a few hundred yards ahead of him, with a tail of torn cobweb trailing behind him, rode the little man on the white horse, still but imperfectly in the saddle. The reeds bent before them, the wind blew fresh and strong, over his shoulder the master could see the webs hurrying to overtake...

He was so intent to escape the spiders' webs that only as his horse gathered together for a leap did he realise the ravine ahead. And then he realised it only to misunderstand and interfere. He was leaning forward on his horse's neck and sat up and back all too late.

But if in his excitement he had failed to leap, at any rate he had not forgotten how to fall. He was horseman again in mid-air. He came off clear with a mere bruise upon his shoulder, and his horse rolled, kicking spasmodic legs, and lay still. But the master's sword drove its point into the hard soil, and snapped clean across, as though Chance refused him any longer as her Knight, and the splintered end missed his face by an inch or so.

He was on his feet in a moment, breathlessly scanning the onrushing spider-webs. For a moment he was minded to run, and then thought of the ravine, and turned back. He ran aside once to dodge one drifting terror, and then he was swiftly clambering down the precipitous sides, and out of the touch of the gale.

There under the lee of the dry torrent's steeper banks he might crouch, and watch these strange, grey masses pass and pass in safety till the wind fell, and it became possible to escape. And there for a long time he crouched, watching the strange, grey, ragged masses trail their streamers across his narrowed sky.

Once a stray spider fell into the ravine close beside him—a full foot it measured from leg to leg, and its body was half a man's hand—and after he had watched its monstrous alacrity of search and escape for a little while, and tempted it to bite his broken sword, he lifted up his iron heeled boot and smashed it into a pulp. He swore as he did so, and for a time sought up and down for another.

Then presently, when he was surer these spider swarms could not drop into the ravine, he found a place where he could sit down, and sat and fell into deep thought and began after his manner to gnaw his knuckles and bite his nails. And from this he was moved by the coming of the man with the white horse.

He heard him long before he saw him, as a clattering of hoofs, stumbling footsteps, and a reassuring voice. Then the little man appeared, a rueful figure, still with a tail of white cobweb trailing behind him. They approached each other without speaking, without a salutation. The little man was fatigued and shamed to the pitch of hopeless bitterness, and came to a stop at last, face to face with his seated master. The latter winced a little under his dependant's eye. "Well?" he said at last, with no pretence of authority.

"You left him?"

"My horse bolted."

"I know. So did mine."

He laughed at his master mirthlessly.

"I say my horse bolted," said the man who once had a silver-studded bridle.

"Cowards both," said the little man.

The other gnawed his knuckle through some meditative moments, with his eye on his inferior.

"Don't call me a coward," he said at length.

"You are a coward like myself."

"A coward possibly. There is a limit beyond which every man must fear. That I have learnt at last. But not like yourself. That is where the difference comes in."

"I never could have dreamt you would have left him. He saved your life two minutes before...Why are you our lord?"

The master gnawed his knuckles again, and his countenance was dark.

"No man calls me a coward," he said. "No. A broken sword is better than none...One spavined white horse cannot be expected to carry two men a four days' journey. I hate white horses, but this time it cannot be helped. You begin to understand me...? I perceive that you are minded, on the strength of what you have seen and fancy, to taint my reputation. It is men of your sort who unmake kings. Besides which—I never liked you."

"My lord!" said the little man.

"No," said the master. "No!"

He stood up sharply as the little man moved. For a minute perhaps they faced one another. Overhead the spiders' balls went driving. There was a quick movement among the pebbles; a running of feet, a cry of despair, a gasp and a blow...

Towards nightfall the wind fell. The sun set in a calm serenity, and the man who had once possessed the silver bridle came at last very cautiously and by an easy slope out of the ravine again; but now he led the white horse that once belonged to the little man. He would have gone back to his horse to get his silver-mounted bridle again, but he feared night and a quickening breeze might still find him in the valley, and besides he disliked greatly to think he might discover his horse all swathed in cobwebs and perhaps unpleasantly eaten.

And as he thought of those cobwebs and of all the dangers he had been through, and the manner in which he had been preserved that day, his hand sought a little reliquary that hung about his neck, and he clasped it for a moment with heartfelt gratitude. As he did so his eyes went across the valley.

"I was hot with passion," he said, "and now she has met her reward. They also, no doubt—"

And behold! Far away out of the wooded slopes across the valley, but in the clearness of the sunset distinct and unmistakable, he saw a little spire of smoke.

At that his expression of serene resignation changed to an amazed anger. Smoke? He turned the head of the white horse about, and hesitated. And as he did so a little rustle of air went through the grass about him. Far away upon some reeds swayed a tattered sheet of grey. He looked at the cobwebs; he looked at the smoke.

"Perhaps, after all, it is not them," he said at last.

But he knew better.

After he had stared at the smoke for some time, he mounted the white horse.

As he rode, he picked his way amidst stranded masses of web. For some reason there were many dead spiders on the ground, and those that lived feasted guiltily on their fellows. At the sound of his horse's hoofs they fled.

Their time had passed. From the ground without either a wind to carry them or a winding sheet ready, these things, for all their poison, could do him little evil. He flicked with his belt at those he fancied came too near. Once, where a number ran together over a bare place, he was minded to dismount and trample them with his boots, but this impulse he overcame. Ever and again he turned in his saddle, and looked back at the smoke.

"Spiders," he muttered over and over again. "Spiders! Well, well... The next time I must spin a web."

44

The Country of the Blind

Three hundred miles and more from Chimborazo, one hundred from the snows of Cotopaxi, in the wildest wastes of Ecuador's Andes, there lies that mysterious mountain valley, cut off from all the world of men, the Country of the Blind. Long years ago that valley lay so far open to the world that men might come at last through frightful gorges and over an icy pass into its equable meadows, and thither indeed men came, a family or so of Peruvian half-breeds fleeing from the lust and tyranny of an evil Spanish ruler. Then came the stupendous outbreak of Mindobamba, when it was night in Quito for seventeen days, and the water was boiling at Yaguachi and all the fish floating dying even as far as Guayaquil; everywhere along the Pacific slopes there were landslips and swift thawings and sudden floods, and one whole side of the old Arauca crest slipped and came down in thunder, and cut off the Country of the Blind for ever from the exploring feet of men. But one of these early settlers had chanced to be on the hither side of the gorges when the world had so terribly shaken itself, and he perforce had to forget his wife and his child and all the friends and possessions he had left up there, and start life over again in the lower world. He started it again but ill, blindness overtook him, and he died of punishment in the mines; but the story he told begot a legend that lingers along the length of the Cordilleras of the Andes to this day.

He told of his reason for venturing back from that fastness, into which he had first been carried lashed to a llama, beside a vast bale of gear, when he was a child. The valley, he said, had in it all that the heart of man could desire—sweet water, pasture, an even climate, slopes of rich brown soil with tangles of a shrub that bore an excellent fruit, and on one side great hanging forests of pine that held the avalanches high. Far overhead, on three sides, vast cliffs of grey-green rock were capped by cliffs of ice; but the glacier stream came not to them, but flowed away by the farther slopes, and only now and then huge ice masses fell on the valley side. In this valley it neither rained nor snowed, but the abundant springs gave a rich green pasture, that irrigation would spread over all the valley space. The settlers did well indeed there. Their beasts did well and multiplied, and but one thing marred their happiness. Yet it was enough to mar it greatly. A strange disease had come upon them and had made all the children born to them there—and indeed, several older children also—blind. It was to seek some charm or antidote against this plague of blindness that he had with fatigue and danger and difficulty returned down the gorge. In those days, in such cases, men did not think of germs and infections, but of sins, and it seemed to him that the reason of this affliction must he in the negligence of these priestless immigrants to set up a shrine so soon as they entered the valley. He wanted a shrine—a handsome, cheap, effectual shrine—to be erected in the valley; he wanted relics and suchlike potent things of faith, blessed objects and mysterious medals and prayers. In his wallet he had a bar of native silver for which he would not account; he insisted there was none in the valley with something of the insistence of an inexpert liar. They had all clubbed their money and ornaments together, having little need for such treasure up there, he said, to buy them holy help against their ill. I figure this dim-eyed young mountaineer, sunburnt, gaunt, and anxious, hat brim clutched feverishly, a man all unused to the ways of the lower world, telling this story to some keen-eyed, attentive priest before the great convulsion; I can picture him presently seeking to return with pious and infallible remedies against that trouble, and the infinite dismay with which he must have faced the tumbled vastness where the gorge had once come out. But the rest of his story of mischances is lost to me, save that I know of his evil death after several years. Poor stray from that remoteness! The stream that had once made the gorge now bursts from the mouth of a rocky cave, and the legend his poor, ill-told story set going developed into the legend of a race of blind men somewhere "over there" one may still hear to-day.

And amidst the little population of that now isolated and forgotten valley the disease ran its course. The old became groping, the young saw but dimly, and the children that were born to them never saw at all. But life was very easy in that snow-rimmed basin, lost to all the world, with neither thorns nor briers, with no evil insects nor any beasts save the gentle breed of llamas they had lugged and thrust and followed up the beds of the shrunken rivers in the gorges up which they had come. The seeing had become purblind so gradually that they scarcely noticed their loss. They guided the sightless youngsters hither and thither until they knew the whole valley marvellously, and when at last sight died out among them the race lived on. They had even time to adapt themselves to the blind control of fire, which they made carefully in stoves of stone. They were a simple strain of people at the first, unlettered, only slightly touched with the Spanish civilisation, but with something of a tradition of the arts of old Peru and of its lost philosophy. Generation followed generation. They forgot many things; they devised many things. Their tradition of the greater world they came from became mythical in colour and uncertain. In all things save sight they were strong and able, and presently chance sent one who had an original mind and who could talk and persuade among them, and then afterwards another. These two passed, leaving their effects, and the little community grew in numbers and in understanding, and met and settled social and economic problems that arose. Generation followed generation. Generation followed generation. There came a time when a child was born who was fifteen generations from that ancestor who went out of the valley with a bar of silver to seek God's aid, and who never returned. There about it chanced that a man came into this community from the outer world. And this is the story of that man.

He was a mountaineer from the country near Quito, a man who had been down to the sea and had seen the world, a reader of books in an original way, an acute and enterprising man, and he was taken on by a party of Englishmen who had come out to Ecuador to climb mountains, to replace one of their three Swiss guides who had fallen ill. He climbed here and he climbed there, and then came the attempt on Parascotopetl, the Matterhorn of the Andes, in which he was lost to the outer world. The story of that accident has been written a dozen times. Pointer's narrative is the best. He tells how the little party worked their difficult and almost vertical way up to the very foot of the last and greatest precipice, and how they built a night shelter amidst the snow upon a little shelf of rock, and with a touch of real dramatic power, how presently they found Nunez had gone from them. They shouted, and there was no reply; shouted and whistled, and for the rest of that night they slept no more.

As the morning broke they saw the traces of his fall. It seems impossible he could have uttered a sound. He had slipped eastward towards the unknown side of the mountain; far below he had struck a steep slope of snow, and ploughed his way down it in the midst of a snow avalanche. His track went straight to the edge of a frightful precipice, and beyond that everything was hidden. Far, far below, and hazy with distance, they could see trees rising out of a narrow, shut-in valley—the lost Country of the Blind. But they did not know it was the lost Country of the Blind, nor distinguish it in any way from any other narrow streak of upland valley. Unnerved by this disaster, they abandoned their attempt in the afternoon, and Pointer was called away to the war before he could make another attack. To this day Parascotopetl lifts an unconquered crest, and Pointer's shelter crumbles unvisited amidst the snows.

And the man who fell survived.

At the end of the slope he fell a thousand feet, and came down in the midst of a cloud of snow upon a snow slope even steeper than the one above. Down this he was whirled, stunned and insensible, but without a bone broken in his body; and then at last came to gentler slopes, and at last rolled out and lay still, buried amidst a softening heap of the white masses that had accompanied and saved him. He came to himself with a dim fancy that he was ill in bed; then realized his position with a mountaineer's intelligence and worked himself loose and, after a rest or so, out until he saw the stars. He rested flat upon his chest for a space, wondering where he was and what had happened to him. He explored his limbs, and discovered that several of his buttons were gone and his coat turned over his head. His knife had gone from his pocket and his hat was lost, though he had tied it under his chin. He recalled that he had been looking for loose stones to raise his piece of the shelter wall. His ice-axe had disappeared.

He decided he must have fallen, and looked up to see, exaggerated by the ghastly light of the rising moon, the tremendous flight he had taken. For a while he lay, gazing blankly at the vast, pale cliff towering above, rising moment by moment out of a subsiding tide of darkness. Its phantasmal, mysterious beauty held him for a space, and then he was seized with a paroxysm of sobbing laughter...

After a great interval of time he became aware that he was near the lower edge of the snow. Below, down what was now a moonlit and practicable slope, he saw the dark and broken appearance of rock-strewn turf. He struggled to his feet, aching in every joint and limb, got down painfully from the heaped loose snow about him, went downward until he was on the turf, and there dropped rather than lay beside a boulder, drank deep from the flask in his inner pocket, and instantly fell asleep...

He was awakened by the singing of birds in the trees far below.

He sat up and perceived he was on a little alp at the foot of a vast precipice that sloped only a little in the gully down which he and his snow had come. Over against him another wall of rock reared itself against the sky. The gorge between these precipices ran east and west and was full of the morning sunlight, which lit to the westward the mass of fallen mountain that closed the descending gorge. Below him it seemed there was a precipice equally steep, but behind the snow in the gully he found a sort of chimney-cleft dripping with snow-water, down which a desperate man might venture. He found it easier than it seemed, and came at last to another desolate alp, and then after a rock climb of no particular difficulty, to a steep slope of trees. He took his bearings and turned his face up the gorge, for he saw it opened out above upon green meadows, among which he now glimpsed quite distinctly a cluster of stone huts of unfamiliar fashion. At times his progress was like clambering along the face of a wall, and after a time the rising sun ceased to strike along the gorge, the voices of the singing birds died away, and the air grew cold and dark about him. But the distant valley with its houses was all the brighter for that. He came presently to talus, and among the rocks he noted—for he was an observant man—an unfamiliar fern that seemed to clutch out of the crevices with intense green hands. He picked a frond or so and gnawed its stalk, and found it helpful.

About midday he came at last out of the throat of the gorge into the plain and the sunlight. He was stiff and weary; he sat down in the shadow of a rock, filled up his flask with water from a spring and drank it down, and remained for a time, resting before he went on to the houses.

They were very strange to his eyes, and indeed the whole aspect of that valley became, as he regarded it, queerer and more unfamiliar. The greater part of its surface was lush green meadow, starred with many beautiful flowers, irrigated with extraordinary care, and bearing evidence of systematic cropping piece by piece. High up and ringing the valley about was a wall, and what appeared to be a circumferential water-channel, from which the little trickles of water that fed the meadow plants came, and on the higher slopes above this flocks of llamas cropped the scanty herbage. Sheds, apparently shelters or feeding-places for the llamas, stood against the boundary wall here and there. The irrigation streams ran together into a main channel down the centre of the valley, and this was enclosed on either side by a wall breast high. This gave a singularly urban quality to this secluded place, a quality that was greatly enhanced by the fact that a number of paths paved with black and white stones, and each with a curious little kerb at the side, ran hither and thither in an orderly manner. The houses of the central village were quite unlike the casual and higgledy-piggledy agglomeration of the mountain villages he knew; they stood in a continuous row on either side of a central street of astonishing cleanness, here and there their parti-coloured facade was pierced by a door, and not a solitary window broke their even frontage. They were parti-coloured with extraordinary irregularity, smeared with a sort of plaster that was sometimes grey, sometimes drab, sometimes slate-coloured or dark brown; and it was the sight of this wild plastering first brought the word "blind" into the thoughts of the explorer. "The good man who did that," he thought, "must have been as blind as a bat."

He descended a steep place, and so came to the wall and channel that ran about the valley, near where the latter spouted out its surplus contents into the deeps of the gorge in a thin and wavering thread of cascade. He could now see a number of men and women resting on piled heaps of grass, as if taking a siesta, in the remoter part of the meadow, and nearer the village a number of recumbent children, and then nearer at hand three men carrying pails on yokes along a little path that ran from the encircling wall towards the houses. These latter were clad in garments of llama cloth and boots and belts of leather, and they wore caps of cloth with back and ear flaps. They followed one another in single file, walking slowly and yawning as they walked, like men who have been up all night. There was something so reassuringly prosperous and respectable in their bearing that after a moment's hesitation Nunez stood forward as conspicuously as possible upon his rock, and gave vent to a mighty shout that echoed round the valley.

The three men stopped, and moved their heads as though they were looking about them. They turned their faces this way and that, and Nunez gesticulated with freedom. But they did not appear to see him for all his gestures, and after a time, directing themselves towards the mountains far away to the right, they shouted as if in answer. Nunez bawled again, and then once more, and as he gestured ineffectually the word "blind" came up to the top of his thoughts. "The fools must be blind," he said.

When at last, after much shouting and wrath, Nunez crossed the stream by a little bridge, came through a gate in the wall, and approached them, he was sure that they were blind. He was sure that this was the Country of the Blind of which the legends told. Conviction had sprung upon him, and a sense of great and rather enviable adventure. The three stood side by side, not looking at him, but with their ears directed towards him, judging him by his unfamiliar steps. They stood close together like men a little afraid, and he could see their eyelids closed and sunken, as though the very balls beneath had shrunk away. There was an expression near awe on their faces.

"A man," one said, in hardly recognisable Spanish—"A man it is—a man or a spirit—coming down from the rocks."

But Nunez advanced with the confident steps of a youth who enters upon life. All the old stories of the lost valley and the Country of the Blind had come back to his mind, and through his thoughts ran this old proverb, as if it were a refrain—

"In the Country of the Blind the One-Eyed Man is King."

"In the Country of the Blind the One-Eyed Man is King."

And very civilly he gave them greeting. He talked to them and used his eyes.

"Where does he come from, brother Pedro?" asked one.

"Down out of the rocks."

"Over the mountains I come," said Nunez, "out of the country beyond there—where men can see. From near Bogota, where there are a hundred thousands of people, and where the city passes out of sight."

"Sight?" muttered Pedro. "Sight?"

"He comes," said the second blind man, "out of the rocks."

The cloth of their coats, Nunez saw was curious fashioned, each with a different sort of stitching.

They startled him by a simultaneous movement towards him, each with a hand outstretched. He stepped back from the advance of these spread fingers.

"Come hither," said the third blind man, following his motion and clutching him neatly.

And they held Nunez and felt him over, saying no word further until they had done so.

"Carefully," he cried, with a finger in his eye, and found they thought that organ, with its fluttering lids, a queer thing in him. They went over it again.

"A strange creature, Correa," said the one called Pedro. "Feel the coarseness of his hair. Like a llama's hair."

"Rough he is as the rocks that begot him," said Correa, investigating Nunez's unshaven chin with a soft and slightly moist hand. "Perhaps he will grow finer."

Nunez struggled a little under their examination, but they gripped him firm.

"Carefully," he said again.

"He speaks," said the third man. "Certainly he is a man."

"Ugh!" said Pedro, at the roughness of his coat.

"And you have come into the world?" asked Pedro.

"Out of the world. Over mountains and glaciers; right over above there, halfway to the sun. Out of the great, big world that goes down, twelve days' journey to the sea."

They scarcely seemed to heed him. "Our fathers have told us men may be made by the forces of Nature," said Correa. "It is the warmth of things, and moisture, and rottenness—rottenness."

"Let us lead him to the elders," said Pedro.

"Shout first," said Correa, "lest the children be afraid. This is a marvellous occasion."

So they shouted, and Pedro went first and took Nunez by the hand to lead him to the houses.

He drew his hand away. "I can see," he said.

"See?" said Correa.

"Yes; see," said Nunez, turning towards him, and stumbled against Pedro's pail.

"His senses are still imperfect," said the third blind man. "He stumbles, and talks unmeaning words. Lead him by the hand."

"As you will," said Nunez, and was led along laughing.

It seemed they knew nothing of sight.

Well, all in good time he would teach them.

He heard people shouting, and saw a number of figures gathering together in the middle roadway of the village.

He found it tax his nerve and patience more than he had anticipated, that first encounter with the population of the Country of the Blind. The place seemed larger as he drew near to it, and the smeared plasterings queerer, and a crowd of children and men and women (the women and girls he was pleased to note had, some of them, quite sweet faces, for all that their eyes were shut and sunken) came about him, holding on to him, touching him with soft, sensitive hands, smelling at him, and listening at every word he spoke. Some of the maidens and children, however, kept aloof as if afraid, and indeed his voice seemed coarse and rude beside their softer notes. They mobbed him. His three guides kept close to him with an effect of proprietorship, and said again and again, "A wild man out of the rocks."

"Bogota," he said. "Bogota. Over the mountain crests."

"A wild man—using wild words," said Pedro. "Did you hear that—Bogota? His mind has hardly formed yet. He has only the beginnings of speech."

A little boy nipped his hand. "Bogota!" he said mockingly.

"Aye! A city to your village. I come from the great world—where men have eyes and see."

"His name's Bogota," they said.

"He stumbled," said Correa, "stumbled twice as we came hither."

"Bring him in to the elders."

And they thrust him suddenly through a doorway into a room as black as pitch, save at the end there faintly glowed a fire. The crowd closed in behind him and shut out all but the faintest glimmer of day, and before he could arrest himself he had fallen headlong over the feet of a seated man. His arm, outflung, struck the face of someone else as he went down; he felt the soft impact of features and heard a cry of anger, and for a moment he struggled against a number of hands that clutched him. It was a one-sided fight. An inkling of the situation came to him and he lay quiet.

"I fell down," he said; "I couldn't see in this pitchy darkness."

There was a pause as if the unseen persons about him tried to understand his words. Then the voice of Correa said: "He is but newly formed. He stumbles as he walks and mingles words that mean nothing with his speech."

Others also said things about him that he heard or understood imperfectly.

"May I sit up?" he asked, in a pause. "I will not struggle against you again."

They consulted and let him rise.

The voice of an older man began to question him, and Nunez found himself trying to explain the great world out of which he had fallen, and the sky and mountains and suchlike marvels, to these elders who sat in darkness in the Country of the Blind. And they would believe and understand nothing whatever that he told them, a thing quite outside his expectation. They would not even understand many of his words. For fourteen generations these people had been blind and cut off from all the seeing world; the names for all the things of sight had faded and changed; the story of the outer world was faded and changed to a child's story; and they had ceased to concern themselves with anything beyond the rocky slopes above their circling wall. Blind men of genius had arisen among them and questioned the shreds of belief and tradition they had brought with them from their seeing days, and had dismissed all these things as idle fancies and replaced them with new and saner explanations. Much of their imagination had shrivelled with their eyes, and they had made for themselves new imaginations with their ever more sensitive ears and finger-tips. Slowly Nunez realised this: that his expectation of wonder and reverence at his origin and his gifts was not to be borne out; and after his poor attempt to explain sight to them had been set aside as the confused version of a new-made being describing the marvels of his incoherent sensations, he subsided, a little dashed, into listening to their instruction. And the eldest of the blind men explained to him life and philosophy and religion, how that the world (meaning their valley) had been first an empty hollow in the rocks, and then had come first inanimate things without the gift of touch, and llamas and a few other creatures that had little sense, and then men, and at last angels, whom one could hear singing and making fluttering sounds, but whom no one could touch at all, which puzzled Nunez greatly until he thought of the birds.

He went on to tell Nunez how this time had been divided into the warm and the cold, which are the blind equivalents of day and night, and how it was good to sleep in the warm and work during the cold, so that now, but for his advent, the whole town of the blind would have been asleep. He said Nunez must have been specially created to learn and serve the wisdom they had acquired, and that for all his mental incoherency and stumbling behaviour he must have courage and do his best to learn, and at that all the people in the doorway murmured encouragingly. He said the night—for the blind call their day night—was now far gone, and it behooved everyone to go back to sleep. He asked Nunez if he knew how to sleep, and Nunez said he did, but that before sleep he wanted food.

They brought him food—llama's milk in a bowl and rough salted bread—and led him into a lonely place to eat out of their hearing, and afterwards to slumber until the chill of the mountain evening roused them to begin their day again. But Nunez slumbered not at all.

Instead, he sat up in the place where they had left him, resting his limbs and turning the unanticipated circumstances of his arrival over and over in his mind.

Every now and then he laughed, sometimes with amusement and sometimes with indignation.

"Unformed mind!" he said. "Got no senses yet! They little know they've been insulting their heaven-sent king and master. I see I must bring them to reason. Let me think—Let me think."

He was still thinking when the sun set.

Nunez had an eye for all beautiful things, and it seemed to him that the glow upon the snowfields and glaciers that rose about the valley on every side was the most beautiful thing he had ever seen. His eyes went from that inaccessible glory to the village and irrigated fields, fast sinking into the twilight, and suddenly a wave of emotion took him, and he thanked God from the bottom of his heart that the power of sight had been given him.

He heard a voice calling to him from out of the village.

"Ya ho there, Bogota! Come hither!"

At that he stood up, smiling. He would show these people once and for all what sight would do for a man. They would seek him, but not find him.

"You move not, Bogota," said the voice.

He laughed noiselessly and made two stealthy steps aside from the path.

"Trample not on the grass, Bogota; that is not allowed."

Nunez had scarcely heard the sound he made himself. He stopped, amazed.

The owner of the voice came running up the piebald path towards him.

He stepped back into the pathway. "Here I am," he said.

"Why did you not come when I called you?" said the blind man. "Must you be led like a child? Cannot you hear the path as you walk?"

Nunez laughed. "I can see it," he said.

"There is no such word as see," said the blind man, after a pause. "Cease this folly and follow the sound of my feet."

Nunez followed, a little annoyed.

"My time will come," he said.

"You'll learn," the blind man answered. "There is much to learn in the world."

"Has no one told you, 'In the Country of the Blind the One-Eyed Man is King'?"

"What is blind?" asked the blind man, carelessly, over his shoulder.

Four days passed and the fifth found the King of the Blind still incognito, as a clumsy and useless stranger among his subjects.

It was, he found, much more difficult to proclaim himself than he had supposed, and in the meantime, while he meditated his coup d'etat, he did what he was told and learnt the manners and customs of the Country of the Blind. He found working and going about at night a particularly irksome thing, and he decided that, that should be the first thing he would change.

They led a simple, laborious life, these people, with all the elements of virtue and happiness as these things can be understood by men. They toiled, but not oppressively; they had food and clothing sufficient for their needs; they had days and seasons of rest; they made much of music and singing, and there was love among them and little children.

It was marvellous with what confidence and precision they went about their ordered world. Everything, you see, had been made to fit their needs; each of the radiating paths of the valley area had a constant angle to the others, and was distinguished by a special notch upon its kerbing; all obstacles and irregularities of path or meadow had long since been cleared away; all their methods and procedure arose naturally from their special needs. Their senses had become marvellously acute; they could hear and judge the slightest gesture of a man a dozen paces away—could hear the very beating of his heart. Intonation had long replaced expression with them, and touches gesture, and their work with hoe and spade and fork was as free and confident as garden work can be. Their sense of smell was extraordinarily fine; they could distinguish individual differences as readily as a dog can, and they went about the tending of llamas, who lived among the rocks above and came to the wall for food and shelter, with ease and confidence. It was only when at last Nunez sought to assert himself that he found how easy and confident their movements could be.

He rebelled only after he had tried persuasion.

He tried at first on several occasions to tell them of sight. "Look you here, you people," he said. "There are things you do not understand in me."

Once or twice one or two of them attended to him; they sat with faces downcast and ears turned intelligently towards him, and he did his best to tell them what it was to see. Among his hearers was a girl, with eyelids less red and sunken than the others, so that one could almost fancy she was hiding eyes, whom especially he hoped to persuade. He spoke of the beauties of sight, of watching the mountains, of the sky and the sunrise, and they heard him with amused incredulity that presently became condemnatory. They told him there were indeed no mountains at all, but that the end of the rocks where the llamas grazed was indeed the end of the world; thence sprang a cavernous roof of the universe, from which the dew and the avalanches fell; and when he maintained stoutly the world had neither end nor roof such as they supposed, they said his thoughts were wicked. So far as he could describe sky and clouds and stars to them it seemed to them a hideous void, a terrible blankness in the place of the smooth roof to things in which they believed—it was an article of faith with them that the cavern roof was exquisitely smooth to the touch. He saw that in some manner he shocked them, and gave up that aspect of the matter altogether, and tried to show them the practical value of sight. One morning he saw Pedro in the path called Seventeen and coming towards the central houses, but still too far off for hearing or scent, and he told them as much. "In a little while," he prophesied, "Pedro will be here." An old man remarked that Pedro had no business on path Seventeen, and then, as if in confirmation, that individual as he drew near turned and went transversely into path Ten, and so back with nimble paces towards the outer wall. They mocked Nunez when Pedro did not arrive, and afterwards, when he asked Pedro questions to clear his character, Pedro denied and outfaced him, and was afterwards hostile to him.

Then he induced them to let him go a long way up the sloping meadows towards the wall with one complaisant individual, and to him he promised to describe all that happened among the houses. He noted certain goings and comings, but the things that really seemed to signify to these people happened inside of or behind the windowless houses—the only things they took note of to test him by—and of those he could see or tell nothing; and it was after the failure of this attempt, and the ridicule they could not repress, that he resorted to force. He thought of seizing a spade and suddenly smiting one or two of them to earth, and so in fair combat showing the advantage of eyes. He went so far with that resolution as to seize his spade, and then he discovered a new thing about himself, and that was that it was impossible for him to hit a blind man in cold blood.

He hesitated, and found them all aware that he had snatched up the spade. They stood all alert, with their heads on one side, and bent ears towards him for what he would do next.

"Put that spade down," said one, and he felt a sort of helpless horror. He came near obedience.

Then he had thrust one backwards against a house wall, and fled past him and out of the village.

He went athwart one of their meadows, leaving a track of trampled grass behind his feet, and presently sat down by the side of one of their ways. He felt something of the buoyancy that comes to all men in the beginning of a fight, but more perplexity. He began to realise that you cannot even fight happily with creatures who stand upon a different mental basis to yourself. Far away he saw a number of men carrying spades and sticks come out of the street of houses and advance in a spreading line along the several paths towards him. They advanced slowly, speaking frequently to one another, and ever and again the whole cordon would halt and sniff the air and listen.

The first time they did this Nunez laughed. But afterwards he did not laugh.

One struck his trail in the meadow grass and came stooping and feeling his way along it.

For five minutes he watched the slow extension of the cordon, and then his vague disposition to do something forthwith became frantic. He stood up, went a pace or so towards the circumferential wall, turned, and went back a little way. There they all stood in a crescent, still and listening.

He also stood still, gripping his spade very tightly in both hands. Should he charge them?

The pulse in his ears ran into the rhythm of "In the Country of the Blind the One-Eyed Man is King."

Should he charge them?

He looked back at the high and unclimbable wall behind—unclimbable because of its smooth plastering, but withal pierced with many little doors and at the approaching line of seekers. Behind these others were now coming out of the street of houses.

Should he charge them?

"Bogota!" called one. "Bogota! Where are you?"

He gripped his spade still tighter and advanced down the meadows towards the place of habitations, and directly he moved they converged upon him. "I'll hit them if they touch me," he swore; "by Heaven, I will. I'll hit." He called aloud, "Look here, I'm going to do what I like in this valley! Do you hear? I'm going to do what I like and go where I like."

They were moving in upon him quickly, groping, yet moving rapidly. It was like playing blind man's buff with everyone blindfolded except one. "Get hold of him!" cried one. He found himself in the arc of a loose curve of pursuers. He felt suddenly he must be active and resolute.

"You don't understand," he cried, in a voice that was meant to be great and resolute, and which broke. "You are blind and I can see. Leave me alone!"

"Bogota! Put down that spade and come off the grass!"

The last order, grotesque in its urban familiarity, produced a gust of anger. "I'll hurt you," he said, sobbing with emotion. "By Heaven, I'll hurt you! Leave me alone!"

He began to run, not knowing clearly where to run. He ran from the nearest blind man, because it was a horror to hit him. He stopped, and then made a dash to escape from their closing ranks. He made for where a gap was wide, and the men on either side, with a quick perception of the approach of his paces, rushed in on one another. He sprang forward, and then saw he must be caught, and Swish! The spade had struck. He felt the soft thud of hand and arm, and the man was down with a yell of pain, and he was through.

Through! And then he was close to the street of houses again, and blind men, whirling spades and stakes, were running with a reasoned swiftness hither and thither.

He heard steps behind him just in time, and found a tall man rushing forward and swiping at the sound of him. He lost his nerve, hurled his spade a yard wide of this antagonist, and whirled about and fled, fairly yelling as he dodged another.

He was panic-stricken. He ran furiously to and fro, dodging when there was no need to dodge, and in his anxiety to see on every side of him at once, stumbling. For a moment he was down and they heard his fall. Far away in the circumferential wall a little doorway looked like Heaven, and he set off in a wild rush for it. He did not even look round at his pursuers until it was gained, and he had stumbled across the bridge, clambered a little way among the rocks, to the surprise and dismay of a young llama, who went leaping out of sight, and lay down sobbing for breath.

And so his coup d'etat came to an end.

He stayed outside the wall of the valley of the blind for two nights and days without food or shelter, and meditated upon the unexpected. During these meditations he repeated very frequently and always with a profounder note of derision the exploded proverb: "In the Country of the Blind the One-Eyed Man is King." He thought chiefly of ways of fighting and conquering these people, and it grew clear that for him no practicable way was possible. He had no weapons, and now it would be hard to get one.

The canker of civilisation had got to him even in Bogota, and he could not find it in himself to go down and assassinate a blind man. Of course, if he did that, he might then dictate terms on the threat of assassinating them all. But—Sooner or later he must sleep...!

He tried also to find food among the pine trees, to be comfortable under pine boughs while the frost fell at night, and—with less confidence—to catch a llama by artifice in order to try to kill it—perhaps by hammering it with a stone—and so finally, perhaps, to eat some of it. But the llamas had a doubt of him and regarded him with distrustful brown eyes and spat when he drew near. Fear came on him the second day and fits of shivering. Finally he crawled down to the wall of the Country of the Blind and tried to make his terms. He crawled along by the stream, shouting, until two blind men came out to the gate and talked to him.

"I was mad," he said. "But I was only newly made."

They said that was better.

He told them he was wiser now, and repented of all he had done.

Then he wept without intention, for he was very weak and ill now, and they took that as a favourable sign.

They asked him if he still thought he could see."

"No," he said. "That was folly. The word means nothing—less than nothing!"

They asked him what was overhead.

"About ten times ten the height of a man there is a roof above the world—of rock—and very, very smooth..." He burst again into hysterical tears. "Before you ask me any more, give me some food or I shall die!"

He expected dire punishments, but these blind people were capable of toleration. They regarded his rebellion as but one more proof of his general idiocy and inferiority, and after they had whipped him they appointed him to do the simplest and heaviest work they had for anyone to do, and he, seeing no other way of living, did submissively what he was told.

He was ill for some days and they nursed him kindly. That refined his submission. But they insisted on his lying in the dark, and that was a great misery. And blind philosophers came and talked to him of the wicked levity of his mind, and reproved him so impressively for his doubts about the lid of rock that covered their cosmic casserole that he almost doubted whether indeed he was not the victim of hallucination in not seeing it overhead.

So Nunez became a citizen of the Country of the Blind, and these people ceased to be a generalised people and became individualities to him, and familiar to him, while the world beyond the mountains became more and more remote and unreal. There was Yacob, his master, a kindly man when not annoyed; there was Pedro, Yacob's nephew; and there was Medina-sarote, who was the youngest daughter of Yacob. She was little esteemed in the world of the blind, because she had a clear-cut face and lacked that satisfying, glossy smoothness that is the blind man's ideal of feminine beauty, but Nunez thought her beautiful at first, and presently the most beautiful thing in the whole creation. Her closed eyelids were not sunken and red after the common way of the valley, but lay as though they might open again at any moment; and she had long eyelashes, which were considered a grave disfigurement. And her voice was weak and did not satisfy the acute hearing of the valley swains. So that she had no lover.

There came a time when Nunez thought that, could he win her, he would be resigned to live in the valley for all the rest of his days.

He watched her; he sought opportunities of doing her little services and presently he found that she observed him. Once at a rest-day gathering they sat side by side in the dim starlight, and the music was sweet. His hand came upon hers and he dared to clasp it. Then very tenderly she returned his pressure. And one day, as they were at their meal in the darkness, he felt her hand very softly seeking him, and as it chanced the fire leapt then, and he saw the tenderness of her face.

He sought to speak to her.

He went to her one day when she was sitting in the summer moonlight spinning. The light made her a thing of silver and mystery. He sat down at her feet and told her he loved her, and told her how beautiful she seemed to him. He had a lover's voice, he spoke with a tender reverence that came near to awe, and she had never before been touched by adoration. She made him no definite answer, but it was clear his words pleased her.

After that he talked to her whenever he could take an opportunity. The valley became the world for him, and the world beyond the mountains where men lived by day seemed no more than a fairy tale he would some day pour into her ears. Very tentatively and timidly he spoke to her of sight.

Sight seemed to her the most poetical of fancies, and she listened to his description of the stars and the mountains and her own sweet white-lit beauty as though it was a guilty indulgence. She did not believe, she could only half understand, but she was mysteriously delighted, and it seemed to him that she completely understood.

His love lost its awe and took courage. Presently he was for demanding her of Yacob and the elders in marriage, but she became fearful and delayed. And it was one of her elder sisters who first told Yacob that Medina-sarote and Nunez were in love.

There was from the first very great opposition to the marriage of Nunez and Medina-sarote; not so much because they valued her as because they held him as a being apart, an idiot, incompetent thing below the permissible level of a man. Her sisters opposed it bitterly as bringing discredit on them all; and old Yacob, though he had formed a sort of liking for his clumsy, obedient serf, shook his head and said the thing could not be. The young men were all angry at the idea of corrupting the race, and one went so far as to revile and strike Nunez. He struck back. Then for the first time he found an advantage in seeing, even by twilight, and after that fight was over no one was disposed to raise a hand against him. But they still found his marriage impossible.

Old Yacob had a tenderness for his last little daughter, and was grieved to have her weep upon his shoulder.

"You see, my dear, he's an idiot. He has delusions; he can't do anything right."

"I know," wept Medina-sarote. "But he's better than he was. He's getting better. And he's strong, dear father, and kind—stronger and kinder than any other man in the world. And he loves me—and father, I love him."

Old Yacob was greatly distressed to find her inconsolable, and besides—what made it more distressing—he liked Nunez for many things. So he went and sat in the windowless council-chamber with the other elders and watched the trend of the talk, and said, at the proper time, "He's better than he was. Very likely, some day, we shall find him as sane as ourselves."

Then afterwards one of the elders, who thought deeply, had an idea. He was a great doctor among these people, their medicine-man, and he had a very philosophical and inventive mind, and the idea of curing Nunez of his peculiarities appealed to him. One day when Yacob was present he returned to the topic of Nunez. "I have examined Nunez," he said, "and the case is clearer to me. I think very probably he might be cured."

"This is what I have always hoped," said old Yacob.

"His brain is affected," said the blind doctor.

The elders murmured assent.

"Now, what affects it?"

"Ah!" said old Yacob.

"This," said the doctor, answering his own question. "Those queer things that are called the eyes, and which exist to make an agreeable depression in the face, are diseased, in the case of Nunez, in such a way as to affect his brain. They are greatly distended, he has eyelashes, and his eyelids move, and consequently his brain is in a state of constant irritation and distraction."

"Yes?" said old Yacob. "Yes?"

"And I think I may say with reasonable certainty that, in order to cure him complete, all that we need to do is a simple and easy surgical operation—namely, to remove these irritant bodies."

"And then he will be sane?"

"Then he will be perfectly sane, and a quite admirable citizen."

"Thank Heaven for science!" said old Yacob, and went forth at once to tell Nunez of his happy hopes.

But Nunez's manner of receiving the good news struck him as being cold and disappointing.

"One might think," he said, "from the tone you take that you did not care for my daughter."

It was Medina-sarote who persuaded Nunez to face the blind surgeons.

"You do not want me," he said, "to lose my gift of sight?"

She shook her head.

"My world is sight."

Her head drooped lower.

"There are the beautiful things, the beautiful little things—the flowers, the lichens amidst the rocks, the light and softness on a piece of fur, the far sky with its drifting dawn of clouds, the sunsets and the stars. And there is you. For you alone it is good to have sight, to see your sweet, serene face, your kindly lips, your dear, beautiful hands folded together...It is these eyes of mine you won, these eyes that hold me to you, that these idiots seek. Instead, I must touch you, hear you, and never see you again. I must come under that roof of rock and stone and darkness, that horrible roof under which your imaginations stoop...No; you would not have me do that?"

A disagreeable doubt had arisen in him. He stopped and left the thing a question.

"I wish," she said, "sometimes—" She paused.

"Yes?" he said, a little apprehensively.

"I wish sometimes—you would not talk like that."

"Like what?"

"I know it's pretty—it's your imagination. I love it, but now—"

He felt cold. "Now?" he said, faintly.

She sat quite still.

"You mean—you think—I should be better, better perhaps—"

He was realising things very swiftly. He felt anger perhaps, anger at the dull course of fate, but also sympathy for her lack of understanding—a sympathy near akin to pity.

"Dear," he said, and he could see by her whiteness how tensely her spirit pressed against the things she could not say. He put his arms about her, he kissed her ear, and they sat for a time in silence.

"If I were to consent to this?" he said at last, in a voice that was very gentle.

She flung her arms about him, weeping wildly. "Oh, if you would," she sobbed, "if only you would!"

For a week before the operation that was to raise him from his servitude and inferiority to the level of a blind citizen Nunez knew nothing of sleep, and all through the warm, sunlit hours, while the others slumbered happily, he sat brooding or wandered aimlessly, trying to bring his mind to bear on his dilemma. He had given his answer, he had given his consent, and still he was not sure. And at last work-time was over, the sun rose in splendour over the golden crests, and his last day of vision began for him. He had a few minutes with Medina-sarote before she went apart to sleep.

"To-morrow," he said, "I shall see no more."

"Dear heart!" she answered, and pressed his hands with all her strength.

"They will hurt you but little," she said; "and you are going through this pain—you are going through it, dear lover, for me... Dear, if a woman's heart and life can do it, I will repay you. My dearest one, my dearest with the tender voice, I will repay."

He was drenched in pity for himself and her.

He held her in his arms, and pressed his lips to hers and looked on her sweet face for the last time. "Good-bye!" he whispered to that dear sight, "Good-bye!"

And then in silence he turned away from her.

She could hear his slow retreating footsteps, and something in the rhythm of them threw her into a passion of weeping.

He walked away.

He had fully meant to go to a lonely place where the meadows were beautiful with white narcissus, and there remain until the hour of his sacrifice should come, but as he walked he lifted up his eyes and saw the morning, the morning like an angel in golden armour, marching down the steeps...

It seemed to him that before this splendour he and this blind world in the valley, and his love and all, were no more than a pit of sin.

He did not turn aside as he had meant to do, but went on and passed through the wall of the circumference and out upon the rocks, and his eyes were always upon the sunlit ice and snow.

He saw their infinite beauty, and his imagination soared over them to the things beyond he was now to resign for ever!

He thought of that great free world that he was parted from, the world that was his own, and he had a vision of those further slopes, distance beyond distance, with Bogota, a place of multitudinous stirring beauty, a glory by day, a luminous mystery by night, a place of palaces and fountains and statues and white houses, lying beautifully in the middle distance. He thought how for a day or so one might come down through passes drawing ever nearer and nearer to its busy streets and ways. He thought of the river journey, day by day, from great Bogota to the still vaster world beyond, through towns and villages, forest and desert places, the rushing river day by day, until its banks receded, and the big steamers came splashing by and one had reached the sea—the limitless sea, with its thousand islands, its thousands of islands, and its ships seen dimly far away in their incessant journeyings round and about that greater world. And there, unpent by mountains, one saw the sky—the sky, not such a disc as one saw it here, but an arch of immeasurable blue, a deep of deeps in which the circling stars were floating...

His eyes scrutinised the great curtain of the mountains with a keener inquiry.

For example; if one went so, up that gully and to that chimney there, then one might come out high among those stunted pines that ran round in a sort of shelf and rose still higher and higher as it passed above the gorge. And then? That talus might be managed. Thence perhaps a climb might be found to take him up to the precipice that came below the snow; and if that chimney failed, then another farther to the east might serve his purpose better.

And then? Then one would be out upon the amber-lit snow there, and halfway up to the crest of those beautiful desolations. And suppose one had good fortune!

He glanced back at the village, then turned right round and regarded it with folded arms.

He thought of Medina-sarote, and she had become small and remote.

He turned again towards the mountain wall down which the day had come to him.

Then very circumspectly he began his climb.

When sunset came he was no longer climbing, but he was far and high. His clothes were torn, his limbs were blood-stained, he was bruised in many places, but he lay as if he were at his ease, and there was a smile on his face.

From where he rested the valley seemed as if it were in a pit and nearly a mile below. Already it was dim with haze and shadow, though the mountain summits around him were things of light and fire. The mountain summits around him were things of light and fire, and the little things in the rocks near at hand were drenched with light and beauty, a vein of green mineral piercing the grey, a flash of small crystal here and there, a minute, minutely beautiful orange lichen close beside his face. There were deep, mysterious shadows in the gorge, blue deepening into purple, and purple into a luminous darkness, and overhead was the illimitable vastness of the sky. But he heeded these things no longer, but lay quite still there, smiling as if he were content now merely to have escaped from the Valley of the Blind, in which he had thought to be King. And the glow of the sunset passed, and the night came, and still he lay there, under the cold, clear stars.

45

The Empire of the Ants

1.

When Captain Gerilleau received instructions to take his new gunboat, the Benjamin Constant, to Badama on the Batemo arm of the Guaramadema and there assist the inhabitants against a plague of ants, he suspected the authorities of mockery. His promotion had been romantic and irregular, the affections of a prominent Brazilian lady and the captain's liquid eyes had played a part in the process, and the Diario and O Futuro had been lamentably disrespectful in their comments. He felt he was to give further occasion for disrespect.

He was a Creole, his conceptions of etiquette and discipline were pure-blooded Portuguese, and it was only to Holroyd, the Lancashire engineer, who had come over with the boat, and as an exercise in the use of English—his "th" sounds were very uncertain—that he opened his heart.

"It is in effect," he said, "to make me absurd! What can a man do against ants? Dey come, dey go."

"They say," said Holroyd, "that these don't go. That chap you said was a Sambo—"

"Zambo—it is a sort of mixture of blood."

"Sambo. He said the people are going!"

The captain smoked fretfully for a time. "Dese things 'ave to happen," he said at last. "What is it? Plagues of ants and suchlike as God wills. Dere was a plague in Trinidad—the like ants that carry leaves. Orl der oranges-trees, all der mangoes! What does it matter? Sometimes ant armies come into your houses—fighting ants; a different sort. You go and they clean the house. Then you come back again;—the house is clean, like new! No cockroaches, no fleas, no jiggers in the floor."

"That Sambo chap," said Holroyd, "says these are a different sort of ant."

The captain shrugged his shoulders, fumed, and gave his attention to a cigarette.

Afterwards he reopened the subject. "My dear 'Olroyd, what am I to do about des infernal ants?"

The captain reflected. "It is ridiculous," he said. But in the afternoon he put on his full uniform and went ashore, and jars and boxes came back to the ship and subsequently he did. And Holroyd sat on deck in evening coolness and smoked profoundly and marvelled at Brazil. They were six days up the Amazon, some hundreds of miles from the ocean, and east and west of him there was horizon like the sea, and to the south nothing but a sand-bank island with some tufts of scrub. The water was always running like a sluice, thick with dirt, animated with crocodiles and hovering birds, and fed by some inexhaustible source of tree trunks; and the waste of it, the headlong waste of it, filled his soul. The town of Alemquer, with its meagre church, its thatched sheds for houses, its discoloured ruins of ampler days, seemed a little thing lost in this wilderness of Nature, a sixpence dropped on Sahara. He was a young man, this was his first site of the tropics, he came straight from England, where Nature is hedged, ditched, and drained into the perfection of submission, and he had suddenly discovered the insignificance of man. For six days they had been steaming up the sea by unfrequented channels, and man had been as rare as a rare butterfly. One saw one day a canoe, another day a distant station, the next no men at all. He began to perceive that man is indeed a rare animal, having but a precarious hold upon this land.

He perceived it more clearly as the days passed, and he made his devious way to the Batemo, in the company of this remarkable commander, who ruled over one big gun, and was forbidden to waste his ammunition. Holroyd was learning Spanish industriously, but he was still in the present tense and substantive stage of speech, and the only other person who had any words of English was a negro stoker, who had them all wrong. The second in command was a Portuguese, da Cunha, who spoke French, but it was a different sort of French from the French Holroyd had learned in Southport, and their intercourse was confined to politenesses and simple propositions about weather. And the weather, like everything else in this amazing new world, the weather had no human aspect, and was hot by night and hot by day, and the air steam, even the wind was hot steam, smelling of vegetation in decay: and the alligators and the strange birds, the flies of many sorts and sizes, the beetles, the ants, the snakes and monkeys seemed to wonder what man was doing in an atmosphere that had no gladness in its sunshine and no coolness in its night. To wear clothing was intolerable, but to cast it aside was to scorch by day, and expose an ampler area to the mosquitoes by night; to go on deck by day was to be blinded by glare and to stay below was to suffocate. And in the daytime came certain flies, extremely clever and noxious about one's wrist and ankle. Captain Gerilleau, who was Holroyd's sole distraction from these physical distresses, developed into a formidable bore, telling the simple story of his heart's affections day by day, a string of anonymous women, as if he was telling beads. Sometimes he suggested sport, and they shot at alligators, and at rare intervals they came to human aggregations in the waste of trees, and stayed for a day or so, and drank and sat about; and one night, danced with Creole girls, who found Holroyd's poor elements of Spanish, without either past tense or future, amply sufficient for their purposes. But these were mere luminous chinks in the long grey passage of the streaming river, up which the throbbing engines beat. A certain liberal heathen deity, in the shape of demi-john, held seductive court aft, and it is probable, forward.

But Gerilleau learned things about the ants, more things and more, at this stopping-place and that, and became interested in his mission.

"Dey are a new sort of ant," he said. "We have got to be—what do you call it—? Entomologie? Big. Five centimetres! Some bigger! It is ridiculous. We are like monkeys—sent to pick insects...But dey are eating up the country."

He burst out indignantly. "Suppose—suddenly, there are complications with Europe. Here am I—soon we shall be above the Rio Negro—and my gun, useless!"

He nursed his knee and mused.

"Dose people who were dere at de dancing place, dey 'ave come down. Dey 'ave lost all they got. De ants come to deir house one afternoon. Everyone run out. You know when de ants come one must—every one runs out and they go over the house. If you stayed they'd eat you. See? Well, presently dey go back; dey say, 'The ants 'ave gone...' De ants 'aven't gone. Dey try to go in—de son, 'e gose in. De ants fight."

"Swarm over him?"

"Bite 'im. Presently he comes out again—screaming and running. He runs past them to river. See? He get into de water and drowns de ants—yes." Gerilleau paused, brought his liquid eyes close to Holroyd's face, tapped Holroyd's knee with his knuckle. "That night he dies, just as if he was stung by snake."

"Poisoned—by the ants?"

"Who knows?" Gerilleau shrugged his shoulders. "Perhaps they bit him badly...When I joined dis service I joined to fight men. Dese things, dese ants, dey come and go. It is no business for men."

After that he talked frequently of ants to Holroyd, and whenever they chanced to drift against any speck of humanity in that waste of water and sunshine and distant trees, Holroyd's improving knowledge of the language enabled him to recognise the ascendant word Sauba, more and more completely dominating the whole.

He perceived the ants were becoming interesting, and the nearer he drew to them the more interesting they became. Gerilleau abandoned his old themes almost suddenly, and the Portuguese lieutenant became a conversational figure; he knew something about the leaf-cutting ant, and expanded his knowledge. Gerilleau sometimes rendered what he had to tell to Holroyd. He told of the little workers that swarm and fight, and the big workers that command and rule, and how these latter always crawled to the neck and how their bites drew blood. He told how they cut leaves and made fungus beds, and how their nests in Caracas are sometimes a hundred yards across. Two days the three men spent disputing whether ants have eyes. The discussion grew dangerously heated on the second afternoon, and Holroyd saved the situation by going ashore in a boat to catch ants and see. He captured various specimens and returned and some had eyes and some hadn't. Also, they argued, do ants bite or sting?

"Dese ants," said Gerilleau, after collecting information at a rancho, "have big eyes. They don't run about blind—not as most ants do. No! Dey get in corners and watch what you do."

"And they sting?" asked Holroyd.

"Yes. Dey sting. Dere is poison in the sting." He meditated. "I do not see what men can do against ants. Dey come and go."

"But these don't go."

"They will," said Gerilleau.

Past Tamandu there is a long low coast of eighty miles without any population, and then ones comes to the confluence of the main river and the Batemo arm, like a great lake, and then the forest came nearer, came at last intimately near. The character of the channel changes, snags abound, and the Benjamin Constant moored by a cable that night, under the very shadow of dark trees. For the first time for many days came a spell of coolness, and Holroyd and Gerilleau sat late, smoking cigars and enjoying this delicious sensation. Gerilleau's mind was full of ants and what they could do. He decided to sleep at last, and lay down on a mattress on deck, a man hopelessly perplexed; his last words, when he already seemed asleep, were to ask, with a flourish of despair: "What can one do with ants...? De whole thing is absurd."

Holroyd was left to scratch his bitten wrists, and meditate alone.

He sat on the bulwark and listened to changes in Gerilleau's breathing until he was fast asleep, and then the ripple and lap of stream took his mind, and brought back that sense of immensity that had been growing upon him since first he had left Para and come up the river. The monitor showed but one small light, and there was first a little talking forward and then stillness. His eyes went from the dim black outlines of the middle works of the gunboat towards the bank, to the black overwhelming mysteries of forest, lit now and then by a fire-fly, and never still from the murmur of alien and mysterious activities...

It was the inhuman immensity of this land that astonished and oppressed him. He knew the skies were empty of men, the stars were specks in an incredible vastness of space; he knew the ocean was enormous and untamable, but in England he had come to think of the land as man's. In England it is indeed man's, the wild things live by sufferance, grow on lease, everywhere the roads, the fences, and absolute security runs. In an atlas, too, the land is man's, and all coloured to show his claim to it—in vivid contrast to the universal independent blueness of the sea. He had taken it for granted that a day would come when everywhere about the earth, plough and culture, light tramways, and good roads, an ordered security, would prevail. But now he doubted.

This forest was interminable, it had an air of being invincible, and Man seemed at best an infrequent precarious intruder. One travelled for miles amidst the still silent struggle of giant trees, of strangulating creepers, of assertive flowers, everywhere the alligator, the turtle, and endless varieties of bird and insects seemed at home, dwelt irreplaceable—but man, man at most held a footing upon resentful clearings, fought weeds, fought beasts and insects for the barest foothold, fell a prey to snake and beast, insects and fever, and was presently carried away. In many places down the river he had been manifestly driven back, this deserted creek or that preserved the name of a casa, and here and there ruinous white walls and shattered towers enforced the lesson. The puma, the jaguar, were more the masters here...

Who are the real masters?

In a few miles of this forest there must be more ants than there are men in the world! This seemed to Holroyd a perfectly new idea. In a few thousand years men had emerged from barbarism to a stage of civilisation that made them feel lords of the future and masters of earth! But what was to prevent ants evolving also? Such ants as one knew lived in little communities of a few thousand individuals, made no concerted efforts against the greater world. But they had a language, they had an intelligence! Why should things stop at that any more then men had stopped at the barbaric stage? Suppose presently the ants began to store knowledge, just as men had done by means of books and records, use weapons, form great empires, sustain a planned and organised war?

Things came back to him that Gerilleau had gathered about these ants they were approaching. They used a poison like the poison of snakes. They obeyed greater leaders even as the leaf-cutting ants do. They were carnivorous, and where they came they stayed...

The forest was very still. The water lapped incessantly against the side. About the lantern overhead there eddied a noiseless whirl of phantom moths.

Gerilleau stirred in the darkness and sighed. "What can one do?" he murmured, and turned over and was still again.

Holroyd was roused from meditations that were becoming sinister by the hum of a mosquito.

2.

The next morning Holroyd learned they were within forty kilometers of Badama, and his interest in the banks intensified. He came up whenever an opportunity offered to examine his surroundings. He could see no signs of human occupation whatever, save for a weedy ruin of a house and green-stained facade of the long-deserted monastery at Moju, with a forest tree growing out of a vacant window space, and great creepers netted across its vacant portals. Several flights of strange yellow butterflies with semi-transparent wings crossed the river that morning, and many alighted on the monitor and were killed by men. It was towards afternoon that they came upon the derelict cuberta.

She did not at first appear to be derelict; both her sails were set and hanging slack in the afternoon calm, and there was the figure of a man sitting on the fore planking beside the shipped sweeps. Another man appeared to be sleeping face downwards on the sort of longitudinal bridge, these big canoes have in the waist. But it was presently apparent, from the sway of her rudder and the way she drifted into the course of the gunboat, that something was out of order with her. Gerilleau surveyed her through a field-glass, and became interested in queer darkness of the face of the sitting man, a red-faced man he seemed, without a nose—crouching he was rather than sitting, and the longer the captain looked the less he liked to look at him, and the less able he was to take his glasses away.

But he did so at last, and went a little way to call up Holroyd. Then he went back to hail the cuberta. He hailed her again, and so she drove past him. Santa Rosa stood out clearly as her name.

As she came by and into the wake of the monitor, she pitched a little, and suddenly the figure of the crouching man collapsed as though all it's joints had given way. His hat fell off, his head was not nice to look at, and his body flopped lax and rolled out of sight behind the bulwarks.

"Caramba!" cried Gerilleau, and resorted to Holroyd forthwith.

Holroyd was halfway up the companion. "Did you see dat?" said the captain.

"Dead!" said Holroyd. "Yes. You'd better send a boat aboard. There's something wrong."

"Did you—by any chance—see his face?"

"What was it like?"

"It was—ugh—! I have no words." And the captain suddenly turned his back on Holroyd and became a active and strident commander.

The gunboat came about, steamed parallel to the erratic course of the canoe, and dropped the boat with Lieutenant da Cunha and three sailors to board her. Then the curiosity of the captain made him draw up almost alongside as the lieutenant got aboard, so that the whole of the Santa Rosa deck and hold, was visible to Holroyd.

He saw now clearly that the sole crew of the vessel was these two dead men, and though he could not see their faces, he saw by their outstretched hands, which were all of ragged flesh, that they had been subjected to some strange exceptional process of decay. For a moment his attention, concentrated on these two enigmatical bundles of dirty cloths and laxly flung limbs, and then his eyes went forward to discover the open hold piled high with trunks and cases, and aft, to where the little cabin gaped inexplicably empty. Then he became aware that the planks of the middle decking were dotted with moving black specks.

His attention was riveted by these specks. They were all walking in directions radiating from the fallen man in a manner—the image came unsought to his mind—like the crowd dispersing from a bull-fight.

He became aware of Gerilleau beside him. "Capo," he said, "have you your glasses? Can you focus as closely as those planks there?"

Gerilleau made an effort, grunted, and handed him the glasses.

There followed a moment of scrutiny. "It's ants," said the Englishman, and handed the focused field-glasses back to Gerilleau.

His impression of them was of a crowd of large black ants, very like ordinary ants except for size, and for the fact some of the larger of them bore a sort of clothing of grey. But at the time his inspection was too brief for particulars. The head of Lieutenant da Cunha appeared over the side of the cuberta, and a brief colloquy ensued.

"You must go aboard," said Gerilleau.

The lieutenant objected that the boat was full of ants.

"You have your boots," said Gerilleau.

The lieutenant changed the subject. "How did these men die?" he asked.

Captain Gerilleau embarked upon speculation that Holroyd could not follow, and the two men disputed with a certain vehemence. Holroyd took up the field-glass and resumed his scrutiny, first of ants and then of the dead man amidships.

He has described these ants to me very particularly.

He says they were as large as any ants he has ever seen, black and moving with a steady deliberation very different from the mechanical fussiness of the common ant. About one in twenty was much larger than it's fellows, and with an exceptionally large head. These reminded him at once of the master workers who are said to rule over the leaf-cutter ants; like them they seemed to be directing and co-ordinating the general movements. They tilted their bodies back in a manner altogether singular, as if they made some use of the fore feet. And he had a curious fancy, that he was too far off to verify, that most of these ants of both kinds were wearing accoutrements, had things strapped about their bodies by bright white bands like white metal threads...

He put down the glasses abruptly, realising that the question of discipline between the captain and his subordinate had become acute.

"It is your duty," said the captain, "to go aboard. It is my instructions."

The lieutenant seemed on the verge of refusing. The head of one of the mulatto sailors appeared beside him.

"I believe these men were killed by ants," said Holroyd abruptly in English.

The captain burst into rage. He made no answer to Holroyd. "I have commanded you to go aboard," he screamed to his subordinate in Portuguese. "If you do not go aboard forthwith it is mutiny—rank mutiny. Mutiny and cowardice! Where is the courage that should animate us? I will have you in irons, I will have you shot like a dog." He began a torrent of abuse and curses, he danced to and fro. He shook his fists, he behaved as if beside himself with rage, and the lieutenant, white and still, stood looking at him. The crew appeared forward, with amazed faces.

Suddenly, in a pause of this outbreak, the lieutenant came to some heroic decision, saluted, drew himself together and clambered upon the deck of the cuberta.

"Ah!" said Gerilleau, and his mouth shut like a trap. Holroyd saw the ants retreating before da Cunha's boots. The Portuguese walked slowly to the fallen man, stooped down, hesitated, clutched his coat and turned him over. A black swarm of ants rushed out of the clothes, and da Cunha stepped back very quickly and trod two or three times on the deck.

Holroyd put up the glasses. He saw the scattered ants about the invader's feet, and doing what he had never seen ants doing before. They had nothing of the blind movements of the common ant; they were looking at him—as a rallying crowd of men might look at some gigantic monster that had dispersed it.

"How did he die?" the captain shouted.

Holroyd understood the Portuguese to say the body was too much eaten to tell.

"What is there forward?" asked Gerilleau.

The lieutenant walked a few paces, and began his answer in Portuguese. He stopped abruptly and beat off something from his leg. He made some peculiar steps as if he was trying to stamp on something invisible, and went quickly towards the side. Then he controlled himself, turned about, walked deliberately forward to the hold, clambered up to the fore decking, from which the sweeps are worked, stooped for a time over the second man, groaned audibly, and made his way back and aft to the cabin; moving very rigidly. He turned and began a conversation with his captain, cold and respectful in tone on either side, contrasting vividly with the wrath and insult of a few moments before. Holroyd gathered only fragments of it's purport.

He reverted to the field-glass, and was surprised to find the ants had vanished from all exposed surfaces of the deck. He turned towards the shadow beneath the decking, and it seemed to him they were full of watching eyes.

The cuberta, it was agreed, was derelict, but too full of ants to put men aboard to sit and sleep: it must be towed. The lieutenant went forward to take in and adjust the cable, and the men in the boat stood up to be ready to help him. Holroyd's glasses searched the canoe.

He became more and more impressed by the fact that a great if minute and furtive activity was going on. He perceived that a number of gigantic ants—they seemed nearly a couple of inches in length—carrying oddly-shaped burthens for which he could imagine no use—were moving in rushes from one point of obscurity to another. They did not move in columns across the exposed places, but in open, spaced-out lines, oddly suggestive of the rushes of modern infantry advancing under fire. A number were taking cover under the dead man's clothes, and a perfect swarm was gathering along the side over which da Cunha must presently go.

He did not see them actually rush for the lieutenant as he returned, but he has no doubt they did make a concerted rush. Suddenly the lieutenant was shouting and cursing and beating at his legs. "I'm stung!" he shouted, with a face of hate and accusation towards Gerilleau.

Then he vanished over the side, dropped into his boat, and plunged at once into the water. Holroyd heard the splash.

The three men in the boat pulled him out and brought him aboard, and that night he died.

3.

Holroyd and the captain came out of the cabin in which the swollen and contorted body of the lieutenant lay, and stood together at the stern of the monitor, staring at the sinister vessel they trailed behind them. It was a close, dark night that had only phantom flickers of sheet lightning to illuminate it. The cuberta, a vague black triangle, rocked about in the steamer's wake, her sails bobbing and flapping, and the black smoke from the funnels, spark-lit ever and again, streamed over her swaying masts.

Gerilleau's mind was inclined to run on the unkind things the lieutenant had said in the heat of his last fever.

"He says I murdered 'im," he protested. "It is simply absurd. Someone 'ad to go aboard. Are we to run away from these confounded ants whenever they show up?"

Holroyd said nothing. He was thinking of a disciplined rush of little black shapes across bare sunlit planking.

"It was his place to go," harped Gerilleau. "He died in the execution of his duty. What has he to complain of? Murdered...! But the poor fellow was—what is it—? Demented. He was not in his right mind. The poison swelled him...U'm."

They came to a long silence.

"We will sink that canoe—burn it."

"And then?"

The inquiry irritated Gerilleau. His shoulders went up, his hands flew out at right angles from his body. "What is one to do?" he said, his voice going up to an angry squeak.

"Anyhow," he broke out vindictively, "every ant in dat cuberta—! I will burn dem alive!"

Holroyd was not moved to conversation. A distant ululation of howling monkeys filled the sultry night with foreboding sounds, and as the gunboat drew near the black mysterious banks this was reinforced by a depressing clamour of frogs.

"What is one to do?" the captain repeated after a vast interval, and suddenly becoming active and savage and blasphemous, decided to burn the Santa Rosa without further delay. Everyone aboard was pleased by that idea, everyone helped with zest; they pulled in the cable, cut it, and dropped the boat and fired her with tow and kerosene, and soon the cuberta was crackling and flaring merrily amidst the immensities of the tropical night. Holroyd watched the mounting yellow flare against the blackness, and the livid flashes of sheet lightning that came and went above the forest summits, throwing them into momentary silhouette, and his stoker stood behind him watching also.

The stoker was stirred to the depths of his linguistics. "Sauba go pop, pop," he said. "Wahaw!" and laughed richly.

But Holroyd was thinking that these little creatures on the decked canoe had also eyes and brains.

The whole thing impressed him as incredibly foolish and wrong, but—what was one to do? This question came back enormously reinforced on the morrow, when at last the gunboat reached Badama.

This place, with its leaf-thatch-covered houses and sheds, its creeper-invaded sugar-mill, its little jetty of timber and canes, was very still in the morning heat, and showed never a sign of living men. Whatever ants there were at that distance were too small to see.

"All the people have gone," said Gerilleau, "but we will do one thing anyhow. We will 'oot and vissel."

So Holroyd hooted and whistled.

Then the captain fell into a doubting fit of the worst kind. "Dere is one thing we can do," he said presently.

"What's that?" said Holroyd.

"'Oot and vissel again."

So they did.

The captain walked his deck and gesticulated to himself. He seemed to have many things on his mind. Fragments of speeches came from his lips. He appeared to be addressing some imaginary public tribunal either in Spanish or Portuguese. Holroyd's improving ear detected something about ammunition. He came out of these preoccupations suddenly into English. "My dear 'Olroyd!" he cried, and broke off with "But what can one do?"

They took the boat and field-glasses, and went close in to examine the place. They made out a number of big ants, whose still postures had a certain effect of watching them, dotted about the edge of the rude embarkation jetty. Gerilleau tried ineffectual pistol shots at these. Holroyd thinks he distinguished curious earthworks running between the nearer houses, that may have been the work of insect conquerors of those human habitations. The explorers pulled past the jetty, and became aware of a human skeleton wearing a loin cloth, and very bright and clean and shining, lying beyond. They came to a pause regarding this...

"I 'ave all dose lives to consider," said Gerilleau suddenly.

Holroyd turned and stared at the captain, realising slowly that he referred to the unappetising mixture of races that constituted his crew.

"To send a landing party—it is impossible—impossible. They will be poisoned, they will swell, they will swell up and abuse me and die. It is totally impossible...If we land, I must land alone, alone in thick boots and with my life in my hand. Perhaps I should live. Or again—I might not land. I do not know. I do not know."

Holroyd thought he did, but he said nothing.

"De whole thing," said Gerilleau suddenly, "'as been got up to make me ridiculous. De whole thing!"

They paddled about and regarded the clean white skeleton from various points of view, and then they returned to the gunboat. Then Gerilleau's indecisions became terrible. Steam was got up, and in the afternoon the monitor went on up the river with an air of going to ask somebody something, and by sunset came back again, and anchored. A thunderstorm gathered and broke furiously, and then the night became beautifully cool and quiet and everyone slept on deck. Except Gerilleau, who tossed about and muttered. In the dawn he awakened Holroyd.

"Lord!" said Holroyd, "what now?"

"I have decided," said the captain.

"What—to land?" said Holroyd, sitting up brightly.

"No!" said the captain, and was for a time very reserved. "I have decided," he repeated, and Holroyd manifested symptoms of impatience.

"Well—yes," said the captain. "I shall fire de big gun!"

And he did! Heaven knows what the ants thought of it, but he did. He fired it twice with great sternness and ceremony. All the crew had wadding in their ears, and there was effect of going into action about the whole affair, and first hit and wrecked the old sugar-mill, and then they smashed the abandoned store behind the jetty. And then Gerilleau experienced the inevitable reaction.

"It is no good," he said to Holroyd; "no good at all. No sort of bally good. We must go back—for instructions. Dere will be de devil of a row about dis ammunition—oh! De devil of a row! You don't know, 'Olroyd..."

He stood regarding the world in infinite perplexity for a space.

"But what else was there to do?" he cried.

In the afternoon the monitor started down stream again, and in the evening a landing party took the body of the lieutenant and buried it on the bank upon which the new ants have so far not appeared...

4.

I heard this story in a fragmentary state from Holroyd not three weeks ago. These new ants have got into his brain, and he has come back to England with the idea, as he says, of "exciting people" about them "before it is too late." He says they threaten British

Guiana, which cannot be much over a trifle of a thousand miles from their present sphere of activity, and that the Colonial Office ought to get to work upon them at once. He declaims with great passion: "These are intelligent ants. Just think what that means!"

There can be no doubt they are a serious pest, and that the Brazilian Government is well advised in offering a prize of five hundred pounds for some effectual method of extirpation. It is certain too, that since they first appeared in the hills beyond Badama, about three years ago, they have achieved extraordinary conquests. The whole of the south bank of the Batemo River, for nearly sixty miles, they have in their effectual occupation; they have driven men out completely, occupied plantations and settlements, and boarded and captured at least one ship. It is even said they have in some inexplicable way bridged the very considerable Capuarana arm and pushed many miles towards the Amazon itself. There can be little doubt that they are far more reasonable and with a far better social organisation then any previously known ant species; instead of being dispersed societies they are organised into what is in effect a single nation; but their peculiar and immediate formidableness lies not so much in this as in the intelligent use they make of poison against their enemies. It would seem this poison of theirs is closely akin to snake poison, and it is highly probable they actually manufacture it, and that the larger individuals among them carry the needle-like crystals of it in their attacks upon men.

Of course it is extremely difficult to get any detailed information about these new competitors for sovereignty of the globe. No eye-witnesses of their activity, except for such glimpses as Holroyd's, have survived the encounter. The most extraordinary legends of their prowess and capacity are in circulation in the region of the Upper Amazon, and grow daily as the steady advance of the invader stimulates men's imaginations through their fears. These strange little creatures are credited not only with the use of implements and knowledge of fire and metals and with organised feats of engineering that stagger our Northern minds—used as we are to such feats as that of the Saubas of Rio de Janeiro, who, in 1841, drove a tunnel under Parahyba, where it is as wide as the Thames at London Bridge—but with an organised and detailed method of record and communication analogous to our books. So far their action has been a steady progressive settlement, involving the flight or slaughter of every human being in the new areas they invade. They are increasing rapidly in numbers, and Holroyd at least is firmly convinced that they will finally dispossess man over the whole of tropical South America.

And why should they stop at tropical South America?

Well, there they are, anyhow. By 1911 or thereabouts, if they go on as they are going, they ought to strike the Capuarana Extension Railway, and force themselves upon the attention of the European capitalist.

By 1920 they will be halfway down the Amazon. I fix 1950 or '60 at least for the discovery of Europe.

46

The Beautiful Suit

There was once a little man whose mother made him a beautiful suit of clothes. It was green and gold, and woven so that I can not describe how delicate and fine it was, and there was a tie of orange fluffiness that tied up under his chin. And the buttons in their newness shone like stars. He was proud and pleased by his suit beyond measure, and stood before the long looking-glass when first he put it on, so astonished and delighted with it that he could hardly turn himself away.

He wanted to wear it everywhere, and show it to all sorts of people. He thought over all the places he had ever visited, and all the scenes he had ever heard described, and tried to imagine what the feel of it would be if he were to go now to those scenes and places wearing his shining suit, and he wanted to go out forthwith into the long grass and hot sunshine of the meadow wearing it. Just to wear it! But his mother told him "No," She told him he must take great care of his suit, for never would he have another nearly so fine; he must save it and save it, and only wear it on rare great occasions. It was his wedding-suit, she said. And she took the buttons and twisted them up with tissue paper for fear their bright newness should be tarnished, and she tacked little guards over the cuffs and elbows, and wherever the suit was most likely to come to harm. He hated and resisted these things, but what could he do? And at last her warnings and persuasions had effect, and he consented to take off his beautiful suit and fold it into its proper creases, and put it away. It was almost as though he gave it up again. But he was always thinking of wearing it, and of the supreme occasions when some day it might be worn without the guards, without the tissue paper on the buttons, utterly and delightfully, never caring, beautiful beyond measure.

One night, when he was dreaming of it after his habit, he dreamt he took the tissue paper from one of the buttons, and found its brightness a little faded, and that distressed him mightily in his dream. He polished the poor faded button and polished it, and if anything, it grew duller. He woke up and lay awake, thinking of the brightness slightly dulled, and wondering how he would feel if perhaps when the great occasions (whatever it might be) should arrive, one button should chance to be ever so little short of its first glittering freshness, and for days and days that thought remained with him distressingly. And when next his mother let him wear his suit, he was tempted and nearly gave way to the temptation just to fumble off a bit of tissue paper and see if indeed the buttons were keeping as bright as ever.

He went trimly along on his way to church, full of this wild desire. For you must know his mother did, with repeated and careful warnings, let him wear his suit at times, on Sundays, for example, to and fro from church, when there was no threatening of rain, no dust blowing, nor anything to injure it, with its buttons covered and its protections tacked upon it, and a sunshade in his hand to shadow it, if there seemed too strong a sunlight for its colours. And always, after such occasions, he brushed it over and folded it exquisitely as she had taught him, and put it away again.

Now all these restrictions his mother set to the wearing of his suit he obeyed, always he obeyed them, until one strange night he woke up and saw the moonlight shining outside his window. It seemed to him the moonlight was not common moonlight, nor the night a common night, and for a while he lay quite drowsily, with this odd persuasion in his mind. Thought joined on to thought like things that whisper warmly in the shadows. Then he sat up in his little bed suddenly very alert, with his heart beating very fast, and a quiver in his body from top to toe. He had made up his mind. He knew that now he was going to wear his suit as it should be worn. He had no doubt in the matter. He was afraid, terribly afraid, but glad, glad.

He got out of his bed and stood for a moment by the window looking at the moonshine-flooded garden, and trembling at the thing he meant to do. The air was full of a minute clamour of crickets and murmurings, of the infinitesimal shouting of little living things. He went very gently across the creaking boards, for fear that he might wake the sleeping house, to the big dark clothes-press wherein his beautiful suit lay folded, and he took it out garment by garment, and softly and very eagerly tore off its tissue-paper covering and its tacked protections until there it was, perfect and delightful as he had seen it when first his mother had given it to him—a long time it seemed ago. Not a button had tarnished, not a thread had faded on this dear suit of his; he was glad enough for weeping, as in a noiseless hurry he put it on. And then back he went, soft and quick, to the window that looked out upon the garden, and stood there for a minute, shining in the moonlight, with his buttons twinkling like stars, before he got out on the sill, and making as little of a rustling as he could, clambered down to the garden path below. He stood before his mother's house, and it was white and nearly as plain as by day, with every window-blind but his own shut like an eye that sleeps. The trees cast still shadows like intricate black lace upon the wall.

The garden in the moonlight was very different from the garden by day; moonshine was tangled in hedges and stretched in phantom cobwebs from spray to spray. Every flower was gleaming white or crimson black, and the air was a-quiver with the thridding of small crickets and nightingales singing unseen in the depths of the trees.

There was no darkness in the world, but only warm, mysterious shadows, and all the leaves and spikes were edged and lined with iridescent jewels of dew. The night was warmer than any other night had ever been; the heavens by some miracle at once vaster and nearer, and in spite of the great ivory-tinted moon that ruled the world, the sky was full of stars.

The little man did not shout nor sing for all his infinite gladness. He stood for a time like one awe-stricken, and then with a queer small cry and holding out his arms, he ran out as if he would embrace at once the whole round immensity of the world. He did not follow the neat set paths that cut the garden squarely, but thrust across the beds and through the wet, tall, scented herbs, though the night-stock and the nicotine and the clusters of phantom white mallow flowers and through the thickets of southernwood and lavender, and knee-deep across a wide space of mignonette.

He came to the great hedge, and he thrust his way through it; and though the thorns of the brambles scored him deeply and tore threads from his wonderful suit, and though burrs and goose-grass and havers caught and clung to him, he did not care. He did not care, for he knew it was all part of the wearing for which he had longed. "I am glad I put on my suit," he said; "I am glad I wore my suit."

Beyond the hedge he came to the duck-pond, or at least to what was the duck-pond by day. But by night it was a great bowl of silver moonshine all noisy with singing frogs, of wonderful silver moonshine twisted and clotted with strange patternings, and the little man ran down into its waters between the thin black rushes, knee-deep and waist-deep and to his shoulders, smiting the water to black and shining wavelets with either hand, swaying and shivering wavelets, amidst which the stars were netted in the tangled reflections of the brooding trees upon the bank. He waded until he swam, and so he crossed the pond and came out upon the other side, trailing, as it seemed to him, not duckweed, but very silver in long, clinging, dripping masses. And up he went through the transfigured tangles of the willow-herb and the uncut seeding grasses of the farther bank. He came glad and breathless into the high road. "I am glad," he said, "beyond measure, that I had clothes that fitted this occasion."

The high-road ran straight as an arrow flies, straight into the deep-blue pit of the sky beneath the moon, a white and shining road between the singing nightingales, and along it he went, running now and leaping, and now walking and rejoicing, in the clothes his mother had made for him with tireless, loving hands. The road was deep in dust, but that for him was only soft whiteness; and as he went a great dim moth came fluttering round his wet and shimmering and hastening figure. At first he did not heed the moth, and then he waved his hands at it, and made a sort of dance with it, as it circled round his head. "Soft moth!" he cried, "Dear moth! And wonderful night, wonderful night of the world! Do you think my clothes are beautiful, dear moth? As beautiful as your scales and all this silver vesture of the earth and sky?"

And the moth circled closer and closer until at last its velvet wings just brushed his lips...

And next morning they found him dead, with his neck broken, in the bottom of the stone pit, with his beautiful clothes a little bloody, and foul and stained with the duckweed from the pond. But his face was a face of such happiness that, had you seen it, you would have understood indeed how that he had died happy, never knowing that cool and streaming silver for the duckweed in the pond.

47

THE DOOR IN THE WALL

1.

One confidential evening, not three months ago, Lionel Wallace told me this story of the Door in the Wall. And at the time I thought that so far as he was concerned it was a true story.

He told it me with such a direct simplicity of conviction that I could not do otherwise than believe in him. But in the morning, in my own flat, I woke to a different atmosphere, and as I lay in bed and recalled the things he had told me, stripped of the glamour of his earnest slow voice, denuded of the focused shaded table light, the shadowy atmosphere that wrapped about him and the pleasant bright things, the dessert and glasses and napery of the dinner we had shared, making them for the time a bright little world quite cut off from everyday realities, I saw it all as frankly incredible. "He was mystifying!" I said, and then: "How well he did it...! It isn't quite the thing I should have expected him, of all people, to do well."

Afterwards, as I sat up in bed and sipped my morning tea, I found myself trying to account for the flavour of reality that perplexed me in his impossible reminiscences, by supposing they did in some way suggest, present, convey—I hardly know which word to use—experiences it was otherwise impossible to tell.

Well I don't resort to that explanation now. I have got over my intervening doubts. I believe now, as I believed at the moment of telling, that Wallace did to the very best of his ability strip the truth of his secret for me. But whether he himself saw, or only thought he saw, whether he himself was the possessor of an inestimable privilege, or the victim of a fantastic dream, I cannot pretend to guess. Even the facts of his death, which ended my doubts forever, throw no light on that. That much the reader must judge for himself.

I forget now what chance comment or criticism of mine moved so reticent a man to confide in me. He was I think, defending himself against an imputation of slackness and unreliability I had made in relation to a great public movement in which he had disappointed me. But he plunged suddenly. "I have" he said, "a preoccupation—

"I know," he went on, after a pause that he devoted to the study of his cigar ash, "I have been negligent. The fact is—it isn't a case of ghosts or apparitions—but—it's an odd thing to tell of, Redmond—I am haunted. I am haunted by something—that rather takes the light out of things, that fills me with longings..."

He paused, checked by that English shyness that so often overcomes us when we would speak of moving or grave or beautiful things. "You were at Saint Althelstan's all through," he said, and for a moment that seemed to me quite irrelevant. "Well—" and he paused. Then very haltingly at first, but afterwards more easily, he began to tell of the thing that was hidden in his life, the haunting memory of a beauty and a happiness that filled his heart with insatiable longings that made all the interests and spectacle of worldly life seem dull and tedious and vain to him.

Now that I have the clue to it, the thing seems written visibly in his face. I have a photograph in which that look of detachment has been caught and intensified. It reminds me of what a woman once said of him—a woman who had loved him greatly. "Suddenly," she said, "the interest goes out of him. He forgets you. He doesn't care a rap for you—under his very nose..."

Yet the interest was not always out of him, and when he was holding his attention to a thing Wallace could contrive to be an extremely successful man. His career, indeed, is set with successes. He left me behind him long ago; he soared up over my head, and cut a figure in the world that I couldn't cut—anyhow. He was still a year short of forty, and they say now that he would have been in office and very probably in the new Cabinet if he had lived. At school he always beat me without effort—as it were by nature. We were at school together at Saint Althelstan's College in West Kensington for almost all our school-time. He came into the school as my co-equal, but he left far above me, in a blaze of scholarships and brilliant performance. Yet I think I made a fair average running. And it was at school I heard first of the "Door in the Wall—" that I was to hear of a second time only a month before his death.

To him at least the Door in the Wall was a real door leading through a real wall to immortal realities. Of that I am now quite assured.

And it came into his life early, when he was a little fellow between five and six. I remember how, as he sat making his confession to me with a slow gravity, he reasoned and reckoned the date of it. "There was," he said, "a crimson Virginia creeper in it—all one bright uniform crimson in a clear amber sunshine against a white wall. That came into the impression somehow, though I don't clearly remember how, and there were horse-chestnut leaves upon the clean pavement outside the green door. They were blotched yellow and green, you know, not brown nor dirty, so that they must have been new fallen. I take it that means October. I look out for horse-chestnut leaves every year, and I ought to know."

"If I'm right in that, I was about five years and four months old."

He was, he said, rather a precocious little boy—he learned to talk at an abnormally early age, and he was so sane and "old-fashioned," as people say, that he was permitted an amount of initiative that most children scarcely attain by seven or eight. His mother died when he was born, and he was under the less vigilant and authoritative care of a nursery governess. His father was a stern, preoccupied lawyer, who gave him little attention, and expected great things of him. For all his brightness he found life a little grey and dull I think. And one day he wandered.

He could not recall the particular neglect that enabled him to get away, nor the course he took among the West Kensington roads. All that had faded among the incurable blurs of memory. But the white wall and the green door stood out quite distinctly.

As his memory of that remote childish experience ran, he did at the very first sight of that door experience a peculiar emotion, an attraction, a desire to get to the door and open it and walk in.

And at the same time he had the clearest conviction that either it was unwise or it was wrong of him—he could not tell which—to yield to this attraction. He insisted upon it as a curious thing that he knew from the very beginning—unless memory has played him the queerest trick—that the door was unfastened, and that he could go in as he chose.

I seem to see the figure of that little boy, drawn and repelled. And it was very clear in his mind too, though why it should be so was never explained, that his father would be very angry if he went through that door.

Wallace described all these moments of hesitation to me with the utmost particularity. He went right past the door, and then with his hands in his pockets, and making an infantile attempt to whistle, strolled right along beyond the end of the wall. There he recalls a number of mean, dirty shops, and particularly that of a plumber and decorator, with a dusty disorder of earthenware pipes, sheet lead ball taps, pattern books of wall paper, and tins of enamel. He stood pretending to examine these things, and coveting, passionately desiring the green door.

Then he said, he had a gust of emotion. He made a run for it, lest hesitation should grip him again, he went plump with outstretched hand through the green door and let it slam behind him. And so, in a trice, he came into the garden that has haunted all his life.

It was very difficult for Wallace to give me his full sense of that garden into which he came.

There was something in the very air of it that exhilarated, that gave one a sense of lightness and good happening and well-being; there was something in the sight of it that made all its colour clean and perfect and subtly luminous. In the instant of coming into it one was exquisitely glad—as only in rare moments and when one is young and joyful one can be glad in this world. And everything was beautiful there...

Wallace mused before he went on telling me. "You see," he said, with the doubtful inflection of a man who pauses at incredible things, "there were two great panthers there...Yes, spotted panthers. And I was not afraid. There was a long wide path with marble-edged flower borders on either side, and these two huge velvety beasts were playing there with a ball. One looked up and came towards me, a little curious as it seemed. It came right up to me, rubbed its soft round ear very gently against the small hand

I held out and purred. It was I tell you, an enchanted garden. I know. And the size? Oh! it stretched far and wide, this way and that. I believe there were hills far away. Heaven knows where West Kensington had suddenly got to. And somehow it was just like coming home."

"You know, in the very moment the door swung to behind me, I forgot the road with its fallen chestnut leaves, its cabs and tradesmen's carts, I forgot the sort of gravitational pull back to the discipline and obedience of home, I forgot all hesitations and fear, forgot discretion, forgot all the intimate realities of this life. I became in a moment a very glad and wonder-happy little boy—in another world. It was a world with a different quality, a warmer, more penetrating and mellower light, with a faint clear gladness in its air, and wisps of sun-touched cloud in the blueness of its sky. And before me ran this long wide path, invitingly, with weedless beds on either side, rich with untended flowers, and these two great panthers. I put my little hands fearlessly on their soft fur, and caressed their round ears and the sensitive corners under their ears, and played with them, and it was as though they welcomed me home. There was a keen sense of home-coming in my mind, and when presently a tall, fair girl appeared in the pathway and came to meet me, smiling, and said 'Well?' to me, and lifted me, and kissed me, and put me down, and led me by the hand, there was no amazement, but only an impression of delightful rightness, of being reminded of happy things that had in some strange way been overlooked. There were broad steps, I remember, that came into view between spikes of delphinium, and up these we went to a great avenue between very old and shady dark trees. All down this avenue, you know, between the red chapped stems, were marble seats of honour and statuary, and very tame and friendly white doves..."

"And along this avenue my girl-friend led me, looking down—I recall the pleasant lines, the finely-modelled chin of her sweet kind face—asking me questions in a soft, agreeable voice, and telling me things, pleasant things I know, though what they were I was never able to recall...And presently a little Capuchin monkey, very clean, with a fur of ruddy brown and kindly hazel eyes, came down a tree to us and ran beside me, looking up at me and grinning, and presently leapt to my shoulder. So we went on our way in great happiness..."

He paused.

"Go on," I said.

"I remember little things. We passed an old man musing among laurels, I remember, and a place gay with paroquets, and came through a broad shaded colonnade to a spacious cool palace, full of pleasant fountains, full of beautiful things, full of the quality and promise of heart's desire. And there were many things and many people, some that still seem to stand out clearly and some that are a little vague, but all these people were beautiful and kind. In some way—I don't know how—it was conveyed to me that they all were kind to me, glad to have me there, and filling me with gladness by their gestures, by the touch of their hands, by the welcome and love in their eyes. Yes—"

He mused for awhile. "Playmates I found there. That was very much to me, because I was a lonely little boy. They played delightful games in a grass-covered court where there was a sun-dial set about with flowers. And as one played one loved...

"But—it's odd—there's a gap in my memory. I don't remember the games we played. I never remembered. Afterwards as a child, I spent long hours trying, even with tears, to recall the form of that happiness. I wanted to play it all over again—in my nursery—by myself. No! All I remember is the happiness and two dear playfellows who were most with me...Then presently came a sombre dark woman, with a grave, pale face and dreamy eyes, a sombre woman wearing a soft long robe of pale purple, who carried a book and beckoned and took me aside with her into a gallery above a hall—though my playmates were loth to have me go, and ceased their game and stood watching as I was carried away. 'Come back to us!' they cried. 'Come back to us soon!' I looked up at her face, but she heeded them not at all. Her face was very gentle and grave. She took me to a seat in the gallery, and I stood beside her, ready to look at her book as she opened it upon her knee. The pages fell open. She pointed, and I looked, marvelling, for in the living pages of that book I saw myself; it was a story about myself, and in it were all the things that had happened to me since ever I was born...

"It was wonderful to me, because the pages of that book were not pictures, you understand, but realities."

Wallace paused gravely—looked at me doubtfully.

"Go on," I said. "I understand."

"They were realities—yes, they must have been; people moved and things came and went in them; my dear mother, whom I had near forgotten; then my father, stern and upright, the servants, the nursery, all the familiar things of home. Then the front door and the busy streets, with traffic to and fro: I looked and marvelled, and looked half doubtfully again into the woman's face and turned the pages over, skipping this and that, to see more of this book, and more, and so at last I came to myself hovering and hesitating outside the green door in the long white wall, and felt again the conflict and the fear.

"'And next?' I cried, and would have turned on, but the cool hand of the grave woman delayed me.

"'Next?' I insisted, and struggled gently with her hand, pulling up her fingers with all my childish strength, and as she yielded and the page came over she bent down upon me like a shadow and kissed my brow.

"But the page did not show the enchanted garden, nor the panthers, nor the girl who had led me by the hand, nor the playfellows who had been so loth to let me go. It showed a long grey street in West Kensington, on that chill hour of afternoon before the lamps are lit, and I was there, a wretched little figure, weeping aloud, for all that I could do to restrain myself, and I was weeping because I could not return to my dear playfellows who had called after me, 'Come back to us! Come back to us soon!' I was there. This was no page in a book, but harsh reality; that enchanted place and the restraining hand of the grave mother at whose knee I stood had gone—whither have they gone?"

He halted again, and remained for a time, staring into the fire.

"Oh! The wretchedness of that return!" he murmured.

"Well?" I said after a minute or so.

"Poor little wretch I was—! Brought back to this grey world again! As I realised the fullness of what had happened to me, I gave way to quite ungovernable grief. And the shame and humiliation of that public weeping and my disgraceful home-coming remain with me still. I see again the benevolent-looking old gentleman in gold spectacles who stopped and spoke to me—prodding me first with his umbrella. 'Poor little chap,' said he; 'and are you lost then—?' And me a London boy of five and more! And he must needs bring in a kindly young policeman and make a crowd of me, and so march me home. Sobbing, conspicuous and frightened, I came from the enchanted garden to the steps of my father's house.

"That is as well as I can remember my vision of that garden—the garden that haunts me still. Of course, I can convey nothing of that indescribable quality of translucent unreality, that difference from the common things of experience that hung about it all; but that—that is what happened. If it was a dream, I am sure it was a daytime and altogether extraordinary dream...H'm—! Naturally there followed a terrible questioning, by my aunt, my father, the nurse, the governess—everyone...

"I tried to tell them, and my father gave me my first thrashing for telling lies. When afterwards I tried to tell my aunt, she punished me again for my wicked persistence. Then as I said, everyone was forbidden to listen to me, to hear a word about it. Even my fairy tale books were taken away from me for a time—because I was too 'imaginative.' Eh? Yes, they did that! My father belonged to the old school...And my story was driven back upon myself. I whispered it to my pillow—my pillow that was often damp and salt to my whispering lips with childish tears. And I added always to my official and less fervent prayers this one heartfelt request: 'Please God I may dream of the garden. Oh! Take me back to my garden! Take me back to my garden!'

"I dreamt often of the garden. I may have added to it, I may have changed it; I do not know...All this you understand is an attempt to reconstruct from fragmentary memories a very early experience. Between that and the other consecutive memories of my boyhood there is a gulf. A time came when it seemed impossible I should ever speak of that wonder glimpse again."

I asked an obvious question.

"No," he said. "I don't remember that I ever attempted to find my way back to the garden in those early years. This seems odd to me now, but I think that very probably a closer watch was kept on my movements after this misadventure to prevent my going astray. No, it wasn't until you knew me that I tried for the garden again. And I believe there was a period—incredible as it seems now—when I forgot the garden altogether—when I was about eight or nine it may have been. Do you remember me as a kid at Saint Althelstan's?"

"Rather!"

"I didn't show any signs did I in those days of having a secret dream?"

2.

He looked up with a sudden smile.

"Did you ever play North-West Passage with me...? No, of course you didn't come my way!

"It was the sort of game," he went on, "that every imaginative child plays all day. The idea was the discovery of a North-West Passage to school. The way to school was plain enough; the game consisted in finding some way that wasn't plain, starting off ten minutes early in some almost hopeless direction, and working one's way round through unaccustomed streets to my goal. And one day I got entangled among some rather low-class streets on the other side of Campden Hill, and I began to think that for once the game would be against me and that I should get to school late. I tried rather desperately a street that seemed a cul de sac, and found a passage at the end. I hurried through that with renewed hope. 'I shall do it yet,' I said, and passed a row of frowsy little shops that were inexplicably familiar to me, and behold! There was my long white wall and the green door that led to the enchanted garden!

"The thing whacked upon me suddenly. Then after all, that garden, that wonderful garden, wasn't a dream...!"

He paused.

"I suppose my second experience with the green door marks the world of difference there is between the busy life of a schoolboy and the infinite leisure of a child. Anyhow this second time I didn't for a moment think of going in straight away. You see—For one thing my mind was full of the idea of getting to school in time—set on not breaking my record for punctuality. I must surely have felt some little desire at least to try the door—yes, I must have felt that...But I seem to remember the attraction of the door mainly as another obstacle to my overmastering determination to get to school. I was immediately interested by this discovery I had made, of course—I went on with my mind full of it—but I went on. It didn't check me. I ran past tugging out my watch, found I had ten minutes still to spare, and then

I was going downhill into familiar surroundings. I got to school, breathless, it is true, and wet with perspiration, but in time. I can remember hanging up my coat and hat... Went right by it and left it behind me. Odd, eh?"

He looked at me thoughtfully. "Of course, I didn't know then that it wouldn't always be there. School boys have limited imaginations. I suppose I thought it was an awfully jolly thing to have it there, to know my way back to it, but there was the school tugging at me. I expect I was a good deal distraught and inattentive that morning, recalling what I could of the beautiful strange people I should presently see again. Oddly enough I had no doubt in my mind that they would be glad to see me... Yes, I must have thought of the garden that morning just as a jolly sort of place to which one might resort in the interludes of a strenuous scholastic career.

"I didn't go that day at all. The next day was a half holiday, and that may have weighed with me. Perhaps too, my state of inattention brought down impositions upon me and docked the margin of time necessary for the detour. I don't know. What I do know is that in the meantime the enchanted garden was so much upon my mind that I could not keep it to myself.

"I told—What was his name—? A ferrety-looking youngster we used to call Squiff."

"Young Hopkins," said I.

"Hopkins it was. I did not like telling him, I had a feeling that in some way it was against the rules to tell him, but I did. He was walking part of the way home with me; he was talkative, and if we had not talked about the enchanted garden we should have talked of something else, and it was intolerable to me to think about any other subject. So I blabbed.

"Well, he told my secret. The next day in the play interval I found myself surrounded by half a dozen bigger boys, half teasing and wholly curious to hear more of the enchanted garden. There was that big Fawcett—you remember him—? And Carnaby and Morley Reynolds. You weren't there by any chance? No, I think I should have remembered if you were...

"A boy is a creature of odd feelings. I was, I really believe, in spite of my secret self-disgust, a little flattered to have the attention of these big fellows. I remember particularly a moment of pleasure caused by the praise of Crawshaw—you remember

Crawshaw major, the son of Crawshaw the composer—? Who said it was the best lie he had ever heard. But at the same time there was a really painful undertow of shame at telling what I felt was indeed a sacred secret. That beast Fawcett made a joke about the girl in green—"

Wallace's voice sank with the keen memory of that shame. "I pretended not to hear," he said. "Well, then Carnaby suddenly called me a young liar and disputed with me when I said the thing was true. I said I knew where to find the green door, could lead them all there in ten minutes. Carnaby became outrageously virtuous, and said I'd have to—and bear out my words or suffer. Did you ever have Carnaby twist your arm? Then perhaps you'll understand how it went with me. I swore my story was true. There was nobody in the school then to save a chap from Carnaby though Crawshaw put in a word or so. Carnaby had got his game. I grew excited and red-eared, and a little frightened, I behaved altogether like a silly little chap, and the outcome of it all was that instead of starting alone for my enchanted garden, I led the way presently—cheeks flushed, ears hot, eyes smarting, and my soul one burning misery and shame—for a party of six mocking, curious and threatening schoolfellows."

"We never found the white wall and the green door..."

"You mean—?"

"I mean I couldn't find it. I would have found it if I could.

"And afterwards when I could go alone I couldn't find it. I never found it. I seem now to have been always looking for it through my school-boy days, but I've never come upon it—again."

"Did the fellows—make it disagreeable?"

"Beastly...Carnaby held a council over me for wanton lying. I remember how I sneaked home and upstairs to hide the marks of my blubbering. But when I cried myself to sleep at last it wasn't for Carnaby, but for the garden, for the beautiful afternoon I had hoped for, for the sweet friendly women and the waiting playfellows and the game I had hoped to learn again, that beautiful forgotten game...

"I believed firmly that if I had not told—...I had bad times after that—crying at night and wool-gathering by day. For two terms I slackened and had bad reports. Do you remember? Of course you would! It was you—your beating me in mathematics that brought me back to the grind again."

3.

For a time my friend stared silently into the red heart of the fire. Then he said: "I never saw it again until I was seventeen."

"It leapt upon me for the third time—as I was driving to Paddington on my way to Oxford and a scholarship. I had just one momentary glimpse. I was leaning over the apron of my hansom smoking a cigarette, and no doubt thinking myself no end of a man of the world, and suddenly there was the door, the wall, the dear sense of unforgettable and still attainable things.

"We clattered by—I too taken by surprise to stop my cab until we were well past and round a corner. Then I had a queer moment, a double and divergent movement of my will: I tapped the little door in the roof of the cab, and brought my arm down to pull out my watch. 'Yes, sir!' said the cabman, smartly. 'Er—well—it's nothing,' I cried. 'My mistake! We haven't much time! Go on!' And he went on...

"I got my scholarship. And the night after I was told of that I sat over my fire in my little upper room, my study in my father's house, with his praise—his rare praise—and his sound counsels ringing in my ears, and I smoked my favourite pipe—the formidable bulldog of adolescence—and thought of that door in the long white wall. 'If I had stopped,' I thought, 'I should have missed my scholarship, I should have missed Oxford—muddled all the fine career before me! I begin to see things better!' I fell musing deeply, but I did not doubt then this career of mine was a thing that merited sacrifice.

"Those dear friends and that clear atmosphere seemed very sweet to me, very fine, but remote. My grip was fixing now upon the world. I saw another door opening—the door of my career."

He stared again into the fire. Its red lights picked out a stubborn strength in his face for just one flickering moment, and then it vanished again.

"Well", he said and sighed, "I have served that career. I have done—much work, much hard work. But I have dreamt of the enchanted garden a thousand dreams, and seen its door, or at least glimpsed its door, four times since then. Yes—four times. For a while this world was so bright and interesting, seemed so full of meaning and opportunity that the half-effaced charm of the garden was by comparison gentle and remote. Who wants to pat panthers on the way to dinner with pretty women and distinguished men? I came down to London from Oxford, a man of bold promise that I have done something to redeem. Something—and yet there have been disappointments...

"Twice I have been in love—I will not dwell on that—but once, as I went to someone who, I know, doubted whether I dared to come, I took a short cut at a venture through an unfrequented road near Earl's Court, and so happened on a white wall and a familiar green door. 'Odd!' said I to myself, 'But I thought this place was on Campden Hill. It's the place I never could find somehow—like counting Stonehenge—the place of that queer day dream of mine.' And I went by it intent upon my purpose. It had no appeal to me that afternoon.

"I had just a moment's impulse to try the door, three steps aside were needed at the most—though I was sure enough in my heart that it would open to me—and then I thought that doing so might delay me on the way to that appointment in which I thought my honour was involved. Afterwards I was sorry for my punctuality—I might at least have peeped in I thought, and waved a hand to those panthers, but I knew enough by this time not to seek again belatedly that which is not found by seeking. Yes, that time made me very sorry...

"Years of hard work after that and never a sight of the door. It's only recently it has come back to me. With it there has come a sense as though some thin tarnish had spread itself over my world. I began to think of it as a sorrowful and bitter thing that I should never see that door again. Perhaps I was suffering a little from overwork—perhaps it was what I've heard spoken of as the feeling of forty. I don't know. But certainly the keen brightness that makes effort easy has gone out of things recently, and that just at a time—ith all these new political developments—when I ought to be working. Odd isn't it? But I do begin to find life toilsome, its rewards, as I come near them, cheap. I began a little while ago to want the garden quite badly. Yes—and I've seen it three times."

"The garden?"

"No—The door! And I haven't gone in!"

He leaned over the table to me, with an enormous sorrow in his voice as he spoke. "Thrice I have had my chance—thrice! If ever that door offers itself to me again, I swore, I will go in out of this dust and heat, out of this dry glitter of vanity, out of these toilsome futilities. I will go and never return. This time I will stay...I swore it and when the time came—I didn't go.

"Three times in one year have I passed that door and failed to enter. Three times in the last year."

"The first time was on the night of the snatch division on the Tenants' Redemption Bill, on which the Government was saved by a majority of three. You remember? No one on our side—perhaps very few on the opposite side—expected the end that night. Then the debate collapsed like eggshells. I and Hotchkiss were dining with his cousin at Brentford, we were both unpaired, and we were called up by telephone, and set off at once in his cousin's motor. We got in barely in time, and on the way we passed my wall and door—livid in the moonlight, blotched with hot yellow as the glare of our lamps lit it, but unmistakable. 'My God!' cried I. 'What?' said Hotchkiss. 'Nothing!' I answered, and the moment passed."

"'I've made a great sacrifice,' I told the whip as I got in. 'They all have,' he said, and hurried by.

"I do not see how I could have done otherwise then. And the next occasion was as I rushed to my father's bedside to bid that stern old man farewell. Then too, the claims of life were imperative. But the third time was different; it happened a week ago. It fills me with hot remorse to recall it. I was with Gurker and Ralphs—it's no secret now you know that I've had my talk with Gurker. We had been dining at Frobisher's, and the talk had become intimate between us. The question of my place in the reconstructed ministry lay always just over the boundary of the discussion. Yes—yes. That's all settled. It needn't be talked about yet, but there's no reason to keep a secret from you... Yes—Thanks! Thanks! But let me tell you my story.

"Then, on that night things were very much in the air. My position was a very delicate one. I was keenly anxious to get some definite word from Gurker, but was hampered by Ralphs' presence. I was using the best power of my brain to keep that light and careless talk, not too obviously, directed to the point that concerns me. I had to. Ralphs' behaviour since has more than justified my caution...Ralphs I knew, would leave us beyond the Kensington High Street, and then I could surprise Gurker by a sudden frankness. One has sometimes to resort to these little devices...And then it was that in the margin of my field of vision I became aware once more of the white wall, the green door before us down the road."

"We passed it talking. I passed it. I can still see the shadow of Gurker's marked profile, his opera hat tilted forward over his prominent nose, the many folds of his neck wrap going before my shadow and Ralphs' as we sauntered past.

"I passed within twenty inches of the door. 'If I say good-night to them, and go in,' I asked myself, 'what will happen?' And I was all a-tingle for that word with Gurker.

"I could not answer that question in the tangle of my other problems. 'They will think me mad,' I thought. 'And suppose I vanish now—! Amazing disappearance of a prominent politician!' That weighed with me. A thousand inconceivably petty worldlinesses weighed with me in that crisis."

Then he turned on me with a sorrowful smile, and speaking slowly; "Here I am!" he said.

"Here I am!" he repeated, "and my chance has gone from me. Three times in one year the door has been offered me—the door that goes into peace, into delight, into a beauty beyond dreaming, a kindness no man on earth can know. And I have rejected it, Redmond, and it has gone—"

"How do you know?"

"I know. I know. I am left now to work it out, to stick to the tasks that held me so strongly when my moments came. You say, I have success—this vulgar, tawdry, irksome, envied thing. I have it." He had a walnut in his big hand. "If that was my success," he said, and crushed it, and held it out for me to see.

"Let me tell you something, Redmond. This loss is destroying me. For two months, for ten weeks nearly now, I have done no work at all, except the most necessary and urgent duties. My soul is full of inappeasable regrets. At nights—when it is less likely I shall be recognised—I go out. I wander. Yes. I wonder what people would think of that if they knew. A Cabinet Minister, the responsible head of that most vital of all departments, wandering alone—grieving—sometimes near audibly lamenting—for a door, for a garden!"

4.

I can see now his rather pallid face, and the unfamiliar sombre fire that had come into his eyes. I see him very vividly to-night.

I sit recalling his words, his tones, and last evening's Westminster Gazette still lies on my sofa, containing the notice of his death. At lunch to-day the club was busy with him and the strange riddle of his fate.

They found his body very early yesterday morning in a deep excavation near East Kensington Station. It is one of two shafts that have been made in connection with an extension of the railway southward. It is protected from the intrusion of the public by a hoarding upon the high road, in which a small doorway has been cut for the convenience of some of the workmen who live in that direction. The doorway was left unfastened through a misunderstanding between two gangers, and through it he made his way...

My mind is darkened with questions and riddles.

It would seem he walked all the way from the House that night—he has frequently walked home during the past Session—and so it is I figure his dark form coming along the late and empty streets, wrapped up, intent. And then did the pale electric lights near the station cheat the rough planking into a semblance of white? Did that fatal unfastened door awaken some memory?

Was there, after all, ever any green door in the wall at all?

I do not know. I have told his story as he told it to me. There are times when I believe that Wallace was no more than the victim of the coincidence between a rare but not unprecedented type of hallucination and a careless trap, but that indeed is not my profoundest belief. You may think me superstitious if you will, and foolish; but indeed, I am more than half convinced that he had in truth, an abnormal gift, and a sense, something—I know not what—that in the guise of wall and door offered him an outlet, a secret and peculiar passage of escape into another and altogether more beautiful world. At any rate, you will say, it betrayed him in the end. But did it betray him? There you touch the inmost mystery of these dreamers, these men of vision and the imagination.

We see our world fair and common, the hoarding and the pit. By our daylight standard he walked out of security into darkness, danger and death. But did he see like that?

48

The Grisly Folk

"Can these bones live?"

Could anything be more dead, more mute and inexpressive to the inexpert eye than the ochreous fragments of bone and the fractured lumps of flint that constitute the first traces of something human in the world? We see them in the museum cases, sorted out in accordance with principles we do not understand, labelled with strange names. Chellean, Mousterian, Solutrian and the like, taken mostly from the places Chelles, La Moustier, Solutre, and so forth where the first specimens were found. Most of us stare through the glass at them, wonder vaguely for a moment at that half-savage, half-animal past of our race, and pass on. Primitive man, we say. Flint implements. The mammoth used to chase him. Few of us realise yet how much the subtle indefatigable cross-examination of the scientific worker has been extracting from the evidence of these rusty and obstinate witnesses during the last few years.

One of the most startling results of this recent work is the gradual realisation that great quantities of these flint implements and some of the earlier fragments of bone that used to be ascribed to humanity are the vestiges of creatures, very manlike in many respects, but not, strictly speaking, belonging to the human species. Scientific men call these vanished races man (Homo), just as they call lions and tigers cats (Felis), but there are the soundest reasons for believing that these earlier so-called men were not of our blood, not our ancestors, but a strange and vanished animal, like us, akin to us, but different from us, as the mammoth was like, and akin to, and yet different from, the elephant. Flint and bone implements are found in deposits of very considerable antiquity; some in our museums may be a million years old or more, but the traces of really human creatures, mentally and anatomically like ourselves, do not go back much earlier than twenty or thirty thousand years ago. True men appeared in Europe then, and we do not know whence they came. These other tool-using, fire-making animals, the things that were like men and yet were not men, passed away before the faces of the true men.

Scientific authorities already distinguish four species of these pseudo-men, and it is probable that we shall learn from time to time of other species. One strange breed made the implements called Chellean. These are chiefly sole-shaped blades of stone found in deposits of perhaps 300,000 or 400,000 years ago. Chellean implements are to be seen in any great museum. They are huge implements, four or five times as big as those made by any known race of true men, and they are not ill made. Certainly some creature with an intelligent brain made them. Big clumsy hands must have gripped and used these rocky chunks. But so far only one small fragment of a skeleton of this age has been found, a very massive chinless lower jawbone, with teeth rather more specialised than those of men to-day. We can only guess what strange foreshadowing of the human form once ate with that jaw, and struck at its enemies with those big but not unhandy flint blades. It may have been a tremendous fellow, probably much bigger in the body than a man. It may have been able to take bears by the scruff and the sabre-toothed lion by the throat. We do not know. We have just these great stone blades and that bit of a massive jaw and—the liberty to wonder.

Most fascinating riddle of all these riddles of the ages of ice and hardship, before the coming of the true men, is the riddle of the Mousterian men, because they were perhaps still living in the world when the true man came wandering into Europe. They lived much later than those unknown Chellean giants. They lived thirty or forty thousand years ago—a yesterday compared with the Chellean time. These Mousterians are also called Neandertalers. Until quite recently it was supposed that they were true men like ourselves. But now we begin to realise that they were different, so different that it is impossible that they can be very close relations of ours. They walked or shambled along with a peculiar slouch, they could not turn their heads up to the sky, and their teeth were very different from those of true men. One oddity about them is that in one or two points they were less like apes than we are. The dog tooth, the third tooth from the middle, which is so big in the gorilla, and which in man is pointed and still quite distinct from the other teeth, is not distinct at all in the Neandertaler. He had a very even row of teeth, and his cheek teeth also were very unlike ours, and less like the apes' than ours. He had more face and less brow than true men, but that is not because he had a lesser brain; his brain was as big as a modern man's but it was different, bigger behind and smaller in front, so that probably he thought and behaved differently from us. Perhaps he had a better memory and less reasoning power than real men, or perhaps he had more nervous energy and less intelligence. He had no chin, and the way his jawbones come together below make it very doubtful if he could have used any such sounds in speech as we employ. Probably he did not talk at all. He could not hold a pin between his finger and thumb. The more we learn about this beast-man the stranger he becomes to us and the less like the Australoid savage he was once supposed to be.

And as we realise the want of any close relationship between this ugly, strong, ungainly, manlike animal and mankind, the less likely it becomes that he had a naked skin and hair like ours and the more probable that he was different, and perhaps bristly or hairy in some queer inhuman fashion like the hairy elephant and the woolly rhinoceros who were his contemporaries. Like them he lived in a bleak land on the edge of the snows and glaciers that were even then receding northward. Hairy or grisly, with a big face like a mask, great brow ridges and no forehead, clutching an enormous flint, and running like a baboon with his head forward and not, like a man, with his head up, he must have been a fearsome creature for our forefathers to come upon.

Almost certainly they met, these grisly men and the true men. The true man must have come into the habitat of the Neandertaler, and the two must have met and fought. Some day we may come upon the evidences of this warfare.

Western Europe, which is the only part of the world that has yet been searched with any thoroughness for the remains of early men, was slowly growing warmer age by age; the glaciers that had once covered half the continent were receding, and wide stretches of summer pasture and thin woods of pine and birch were spreading slowly over the once icy land. South Europe then was like northern Labrador to-day. A few hardy beasts held out amidst the snows; the bears hibernated. With the spring grass and foliage came great herds of reindeer, wild horses, mammoth, elephant, and rhinoceros, drifting northward from the slopes of the great warm valley that is now filled up with water—the Mediterranean Sea. It was in those days before the ocean waters broke into the Mediterranean that the swallows and a multitude of other birds acquired the habit of coming north, a habit that nowadays impels them to brave the passage of the perilous seas that flow over and hide the lost secrets of the ancient Mediterranean valleys. The grisly men rejoiced at the return of life, came out of the caves in which they had lurked during the winter, and took their toll of the beasts.

These grisly men must have been almost solitary creatures.

The winter food was too scanty for communities. A male may have gone with a female or so; perhaps they parted in the winter and came together in the summer; when his sons grew big enough to annoy him, the grisly man killed them or drove them off. If he killed them he may have eaten them. If they escaped him they may have returned to kill him. The grisly folk may have had long unreasoning memories and very set purposes.

The true men came into Europe, we know not whence, out of the South. When they appeared in Europe their hands were as clever as ours; they could draw pictures we still admire, they could paint and carve; the implements they made were smaller than the Mousterian ones, far smaller than the Chellean, but better made and more various. They wore no clothes worth speaking of, but they painted themselves and probably they talked. And they came in little bands. They were already more social than the Neandertaler; they had laws and self-restraints; their minds had travelled a long way along that path of adaptation and self-suppression which has led to the intricate mind of man to-day with its concealed wishes, its confusions, and laughter and the fantasies and reveries and dreams. They were already held together, these men, and kept in order by the strange limitations of tabu.

They were still savages, very prone to violence and convulsive in their lusts and desires; but to the best of their poor ability they obeyed laws and customs already immemorably ancient, and they feared the penalties of wrong-doing. We can understand something of what was going on in their minds, those of us who can remember the fears, desires, fancies and superstitions of our childhood. Their moral struggles were ours—in cruder forms. They were our kind. But the grisly folk we cannot begin to understand. We cannot conceive in our different minds the strange ideas that chased one another through those queerly shaped brains. As well might we try to dream and feel as a gorilla dreams and feels.

We can understand how the true men drifted northward from the lost lands of the Mediterranean valley into the high Spanish valleys and the south and centre of France, and so on to what is now England—for there was no Channel then between England and France—and eastward to the Rhineland and over the broad wilderness which is now the North Sea, and the German plain. They would leave the snowy wilderness of the Alps, far higher then and covered with great glaciers, away on their right. These people drifted northward for the very good reason that their kind was multiplying and food diminishing. They would be oppressed by feuds and wars. They had no settled homes; they were accustomed to drift with the seasons, every now and then some band would be pushed by hunger and fear a little farther northward into the unknown.

We can imagine the appearance of a little group of these wanderers, our ancestors, coming over some grassy crest into these northern lands. The time would be late spring or early summer, and they would probably be following up some grazing beasts, a reindeer herd or horses.

By a score of different means our anthropologists have been able to reconstruct the particulars of the appearance and habits of these early pilgrim fathers of mankind.

They would not be a very numerous band, because if they were there would be no reason why they should have been driven northward out of their former roving grounds. Two or three older men of thirty or so, eight or ten women and girls with a few young children, a few lads between fourteen and twenty, might make up the whole community. They would be a brownish brown-eyed people with wavy dark hair; the fairness of the European and the straight blue-black hair of the Chinaman had still to be evolved in the world. The older men would probably lead the band, the women and children would keep apart from the youths and men, fenced off by complex and definite tabus from any close companionship. The leaders would be tracking the herd they were following. Tracking was then the supreme accomplishment of mankind. By signs and traces that would be invisible to any modern civilised eye, they would be reading the story of the previous day's trek of the herd of sturdy little horses ahead of them. They would be so expert that they would go on from one faint sign to another with as little delay as a dog who follows a scent.

The horses they were following were only a little way ahead—so the trackers read the signs—they were numerous and nothing had alarmed them. They were grazing and moving only very slowly. There were no traces of wild dog or other enemies to stampede them. Some elephants were also going north, and twice our human tribe had crossed the spoor of woolly rhinoceros roaming westward.

The tribe travelled light. They were mainly naked, but all of them were painted with white and black and red and yellow ochre. At this distance of time it is difficult to see whether they were tattooed. Probably they were not. The babies and small children were carried by the women on their backs in slings or bags made of animal skins, and perhaps some or all of them wore mantles and loin bands of skin and had pouches and belts of leather. The men had stone-pointed spears, and carried sharpened flints in their hands.

There was no Old Man who was lord and master and father of this particular crowd. Weeks ago the Old Man had been charged and trampled to a jelly by a great bull in the swamp far away. Then two of the girls had been waylaid and carried off by the young men of another larger tribe. It was because of these losses that this remnant was now seeking new hunting grounds.

The landscape that spread before the eyes of this little band as they crested the hill was a bleaker, more desolate and altogether unkempt version of the landscape of western Europe to-day. About them was a grassy down athwart which a peewit flew with its melancholy cry. Before them stretched a great valley ridged with transverse purple hills over which the April cloud-shadows chased one another. Pinewoods and black heather showed where these hills became sandy, and the valleys were full of brown brushwood, and down their undrained troughs ran a bright green band of peaty swamps and long pools of weedy water. In the valley thickets many beasts lurked unseen, and where the winding streams had cut into the soil there were cliffs and caves. Far away along the northern slopes of the ridge that were now revealed, the wild ponies were to be seen grazing.

At a sign from the two leaders the little straggle of menfolk halted, and a woman who had been chattering in subdued tones to a little girl became silent. The brothers surveyed the wide prospect earnestly.

"Ugh!" said one abruptly and pointed.

"Ugh!" cried his brother.

The eyes of the whole tribe swung round to the pointing finger.

The group became one rigid stare.

Every soul of them stood still, astonishment had turned them into a tense group of statuettes.

Far away down the slope with his body in profile and his head turned towards them, frozen by an equal amazement, stood a hunched grey figure, bigger but shorter than a man. He had been creeping up behind a fold in the ground to peer at the ponies; and suddenly he had turned his eyes and seen the tribe. His head projected like a baboon's. In his hand he carried what seemed to the menfolk a great rock.

For a little while this animal scrutiny held discoverers and discovered motionless. Then some of the women and children began to stir and line out to see the strange creature better. "Man!" said an old crone of forty. "Man!" At the movement of the women the grisly man turned, ran clumsily for a score of yards or so towards a thicket of birch and budding thorn. Then he halted again for a moment to look at the newcomers, waved an arm strangely, and then dashed into cover.

The shadows of the thicket swallowed him up, and by hiding him seemed to make him enormous. It identified itself with him, and watched them with his eyes. Its tree stems became long silvery limbs, and a fallen trunk crouched and stared.

It was still early in the morning, and the leaders of the tribe had hoped to come up with the wild ponies as the day advanced and perhaps cut one off and drive it into difficulties among the bushes and swampy places below, and wound it and follow it up and kill it. Then they would have made a feast, and somewhere down in the valley they would have found water and dry bracken for litter and a fire before night. It had seemed a pleasant and hopeful morning to them until this moment. Now they were disconcerted. This grey figure was as if the sunny morning had suddenly made a horrible and inexplicable grimace.

The whole expedition stood gazing for a time, and then the two leaders exchanged a few words. Waugh, the elder, pointed. Click, his brother, nodded his head. They would go on, but instead of slanting down the slopes towards the thickets they would keep round the ridge.

"Come," said Waugh, and the little band began to move again. But now it marched in silence. When presently a little boy began a question his mother silenced him by a threat. Everybody kept glancing at the thickets below.

Presently a girl cried out sharply and pointed. All started and stopped short.

There was the grisly thing again. It was running across an open space, running almost on all fours, in joltering leaps. It was hunchbacked and very big and low, a grey hairy wolf-like monster. At times its long arms nearly touched the ground. It was nearer than it had been before. It vanished amidst the bushes again. It seemed to throw itself down among some red dead bracken...

Waugh and Click took counsel.

A mile away was the head of the valley where the thickets had their beginning. Beyond stretched the woldy hills, bare of cover. The horses were grazing up towards the sun, and away to the north the backs of a herd of woolly rhinoceros were now visible on a crest—just the ridges of their backs showing like a string of black beads.

If the tribe struck across those grassy spaces, then the lurking prowler would have either to stay behind or come into the open. If he came into the open the dozen youths and men of the tribe would know how to deal with him.

So they struck across the grass. The little band worked round to the head of the valley, and there the menfolk stayed at the crest while the women and children pushed on ahead across the open.

For a time the watchers remained motionless, and then Waugh was moved to gestures of defiance. Click was not to be outdone. There were shouts at the hidden watcher, and then one lad, who was something of a clown, after certain grimaces and unpleasant gestures, obliged with an excellent imitation of the grey thing's lumbering run. At that, scare gave place to hilarity.

In those days laughter was a social embrace. Men could laugh, but there was no laughter in the grisly pre-man who watched and wondered in the shadow. He marvelled. The men rolled about and guffawed and slapped their thighs and one another. Tears ran down their faces.

Never a sign came from the thickets.

"Yahah," said the menfolk. "Yahah! Bzzzz. Yahah! Yah!"

They forgot altogether how frightened they had been.

And when Waugh thought the women and children had gone on a sufficient distance, he gave the word for the men to follow them.

In some such fashion it was that men, our ancestors, had their first glimpse of the pre-men of the wilderness of western Europe.

The two breeds were soon to come to closer quarters.

The newcomers were pushing their way into the country of these grisly men. Presently came other glimpses of lurking semi-human shapes and grey forms that ran in the twilight. In the morning Click found long narrow footprints round the camp...

Then one day, one of the children, eating those little green thorn-buds that rustic English children speak of as bread and cheese, ventured too far from the others. There was a squeal and a scuffle and a thud, and something grey and hairy made off through the thickets carrying its victim, with Waugh and three of the younger men in hot pursuit. They chased the enemy into a dark gully, very much overgrown. This time it was not a solitary Neandertaler they had to deal with. Out of the bushes a big male came at them to cover the retreat of his mate, and hurled a rock that bowled over the youth it hit like a nine-pin, so that thereafter he limped always. But Waugh with his throwing spear got the grey monster in the shoulder, and he halted snarling.

No further sound came from the stolen child.

The female showed herself for a moment up the gully, snarling, bloodstained, and horrible, and the menfolk stood about afraid to continue their pursuit, and yet not caring to desist from it. One of them was already hobbling off with his hand to his knee.

How did that first fight go?

Perhaps it went against the men of our race. Perhaps the big Neandertaler male, his mane and beard bristling horribly, came down the gully with a thunderous roar, with a great rock in either hand. We do not know whether he threw those big discs of flint or whether he smote with them. Perhaps it was then that Waugh was killed in the act of running away. Perhaps it was bleak disaster then for the little tribe. Short of two of its members it presently made off over the hills as fast as it could go, keeping together for safety, and leaving the wounded youth far behind to limp along its tracks in lonely terror.

Let us suppose that he got back to the tribe at last—after nightmare hours.

Now that Waugh had gone, Click would become Old Man, and he made the tribe camp that night and build their fire on the high ridges among the heather far away from the thickets in which the grisly folk might be lurking.

The grisly folk thought we knew not how about the menfolk, and the men thought about the grisly folk in such ways as we can understand; they imagined how their enemies might act in this fashion or that, and schemed to circumvent them. It may have been Click who had the first dim idea of getting at the gorge in which the Neandertalers had their lair, from above. For as we have said, the Neandertaler did not look up. Then the menfolk could roll a great rock upon him or pelt him with burning brands and set the dry bracken alight.

One likes to think of a victory for the human side. This Click we have conjured up had run in panic from the first onset of the grisly male, but as he brooded by the fire that night, he heard again in imagination the cry of the lost girl, and he was filled with rage. In his sleep the grisly male came to him and Click fought in his dreams and started awake stiff with fury. There was a fascination for him in that gorge in which Waugh had been killed. He was compelled to go back and look again for the grisly beasts, to waylay them in their tracks, and watch them from an ambush. He perceived that the Neandertalers could not climb as easily as the menfolk could climb, nor hear so quickly, nor dodge with the same unexpectedness. These grisly men were to be dealt with as the bears were dealt with, the bears before whom you run and scatter, and then come at again from behind.

But one may doubt if the first human group to come into the grisly land was clever enough to solve the problems of the new warfare. Maybe they turned southward again to the gentler regions from which they had come, and were killed by or mingled with their own brethren again. Maybe they perished altogether in that new land of the grisly folk into which they had intruded. Yet the truth may be that they even held their own and increased. If they died there were others of their kind to follow them and achieve a better fate.

That was the beginning of a nightmare age for the little children of the human tribe. They knew they were watched.

Their steps were dogged. The legends of ogres and man-eating giants that haunt the childhood of the world may descend to us from those ancient days of fear. And for the Neandertalers it was the beginning of an incessant war that could end only in extermination.

The Neandertalers, albeit not so erect and tall as men, were the heavier, stronger creatures, but they were stupid, and they went alone or in twos and threes; the menfolk were swifter, quicker-witted, and more social—when they fought they fought in combination. They lined out and surrounded and pestered and pelted their antagonists from every side. They fought the men of that grisly race as dogs might fight a bear. They shouted to one another what each should do, and the Neandertaler had no speech; he did not understand. They moved too quickly for him and fought too cunningly.

Many and obstinate were the duels and battles these two sorts of men fought for this world in that bleak age of the windy steppes, thirty or forty thousand years ago. The two races were intolerable to each other. They both wanted the caves and the banks by the rivers where the big flints were got. They fought over the dead mammoths that had been bogged in the marshes, and over the reindeer stags that had been killed in the rutting season. When a human tribe found signs of the grisly folk near their cave and squatting place, they had perforce to track them down and kill them; their own safety and the safety of their little ones was only to be secured by that killing. The Neandertalers thought the little children of men fair game and pleasant eating.

How long the grisly folk lived on in that chill world of pines and silver birch between the steppes and the glaciers, after the true menfolk came, we do not know. For ages they may have held out, growing more cunning and dangerous as they became rare. The true men hunted them down by their spoor and by their tracks, and watched for the smoke of their fires, and made food scarce for them.

Great Paladins arose in that forgotten world, men who stood forth and smote the grey man-beast face to face and slew him. They made long spears of wood, hardened by fire at the tips; they raised shields of skin against his mighty blows. They struck at him with stones on cords, and slung them at him with slings. And it was not simply men who withstood the grisly beast but women. They stood over their children; they stood by their men against this eerie thing that was like and yet not like mankind. Unless the savants read all the signs awry, it was the women who were the makers of the larger tribes into which human families were already growing in those ancient times. It was the woman's subtle, love-guided wits which protected her sons from the fierce anger of the Old Man, and taught them to avoid his jealousy and wrath, and persuaded him to tolerate them and so have their help against the grisly enemy. It was woman, says Atkinson, in the beginning of things human, who taught the primary tabus, that a son must go aside out of the way of his stepmother, and get himself a wife from another tribe, so as to keep the peace within the family. She came between the fratricides, and was the first peacemaker. Human societies in their beginnings were her work, done against the greater solitariness, the lonely fierceness of the adult male. Through her, men learnt the primary co-operation of sonship and brotherhood. The grisly folk had not learnt even the rudest elements of co-operation, and mankind had already spelt out the alphabet of a unity that may some day comprehend the whole earth. The menfolk kept together by the dozen and by the score. By ones and twos and threes therefore the grisly folk were beset and slain, until there were no more of them left in the world.

Generation after generation, age after age, that long struggle for existence went on between these men who were not quite men and the men, our ancestors, who came out of the South into western Europe. Thousands of fights and hunts, sudden murders and headlong escapes there were amidst the caves and thickets of that chill and windy world between the last age of glaciers and our own warmer time. Until at length the last poor grisly was brought to bay and faced the spears of his pursuers in anger and despair.

What leapings of the heart were there not throughout that long warfare! What moments of terror and triumph! What acts of devotion and desperate wonders of courage! And the strain of the victors was our strain; we are lineally identical with those sun-brown painted beings who ran and fought and helped one another, the blood in our veins glowed in those fights and chilled in those fears of the forgotten past. For it was forgotten. Except perhaps for some vague terrors in our dreaming life and for some lurking element of tradition in the legends and warnings of the nursery, it has gone altogether out of the memory of our race. But nothing is ever completely lost. Seventy or eighty years ago a few curious savants began to suspect that there were hidden memories in certain big chipped flints and scraps of bone they found in ancient gravels. Much more recently others have begun to find hints of remote strange experiences in the dreams and odd kinks in modern minds. By degrees these dry bones begin to live again.

This restoration of the past is one of the most astonishing adventures of the human mind. As humanity follows the gropings of scientific men among these ancient vestiges, it is like a man who turns over the yellow pages of some long-forgotten diary, some engagement book of his adolescence. His dead youth lives again. Once more the old excitements stir him, the old happiness returns. But the old passions that once burnt, only warm him now, and the old fears and distresses signify nothing.

A day may come when these recovered memories may grow as vivid as if we in our own persons had been there and shared the thrill and the fear of those primordial days; a day may come when the great beasts of the past will leap to life again in our imaginations, when we shall walk again in vanished scenes, stretch painted limbs we thought were dust, and feel again the sunshine of a million years ago.

49

THE PEARL OF LOVE

The pearl is lovelier than the most brilliant of crystalline stones, the moralist declares, because it is made through the suffering of a living creature. About that I can say nothing because I feel none of the fascination of pearls. Their cloudy lustre moves me not at all. Nor can I decide for myself upon that age-long dispute whether the Pearl of Love is the cruellest of stories or only a gracious fable of the immortality of beauty.

Both the story and the controversy will be familiar to students of mediaeval Persian prose. The story is a short one, though the commentary upon it is a respectable part of the literature of that period. They have treated it as a poetic invention and they have treated it as an allegory meaning this, that, or the other thing. Theologians have had their copious way with it, dealing with it particularly as concerning the restoration of the body after death, and it has been greatly used as a parable by those who write about aesthetics. And many have held it to be the statement of a fact, simply and baldly true.

The story is laid in North India, which is the most fruitful soil for sublime love stories of all the lands in the world. It was in a country of sunshine and lakes and rich forests and hills and fertile valleys; and far away the great mountains hung in the sky, peaks, crests, ridges of inaccessible and eternal snow. There was a young prince, lord of all the land; and he found a maiden of indescribable beauty and delightfulness and he made her his queen and laid his heart at her feet. Love was theirs, full of joys and sweetness, full of hope, exquisite, brave and marvellous love, beyond anything you have ever dreamt of love. It was theirs for a year and part of a year, and then suddenly, because of some venomous sting that came to her in a thicket, she died.

She died and for a while the prince was utterly prostrated. He was silent and motionless with grief. They feared he might kill himself, and he had neither sons nor brothers to succeed him. For two days and nights he lay upon his face, fasting, across the foot of the couch which bore her calm and lovely body. Then he arose and ate, and went about very quietly like one who has taken a great resolution. He caused her body to be put in a coffin of lead mixed with silver, and for that he had an outer coffin made of the most precious and scented woods wrought with gold, and about that there was to be a sarcophagus of alabaster, inlaid with precious stones. And while these things were being done he spent his time for the most part by the pools and in the garden-houses and pavilions and groves and in those chambers in the palace where they two had been most together, brooding upon her loveliness. He did not rend his garments nor defile himself with ashes and sackcloth as the custom was, for his love was too great for such extravagances. At last he came forth again among his councillors and before the people, and told them what he had a mind to do.

He said he could never more touch woman, he could never more think of them, and so he would find a seemly youth to adopt for his heir and train him to his task, and that he would do his princely duties as became him; but that for the rest of it, he would give himself with all his power and all his strength and all his wealth, all that he could command, to make a monument worthy of his incomparable, dear, lost mistress. A building it should be of perfect grace and beauty, more marvellous than any other building had ever been or could ever be, so that to the end of time it should be a wonder, and men would treasure it and speak of it and desire to see it and come from all lands of the earth to visit and recall the name and memory of his queen. And this building he said was to be called the Pearl of Love.

And this his councillors and people permitted him to do, and so he did.

Year followed year, and all the years he devoted himself to building and adorning the Pearl of Love. A great foundation was hewn out of the living rock in a place whence one seemed to be looking at the snowy wilderness of the great mountains across the valley of the world. Villages and hills there were, a winding river, and very far away three great cities. Here they put the sarcophagus of alabaster beneath a pavilion of cunning workmanship; and about it there were set pillars of strange and lovely stone and wrought and fretted walls, and a great casket of masonry bearing a dome and pinnacles and cupolas, as exquisite as a jewel. At first the design of Pearl of Love was less bold and subtle than it became later. At first it was smaller and more wrought and encrusted; there were many pierced screens and delicate clusters of rosy-hued pillars, and the sarcophagus lay like a child that sleeps among flowers. The first dome was covered with green tiles, framed and held together by silver, but this was taken away again because it seemed close, because it did not soar grandly enough for the broadening imagination of the prince.

For by this time he was no longer the graceful youth who had loved the girl queen. He was now a man, grave and intent, wholly set upon the building of the Pearl of Love. With every year of effort he had learnt new possibilities in arch and wall and buttress; he had acquired greater power over the material he had to use and he had learnt of a hundred stones and hues and effects that he could never have thought of in the beginning. His sense of colour had grown finer and colder; he cared no more for the enamelled gold-lined brightness that had pleased him first, the brightness of an illuminated missal; he sought now for blue colouring like the sky and for the subtle hues of great distances, for recondite shadows and sudden broads floods of purple opalescence and for grandeur and space. He wearied altogether of carvings and pictures and inlaid ornamentation and all the little careful work of men. "Those were pretty things," he said of his earlier decorations; and had them put aside into subordinate buildings where they would not hamper his main design. Greater and greater grew his artistry. With awe and amazement people saw the Pearl of Love sweeping up from its first beginnings to a superhuman breadth and height and magnificence. They did not know clearly what they had expected, but never had they expected so sublime a thing as this. "Wonderful are the miracles," they whispered, "that love can do," and all the women in the world, whatever other loves they had, loved the prince for the splendour of his devotion.

Through the middle of the building ran a great aisle, a vista, that the prince came to care for more and more. From the inner entrance of the building he looked along the length of an immense pillared gallery and across the central area from which the rose-hued columns had long since vanished, over the top the pavilion under which lay the sarcophagus, through a marvellously designed opening, to the snowy wilderness of the great mountain, the lord of all mountains, two hundred miles away. The pillars and arches and buttresses and galleries soared and floated on either side, perfect yet unobtrusive, like great archangels waiting in the shadows about the presence of God. When men saw that austere beauty for the first time they were exalted, and then they shivered and their hearts bowed down. Very often would the prince come to stand there and look at that vista, deeply moved and not yet fully satisfied. The Pearl of Love had still something for him to do, he felt, before his task was done. Always he would order some little alteration to be made or some recent alteration to be put back again. And one day he said that the sarcophagus would be clearer and simpler without the pavilion; and after regarding it very steadfastly for a long time, he had the pavilion dismantled and removed.

The next day he came and said nothing, and the next day and the next. Then for two days he stayed away altogether. Then he returned, bringing with him an architect and two master craftsmen and a small retinue.

All looked, standing together silently in a little group, amidst the serene vastness of their achievement. No trace of toil remained in its perfection. It was as if God of nature's beauty had taken over their offspring to himself.

Only one thing there was to mar the absolute harmony. There was a certain disproportion about the sarcophagus. It had never been enlarged, and indeed how could it have been enlarged since the early days? It challenged the eye; it nicked the streaming lines. In that sarcophagus was the casket of lead and silver, and in the casket of lead and silver was the queen, the dear immortal cause of all this beauty. But now that sarcophagus seemed no more than a little dark oblong that lay incongruously in the great vista of the Pearl of Love. It was as if someone had dropped a small valise upon the crystal sea of heaven.

Long the prince mused, but no one knew the thoughts that passed through his mind.

At last he spoke. He pointed.

"Take that thing away," he said.

50

The Queer Story of Brownlow's Newspaper

1

I call this a Queer Story because it is a story without an explanation. When I first heard it, in scraps, from Brownlow I found it queer and incredible. But—it refuses to remain incredible. After resisting and then questioning and scrutinizing and falling back before the evidence, after rejecting all his evidence as an elaborate mystification and refusing to hear any more about it, and then being drawn to reconsider it by an irresistible curiosity and so going through it all again, I have been forced to the conclusion that Brownlow, so far as he can tell the truth, has been telling the truth. But it remains queer truth, queer and exciting to the imagination. The more credible his story becomes the queerer it is. It troubles my mind. I am fevered by it, infected not with germs but with notes of interrogation and unsatisfied curiosity.

Brownlow is, I admit, a cheerful spirit. I have known him tell lies. But I have never known him do anything so elaborate and sustained as this affair, if it is a mystification, would have to be. He is incapable of anything so elaborate and sustained. He is too lazy and easy-going for anything of the sort. And he would have laughed. At some stage he would have laughed and given the whole thing away. He has nothing to gain by keeping it up. His honour is not in the case either way. And after all there is his bit of newspaper in evidence—and the scrap of an addressed wrapper....

I realize it will damage this story for many readers that it opens with Brownlow in a state very definitely on the gayer side of sobriety. He was not in a mood for cool and calculated observation, much less for accurate record. He was seeing things in an exhilarated manner. He was disposed to see them and greet them cheerfully and let them slip by out of attention. The limitations of time and space lay lightly upon him. It was after midnight. He had been dining with friends.

I have inquired what friends—and satisfied myself upon one or two obvious possibilities of that dinner party. They were, he said to me, "just friends. They hadn't anything to do with it." I don't usually push past an assurance of this sort, but I made an exception in this case. I watched my man and took a chance of repeating the question. There was nothing out of the ordinary about that dinner party, unless it was the fact that it was an unusually good dinner party. The host was Redpath Baynes, the solicitor, and the dinner was in his house in St. John's Wood. Gifford, of the *Evening Telegraph*, whom I know slightly, was, I found, present, and from him I got all I wanted to know. There was much bright and discursive talk and Brownlow had been inspired to give an imitation of his aunt, Lady Clitherholme, reproving an inconsiderate plumber during some re-building operations at Clitherholme. This early memory had been received with considerable merriment—he was always very good about his aunt, Lady Clitherholme—and Brownlow had departed obviously elated by this little social success and the general geniality of the occasion. Had they talked, I asked, about the Future, or Einstein, or J.W. Dunne, or any such high and serious topic at that party? They had not. Had they discussed the modern newspaper? No. There had been nobody whom one could call a practical joker at this party, and Brownlow had gone off alone in a taxi. That is what I was most desirous of knowing. He had been duly delivered by his taxi at the main entrance to Sussex Court.

Nothing untoward is to be recorded of his journey in the lift to the fifth floor of Sussex Court. The liftman on duty noted nothing exceptional. I asked if Brownlow said, "Good night." The liftman does not remember. "Usually he says Night O," reflected the liftman—manifestly doing his best and with nothing particular to recall. And there the fruits of my inquiries about the condition of Brownlow on this particular evening conclude. The rest of the story comes directly from him. My investigations arrive only at this: he was certainly not drunk. But he was lifted a little out of our normal harsh and grinding contact with the immediate realities of existence. Life was glowing softly and warmly in him, and the unexpected could happen brightly, easily, and acceptably.

He went down the long passage with its red carpet, its clear light, and its occasional oaken doors, each with its artistic brass number. I have been down that passage with him on several occasions. It was his custom to enliven that corridor by raising his hat gravely as he passed each entrance, saluting his unknown and invisible neighbours, addressing them softly but distinctly by playful if sometimes slightly indecorous names of his own devising, expressing good wishes or paying them little compliments.

He came at last to his own door, number 49, and let himself in without serious difficulty. He switched on his hall light. Scattered on the polished oak floor and invading his Chinese carpet were a number of letters and circulars, the evening's mail. His parlourmaid-housekeeper who slept in a room in another part of the building, had been taking her evening out, or these letters would have been gathered up and put on the desk in his bureau. As it was, they lay on the floor. He closed his door behind him or it closed of its own accord; he took off his coat and wrap, placed his hat on the head of the Greek charioteer whose bust adorns his hall, and set himself to pick up his letters.

This also he succeeded in doing without misadventure. He was a little annoyed to miss the *Evening Standard*. It is his custom, he says, to subscribe for the afternoon edition of the Star to read at tea-time and also for the final edition of the *Evening Standard* to turn over the last thing at night, if only on account of Low›s cartoon. He gathered up all these envelopes and packets and took them with him into his little sitting-room. There he turned on the electric heater, mixed himself a weak whisky-and-soda, went to his bedroom to put on soft slippers and replace his smoking jacket by a frogged jacket of llama wool, returned to his sitting-room, lit a cigarette, and sat down in his arm-chair by the reading lamp to examine his correspondence. He recalls all these details very exactly. They were routines he had repeated scores of times.

Brownlow's is not a preoccupied mind; it goes out to things. He is one of those buoyant extroverts who open and read all their letters and circulars whenever they can get hold of them. In the daytime his secretary intercepts and deals with most of them, but at night he escapes from her control and does what he pleases, that is to say, he opens everything.

He ripped up various envelopes. There was a formal acknowledgment of a business letter he had dictated the day before, there was a letter from his solicitor asking for some details about a settlement he was making, there was an offer from some unknown gentleman with an aristocratic name to lend him money on his note of hand alone, and there was a notice about a proposed new wing to his club. "Same old stuff," he sighed. "Same old stuff. What bores they all are!" He was always hoping, like every man who is proceeding across the plains of middle-age, that his correspondence would contain agreeable surprises—and it never did. Then, as he put it to me, *inter alia*, he picked up the remarkable newspaper.

2

It was different in appearance from an ordinary newspaper, but not so different as not to be recognizable as a newspaper, and he was surprised, he says, not to have observed it before. It was enclosed in a wrapper of pale green, but it was unstamped; apparently it had been delivered not by the postman, but by some other hand. (This wrapper still exists; I have seen it.) He had already torn it off before he noted that he was not the addressee.

For a moment or so he remained looking at this address, which struck him as just a little odd. It was printed in rather unusual type: "Evan O'Hara Mr., Sussex Court 49."

"Wrong name," said Mr. Brownlow; "Right address. Rummy. Sussex Court 49. ... 'Spose he's got my Evening Standard. ... 'Change no robbery."

He put the torn wrapper with his unanswered letters and opened out the newspaper.

The title of the paper was printed in large slightly ornamental black-green letters that might have come from a kindred fount to that responsible for the address. But, as he read it, it was the *Evening Standard!* Or, at least, it was the "Even Standrd." "Silly," said Brownlow. "It›s some damn Irish paper. Can›t spell—anything—these Irish. ..."

He had, I think, a passing idea, suggested perhaps by the green wrapper and the green ink, that it was a lottery stunt from Dublin.

Still, if there was anything to read he meant to read it. He surveyed the front page. Across this ran a streamer headline: "WILTON BORING REACHES SEVEN MILES: SUCCES ASSURED."

"No," said Brownlow. "It must be oil. ... Illiterate lot these oil chaps—leave out the 's' in 'success.'"

He held the paper down on his knee for a moment, reinforced himself by a drink, took and lit a second cigarette, and then leant back in his chair to take a dispassionate view of any oil-share pushing that might be afoot.

But it wasn't an affair of oil. It was, it began to dawn upon him, something stranger than oil. He found himself surveying a real evening newspaper, which was dealing, so far as he could see at the first onset, with the affairs of another world.

He had for a moment a feeling as though he and his arm-chair and his little sitting-room were afloat in a vast space and then it all seemed to become firm and solid again.

This thing in his hands was plainly and indisputably a printed newspaper. It was a little odd in its letterpress, and it didn't feel or rustle like ordinary paper, but newspaper it was. It was printed in either three or four columns—for the life of him he cannot remember which—and there were column headlines under the page streamer. It had a sort of art-nouveau affair at the bottom of one column that might be an advertisement (it showed a woman in an impossibly big hat), and in the upper left-hand corner was an unmistakable weather chart of Western Europe, with *coloured* isobars, or isotherms, or whatever they are, and the inscription: "To-morrow›s Weather."

And then he remarked the date. The date was November 10th, 1971!

"Steady on," said Brownlow. "Damitall! Steady on."

He held the paper sideways, and then straight again. The date remained November 10th, 1971.

He got up in a state of immense perplexity and put the paper down. For a moment he felt a little afraid of it. He rubbed his forehead. "Haven't been doing a Rip Van Winkle, by any chance, Brownlow, my boy?" he said. He picked up the paper again, walked out into his hall and looked at himself in the hall mirror. He was reassured to see no signs of advancing age, but the expression of mingled consternation and amazement upon his flushed face struck him suddenly as being undignified and unwarrantable. He laughed at himself, but not uncontrollably. Then he stared blankly at that familiar countenance. "I must be half-way *tordu*" he said, that being his habitual facetious translation of "screwed." On the console table was a little respectable-looking adjustable calendar bearing witness that the date was November 10th, 1931.

"D'you see?" he said, shaking the queer newspaper at it reproachfully. "I ought to have spotted you for a hoax ten minutes ago. 'Moosing trick, to say the least of it. I suppose they've made Low editor for a night, and he's had this idea. Eh?"

He felt he had been taken in, but that the joke was a good one. And, with quite unusual anticipations of entertainment, he returned to his arm-chair. A good idea it was, a paper forty years ahead. Good fun if it was well done. For a time nothing but the sounds of a newspaper being turned over and Brownlow's breathing can have broken the silence of the flat.

3

Regarded as an imaginative creation, he found the thing almost too well done. Every time he turned a page he expected the sheet to break out into laughter and give the whole thing away. But it did nothing of the kind. From being a mere quip, it became an immense and amusing, if perhaps a little over-elaborate, lark. And then, as a lark, it passed from stage to stage of incredibility until, as any thing but the thing it professed to be, it was incredible altogether. It must have cost far more than an ordinary number. All sorts of colours were used, and suddenly he came upon illustrations that went beyond amazement; they were in the colours of reality. Never in all his life had he seen such colour printing—and the buildings and scenery and costumes in the pictures were strange. Strange and yet credible. They were colour photographs of actuality forty years from now. He could not believe anything else of them. Doubt could not exist in their presence.

His mind had swung back, away from the stunt-number idea altogether. This paper in his hand would not simply be costly beyond dreaming to produce. At any price it could not be produced. All this present world could not produce such an object as this paper he held in his hand. He was quite capable of realizing that.

He sat turning the sheet over and—quite mechanically—drinking whisky. His sceptical faculties were largely in suspense; the barriers of criticism were down. His mind could now accept the idea that he was reading a newspaper of forty years ahead without any further protest.

It had been addressed to Mr. Evan O'Hara, and it had come to him. Well and good. This Evan O'Hara evidently knew how to get ahead of things. ...

I doubt if at that time Brownlow found anything very wonderful in the situation.

Yet it was, it continues to be, a very wonderful situation. The wonder of it mounts to my head as I write. Only gradually have I been able to build up this picture of Brownlow turning over that miraculous sheet, so that I can believe it myself. And you will understand how, as the thing flickered between credibility and incredibility in my mind, I asked him, partly to justify or confute what he told me, and partly to satisfy a vast expanding and, at last, devouring curiosity: "What was there in it? What did it have to say?" At the same time, I found myself trying to catch him out in his story, and also asking him for every particular he could give me.

What was there in it? In other words, What will the world be doing forty years from now? That was the stupendous scale of the vision, of which Brownlow was afforded a glimpse. The world forty years from now! I lie awake at nights thinking of all that paper might have revealed to us. Much it did reveal, but there is hardly a thing it reveals that does not change at once into a constellation of riddles. When first he told me about the thing I was—it is, I admit, an enormous pity—intensely sceptical. I asked him questions in what people call a "nasty" manner. I was ready—as my manner made plain to him—to jump down his throat with "But that's preposterous!" at the very first slip. And I had an engagement that carried me off at the end of half an hour. But the thing had already got hold of my imagination, and I rang up Brownlow before tea-time, and was biting at this "queer story" of his again. That afternoon he was sulking because of my morning's disbelief, and he told me very little. "I was drunk and dreaming, I suppose," he said. "I'm beginning to doubt it all myself." In the night it occurred to me for the first time that, if he was not allowed to tell and put on record what he had seen, he might become both confused and sceptical about it himself. Fancies might mix up with it. He might hedge and alter to get it more credible. Next day, therefore, I lunched and spent the afternoon with him, and arranged to go down into Surrey for the week-end. I managed to dispel his huffiness with me. My growing keenness restored his. There we set ourselves in earnest, first of all to recover everything he could remember about his newspaper and then to form some coherent idea of the world about which it was telling.

It is perhaps a little banal to say we were not trained men for the job. For who could be considered trained for such a job as we were attempting? What facts was he to pick out as important and how were they to be arranged? We wanted to know everything we could about 1971; and the little facts and the big facts crowded on one another and offended against each other.

The streamer headline across the page about that seven-mile Wilton boring, is, to my mind, one of the most significant items in the story. About that we are fairly clear. It referred, says Brownlow, to a series of attempts to tap the supply of heat beneath the surface of the earth. I asked various questions. "It was *explained*, y'know," said Brownlow, and smiled and held out a hand with twiddling fingers. "It was explained all right. Old system, they said, was to go down from a few hundred feet to a mile or so and bring up coal and burn it. Go down a bit deeper, and there's no need to bring up and burn anything. Just get heat itself straightaway. Comes up of its own accord—under its own steam. See? Simple.

"They were making a big fuss about it," he added. "It wasn't only the streamer headline; there was a leading article in big type. What was it headed? Ah! The Age of Combustion has Ended!"

Now that is plainly a very big event for mankind, caught in mid-happening, November 10th, 1971. And the way in which Brownlow describes it as being handled, shows clearly a world much more preoccupied by economic essentials than the world of to-day, and dealing with them on a larger scale and in a bolder spirit.

That excitement about tapping the central reservoirs of heat, Brownlow was very definite, was not the only symptom of an increase in practical economic interest and intelligence. There was much more space given to scientific work and to inventions than is given in any contemporary paper. There were diagrams and mathematical symbols, he says, but he did not look into them very closely because he could not get the hang of them. "*Frightfully* highbrow, some of it," he said.

A more intelligent world for our grandchildren evidently, and also, as the pictures testified, a healthier and happier world.

"The fashions kept you looking," said Brownlow, going off at a tangent, "all coloured up as they were."

"Were they elaborate?" I asked.

"Anything *but*" he said.

His description of these costumes is vague. The people depicted in the social illustrations and in the advertisements seemed to have reduced body clothing—I mean things like vests, pants, socks and so forth—to a minimum. Breast and chest went bare. There seem to have been tremendously exaggerated wristlets, mostly on the left arm and going as far up as the elbow, provided with gadgets which served the purpose of pockets. Most of these armlets seem to have been very decorative, almost like little shields. And then, usually, there was an immense hat, often rolled up and carried in the hand, and long cloaks of the loveliest colours and evidently also of the most beautiful soft material, which either trailed from a sort of gorget or were gathered up and wrapped about the naked body, or were belted up or thrown over the shoulders.

There were a number of pictures of crowds from various parts of the world. "The people looked fine," said Brownlow. "Prosperous, you know, and upstanding. Some of the women—just lovely."

My mind went off to India. What was happening in India?

Brownlow could not remember anything very much about India. "Ankor," said Brownlow. "That's not India, is it?" There had been some sort of Carnival going on amidst "perfectly lovely" buildings in the sunshine of Ankor.

The people there were brownish people but they were dressed very much like the people in other parts of the world.

I found the politician stirring in me. Was there really nothing about India? Was he sure of that? There was certainly nothing that had left any impression in Brownlow's mind. And Soviet Russia? "Not as Soviet Russia," said Brownlow. All that trouble had ceased to be a matter of daily interest. "And how was France getting on with Germany?" Brownlow could not recall a mention of either of these two great powers. Nor of the British Empire as such, nor of the U.S.A. There was no mention of any interchanges, communications, ambassadors, conferences, competitions, comparisons, stresses, in which these governments figured, so far as he could remember. He racked his brains. I thought perhaps all that had been going on so entirely like it goes on to-day—and has been going on for the last hundred years—that he had run his eyes over the passages in question and that they had left no distinctive impression on his mind. But he is positive that it was not like that. "All that stuff was washed out," he said. He is unshaken in his assertion that there were no elections in progress, no notice of Parliament or politicians, no mention of Geneva or anything about armaments or war. All those main interests of a contemporary journal seem to have been among the "washed out" stuff. It isn't that Brownlow didn't notice them very much; he is positive they were not there.

Now to me this is a very wonderful thing indeed. It means, I take it, that in only forty years from now the great game of sovereign states will be over. It looks also as if the parliamentary game will be over, and as if some quite new method of handling human affairs will have been adopted. Not a word of patriotism or nationalism; not a word of party, not an allusion. But in only forty years! While half the human beings already alive in the world will still be living! You cannot believe it for a moment. Nor could I, if it wasn't for two little torn scraps of paper. These, as I will make clear, leave me in a state of—how can I put it?—incredulous belief.

4

After all, in 1831 very few people thought of railway or steamship travel, and in 1871 you could already go round the world in eighty days by steam, and send a telegram in a few minutes to nearly every part of the earth. Who would have thought of that in 1831? Revolutions in human life, when they begin to come, can come very fast. Our ideas and methods change faster than we know.

But just forty years!

It was not only that there was this absence of national politics from that evening paper, but there was something else still more fundamental. Business, we both think, finance that is, was not in evidence, at least upon anything like contemporary lines. We are not quite sure of that, but that is our impression. There was no list of Stock Exchange prices. for example, no City page, and nothing in its place. I have suggested already that Brownlow just turned that page over, and that it was sufficiently like what it is to-day that he passed and forgot it. I have put that suggestion to him. But he is quite sure that that was not the case. Like most of us nowadays, he is watching a number of his investments rather nervously, and he is convinced he looked for the City article.

November 10th, 1971, may have been Monday—there seems to have been some readjustment of the months and the days of the week; that is a detail into which I will not enter now—but that will not account for the absence of any City news at all. That also, it seems, will be washed out forty years from now.

Is there some tremendous revolutionary smash-up ahead, then? Which will put an end to investment and speculation? Is the world going Bolshevik? In the paper, anyhow, there was no sign of, or reference to, anything of that kind. Yet against this idea of some stupendous economic revolution we have the fact that here forty years ahead is a familiar London evening paper still tumbling into a private individual's letter-box in the most uninterrupted manner. Not much suggestion of a social smash-up there. Much stronger is the effect of immense changes which have come about bit by bit, day by day, and hour by hour, without any sort of revolutionary jolt, as morning or springtime comes to the world.

These futile speculations are irresistible. The reader must forgive me them. Let me return to our story.

There had been a picture of a landslide near Ventimiglia and one of some new chemical works at Salzburg, and there had been a picture of fighting going on near Irkutsk. (Of that picture, as I will tell presently, a fading scrap survives.) "Now that was called——" Brownlow made an effort, and snapped his fingers triumphantly. "——'Round-up of Brigands by Federal Police.'"

"*What Federal Police?*" I asked.

"There you have me," said Brownlow. "The fellows on both sides looked mostly Chinese, but there were one or two taller fellows, who might have been Americans or British or Scandinavians.

"What filled a lot of the paper," said Brownlow, suddenly, "was gorillas. There was no end of a fuss about gorillas. Not so much as about that boring, but still a lot of fuss. Photographs. A map. A special article and some paragraphs."

The paper, had, in fact, announced the death of the last gorilla. Considerable resentment was displayed at the tragedy that had happened in the African gorilla reserve. The gorilla population of the world had been dwindling for many years. In 1931 it had been estimated at nine hundred. When the Federal Board took over it had shrunken to three hundred.

"*What* Federal Board?" I asked.

Brownlow knew no more than I did. When he read the phrase, it had seemed all right somehow. Apparently this Board had had too much to do all at once, and insufficient resources. I had the impression at first that it must be some sort of conservation board, improvised under panic conditions, to save the rare creatures of the world threatened with extinction. The gorillas had not been sufficiently observed and guarded, and they had been swept out of existence suddenly by a new and malignant form of influenza. The thing had happened practically before it was remarked. The paper was clamouring for inquiry and drastic changes of reorganization.

This Federal Board, whatever it might be, seemed to be something of very considerable importance in the year 1971. Its name turned up again in an article of afforestation. This interested Brownlow considerably because he has large holdings in lumber companies. This Federal Board was apparently not only responsible for the maladies of wild gorillas but also for the plantation of trees in—just note these names!—Canada, New York State, Siberia, Algiers, and the East Coast of England, and it was arraigned for various negligences in combating insect pests and various fungoid plant diseases. It jumped all our contemporary boundaries in the most astounding way. Its range was world-wide. "In spite of the recent additional restrictions put upon the use of big timber in building and furnishing, there is a plain possibility of a shortage of shelter timber and of rainfall in nearly all the threatened regions for 1985 onwards. Admittedly the Federal Board has come late to its task, from the beginning its work has been urgency work; but in view of the lucid report prepared by the James Commission, there is little or no excuse for the inaggressiveness and over-confidence it has displayed."

I am able to quote this particular article because as a matter of fact it lies before me as I write. It is indeed, as I will explain, all that remains of this remarkable newspaper. The rest has been destroyed and all we can ever know of it now is through Brownlow's sound but not absolutely trustworthy memory.

5

My mind, as the days pass, hangs on to that Federal Board. Does that phrase mean, as just possibly it may mean, a world federation, a scientific control of all human life only forty years from now? I find that idea—staggering. I have always believed that the world was destined to unify—"Parliament of Mankind and Confederation of the World," as Tennyson put it—but I have always supposed that the process would take centuries. But then my time sense is poor. My disposition has always been to under-estimate the pace of change. I wrote in 1900 that there would be aeroplanes "in fifty years' time." And the confounded things were buzzing about everywhere and carrying passengers before 1920.

Let me tell very briefly of the rest of that evening paper. There seemed to be a lot of sport and fashion; much about something called "Spectacle"—with pictures—a lot of illustrated criticism of decorative art and particularly of architecture. The architecture in the pictures he saw was "towering—kind of magnificent. Great blocks of building. New York, but more so and all run together" ... Unfortunately he cannot sketch. There were sections devoted to something he couldn't understand, but which he thinks was some sort of "radio programme stuff."

All that suggests a sort of advanced human life very much like the life we lead to-day, possibly rather brighter and better. But here is something—different.

"The birth-rate," said Brownlow, searching his mind, "was seven in the thousand."

I exclaimed. The lowest birth-rates in Europe now are sixteen or more per thousand. The Russian birth-rate is forty per thousand, and falling slowly.

"It was seven," said Brownlow. "Exactly seven. I noticed it. In a paragraph."

But what birth-rate, I asked. The British? The European?

"It said the birth-rate," said Brownlow. "Just that." That I think is the most tantalizing item in all this strange glimpse of the world of our grandchildren. A birth-rate of seven in the thousand does not mean a fixed world population; it means a population that is being reduced at a very rapid rate—unless the death-rate has gone still lower. Quite possibly people will not be dying so much then, but living very much longer. On that Brownlow could throw no light. The people in the pictures did not look to him an "old lot." There were plenty of children and young or young-looking people about.

"But Brownlow," I said, "wasn't there any crime?"

"Rather," said Brownlow. "They had a big poisoning case on, but it was jolly hard to follow. You know how it is with these crimes. Unless you've read about it from the beginning, it's hard to get the hang of the situation. No newspaper has found out that for every crime it ought to give a summary up-to-date every day—and forty years ahead, they hadn't. Or they aren't going to. Whichever way you like to put it.

"There were several crimes and what newspaper men call stories," he resumed; "personal stories. What struck me about it was that they seemed to be more sympathetic than our reporters, more concerned with the motives and less with just finding someone out. What you might call psychological—so to speak."

"Was there anything much about books?" I asked him.

"I don't remember anything about books," he said. ...

And that is all. Except for a few trifling details such as a possible thirteenth month inserted in the year, that is all. It is intolerably tantalizing. That is the substance of Brownlow's account of his newspaper. He read it—as one might read any newspaper. He was just in that state of alcoholic comfort when nothing is incredible and so nothing is really wonderful. He knew he was reading an evening newspaper of forty years ahead and he sat in front of his fire, and smoked and sipped his drink and was no more perturbed than he would have been if he had been reading an imaginative book about the future.

Suddenly his little brass clock pinged Two.

He got up and yawned. He put that astounding, that miraculous newspaper down as he was wont to put any old newspaper down; he carried off his correspondence to the desk in his bureau, and with the swift laziness of a very tired man he dropped his clothes about his room anyhow and went to bed.

But somewhen in the night he woke up feeling thirsty and grey-minded. He lay awake and it came to him that something very strange had occurred to him. His mind went back to the idea that he had been taken in by a very ingenious fabrication. He got up for a drink of Vichy water and a liver tabloid, he put his head in cold water and found himself sitting on his bed towelling his hair and doubting whether he had really seen those photographs in the very colours of reality itself, or whether he had imagined them. Also running through his mind was the thought that the approach of a world timber famine for 1985 was something likely to affect his investments and particularly a trust he was setting up on behalf of an infant in whom he was interested. It might be wise, he thought, to put more into timber.

He went back down the corridor to his sitting-room. He sat there in his dressing-gown, turning over the marvellous sheets. There it was in his hands complete in every page, not a corner torn. Some sort of auto-hypnosis, he thought, might be at work, but certainly the pictures seemed as real as looking out of a window. After he had stared at them some time he went back to the timber paragraph. He felt he must keep that. I don't know if you will understand how his mind worked—for my own part I can see at once how perfectly irrational and entirely natural it was—but he took this marvellous paper, creased the page in question, tore off this particular article and left the rest. He returned very drowsily to his bedroom, put the scrap of paper on his dressing-table, got into bed and dropped off to sleep at once.

6

When he awoke again it was nine o'clock; his morning tea was untasted by his bedside and the room was full of sunshine. His parlourmaid-housekeeper had just re-entered the room.

"You were sleeping so peacefully," she said; "I couldn't bear to wake you. Shall I get you a fresh cup of tea?"

Brownlow did not answer. He was trying to think of something strange that had happened.

She repeated her question.

"No. I'll come and have breakfast in my dressing-gown before my bath," he said, and she went out of the room.

Then he saw the scrap of paper.

In a moment he was running down the corridor to the sitting-room. "I left a newspaper," he said. "I left a newspaper."

She came in response to the commotion he made.

"A newspaper?" she said. "It's been gone this two hours, down the chute, with the dust and things."

Brownlow had a moment of extreme consternation.

He invoked his God. "I wanted it *kept*!" he shouted. "I wanted it *kept*."

"But how was *I* to know you wanted it kept?"

"But didn't you notice it was a very extraordinary-looking newspaper?"

"I've got none too much time to dust out this flat to be looking at newspapers," she said. "I thought I saw some coloured photographs of bathing ladies and chorus girls in it, but that's no concern of mine. It didn't seem a proper newspaper to me. How was I to know you'd be wanting to look at them again this morning?"

"I must get that newspaper back," said Brownlow. "It's—it's vitally important. ... If all Sussex Court has to be held up I want that newspaper back."

"I've never known a thing come up that chute again," said his housekeeper, "that's once gone down it. But I'll telephone down, sir, and see what can be done. Most of that stuff goes right into the hot-water furnace, they say...."

It does. The newspaper had gone.

Brownlow came near raving. By a vast effort of self-control he sat down and consumed his cooling breakfast. He kept on saying "Oh, my God!" as he did so. In the midst of it he got up to recover the scrap of paper from his bedroom, and then found the wrapper addressed to Evan O'Hara among the overnight letters on his bureau. That seemed an almost maddening confirmation. The thing had happened.

Presently after he had breakfasted, he rang me up to aid his baffled mind.

I found him at his bureau with the two bits of paper before him. He did not speak. He made a solemn gesture.

"What is it?" I asked, standing before him.

"Tell me," he said. "Tell me. What are these objects? It's serious. Either——" He left the sentence unfinished.

I picked up the torn wrapper first and felt its texture. "Evan O'Hara, Mr.," I read.

"Yes. Sussex Court, 49. Eh?"

"Right," I agreed and stared at him.

"*That's* not hallucination, eh?"

I shook my head.

"And now this?" His hand trembled as he held out the cutting. I took it.

"Odd," I said. I stared at the black-green ink, the unfamiliar type, the little novelties in spelling. Then I turned the thing over. On the back was a piece of one of the illustrations; it was, I suppose, about a quarter of the photograph of that "Round-up of Brigands by Federal Police" I have already mentioned.

When I saw it that morning it had not even begun to fade. It represented a mass of broken masonry in a sandy waste with bare-looking mountains in the distance. The cold, clear atmosphere, the glare of a cloudless afternoon were rendered perfectly. In the foreground were four masked men in a brown service uniform intent on working some little machine on wheels with a tube and a nozzle projecting a jet that went out to the left, where the fragment was torn off. I cannot imagine what the jet was doing. Brownlow says he thinks they were gassing some men in a hut. Never have I seen such realistic colour printing.

"What on earth is this?" I asked.

"It's *that*" said Brownlow. "I'm not mad, am I? It's really *that*."

"But what the devil is it?"

"It's a piece of a newspaper for November 10th, 1971."

"You had better explain," I said, and sat down, with the scrap of paper in my hand, to hear his story. And, with as much elimination of questions and digressions and repetitions as possible, that is the story I have written here.

I said at the beginning that it was a queer story and queer to my mind it remains, fantastically queer. I return to it at intervals, and it refuses to settle down in my mind as anything but an incongruity with all my experience and beliefs. If it were not for the two little bits of paper, one might dispose of it quite easily. One might say that Brownlow had had a vision, a dream of unparalleled vividness and consistency. Or that he had been hoaxed and his head turned by some elaborate mystification. Or, again, one might suppose he had really seen into the future with a sort of exaggeration of those previsions cited by Mr. J.W. Dunne in his remarkable "Experiment with Time." But nothing Mr. Dunne has to advance can account for an actual evening paper being slapped through a letter-slit forty years in advance of its date.

The wrapper has not altered in the least since I first saw it. But the scrap of paper with the article about afforestation is dissolving into a fine powder and the fragment of picture at the back of it is fading out; most of the colour has gone and the outlines have lost their sharpness. Some of the powder I have taken to my friend Ryder at the Royal College, whose work in micro-chemistry is so well known. He says the stuff is not paper at all, properly speaking. It is mostly aluminium fortified by admixture with some artificial resinous substance.

7

Though I offer no explanation whatever of this affair I think I will venture on one little prophesy. I have an obstinate persuasion that on November 10th, 1971, the name of the tenant of 49, Sussex Court, will be Mr. Evan O'Hara. (There is no tenant of that name now in Sussex Court and I find no evidence in the Telephone Directory, or the London Directory, that such a person exists anywhere in London.) And on that particular evening forty years ahead, he will not get his usual copy of the *Even Standrd*: instead he will get a copy of the *Evening Standard* of 1931. I have an incurable fancy that this will be so.

There I may be right or wrong, but that Brownlow really got and for two remarkable hours, read, a real newspaper forty years ahead of time I am as convinced as I am convinced that my own name is Hubert G. Wells. Can I say anything stronger than that?

Other Titles In This Series